Amanda Brookfield

Amanda Brookfield gained a First Class Honours Degree
from Oxford before working at an advertising agency for
several years. She wrote her first novel while living in
Buenos Aires with her diplomat husband, and her second
while in Washington, D.C. She has two young sons and
now lives in London and divides her time between
writing fiction and looking after her family.

Godmother
Marriage Games

Amanda Brookfield

SCEPTRE

THE GODMOTHER

For Edward

With special thanks to Kevin Duncan, Gyll Foster, Sara Westcott and Edward Brookfield for their patient and generous responses to all my questions.

'Give him to Rachel,' said Joy, pointing with the christening candle across the room.

'Yes, give him to Rachel,' echoed Tony, her husband, emerging from the kitchen with a fresh pitcher of wine. 'Let the godmother have a go.'

The wriggling bundle of yellowing silk, trimmed with cobwebbed lace, was passed from hand to hand along the line of guests, like a parcel at a children's party, thought Rachel, regarding its approach with all the wariness of a native being invited to speak a foreign language.

'He's bound to cry,' she declared, smiling through her fear, feeling all eyes upon her as she laid her white suede handbag on the arm of the sofa and rubbed her hands together in a show of eagerness for the challenge ahead.

But Leo, who was six months old and who had been placed in the woefully haphazard care of his eleven-year-old sister, Isobel, for the last twenty minutes, did not cry upon being delivered to his godmother. He frowned at her instead, twisting his fist into his mouth and kicking out at the restrictions of the long christening robe, now entwined round his stocky legs like clingfilm.

'I'm not sure he approves of his costume very much,' Rachel ventured, cradling the baby in stiff arms, wary of projectile milk-dribble staining the front of her white linen jacket, or, worse still, her chest being mistakenly identified as a source of nutrition. A frisson of repulsion and curiosity had zigzagged through her the day before upon finding Joy with her T-shirt hoicked up unceremoniously over one ripe and veiny bosom, so that Leo could feed while she guided Sam, her dyslexic nine year old, through a French reading book about farms.

'But they all wore that gown,' remarked a brisk, mousy-haired woman with Tony's nose, 'it's family tradition.'

'Oh, I see.' Her arms were aching now. The woman turned away, giving Rachel the chance to step out of the social throng, none of whom she knew anyway, and sit down beside her handbag. Gingerly, she propped the baby up on her lap, straightening the copious folds of the gown as tidily as she could and doing her best to contain the wriggling limbs. For a moment she thought wistfully of her other three godchildren, all of whom had long since acquired mouthfuls of teeth and a taste for beautifully undemanding, postable activities like video games and Barbie dolls. 'Bad luck Leo,' she whispered, giving the voluminous family heirloom another tug, 'I should hate it too.' The baby offered a feisty kick by way of concurrence and then promptly put his head in the crook of her arm and closed his eyes. Hardly daring to move for fear of interrupting this astonishingly rapid – and most welcome – submission to the pull of sleep, Rachel lifted her eyes for a few moments in order to study the room.

It was still only a few months since Joy and Tony had made their daring exit from the London rat race, transplanting the family from a four-bedroomed semi in Wimbledon to a charming but dilapidated farmhouse a few miles outside Turon, a medieval town that nestled in the upper regions of the Loire valley. A daring move indeed. Something to be admired as an attempt to make a dream come true, one of those life moves about which most mortals end up doing nothing more than talking. Upon studying the undisguisable chaos of the Daltons' new sitting room, however, the peeling wallpaper, the bunches of wires sticking out of the walls like skeletal fingers, the scores of boxes stacked along every spare inch of wall, Rachel could not resist a shiver of relief that the experience was being endured by Joy and not herself. Leo hadn't been part of their plan either, she remembered, casting a wary eye at her lap, her godson's conception apparently having occurred quite by accident during the chaotic and unforseeably long business of trying to sell the house and settle all their affairs in England. Joy, while professing to be appalled at the discovery of this unscheduled pregnancy, had seemed to revel in it too, perhaps, thought Rachel wickedly, because she was secretly thrilled to have proved that a fifteen-year marriage could still muster enough passion to overlook the use of sexual prophylactics.

'Well, if it is such a disaster, why not consider your options?' Rachel had asked, trying to be blunt but kind, when Joy first broke the news, weeping into a glass of wine which she said she really shouldn't have, but from which she nevertheless gulped with unabashed need.

'Christ, Rachel,' she had gasped, hugging the small hump still easily disguised by a generous sweatshirt, 'there's a child in there. At twelve weeks it's got all its bits. I know it may be hard for you to understand, not having children and so on, but to have its life terminated, even now, would be tantamount to murder.'

'OK, OK – sorry I spoke.' Rachel held both hands up. 'Though I do remember,' she couldn't resist muttering, 'there was a time when you waved a banner for abortion rights . . .'

'That was years ago, for God's sake. It's different when you've had children, believe me. The very thought that . . . Oh, it's impossible to explain.'

Rachel had nodded in a show of empathy, hating the familiar, unspoken criticism for the fact that she herself had not borne any children, that she had committed the unmentionable sin of choosing to remain single, to nurture a career instead of a family. Once, friends like Joy had challenged her openly about such things, expressing either pity or fascination with her single status, teasing her with suggestions for life partners and having late babies. Now they no longer did so. An omission which Rachel suspected was connected directly to the fact that, at thirty-nine, she was now perilously close to the category of spinster as opposed to unmarried woman, an age well past the point where acquaintances expected or even wanted her to change her ways.

Leo yawned, absently pushed a thumb into his eye socket, scowled at the unexpected pain, and then settled back to sleep, the dimpled fingers of one hand closing round the third button of Rachel's suit jacket.

The trouble was, thought Rachel, watching the button being tugged by its cotton roots and not minding, the trouble was, something did feel different these days. Some new, unclassifiable emotion was pushing its way into the perfect bubble of her world, something which she did her best to ignore, but which felt disturbingly like a growing sense of pointlessness behind all that she had created, all that she had achieved. The ebb and flow of such thoughts, apart from being unpredictable and distressing, was also highly inconvenient. As board director of an international advertising agency, earning in excess of a hundred thousand pounds per annum, with a luxurious flat in Chelsea, a soft-topped Audi Cabriolet and her own named parking slot in the underground cubby hole of a directors' car park, Rachel Elliot was not in the habit of entertaining doubts of any kind. As well as being a formidable businesswoman with a string of happy clients and successful campaigns to her credit, she had lovers, she had hobbies, she had friends, she had good health. Dissatisfaction – or whatever it was – had no business creeping up on her like that. How dare it? she thought now, looping her little finger into the cup of Leo's free hand and being surprised at the hungry clench offered in reply.

'Rachel, you are sweet. Thank you so much. I know babies aren't exactly your thing.' Joy held out her arms for her son. 'Both Tony and I are absolutely thrilled that you agreed to be his godmother – and of course that you could come all this way. Really, it means a lot to us . . . friends like you . . .' She sucked in her lower lip and then blew out hard. 'Well, we go back a long way you and I, don't we?'

As Joy took the child Rachel felt the pull on the button increase until, with a yank, the little fingers were forced to let go. 'We certainly do.' She studied Joy's face for a moment, trying to judge whether the veins standing out round her eyes and the straggly limp hair spoke of something more than the exhaustion of moving countries and taking care of children. Though their friendship dated back to the shared horror of an old-fashioned boarding school, testimony to the mutual problem of having fathers in the armed forces, Rachel no longer felt that she really knew Joy very well. In recent years, their meetings had slumped to one or two a year, over the occasional dinner-party table, or a snatched evening at the theatre. Wimbledon was a long way from Chelsea and, as Rachel found with nearly all her girlfriends, marriages to men whom she barely knew and whom she struggled to find obviously endearing, inevitably took their toll on the degree of intimacy which she was able to maintain. 'No second thoughts, I hope?'

'Second thoughts?' Joy rocked Leo gently in her arms, her hips swaying with a practised, unselfconscious ease that made Rachel almost ashamed of her aching arms, ashamed of her timidity over something so small and peaceful.

'About France. About living here.'

Joy's expression tightened into a concentration of brightness. 'But how could I? This is what we've always wanted, what we've both worked towards for years. Tony had absolutely had it with the whole architectural scene in London. Here he's his own boss – converting barns and all that kind of thing. He loves it. And after holidaying round here for so long he's built up scores of useful connections. He's already got more work than he knows what to do with. And oh, Rachel, you should see Tony's plans for this house. It's going to be positively dreamy. We'll have to force relatives and friends like you to join the queue to come and stay. And the school is fine,' she swept on, 'even though the classes are bigger than the children are used to. Isobel is already jabbering like a local, though poor Sammy is obviously going to take a little longer to find his feet. And as for this one . . .' she nuzzled Leo's yellow fuzz of hair, 'he could be on Mars for all he cares, so long as he's got a steady supply of food and a dry bottom . . .'

'Oh, good,' murmured Rachel, wondering if Joy was aware that she had accounted for everyone's state of happiness but her own.

The best thing about being alone was the freedom, mused Rachel, as she glibly fibbed about having an airplane to catch and levered herself out of the squash of the Daltons' cement-floored sitting room in order to escape back to her hotel. Although a light rain was still falling it felt warmer outside, more welcoming. She shivered again at the recollection of the stone walls of the house, the plastic flapping in place of window panes, the way the loo door had refused to close, forcing her to sit awkwardly with one leg outstretched in case any other unsuspecting guest had chosen that moment to barge in. Apart from Joy and Tony she had known no one at all, only close family having been able to make the journey and none of their new local friends being familiar to her.

With a satisfying click the doors of her hired Mercedes obediently unlocked themselves. As she slipped into the driver's seat, Rachel threw a wistful glance at the peachy straw hat in the back. Joy should have warned her. Smart outfits but not a hat in sight. And it had suited her, too, especially with its wide brim pulled ever so slightly down over one temple, so that she could peer out imperiously from underneath, feeling grand and pretty all at the same time. She didn't often get a chance to wear hats these days, weddings and christenings being somewhat a thing of the past.

Although September had barely begun, the imprint of autumn had already touched the landscape bordering the narrow tarmac road on which Rachel sped away: armies of drooping sunflowers smothered the fields to her right and left, their blackened heads nodding in the damp breeze like old men despairing at the ways of the world. Sensing that her good mood was in danger of slipping away, Rachel turned on the radio, tuning into a light, fizzy pop tune that sounded vaguely familiar. She tapped her fingers on the steering wheel and hummed quietly, squinting at the signposts because she had left her spectacles in the hotel. Some ten minutes into her journey an avalanche of grey clouds scudded past like shifting scenery, allowing a new assemblage of fluffy white tufts and a beaming sun to take their place. The sunflowers were replaced by acres of harvested corn, rolled into golden cylinders, their wet surfaces glistening on this new and brilliant stage like giant polished tins.

Turning away from the fields, towards the less dramatic pastures that lined the sides of the Loire itself, Rachel braced herself for the first glimpse of the château in whose environs she was fortunate enough to be staying. It perched on a piece of high ground beside the river like a fairytale castle, complete with Rapunzel-style pointed turrets and vertical slits in its towering walls. The hotel itself was in a converted side-section, where French lords were said to have once stabled their horses. Set further into the extensive grounds, carefully masked behind several rows of tall trees, lay a kidney-shaped swimming pool; flecks of its shimmering azure could just be glimpsed from the four windows of Rachel's second-floor room.

A team of maids had come to close the shutters and turn down the sheets on her bed the evening before, bustling in when she was only just out of the bath, smiling approvingly at the vast white towelling dressing gown in which she emerged, their eyes saying they had seen it all before and much more besides, that such states of undress were entirely expected of such patrons at such times of day.

When she arrived back after the christening the shutters were still open, allowing the rain-washed air to drift in and lighten the oppressively regal atmosphere of the room, of which the four-poster bed formed the centrepiece, its sides decked with sweeping brocaded curtains of the kind that Rachel associated with honeymooning couples in old films.

Settling herself against the wall of embroidered cushions arranged along the tapestried headboard, she took a desultory nibble of the mint chocolate which had been left on her pillow, willing herself to sink into the stupour of self-indulgence which her surroundings demanded. She reached for the telephone beside her bed to dial room service, but changed her mind. There was nothing she wanted after all. Nothing at all.

Beside her lay most of the contents of her small suitcase, rummaged through earlier that day in her hurry not to be late for the church. In her absence, invisible hands had folded and arranged every item into tidy shapes across the bed, the line between assistance and intervention clearly dictating that the repacking of the suitcase itself was not permitted. Rachel picked up a neatly folded pair of white silk stockings and threw them in the direction of the open suitcase. They flew badly, too light to reach their destination, fluttering down instead, like tired wings, on a black leather book near the far edge of the bed. On noticing the book, Rachel rolled over and picked it up. Still lying on her stomach, she extracted a gold ball point pen from its broad spine and began to write, her hand sweeping fluently across and down the lined page.

September 12th

Turon is beautiful. I arrived midday Saturday – such a relief to be out of London – and at this palace of a hotel. Tony and Joy's house is in the most magnificent setting, complete with its very own mini-tributary of the Loire running through the back garden. The children all look suntanned and healthy – even little Leo – far more so than they would after a summer in London. Joy was too busy with arrangements for the christening to talk properly, but she seems very pleased with the move down here.

Rachel paused and sucked the end of her pen. Over her shoulder, slats of afternoon sunshine streamed in through the open windows, illuminating the page to such a degree that the whiteness of it hurt her eyes. Absently, she rubbed one temple, where the edge of a dull pain was surfacing. She should have eaten properly. Instead, she had picked at Joy's home-made pizza squares and triangles of liver pâté, eating enough to be polite, presenting an appearance of sociability while inside she had held herself in check.

Such a forceful entrance of the sun brought with it an irritating sense of obligation to swim. There was no excuse not to. Especially now that the masterful sweep of her hair, so artfully streaked and styled by the formidable Petrona at the hairdresser's, had successfully sailed through the occasion for which it had been designed. It didn't matter what she looked like now. It didn't matter what she looked like until Tuesday, in fact, when she was due back in the office.

But Rachel did not want to go swimming. An apathy that had nothing to do with the late heat of the day was pressing upon her, bringing with it a melancholic longing to be home. The thought of the evening ahead of her, the business of dining alone, of having to sleep amidst the suffocating grandeur of the room, was suddenly deadening.

The mood swing left Rachel exasperated. Like so many of her feelings these days, it was all the more unsettling for being so totally unforeseen. She had deliberately made this weekend a long one. She had been looking forward to bedroom mints and kidney-shaped swimming pools and elegant meals alone. As in the more immediate past of leaving the Daltons' ruin of a farmhouse, she had been looking forward to the prospect of time for herself. And yet now that it had actually arrived, the satisfaction of that prospect seemed to dissolve like a mirage, as if it had been an image of purely false allure. For here she was, right inside the brochure, so to speak, lying in one of the very stately rooms she had found so enticing in its photographic form, only to find it empty. Rachel could hear the seconds ticking by on her gold bracelet of a wristwatch, each one reinforcing the unpleasant notion that the time for which she had yearned as a reward now felt little better than a refined form of punishment.

With a fresh burst of energy, she returned her attention to her diary.

The christening went off beautifully. Hearing it all in French was somehow more romantic and all the godparents spoke together so there was no problem over embarrassment about my accent. Joy and Tony had gone to great trouble over the reception afterwards – very brave of them given the constraints of the house, so many of the rooms still being completely uninhabitable. I did my godmotherly bit, shook hands with the relatives and so on, though, her writing slowed and she gripped the pen harder; *though for some reason I wasn't really in the mood. I held Leo for a while.* She paused again, for longer this time. Then she put a full stop, a large globule of a punctuation mark that took some time.

She closed the book abruptly and cast it to one side. Raising her bottom off the bed she unzipped her skirt and slithered out of it, intending to pull on her bathing costume at once. But she got sidetracked by the sight of her skinny white thighs and the marble slab of her stomach. She ran her hands down the sides of her waist and over the sharp mounds of her hip bones, marking the edges of her like pearly stones. She had always been proud of her slimness, had worn it like a badge of achievement, if she was honest, strutting it in tight suits and tailored shirts at work, as if a sylph-like silhouette spoke volumes for the worth of the person inside. As if it said, 'Trust me, I know how to take care of myself, I am in control.'

But lately Rachel was not so sure. Upon recent examinations of the carved whiteness of her limbs, it was the word 'skinny' which sprang most readily to mind. A word redolent of deprivation and pity; a word suggestive of nothing more glamorous than undernourishment. Between her hips the skin sank in a gentle curve, a blank space that pressed inwards, away from the world. She stroked this space now, trying to imagine it filled. Over the years she had regarded the ballooning bodies of pregnant friends with incredulous curiosity, fascinated and even slightly sickened at their vast waistlines, at the obvious uncontrollability of it all. But now something about the concave ski slope of her belly made her sad. She remembered again the weight of Leo in her lap, the sheer density of him.

Swinging her legs quickly over the side, Rachel got off the bed. Small points of light danced in front of her eyes. She stood still for a moment, trying to collect herself. A swim will clear my head she told herself, starting to undo the mother-of-pearl buttons on her sleeveless cotton blouse. But her movements were arrested once again by the sight of herself in the full-length, gilt-framed mirror beside the bed. Two tubby cherubs eyed her skittishly from its top corners. Beneath their gaze stood a skinny woman of nearly forty. A woman with smart, expensive, fairish hair framing a pale, bony face, saved from mediocrity by the dark brows and lashes which drew attention to the clarity of her grey-blue eyes. Rachel stood quite still, examining the reflection as she might a portrait of a stranger, scouring the map of the body for evidence of happiness.

When the telephone rang she threw herself across the length of the bed, lunging for the receiver like a lifeline. It was probably work, she thought excitedly, some unforeseen crisis, some pre-production muddle which only she could sort out. Frank Alder had probably asked for her personally, said that only Rachel Elliot would do, said that she was the only director in the agency who really understood the skincare market . . .

'Rachel, is that you? Christ, this is a lousy line.'

'Nathan?'

'Can you hear me all right? You're faint as hell.'

'Where are you?'

'Heathrow. Flew in today. Paris on Tuesday. Have we time to meet up?'

The crackles on the line suddenly dissolved. 'Wow, that's better. What the hell are you doing over there? I had to call all over to get your number. Lucky some of your team work weekends or you wouldn't have got me at all.'

'Oh Nathan,' Rachel felt quite breathless, 'it's good to hear you. I'm here for a christening – I'm the unwise choice of godmother – it's an old schoolfriend—'

'Well that's great, Rachel. We'll take a rain-check then . . .'

'Oh no need. We could meet tomorrow.'

'Now you're talking. It will be good to see you.'

'Me too.'

'I'm at The Grosvenor. I'll call you in the morning.'

'Perfect.' Rachel lay on her stomach on the bed, her legs bent up behind her, crossed at the ankle. She rubbed the arches of her feet together as she talked, soothed by the demand to make arrangements, to do something other than think about herself. 'How are things, anyway? How's the world of high finance?'

'Just great, Rachel,' he replied with an easy laugh, 'markets crazy as usual. Hitting the big time in Eastern Europe. I'll tell you all about it tomorrow.'

Her spirits edged down half a notch. Nathan liked to talk about his work. 'Until tomorrow then. Bye now.' After replacing the receiver Rachel pulled her skirt back on, hastily did up the buttons of her shirt and hurried down the cushioned quietness of the corridors to reception with her plane ticket. She would ask them to phone the airline on her behalf. It was pointless staying the night after all. It had been a simple mistake to make, thinking she needed time away when she didn't. It was another joy of being on one's own that altering plans could be indulged in at whim, without the hassle of disappointing or pleasing other people. She could do with a day at home anyway, she told herself a few minutes later, as she made her way back to her room and began packing. She spent too little time there as it was.

Nathan Kramer and Rachel Elliot had first met five years earlier at the home of Rachel's elder brother, a paediatrician who had married an American dental nurse and settled in Washington DC. Rachel was on a visit for the christening of her then four-month-old nephew, Craig, while Nathan was an economist at the World Bank, an institution which he deserted soon afterwards for the more verdant financial pastures of an investment bank in New York. Duncan Elliot's wife, Mary Beth, an eager apprentice in the game of networking dinner parties that defined the slow slither up the Washington social ladder, had arranged a supper party supposedly in Rachel's honour, but which in truth had more to do with showing off her new roomy Bethesda home than wanting to make her sister-in-law feel welcome. Rachel, in Mary Beth's eyes, needed very little help in being made to feel welcome or anything else. Those crystal grey eyes of hers – so unlike dear Duncan's hound-dog brown ones – faced all comers with such unnerving directness that Mary Beth found herself sucking in her stomach and making false announcements about post-maternal career plans just from the sheer pressure of it.

Although the idea of a sit-down dinner for sixteen filled Mary Beth's head with dizzy images of the kind she most treasured in her glossy upmarket magazines, a combination of good sense and cowardice prompted her to opt for a buffet format instead. On the morning of the dinner she made Duncan shift chairs and tables around the ground floor of the house before he left for work, issuing instructions like a novice stage manager anxious about a first night. Carmen, their recently acquired Hispanic maid-cum-child minder, had been treated to a frilly black and white outfit in honour of the occasion, together with several torturous sessions on how to receive coats and flowers.

After observing all these shenanigans from behind copious sections of the *Washington Post* (which Mary Beth retrieved from a plastic bag hurled into the front garden every morning but never actually seemed to read), Rachel decided to make a tactical withdrawal downtown on the pretext of some sightseeing. Though Craig's elder brother had soared in her estimation by his dogged five-year-old attempts to shift all the rearranged furniture into more interesting positions, she still found the strain of being a bystander to family life quite draining. So much noise. So much sudden escalation of mood. So many demands. That Mary Beth was the kind of mother who shrieked at the antics of her offspring and then buried her head in their tiny chests for forgiveness did not make the observation of their habits any easier. She was all extremes, all insecurity herself; quite unfit, in Rachel's eyes, to assist other humans in the business of adapting to the world.

Studying the understated bleakness of the Vietnam War Memorial steadied if not exactly cheered her nerves. More envigorating were the avenues of pastel blossoms lining the parks and roads of Washington's central square mile, like cheerleaders with fistfuls of bright pom-poms. After peering through the railings skirting the sloping lawn of the White House, Rachel wandered back along the glass rectangle of the reflecting pool and up towards the Lincoln Memorial. At the top of the steps she sat down a few feet from the pensive marbled president and gloomily contemplated the prospect of her last evening's entertainment. Her sister-in-law's bejewelled guest list of aspiring politicians and lobbyists had already been the focus of enough dissection and celebration for Rachel to want no part of it. As her eye was caught by an airplane following the busy flight path into the city airport, she toyed enviously with the idea of escaping in the same direction herself that afternoon. Craig's christening had, after all, been dutifully attended. The delights of catching up with a brother to whom she had never felt particularly close and who seemed to be fattening himself on a highly dubious system of medical care, had quickly palled. She longed to go home, back to her lovely new Chelsea flat, then gleaming under fresh coats of paint, and containing no tensions other than those she chose to introduce herself.

Nathan Kramer came as something of an unexpected treat. He had the kind of hairstyle which Rachel associated with American film stars of the eighties, spruce blond spikes that stood effortlessly to attention. Contributing to this impression was something of a rugged jaw line, complete with a faint silvery scar which ran from the lobe of one ear to a point directly below the dimple in his chin. Attracted, against her better judgement, Rachel moved cautiously. While quite within her powers, an eclectic sexual life was not something she had ever managed. She was too busy at work, for one thing. For another, there was always the tedium of self-recrimination afterwards, a silly irrational female reflex which, however hard she tried to quell it, usually got the better of her in the end. Although there had been various sexual liaisons over the years, there had been nothing long term in the relationship department for a good while. Not since Robbie, in fact, from whom Rachel had finally shaken free a decade previously, at the tender age of twenty-five. The pitiable or traumatic state of most of the relationships with which she had grown acquainted in the meantime had hardly been an enticement to join the fray.

Having recently emerged bloodied but undaunted from a highly charged marriage to a fellow economist, Nathan Kramer advertised his availability in the first flash of his blue eyes, the faint swagger of his hips as he strolled nonchalantly across Mary Beth's sherbet-lemon carpet and introduced himself to the most attractive woman at the party. Rachel greeted him with a slight tilt of the head and a faint smile which acknowledged some degree of flattery as well as interest. His kind of woman, Nathan decided at once, helping himself from a tray of drinks and taking on the stare of the intense blue-grey eyes with all the excitement of a hunter embarking on an attainable – but by no means certain – chase.

'I'm in advertising,' Rachel declared by way of an introduction, 'on the board of McKenzie Cartwright. You might have heard of them.'

'You bet I have. Been there long?'

'Five years. Before that I was with Burton, May and Saunders.

A much smaller outfit. Interesting creative work, but no big budgets. I always wanted to try my hand at the international scene.' She spoke with deliberate incisiveness, judging correctly that this would impress him, make him feel safe enough to confirm that the attraction was mutual. It was men's talk really, of the kind at which she had come to be most adept, having quickly discovered during the early stages of her career that the easiest way to beat men at their own game was to talk their language. It was like wearing camouflage.

'McKenzie Cartwright . . . what do they bill these days?'

'Two hundred.'

'I take it that's in millions?' The dimple in his chin changed shape when he smiled.

'What about you?' went on Rachel, deliberately ignoring all knowledge acquired through Mary Beth's weighty pre-dinner briefings. It was his turn to talk; his turn – in this pre-mating ritual – to be allowed to show a few colours.

They slept together just once before she returned to England, between midnight and two o'clock that morning, after leaving the tail end of Mary Beth's party on the pretext of going to a club. Rachel had enjoyed her sister-in-law's expression of undisguised shock when she asked for a house key, though Duncan's surly nod brought back less pleasant memories of censorial elder brothers and parents, of running the gamut of family distrust and old-fashioned judgements about rebellious females forging on alone.

Not wanting to discredit herself entirely, Rachel had insisted on getting back by half past two, a time scale which dictated a certain amount of haste but no mean degree of pleasure. They went straight to Nathan's flat, a smart, if rather clinical two-bedroomed affair just off Dupont Circle. Rachel observed the picture of his wedding day, on a high, undusted shelf in his bedroom, without comment. She knew there had been a wife, just as she knew there had been no children. There seemed little point in probing further. For his part, Nathan displayed an equally forthright lack of curiosity. While a small subterranean part of Rachel might, if it had been allowed to, have found this insulting, it was reassuring too. No questions meant no threat, no possibility of having to surrender control, except in the act of love itself, into which she threw herself with sensual abandon. Love, the emotional counterpart of such pleasure, played not even the shadow of a role in the two hours they spent together. And if it had, Rachel would almost certainly not have handed Nathan Kramer her telephone number, placing it on top of one sculpted pectoral muscle as he lay in bed trying not to fall asleep, before she slipped out of the door and scurried down the curling stairwell to the yellow cab waiting in the street below.

Rachel decoded the alarm, slammed the door shut with her heel and flung her coat across the hall chair. After the fussy grandeur of the Hotel Turon the sight of her own flat was instantly soothing. Kicking off her shoes, she made an almost reverential tour of the rooms, flicking on lights and pulling curtains, savouring the taste of being home. The sitting room was two steps down at the end of the hallway, a long, elegant rectangle that ran the full length of the apartment, all the windows of its furthest wall overlooking the pretty lawn and shrubbery which, theoretically, she shared with other residents, but which always felt like her own. She had used the garden more than ever that summer, sitting out in a reclining seat on her square patio, sipping wine and breathing in the musky smells drifting on the breeze of late evening, glad that her co-residents were either too idle or too shy to do the same.

Her previous residence had been a small but handy one-bedroomed flat between Knightsbridge and Kensington, slightly lacking in character but slick and serviceable – ideal for a resident whose average homecoming was around ten o'clock at night and whose weekends were either spent in a blur of indolence or out visiting friends. While Rachel's work patterns showed no sign of change, her early thirties had seen a burgeoning need for a more comforting domestic backdrop to her hectic life, somewhere that felt less like a living unit and more like a home. The move to McKenzie Cartwright, whose offices took up several floors of a shimmering blue edifice between Covent Garden and The Strand, had presented the obvious moment for change. With the help of Anita, visibly bending under the weight of a then hefty ten-month-old Charlotte, slotted into a contraption the size of a large rucksack, she had flat-hunted her way southwards, finally settling on a street within walking distance of both the King's Road and the Embankment. Though the street contained several rather seedy-looking hotels, it was a part of London that she had always loved, and a mere fifteen-minute drive away from her new employers.

And location was everything, Anita reminded her, as they had surveyed the empty flat together on a wet Saturday shortly after completion, both women equally dismayed at the unsightly pockmarks and stains revealed by the removal of the previous owner's furniture and pictures. On the ceiling above their heads two bare lightbulbs swung gently on a draught cutting in through the crusted window frames overlooking the garden, a detail of dilapidation which on all of Rachel's previous visits had been masked by several pairs of handsome green velvet curtains.

'And I thought I could live here,' she muttered, tearing off a loose section of faded William Morris wallpaper flapping near at hand. 'It's a fucking pigsty.' She offered an apologetic scowl at her goddaughter, who, too young even to mimic the more ill-advised phrases of her seniors, was at that moment enjoying the unmatchable solace of a pink lollipop. 'And he never said anything about taking the carpets,' she added, digging the toe of her shoe into one of the gaping crevasses separating the floorboards.

'It's only cosmetic.' Anita waved her arms at the room. 'The survey was fine, remember?'

'I'm not sure I believe it any longer.'

'What you need is Priscilla Pargiter,' declared Anita, retrieving her daughter's sweet from the floor and licking off the dust before handing it back over her shoulder. 'Don't be put off by the name. Everyone says she's marvellous. When Giles and I win the pools and move to a twelve-roomed mansion on Highgate Hill, she'll be the one I call.' She scribbled a phone number on the back of an old shopping list and pressed it into Rachel's reluctant hand. 'And don't tell me you can't afford it with that spanking new job of yours, because I shan't listen to a word.'

Five years on Rachel had no regrets about taking Anita's advice. Priscilla Pargiter, clad in a tank-sized kaftan dress and tinkling like a wind charm, had breezed into the flat with gushing visions about upholstery and wallpaper that made Rachel secretly afraid. She sketched pictures with her arms as she talked, enthusing about colours and materials whose names sounded like the roll-call of an exotic menu. Rachel, who had been both too desperate and too busy at work to resist, watched from the sidelines as her bomb site of a home was transformed into effortlessly stunning schemes of colour and design. Too pleased with the results to mind that the realisation of such an achievement had required the intervention of an imagination other than her own, she found herself entering a new phase of satisfaction with life in general; a plateau of contentment that bordered on the smug.

Her circle of female friends meanwhile, all of whom had by then entered the long and in some cases bewildering tunnel of motherhood, latched onto Rachel's new surroundings with equal relish. All sparks of envy were quickly defused by gratitude at having access to such a refuge from the domestic hubbub of their own homes, somewhere they could uncoil from family tensions, soaking up the decor and Rachel's wine stocks with equal relish. Any sense on Rachel's part of being invaded rather than complimented by such attentions, was purely momentary. She had seen quite enough of the clutter in the lives of such friends – the way that family rubble had to be cleared and stacked to make room for basic necessities like eating and sitting down – to sympathise deeply with their need to escape. After a spell at the homes of Anita or Joy, she herself would return to her flat like a monk in retreat, welcoming the cool silence of its empty space, the knowledge that all imprints upon its surfaces were hers and hers alone.

Rachel dropped the brochure hailing the attractions of the Hotel Turon into the kitchen bin and pressed the play button on her answering machine. While the tape was rewinding she poured herself a glass of white wine and leant back against the fridge, closing her eyes.

Two clicks.

'Hey Rachel, it's Nathan. Just to say I'm in town for a couple of days and would like to see you. I guess you're at work. I'll call you there. Ciao till later . . .'

Typical Nathan: succinct and unstumbling. Rachel sipped her wine, which had seen better days, but which was at least cold.

'Rachel, Anita here . . . just calling for a chat really. Actually no, what I'd really like is to invite myself round – if that's OK – I mean I know you're frantically busy and all that. It's just that things are looking a bit bleak at the moment . . . could do with a break to be honest. .After playing the hero amongst all those Russian rebels Giles seems to expect the entire family to go into worship-mode – he bellows at the children for not being perfect and at me for . . . oh anything that takes his fancy. And I've been trying to do that piece on leisure centres I told you about – OK so it's not as glamorous as covering wars but someone has to fill the cereal bowls in the morning . . . Charlotte's been waking and coming into our bed at all hours of the night and the twins are in this chronic phase of thinking their day starts at five o'clock . . .'

There was a short pause and a sigh. *'You're going to run out of tape. Sorry. Feeling low and all that. Could I come round some time? Giles is on early shifts soon and could field the kids. Let me know. Thanks so much . . .'*

Rachel put down her glass of wine and returned her attentions to the fridge. There was a pot of taramasalata, whose sell-by date had recently passed but which smelt all right, and a packet of mini wholemeal pitta bread which might be revived by a few seconds in the microwave. Behind her, the answering machine continued to play.

'Ah, so you're not there,' said the quiet, but subtly accusatory voice of her mother. *'Just ringing to see how you were, dear. We had your big brother to stay over the bank holiday – they all came down by train – they've got one of these family rail cards, Ian said – so much cheaper and easier than using the car. They seemed very well, even little Malcolm, who as you know suffers terribly with his ears. Ian seems to be running several Scottish hospitals single-handed and Clare is back doing something part-time in a library which she says she enjoys. I can't think how she manages it with the children to look after. They asked after you of course . . . I said you were fine as far as we knew. It's high time you came to see us, dear, it's been ever such a long time. Do you think you could manage a Sunday lunch? I do know how terribly busy you are. I'll call you later in the week . . . Oh and your father sends his love.'*

Rachel dipped her index finger deep into the soft pink paste and scooped an unseemly clod into her mouth, savouring the garlic-fishy flavours as she swallowed. The circles of pitta bread had only responded in part to the reinvigorating effects of intense heat, their centres going soft while their edges had turned testingly brittle. With the determination born of real hunger, Rachel ate steadily, using the stale bread as a spoon and sucking the taramasalata off the bits that were too impossibly hard to bother with.

When her answering machine stopped she became aware of rain drumming on the patio outside. Licking her fingers, she went back into her sitting room, her stockinged feet slipping on the sections of parquet floor between the rugs. There the noise was louder than ever, thanks to a whisking wind driving directly against the windows. As she listened, she began to distinguish another sound too, a high-pitched whining that sent shivers across her scalp. An animal of some kind. A fox maybe. Something suffering. She frowned, curious but reluctant to be drawn to any drama being enacted in the sodden darkness outside. Foxes could get painfully locked in the act of copulation, she remembered, this compelling fact flitting into her head from nowhere, sliding unexpectedly out of the dark recesses of her memory reserved for such trivia.

Still resisting the mounting urge to peer outside, Rachel crossed over to the mahogany shelves that housed her music centre and began trailing a finger along the library of CDs. Behind her the whining stopped briefly and then started up again, more loudly this time. Apprehensive, her imagination grappling with unappealing images of interlocking foxes, Rachel strode across the room and lifted the bottom corner of one of the long blue curtains covering the glass-panelled door leading into the garden.

Either because it was intelligent enough to know – even from its limited vantage point in the dank darkness – that this was the entrance to the room, or because it had glimpsed Rachel approaching and darted into a position from which it would be seen, the cat was sitting waiting for her right beside the door. On seeing Rachel, it reduced its yowl to a pitiful mew. Her first instinct was to drop the curtain. She did not like animals particularly. Though they were all right in other people's houses – even quite pleasant sometimes – she had always shied away from adopting a similar burden for herself, her mind associating such things with unwanted smells and coatings of hoover-resistant fur.

Upon finding the snapshot of a warm dry sanctuary blacked out, the cat immediately reverted to its high-pitched wail.

The curtain was lifted again, more brusquely this time.

'Go away.' She mouthed the words with exaggerated care, glaring hard through the rain-smeared glass.

The cat, which was black, with white patches circling its eyes and white tips to its ears, cocked its head and opened its mouth very wide in return, making no sound now, as if it too was merely framing words rather than audibly expressing any views.

'Buggeration.' Rachel wrenched back the curtain and unlocked the door. 'I don't want you, puss,' she said, as he darted in between her legs and trotted, tail high, over towards the hand-woven Peruvian rug which Anita had helped her choose from an intimidatingly chic and cramped carpet shop in the Brompton Road. The cat sat down and began licking its stomach in a businesslike way, its pink tongue pushing the fur into manicured tufts.

'Just for tonight then,' said Rachel, returning her attentions to her CD player and opting for a Fauré piano quartet. 'And that's it. So don't go getting any ideas.'

Determined to ignore her intruder, Rachel settled herself on her sofa with her briefcase on her lap and a full wine glass at her side. As one of the more senior board directors at the agency, she had overall responsibility for two accounts, Mallarmé Skincare Products plc, which billed a mighty eighty million worldwide and of which she was inordinately proud and fond, and a national chain of DIY shops called Blackers, which was in the throes of financial crisis and from which she had been hoping to extricate herself – and the agency – for several months. The papers she removed from her briefcase related not to client business however, but to a general presentation on the staffing and recruiting policies of the agency. While the presentation itself contained many ideas of which she was justly proud, its creation related directly to the plum and soon-to-be vacant post of Head of Account Management. The extra work would be daunting, but it was time her career took another pace forward. To become a departmental head was the obvious step. Alan Jarvis had all but said as much himself many times in the past.

She held up the sheaf of papers, squinted at the print and then threw them to one side in annoyance.

'Glasses, bloody glasses – where the hell are you?' Quite used to talking to herself when the occasion demanded, Rachel did not notice the cat casting her a wary eye from its cosy corner of the rug, while she rummaged ineffectually in her briefcase before extending her search to the hall. Having located the glasses in the side pocket of her handbag, still parked on the hall floor beside her suitcase, she sank back onto the sofa and closed her eyes. She was tired. Flying, however short the distance, always wore her out. It dried her skin too, she reflected, touching one cheek morosely with the tips of her fingers. The presentation could wait. Perhaps it wasn't even necessary. It was her turn for promotion, and Jarvis knew it.

Stealthy, on velvet, freshly prinked paws, the cat hopped up onto the sofa and crept towards the vacant lap. Half-asleep, Rachel felt the warm cushion of its body arrive. It turned just once, before settling itself across her stomach and thighs. Her dreaming self welcomed the heat and weight of it, slipping easily from sensations of the present moment to recollections of a similar pleasantness earlier in the day; until the cat had become a baby, pushing up from the deep heart of her like a blossoming flower.

Clothes have to work harder these days, thought Rachel, grimacing at her reflection in the mirrored walls of the lift before striding
out onto the fourth floor. She was wearing one of her favourite
suits, of soft creamy wool with a pencil-shaped, knee-length skirt
and a flatteringly tailored jacket, trimmed with triangular black
velvet lapels.

'Morning, Rachel,' trilled Kath, McKenzie Cartwright's main
receptionist, flicking her pretty brown eyes up from the gossip
page of the *Daily Mail*.

'Morning, Kath, hard at work I see,' observed Rachel dryly,
but smiling to show she meant no harm.

She strode off down the maze of corridors, exchanging brief
pleasantries with several colleagues, before arriving at the open-
plan square of four desks that housed a gaggle of secretaries, two
rubber plants and a photocopying machine. Melissa, Rachel's
own secretary, smiled at once and then frowned.

'What are you doing here? You're supposed to be in France.'

'Too much to do.'

Melissa, who had a plump but pretty face, with smudged freckles
and glossy dark hair, followed Rachel into her office. 'And there's
me thinking I'm going to get an easy day for once. Coffee?'

She began fiddling with the cappuccino machine that lived
on a table in the corner of the room, a prized possession of
Rachel's whose services were much sought after by the rest of
the department.

'And have one yourself,' Rachel murmured, flicking through
the pile of post on her desk with one hand, while the other
moved deftly over the keys of her computer.

'Put a call through to Frank Alder at Mallarmé, could you? Tell him I'm around if he needs me. Then tell Felicity downstairs I'll want a progress report on pre-production for the Allday Sunlotion launch – the shoot's going to be in Bermuda not Florida now and we've only a few weeks to go. And could you retype this little lot,' she held out the file containing her presentation on account management policy, 'by eleven o'clock, if possible, so I can talk it through with Alan before lunch. Which means I'll need a ten-minute slot with him. If Julie gives you a hard time, let me know.' Julie Stern, the managing director's tiger of a PA, had been known to reduce some of the humbler secretaries to tears for daring to make demands upon her boss's precious allocations of time.

Melissa placed a cup of frothy coffee on Rachel's desk and turned to retrieve her own.

'Any messages?'

'No, apart from a . . .' Melissa studied some writing on the palm of her left hand, '. . . Mr Will Raphael. Something about photography lessons. Said you had his number.' She looked up. 'Thinking of a new career?'

'Bloody hell, I forgot – I was supposed to call ages ago – back in August when things looked quiet enough for me to take up a hobby.' She gave a wry smile. 'Steve Betts, the Allday director, recommended him. Damn.'

'I'll call him back if you like,' Melissa offered, remembering the friendly and deferential voice of Mr Raphael with some warmth.

'That's very sweet of you, Mel, but I really feel I ought to do it myself, seeing as I've already left it embarrassingly late. I can't remember where the hell I put his number . . .' Rachel began rifling through the drawer on her right, where she kept receipts and other personal odds and ends.

'Anything else?' Melissa stood in the doorway, coffee in hand, trying not to look disappointed that her quiet Monday had fallen to pieces, while a part of her felt sorry for a woman who had nothing better to do on a day off than come into the office. Not everybody liked Rachel Elliot. She was too smart in every sense, too self-contained for most people's tastes. In the two years that Melissa had worked for her, however, she had developed something of a protective fondness for the woman, based on a recognition that behind the cool and brisk exterior lay a scrupulous sense of fair play and an appealingly dry sense of humour. There were no tricks up her sleeve, no hidden agendas. Unlike some of her fellow directors, who seemed to relish dodging deadlines and dicing with uncertainty, Rachel had a reputation for down-the-line directness and reliability. She fought for creative ideas that she believed in and rejected others out of hand. She made no secret of her ambitions either, a fact which clearly intimidated her male colleagues and which earned her few friends amongst those of her own sex. That she was easily the most senior – and among the most attractive – of the female executives did not exactly help. Nor, in Melissa's view, did it count in her boss's favour that she was so irrefutably single. Unfair though it was, getting as far as Rachel had without publicly shackling herself to a member of the opposite sex seemed to be regarded by her less independent sisters in the business as a form of cheating. The more vitriolic amongst them even liked to rumour, during hair-combing and lipstick sessions in the ladies' lavatory, that the ambitious Ms Elliot had slept her way to the top, via Jarvis and a string of others. Melissa, who knew better than most quite how hard her boss drove herself, and who suspected the existence of a man in New York, doubted this very much indeed. In addition to which, she retained a particularly vivid and poignant image of Rachel alone in her office late one Friday night, crumpled and heaving over a box of tissues. Melissa, who had popped back upstairs from a party in the bar in order to retrieve her make-up bag from the bottom drawer of a filing cabinet, had crept away empty handed, her heart pounding with the guilty sense of having stumbled upon a secret. It wasn't right for anyone to look so alone and sad, especially not on a Friday night. The thought of offering comfort herself flickered and died. Rachel Elliot was not the cry-on-your-shoulder type, not at all. It would have felt like cruelty to intervene.

Jimmy Chartsworth appeared behind Melissa, looking unkempt but somehow dashing, as was his wont, the ashen colour of his face suggesting a weekend of intense social activity, but the sparkle in his eyes telling the world that such habits were to be envied rather than give cause for concern. His office, from where he directed operations on a number of small but flourishing accounts, was opposite Rachel's, on the other side of the quadrille of secretaries, a geographical fact which meant that he was regularly to be found batting his handsome eyelashes shamelessly between the trailing fronds of the pot plants. Melissa, who suffered irritating heart palpitations when it came to Jimmy, sauntered with careful nonchalance across to her desk.

'Good morning, Melissa, my darling.'

'Good morning, Jimmy.'

'Do you really want that delicious cup of foaming caffeine, or are you prepared to donate it to a worthier cause?' He placed both hands on either side of her computer screen and leant right over the desk.

'Stop harassing my secretary, Chartsworth,' called Rachel cheerfully from her office, 'she's got work to do. Come and help yourself if you want.'

Jimmy straightened himself, shoved both hands deep into the pockets of his jacket and offered Rachel a brief bow. 'I might just do that, thank you.' He winked at Melissa before going off in search of a clean mug.

Rachel doodled in the margin of her pad while Frank Alder, European Managing Director of Mallarmé Skincare Products plc, talked at considerable length about the spectrum of marketing and advertising issues facing the company, his gravelly voice reiterating points from presentations she herself had made.

Rachel was beginning to wonder why she had bothered to come into work, why, instead of lounging in bed with tea and papers, she had woken with a start at 6 o'clock, fizzing with energy and impatience. She felt inclined to blame the cat, guileless though it looked, curled up on the end of her bed, its handsome bush of a tail tucked round one broad cheek like a feather pillow. Rachel had wiggled her toes to awaken it and then shooed it out into the dripping brilliance of the garden. Clearly having imagined that hospitality might include breakfast, the cat exited with haughty reluctance, taking up a stiff-backed position just a few feet from the sitting-room door, its glassy green eyes brimming with reproach. Rachel, who feared that feeding itinerant pets might only discourage them from returning to their rightful owners, had observed these reactions with stony resolution, roughly pulling the curtains shut and marching back to her bedroom, where she pretended to enjoy tossing amongst the pillows until the boredom and discomfort grew too much and she got up to run herself a bath.

There was something mildy upsetting about the fact that no one but Melissa seemed to have remembered that she wasn't supposed to be at work at all. Instead of having one of those catch-up days that she had intended, usually only possible on a weekend or bank holiday, she had found herself sucked into the hubbub of account management life. Managers on all the products for which she was responsible buzzed in and out of her office with questions and problems. Ever wary of losing touch with the real business for which she was employed (she had seen colleagues stumble from divorcing themselves too much from the nitty-gritty of account handling) and also being of a nature that found it wrenchingly hard to surrender control of anything, Rachel went with the flow, skipping lunch in the process.

Alan Jarvis was apparently out of bounds until after six o'clock. Waiting to see him was going to make her late for Nathan, whom she had agreed to meet at six-thirty in the foyer of his hotel. She probably wouldn't have bothered – would have asked Melissa to fix something for later in the week – if she hadn't observed for herself that 'out of bounds' meant engrossed in a one-to-one with Cliff Weybourne, the agency's new board director, imported at some considerable expense – transferred like a footballer for an obscene fee – from one of the hotshop agencies that had sprung up on the heels of the recession. What was more, he had been recruited for the specific purpose of leading new business pitches, the agency's record for winning fresh accounts having fallen somewhat over the last year. Rachel, who knew that leading the bid for the Mallarmé account had been the making of her and who believed that going after new business was a treat that should be shared fairly amongst directors suffering the daily grind of servicing difficult accounts, had been sceptical about this appointment from the first. Further acquaintance with the new arrival had done nothing to allay her fears.

Frank Alder had moved onto a meandering analysis of the

imminent launch of Allday Sunlotion. Rachel, while making suitable noises of concurrence, found her thoughts drifting in not altogether professional directions. Bermuda in November. Even after fifteen years in the business it was impossible not to be excited. In these days of tight budgets, shoots in anything beyond converted warehouses were a rare treat. Abandoning her doodle, which had begun as a spider's web but turned into a fat animal face with pointed ears, she cleared her throat in preparation to interrupt. Frank, dear man though he was, could ramble for hours if not taken in hand; he liked to end on a point of impressive gravitas, but sometimes seemed to have trouble finding it.

Rachel seized upon a pause. 'The pre-production meeting is set for the third week in October Frank, just as we agreed. The final draft of the media plan is being drawn up as we speak – a few spots in January to catch the winter sun-seekers and then a real blitz in May and June. It's looking good Frank. All of us on this side of the fence are very excited.'

Nathan Kramer did not like to be kept waiting, especially not when he was jet-lagged and hungry and trying not to drink because he wanted to enjoy wine with dinner and have a clear head for Paris the next day. Though Rachel had rung to explain, very sweetly, that she was running late, he still felt annoyed. They should have skipped meeting up this time after all, he thought, his eyes aimlessly perusing the by now very familiar front page of the *New York Times*, while his stomach whined for food.

But the moment he caught sight of her, emerging head high and eyes alert through the grand swing doors, he changed his mind. Nathan liked powerful women, women whose body language reflected their inner confidence, their soaring levels of self-esteem. His wife had been of a similar mould, too much so, in fact, for the marriage ever to have had a hope of success. Their egos had clashed like Titans. He still saw Melanie sometimes, when business took her to New York; they would lunch in civilised fashion, while he tried to quell the abdominal flutters that the sight of her long, stilettoed legs still provoked, calming them with recollections of how domestic stress had once intervened to turn things sour.

'Hello, Nathan. You look well.' Rachel kissed him on the cheek with cool, unhurried lips that made him instantly want more of the same. 'Sorry about the delay. Office politics, I'm afraid.' She slipped off her jacket and slung it over the arm that was carrying her briefcase. 'Shall we go for a drink somewhere first?'

'Sure, if you like.' He touched her shoulder to bring her attention back to his face. Her eyes looked tired, he thought, noting the faint pouches of fatigue with a little twist of dismay. 'We could go upstairs,' he said quietly, 'you know, do the room service thing. Would you like that?' Rachel, who was struggling with the by now discomfortingly familiar sensation of having arrived at something to which she was looking forward enormously, only to find that it tasted of nothing once she got there, smiled briefly. She was not in the mood for the 'room service thing' at all. Nor was she in the mood for Nathan's all-American-boy grin, telling her he wanted to have sex before dinner. As at the office, she began to wonder what she was doing there, what strange motives had impelled her to come at all.

'I'd like a drink and a sit-down meal, if you don't mind, Nathan. Sorry to be dull. I've had a bit of a day.'

'That's fine, just fine.' His smile tightened into a mask of disappointment. 'Got anywhere in mind?'

'The new Logan place is supposed to be very good. I've been wanting to try it for months,' she lied. 'We could walk it easily from here.'

'Great. Let's go.' He clapped his hands with a heartiness that told her his ego was still bruised and followed her out into the street.

She linked her arm through his for the walk, taking extra care to match her pace to his long strides, wanting to do everything she could to re-establish harmony. While she asked him about work, her mind motored down sliproads of its own. The artificiality of their relationship – the safe containability which had so attracted her five years before – was at last beginning to get her down, she realised, gripping his arm harder as if to hide the thought. She knew herself too well to worry that this might be a sign that she was falling in love with Nathan Kramer or that she wished him to grow emotionally more passionate with her. She associated it instead with the general malaise with which she had been affected in recent weeks, the distinct sense that wherever she longed to be, once she got there, there was nothing but emptiness to hold her hand.

They ate quite quickly, taking up and pursuing lines of communication with professional determination, each wrapped up in preoccupations that felt impossible to share. The restaurant was furnished in the convenient but elegant style that characterised all of Logan's eating haunts, with a menu that was short and expensive enough to make patrons feel they were getting something special. Rachel ate a colourful heap of goat's cheese, chicken and pasta which sat in her stomach afterwards with mystifying obstinacy, dissuading her from joining Nathan with a dessert and thereby contributing to the shadow of a pout that lurked beneath the polite expressions on his handsome face. To make up for it, she invited him back to her flat afterwards, suddenly unable to face the sterile prospect of his hotel room, with the usual clinical brightness of the bathroom and the uncomfortable awareness that other couples, many many other couples, had heaved their way towards sexual climax on its gently creaking bed.

As Rachel led the way into her flat she found herself looking out for the cat. She drew the sitting room curtains more tentatively than usual, her eyes scanning the darkness for any signs of movement. But all was still and quiet. She poured two whiskies, flicked Fauré back into action and went to sit beside Nathan on the sofa.

Nathan felt he had been made to wait a long time, long enough not to be reticent about turning his attentions, after only one sip of whisky, to the pink buttons down the front of Rachel's shirt, each one as enticing as the sugared topping of an iced gem. He used his teeth as well as his hands, licking the skin of her cleavage in a way that Rachel – unless she had fought the emotion hard – might even have found ridiculous.

'I'd better go to the bathroom,' she whispered after a few moments, this being her customary euphemism for inserting her cap.

'Sure, baby, sure.' He lifted his tousled head from her chest, his eyes glazed with a drugged look of arousal. 'I'll wait for you in there, shall I?' He motioned towards her bedroom with his head, his fingers fumbling with the buttons on his own shirt whose badly creased untucked ends reached almost to his knees.

'Yes, if you like.' Rachel picked up her handbag and walked quickly from the room. Once inside the bathroom she closed and bolted the door before leaning back against it, taking deep breaths in through her nose and inwardly cursing the fact that this voluntarily adopted system of irregular sexual encounters offered no guarantee for being in the mood when the possibilities presented themselves. It did not help that her period was due. Her stomach felt unpleasantly bloated and tight; her skin, shining in the bright mirror-light, looked – to Rachel's habitually self-critical eyes – as greasy and blotched as that of a ripening teenager. She got out her powder compact and dabbed hastily across her cheeks, frowning at the realisation that without a sense of her own desirability she could feel little desire. The sight of her cap, with its saggy rubber middle, did little to fast-forward her libido. She sank down onto the bathroom stool for a moment, regarding the contraceptive with distaste, overcome by a sense of absurdity that such an ugly, flimsy thing could mean the difference between conception and sterility, between life and nothing at all.

'You were a long time,' drawled Nathan, trying to keep a sense of injustice from his tone.

'Was I? Sorry.' She slipped into bed beside him and pressed her face to his chest, wanting to stifle the images playing leap-frog inside her head. A faint smell of rubber lingered on her fingertips, reminding her that there was sex and there was procreation, the same act, but worlds apart. While Nathan's mind zigzagged in colourful streaks of its own, unburdened by intellectual preoccupations of any kind, Rachel fought and lost the battle between sensation and thought, her mind homing in instead on an almost palpable sense of the slim rubber barrier planted deep inside. And when, a little later, she cried out, a strange gutteral sound flying from the back of her throat, her lover could not have known that this was no prompt for the celebratory, pumping finale that he offered in response, but rather a cry of protest that the barrier was there at all.

Nathan fell asleep almost at once. Rachel quietly left the bed and returned to the bathroom, feeling strangely tranquil and alert. Her period had come. Usually it was a nuisance; but this time it reassured her. She sat at her kitchen table, both hands rubbing the slight curve of her stomach as the cramps came and went. She could have a child if she wanted to. She was not yet forty. There was still time. She had money. She even had a partner . . . but here the steady march of her thoughts faltered. It was somewhat ironic, she mused ruefully, getting up to fill the kettle, that just as she was facing up to the fact that she had little in common with Nathan Kramer beyond a preference for chocolate-chip ice cream, her heart should take it upon itself to have a volte-face about motherhood. But Nathan was all she had.

Sitting back at the kitchen table, Rachel reached for her shopping list pad and began to draft something of a time-plan. Bermuda in November. Pregnant by December. Baby the following autumn. Three months' maternity leave . . . She stopped abruptly, faintly appalled by her own eagerness to make such crude calculations and by the audacity with which she was banking on Nathan's cooperation. But then Nathan had made no secret of the fact that he did not want children. Which did rather simplify things. She would just have to ask him straight out. Invite him to be an honorary parent – no strings attached. Just how he liked it. She couldn't help smiling. He might even be flattered.

She returned her attentions to her pad. Back to work by the following January at the latest. Aged forty-one. She would be sixty-one when her child was twenty. A young sixty-one, she reassured herself. Not like her own mother, who though a much younger parent, had clearly burnt all bridges with her younger self. Rachel shivered and got up to squeeze out her teabag over the sink. Tiny droplets of brown splashed up its white sides, before starting to dribble down again, like muddy tears. Rachel watched them absently, assailed by familiar, ineradicable childhood memories of not fitting in, of repeatedly disappointing those whose love one needed most.

The spare bedroom could accommodate a nanny. It was large enough for one corner to be sequestered for a shower cubicle. If she moved her computer and desk into the sitting room – there was plenty of unused space down the far end – the study could be transformed into a nursery. The memory of Priscilla Pargiter loomed large. With her help, anything would be possible. But not yet. One step at a time.

Still restless, Rachel padded through into the sitting room and curled up at one end of the sofa, bringing her knees up to her chin and tucking her hands into her armpits. The sense of emptiness, the dissatisfactions of recent weeks, all suddenly seemed to make sense. She had been in denial, as Nathan would have put it, stifling a longing that had at last burst through. She took these last thoughts back to bed with her, where the most vital component of her speculations lay spreadeagled on top of the duvet, small buzzing sounds coming from his nose. He cooperated with the sweetness of a sleeping infant as she gently pushed him over to one side and pulled the duvet up around her shoulders. After one final snort the snoring stopped altogether. Although he had curled up a couple of feet away from her, Rachel could feel the heat of his body spreading through the bed. Having sat for so long in the relative chill of her sitting room, this warmth was welcome indeed, though it triggered no impulses in her to nestle any closer. But it would be nice to want to, she thought sleepily, bringing her knees up to her chest and closing her eyes; it would be nice to want the man as well as the child.

Rachel was awakened by faint grunting sounds coming from the floor. Nathan was doing his exercises, a daily programme of fifty press-ups, fifty sit-ups and some curious hip-swivels done at breakneck speed with his elbows cartwheeling around his ears. Wanting to tease, but warier than usual of bruising her lover's highly sensitised male pride, Rachel sidled past in order to retrieve her dressing gown from the peg on the back of the bedroom door.

'Coffee?'

'Uh.'

'I'll take that as a yes. I can stretch to toast as well, if you like?'

Nathan, at that moment having completed the last of a series of fifty, jumped to his feet and clapped his hands. 'Toast would be great, Rachel.' Sweat was running freely down his nose and temples. A small dark wet patch at the top of his briefs bore testimony to the exertions suffered by the admirable scrubbing board muscles of his torso. Catching sight of himself in Rachel's full-length mirror, he took up a body-building pose. 'Not bad, huh, for a guy who's kissed goodbye to forty?'

'Marvellous,' she replied, smiling as she was meant to, while inwardly she wondered whether it was just nerves, lack of sleep or plain sod's law that was making Nathan suddenly appear so childish and unappealing. 'You're just a little boy at heart, aren't you,' she accused gently, planting a kiss on a dry section of his shoulder.

'They say that's my greatest asset.' He grinned at her before burying his head in a towel and rubbing vigorously.

As she made to leave the room he caught her hand. 'Have we got time . . . ?'

'No, we haven't,' she whispered, putting her mouth to his ear to explain that her period had arrived in the small hours.

Nathan let go at once. He wasn't good with the monthly business; it didn't fit in with any part of the aspect of women that turned him on. It wasn't just the thought of all the blood, it was deeper than that, something to do with the notion that deliciously cool and powerful creatures like Rachel Elliot weren't ultimately in control after all, that in this one aspect they were victims like any ordinary female.

'I'll take a shower.'

Rachel hummed quietly to herself as she moved round the kitchen in bare feet, absently rummaging for breakfast things, while her thoughts floated along in a bubble of their own. Thousands of women had babies without partners. It would be easy. It would be perfect. Problems – as she had learnt from countless husband-related confidences over the years – came from fathers. Even Anita had been known to say it was easier to be a mother when Giles was abroad. When he was around she nagged him to do things, she explained. Whereas, when he was away she was quite happy to cope alone. Husbands who cared more about football results than their families, husbands who preferred pubs to helping with bath-time, husbands who got jealous of their children – Rachel had heard it all. A thousand times.

Of all the relationships with which she was acquainted, the only one which seemed to have arrived at a plateau of mutual satisfaction was between a couple called Naomi and Graham Fullerton, whom Rachel had met in her twenties. Naomi had been a highly respected media buyer at Rachel's first agency, but threw it all in to marry Graham, a premature grandfather of a man with a bushy beard and an infectious throaty laugh. Shortly afterwards they had moved to a small town in Suffolk, where Graham joined a practice of country solicitors while Naomi concentrated on producing a family. They had four girls, the second one of whom, Jessica, was another of Rachel's godchildren. The Fullertons' marital contentment seemed to Rachel, from two decades of biannual weekend visits, to reside with a clear definition of roles. While Graham paid the bills,

Naomi applied all the energy which had once so impressed her bosses into running her home and family. The children emerged from their bedrooms each morning as immaculate as handcrafted dolls, wearing colour-coordinated embroidered smocks and with pretty ribbons neatly securing their glossy plaits and curls. The house itself had been extended, remoulded and improved several times over, while the garden boasted toy-town grids of paths and flowers and climbing frames – not covered in rust and mud like the toppling structure stuffed into one corner of Anita's garden, but each edge and line gleaming with vibrance and colour.

That Naomi Fullerton had made a career out of her family was a fact which had dawned on Rachel many years back. While admiring her friend for the sheer feat of such an achievement, Rachel had never been foolish enough to imagine that she could be happy with such a scenario herself. Somehow, Naomi had learnt to live for the pleasure of other people; for the clockwork precision of domestic routine; for the reward of an appreciative bear hug from her husband at the end of the day. Such selflessness, as Rachel well knew, was simply not within her power. She would have been more like the Anitas of the world, kicking and screaming to the bitter end. Which was probably why she liked Anita better, she thought with a sigh, absently scraping a charred corner of a piece of toast into the pedal bin and making a mental note to call her back that day. Dear, desperate, career-juggling Anita, compromising on all fronts and winning on none. What would she say when Rachel told her of her plans to have a child? The thought was not exactly appealing. Telling people was going to be the hardest part, she realised. Especially at work. Rachel shuddered, for a moment daunted by the prospect of seeing it through.

'Is that for me?' Nathan took the piece of toast from her hand and put it on his plate. 'Sleep OK?'

'Fine, thanks.' She put the butter in front of him and busied herself with chasing truant coffee grains round her mug with a teaspoon.

'Paris should be good.' Nathan spoke energetically through a mouthful of buttered toast. 'We'll be talking about new budgets for old countries. Emerging markets is most definitely where it's at. The opportunities for investment there are fantastic.' His Adam's apple jigged as he swallowed.

'It sounds brilliant,' Rachel enthused, mustering a herculean effort of will to clamber somewhere in the region of his wavelength. 'It's the same with advertising. All our big clients are opening factories over there – Prague, Budapest, Moscow – you name it. We're looking at how to adapt campaigns for those markets all the time. There are millions to be made.'

'You said it. Billions, even.' His eyes twinkled with reassurance. Nathan liked to talk about money. It was something one could latch on to, something to be measured by and feel sure of. 'So when can we do this again?' He licked away a fleck of butter from the corner of his lips and winked at her. 'Not so rushed next time, uh?' He glanced at his watch. 'Shoot, I've got to go. Any chance of a taxi, babe?'

'I'm due for a trip to the States in November,' Rachel offered casually, reaching for the telephone. 'A stop-over on the way to Bermuda. We're shooting a suncream film there. I was planning to see my brother, but if you could make it down from New York . . . save me from my thuggish godson . . .'

'Sounds good to me. Call me soon so we can talk dates. I'll fix something up. Something special, perhaps.'

'Oh, I don't need anything special,' she said quietly, putting down the phone and cupping her hands round the back of his neck. 'Just bring yourself.' At the thought of her deviousness her mouth creased into a small, guilty smile. It would be such a relief to tell him of her plan. When the time was right.

Nathan, who interpreted the wickedness of the smile along quite different lines, increased the pressure of his arms around her back.

'You be a good girl now, you hear?' he said huskily, holding her close. 'You're very special to me, Rachel, very special indeed.'

Anita Cavanagh, aware that the twins were applying paint not only to the paper she had pinned on each side of their easel but also to all reachable sections of the kitchen wall, told herself that it did not matter, that a writer of her experience and calibre could rise above such distractions in order to finish composing a witty feature on the range of facilities offered by London leisure centres.

The background green of her laptop screen shimmered unhelpfully. Outside, the rain danced off the windowsill; beyond, she could see the thinning grass of their meagre lawn, rapidly being converted to a sea of mud. The twins would love it, she thought glumly, recalling their recent clamour to be let out of the house, how their breath had steamed up the glass panels of the back door as they scrabbled to be released, like puppies wanting a walk. Only four more months, she told herself, before the blissful release of nursery school and the unimaginably wonderful prospect of five mornings to herself.

Bored of flat surfaces, the twins had begun painting each other, beginning with their faces and hands and then moving on to their clothes. Anita glanced up at the clock. Almost twelve, thank God. Almost the witching hour. Two minutes early wouldn't harm. It had been a hellish morning after all. The wine box sat on a shelf above the washing machine in the utility room. Taking a tumbler from the dishwasher she slipped out of the kitchen, willing the twins not to follow. Resisting the urge to swig, she took several sips in quick succession, standing alone with only the whirr of spinning sheets beside her and the sound of rain on the roof overhead. A few seconds' peace. Exquisite.

'Me and Eddie are tigers,' roared Laura when their mother reappeared a few minutes later. They growled and leapt under the skirts of the kitchen tablecloth while she managed to pretend to be scared and to tap out a few quite incisive sentences all at the same time.

'You tigers are going to need a bath,' she said, laughing in spite of herself at the sight of their round smeary faces and matted hair and shooing them upstairs.

Leaving her offspring splashing noisily amongst a fleet of plastic vehicles, Anita slipped back down to the kitchen and gave herself a refill before settling down to call Rachel. Supremely cool, terrifyingly successful and wonderfully kind Rachel, whom she couldn't help liking enormously, even if being near her was inclined to make one feel like a rough pebble beside a polished stone. Rachel was her oasis of sanity, a tireless fount of objectivity and strength, someone to help crisis-lurching part-time mothers get everything back in perspective again.

They had met back in the late seventies, in the days when Rachel was still buying space in magazines and Anita was writing articles for *Campaign*, the magazine which agencies loved to slander, but to which they all pandered shamelessly none the less. Having come to interview Rachel for a tiny and uninspired piece on the escalating costs of media space, she ended up taking her out for a long and very enjoyable lunch. They talked with that ease peculiar to women who sense interests in common; Anita made no secret of her long-term hopes, how she was using *Campaign* as a ladder rung towards much dizzier heights of journalistic achievement. Rachel, though more guarded about her own ambitions, had been wonderfully receptive and encouraging, quite unafraid to speak her mind.

But Anita's career plans had not counted on the knee-knocking charms of one Giles Cavanagh, a keen young political journalist with an ambitious agenda of his own. From almost the moment they met, Anita somehow found herself subjugating the needs of her career to that of her lover's, initially because she was besotted, and then later because a pattern had been set and she was terrified of being deserted. Even before they eventually got married, given the choice of regular work in London or accompanying Giles on a spell abroad, Anita would invariably choose the latter, thereby securing the continuance of the relationship but at an immeasurable cost to herself. Gradually the demand for her work dwindled. Hardly surprising for a freelance without a speciality who was seldom there.

The Cavanaghs' first child, Charlotte, to whom Rachel was godmother, was born when Anita was thirty-three and desperate for something to fill the disappointment left by the failings of her career. Although motherhood certainly provided consolation of a kind, it came as quite a shock too; not just because Charlotte's three-hour colic-screaming sessions lasted for four solid months, but also because of the unutterable enslavement of it all. That Giles could continue flying out to hot spots at a moment's notice, while his wife was tied to a treadmill of on-tap feeding and broken nights, only served to heighten this sense of entrapment. Given such a context, the decision to have a second child was hard. But Anita, having suffered as an only child herself, was adamant that Charlotte should not have to do the same. The news that she was pregnant with twins was a shock of almost catastrophic proportions, the sole redeeming feature being that Giles, deeply affected himself, came up trumps by engineering an admirable phase of home-based work that lasted well into Eddie and Laura's second year. While doing a lot in terms of acquainting their father with the delights of caring for small infants, it was not so helpful where the marriage itself was concerned. It often seemed to Anita that the two of them now sat on opposite ends of an unstoppable see-saw of resentment and envy, typically characterised by spiralling arguments-cum-discussions as to whose suffering was the greatest. A large mortgage taken out on a dilapidated Camden maisonette during the late eighties meant there was little prospect of alleviating the mundane miseries of their situation with extravagances like nannies and second cars. It was all they could do to manage two weeks a year on an English beach.

'If it wasn't for you,' Anita reminded Rachel on the phone on the morning of the twins' spectacularly creative painting session, 'I think I would go barmy.' Guilt at having left the children unattended in the bath for too long was making her gabble. 'The twins between them have just about repainted the kitchen walls – limey green and orange – it's quite ghastly.' The thought of Rachel sitting in a broad-backed swivel-chair before a vast, orderly desk prompted a fresh gulp of wine.

'Poor Anita,' murmured Rachel, unable to resist the thought that alternative and more acceptable forms of entertainment could have been found for bored three year olds and that it was typical of Anita to have let a situation slip beyond her control. She began to flick through the pages of her diary in order to settle upon a suitable evening on which to meet. It was not easy. A reputation for working late led inevitably to the arrangement of early-evening meetings, which could run on until all hours. Saturday night was free, but she had promised to drive to her parents for lunch on the Sunday and did not want to be up till all hours the night before. 'How about next Thursday?' she suggested, making a mental note to tell Melissa not to book anything for after six that afternoon.

'Next Thursday. Wonderful. Perfect. I'll stay the night, if that's OK.'

'Would you like to check it with Giles . . . ?'

'Absolutely not.' There was something faintly reckless in Anita's tone which triggered the jangle of old alarm bells.

'We could make it sooner if you like . . . I could do Saturday . . .'

'Nope. Thursday's great. Better fish the kids out of the bath. 'Spect it will be dyed yellow like the walls. Bye for now.' There was a giggle before the line went dead.

'Shit,' said Rachel, loud enough for Melissa, who sat closest to her open door, to turn and raise an eyebrow at a colleague. 'Stupid, stupid girl.' Rachel gathered up the papers she needed for Jarvis's bi-weekly board meeting and left her office still muttering under her breath. Should she phone Giles, she wondered, or pretend she hadn't noticed? It was so hard to know how far to interfere or leave well alone. Besides which, Anita would deny it, like she always did, before shame or common sense or God knows what prompted her to dry herself out again.

As Rachel strode down the stretch of lush, cornflower carpeting that led towards the most salubrious of the agency's conference rooms, the one that Alan Jarvis rather pompously insisted on using for any meeting that required his presence, she caught herself wishing for someone in whom she could confide. Friends like Anita were so needy, so brimming over with intimate revelations of their own, that it was hard to reverse the process, especially for one more inclined to cope with emotional dramas on her own. It was so much easier to be depended on, she thought with a sigh, taking her seat at the middle of the long, polished mahogany table, so much easier being the one to listen instead of the one to speak. The only person with whom anything like the reverse had been true was Robbie Dexter, the boyfriend of two decades ago whom she had finally jettisoned during a damp camping holiday in Wales. Dear Robbie, so dogged and unjudgemental, so eager – even at the tender age of twenty-five – to dig in and settle down. As the first grand passion of both their lives and with a history of courtship that stretched back to their teens, breaking up had been hard. The reassurance of such unquestioning love, which had so eased the passage from late teens to adulthood, from school to work, from home to living in a bed-sit in London, was something for which Rachel would always be grateful. The crunch had come with Robbie's decision to start his own landscape gardening business in Cornwall and an invitation for her to accompany him. After a few weeks of cowardly prevarication, Rachel finally settled matters in a leaky two-man tent at the bottom of a verdant Welsh valley. Hurt, but pitiably forgiving, Robbie had sloped off into his new life like a beaten dog. A trickle of cryptic postcards featuring geographical highlights of the Lizard Peninsula followed for a while; but after a few months even these brief connections had faltered and died.

Rachel smiled absently at the other senior members of the agency drifting in to take their seats, her thoughts meandering from peculiarly tender recollections of Robbie to her forth-coming trip. She twisted the pencil in her fingers. As far as her cycle was concerned, the dates were unbelievably perfect. One encounter with Nathan might even be enough. If luck was on her side. She sipped some water, suppressing a smile.

'Are you with us, Rachel?'

She glanced up, blinking the dreaminess from her eyes. 'Not remotely, Alan, but do go ahead. I'll join you when I'm ready.'

Alan Jarvis chortled, appreciating as always the cool self-possession of the one female in the agency senior enough to attend his board meetings. He rapped his knuckles on the table and cleared his throat, before rattling through the agenda with characteristic haste.

When it came to the matter of problem accounts Rachel spoke up unhesitatingly about Blackers, using the direct approach which she knew was the one most likely to be respected.

'Alan, we've been too generous for too long. Blackers is nothing but trouble and a time-consuming one at that. It's time to resign the business. They have no budget for next year. They do nothing but phone up with absurd requests for data and analyses which their own marketing people should be perfectly capable of producing. There's still the question of Quantum's research – which they commissioned and now say we should pay for. I say we cut our losses and get out.'

Alan Jarvis eyed her over the top of his half-moon spectacles. 'Not like you to turn from a fight, Rachel.'

She swallowed hard. 'It's not a fight worth winning. They've got nothing in the pipeline. They're in deep financial trouble. They'll be out of business by Christmas and in the meantime we are just wasting our time.'

'The word is they're about to be taken over. Could be a very good prospect indeed a few months from now.' It was Cliff Weybourne, the new recruit, who spoke. His head was angled towards the top end of the table so that Rachel could only see the side of his face and not its full expression. There was a puffiness to his cheeks and neck, bearing out the rumours of too much good living. Though cleverly tailored to disguise the curving bulge of his torso, it was clear that he was considerably overweight. As if sensitive of these physical imperfections, he had a habit of constantly adjusting his wide power-ties as he talked, tweaking them down over the buttons of his shirt, as if hoping to conceal some of the expanse that heaved behind.

'You're welcome to take them on, Cliff,' Rachel said sweetly, fixing her eyes on his face until he was forced to turn and acknowledge her presence. She held out both hands. 'Blackers are all yours. With my love.'

'That's very kind, Rachel, but I've got a lot on my plate.'

'Ah ... yes of course. New business. Silly me.' She returned her attention to the head of the table, aware that the chill in the atmosphere was now obvious to everyone else in the room. It made her afraid, but she pressed on. 'I want out, Alan. Mallarmé is launching new products all over the place – you've seen Alder's five-year plan – I really think my time would be better spent concentrating on servicing them. Their advertising spend could literally double in the next couple of years.'

'Yes, yes. I was coming to Mallarmé.' Alan Jarvis placed both hands on the table and leant forward. 'We seem to have finished apart from that. If there's no other business,' he removed his glasses and began polishing them with one of the paper napkins stacked beside the plate of biscuits in the middle of the table, 'perhaps the rest of you would be happy to leave. I know you're all busy. If Rachel and Cliff could give me just a few moments longer. Thank you all so much.' He slotted his glasses back into the dent on his nose and examined the end of his pencil while the other directors trooped out.

'The Mallarmé Christmas weekend thing. I'd like Cliff to be involved.'

'Whatever for?' For the last five years Rachel had organised what she jokingly called her annual 'bonding session' with Frank Alder, when sixteen representatives from the client and agency were invited to spend two days billeted in a country hotel, getting to know each other over pleasant food and hearty, fashionable activities like go-cart racing and clay pigeon shooting. It had been Rachel's idea in the first place, after a dicey year in which client–agency relations had grown dangerously strained over a botched launch of a product that turned out to cause allergic rashes if used too generously on dry skins. The first weekend had been such a success that it was now a regular feature in the hectic December schedule.

Cliff Weybourne, blinking expressionless eyes at the print of Impressionist waterlilies above Rachel's head, remained silent. His eyelashes were very short, Rachel noticed, hardly visible at all.

Alan Jarvis was firm. 'You're right, they are expanding rapidly. I don't want them giving business to other agencies. Cliff has a lot of experience launching new products in this market. I think it would be useful for him to get to know some of the Mallarmé team.'

'They can have lunch, then. I'll arrange it.'

'Rachel, Rachel,' Alan Jarvis's tone was growing weary. He had been in the business long enough to know that women were more prone to displays of emotion than men, but he was not in the mood for pussyfooting around feelings, especially not Rachel Elliot's, a lady with enough experience to know better. 'Rachel, I forbid you to take this personally. It's pure business sense. By all means introduce them beforehand if you want to, my dear. But that weekend is in Cliff's diary and I want it to stay there.'

She hated it when he called her 'my dear', the element of patronage in his tone redolent not just of his ultimate, inarguable seniority, but also of his maleness. There was no equivalent to a 'my dear' for any of the men who sat round that table, she thought furiously, stacking her papers to hide the tremble in her hands.

'And there's to be no ill-feeling about this, Rachel. You know as well as I do that any whiff of dissension in the home ranks can be the cause of the most terrible trouble.'

'No ill-feeling at all, Alan.' Her eyes glittered. 'I'll tell Frank Alder immediately. He'll be thrilled.'

'As indeed am I, Rachel.' Cliff Weybourne extended his hand across the table, reaching so far that the swell of his belly rested on its polished surface. Rachel accepted the hand without meeting the triumphant gaze of the small black eyes. Her dislike of the man intensified in those moments, extending beyond professional distrust of his motives and methods, to something infinitely more personal and instinctive. She squeezed the fat fingers only briefly, before slipping free and leaving the room.

Stuck to her desk was a yellow post-it note in Melissa's writing.

'Will Raphael called again. No message.'

'Damn,' Rachel murmured, screwing the piece of paper up into a tiny ball and then flicking it towards an ashtray full of paper-clips. She still hadn't called back. How unforgivably rude. With fresh determination, she dug around the drawers of her desk for his number, before spotting it pinned under the pot in which she kept her pens and pencils. Photography lessons indeed, she thought, pressing the digits; who had she been trying to fool?

Impatient now to get the call over with, she took two deep breaths while waiting for the receiver to be picked up. But the rings were abruptly interrupted by a recorded message.

'*This is Will. Please talk to me.*' There followed a short beep, so short that Rachel found herself hesitating.

'Er . . . Rachel Elliot speaking – Steve Betts' colleague at McKenzie Cartwright. Returning your call – sorry for not having got back to you sooner – thank you so much for offering to help, but actually I've changed my mind – I mean I simply do not have time to learn about photography or anything else outside work at the moment. Sorry to have bothered you unnecessarily and . . . um . . . thanks again – very much.'

She replaced the receiver, slightly disappointed at her own incoherence, but relieved that the whole matter had at last been resolved without the potentially awkward necessity of personal contact.

She took several more deep breaths before picking up the phone again. Calling Frank Alder was going to be much harder. The man knew her well. If she was not to give away any hint of dissatisfaction with regard to Cliff Weybourne's involvement in the account, she was going to have to deliver a very tight performance indeed. Alan Jarvis was right if only in that respect alone; one hint of agency discord was enough to send clients scurrying for cover; and before you knew it all sorts of destructive rot could set in.

Margaret Elliot flicked the kettle switch on, waited ten seconds and then fed two slices of thick white bread into the toaster. She had been married to Henry Elliot too long to think it inconvenient or odd that it gave her husband pleasure to see the kettle boil and the toast pop at the same time. Wanting to grant her spouse the prospect of the simultaneous enjoyment of warm toast and slurpable tea was one of innumerable small rituals which had become embedded in the routine of the Elliots' daily life; using the flowered crockery at breakfast was another, the striped cups having, at some indefinable juncture in their lives, been consigned to the demands of tea-time, together with the restorative powers of two digestive biscuits, balanced on the left-hand side of the saucer, opposite the teaspoon. Cake, like church and apple crumble, was for Sundays. Deep down, Margaret Elliot acknowledged the comfort of such rituals, the way they precluded the necessity of choice-making and self-doubt. Time had to be managed very carefully, she found, especially after a certain age. The awful business of Henry's early retirement had taught her that, if nothing else. All those dreadful days of door-slamming and angry silences, underlined by the shouting but unmentioned feeling that she, Margaret Bowling, was not enough, that without the British Army to sustain him, Henry believed his life to be worthless. Echoes of such feelings, the sense of time dragging till it hurt, still reverberated at the back of her mind, reminders, if she ever needed them, that the present system, regimented and inflexible though it was, was infinitely preferable in every respect.

She gave the teabags one good stir before placing both the pot and the toast rack on the table. Though she was looking forward to seeing her daughter, she felt apprehensive too. Rachel was always so fiery and unpredictable, so prone to speak her mind. It drove Henry mad. Visits from her brothers, even now, with wives and children in tow, always seemed to pass off so much more smoothly. But then, as Margaret had said and thought many times in her life, boys were easier than girls right from the start: big appetites and big hearts. None of those impenetrable, cunning sulks which had so punctuated Rachel's girlhood; none of that baffling unhappiness, the selfish obstinacy to go her own way no matter what.

'Jam or marmalade, dear?' she asked, pouring tea into the large, bone china cup beside her husband and substituting a plate for the cereal bowl which had contained the spoonful of prunes which Henry consumed in the interests of keeping himself regular. Margaret herself had recently developed a bold preference for cod liver oil capsules to achieve the same purpose. Though it was a question she had posed most mornings of the forty-seven years of their married life, the answer was one that she had never mastered the art of anticipating.

'Jam, I think.' Henry Elliot patted his moustache with his napkin and folded the paper for a better view of the columns on the lower half. 'Blackberry.'

'Blackberry? Ah yes, there's a little left, just enough. I'll put it on the list for tomorrow.'

'Very good.'

Margaret wanted to talk about lunch, about which she was feeling increasingly nervous. In the days when Henry had been a lieutenant-colonel she had prepared meals on a grand scale as a matter of course. She had kept a red leather notebook in which she wrote the names of the guests and details of what she had served, so as to preclude the possibility of lumbering any second-time visitor with the burden of having to consume the same dish. There had been another book, too, a gift from Henry's dear mother, all about place settings and how to make napkins look like doves, and which side to serve and take away. Coming from very humble origins herself, Margaret had been quite overwhelmed by the glamour of it all, painfully aware of the importance of not letting Henry down, of not getting in the way – as bad wives were rumoured to do – of promotion. Such books were now stowed away in a plastic box on one of the spotless shelves in their spacious attic, in between Duncan's train set and Henry's camera equipment, dating back to the now unmentionable difficult patch, when cameras had been one of the many instruments taken up and abandoned during that first shocking emptiness of retirement.

Margaret spread a thin layer of marmalade across the swathe of butter she had applied to her own toast and began eating, all the while watching for a break in Henry's concentration on the headlines, a chink that would allow her in, allow her to say that she was nervous about the day. It wasn't just the thought of Rachel that made her so, for there were to be other guests too. The new vicar was coming, together with his son, whom she had heard was a delight, but whom she had only ever eyed from a distance. It was the notion of the son which now troubled her, since the invitation had been extended to him with Rachel in mind, a fact of which she feared Rachel could not fail to be aware and about which she was now having severe second thoughts. But it was so hard to stop trying, so hard to give up on hopes of happiness where one's closest family was concerned.

At the petrol station Rachel bought some flowers and a box of assorted chocolates. Though there was a distinctly autumnal chill in the air she had decided to drive with the roof down, so as to make the most of the sunshine. While waiting to sign for her purchases she fiddled with the loose corners of the green silk scarf which she had wrapped around her head to protect her hair from the wind, tucking it into the polo neck of her bottle-green jumper – a favourite old cashmere that went well with the dark caramel of her corduroy trousers. That her parents made a habit of dressing up on Sundays had always induced in her the wicked urge to do the opposite.

The man at the cash till winked when he handed Rachel her credit card and receipt. Rachel offered a weak smile in return, uncertain whether the facial gesture was friendly or lascivious. At thirty-nine it was no longer possible to be sure of one's judgement about such things. Upon reaching her car, she glanced back in his direction to see if the look had been followed up by a more sustained show of appreciation; but the man's attention was focused on his next customer. Chiding herself for caring even a little, Rachel carefully laid the freesias and chocolates on the passenger seat and continued on her way.

As she sped through the bedraggled suburbs of west London she could not help wishing that she was driving somewhere other than Gerrard's Cross, somewhere altogether more suited to the inspiring crispness of the day, the sense that life, after all, might be full of new beginnings. The thought of seeing her parents again engendered the usual mesh of complicated feelings, not the least of these being a tireless hope that this time it would go well, that this time there would be no disappointment, no sense that, deep down, they cared for nothing but themselves.

'Hello, Mother. How are you?'

'Not so bad, thank you dear.' There followed a fractional pause, a pause that seemed to embrace the whole flawed history of their relationship, as Margaret took in her daughter's appearance before holding out both arms for an embrace. 'But darling, how lovely to see you, and looking so ... so ... *fashionable* too. Flowers *and* chocolates – how sweet. Come in. Your father's in the drawing room.'

As Rachel stepped inside she was assailed by the familiar, uncategorisable scents of her childhood, together with the usual discomforting sense of not being at home. The Gerrard's Cross house, to which her parents had moved shortly after her father's retirement, had always struck her as the most soulless of resting places, not just because the house itself was of unattractive grey brick, with big, unimaginative square rooms, but also because it was surrounded by expensive, spacious residences equally lacking in interest or originality. A roost for the disappointed middle-class, Robbie had called it once, encapsulating her thoughts with that knack he sometimes had.

'Rachel, my dear.' Henry Elliot put down his pipe and levered himself out of his armchair. 'Good to see you, good to see you.' The thatch of his moustache prickled her cheek in exactly the spot it always did. The sweet smell of his tobacco hung not only in the air but also in the tweed of his jacket, in the folds of skin visible over the top of his shirt collar. He wore a dark blue and green striped tie with some military emblem stitched into the middle of it. 'Shall we have sherry now, Margaret, or wait for the others?'

'The others?'

Margaret Elliot wrung her hands under the crisp white front of her apron. 'Just the vicar. And his son.'

'I didn't know Reverend Timms had a son.'

'No, he doesn't. This is a new one. Reverend Berenson. Your father and I like him very much, don't we, Henry? Not so lively as Reverend Timms, but terribly clever. His wife passed away several years ago. Stomach cancer.'

'How sad,' Rachel murmured.

'His faith helped him through,' added her mother soulfully. She extracted her hands from their hiding place and pressed them together in a movement suggestive of prayer.

'I'll get the sherry, then,' put in Henry, using brisk tones reserved for any occasion threatened by the intrusion of sentimentality.

'Could I have wine instead? Would you mind, Dad?' Rachel shuddered at the thought of the sweet sherry which constituted her parents' favourite pre-prandial tipple. 'Only if you've a bottle going, of course. I'm really not bothered.'

'We've got the one for lunch . . .' began Margaret, casting a questioning look at her husband.

'No matter, no matter. I'll fetch another from the cellar.'

'No honestly, I'll leave it. Please, don't go to any trouble, Dad.'

But her father was already on his way to examine his precious wine stocks, under the guise of wanting to please, but the set of his body telling Rachel that, only minutes after her arrival in the house, old rhythms were re-establishing themselves, that no matter how she hoped and tried, there would never be any escape from the repressive cycles which had spun through the phases of her youth. She had her role and she was stuck with it: difficult Rachel, aged thirty-nine, going on twelve.

Reverend Berenson worked so hard at giving the impression of erudition that Rachel found herself suspecting a history of frustrated scholarliness, a shadow of a sense that deep down the vicar believed himself more suited to ministering to the needs of an Oxford college than the cultural wasteland of a suburban metropolis. While giving the impression of conversing, he in fact dominated the lunch table to an almost offensive degree, steering each subject and sentence towards his own aims, using every attempt of Rachel's to expand the dialogue as a platform for further anecdotes or expostulations of his own. Her parents clucked and swooned appreciatively, clearly happy to labour under the illusion that they were basking in the presence of an intellect far superior to their own. Their daughter, however, found herself chewing unnecessarily hard on her thin slices of roast beef, forcing herself not to step out of line and pondering bitterly on the pitiable lack of conversational energy being shown by the wordless, bespectacled, thirty-something son, so thoughtfully positioned opposite her.

There were enough established channels of contention on the subject of her single status for Rachel to perceive at once that Luke Berenson had been invited with her own interests very much in mind, and for her at the same time to manage to rise above the appalling implications behind this fact in order to defy her mother with indifference. Lack of skill or success in this particular branch of social engineering had never deterred Mrs Elliot's persistence: there had been other sons in the past, other brothers or cousins, invited along under the pretext of being granted the privilege of sampling Mrs Elliot's home cooking, but in reality to be viewed as prospective husbands for her daughter. Rachel was far too inured to these clumsy Mrs Bennet-style tactics to care. What she did not, and could not forgive her parents for, was their unshakeable belief that it was some failing in her that had resulted in the kind of life she led, that it was because no man had felt able to take her on, that caused her to remain single. On occasions they still referred regretfully to the departure of Robbie, all subsequent evidence of their daughter's love life being so paltry as to convince them that she had thrown away her best chance at twenty-five.

'Do you stay with your father often, Luke?' Rachel asked now, handing over the cream jug and using a sugary voice which she reserved for those she despised most.

He raised his eyes from an intimidatingly full bowl of stodgy raisin and apple crumble and smiled for the first time since they had all sat down. It was a nice smile too, broad enough to cause the large wire frames of his spectacles to shift position where they rested on his cheeks.

'Now and then, like any dutiful child.' His voice was flat and dry. Doing justice to the dessert presented a new pretext for absorbing all his energies. She wondered exactly how old he was. In spite of a fresh, almost cherubic face, there were wires of grey running through the sweep of sandy hair pushed back off his forehead and in the more closely shaven section just above his ears.

'Luke works in the Inner Temple,' put in Margaret, her eyes bright with admiration.

'How nice for him.' Rachel, reckless with disappointment and irritation, could feel herself in danger of being rude. 'The Inner Temple. Wow.'

'Both our boys are doctors,' put in Henry quickly, 'one in Scotland and the other in Washington DC.'

'Marvellous,' exclaimed the reverend. 'And what do you do, Rachel, to keep the wolf from the door?'

'There are no wolves at my door, reverend,' she replied, thinking for some reason of the cat. 'I work in advertising. I'm a board dir—'

'Advertising, eh?' He put down his spoon, his beady brown eyes twinkling in an unbecomingly adversarial way which put Rachel on her guard. 'That must be very . . . stimulating for you.'

'Stimulating? It's hard work, certainly.' Keep calm, she told herself, keep calm. There was no point in minding whether she impressed this man or not. It did not matter what he thought of her or her profession. She knew all the arguments backwards, having defended herself round countless tables, where people with less interesting, less well paid but traditionally more revered professions began by discussing their favourite adverts, asked her if she was responsible for any of them and then concluded with a jolly round of – invariably ill-informed – slating of the industry as a whole.

'A lot of wasted talent in advertising, so they say.'

'Do they?'

'Well, it's no secret that we've always felt Rachel could have done a lot better for herself. But there you are,' Henry folded his napkin into a neat square which he lined up exactly parallel to his place mat, 'that's children for you.'

'They will go their own way, won't they?' chimed Margaret, nodding her head at Rachel in a show of fond maternal despair.

'Thoughtless of us, isn't it,' agreed Rachel, her eyes ablaze.

'Now Rachel,' warned her father, detecting the same spirit of confrontation which had prompted defiant nocturnal cot-clambering some thirty-eight years before.

'I'd love to be in advertising,' said Luke Berenson, quietly, but with great determination. 'Those beer ones are my favourite, the ones with the eskimo and the talking polar bear. Brilliant. Have me in stitches every time. I don't care whether it sells more of the stuff, it's like comedy in its own right.'

'Thank you,' breathed Rachel, sinking back into her chair, forcing herself to remain calm.

At which point their spiritual elder, clearly unimpressed by the turn the conversation was taking, embarked upon a short account of his passion for the writings of Matthew Arnold, concluding with a recitation of the final stanza from 'Dover Beach'. Throughout this discourse Rachel noticed how Luke concentrated on arranging his spoon and fork over the top of a wedge of uneaten pudding, pushing down hard, as if hoping to compress the remains out of sight entirely.

Margaret Elliot, apparently not having witnessed anything to discourage the prospect of a relationship between her daughter and the vicar's son, suggested that the 'young ones' take themselves on a walk, while the less advantaged supped a glass of port. It reminded Rachel of being commandeered to play as a child, usually with a strange and unfriendly-looking counterpart, as if having fun was something that could be taken up and dispensed with at will, without effort or cost or inspiration.

But it was wonderful to get out of the house. Luke led the way down the narrow gravel path to the front gate, his hands thrust deep into the pockets of his blue chino trousers, his shoulders and neck hunched, as if in preparation for a low-beamed door. When he reached the pavement he stopped and waited for her to catch up. Behind them Margaret waved before closing the door.

'Christ, I'm sorry.' He shook his head miserably. 'Insufferable. I should never have agreed to come. Sorry.'

Rachel, delighted by the revelation of emotions that matched her own, burst out laughing. 'Oh sod them all. Let's walk.'

'And he got poor old Matthew Arnold all wrong,' he added, as they set off down the street, scuffling through the shallow trail of curling brown leaves. 'He always says "vast edges blear" instead of "drear" – it drives me nuts every time. But there's no point in saying anything. He won't listen. He never does. Never has. Too many sermons perhaps,' he muttered, kicking a stone. 'Too much time telling other people how to live their lives.'

They walked on in silence for a bit. The air was thick with the sweet smell of rotting leaves. Rachel concentrated on her breathing, matching each exhalation to every stride, restraining herself from an eager concurrence with these opinions. In her experience criticising parents was the prerogative of their children. Outsiders had to be very careful indeed.

'I suppose I was invited for you, sort of thing,' he said at length.

She grinned, in spite of herself. 'Yes, I think that just about sums it up.'

'Sorry.'

'I wish you'd stop apologising. It's hardly your fault. Although I'm nearly forty my mother has retained the flattering habit of regarding me as a reluctant wallflower who needs help filling her dance card. Dad's not much better. I should apologise to you. Parents like mine are a rare treat.'

Having crossed several tree-lined roads, they arrived at some railings guarding a large rectangle of green, the near corner of which housed a metal climbing frame in the shape of a pirate ship. A wet start to October had allowed the grass to recover some lushness after the ravages of a peculiarly tropical summer, while the foliage of the trees skirting its edges blinked prettily with spots of red and burnished gold.

'There's just one snag,' remarked Luke, holding open the gate for her and standing to one side to let her through, 'of which I suspect your mother is unaware.'

'One snag to what?'

'To any joyful coupling that she may have in mind.'

'And what's that?'

It was his turn to laugh, all the strains of lunch clearly far from his mind. 'I'm gay.'

Rachel slapped her thigh and let out a whoop of mirth. 'Oh great – oh I love it – that has absolutely made my day – I'd give anything to tell her.'

His face crumpled with dismay. 'I'd rather you didn't . . .'

'Don't worry.' She swallowed the laugh at once, reading genuine alarm in his sombre brown eyes. 'Of course I won't. I wouldn't dream of breathing a word.'

As they strolled round the perimeter of the playing field, half under the verdant awning of trees, a quieter mood settled upon them, bringing with it a quite unexpected sense of intimacy.

'My mother would have understood, but I hadn't come to terms with it myself when she was alive. As for my father . . . well you saw for yourself. I've done my best for him – I don't really like the law, but it earns me a good living and it keeps him of my back. I'd really like to be a nurse – something more caring – though I know it sounds corny and you're probably creasing up inside.'

'No, no I'm not at all. There are heaps of things I could never say to my parents, things they could never understand . . .'

'Like?'

'Like I'm nearly forty and I want a child but not a husband.'

'Brilliant. Go for it.'

She stopped and turned. 'I'm going to.' She laughed, brushing the hair back from her eyes and shaking her face at the wintry blue sky. 'I'm really going to.'

They arrived at the pirate ship just as a cluster of whining children were being herded back out into the street. Luke climbed to the top of the metal ladder-cum-mast and swung himself out to one side, holding on with only one arm. 'You can buy brochures on genetically suitable partners these days, can't you?'

Rachel, who was leaning up against the rungs beneath him, secretly marvelling at the looseness of her tongue before a virtual stranger, caught herself grappling with the impulse to say even more. But at the same time she distrusted it.

'I have a suitable partner in mind, actually . . .' she ventured.

'That's lucky.' He began to clamber down.

The sun seemed to be pulling back from the world, not so much lowering itself as withdrawing, taking with it what was left of the warmth of the afternoon. Rachel shivered and burrowed her hands into the sleeves of her jumper, the fingers of each hand gripping the wrists of the other for warmth. 'I could not do it the clinical way,' she began. 'I . . . I don't know why, I just . . . couldn't.' She shuddered. 'Not my style.'

'I suppose you are sure, are you? I mean, there might be other reasons why—'

'Absolutely sure,' she cut in at once, riled by this odd combination of timidity and presumption. 'I've always been one to know my own mind.'

'Yes, I can believe that all right,' he murmured, his eyes twinkling behind the large circles of his glasses.

'And I have every reason to believe that I shall succeed. We Elliot women are very fertile, you know,' she declared stoutly, shaking her hands free of her jumper sleeves and blowing on her fingers. 'My mother,' she added with a scowl, 'has been known to take pleasure in reminding me of the fact.'

'Your mother . . . there's an intriguing thought. How will she take it, do you suppose?'

'My mother will be appalled. So will my father.'

'You're braver than me,' he said quietly, linking his arm through hers as they walked back to the park gate. 'I've got friends who have told their parents they're homosexual and, with a few beautiful exceptions, it's been very hard for all concerned. My . . . my partner was one of the lucky ones. His parents are wonderful.'

'Does he work in the Inner Temple too?' she asked, mimicking the hallowed tones adopted earlier on by her mother, in the hope of erasing some of the seriousness from his face.

'He died.'

'Oh dear, I'm so sorry.' She looked at her feet, cursing herself for being inept, for not reading the signs with more care.

'Yeah, so am I. Not yet ready to talk about it, I'm afraid. Not cross or anything. Just can't talk.'

She saw that he was swallowing and looked away.

'Better get back.'

'Yeah.'

'I'll tell my parents we fell in love and want a spring wedding.'

He chuckled at that, but did not look at her again.

By the time they arrived back at the dejected remains of a fuschia that tumbled along the low wall bordering her parents' front garden, Luke had recovered his composure. Rachel plucked off one of the drooping crimson flowers and squeezed it between her fingers. 'Er . . . thank you,' she muttered, flicking the crushed petals to the ground, 'usually my role is something akin to the Marj Proops of middle-class England. I don't tell people things.'

Behind him the sun was just sinking below the roofs of the houses on the opposite side of the street, illuminating their edges with a fiery orange glow. The effect was to make Luke look paler than ever, and much younger suddenly. Clearly embarrassed by the compliment, he took off his glasses and began polishing them on the baggy hem of his jumper. His eyes were a pretty almond shape, she noticed, trimmed with absurdly long sandy lashes.

'Well, we made friends, didn't we?' he remarked, slipping his glasses back on and leading the way up the path. 'Just like we were supposed to. And no hanky panky at all,' he added with a chuckle.

'There's still time,' she said, the sight of her mother's pale face bobbing behind a curtain, stirring her, as always, towards mischief.

I have decided to have a child.

Rachel had been avoiding her diary for days, deterred by some deep reflexive fear of committing such an enormous decision to the concrete whiteness of the page. Even now she had deliberately picked a moment that was hurried, a snatched slot of time before the door bell went, heralding the appearance of Anita with that striking swathe of grey ripping through the middle of her short black hair – the twins' calling card, she liked to call it – and that worryingly hysterical enthusiasm at having escaped her family.

Rachel paused, aware, as always, that she wrote for an invisible audience, one that heard and judged. It was important to sound lucid.

I have decided to ask Nathan to do the honours (!) when we meet in a few weeks' time on my way to Bermuda. The timing of the Mallarmé shoot really couldn't be more convenient . . . I can't help feeling confident – utterly sure – that I am doing the right thing. This flat will accommodate a baby very easily, and a nanny too. It will be nice to have . . . but there she stopped and put a line through the last six words. She had written enough. What mattered was the decision itself, not the labyrinthine, ineluctable emotions that had prompted it. She thrust the book to one side and let out a great sigh. It would be so much easier when she was pregnant, when everything was to be done rather than thought about. Waiting for things to happen was always hateful.

Thanks to a double dose of chickenpox visited upon the poor twins, the rendezvous with Anita had been postponed to a Friday evening in late October. Rachel had been writing her diary in the sitting room, having had a quick shower and changed into black leggings and an electric-blue polo neck jumper that hung almost to her knees. The colour brought out the shimmers of blue in her irises, the softness engrained in the steely grey. Her hair, she noted wistfully, while trying to comb some sense into it in front of the bathroom mirror, was in need of attention again: the streaks of blonde were growing out already and the swept-back shape was now too heavy to stay in place for long. A similar exasperation earlier in the week had prompted the unprecedented purchase of some aerosol hairspray, an expensive gold-canned product promising 'natural body and hold', which had since between consigned to the bin. Its fragrant mist had settled upon her hair with quite unnatural efficacy, bestowing the kind of lifeless sheen which Rachel had always disparagingly associated with wigs. To make up for her hair she had spent longer than usual on her eyes, drawing a careful line of blue across the top of her lids and then painstakingly teasing out her long fine lashes with some black mascara. It was not for Anita's benefit that she took such trouble, but for her own. If she couldn't face herself in the mirror, she certainly couldn't face anyone else.

On the low table at one end of the sofa was a glass of water from which Rachel sipped absently, doing little more than wetting her lips. She had wanted a proper drink, but had somehow found herself deterred from the idea of indulging alone by suspicions about the possibility of Anita's renewed acquaintance with the bottle. While fearing the worst, she none the less hoped for the best. Over the last five years or so Anita's behaviour towards drink had displayed the spasms of absolute love or hate that are the preserve of the true addict. It was impossible to know what to expect, which part of the downward or upward curve she would be riding on any particular day.

Supper had been selected from the extensive freezer section of an expensive supermarket during her lunch hour. The chore of shopping had been exacerbated by particularly rebellious trolley wheels and an inability to focus. Segments of time whizzed by while Rachel found herself standing dazed and confounded before chests of microwaveable feasts and aisles of bread and vegetables. Colours and prices swarmed in a blur of nonsense, while her hands hovered over items and then lost their nerve. Never having taken much pleasure over the purchase of food, the realisation that she was dawdling ineffectually, that an activity which normally took her fifteen minutes was taking five times that long, was disturbing. As a result she bought much more than she needed to, coping with the inability to choose by selecting several things where one would have done as well. In the queue at the checkout Rachel eyed her full trolley with something like incredulity, examining the contents as she sometimes did a stranger's, as if a perusal of the packets and tins on which individuals chose to sustain themselves might offer up a glimpse of their personalities, a taste of the private domestic dramas being enacted in their homes. Anyone studying her own groceries, she thought ruefully, would assume she was feeding a large family with expensive tastes, a lack of interest in cooking and a collective penchant for unusual bread-types.

In front of her a chinless barrel of an infant was seizing each thing as it was placed on the conveyor belt and hurling it back into the trolley, while its mother smiled, shaking her head at the checkout girl, clearly too overcome by love to muster the energy for reprimand.

'He loves shopping,' she murmured, catching Rachel's eye.

Rachel offered a generous smile in return, inwardly marvelling at the separation of emotions in her own heart, at the way she could feel such determination to produce a child herself and at the same time experience nothing but guarded revulsion for the toddler wedged into the trolley in front of her.

She was truly astonished at quite how many babies and pregnant mothers now seemed to populate the world. Having until recently passed prams and pushchairs with unseeing or, at best, impatient eyes, it now felt as if they were everywhere, as if some shadowy force was bent upon reminding her at every possible moment of every day, of the new avenue down which her instincts were being drawn.

Common sense had prompted Rachel that afternoon – albeit reluctantly – to take the precaution of booking herself an appointment with a Harley Street gynaecologist, deliberately taking her custom to a doctor completely unacquainted with the history of her life or her body. She wanted a straightforward

analysis, without the burden of chit-chat or judgements of any
kind. She would get enough of that from other sources, she
thought dryly, bending to retrieve a large bag of fresh spinach
which the porky-faced child had slung at her feet. Imagining her
parents' mutual horror at their daughter managing to produce a
baby but not a husband, made Rachel smile with fear and then
hate herself the instant after. She had never pleased them in
anything; how puerile to think she could change the habit of
a lifetime now; how belittling even to care.

A selection of boxes and one loaf of red-pepper bread now
sat beside the sleek, black-faced microwave in Rachel's kitchen.
Seven minutes to produce four exotic dishes. Not bad at all. She
checked the cooking instructions for the third time and then
pressed the replay button on her answering machine. There
were a series of promising clicks but only one short message.

'Will Raphael speaking. What do you mean, you've changed your
mind?'

His voice was low, and teasingly indignant. Almost as if he'd
sensed the relief behind the delivery of her message and was
deliberately making complications.

'Bloody cheek,' she exclaimed out loud, before pulling out
the bottle of Chablis she had wedged into the freezer half an
hour before and filling up one of the two empty glasses that sat
beside a bread basket full of coral-coloured poppadums. 'I mean
I've changed my mind,' she declared to the machine. 'I'm too
busy. Period.'

These one-sided expostulations were interrupted by the door
buzzer.

When Rachel leant forward to greet her, Anita took a dramatic leap backwards, making a big show of trumpeting into a
handkerchief and waving her hands across her face. 'Horrible
head cold,' she sniffed, flapping the hanky and shaking her head.
'Only thing keeping me going is whisky and Disprin. Been like it
all week. Think it's connected to the chickenpox but can't prove
a thing.'

Rachel, who lived with the firm conviction that people with
horrible head colds or any similar afflictions should not be
so generous as to consider stepping beyond the quarantined
confines of their own homes, instinctively shuffled backwards.

Then she remembered that Anita was almost certainly drinking again and that alcoholics, especially lapsed ones with a history of broken resolutions to their credit, could be fantastically cunning. She found herself studying her friend's nose for signs of handkerchief abuse and listening out for a telltale nasal twang. But Anita's nostrils looked markedly untroubled, as did the rest of her face – her eyes black and clear, her skin its usual alabaster, a fashionable pallor which she liked to heighten by the application of garish lipstick. The handkerchief, meanwhile, looked decidedly unglued and fresh.

'Whisky and Disprin, eh?' she remarked, her heart softening as it always did when she actually saw Anita instead of just thought about her.

'I hope you're not going to be a bully, because I don't think I could bear it.'

Rachel opened the door wider and stood to one side. 'No, I'm not in the mood. How does Chablis and Disprin sound?'

'Just to be here is bliss,' sighed Anita, stuffing the handkerchief into the side pocket of her red woollen jacket and stepping into the hall with a look of grateful awe across her face. Rachel, pleased to see her pleased, as always, led the way through into the sitting room, where Anita promptly flung herself into one end of the sofa with a theatrical sigh, throwing one arm along its smooth leather back. 'You look so well, Rachel – I always say blue is your best colour – so sickeningly unstressed, so unlike the rest of us cronies. I'm in need of a *very* long moan by the way, I hope you don't mind. Giles has plummeted new depths of irascibility and uncooperativeness – is that a word? – and the twins have picked every scab they can reach and are bound to be scarred for life. I don't mind about Eddie so much – scars can be quite becoming on a man, don't you think? – but Laura, with that version of Giles's nose for a plonker, is going to need every bit of help she can get. And, just to cap it all, your goddaughter is being monstrous. Firstly,' she held up her fingers to count off the points, 'she has declared herself to be jealous of the twins' spots – of all things. Secondly, she wants hair as long as a poisonous child called Nigella, whose mother clearly has nothing better to do in the mornings than weave horribly impeccable French plaits, and thirdly, she flew into a tantrum about my coming to see you. I'd have slit my wrists days ago if I'd thought Giles could cope with the mess. Can you believe little Charlotte thinking, at the ripe old age of six, that she's every right to join me for dinner with her godmother? After an early Christmas present I expect, the little vixen.'

Anita's habit of putting down her own children, a form of self-deprecation once removed which Rachel associated with the more keenly disappointed of her friends, could at times be quite entertaining. She smiled, as she was meant to, at the same time handing over a glass of wine and sitting down next to her. 'Dinner's just an electromagnetic wave or two away from being edible. Tell me when you're hungry and I'll press the necessary buttons. It's good to see you,' she said with genuine warmth, 'it's been far too long as usual. Sounds as though things have been rather tough.'

'Pure hell,' agreed Anita, with a cheerful grin. 'I even suffered the humiliation of having my latest piece sent back . . .' She pressed her lips together hard, faintly smudging the neat outline of her lipstick. 'Fucking embarrassing actually.' She glowered at her drink. 'What a boring subject, though. I mean, leisure centres, I ask you – no wonder I came up with a load of crap.' She let out a loose throaty laugh for which she had once been famous, and raised her glass. 'Sod them all.'

Rachel laughed too, refreshed and comforted as always by Anita's frank admission that life was hard and full of disappointment. It made a welcome change from the usual human predilection – of which Rachel knew herself to be guilty – for exaggerating one's state of happiness. Why was it, she wondered, taking a sip of wine, that humans so often felt the need to present a bold front to each other, as if happiness was not an emotion but a measure of success?

'And how are you Rachel, how are things?'

'Not bad.' She beamed, tucking her legs up to one side of her and resting her glass on her knees. Anita, she noticed, had not yet touched her own drink, but was fiddling with the stem and running her index finger round the rim.

'Oh God, what the—' Anita jerked forwards, spilling a few drops of wine on her lap, as the cat, appearing from nowhere, landed beside her arm. Unperturbed by Anita's shriek, it began massaging the soft leather with its paws, clearly sizing up the possibilities of claiming a seat on the sofa itself. 'I didn't know you had acquired a pet,' she gasped, putting one hand to her chest as if to steady her breathing. 'Gave me such a fright.' She swigged from her glass. 'Sorry. Phew! That's better. Nice puss. What's your name? Mind my bloody drink.' The cat was now making its way towards Rachel, picking its way daintily through an obstacle course of bags and cushions.

Not having seen the animal since its one night stay several weeks before, Rachel was quite as surprised as Anita. 'The little devil. It must have slipped in when I opened the front door just now.' She stroked the soft fur, feeling its back arch in appreciation. 'It's not mine at all. It must belong to a neighbour. I'll put it out.'

'Oh no, don't. He's rather fine.' Anita reached out to rub the cat under one ear. It leant towards her, its wide face set in an inviting grin. 'I'd say he's got some Persian in him – look at the shape of his face and that wonderfully fluffy tail.'

'How do you know it's a him?'

Anita pursed her lips and made a squeaky noise aimed at reclaiming the attention of their intruder, who had straightened itself and was now walking round in small circles on Rachel's lap. 'Of course he's a he – all butch and pleased with himself, like any normal male.' She chuckled. 'Though if you think I'm going to check you've got another think coming – have you seen the size of those claws?'

'Ow, yes.' Rachel stood up, tipping the animal to the floor, where it recovered its composure huffily, before stalking over to the rug on which it had curled up on its previous visit. 'I'll catch him. You open the door.'

'Oh, let's leave him for a bit. He's not doing any harm.' Anita bent down and began crooning again, holding out her hand while the cat cocked its head in a show of playing hard to get. 'Cats are fine, so long as you're not pregnant of course. There's this disease you can get,' she went on, warming to her subject, 'I did an article on it once – toxoplasmosis – symptoms like flu and nothing to worry about so long as you don't happen to be carrying a foetus inside you. Hardly something which is likely to worry you.' She returned her attentions to the cat which was now lying on its back with a dreamy look in its eyes. 'What a flirt,' she laughed, 'just look at him—'

'Why, what happens if you're pregnant?'

'Oh, everything. Blindness, encephalitis, brain damage – a real picnic. Comes from the faeces apparently,' she concluded cheerfully, leaving the cat and picking up her glass before going over to study an impressive black-and-white photograph of a suspension bridge, which hung above the mantelpiece. Behind her, Rachel sneaked a wary look at her uninvited guest, who closed one eye.

'I've always loved this – all those luxuriant shadows and elegant lines – so simple and yet so refined. Hey,' she spun round, 'weren't you going to do a photography course or something? Have you started yet?'

'Oh, I changed my mind,' replied Rachel airily, her thoughts still on brain-damaged foetuses and whether Anita might be doing her thing of exaggerating a story for effect. 'Work is ridiculously hectic at the moment. Everybody always uses Christmas as the deadline by which they want everything and then of course I've got my trip to America and Bermuda for that shoot I told you about—'

'It's a hard life eh, Rachel?'

'You know as well as I do it's not as glamorous as it sounds . . .'

'Oh, do I?' Anita raised her dark eyebrows and then dangled her empty glass. 'Any more of this?'

'Heaps. Let's eat, too.'

The two women retreated into the kitchen, leaving the cat curled in a ball before the authentically darting flames of Rachel's coal-gas fire, watched over by a photograph on the mantelpiece – a much darker-haired, rounder-faced version of Rachel which Robbie had immortalised with an instamatic and which had somehow established itself as one of the immovable archives with which she lived.

Not long afterwards, without exactly intending to, Rachel found herself crossing the invisible border into that alluring territory where not even the prospect of a hangover is enough to deter the refilling of a glass. It had been a long time since she got drunk. A very long time. And Anita was the best of drinking partners, since, regardless of her problems, she had a famous capacity for arriving at a point of happy intoxication and staying there for a long time before toppling less happily down the other side. It was, as always, unwise and certainly – given Anita's history – irresponsible. But it felt that night as if it was the only way in which she was truly going to relax herself; so much was bottled up inside, none of it was going to be uncorked without a bit of help.

As it turned out, things were uncorked on every front, spurred on by a second bottle of Chablis – less chilled than the first but consumed even more quickly – and Rachel's eventual impatience with the subject of Anita's unsatisfactory home life. Timid of confessing outright to her recent decisions about her own future, Rachel did her best to steer the conversation in the right direction, hoping Anita might work things out for herself.

But Anita was in no mood for working out anything. 'Christ, I need a cigarette,' she declared, ignoring Rachel's second throwaway remark about late motherhood and sighing deeply at the desire – invariably experienced some way through the second bottle – for nicotine. She began rummaging furiously through her handbag.

'You just say children are awful because you've got some.'

'They are awful.' She punched her bag with both fists. 'Shit.'

'Well, perhaps I'm not prepared to take your word for it.'

'Is there an off-licence round here?' Anita seized her purse and then put it down again, very slowly. 'What did you say?'

'I said,' Rachel repeated, 'perhaps I am no longer prepared to take your word for it.'

Anita folded her arms and frowned, sticking out her jaw like Giles sometimes did when defending one of his lefty political viewpoints. 'I hope that doesn't mean what I think it means.'

'And what do you think it means?'

'That you might, possibly, be considering, at some stage, having a child.'

'Of course I bloody well might. And I think it's bloody arrogant of you to assume otherwise.'

Anita let out a laugh of undisguised incredulity. 'You can hardly blame me for that, Rachel my dearest.' She pushed her handbag to one side and leant across the table. 'All that matters,' she went on more tenderly, 'is that you don't make a mistake.'

Her lipstick was still vibrantly red, Rachel noticed, an observation which deflected her outrage for a moment, making her wonder, tipsily, what component made it so resistant to napkins and food, and whether it came off on the rare occasion that she embraced her husband. They hadn't made love for three months, she had confided earlier on, a typical Anita-style revelation which had left Rachel secretly marvelling at the fact that she probably had sex more often than many women with partners resident in the same bed.

'You would be mad, quite mad, to have a child, Rachel,' Anita was declaring now. 'Children are parasites from the word go. You would go grey overnight, you would lose that sylph-like figure, you would lose – most important of all – your independence. You may have sufficient funds to employ the best nanny that money can buy, but it's not that simple, believe me. You would feel torn in two. You would long to get away, to work, to anywhere – for peace, for sanity and all the elements of life that you now take for granted. And yet you would feel the compulsion to stay at home too, not just because your breasts have swollen to the size of ripe watermelons, but also thanks to that mysterious, damnable bond which ensures that every reproductive female on this planet drags a millstone of guilt round her neck every time she absents herself from the little darlings for more than a nanosecond. Nannies do not solve this problem. You have a perfect life Rachel. Do not, I repeat, do not, fuck it up now.'

'Well, thank you for your support, Anita.' Rachel's voice was breathy with indignation. 'I'll bear all that in mind, of course. How could I not, since you are such an unarguably fine representative of motherhood, so intimately acquainted with its challenges, so admirably on top of things.' She picked up the second empty wine bottle and marched with it to the bin, knowing that Anita would know what she meant by the gesture, knowing that it would cut deep. 'I'll keep my ideas to myself in future,' she muttered, thinking suddenly of Luke Berenson and the absurd fact that she had received more emotional encouragement from a total stranger than from one of her oldest friends.

'We can't change what we are,' said Anita fiercely, fighting her corner with a last flutter of energy which even Rachel, through her fury, recognised as bordering on the courageous.

'Oh yes we can.' Her voice was all determination and hope, very quiet. 'We can. We can be what we want to be, every one of us. Otherwise . . . otherwise there's no point.'

'Maybe.' Anita hung her head in defeat. She longed for one more drink, but did not dare to ask. 'I'm going to buy some cigarettes,' she mumbled, thinking that at the same time she could treat herself to a little something, just a couple of swigs to see her through till bedtime. 'Shall I take a taxi home afterwards?'

'No, no.' Rachel shook her head wearily. 'Of course not, you twit. I'll leave the door on the latch. And Anita,' she looked at the floor. 'Sorry if I've been mean. I'm all uptight at the moment . . .'

'Me too. It's just that . . . you know I love the children, you know I'd die for them, but at times . . . at times they've almost destroyed me too. I would hate to see you crushed by anything, Rachel, you're so strong, it wouldn't be right.'

'Go and get your fags, before you have me in tears. I'll put on the coffee. Oh, Anita, just cigarettes, eh, there's a good girl. We're drunk enough already.'

'Sure,' she replied, thinking that one of those airplane-style mini-bottles could be despatched on the way back, and that, for by no means the first time in her life, the famous undetectability of vodka was a blessing indeed.

While Rachel knew that some of the best gynaecologists in the world were reputed to be male, she had always preferred any scrutiny of the more private areas of her body to be undertaken by women. Anita, who raved about the swarthy Latin looks of the doctor at her local family planning clinic, took a rather different view. 'People make judgements about each other all the time, whatever they do,' she claimed. 'Doctors of either sex will secretly be deciding whether someone is fat or pretty, just like the rest of us do. Wear your best frock and enjoy it, that's my attitude.'

'But it's not mine,' murmured Rachel to herself as she slipped out of the office in the middle of the morning in order to keep her appointment in Harley Street. Once safely settled inside the cab, she pulled out her mobile from the side pocket of her handbag and dialled her own number at work.

'Melissa, it's me. I had to pop out for something – decided I'd better tell you in case you thought I'd got locked in a lavatory or a lift. It's some family business. Nothing terrible or urgent.'

'Fine,' replied her secretary, secretly wondering what kind of business could crop up so unexpectedly without being either of those things. 'Will you be back in time for your three o'clock?'

'Oh goodness, yes. And remember, tea as well as coffee, and see if you can rustle up some of those biscuits we had last week, the ones with the raisins in – Frank Alder ate nearly the entire plateful.' It was the final pre-production meeting before the shoot in Bermuda and her client was showing typical last-minute nerves about details which had been agreed for weeks. The film required the services of two models, one black and one white, lying side by side on their stomachs in the shallows of a beach. They were to be topless, but not exuberantly so. While the question of degrees of nudity seemed at last to have been settled, there were fresh worries about the chosen colours for the bikini bottoms. Rachel had promised to try a couple more options, but was fearful that too great a choice would only lead to greater indecision.

Though tedious, the inevitable bustle of sorting out such last-minute issues was providing a welcome distraction from other, less controllable aspects of office life. Ever since her minor showdown with Cliff Weybourne, Rachel had been suffering the disquieting sense that she was being edged out of the sphere of influence to which she had grown accustomed. That there was no tangible evidence for these suspicions, nothing she could quite put her finger on, only made it worse. Meanwhile, the matter of the new departmental head was still unresolved, an unnecessary prevarication which Rachel felt was bad for the agency as a whole, but about which – given her overtly personal interest in the matter – she felt it would be inappropriate to complain.

'And check my plane tickets are on the way, could you Melissa? I'd prefer to get my hands on them days as opposed to hours before take-off.'

'Will do. See you later.'

Rachel slipped her phone into her bag and leant her head back against the weathered upholstery of the cab. The prospect of getting away was growing increasingly attractive. America. Nathan. Her stomach tightened. Bermuda. Lots of work, but sunshine and luxury too. The hotel looked spectacular. It could be brilliant.

Thinking again of her appointment, she crossed her legs. Anything to do with gleaming metal instruments and smells of disinfectant made Rachel sicker at heart than most. While her mother liked to blame it on a prolonged stay in hospital for a life-threatening bout of double pneumonia at the age of five, Rachel herself believed that it went much deeper than that, that a fear of medical practices was something she had been born with, like grey eyes and having a second toe longer than a first. If anything, her phobia had grown worse over the years: doctors, with all their intimate knowledge of corporeal failings and functions, made her feel ignorant, and therefore vulnerable. Nothing, in Rachel's experience, was quite so disempowering as ignorance: it removed the possibility of judgement and choice; it made people pliant and afraid.

'So, Miss Elliot, you want to have a baby.' The leathery round face of the doctor, with its androgenous clumps of thick grey hair, was not what Rachel had been expecting at all. She's not my kind of woman, she thought at once, her heart sinking as she extended her hand to meet the hearty grip. She waited for instructions to remove her clothes, eyeing with distaste the white pallet of a bed poking out from behind the half open door of an adjoining room.

'Cup of tea? I'm having one.'

'Tea? Well – oh yes – thank you.'

A tray of cups and a small teapot was brought in by a young girl in a tartan skirt and red jumper.

'And no calls, thank you, Jennifer,' instructed Doctor Abbot, proceeding to pour tea and offer sugar, behaving for all the world as if they were two cosy members of a WI group, meeting for a chat about church flowers and the takings on the last bring-and-buy sale.

'I'm quite pushed for time . . .' Rachel began.

'And so am I, Miss Elliot, I assure you. But when it comes to discussing babies I have all the time in the world. Congratulations, by the way. It is a wonderfully exciting thing to want a child. You must be very pleased with yourself.'

Rachel, caught off guard by such kind enthusiasm, found a lump blocking her throat. 'Thank you,' she managed, blinking hard.

Dr Abbot pushed the tea closer and selected a pen from a small ceramic pot beside her telephone. 'Now, as you probably expected, there are certain questions I need to ask in order to carry out the check-up that you have requested. Lots of women don't bother, you know, which does make things difficult if they run into problems. This way we can bash anything on the head before it gets out of hand. You look quite splendidly fit, so I'm sure we'll whizz through most of this.' She tapped her pen on the pile of papers in front of her. 'But let's get the basics out of the way first.'

Rachel began undoing the buttons of her shirt.

'That won't be necessary, Miss Elliot. If you could just roll up your sleeve. That's it. Perfect. There we are. This might get to feel a little tight, that's all.' She studied her watch for a few moments before and after pumping. 'Blood pressure fine. Now let's get you on the scales. Slip your shoes off. Lovely. Could do with a few more pounds on you, but not to worry. Off you get now. Thank you. And now I'll need a sample of your urine. I don't ask people while they're in the waiting room; I always think it can be embarrassing – disappearing into the loo with a plastic jar and having to come out again.' She handed Rachel a plastic bag containing a conical see-through pot with a lid and showed her to a toilet adjoining the consulting room. 'Take your time,' she called cheerily, as Rachel closed the door. 'I know it doesn't always happen the moment you want it to.'

When Rachel reappeared the doctor was back behind her desk, spectacles on the top of her broad nose, bat-wing handwriting flying across a page.

'Splendid. Good girl. I'll give that to my nurse while we finish our chat.'

The questions were mostly quite straightforward, as indeed were Rachel's answers. Yes, her periods had always been regular; yes she did notice vaginal discharge about halfway through her cycle; no she was not taking any kind of drugs; no she didn't smoke; yes she kept to a sensible diet. The warm tea and Dr Abbot's cosy approach made it very easy, so easy that even when the difficult questions came they were not nearly as hard to answer as she had feared.

'Do you have any children?'

'No.' The pen scurried as they talked.

'Have you been pregnant before?'

Rachel cleared her throat before answering. 'Yes. When I was twenty-two. I had an abortion at nine weeks.'

'Any pain or bleeding afterwards?'

'A little . . . not much pain, a bit of blood.'

'Anything that required antibiotics to sort out?'

Rachel shook her head, reliving for a second the brilliant relief of stepping out of the sterile whiteness of the clinic into the afternoon sunshine, how beautifully unencumbered she had felt, how free.

'Nearly there.' Dr Abbot peered over the top of her glasses and delivered the most heartwarming of smiles. 'Experience has taught me that every question, even the most obvious, has to be asked. I have had women begging to be referred to infertility clinics when the only thing wrong was their technique. The human body is blessed with several orifices; some people get quite confused as to quite what to do with them all.'

Rachel couldn't help laughing out loud, though the doctor restricted herself to a broad smile.

'Right. Where were we? . . . Ah yes. Do you have a partner?'

'Yes.' Rachel felt the blood ebb from her cheeks. Suddenly the room didn't seem quite so warm after all. Lying to this woman did not come naturally. But the idea of the truth scared her too; it would sound too calculated, too weird. And she did have a partner. Nathan. And yes, he was healthy, non-smoking and all those other things that mattered as far as the doctor was concerned.

'Has he fathered a child before?'

'No.'

'Does he ejaculate inside you?'

It was hard not to squirm. 'Yes.'

'Common problem,' the doctor murmured, 'you'd be surprised.'

Suddenly it was over. Dr Abbot pushed her pad of paper to one side and came round to perch on the side of her desk.

'It all sounds marvellous.'

'The . . . the abortion doesn't matter, then?'

She made a clucking noise. 'No, no. If you'd had a post-operative infection of some kind then maybe. Infections and scarring can result in blocked tubes. But in your case there was nothing of the kind. You've no history of family problems. You're clearly ovulating beautifully. Time intercourse for twelve to eighteen days after the start of your period and keep your fingers crossed. Lady Luck, I'm afraid, will always play a large part in the proceedings. None of us can do anything about that. But then that's what makes the whole business such fun, I always think.' She rubbed her hands together gleefully. 'Gives us all an excuse to practise hard.'

Rachel, who found it difficult to imagine this friendly barrel of a woman in the embrace of anything more erotic than an armchair, caught herself scanning the room for signs of a family. There was only one picture on the desk, of a smiling, bald-headed man with spectacles and gaps between his teeth.

'Is that your husband?' she asked, the question slipping out before a sense of impropriety could get the better of her.

'Yes, that's my Geoffrey. We tried for years and years.' Her beaming face showed no signs of strain at the admission. 'That's the way it is sometimes. He died a few years back. Heart condition. Smoked like a chimney, the silly love, though we're not sure that's what finally shut everything down. Now then,' she had sat back down behind her desk and begun scribbling on a pad, 'by no means compulsory, but I do recommend them.' She tore off the prescription and handed it to Rachel, who was struggling with the impulse to express sympathy, coupled with the sense that the moment for doing so might already have passed. She frowned at the handwriting on the page before her, which resembled a series of Impressionist seagulls.

'Folate supplements,' explained Doctor Abbot. 'One tablet a day reduces the incidences of neural tube defects.'

'Neural tube defects?'

'Spina bifida and so on. Don't look so worried, Miss Elliot. Healthy babies are born to women of all ages every day of the week. The most important thing is that you want to have a child and that you give yourself the very best possible chance of doing so. You can buy these tablets in any chemist actually, you don't even need a prescription. I should see which works out cheaper and go for that.' She stood up and held out her hand. Her own cup of tea, Rachel noticed, had barely been touched.

Rachel took the hand with considerably more enthusiasm than she had at the beginning of the interview. 'Thank you. You've been very kind.'

'Not at all. And the very best of luck. Come back and see me when you strike lucky.'

In Rachel's experience, no method for crossing the Atlantic was
entirely satisfactory. Though she had colleagues who swore by
double whiskies and knock-out pills, in her view the time
allowed for sleeping was too short, too readily interrupted by
unwanted sing-song announcements about landing cards and
duty free perfumes, to be restorative in any sense. She opted
on this occasion for an early evening flight, resigning herself to
the dazed exhaustion that lay ahead, followed by the frustration
of waking with a racing pulse five hours before the next day was
supposed to have started.

Rachel sighed and took another sip of her complimentary
champagne. It was foolish to drink, she knew, but on the
other hand she felt she owed it to herself – both as a small,
anticipatory celebration for what lay ahead, and as a reward
for having successfully survived all sorts of last-minute complications without losing her temper or missing the plane. Not only
had Steve Betts, the director, been struck down with shingles,
but one of the models had twisted her ankle in a nightclub.
While lying in the ebb-tide of a pearly pink beach required
little from an ankle, the question of a replacement director
at such short notice had been taxing almost to the point of
impossible. A substitute had at last been found – someone
highly recommended and expensive, whom Rachel had taken
care to sell to Frank Alder in the most glowing and confident of
terms. But inside she worried still. Bringing a storyboard to life
could be a complicated business. A little magic was invariably
required, even on a Bermudan beach.

That the flight was delayed one hour by the last-minute

discovery of an electrical fault did little to allay a hovering sense of doom. As the airplane taxied back from the runway, Rachel reminded herself that such inconvenience was infinitely preferable to an unscheduled landing in the middle of the Atlantic Ocean. But the reality of such a prospect shimmered hopelessly out of reach. As did the good humour which had been beaten out of her by the whirlwind rush in which she eventually left the flat earlier that afternoon. Having popped home intending only to shower and change, she had been assailed by a series of unwanted calls, the more unexpected among them coming from Naomi Fullerton.

'What a treat. I was expecting your voice box. How are you, Rachel? It's been ages.'

An unhelpful picture sprang to mind, of Naomi curled up in the broad creaky arms of the straw rocking chair beside her beloved black beast of an Aga, cup of tea in hand, open magazine on her lap, her various children despatched to tea parties or settled round her in prettily coordinated outfits and hair bobbles. Anita would have been easier to reject. But Naomi was different. Partly because she rang so seldom (invariably making Rachel feel guilty for not having got there first) and partly because of the determined ostentation with which she played her role as mother. As a female still very much on the opposite end of such a spectrum, Rachel had learnt to be very careful about not saying anything that might suggest she considered herself superior, or busier, or more fulfilled in any way.

'Naomi – lovely to hear you, but I'm afraid this is a bit of a bad time. I'm in danger of being late for an airplane.'

'Oh, that sounds exciting. Where are you going?'

'America – Washington then Bermuda.'

'Really?' The word, though innocent enough, seemed to Rachel to contain accusatory overtones, as if Naomi believed that, as an old friend, she had every right to be informed of such large-scale manoeuvres before they occurred. 'Any chance of getting you over here before Christmas? Graham and I would love to see you. And so would Jessica, of course. She's taking her grade II piano this term.'

'Is she?' Rachel felt herself growing faintly hysterical. 'That's fantastic. Tell her best of luck and everything.'

Jessica, the third of Graham and Naomi's four girls, was by far the most precocious and accomplished of her various godchildren, having, at the tender age of seven, already taken up two instruments, elocution lessons and ballet. She wanted to have her own television show when she grew up, she said, one that had dancing and news. Rachel could be quite enchanted by such revelations when in the mood. But standing in a bath towel with wet hair trickling unpleasantly down her neck and the hands of the kitchen clock racing at twice their usual speed, made her less receptive to such disclosures. 'And I'd love to see you all – terribly soon. Let's talk when I get back. Tell Jessica I'll get her something special for Christmas from America.'

'So you'll call me, will you?' Naomi sounded sceptical.

'Yes. Absolutely. Soon as I get back.'

As Rachel scurried back towards the bathroom her fax machine whirred into life. Grabbing a towel and rubbing at her wet hair – she had tried and failed to get to the hairdresser's that afternoon – she returned to the study, her bare feet squeaking faintly on the polished wood floor. A single page had emerged from the machine, with just one line written across the top of it.

I said, why have you changed your mind? W.R. Fax: 01813687551

Rachel screwed the message up into a ball which she lobbed, with satisfying accuracy, into the wastepaper basket beside her desk. By the time she had finished getting dressed yet another message had arrived. This time from Melissa.

Just signing off and wishing you luck. No more last-minute panics unless you count an urgent-sounding call from your favourite client of Blackers Inc . . . I put him through to AJ. Julie says they fixed a lunch. Send us a p-c. Yrs enviously, Mel. PS Jo says to tell you the ankle hardly looks swollen at all so DON'T WORRY.

Rachel, smiling to herself, crumpled this missive in her fist and hurled it in the direction of the last one. This time she missed. On going over to retrieve it, she caught sight of Will Raphael's note, now half-unfurled in the bottom of the bin. His fax number was just visible on the top right-hand corner of the page. With a feeling akin to the irritation with which one bats a persistent fly, she tore off the corner and marched over to her fax machine.

Because I am busy. Because I am entitled to. Because I'd make a lousy photographer. RE.

From the retrospective vantage point of the airplane, Rachel felt rather pleased with this reply. It contained a certain curt cleverness, she decided, sipping the last of her champagne, of the kind that invariably eluded her in the cut and thrust of real conversation.

After a bad spell of turbulence that left Rachel with the unsettling sensation that bubbles were forming in the innermost recesses of her ears, she remembered the morning's post, stuffed at the last minute into the zip pocket of her overnight bag. There had been something that looked interesting, she recalled, eagerly pulling out the wadge of envelopes and sifting through it. A bank statement, a Christmas appeal from Save The Children, a catalogue from a warehouse clothes company and – here it was – a letter from France. Rachel smiled at Joy's self-consciously spaced and tidy handwriting, a hangover from her days as primary school teacher, when she liked to swear that handling classfuls of rowdy children quite put her off ever having any of her own.

As she ran her thumb under the gummed seal of the envelope, it occurred to Rachel that the Daltons may already have responded to exactly the same kind of teasing urgency with which she herself now wrestled, the overpowering sense that now was the time to effect a life-change, that soon it would be too late. Having a child was going to be her volte-face, she decided, pressing out the creases in the letter, her version of running from London and working to make a dream come true.

Dear Rachel,

I hope you are well and not too busy at work. How's that lovely flat? It was fantastic of you to come over for Leo's christening – both Tony and I really appreciated it – and so will Leo when he's a bit older! I can't believe it was so many weeks ago already and that Christmas is just around the corner.

We'd never spent time down here during the winter before and I have to say it has been a bit of an eye-opener! We've had so much rain all the Brits keep saying how much it reminds them of home. There's an amazingly large group of English people in the area, we've discovered, and even though we have by no means given up on our resolution of integrating ourselves with our French neighbours, I have to admit that there is nothing to beat having a jolly good moan with someone who misses the same things you do and who has the wherewithal to make a decent cup of tea. You wouldn't believe how tasteless French teabags are – everyone agrees – and the milk is mostly that longlife stuff, which the children can't bear and use as an excuse to dollop ten spoonfuls of sugar on their cornflakes! Talking of the children, your godson continues to go from strength to strength (literally). You would not believe how enormous he is – and how demanding. He makes the other two – or at least my recollections of them at this age – seem placid beyond belief. I'm still up at least three times every night. I've tried him on formula milk but he's just not interested, so I'm still wandering round with my buttons undone all the time. It is beginning to get me down just a bit. Especially now we're heading into winter. Apparently it's very common that late children are more of a handful. They are more likely to be geniuses too, apparently – we shall see!

The good news is that Tony continues to have more work than he knows what to do with – mostly, as I say, from English people doing up places of their own. This means, of course, that our own house is still very much in the condition that you saw it at the end of the summer. Tony keeps meaning to get to it at weekends, but he is usually so bushed I don't like to bully him too much. The only real problem is that now that it's so cold and damp, we really are beginning to feel all those unfilled cracks and crannies. A hell of a wind can blow in these parts, we've discovered, and of course since the house is exposed on all sides, we do rather get the brunt of it.

Isobel's French is practically fluent and even Sam is beginning to get the gist of things, which is a great relief. Tony, as you know, was always pretty good anyway, so it's just yours truly who is still struggling to make herself understood by the natives. I've bought a few grammar books and do try and do an hour or so every day, but it is hard to concentrate with Leo around and so much to do about the place. Je veux parler très bien mais je ne peux pas! How's that? Only took me ten minutes with a dictionary (just joking).

I wonder if you could do me a favour, Rachel. I know you're busy and it's a cheek of me to ask, but would you mind awfully finding out if I could subscribe to Good Housekeeping over here – how much it would cost to have it sent over and so on. I would ask my family, but they are already providing a steady supply of all those things – like teabags! – that I miss so dreadfully from Tesco's. I know it sounds silly, but it would be such a treat – it's such an attractive magazine and full of so much – and besides which it might help me with some ideas for this building site we call home!

How many exclamation marks would it take, Rachel wondered angrily, scanning the last lines of the letter, before Joy dared to admit that she was unhappy.

I keep telling myself that with Tony's business going so well one day we'll be able to afford to retire somewhere really tropical and easy, where leaky roofs won't matter and I'll have servants to sweep away the cobwebs. But then we all have to dream.

Yes, we do, thought Rachel, puzzling over the depressing possibility that dreams were not designed to come true, and that when they did they invariably needed replacing with something new. Would having a child bring with it a similar sense of disappointment for her? She tried to imagine what it would feel like to cherish her own baby, to embark on that juggling act she had heard so much about, flying between hearth and office, effortlessly producing nappies and documents like some fairy godmother with a wand. But all that came was a fuzzy warm feeling in the pit of her stomach, a gush of irrational conviction that in her case all would work out for the best.

As Rachel gingerly pressed the tip of her spoon into a small square of lemon-coloured dessert, she experienced, not for the first time, a pang of guilt at having omitted to notify Duncan and Mary Beth of her impending stay in their territory. She was booked instead into the Omnivera Hotel in Georgetown, a white-fluffy-bathrobe type of place, just a few miles from Duncan and Mary Beth's handsome oak front door. After careful consideration she had decided to devote all of her spare time in Washington to Nathan, who was flying down from New York specially and who – almost as if he had picked up on some of the momentous significance for her in this particular visit – had promised a surprise that would 'blow her mind'. If they wrapped up early in Bermuda she would call in on Duncan on the way back, she told herself, blinking heavy eyelids at the lemon pudding, which wobbled disconcertingly, and which had begun to leak a suspiciously colourless tributary of fluid from underneath its edges. On the screen in front of her the opening credits were rolling for a submarine thriller which she had seen with Nathan earlier in the year. She started to put on her headphones but changed her mind, closing her eyes instead and starting to count, for the hundredth time, the number of days since the beginning of her last period. Thirteen; unlucky for some, she thought, smiling to herself as the blank weightlessness of sleep intervened.

Nathan's surprise took the form of a wood and concrete enclave, nestling amongst the high, fir-lined niches of the Virginia mountains. Swiss-style chalets clustered around a massive, sprawling central complex containing every amenity currently in fashionable demand for individuals fortunate enough to reside in a certain income bracket. Ethnic restaurants, two heated swimming pools, a fitness centre, a massage parlour, beauty salons, a bowling alley and a cinema were among the more prominent attractions advertised on the billboard in reception. Nathan was effusively impressed, a reaction which triggered in Rachel an unforgivable desire to appear perversely British and nonchalant, a desire which she put down to the grouchiness of intense fatigue and mounting nervousness about revealing the real ulterior motive behind her stop-over on the East Coast.

The chalets contained none of the rustic accoutrements suggested by their carefully rugged exteriors. Instead, Rachel found herself wading through the lush pile of absurdly silky carpets, strewn with heavy reproduction furniture and framed by yards of velveteen curtains with elaborate pelmet and side cord arrangements. The kitchen, crammed with every device imaginable for the preparation, storage and disposal of food and crockery, had Rachel cowering in the doorway, her jet-lagged brain flicking unhelpfully to thoughts of airplane cockpits and the unpleasant bumpiness with which they had finally made contact with the tarmac of Dulles airport. Some of the more hysterical passengers had actually clapped.

'Not bad, huh?' Nathan came up behind her and placed one proprietorial hand on each breast, while performing a gentle pelvic tilt in the region of her lower back. Rachel prised herself free with a nervous laugh, feeling suddenly like an imposter. The fact that her mental clock was still ticking several hours out of step was doing nothing to help her composure. She had awoken at four o'clock that morning, rolling from one side of her beautiful five-star bed to the other, trying every variation on the sheep-counting theme she had ever heard of, and much more esides. Breakfast and a head-drilling shower had helped. But after a perky patch during which she had walked several blocks to find an English newspaper, her limbs suddenly seemed to quadruple in weight and a thumping headache started. Retiring to her room with the intention of grabbing a nap before Nathan arrived, she had found herself hooked onto the phone instead. The crew, due to fly out the next day, were now showing more signs of nerves than the clients themselves. The sprained ankle was causing particular anxiety for the new director. What about artistic freedom? he complained, many times. What if he chose to do a close-up of the girls' feet? How could he be expected to work with constraints like damaged joints? It wasn't professional.

It was with some weariness, therefore, that Rachel pulled on her shoes and hastily touched up the fading lines of her make-up before venturing down to reception to greet the man whom she hoped would father her child. Nathan, oblivious both to the extent of her exhaustion and the nervous preoccupation burning in her mind, welcomed her with his usual bracing cheeriness. They were headed for the mountains, he told her proudly, in a monster of a four-wheeler that he had hired specially for the occasion. They were to set off at once. Used to an automatic, Nathan ground the gears so frequently during their laborious stop-start progress through the dense traffic of downtown Washington, that Rachel's whole body was clenched with tension by the time they finally hit the clear open road that took them north. They cruised pleasantly enough after that, past white-gated fields of vast properties, and colonial-style mansions with names like The Homestead painted in handsome letters on their roadside mail boxes. The drive took well over three hours, the last part involving a torturous zigzag up through the Virginian mountains. Nathan, tired himself by this stage, talked in a desultory way about the grip of superior rubber on tarmac, while Rachel sleepily eyed the dense squadrons of towering trunks, wondering where all the famous blue ridges were and who had thought up such a description in the first place.

'It's super, Nathan, really super,' she exclaimed, after they had been left alone with a set of keys and several colourful booklets on facilities and mealtimes. 'A super surprise. You clever thing.' She turned and kissed him, registering a pleasant hint of a new aftershave. 'Does your cleverness extend to mastering any of these machines? Could you, for example, rustle up a cup of strong black coffee for a girl who's been awake since the early hours and who doesn't want to ruin the evening by falling asleep at the wrong moment?'

'Poor baby. Is she tired?' He stroked her hair gently, using the movement to draw her face closer still. For a few moments Rachel allowed herself to drift on the pull of his arms, before reality awoke her with a jerk. It would be wrong not to tell him first. She needed to tell him before they made love. 'Coffee,' she whispered, giving him a little push. 'Please.'

Nathan, it had to be said, excelled himself amongst the hi-tech gadgetry of the kitchen, emerging not only with a jug of coffee, but a trayful of food as well, together with a bottle of champagne which had been left in an ice-bucket as a welcome gift. He was wearing a dressing gown, Rachel noticed with a start, not until that moment aware that he had slipped off to change. In view of this attire, it was with some surprise that she found herself being led not upstairs to the bedroom, but out onto a wooden porch at the back of the chalet.

'Nathan, really, it's cold and dark,' she began, pulling her cardigan about her more tightly.

But Nathan, humming a fanfare, put down the tray and pulled off a tarpaulin covering something in the far corner of the balcony. Steam billowed into the chilly night air.

'A hot tub.'

'A what?'

'Bubbling hot water. We sit in it and look at the stars. What do you think?' He was already undoing his dressing gown. 'It's what sold the place to me. My folks used to have one of these when I was a kid. The whole family would pile in it sometimes after dinner, tell ghost stories and that kind of thing. I tell you, they're great for atmosphere.' His body looked faintly luminous in the dim light as he slipped into the water. In an instant he was submerged up to his neck. His teeth gleamed through his smile. 'Hey, could you push the tray a little closer do you think? Now get in for Christ's sake – you're shivering to death.'

Hurriedly Rachel slipped off her clothes. Her bare flesh tingled to attention at the shock of the mountain air. Tiptoeing to minimise contact with the icy wooden boards, she scurried over to join him, hugging herself from a combination of cold and modesty. She felt skeleton-thin, transparent through to the bone. For a moment the heat of the water took her breath away. Then her body began to ease into the deep embrace of the wet warmth. Overhead the sky was a bed of black velvet, bejewelled with light.

'It's beautiful, Nathan,' she gasped, craning her neck upwards and stretching her limbs out in slow swimming motions, gaining confidence as the blanket of water drew her in. 'Oh God, it's beautiful.' She thought of what she had to say, of how easy it would be.

Nathan was eating crab sticks, dipping them into a tub of mayonnaise and popping them into his mouth like sweets. He had ordered the food in advance, he explained, chewing hungrily, pointing out zuccini wedges and onion rings and other delicacies piled high on the plates. 'Quite a feast,' he added, licking away an errant blob of mayonnaise near the dimple in his chin. 'Get stuck in Rachel, it's all getting cold. I only gave these things a couple of minutes in the micro and it's kind of arctic out here. Wow, this is so good.' An exploratory foot felt its way under the water over to her side of the tub. She seized it playfully, making as if to pull him under the water.

'Eat,' he said, laughing, keeping his balance sufficiently to hold out a plate of food. Rachel, who believed that vegetables of any kind tasted better without generous coatings of deep-fried breadcrumbs, opted for one of the fleshy tubes of crab-meat, secretly sure that its chewy texture – though greatly enhanced by the addition of mayonnaise – had never enjoyed a close acquaintance with shellfish of any kind.

'Nathan, there's something I need to ask you.' She licked her fingers, resisting the temptation to rinse her hands in the water lapping round her chin.

'Ask away.' He had placed one foot on each of her bent legs and was absently kneading her kneecaps with his toes while he ate.

'I know this might come as something of a shock but . . . the thing is I have a favour to ask you. Rather a big favour, I suppose. I hope you'll try to understand . . .'

'Anything within my power, baby, you know that.' He reached out to pour the champagne. A mini tidal wave washed over the edges of the tub and slapped onto the wooden floor.

'It's just that,' Rachel clasped her hands under the surface. She was hot now, almost feverish. It was odd to feel sweaty, with cold so close at hand. Her hair was sticking to the sides of her cheeks and temples. She brushed it back with wet hands, feeling a shiver of relief as a breeze drifted across the balcony, cooling her head. 'I would be most honoured – flattered – pleased—' this was hard after all – 'if you would consider fathering my child.'

'Your what?' Nathan pulled his feet away and sat up. 'You're pregnant?'

'No, no.' It was a relief to laugh. Of course such a sudden mention of babies was bound to make a man like Nathan nervous. 'I'm not expecting anything more than the act itself,' she explained eagerly, leaning towards him, the water slopping up around her shoulders. 'I have decided that I would like to have a child. I *want* to do it on my own. There would be no recriminations afterwards, no crawling back for money or commitment from you. You'd be quite free, I promise.'

To her immense surprise, Nathan responded to these reassurances by hurling his glass at the balustrades a few feet to their right. There was a chiming explosion as the glass shattered, spraying invisible shards into darkness. 'How dare you, Rachel Elliot.' He heaved his torso out of the water and sat on the very edge of the tub. Steam rose from every pore of his skin, giving the impression that he was about to burst into flame.

'I'm only asking . . .'

He shook his wet fringe from his eyes. 'You are only asking me to screw you – deposit my stuff – and ciao. Auf wiedersehen. And I'm not supposed to mind? Like I can plant babies all over the place and it doesn't matter? Like I'm some kind of stud? Like I've got no heart?'

'I thought you weren't interested in children . . .' she faltered.

'I'm not,' he snapped. 'But that does not give you the right to ask me such a thing.'

'I'm sorry.' She felt trapped in the water. Though her body was too hot, the air was too cold. There were no towels. 'I'm sorry, I had no idea . . .'

'You know what? You're crazy. What do you want to wreck yourself with a kid for anyway?'

'That's my business.'

'You're telling me. Leave me out of it Rachel.' He gave a bitter laugh. 'Though don't imagine that you getting pregnant wouldn't affect things between us. I mean, Christ – do you think we could just carry on as before with a kid crying all over the goddam place? Give me a break.'

In spite of the cold Nathan was still sitting on the edge of the hot tub, heedless both of his nudity and the cold. Steam was rising only from his legs now, the rest of his body having cooled to meet the chill temperatures of the mountain air. 'Hell, I'm going inside.' He slung on his dressing gown and stooped to pick up the tray of food. The pot of coffee she had requested sat untouched, cold as stone. 'I am truly sorry you did this, Rachel. Truly sorry.' He shook his head.

After he had gone Rachel turned her face up towards the tapestry of stars and stared hard at the pinpoints of light till their edges blurred. The caress of the wind through the trees sounded like whispered laughter. A faint trace of creamy scum was forming on the surface of the water. The towel landed with a dull thump beside the tub, flung with a mute anger that ruled out negotiation or reconciliation of any kind.

They found their way to different bedrooms, knowing that the next morning they would part company for good. Rachel's request had taken them into emotional terrain from which it would have been impossible to withdraw and in which they could not coexist.

As Rachel lay awake, her mind galloping obstinately on, refusing to let her body rest, a deep sense of failure began to mushroom inside. To have miscalculated so badly was upsetting, deeply shocking in fact. She wanted to go home, to retreat and regroup. The thought of Bermuda, of having to maintain control, perform the usual tightrope act of keeping all parties happy, made her suddenly quite sick with apprehension. It felt like a stage-call for an actress who had lost her nerve. The uncrackable Rachel Elliot would be required. Her teeth chattered at the thought. For, as a grey dawn crept up over the green ridges of the mountains, it seemed to her that the uncrackable Rachel Elliot was full of cracks, deep invisible fissures that made her afraid.

Just before she finally drifted off to sleep the comforting face of Dr Abbot swam into view, bringing with it an echo of a voice that had wished her luck. All the luck in the world was no use to her now, she thought bitterly, considering and rejecting the possibility of slipping into Nathan's room and trying to make it up. He wouldn't trust her now, or ever again. The stormy set of his big square face, the disappointment in his eyes, had told her more plainly than words ever could how badly she had underestimated him, how selfishly naive she had been all along.

It rained every day. Sometimes only for twenty minutes, sometimes for two hours. It was impossible, everyone said, unprecedented; it couldn't continue. But continue it did, day after day, until Rachel stopped bothering to listen to the forecast or to quiz the hotel staff as to their opinions on the shapes and sizes of the shifting clouds, forming and merging round the island like malevolent shades.

Rain itself was a technical problem that could be overcome, as Rachel knew from previous unhappy clashes with the calamitously unreliable moods of the British climate. A bit of post-production dabbling with the right instruments could work wonders on grey skies and sodden grass. The hailstorm effect of torrential rain on coral beaches and turquoise seas, however, was another matter entirely. Not only was filming impossible in such conditions, but the aftermath of each heavenly outburst was not unlike that of a ferocious bombing campaign. The moment the skies cleared, scores of locals – hired specially for the task – would leap into action with leaf brushes and rakes, smoothing over the pockmarked shore and scattering bucketfuls of dry sand (laboriously collected whenever such a rare opportunity presented itself) to cover the worst areas.

Meanwhile, the models sulked under umbrellas, chain-smoking and picking their spots. The one with the bad ankle insisted on having a footstool as well as a deck chair brought onto the set, though the joint in question looked to Rachel to be perfectly shapely and undamaged. The two girls would stroll nonchalantly to take up their positions in the water whenever required, too aware of the unarguable splendour of their long limbs and pretty curves to be modest. The dark-skinned one was particularly beautiful, Rachel thought, noting with more than a trace of wistfulness how smoothly stretched a teenaged skin could be, how invitingly flawless and pert. She restricted any comparable states of undress of her own to the rectangular confines of the hotel swimming pool, wise enough to absent herself from arenas in which she knew she could not compete. The persistent mess of her hair, another calamity of the damp air, the intermittent downpours and life-sapping sun, she kept hidden under a broad-brimmed straw hat, which at least, she felt, granted her some vestige of style, something to hide under if nothing else.

After witnessing the sorry state of play for himself for a couple of days, Frank Alder tactfully jetted out of the proceedings. He left an overwrought product manager in his stead, a young man whose petty concerns over issues largely irrelevant to the hourly challenges being faced by the film crew caused Rachel to resort to the uncharacteristically cowardly tactic of avoiding him altogether. If ever forced into direct conversation she agreed with everything he said and made a point of forgetting it the moment after. Instead, she faxed Frank Alder directly each day, restricting herself to brief but honest progress reports, operating with the detached surface of her mind that she reserved as her last shield against panic. A lot of money had been invested by Mallarmé in these two weeks. Five hundred thousand pounds to be exact. Not to mention the media budget of five million, most of which had already been committed to airtime over the coming year. Too much money for mistakes. Too much money for a botched job.

As the days wore on, and the business of huddling under umbrellas and staring at the leaden skies with the crazed intensity of madmen began to feel almost normal, Rachel found herself longing for the cool pragmatism of Steve Betts. His substitute, a much younger man with a tight blond perm and a twitchy mouth, continued to go through the verbal motions of his job, but with a dazed expression and flailing hands that seemed to communicate an inexpressible terror going on inside.

At the beginning of each day the most senior members of the shoot would gather to examine the rushes and decide which, if any, could be used. Dark clouds were as much of a concern as the rain itself, since they badly affected the light and the atmosphere, and could take a torturously long time to disperse afterwards – almost, thought Rachel, as if they were lingering to mock the petty goings-on of the poor forked beasts below. As the talk of what could be achieved in the cutting room increased, so did a sense of doomed camaraderie. Alcohol consumption was reaching record levels. And drugs, too, though there was less proof of that.

During the second week a bad atmosphere was worsened by the inevitable flurry of sexual liaisons between inappropriate parties. A member of the lighting crew, who had been married only a few months, was sleeping with a young waitress whose pretty black eyes had also been admired by several unmarried colleagues. Similar problems of camp rivalry were surfacing over the two models, rumoured to have bestowed sexual favours upon various members of the entourage but who seemed to thrive on switching their affections and sitting back to study the reactions.

Only two more days to go, Rachel wrote in her diary, one evening towards the end of the second week, *and the nightmare will end. We had a record four hours of uninterrupted sunshine this morning, though the afternoon squall was as bad as ever. I have decided we should reduce the film from forty to thirty seconds and increase the number of product shots from two to four. Frank Alder is willing, though the creative team are threatening to mutiny. But then they are not going to have to suffer the consequences quite as I am.* On a new line she wrote: *Still no reply from Nathan.*

She had composed a letter to Nathan on the very first day of the shoot, apologising for her misjudgement and inviting reconciliation. Not because she entertained any serious hopes of rekindling their relationship, but because she could not bear the sense of unfinished business that their method of parting had created. A silent, interminable drive back to Washington, followed by not even a handshake of a goodbye. They had known each other – albeit sporadically – for almost five years. It seemed wrong – it felt like even more failure – not to be able to round things off properly, without some form of civilised affection at least.

For once, writing the diary did not help. A sense of order on the page was irrelevant, she realised, quite futile in fact, when it came to the new confusions of her real life. Still holding her pen, she strolled outside and leant her elbows on the railings of the window-box balcony adjoining her room. With perfect grand irony, each night had been cloudless and still, unveiling a seamless canopy of stars that seemed quite unconnected to the elemental tantrums of the day.

With work there always was an answer in the end, she thought, peering into the darkness, down towards the sea, straining her eyes to match shapes to the snatches of laughter. With work there was always some compromise that could eventually be reached, like a longer pack shot or a shorter film; nothing was insoluble. But in this other matter,. the matter of a baby, she could think of no answers at all. Worse still, with Nathan gone, a new pulse of urgency had arrived, drumming inside her head like the pendulum of a boxed clock.

A breeze rippled through the palm trees edging the compound of the hotel. Their arched trunks, bent in submission to years of onshore winds, were just visible in the moonlight, like giant limbs thrusting up through the sand. The laughter on the beach, the strains of music drifting up from the open window of the bar below, seemed to come from another world. There will be another month, she told herself, gripping the railings with such passion that the pen slipped from her grasp and disappeared into the foliage below. There will be another cycle, another man. There had to be.

A little later, after she had crawled between the two sheets covering her bed, her mind, as if keen to escape the insoluble conundrums of the present, switched immediately to the past. There she saw a simpler version of herself, a vibrant, confident, blossoming version, who tossed her head dismissively at the world. How easy life had once seemed. How sure she had been. How beautifully unafraid. Rachel smiled to herself as Robbie Dexter plodded into view, a part of that old unwavering self, his hair ruffled, the worn patches on the knees of his interminable jeans.

With a start Rachel blinked open her eyes and sat up in the dark, as the fear throbbed inside her chest. For a few moments she could barely breathe. Adrenalin pumped through her veins, filling her with that crisis energy which is the last resort of human strength. Yet there was nothing for the adrenalin to do, nothing on which to focus. She tried to channel her thoughts towards identifiable problems – towards images of rain and rushes and children – but nothing took hold. The anxiety was without shape or solution, a nameless darkness to do with getting older, more uncertain, more alone. The attack stopped as quickly as it had come, the charge of energy leaving her in a state of near exhaustion as it flooded out of her body. Rachel let her head fall back onto her pillow, gulping in air as if strangling fingers had been released from her throat. 'Stupid woman,' she gasped out loud. 'You stupid old woman.'

With rough, angry movements, she pulled on the clothes that lay across her chair and sketched some colour onto her face. Eat, drink and be merry for tomorrow we die, sang her mind, while her lips pursed themselves for a dash of pink and her eyelids fluttered under dabs of crystal blue. A drink and a bit of company was the thing – the only thing – she told herself, slamming the door behind her and striding down the corridor towards the sounds of merriment emanating from the hotel bar.

14

'I thought you'd be browner,' remarked Anita when they met for a drink in the agency a week or so after Rachel's return.

'I told you, it was work – I wasn't there for a bloody holiday.'

'Pardon me.' Anita lit a cigarette and blew a tunnel of smoke rings at the ceiling. She had poured her first glass at eleven o'clock that morning and was feeling deliciously mellow in consequence. Such placidity was close to bliss, she thought lazily, eyeing Rachel through a screen of grey smoke and thinking that she was being tediously crotchety and middle-aged.

Rachel, whose heart had sunk upon registering the faintly aromatic scent of Anita's breath and the dreamy smile that accompanied it, felt all her sympathies crushed by a great sense of weariness. Instead of mustering all efforts towards a tactful offering of help – as she had intended – she found herself ignoring the subject altogether.

The noisy and packed environs of the McKenzie Cartwright in-house bar were hardly suitable for a heart-to-heart of any kind. Rachel had managed to secure a small round table in the furthest corner, near the wall of windows that overlooked a granite no man's land strewn with paper litter and mangled plastic bags. But there was no avoiding the strains of Bryan Ferry's 'Jealous Guy', which a young copywriter with floppy bleached hair had played several times in succession, draped over the side of the juke-box in a disconsolate fashion suggestive of personal identification with the song's theme. At the table next to them an art director in dark Buddy Holly spectacles was holding forth to a bored-looking account manager on the subject of creative autonomy. Beside them a new secretary with an engaging smile was enjoying the competitive attentions of three media buyers. 'It's like a real party,' sighed Anita happily, 'and with some scrumptious men too. No wonder you work such long hours, you wicked girl.'

Rachel, who knew her friend was too far down the road towards total inebriation to be taken seriously on any level, merely rolled her eyes. 'You've got a one-track mind, Anita, did you know that?' As she spoke, she caught sight of Cliff Weybourne entering the room amongst a crowd of mostly unfamiliar faces. Hastily, Rachel adjusted her position, using Anita's frame to block the new arrivals from view. 'Drink up,' she urged, swigging from her own glass, 'it's getting late.' Two minutes, she told herself, and they'd be gone.

The Bermuda footage was proving salvageable, thanks to a final twenty-four hours of brilliant sunshine and some extremely advanced – and expensive – post-production work farmed out by the agency's creative team to a company called Filmstyle. It was work which the agency was going to have to pay for, however, and which would take a considerable chunk out of the project's profits. Though it looked as though Frank Alder would get his forty-second commercial after all and not too far below the standard he had been led to expect, it was no secret that the shoot had been dogged by bad luck and problems. Rachel had endured something of a rough ride in consequence, keeping all parties calm, presenting endless versions of the re-cut film and enduring the sympathies of her colleagues. Being pitied was something she had always found insufferable.

'Still keen on the baby business?'

'The baby business?' Rachel, aware not only of Anita's but Cliff's eyes upon her across the room, managed a careless laugh. 'Hardly. Besides, I've got a cat. The two don't mix, if I remember correctly.' The cat had been waiting for her upon her return from the shoot, posing beside the garden door like some kind of fireside ornament, its ears pricked and its tail curled neatly round its front paws. Instead of minding, Rachel had thrown down her bags and scooped it up in her arms, overcome with pleasure at finding something to welcome her home. As if baffled by the erratic behaviour of humans, the cat had held itself stiffly throughout this fond embrace, and then shaken out its fur several times after being deposited back on the ground. When Rachel pushed open the door for it to enter, the animal hesitated for a moment or two, as if such a decision was not to be undertaken lightly.

'You can borrow Giles if you want,' drawled Anita, now seriously drunk. 'He hasn't laid a finger on me for months – might as well put his dick to some use—'

'Excuse me butting in.' It was Cliff Weybourne, bending down towards them, his lizard eyes wide and unsmiling, his jet hair prinked to perfection. 'Rachel.' He held out his hand. 'I wanted to say well done.'

'Well done?' She was caught off guard.

Anita, picking up on the theme, rubbed her hands together gleefully. 'Is it something to celebrate? Oh, goody – I love celebrations.'

'This is Anita Cavanagh, my friend from—'

'Ah yes, how do you do.' He flicked the most cursory of glances across the table before returning his attention to Rachel. 'Well done indeed, for pulling it out of the bag. I've just been talking to one of the directors of Filmstyle. He says the film is looking excellent. The worst November weather in Bermuda since records began and you come home with a sunlotion commercial. Impressive.'

Rachel pressed her lips together, not trusting herself to speak, falling back on the hope that he would get bored and go away. In the background, at last weary of Bryan Ferry, the copywriter had begun wailing his own version of the song: *I didn't mean to hurt you, I'm sorry that . . .*

There was a chorus of expletives and groans from those seated nearest to him.

Cliff gestured with his head at the bar. 'The man's here, as it happens. Not involved in the film personally, but says he'd like to meet you.' He tweaked his eyebrows suggestively. 'Will Raphael, he's called. Quite a talented photographer, they say.' He turned and beckoned at someone in the group.

That Cliff Weybourne should know anything at all about the personnel involved in the frenzied damage-limitation exercises being conducted in Soho dark rooms was galling in itself. That

Will Raphael, of all people, should be even remotely involved added another unpleasant twist to the situation.

Rachel cast a longing glance at the door while the tallest of the men grouped at the bar, a slim, dark-haired man in white drainpipe trousers and a black leather jacket, nodded at Cliff and stepped off his bar stool. His hair was long and smooth, brushed straight back off his face, revealing a high forehead and large brown eyes. As he approached, Rachel, determined not to appear put out, eyed him steadily over the rim of her glass. She was on the point of extending a dignified hand when Anita let out a small but piercing shriek. 'I told you there were some gorgeous men in here,' she squeaked, 'I told you.' She got to her feet first, elbowing past Rachel and Cliff in her eagerness to be welcoming.

'Anita Cavanagh – not in this business at all, but a very close member of the family, so to speak.' Her words were noticeably slurred now, running off her tongue in breathless cadences, while her eyes gazed but did not seem to see. 'Delighted to meet you. Delicious jacket, by the way. Positively delicious.' She chewed the last word like a mouthful of food.

Rachel's attention was momentarily diverted by the evident smirk of distaste with which Cliff looked away. A deep reflex of defensive loyalty surged inside. She had to get them out, before poor Anita unwittingly gave any more cause for such disdain.

'Well, thank you very much,' Will replied, ignoring Cliff's look of complicitous horror and patting the leather which had been so exuberantly admired. 'It's an old favourite.' His ears moved when he smiled.

'We were just going, actually,' Rachel blurted.

'What a shame.' He turned to her and bowed his head very slightly. 'Rachel Elliot. How do you do, at last.'

'Mr Raphael. Good to meet you.' Rachel seized Anita's elbow and flashed her most sparkling smile at no one in particular. 'I'm afraid we really must be on our way. Thank you, Mr Raphael, for all your sterling work on my client's behalf – Cliff has just told me—'

'Oh, I've done nothing. My involvement in Filmstyle is purely managerial these days.'

'Oh, I see – well thanks anyway.' She managed to keep

her gaze somewhere in the region of his collar, which wasn't particularly hard since he was so tall. Beside her, Anita had worked her arm free and, with the puzzled look of a hurt child, was massaging the spot where Rachel's fingers had pinched the skin.

'It was my pleasure.' His voice sounded lower than she had remembered it from the telephone and full of a formality which now – she was certain – reflected a strong desire to be allowed to return to his colleagues. A quick glance at his face for verification of this fact, however, found him watching Anita, who had sunk back down into her chair and taken up a head-on-arms position that looked worryingly conducive to sleep. 'I only do my own work these days,' he said slowly, swivelling his gaze back to Rachel. 'Apart from giving a few private lessons. But then you know that.'

Rachel had hoped to avoid discussion of the aborted photography lessons altogether. 'As I tried to explain . . .' she began.

'Oh, you explained all right.' Though his tone was accusatory, his eyes were full of amusement. 'A woman of very few words, clearly.'

Rachel was in no mood to be laughed at. While her mind thrashed around for some appropriately feisty response, in her heart she felt nothing but flat and weak. It did not help that Cliff was shuffling his feet and looking longingly at the bar, clearly bored of the game which he had stage-managed thus far, and that Anita was now tossing her head and moaning.

'If you'll excuse us,' she stammered, tapping Anita on the back and beginning to gather up their bags and coats. 'Come on, Anita, please,' she pleaded, noting out of the corner of her eye that Cliff Weybourne was sloping away and praying that Will Raphael would follow suit. 'Nice to have met you,' she called airily over her shoulder, not looking round. Anita, though upright, was now clinging to the back of her chair and swaying dangerously.

'We must go *now* . . .' Rachel hissed, horrified to find herself almost gagging on the words. With a monumental effort of will she swallowed the tears away. It was the culmination of a tough few weeks, she told herself, still juggling ineffectually with coats and bags, beginning now to feel uncomfortably hot and close to panic. It was just a question of coaxing Anita outside. No one was looking at them. There was no question of a spectacle. Not yet, anyway.

'Can I help?'

Christ, he still hadn't gone. 'No, no, we're fine, honestly. She's just a little . . .'

'Tired?' His brown eyes were not laughing now, but very grave. 'Here, let me.'

Somehow Will Raphael got his arm round Anita in such a way that she could give the appearance of walking whilst having to employ only the minimum of effort herself. Rachel took up the rear, clasping their belongings, keeping her eyes firmly fixed upon the back of his trousers, noting two stray white threads that hung from the left back pocket, dangling below the hem of his jacket.

The sight of two taxis emerging round the corner, yellow lights glaring, at precisely the moment that the agency doors swung shut behind them, lifted Rachel's spirits immeasurably, as did the brilliant chill of the December air. It woke Anita up a bit too, though she had to be prised free from Will's jacket, to which she was clinging with white-knuckled determination.

'Sorry and all that,' she mumbled, as they eased her onto the seat of the cab.

'I'll call home,' said Rachel, tucking Anita's coat round her lap as if she were an old lady and kissing her tenderly on the cheek. 'Let Giles know you're on the way . . .'

'Tell him the bitch is drunk again, you mean . . .'

'Shush now. You'll be better for some sleep. I'll call you tomorrow.'

She backed out onto the pavement to find that Will was holding open the door of the other taxi.

'Where shall I tell him?'

'Chelsea. Near the Embankment.'

'You must live near me, then.' For a minute she thought he was going to ask to share the ride, but instead he put his head inside the window to pass on the directions to the driver.

'Thank you very much,' she said, embarrassment flooding in from nowhere, reddening her cheeks in spite of the cold.

'Would you like me to phone her husband?' He was all businesslike. His breath made little clouds that hid his face.

'No, no, it's quite all right.' She patted her bag. 'I've got a mobile.'

'Ah yes, of course, you would have. A mobile. Good.' He grinned. His teeth were very long, she noticed, and neatly packed. The taxi driver tapped impatiently on the glass window. 'Well, good to have met you,' he called as the door swung shut. 'Good to put a face to a voice.'

He turned away immediately, tugging his jacket collar up round his ears and striding quickly up the street.

Watching from the back of the taxi, Rachel could not help experiencing some paltry relief that he was heading away from the entrance to the agency, that there would be no possibility, that night at least, of Will Raphael sharing any of the juicy tidbits of gossip no doubt being savoured inside. Her face burned again at the very thought. A drunken friend and the Bermuda episode were hardly matters likely to entertain the palates of agency gossip-mongers for long, but still it rankled to have given them any fuel at all.

As the taxi sped through the dark streets, Rachel found herself sliding to the middle of the seat, away from the windows, as if fearful of being recognised by the neon snowmen and Father Christmases winking at her from shop windows and lampposts outside.

Not even a five-mile tailback on the M4 could cast a shadow over Rachel's relief to be heading out of London. It confirmed her belief that these days she was only ever happy when on the move, that she had lost touch with the ability to feel settled in the present. Even her flat, her luxury cocoon of a refuge, the place she thought of longingly during every absence, now seemed to lose its allure once she entered it. Quietness, the absence of all thoughts and stimuli but those emanating from her own imagination, were things that these days she seemed only able to cherish in prospect, the reality of acquiring them bringing nothing more than a sort of deep boredom. It was almost as if she had grown too familiar with herself, too familiar with the small library of her own mind.

As she edged along in the heavy Friday night traffic, heading towards the luxury hotel near Bristol that was to play host to the Mallarmé and McKenzie Cartwright Christmas thrash, it occurred to Rachel that she had done something along the lines of falling out of love with herself. There was no self-belief any more, no certainty about anything. Worst of all, there was no desire to be herself, not unless something fundamental changed, something earth-shattering and self-effacing. Like having a baby. The preoccupation with the subject was unbelievably tiring, a relentless wheel of a thought that came round again and again, driven by a mechanism that she could not control. Sometimes her mind ached from being so constantly besieged.

'I must be bored of being selfish,' she murmured, not quite believing it, since the freedom to design the shape of her life was a privilege which she had nurtured very carefully over the years, treasuring it ever more dearly as friends fell foul of compromises and commitments that she could never have imagined for herself. But the luxury of having no limit imposed on the gratification of personal whims was quite meaningless, if one hated oneself and there were no whims, Rachel thought hopelessly, pulling up the handbrake and folding her arms.

Sitting alone in the dark cubicle of her car, she felt a strong urge for the comfort of interruption. She strained her eyes to make out the features of the silhouettes in cars on either side of her. Were they alone too? Were they escaping or returning, longing for solitude or company? She stared so long at the man on her right, that his head turned, some sixth sense roused by her scrutiny. It was too dark to smile, so she nodded instead, a minute salutation from one human being to another. But the man returned his attention to his windscreen, without offering so much as a head-wobble of acknowledgement in return.

Turning to Radio 4 for consolation, Rachel found herself thrust into a confessional on the emotional implications of infertility. One participant admitted to a consultation with a witch doctor while holidaying on the Ivory Coast; another to fantasies about slaughtering puppies. A third confided in hushed tones that two decades of childlessness had been broken by the death of her father. Her firstborn (she had since had three more, all boys) had been conceived on the very night her father died. Possibly at the very same moment. As a breathy round of incredulity hit the airwaves Rachel stabbed the *off* button and reached for her mobile.

She hadn't spoken to Anita since the unhappy fiasco in the agency bar. The hazardous balancing act of offering support without getting in the way grew no easier with time. Giles, when she phoned him that night, had been his usual laconic self, talking in the clipped manner with which he delivered news reports to the background thud of bombs; stiff and stoical in his charcoal flak jacket, firing spurts of information that invited no questions in response, no possibility of interjection or dissent. Anita was on a downward swing, he said, nothing that hadn't been coped with before. His parents had been drafted in to offer domestic reinforcements. Rachel's concern was, as always, greatly appreciated. He would keep her posted as regards any significant developments. Over and out.

Giles' mother, who took the call that Rachel now made from her car, presented a subtler defence based on euphemisms about tiredness and the strain of coping with the arrival of the twins' back molars. It took all Rachel's powers of persuasion before she agreed to fetch Anita herself.

'Rachel?'

'Anita, how are you?'

'Pretty bloody gloomy.' She lowered her voice. 'Giles has called in the green-welly brigade. Can't do a thing.' Rachel was well acquainted with the habits of Anita's in-laws, a pair of hearty seventy year olds who came from a thoroughbred, home-county stock of jolliness and good order. Anita, whose own parents had died a decade before and who, even in her strongest moments, thrived on a much less orthodox lifestyle, had never exactly risen to the challenge of making her in-laws feel at home. The merest sight of their springy grey hair, their crisp no-nonsense smiles, their obvious determination to get a hold of her family life and pummel it into shape, was enough to make her stick a cigarette in her mouth and flick ash into the toilet bowls. It was a subject, given Rachel's differences with her own parents, upon which the two women had enjoyed many years of synchrony.

'Poor you. Hell on earth, I should imagine.'

'Times a million.'

'Your best tack is probably to sort yourself out in that case. Nothing will get rid of them quicker.'

'I know, I know.' Anita sighed. 'God, it's the thought of Christmas that is really getting me down today. I mean, Christmas. All that tinsel and jingle-bloody-bells, playing happy families . . . leaving Santa a pint of beer and a biscuit for fuck's sake. Bloody carrots for the bloody reindeer. It's all just a big lie, isn't it? I mean, what's the good of pretending life is full of tooth fairies and aerodynamic sleighs when actually it's all a pile of shit?'

'Because the children have got plenty of time to discover the shit part for themselves.'

The traffic was at last starting to move. Rachel lodged the telephone between her shoulder and ear in order to get a steadier grip on the wheel.

'Yeah, yeah, yeah. You're right, of course. It'll be turkey and the Queen's speech as usual. The children hate turkey – and mince pies for that matter . . .' She muttered inaudibly for a while, the first real indication that she was not in entire control of her faculties. '. . . Yuletide charades with everyone eyeballing me every time I take a slug of port. My only problem, you know Rachel, is that there's simply too much going on at home.' Her voice had taken on a determined edge, as if she was as intent on persuading herself of the validity of this excuse as Rachel. 'I'm stressed out, that's all. Everything will be fine once the twins start school . . .

Rachel stopped concentrating for a while, partly because she was in danger of being sucked in amongst the spurting tyres of an articulated lorry, and partly because talk of Christmas was distracting her with images of what she had to look forward to herself on that score.· The previous year she had endured the usual family rituals in Gerrard's Cross before catching an airplane to meet Nathan in New York. Looking back on the episode now, it seemed as if it had happened to another person. The city had lain under a pretty sparkle of frozen snow, not enough to produce unseemly black sludge in the streets, but sufficient to outline the bare trees and square rooftops with rims and caps of crystal, like the icing trim on a cake. Nathan's flat was near Times Square, the converted third floor of what had once been a warehouse, with giant windows and ceilings as high as church rafters. For four days they had done nothing but make love, go to movies, sleep late, eat brunch, browse round shops and return to the flat, often to go to bed again. Even the thought of Nathan's electric toothbrush, whirring round the contours of his handsome teeth for five minutes every morning and evening, was not sufficient to cloud the memory. There would be no lox and bagel brunches this year. There wouldn't even be Gerrard's Cross. Her parents were flying out to Washington to be with Duncan and Mary Beth. Rachel had been invited but had declined, unenticed by the prospect of family charades of the kind Anita was so dreading and unwilling to return anywhere near the scene of so much recent personal mess and disappointment. Her eldest brother Ian, no doubt assuming that she had other plans, had not asked her to join them in Scotland. Not that she would have accepted anyway. Clare's side of the family were bound to be there too, with their unignorably large children and all that shrieking Highland mirth.

Instead, for the first time in her life, Rachel faced the possibility of Christmas on her own, a possibility about which she felt faintly incredulous, since, like the rest of the world, she knew herself to be the kind of lady with plans laid in advance for every occasion. There was always Joy or maybe Naomi. But the thought of a draughty French farmhouse was as unappealing as the chocolate-box brand of a family Christmas at which the Fullertons so excelled. Party frocks, mulled wine and kissing the vicar. Rachel shuddered. Besides which, she had recently agreed to visit the Fullertons over Easter. To call back and ask for hospitality at Christmas in the meantime was unthinkable. A woman with plans, a woman envied for her independence and self-possession, does not easily knock on doors and beg to be taken in. Like some kind of latterday Mary, thought Rachel – fighting waves of increasingly hysterical self-deprecation – but without the man at her side or the child in her belly.

'Rachel, are you still there? Don't say you're cross with me too?'

'Cross? No, don't be silly. Just a murderous truck or two. I'd better go. I'm almost at my turn-off. You take care of yourself, you hear.'

'Where are you off to this time?' Anita's voice was sly with envy.

'Somewhere called Great Hampton Lodge. Clay pigeon shoot-ing and go-cart racing with a client. A Christmas treat,' she concluded flatly.

'Christ, you lucky sod.'

'Aren't I just? Lucky is my middle name, Anita, I thought you knew that by now.'

Rachel accelerated past the speed limit, enjoying, in spite of other preoccupations, the way the car surged at the touch of her foot. There was no way but forwards after all, she told herself, her heart filling with fresh resolve to seize all of life's possibilities with both hands and wrestle them under control.

16 ∫

A message at reception to the effect that Mr Cliff Weybourne had been forced to postpone his arrival until the following morning, set the seal on Rachel's good spirits. In the privacy of her room, she performed a little celebratory jig. Frank would not like it at all, she thought gleefully, doing a twirl with a hand towel; he hated to be reminded that any business could be more pressing than his own.

Dinner on the first night took the relaxed form of a cold buffet. Frank Alder waited until the assembled party had laden their plates with food before banging a fork against a glass and gracing them all with his customary speech of welcome. Though his references to the Allday Sunlotion film were hardly effusive, his warm praise for McKenzie Cartwright in general and Rachel in particular sounded genuine enough. Not even mentioning Cliff's absence, he went on to conclude with instructions that speeches were banned for the following night, as was the failure of anyone to have a good time. Joining with the smattering of applause, Rachel allowed herself a smile of satisfaction. Frank Alder had taken several years of careful nurturing. To allow him to play such a leading role in an event which was funded entirely by the agency, was one of the innumerable ways in which she had skilfully pandered to a man whose only weakness was his ego. A little flattery and deference applied in the right areas could work wonders, she had discovered, especially if the originator of such compliments was female and not entirely unattractive. Sometimes she even imagined a hint of a father-daughter thing in his attitude towards her, a decidedly dubious subtext for a business relationship, but one which she deliberately chose not to analyse beyond the fact that it was both manageable and greatly to her own advantage. Alder and Elliot certainly constituted a team with which the wily Cliff Weybourne would have difficulty competing, she reassured herself, catching Frank's eye across the room and raising her glass.

At last it felt good to be somewhere. Her eyes trailed appreciatively round the chattering groups, noting the elegant backdrop of handsome oak wall panels, tastefully littered with oil paintings of sea shores and poppy fields. These were her people, after all. This was her world. The ratio of sexes was no accident either; it made for a better party atmosphere she found, to keep the numbers of men and women roughly equal, particularly given Saturday night, when high spirits of varying origins had been known to lead to a step or two of dancing. At Rachel's suggestion a jazz band had been signed up that year, the idea being that they could perform quietly in the background during dinner and liven things up later on if required. Looking at the polite conversations being conducted now it was hard to imagine that such an investment in entertainment would prove justified. But Rachel knew from past experience that a few shared escapades with bullets and go-carts could lead to the most extreme abandonment of inhibitions. Last year the mousiest of marketing directors had caused a sensation by ripping off his dress shirt and performing ten minutes of gyratory aerobics round a dining-room chair.

Having made a point of saying a few words to everyone, working her way round the room with a polished ease that would have made her socially aspiring American sister-in-law seethe with envy, Rachel slipped away for something of an early night. It would be a long day tomorrow and long days had, increasingly, to be prepared for, she found, if they were to be coped with as deftly as she intended, without the debilitating accompaniment of puffy eyes and a weak heart. Feeling the knives of anxiety twist in her stomach at the mere thought of needing to sleep, Rachel decided to treat herself to a pill from a bottle acquired during a particularly stressful patch a couple of years before. *Not to be taken when pregnant,* the label said, which reminded her that she still hadn't done anything about getting the folate supplements recommended by Dr Abbot. Grimacing at her own ineptitude, she scooped out a fingerful of nightcream and deposited three large blobs on her cheeks and the tip of her nose. She rubbed the cream in with both hands, wondering all the while if middle-aged women dependent on moisturiser and sleeping tablets had any right to flatter themselves with images of pushing prams and being loved. Minutes later the tingling heaviness began, together with the not entirely pleasant sensation of having her veins injected with molten lead.

Cliff Weybourne arrived in time for breakfast, his face as smooth as polished chalk, his black hair freshly cut. Even though olive-green corduroys and a brown mohair jumper offered little camouflage for the generous contours of his figure, there was something sickeningly spritely about the man, Rachel decided, eyeing him over the rim of her coffee cup as he sprang from table to table, firing smiles and shaking hands. He spent longest of all talking to Frank Alder, bending his head confidentially near his ear for one comment, before standing up and slapping his newspaper on his thigh as they both laughed out loud. Rachel tensed, hating the notion that there was a man's club after all, that no matter how hard her outer shell, there was a society that she could never join, a society that would always be more assured, more powerful in the end.

Having helped himself from a buffet of hot-plates, Cliff made his way over towards Rachel, who – in keeping with her aversion to breakfast conversations of any kind – had taken the precaution of seating herself in the furthest corner of the dining room, at a table laid for one. Beside her a large window presented a snapshot of their grand surroundings: gravelled paths and evergreen shrubs skirted an elegant carpet of a croquet pitch, this morning covered with a lacy cloth of white frost. On a terrace below that were two tennis courts, where a keen pair in white track suits and headbands were defying the bitter cold with a set of racy pink tennis balls and rackets with giant heads.

'May I?'

Rachel nodded at the empty seat opposite her. 'Of course.'

'Seen the news?' He smacked his newspaper with the back of his hand. 'Blackers have been taken over by The Glastonbury Group. They're going to invite five agencies to pitch for the business. I was up till all hours with Alan last night. We're on the shortlist apparently. We could get Blackers and a lot more besides.' He put down his plate, on which balanced several toppling pyramids of fried food, and helped himself to a place setting from a neighbouring table.

Jets of fat spurted from the sausage at the prick of his fork. 'It's bloody fantastic. Alan is delighted, as you might well imagine. Not the easiest of markets to advertise.' He had a method of rerouting mouthfuls into one cheek in order to facilitate the business of talking with the section of his mouth that remained vacant. 'Homecare products, do-it-yourself weaponry – there's so bloody much of it and so little to tell them all apart. Going to be a hell of a pitch. Money no object, Alan says – *carte blanche*. Hey, *carte blanche* for Blackers. Not bad, eh?'

Rachel delivered the merest shadow of a smile to acknowledge this witticism before casting her eyes over the newsprint in front of her.

'If we win the business I'll see to it that Alan considers you for the account, of course.' He drove a hefty wadge of fried bread through a pool of egg yolk and tomato skin.

'That's very sweet of you, Cliff, but there's no need, really.' She folded the newspaper and handed it back. 'I would much prefer to concentrate my efforts on Mallarmé, as I have explained to Alan many times. You can keep those power drills and lavatory fittings all to yourself. As you say, a hell of a challenge for all concerned.'

'Absolutely.'

Rachel made a big show of folding her napkin and looking at her watch, thinking all the while how dispiriting it was to fire missiles at such a leathery hide.

'Are you any good with a gun then, Rachel?' There was a hint of a leer to the question, which caught her by surprise.

'Oh yes, Cliff,' she replied coolly, pushing back her chair and standing up. The presence of an as yet undetected speck of encrusted egg yolk to the left of his mouth filled her with a perverse and cheerful optimism for the day ahead. 'I've no problem when it comes to guns.'

'I'm delighted to hear it.' He chuckled, clearly amused rather than warned by the steely look in her eye. 'I look forward to a full demonstration.'

In fact Rachel hated guns. After her first experience of shooting, on a similar weekend four years earlier, vivid pink and purple bruises had sprouted over her right shoulder and upper chest, gradually turning yellow and greeny-blue, like flowers fading past their prime. Though her technique had since improved sufficiently to avoid incurring such physical injuries again, firing bullets at flying discs was not a prospect she had learnt to relish for itself. It was the end results that interested her – the relaxing of business barriers, the curious camaraderie that sharing such experiences allowed.

She smiled at Frank Alder as she passed his table. As usual, he was kitted out in full country squire regalia, complete with a monogrammed cartridge bag, a tweed cap and spotless green hunters, all of which remained suspiciously impervious to the ravages of time. This year there was the addition of a handsome brown leather cartridge belt, which he had placed on display across the table, between his side plate and a glass of orange. The knobs of each bullet gleamed with evidence of polishing. Fancy dress, she thought, broadening her smile. The man was hopelessly pompous – quite unteasable – but really rather sweet, she decided, taking care to admire the belt before going back up to her room.

Before they were allowed to select padded vests and guns, a lecture on safety was barked at them by a veiny-faced man with strikingly protuberant ears that trembled with the delivery of each sentence. There was to be one trap firing, two clays at a time and four stands. Four people at each stand. Twelve bores for the men, sixteen bores for the ladies. Ear plugs were recommended but not compulsory. All beginners would receive as much help as they desired.

As Rachel's turn to take the stand approached, apprehension gave way to a customary determination to appear strong, not to conform to a whimpering female stereotype of any kind. She held the stock tightly into her shoulder as she fired, shouting 'pull' in a voice that hit the still cold air without any trace of the hesitancy lurking inside. Two clays flew out, catapulting into the grey sky and hovering for just an instant before they began to fall, plummeting to the earth like stones. Rachel missed the first three, nicked the fourth and missed the fifth and sixth. Her eyes, watery with cold, squinted at the targets. As she missed and missed again, her mind began to feel as if it was spinning too, firing into nothing, focusing on nothing, adrift on the biting air. A sense of absurdity descended from nowhere, threatening to overwhelm her. What was she doing, on this grey, bitter December Saturday – a day for hot drinks and curling on sofas to watch old films – firing a gun at a blank sky? Both feet had grown quite weightless with cold. An obstinate, unseemly dribble was trickling from her nose, sniff-resistant, tepid on her upper lips. Cold air was snaking into her ears and eye sockets, filling her head with icy pain, blurring her vision until even the sky was no more than a grey fuzz.

She was the last to fire in her group. Several people who had either given up or finished were standing chattering and laughing several yards away, the vapour of their breath mingling with the grey swirls rising from the mouths of the smokers. Even before she started Rachel had caught herself longing to join them, longing to be brave enough to behave as if she did not care. Like the petite brand manager with heart-shaped lips who hadn't even had a go. How sweet it would be to act the sissy for once, to admit defeat with a few girly simpers of distaste and fear. How tiring to be the fearless Rachel Elliot – a match for any man, whatever the game. How utterly futile.

The helper from her stand had fallen back to smoke a cigarette with some of the others. Loading her gun for the last time, Rachel found herself focusing on the prettiness of the grass around her feet, where untrodden blades were still sugar-tipped with frost. Not catching anyone's eye was paramount suddenly; not giving the impression of misery being the least she could do, maybe even the only salvageable achievement of the morning.

Shooting at the next stand was a young account manager called Chlöe, who had flaming red hair and startled blue eyes. Though the hair had begun the morning tucked away up under the brim of a big woollen hat, great tresses of it had since broken free and were now cascading impressively down the quilted back of her protective green vest. Exhilaration shone in the blush of her cheeks, in the confident way in which she swung her gun, aiming it skyward with the ease of a finger pointing at a board. At the third stand, Frank Alder painted an altogether more traditional, if less compelling figure; elegant, but slow. One hit in five, maybe four. Beyond him, the most surprising contributor of all: Cliff Weybourne, as poised and alert as an athlete on the starting block, with split-second reactions that ensured the clash of bullet and target every time. There were no nicking of edges for him, no near misses, but mini explosions of erupting clay, orange shards raining, dark with speed, upon the tops of the black trees clumped along the skyline below. He hit all but one. The ginger-haired Chlöe hit twenty. Frank got eight. Rachel three. Three out of twenty-five.

Once the shoot was over everyone gathered round, blowing into cupped hands for warmth, exchanging jokes and congratulations. The dampness in the air seemed to muffle their voices, sucking out the trill, inducing an urge to shout to be heard at all. Rachel, grey and stiff, clung to her gun, nodding her head with the best of them, only the fear of appearing forlorn giving her the strength to mould her frozen face into something resembling a smile.

'Well tried, Rachel. I like your style. Very promising. I like a woman who tries.' Cliff Weybourne heralded his arrival at her heels with a hearty slap between her shoulder blades. The smack of his hand on her back, so shockingly hard and uninvited, wrought a surge of such irritation that she gasped out loud, digging her nails into her palms in order to prevent herself from hitting back.

'I was bloody awful. Never got my eye in.'

She was rescued by Frank Alder, who appeared on the other side of her. 'Tough conditions today. Though it didn't stop you, Cliff, did it? Most impressive, most impressive. Out of our league, eh Rachel?'

'He certainly is.' When she tried to lick some life back into her lips, the saliva dried in an instant, leaving tiny cracks that felt raw and sore. On impulse, she linked her arm through Frank's, needing suddenly to feel aligned with him, even if it was ineptitude that granted her the privilege.

'You'll get him on the racetrack though, won't you Rachel my dear? If I recall correctly, you're something of a tiger behind a wheel.' He roared with laughter. Rachel, sickened by the realisation that rivalry between her and Cliff should be both so obvious and a cause for such mirth, let go of his arm and moved away.

After a hasty lunch they were herded into a minibus and driven to a tarmac oasis passing under the name of Formula 1 West. This time, insurance waivers had to be signed, promising that if limbs, eyes, or lives were mislaid during the course of the afternoon's entertainment, they had only themselves to blame. A young man with cigarettes and pencils slotted behind his ears then delivered the second safety lecture of the day. Helmets were mandatory, as were grey overalls of curious dimensions that bore little relation to the human shapes for which they were supposedly designed. The most ill-fitted of all was Cliff, whose trouser legs terminated two inches above the tops of his white socks and whose brown mohair tangle peeked through the buttons straining across his belly like stomach hair gone wild. Only Chlöe managed to sport her costume with anything like panache, aided considerably by her flaming film-star tresses and a pair of heavy-soled ankle boots which contributed excellently to the overall effect. In a bid to heighten the atmosphere of the occasion, loud speakers blared 'Simply The Best' as each set of cars took up their positions, adding considerably to the din of engines as they roared away. Rachel, during a faltering set of warm-up laps, found herself grappling for the second time that day with an overpowering sense of the absurd. How had she endured these games before? What on earth had she been playing at?

But when her race started, something clicked into place. All her uncertainties and fear dissolved in the few instants it took to raise her left foot from the brake and press her right hard down on the accelerator. Effortlessly, she cruised past Cliff Weybourne, past the others in her heat, and settled into the lead. The noise of the engines filled her head, adding to the intoxicating impression of speed as the ground, so near at hand, rushed past. It was like flying. She felt immortal. When the marshall waved his chequered flag at the finishing line, her pulse and her go-cart slowed with reluctance. Though Rachel was unaware of it herself, the glow of triumph remained with her for many hours afterwards, greatly heightening the effect of the striking blue evening dress she wore to the dinner that night and lending a vibrance to her appearance, which the more astute among the assembled company realised had been absent for many weeks.

Frank Alder was a good, if slightly lumbering dancer. His answer to the more challengingly rhythmic numbers was to keep time with his hands while his feet played small shuffling games of their own. When it came to slower tunes he steered Rachel round the room in the frame of his arms with a steady elegance that spoke volumes for the ballroom skills of previous generations. The jazz musicians, having been allowed to strum and croon exactly as they pleased throughout the meal, were now called upon to supply a medley of requests quite unrelated to the brand of expertise for which they had originally been hired.

Rachel was old enough to experience a tingle of gratitude as well as pleasure at the way several heads turned in appreciation when she entered the dining room. Where once such appreciation had been a certainty, she was now learning the wisdom of not expecting it.

When exactly did one become an old lady? she had wondered earlier that night, drawing a pencil line round the edges of her lips and pouting in self-mockery at the result. At what point was one supposed to surrender the eyeliner and confront the world with grey hair and a headscarf? How would she avoid joining the pitiable ranks of those who tried too hard, those for whom the very visibility of their efforts undermined any of the beautifying effects achieved? Once upon a time Rachel had been thrilled that the industry in which she worked thrived on an image of youthful ebullience, on the dynamism of its few elderly members. Now it made her secretly afraid. It was all very well feeling good in shimmering dresses, but the daily grind was there too. Children were supposed to keep you young, she thought slyly, remembering Anita's warning and discarding it in the same instant. But the thought of a child was scary too.

She rammed on the lid of her lipstick. Everything scared her these days; it was intolerable. Since she had forgotten to wind the lipstick back into its tube, the lid succeeded only in crushing the contents it was designed to protect. Instead of a smooth torpedo of red, Rachel was left with a sticky, misshapen crayon, like one of the expensive paint sticks she had given Charlotte after the twins had been at them. She dropped the entire mess into the bin beside the dressing table and tried to wipe her fingers clean with a tissue. Though the worst came off easily, a faint pink stain remained on her fingertips; a reminder of the effort behind the costume, the cost of looking good.

But it was impossible not to enjoy herself that night, especially not after the wheels of her own self-respect – and everybody else's – had been thoroughly oiled by several glasses of good wine and four courses of excellent food. Back on the dance floor, opposite Ted Bealey, an old friend from the Planning Department, Rachel felt her body loosen and her blood flow. Dancing with Frank had been an altogether more reserved business, some part of her kept in check by a deep sense of propriety to do with the age gap and a niggle of a worry about the affection lurking in his old-man smile. But with subsequent partners she began to let herself go a little, moving her hips fluidly in time to the music and floating her arms to the front and sides, stretching her fingers as if to feel each pulse more keenly. Ted, clearly inspired by such synchronised abandonment, began to jig more vigorously himself, jerking his hips to the left and right and beckoning Rachel to do the same. Laughing, Rachel joined in the game, moving closer, until the pair of them were nudging alternate hip bones and waving their arms like mad things.

The song had not quite finished when Cliff stepped between them with a hip-thrust of a request to join in the fun. Beads of perspiration glistened on his chalky face; the thick layers of his black hair, usually brushed tidily off his temples, had fallen forwards and were sticking to damp patches on his forehead. He had so far devoted most of the evening to an unabashed courtship of Chlöe, the red-headed account manager, whom he had sat next to at dinner and whose admiration he had since been trying to secure through some peacock-style rituals on the dance floor. While not wanting to pay him the compliment of appearing impressed, Rachel had none the less observed these curiously elegant antics out of the corner of one eye, amazed to note the poise with which the small tidy feet supported the swaying bulk on top.

Patting the left side of his chest in a mime of exhaustion, Ted bowed out. Rachel continued dancing, though with considerably less vigour, letting her eyes rove around the room in a bid to avoid meeting Cliff's look of smug satisfaction while she waited for the tune to end. Instead of pausing for its customary breather between songs however, the band turned the last chord of one song into the first of the next – a much slower one that placed immediate pressure on remaining couples to regroup into more intimate poses. Rachel began backing away but Cliff was too quick for her, springing forward and throwing his arms around her shoulders, his body already swaying in time to the new, heavier rhythm.

'Cliff . . . I'm really tired . . . dropping in fact. I really don't think—'

'Oh, come now Rachel, don't give me that. We could be friends, you know, you and I. We could work very well together. Very well indeed.' His arms pressed harder; they were lower on her back now, pulling her in.

'Really . . . I'd like a drink . . . I'm so hot.' She could feel the damp palms of his hands sticking to the silk covering her back.

'I'm hot too, believe me . . . but everyone's looking, you know, everyone's wondering if we can work this thing out between us. It would be nice to prove them wrong, wouldn't it? Nice to show we're proper grown-ups. No in-fighting. A tight team.'

It was true, their partnership on the dance floor had definitely been noticed. Frank Alder, now reclining in an arm chair with a cigar and a tumbler of brandy, was studying them particularly hard. Cliff was right: it would be cause for even more gossip if she broke away after just a few bars of music. Far better to see it through, to suffer in silence for appearance's sake.

Feeling her resistance lessen, he pulled her closer. In her high heels she was almost as tall as he. He could see the glass freckles of sweat on her bare chest, count every stone in the glittering clusters dangling from her earlobes. Her arms on his shoulders hung loosely, leaving her hands trailing with an insouciance that excited him. A moment of mistiming and their faces touched, a hot brush of cheek on cheek, before she jerked her head back out of range. Some devious shuffling on Cliff's part ensured that their legs touched too, though she managed to keep her hips firmly to herself – an achievement which necessitated a bend at the waist that was almost comic and certainly unnatural.

'Come on, Rachel, relax now. I'm not going to bite, you know. I'm just a man. A man who admires you very much.'

'Oh, and I admire you Cliff, believe me. You are a person of singular abilities.'

'Thank you, Rachel. How generous of you to say so.'

The music seemed endless. Her back, aching from the effort of staying so stiff and separate, gradually began to relent, until only her head remained free, her chin pointing slightly upward, like a swimmer reaching for air.

'I loved today,' he murmured, 'I loved the way you beat me.'

'You beat me, Cliff, remember.' Her voice sounded high pitched and strange. 'The best score of the lot—'

'Ah, but not on the fast track. Christ, you drove like the devil.' His hands, which had travelled even further down her back, arrived at the upper curve of her bottom and squeezed. Energised by repulsion, Rachel pulled away at once. The music stopped in the same instant.

He held up his hands in a mockery of innocence, grinning at the expression on her face before taking her hand and planting a kiss on the knuckles. 'Thank you so much, Rachel, that was delightful.'

When reception telephoned at seven-thirty the next morning, Rachel experienced a few seconds of blissful, unregistering drowsiness before the full horror of the night's event dawned on her again.

'. . . Sleet and snow are forecast for Wales and the Southwest,' declared the radio above her head, 'with temperatures sinking to below freezing tonight. Motorists are warned that driving conditions will be hazardous and are advised to stay at home unless journeys are unavoidable.' Turning down the volume, Rachel lay back and pulled the sheets up to her eyes. In a picture on the wall opposite, St George was slaying a dragon. A willowy princess looked on, suppliant and doey-eyed, waiting for her rescuer to finish off the job.

Cliff Weybourne had tried to have sex with her. The fact of it felt both solid and impossible. He had knocked on her door in the small hours, said he was making an early start for London; said he had important papers about the Blackers takeover; said he was sorry to wake her, said it was important; said . . . she couldn't remember what else. Enough to make her stumble, sleepy and dry-mouthed, to her door, to stand frowning at the passage light, pushing the hair from her eyes as she held out her hand for whatever he had to deliver, her brain in too much of a dozy whir to wonder at the strangeness of such a request. And he was dressed to go, with his black briefcase on the floor at his side and with a sheaf of papers in his hands. But instead of handing them over he had pushed his way in, pushed her too, so that she half-walked, half-stumbled back onto the bed. Before adrenalin gave her strength, his hands were inside her nightie, one up under the hem, the other in through the undone buttons at the front.

'Jesus, Rachel, Jesus,' he grunted, his tongue licking her face.

It was hard to do anything but gasp at first, the attack was so quick, so utterly unexpected.

'You want it,' he grunted, 'I know you want it.'

She tried to kick with her legs, but the weight of him was too much. 'Get out, get out or I'll scream.'

'Oh yes, scream . . . that's fine . . . scream.'

She tried to. She opened her mouth and pushed, but nothing came out, not even air. In the end she used her teeth, biting into the soft roll of flesh pushing over the top of his starched shirt collar, using an energy and venom inspired by fear. He let out a howl and leapt back at once, clutching his neck. In the same instant she rolled free and ran for the door.

'Get out, you bastard.' Her body trembled so much it was hard even to keep a grip on the smooth metal handle of the door.

Cliff was dabbing at his neck with a clean white handkerchief, staring at two rosy specks in horror. 'You bitch.'

'Just get out, now, please.' She could feel her energy begin to sap away, as the surge of adrenalin receded and shock began to take over.

Cliff, the handkerchief still pressed to his neck, was looking round for his briefcase.

'You're not going to get away with this,' she whispered, edging towards the light in the passageway.

'Get away with what? I made a bad call, that's all.' He began adjusting his tie and hair. The bleeding at his neck had stopped, though the skin looked very bruised. 'You gave me the come-on tonight, you can't deny it. Then you let me into your room. You were hot for it Rachel, any man could see that.'

'How dare you . . .'

'How dare I?' He actually laughed, throwing back his head and closing his eyes for a few moments. 'We are grown-ups, my dear. The fact that you went off the idea is not exactly my problem . . .'

'You wait . . . you'll see.'

'Sure, I'll wait and see.' He raised his hand to pat her shoulder but she ducked out of reach. 'My, my, touchy, aren't we? Funny really, I would never have taken you for the frigid spinster type, but then life is full of surprises. Your copy of the documents is over there on the table, by the way. See you Monday. It's been a good weekend, don't you think?'

She watched him walk away, his footsteps soundless on the lilac hallway carpet. Having locked the door, she looked at her watch. Five o'clock in the morning. Outside it was still pitch black, though she could hear a mounting wind signalling the approach of bad weather in the beat of its huge wings. Suddenly icy with cold, she had slipped back between the sheets, pulling them round her neck for warmth while she rubbed her feet together. The movement was soothing, sending heat not only round her legs but across the bed as well.

The aftermath of shock brought an unbelievable sleepiness. As she closed her eyes it dawned on her that, with courage, she now had the wherewithal to eject Cliff Weybourne from her life completely. It offered comfort of sorts. Less comforting was the irony of other, crueller thought associations which tiptoed with her towards the brink of sleep. Would she have kept a baby fathered by Cliff Weybourne? Would rape have been worth a child?

18 ſ

On Christmas Eve Rachel was ambushed by a throng of school-age carol singers on her doorstep. While the elder ones managed only a self-conscious nonchalance, the under-tens belted out the verses with unabashed energy, nudging and smiling happily at each other as they went along. A small crowd gathered, head-nodding encouragement and appreciation, united for a few moments by this shared pleasure, as a blue sky or a fall of snow unites those who smile about it below.

> We wish you a merry Christmas,
> We wish you a merry Christmas,
> We wish you a merry Christmas
> And a happy New Year.
> Glad tidings we bring to you and your king
> We wish you a merry Christmas
> And a happy New Year.

Rachel put her bags down on the pavement and waited for a path to clear to the wide stone steps leading up to the front door of her building. As they launched into the second verse, she caught herself humming and squeezing her toes in time to the music, old echoes of childhood feelings stirring inside. But then it occurred to her that, for adults, Christmas was just a remembered joy, and her toes froze inside her boots.

When they had finished, the smallest child, its sex disguised by a yellow balaclava covering all but two large hazel eyes, stepped forward rattling a blue charity box on the side of which was a handwritten label, saying *Crisis At Christmas*.

'We're collecting for people who are going to have a horrid Christmas,' it said solemnly, jigging the box under Rachel's nose.

'What a worthy cause,' she murmured, slotting a pound coin into the slit.

The leader of the brood, a beaming woman with ruddy cheeks and a floppy-brimmed black velvet hat that bounced over her eyebrows, began herding her protégés away, mouthing 'thank-yous' at the contributions clinking into the box. A few moments later, the strains of 'In The Bleak Mid-Winter', delivered at a cheerfully breakneck speed, started up further down the street.

A wadge of crisp white envelopes sat in her letterbox in the main hall. Thanks to the added burdens of the festive season, the postman had not been arriving at his usual hour. Rachel had caught herself missing their doorstep exchanges, a few pithy comments on the rain or the hazards of British beef having had a mysteriously heartening effect on many a dank morning in the past.

She missed the cat, too. After putting in a brief appearance upon her return from Bermuda, it had vanished, Alice-in-Wonderland-style, apparently for good this time. To miss a cat seemed to Rachel to be quite close to hitting rock bottom. She had never wanted the thing in the first place, had only grown attached to it because of its own impudent persistence. Two tins of gourmet jellied chunks now sat gathering dust on the windowsill. Rabbit and chicken liver. Fifty pence a mouthful. The animal had disappeared the day she bought them, a coincidence that seemed fraught with meanings she did not care to understand.

Having hurled the tins to the back of an empty shelf, she made a cup of tea, turned the central heating dial up several notches and took her post through into the sitting room.

There was a card from Anita. On the front an irate Father Christmas was tugging at a parking ticket wedged into the windscreen of his sleigh. Inside were the usual printed greetings, under which she had scrawled, *In 'Coventry' in the country with G's parents. Being stuffed with food, but at least no cooking which is good. Thanks for Charlotte's parcel (weighs a ton!). Hope Gds Crss is not too gruesome. We're here till Dec 30. See you at the Robsons' New Year thrash as usual?*

Rachel smiled at the expostulating Santa, cheered as always by the faintly anarchic tone of any communication from Anita, and wishing – reluctantly – that she was close at hand. To be in serious need of someone to talk to was a new and highly unenjoyable experience. As was the realisation that isolation and independence were not such poles apart after all.

She also felt a mixture of guilt and alarm at having lied so easily about her whereabouts. Was it entirely normal, she wondered, running her finger under the flap of the next envelope, to find the horror of spending Christmas alone preferable to the admission of any such thing, even to a close friend? Was it so peculiar not to want to give the world permission to feel as sorry for her as she felt herself?

In a last bid to be plucky and make the best of things, she had left work very early that afternoon in order to stop off at an expensive delicatessen on the way home. Without so much as a glance at a price, she had purchased six quails eggs, three strips of smoked eel, two pots of Russian caviar, one bottle of champagne and one of claret, some smoked salmon pâté and two loaves of freshly baked, nutty brown bread, still warm from the oven. At the last minute she threw several jars of delicacies into her basket as well, spurred on by some recommendations from the shop owner and a determination to be as extravagant as possible.

The second card contained the printed message, *Seasonal Greetings from Filmstyle*. Beneath this there were some black loops which, on closer scrutiny, turned out to be an idiosyncratic representation of the name, Will Raphael. The picture on the card was a photograph of a woman, seated at a table alone, head in hands with her eyes closed. The entire scene was black and white, save for a robin, perched on the windowsill behind, and a single red rose, arching out of a slim crystal vase. Rachel studied for a few moments, disliking the image, yet curious as to how effect had been achieved. It was halfway between a pho and a painting. The woman had long straight hair and a face that somehow made up for the emptiness of th the bottom right hand corner were the initials *WR*.

She sipped her tea and added the new cards to the ones already decorating her mantelpiece before turning to Nathan's. It was something of a surprise, after so many weeks, to hear from him at all. It also made her feel guilty for having drawn a thick red line through his presence on her Christmas card list. A colour photograph, of the mass-produced variety, fell out of the envelope, depicting Nathan and a tall blonde girl in ski outfits of dazzling yellow and pink; their mittened hands were waving with puppet-like symmetry at the camera lens. Printed across a section of blue sky in the top left hand corner were the words: *Happy Holidays from Cindy and Nathan. With love to you all.*

Rachel scowled at the fresh-faced slalem star, with her flaw-less, gleaming portals of teeth and her vibrant tumble of hair, looking so yellow against the backdrop of blanket snow. Their happiness looked suspiciously manic, she decided, letting the meanness wash through her, instinctively despising and distrust-ing any brand of love whose proprietors felt the need to advertise it so garishly to the world. She put the card down and then picked it up again. The notion that this Cindy, although more perfectly formed in every respect, might be a younger version of herself, did nothing to fan the embers of her festive spirit. Good teeth, fair hair. They were not so unalike. But what really jarred was the fresh-faced enthusiasm of the girl, the unmistakable glow of a self-conviction which Rachel was beginning to associate with youth and which she had, until so recently, taken for granted herself.

On the other side of the picture there was a faint message, Nathan's biro clearly having had quite a struggle against the laminated surface of the card. *Getting married at New Years. All the best. Nathan.*

So he wasn't just skiing and screwing with the Toothpaste Queen, he was marrying her too. Rachel shook her head in wonder at the exuberant expressions on the tanned faces of the snow-bound pair. True love indeed. She tossed the card to one side and took the cold remains of her tea through into the kitchen.

Images of Anita lurching into the back of a cab assisted greatly in the decision to leave the claret to breathe for a while instead of gulping it down on the spot. Having unpacked her purchases with deliberate briskness, she flicked on the little string of lights entwined round the verdant nylon tree in her hall, ran herself a scalding bath – mountainous with foam – and went to fetch her portable radio from the bedroom. A man with a crooning voice was reading the lesson about the shepherds embarking on the curious challenge of following a star. There followed an inspiring rendition of 'While Shepherds Watched' the unwavering trebles somehow making the old words sound full of fresh meaning, while the notes soared on some impressive acoustics offered by the tiled walls of the bathroom. Just as she was in danger of experiencing a twinge or two of religious fervour, an intermittent buzz started up in the background, as if someone was hoovering a carpet in the choir stalls. The buzz grew louder and nearer until, as the batteries entered their final death throes, the only thing being transmitted was a furious spitting sound. Reaching out a deft, big toe, crested with bubbles, Rachel switched the radio off. This Christmas was going to be one of those times, she told herself, something that had to be lived through, endured, until it stopped, like a bad dream, like getting Cliff Weybourne out of her room.

At the thought of him the water seemed to lose some of its heat. She slipped further down amongst the peaks of foam, seeking more warmth. Nothing was working out these days, absolutely nothing.

All the way back from Bristol, ploughing through horizontal sheets of icy rain, Rachel had exalted at the prospect of turning the horror of recent events to her advantage. The following morning she had marched into Alan Jarvis's spacious office without a moment's hesitation, planting herself in the middle of his creamy sheepskin rug with all the confidence of the truly virtuous.

'Rachel? Is something the matter?'

'You could say that Alan, yes.' She made no attempt to hide her agitation. 'This is not going to be easy . . .'

'Sit down. I'll get Julie on to some coffee—'

'No thank you, not for me.' She inhaled deeply; the room smelt of a mixture of furniture polish and Alan's aftershave, a flowery sweet smell that made her faintly nauseous. 'The simple fact is

that . . . that during the course of the weekend I have been . . .
I was . . . abused by Cliff.'

'Abused? You mean he was rude to you?'

'I mean,' she hesitated for an instant, 'I mean that he harassed
me . . . sexually.'

'You are accusing Cliff Weybourne of sexual harassment?'
There was no hiding the incredulity in his tone. 'Well . . . I
knew that the two of you had something of a personality clash
but really . . .'

'He came into my bedroom, Alan.' The sense that she was
losing his sympathy, that she had never even had it to start
with, gave her the courage to speak more bluntly. 'He threw
himself at me. He assaulted me.'

Alan was rubbing his chin nervously, studying her out of the
corner of his eye. 'This is very . . . very difficult indeed.'

Rachel stood up. 'No, Alan, it is not difficult. Cliff Weybourne
tried to force me to have sex with him. It is intolerable that he
should be allowed to continue working here. He may try again,
he may attack other women . . .' Aware that she was in danger
of sounding hysterical, she sat back down on the slippery edge
of the leather sofa and placed both hands on her knees. After
careful consideration of her wardrobe she had opted for a dark
blue trouser suit with a white shirt buttoned up to her neck:
infallibly chaste, unarguably businesslike.

'Look, Rachel . . .' Alan Jarvis came to sit next to her, lowering
his voice to a pitch of tender concern. '. . . I know Cliff is a hard
man to work with. Believe me, you are not the only person
who has problems with him . . . but he is also a shrewd and
imaginative businessman. Clients love him. He has he been
doing an excellent job on the new business front.' He put
his hands together, interlocking each finger. 'And . . . well, in
simple terms, he would be extremely costly to get rid of.' When
their eyes met he blinked first. 'So, Rachel, I want you to think
very hard for a moment and tell me whether you are absolutely
certain that you wish to persist with this allegation. Sometimes
. . . misunderstandings arise during occasions like these . . . when
everybody is feeling jolly and so on . . .'

'There was no misunderstanding, Alan. I have endured my
quota of uninvited gropes, believe me. I know the difference.

This was attempted sexual assault and, I can assure you, it was not very pleasant.' Her voice trembled.

'No, no,' he soothed, touching her hand for a second, before going back to his desk. He picked up the telephone and held it for a few moments before pressing any numbers. 'You are prepared, I take it, to confront Cliff with these accusations yourself?'

'Oh yes,' she replied quietly, 'I am indeed.' A tight elation was gathering in her stomach. She would hold nothing back, absolutely nothing. The truth was unignorable. Alan Jarvis had his weaknesses – he was a bit of a ditherer, he liked an easy life – but he was also a man of integrity. They had known each other a long time. He trusted her. And she him.

Cliff Weybourne entered the room a few minutes later, his pale face composed but unsmiling. Julie materialised with a tray of coffee behind him, the studied neutrality of her face warning Rachel that the mysteriously osmotic process of in-house gossip had started already. The coffee was poured and passed round, while the two main protagonists arranged themselves between the generous cushions of Alan's handsome three-piece suite, as if preparing to discuss nothing more taxing than a Christmas gift for a client, or the noise problems generated by the recent refurbishment of the ladies' lavatory.

Alan Jarvis kicked off the proceedings, while Rachel chewed the inside of her cheek and studied something invisible on the palm of her right hand.

'Cliff, I'm afraid Rachel has come to me this morning with some very serious allegations of inappropriate conduct on your part during the course of the weekend.'

Cliff sipped his coffee and shook his head, casting a sidelong glance of theatrical regret at Rachel before speaking himself.

'She threatened to do this Alan, but I never thought she would. I really didn't.' He put down his cup and turned to face Rachel. 'Let's leave this here, shall we?' he pleaded. 'We can, you know, Rachel. It's not too late to back down.'

She shook her head, her eyes never leaving his. 'I am accusing you of sexual . . . harassment.'

With a curt laugh Cliff returned his attention to Alan. 'What about this then?' He tilted his chin up so as to give their arbiter a better view of his neck. 'Evidence of quite a passion, I'm sure you'll agree. A lovebite, I believe it's called . . . quite a trophy, I'll admit.' Though the mark was bite-sized, there was no evidence of blood; just innocuous swirls of pink and blue. Cliff leant forwards, resting his elbows on his knees, looking earnest, ignoring Rachel's open-mouthed horror at this easy dismissal of proof on which she herself had been relying. 'Look, Alan, of course I would far rather this had not come out – generally I'm not a believer in relationships crossing the work threshold – but the fact of the matter is Rachel and I' – he had the audacity to shoot her a complicitous smile – 'almost had what you might call a fling. At quite a late stage – for which I apologise Rachel – I changed my mind. I'm afraid it dawned on me quite how unwise it would be, from the work point of view and so on. I pulled back. I returned to London.' He clapped his hands together. 'As far as I'm concerned the matter ended there. I'm just sorry that there seem to be all these hard feelings on Rachel's side.'

'How dare you,' she hissed.

'Now Rachel, it's only fair that he should be allowed to give his version of events.' Alan Jarvis's tone was already weary. The steadily increasing number of reports on sexual harassment cases in the papers had given him neither the appetite nor the confidence for dealing with such issues himself. Rachel Elliot was a good soldier, a very good soldier indeed, but recently she had been showing signs of what Alan Jarvis regarded as typically female distress; she had been moody and preoccupied, not her old self at all. He had even consulted his wife, Hilary, about it, who had mentioned the menopause and said not to worry. In his opinion Rachel still looked a bit on the young side for all that sort of thing, but it did make some sense. He was reminded of quite what a gloomy business Hilary's own hormonal crisis had been, crying and hot flushes all over the shop.

'You have been under a lot of stress recently, Rachel,' he began.

'Stress has nothing to do with this, Alan.' Her voice had gone up a pitch. 'This man,' she glanced at Cliff, reposing beside her, one hand flung across the back of his chair, his legs crossed while he studied her with unblinking eyes, 'this man tried to rape me. He entered my room in the middle of the night—'

'She let me in—'

'You said you had some documents for me—'

'And so I did—'

'Whoa there, please, both of you. First it's sexual harassment and now it's rape. Let's hear it from the start, each in turn, get everybody's cards on the table and take it from there. I want this sorted out quickly and properly. We cannot afford this kind of thing.' In an effort to regain control he had assumed the belittling tone of a reproving headmaster.

Rachel spoke first, doing her best to keep to the absolute facts, and managing to hold her voice steady. She mentioned the dancing that preceded the assault, how Cliff had made unwelcome advances even then, how she had opened her door only because of his insistence that the papers could not wait until the following day. How she had been forced to use her teeth in self-defence.

Cliff gave his reply eagerly. 'This is quite frankly ridiculous. It all started long before the dinner or what happened later. There was a kind of tension between us from the start – a sense of competition. It was exciting, I admit, and I played along with it. It didn't go unnoticed either. We had quite a dance together after dinner. You can be sure that got noticed, too. Ask any witnesses you want – there's a whole roomful to choose from.' He paused and softened his voice. 'Alan, I think I've been a man long enough to know when a female is interested—'

'Jesus Christ, this is intolerable.'

Alan's hand silenced her. 'Go on, Cliff.'

'As I was saying, Rachel here was being quite a flirt with everybody – well, with Frank and a couple of others anyway – but then we'd all had a bit to drink and so that was nothing to write home about. But when the evening broke up I was left under the definite impression that there was more there if I wanted it.' There was a glimpse of a collaborative smile, as if to say we men know about such things. 'I did mention some documents, but only so that she had a pretext for opening the door . . . I mean, it was obvious I could have left them for her at reception, wasn't it? She could easily have yelled at me to go away, not got out of bed at all. Anyway,' Cliff rubbed his hands, 'Rachel opened the door at once . . . and . . . well . . . she wasn't wearing much, if you know what I mean.' He cleared his throat.

'So things got a little . . . hot . . . more or less at once, until, like I said, I changed my mind. And I guess she just couldn't take that.' His eyes, as he met her gaze, were unrepentant, faintly mocking, even.

Alan Jarvis stood up and went to stand beside his window, where he ran his thumbs up and down his braces while he considered what to say next. 'It seems to me there has been a simple case of misunderstanding, a desperately unfortunate misunderstanding. And the best thing would be for both sides to acknowledge that openly, shake hands, and put it behind them.' He turned to present them both with an avuncular smile.

'He tried to assault me, Alan,' said Rachel in a small voice.

'He might have got the wrong idea, but then it seems that you did too . . .'

'I am not a flirt. I do not believe in . . . intimacy . . . of any kind with colleagues at work. In all my time . . .'

'Not what I've heard.'

She turned slowly, more incredulous than afraid of what new lies he might come up with. 'And what have you heard, may I ask, Cliff?'

He tweaked at the handkerchief in his breast pocket as he talked, tucking and tugging it into a neater shape, a lemon triangle, to match the colour of his shirt. 'Bermuda . . . quite a few extracurricular activities of one kind or another, I gather . . .'

'Bermuda?' She spun back to face Alan, who had the grace to wave his hand dismissively.

'There are always rumours like that, Cliff. They are irrelevant here, I think.'

They were both discharged after that, told to go away and think about it, like naughty children being given a second chance. As the door closed behind them Cliff had the temerity to shake her hand, saying that as far as he was concerned there were no hard feelings at all.

The next day Alan announced that Rachel was to be new Head of Account Management and about time too. After a sleepless night rehearsing resignation and revenge, Rachel was momentarily caught off guard. Almost worse than being disbelieved, or being offered a promotion in return for silence, was that Alan Jarvis had clearly failed to see the most basic fact in her defence:

that she would not have had sex with Cliff Weybourne if he had been the last man on earth, if copulation between them had meant the survival of the entire human race.

Without the support of Jarvis, taking the matter further would mean giving evidence in a court of law. While bracing herself to take such a route, Cliff's wily retelling of the tale illuminated the weakness of her position with terrible clarity: she had slow-danced with the man; she had opened her bedroom door to him in the small hours. Rachel could see the faces of the jury now: a middle-aged single woman, going one step too far and then regretting it. A woman scorned, wanting her pound of flesh. It was hopeless.

Unwilling to accept a bribe, yet fearful that resignation might look like an admission of defeat, Rachel had stalled for more time, promising to deliver her answer after the Christmas break. Meanwhile, the agency hummed with the unmistakable drone of rumour, infesting the expressions of colleagues with invisible meanings that left Rachel feeling powerless and wary. Even Melissa felt like the enemy, her looks of baffled curiosity revealing none of the sympathy that bubbled beneath, sympathy that she would have expressed but for the fire in Rachel's eyes, a blaze of warning to any who dared to venture too near.

By the week of Christmas Eve a fresh scandal had broken concerning the agency barman and a young motorbike courier called Leonard. A used condom had been found on top of the cistern in one of the ground-floor lavatories. Cleaning ladies were cited as witnesses, together with a copywriter working late on a storyboard for the Glastonbury new business pitch. Rachel's release from the role of victim was marked by invitations to give her own opinions on this new subject, invitations which she despised but to which she made a show of conforming, driven by a new, keener sense of survival. While the barman laughed it off with camp flicks of his drying up cloth, Rachel found herself feeling bitterly sorry for the boy Leonard, whom she sometimes glimpsed skulking by his motorbike in the car park, his angular face pinched and white, his pretty pink mouth drawing greedily on the stub end of a cigarette.

From the safe and comforting cocoon of her bath, Rachel could feel the whole ugly episode slipping from the spotlight of certainty which had at first burned so brightly in her mind. Perhaps Cliff was right, she thought now, perhaps she had been encouraging. What had actually happened, after all? An unwanted embrace. A rough fumble. Nothing more. Nothing she couldn't handle. Was it really worth resigning over? She flicked at a few snowflakes of foam on her arm and sighed. She felt drained suddenly, quite incapable of anger or anything else.

Bubbles clung to the sides of the tub while the water swirled away. Wrapping a large towel around her chest Rachel padded through to the kitchen to check on the progress of the claret. It wasn't so hard to understand Anita's friendship with the bottle, she thought grimly, taking an appreciative sip and wandering over to study the calendar pinned to the wall above the dishwasher. The line separating chaos from control was a fine one indeed; so much easier to topple down on the wrong side than she had ever previously imagined.

She counted the days of the coming holiday. Only six. Under a week and Anita would be back in town. A second opinion was definitely what she needed, Rachel decided, thumbing through the calendar's library of pictures – a series of stills from famous advertising campaigns, which Melissa had given her for Christmas the year before. She paused at April, the month of her birthday. The page was titled with the slogan from a popular bubble-bath commercial. *Claron. The beginning of a perfect evening*, it said. Underneath these words, a semi-naked model peered wistfully through the curtains of her bedroom window, clearly hopeful of having her flimsy robe ripped off by a handsome passer-by.

Hoicking up her towel, Rachel let the picture drop and cast a wary eye at the undrawn curtain of her own window above the kitchen sink. It would take more than a pint of bubble bath to make her dreams come true, she thought wryly, pulling the curtain across with such a yank that she spilt a drop or two of wine on the floor.

At the sight of Robbie Dexter's tousled hair and eager smile in the middle of her television screen, Rachel gripped the sofa cushion to her stomach and leant forward to get a better look. There were wisps of grey in the hair curling over the tops of his ears, but his figure looked much the same. He wore a round-necked Aran sweater and was standing in a pair of dirty black wellingtons, muddied jeans bunched into the tops of them, his fingers hooked casually through the loops in his waistband. The familiarity of the man and the pose, not seen for over fifteen years and coming on a third full day spent entirely alone, with nothing to do but brood over her multifarious troubles, filled Rachel with an irrational, stomach-flipping sensation of relief.

He was talking about sheep. Charollais sheep. Hurriedly she checked the *Radio Times*. An Animal Special, thirty minutes on unusual breeds, slipped in between a Christmas edition of a soap opera about oil riggers and a comedy quiz special involving a dartboard and a tub of green slime. She knew about the green slime from the trailers, of which there had been several the previous evening. Although it was well into the afternoon, Rachel was still in her dressing gown, encamped on her sofa amongst a medley of coldcare medicines and tissue boxes. The television, usually reserved – like alcohol – for solace and time-filling beyond the watershed hour of six o'clock, had been resorted to as a last weapon against boredom and the rack of self-analysis. On the table beside her sat a pile of newspapers, a sachet of Lemsip, a pot of tea and a jar of pickled walnuts. Though opened, the jar remained untouched, a whimsical repellance having induced her feverish mind to observe the brown convolutions of its contents and be reminded suddenly of brains.

Behind Robbie, scores of broad-backed, long-nosed sheep with pasty pink faces could be seen standing in disconsolate clusters under several towering, leafless oaks, whose black boughs were spread like deep cracks on the surface of the smudgy grey sky. It was raining gently, a fact of which Robbie, typically, seemed to be unaware. He was talking animatedly about dietary supplements and the importance of nurturing delicate breeds with extra gentleness. Rachel, spellbound by the sight of the familiar face, found her thoughts surfing waves of fond recollections. He looked good. Positively attractive, in fact. Her mind scrabbled for a clear recollection of the reasons she had left him, reasons which – thanks to her new circumstances and the passage of time – had grown quite opaque.

The camera angle shifted to reveal a red-bricked cottage with a coil of dark grey smoke curling out of its chimney. Garden tools were leaning up against the wall to the left of the front door, beside a boot-scraper and a . . . The withdrawal of the picture left her feeling robbed. A woman with posy-pink lips and staring eyes appeared in its place, a fat snake slung across her shoulders. Rachel narrowed her eyes at the screen, while a shiver crept down the back of her neck; a shiver which began as repulsion at the reptile but ended as something quite different. Robbie Dexter. She turned the television off. After all these years.

The stuffiness in her head, having enjoyed only temporary bouts of eucalyptus-aided relief, cleared in a couple of instants.

'These creatures need baby-sitting,' Robbie had said with a laugh, 'so it's fortunate that I've friends in Drakeshead who are prepared to man the fort from time to time.'

Rachel got down an atlas, dusted the cover with a clean tissue and found a map of the British Isles. Drakeshead was in Devon. So he had hardly moved at all.

'Robert Dexter,' she said to the man at directory enquiries, 'middle name' – she recalled without any effort at all – 'Timothy. Drakeshead in the West Country.'

A robotic voice recited the number twice. Two minutes later Robbie himself was on the other end of the line.

'Dexter Landscaping,' he said, 'how may I help you?'

'Robbie, it's Rachel – Rachel Elliot.'

'Rachel . . . Rachel – you're joking – wow – Rachel. I mean, hello – how the hell are you?'

'I'm fine,' she began, 'well, actually I'm full of cold and have just spent a boring Christmas cooped up in my flat.'

'You poor old thing, that's too bad.'

'I just saw you on the TV—'

'Oh, you were watching it? A friend in the British Charollais Society set it up – quite a laugh really – just a space filler, but never mind. My goodness, Rachel, what a surprise. What are you up to these days?'

'Same old thing. More money, less time – you know.'

'Married with five kids by any chance?' The chuckle of a laugh that followed was one that she recognised instantly, welcoming it in her heart as an old friend.

'Single as ever. What about you?' Her voice, assisted by the slight husk of ill-health, was a careful study of friendly insouciance.

'There was someone . . . for quite a while . . . but not now. Didn't work out, you know . . .' It sounded for a moment as if he was speaking through clenched teeth.

'I'm sorry to hear that.'

The conversation had reached a point where a sense of direction was required for it to be able to continue. Fifteen years could not be summarised in a few enquiries about rare sheep and the potential existence of life-partners. The attempt either had to be abandoned completely or given a more definitive shape.

'I rang on impulse really, because . . . because I thought it might be fun to catch up sometime . . . you know, meet up in the New Year or something.'

'Why not? Good idea.'

Was that reluctance or shyness, she wondered? It was like moves in a chess game, but with no time to think in between.

'It was just seeing you on the box like that – such a coincidence – I just felt I had to act on it.'

'I'm so glad you did. The trouble is, I don't come to London much . . . I mean, well I don't suppose you fancy a trip to the country, do you?'

'I'd love it.' The words were out before she could stop them, charged with a genuine eagerness to see him, an eagerness that was quite beyond disguise.

'How about this week then?' He sounded slightly breathless. 'Oh, but of course you'll be working—'

'No, I've got the whole Christmas break off. I'm due at a New Year's Eve party back here on Friday. But I've no plans to speak of in the meantime.' Am I making things too easy, she wondered, marvelling at this verbal flinging of herself down a telephone line, but at the same time feeling justified and driven by the extraordinary coincidence that had prompted it, the sweet ease with which everything was falling into place. Two minutes later and she would have missed Robbie's section of the programme entirely.

It was also impossible not to relish the pleasure of speaking to someone who still only knew her as she had been fifteen years before. It made her feel young and interesting. Robbie had always been so unjudgemental and affectionate, so exactly the kind of tonic she needed now.

'I've got a very fast car.'

'Yes, you would have.'

She could hear the smile in his voice.

They made plans for Rachel to drive down the very next afternoon, by tacit agreement leaving the trickier question of the exact duration of her visit undefined. The rest of the conversation was taken up with less arduous practicalities, like how long the drive would take and which landmarks to watch out for during the last couple of miles.

'It sounds like the back of beyond,' she said, laughing at the long scrawl of instructions in front of her, which had begun on the back of an envelope and extended into the margins of an open magazine.

'Perhaps you'd better set off now to be sure.'

'Perhaps I'd better.'

'Will I recognise you?'

'Oh God, I hope so.' Her heart gave a little lurch at the recollection of the dispiriting reflection confronting her in the mirror that morning – a face full of cold, dark suitcases under her eyes, white cracks on her lips, a clown nose. 'The shape of me is much the same,' she faltered.

'That's good to hear. I've gone to seed all over the place.'

'It certainly didn't look like it.'

'Wait till you get a closer look.'

A moment of embarrassment followed as the more intimate implications of these exchanges sank in.

'It'll take me at least a day to straighten the house, so I'd better get cracking, get the spare bed made up and all that sort of thing.'

She was grateful for his hearty tone. 'Oh, anything will do for me – please, don't go to any bother.'

After the phone call Rachel collected up her dirty tissues and punched some life back into the sofa cushions, setting them at pretty angles in the seat corners. After that she tidied up the detritus littering her kitchen, loaded her dishwasher and filled several bags and boxes with bottles and newspapers to take to the recycling dump the next morning. It felt like clearing out a lot more than the clutter of a failed Christmas. It felt like a clearing of something inside her head too, the sort of fundamental reorganisation that precedes a fresh start, a chance, after all, to become something else.

Will Raphael saw Rachel several minutes before she caught sight of him. He hesitated for a moment, half turning back towards the park to check on the child, before returning his gaze to the car park. It was almost empty, with only a handful of cars positioned between the deep wide puddles, each littered with soggy clusters of newspaper pages that had not quite managed the journey from car boot to recycling container. She was wearing red trousers and a green padded coat, the collar of which was turned up, encasing the lower section of her hair and pushing it forwards so that it fell round her cheeks. It looked longer and looser than he remembered, as if it had recently broken free of a hat.

She was struggling with the papers, taking too many at a time, so that it was impossible to lift them up into the high letterbox flap without dropping a few on the way. She kept having to bend down and retrieve the ones that escaped, shaking her head with a happy impatience which assured him he remained unseen. When she had finished with the papers, she got back into the car and drove towards him, or rather, towards the bottle banks, which were situated nearer the tarmacked path and patch of grass which signalled the start of the park.

'It's Rachel Elliot, isn't it?' On his head was a black cap, worn backwards so that the peak stuck out over the upturned collar of his jacket. He gestured at the bags of bottles wedged into the passenger seat of her car. 'What's this, an advertising lady with a conscience?'

Though curiously unsurprised to see him, the remark rankled at once, wiping the smile from her face. 'Aren't advertising ladies supposed to have consciences, then?' The two bottles she had been holding clanked into the bottom of the container. He stood watching her in silence. She wondered if he had heard about the Cliff Weybourne débâcle, whether the two of them had yet shared a drink and a laugh at her expense.

'Good Christmas?'

'Perfectly lovely, thank you,' she replied, wondering why he did not excuse himself from a conversation which was clearly giving neither of them any pleasure, why indeed he had intitiated it in the first place. If ever presented with the danger of an unwanted encounter herself, she had no qualms about hiding behind trees or stopping to study imaginary items on the soles of her shoes.

Oh God, perhaps he wants more gratitude, she thought, busying herself with bottles and forcing out a few sentences of appreciation. 'Mallarmé are thrilled to bits with the film, by the way – brought the TV blitz forward to January.'

'How's your friend?'

'My drunken friend, you mean?' Her eyes glittered. 'Absolutely fine. It was kind of you to help out. We were both very grateful . . .'

'Good, good.' He looked impatient suddenly, shifting his weight from one foot to the other and casting looks over his shoulder.

'Worried about a dog?'

'A child.'

This unexpected remark was followed by shriek of glee from behind. A young boy, aged about five, came tearing towards them, straggly sandy hair streaking back off his face and his small hands pumping the air for added speed.

'This is Jack,' he said, when the boy had arrived, red cheeked and panting at his side.

'Pleased to meet you, Jack.' She rubbed her palms together briskly. 'Well, I've really got to get on . . . I'm off to Devon for a couple of days . . .'

'Devon? How nice. Whereabouts?'

'Er . . . Drakeshead – to see an old friend . . .'

'He can't be that old.'

'I beg your pardon?'

'Or you wouldn't be blushing.'

'I'm not,' she retorted, pressing her palms to her cheeks, furious both at herself and his impudence.

'Lucky you, is all I can say. It's grimy old London for us, isn't it mate?' He put a hand on the boy's shoulder and pulled him closer. 'Can we help with those?'

'Yes please, please, please,' piped the boy, racing round to the open car door and starting to help himself from the remaining bag of empties.

Rachel nodded, fighting an absurd impulse to explain that the quantity of wine bottles related only to the infrequency with which she got round to recycling them.

'Quite a habit you've got here,' remarked Will, lifting up the child so that he could reach the slot in the recycling container.

'I was about to explain,' she began, but stopped at once when she saw that he was laughing at her, his eyes full of mischief.

'I know you were,' he said quietly.

He placed the child back on the ground and then whispered something in his ear. The boy set off running in the direction from which he had come. 'I've given him a two-minute head start,' he confided, as they both stood aside for a cyclist with bulging pink thighs, who appeared from nowhere, bursting past on a rush of wind. 'Used to be three, but he's getting faster.' He swivelled his cap the right way round and pulled some gloves out of his coat pocket.

'How old is he?' asked Rachel, to be polite.

'Six going on thirty-five.' He chuckled, before adding, almost in a whisper, 'I don't suppose you would let me photograph you, would you?' He made a big to-do of putting on the gloves. They looked home-knitted and had Father Christmas faces on each finger. 'Smart, eh?' He held up both hands and grinned. 'Jack gave them to me.'

She couldn't help laughing.

'His mother got earrings – Christmas trees the size of ten-nis balls.'

She was still smiling and shaking her head when he said, 'Would you?' and she knew she hadn't misheard after all. It was such a bizarre request that she laughed again, out of nerves this time. Common sense told her to refuse, not only because it felt curiously personal to be asked such a thing, but also because of all the negative associations already resident inside her head where this man was concerned – the fiasco of the photography lessons, the mess over the Bermuda film, the business with Anita, not to mention his association with Cliff Weybourne.

'I don't make a habit of issuing such invitations. Commissions are more my style.' He beat his gloved hands together and turned to check on the boy, whose concentration on running had been interrupted by the attentions of a large but apparently friendly Alsatian. 'A cheek and all that, I know.'

'Why me?'

He sucked in his breath. 'Now that's more difficult.'

'Well try, then.' She crossed her arms, in a show of having all the time in the world, her curiosity overtaking any flutter of urgency about getting on her way. He was right. It was a cheek, and she wanted some justification for it. 'I'm hardly Miss England material.'

He looked genuinely appalled. 'Oh goodness – no – I mean I wouldn't be remotely interested if you were.'

'Well, thanks very much.'

'No – I didn't mean – it's that . . . I feel you have a story to tell – in your face – there's a lot there. I could show it.' He shrugged, almost with irritation, clearly dissatisfied at this description of the impulsion behind his craft. 'Just a couple of hours. Please? You might even learn something about taking photographs,' he added slyly.

She couldn't help smiling. 'Look, I'm terribly flattered and all that, but the answer is still no. I'm just not the right kind of material – can't sit still for two seconds – always blink when the flash goes—'

'You would be fine—'

'No.' She gave him the most aggressively determined stare, thinking as she did so that he was certainly good looking, as Anita had so crudely observed, and that at the same time there was something guarded in his expression which somehow defused the possible inference of anything improper in the request.

'Well, I guess that's that then.' He tugged at his gloves, stretching the Father Christmas heads until they looked gaunt and pop-eyed. 'Better go. Got a race to run.' Then he turned and sprinted away, calling the boy's name, spurts of mud splashing onto the ankles of his trousers.

Rachel stood watching him go, faintly intrigued in spite of herself. She had always hated being photographed. Ever since she was a little girl every snapshot had induced a prickle of disappointment at the sight of herself, at the realisation that any delusions of film-star beauty existed in her head alone. Yet she felt a curious regret as she watched him charge away, waving and calling to the child. She remembered his Christmas card suddenly, the starkness of it, the hope bursting from the puffed chest of the robin, the suggestion of warmth among the shadows.

As she turned back towards her car, Rachel found herself wondering about the wife. Were they separated or was she the stay-at-home bun-baking sort, happy to absent herself from a spot of male bonding in the park? The thought led her inexorably on towards a glimpse of herself in a similar role, not armed with oven gloves, but with a child that needed fresh air. There followed an outrageous image of Robbie Dexter playing the role of father, an image which good sense told her to quash, but which shimmered obstinately none the less, fuelled by an imagination that had been quite stuffed with solitude and was at last taking its revenge. But there would be an alluring symmetry to it, she reasoned, as the last of her empty bottles crashed into the darkness beneath her hands, a sense of life coming full circle, of making good in the end.

The cockerel crowed five minutes before the ring of the alarm, a sequence of events which was as integral to Robbie's morning routine as picking the sleep from his eyes while he sat on the loo and applying the blade of the razor to his upper lip before he tackled his cheeks. Throwing back the bedclothes, he swung his legs over the side of the bed and sat for a moment with his head in his hands, curling his toes at the cold draughts snaking out between the gaps in the floorboards and up through the thin carpeting. As he stretched, he groaned with the abandonment of one confident that he is alone, his large bony hands reaching with unconscious elegance towards the bare bulb dangling from the middle of the ceiling.

Having splashed cold water on his face from a chipped basin in the corner of the room, Robbie crossed over to the window and lifted one edge of the material which he had pinned up as a temporary curtain some three years before. The darkness of the new day still crouched warily outside. Errol Flynn, the cockerel, named in recognition of its sometimes over-zealous servicing of its harem of ten hens, switched into full throttle once again, its raucous shrieks cutting through the stillness of the morning. There had once been two cockerels, the ebullient Errol and a distant cousin of his, called George, who was, if anything even more enthusiastic when it came to its manly duties concerning the hens. So much so that the hens themselves eventually revolted by refusing to produce any eggs at all. With some reluctance Robbie had donated George to a large farm on the other side of Drakeshead, transporting him in a cardboard box peppered with breathing holes and filling the van with a stench of chicken shit which had lingered for months afterwards. By the following week egg supply and hen-coop harmony had been fully restored, together with a small income from Phil Giddings, the butcher in Drakeshead, who liked to tuck a few egg boxes between his trays of sausages and prime cuts. This income would have been considerably larger if Robbie hadn't eaten quite so many eggs himself, his appetite and a long-established antipathy towards shopping overcoming any fashionable concerns about the clogging effect such habits might be having on his blood vessels.

When Errol had finished his morning chant, the dawn chorus was taken up in a more desultory fashion by a few plaintive bleatings from the sheep, penned into the small field immediately in front of the house. Of the three fields Robbie used in his two-weekly rota, it was the scrubbiest and least satisfactory. But thanks to the fiendish activity of worms, which built up in the soil and could wreak the most terrible havoc in such delicate ruminants' digestive systems, he was forced to use every scrap of land he had.

Robbie sighed, pulling on the T-shirt and pullover that lay on his chair from the day before, and thinking, as he did most mornings, that the Charollais were far too much hard work for a hobby and that he really ought to get shot of them once and for all.

Surveying the chaos of what he had blithely referred to as his spare room on the way downstairs and feeling as always that the demands of his day would never fit into the time allowed for them, made Robbie feel more aggressive towards the sheep than usual. As did a glimpse of the towers of paperwork crowding round the smeary screen of the Apple Mac on the dining-room table. Though he had been meaning, for several months now, to allocate a day a week for admin alone, the intention kept getting overtaken by events. Today, for instance, it was imperative that he make some move towards cleaning the house, towards getting things looking generally shipshape – for Rachel. Rachel. At the thought of her he stopped and caught his breath. Rachel Elliot, who had apparently volunteered to march back into his life with all the panache with which she had once marched out of it. It was impossible not to feel thrilled; yet Robbie was filled with dread as well, as anyone one might dread the re-emergence of something so closely associated with great pain.

What would she look like after so long? How would he feel? How did she feel? What did she want? As Robbie spooned sugar straight from the open packet that lived beside the kettle onto a steep mountain of cornflakes, before tipping half a pint of milk into a moat round its edges, it was this last thought that preoccupied him the most. Rachel, he recalled with some trepidation, was not a lady who drifted into things. She had made up her mind to see him. She wanted to see him. And he, true to form, had agreed at once, had allowed himself to be swept along in the slipstream of her plans, experiencing – in spite of everything – a welcome echo of times past, when the wants of Rachel Elliot had always taken precedence over any meagre desires of his own. Leaving her had been the hardest thing he had ever done in his life, harder even than telling Polly Drayton, as he had back in October, that after seven years of their misshapen zigzag of an alliance, it was time to part for good. The thought of Polly brought with it the usual *frissons* of guilt which no amount of cornflake crunching could suppress entirely. It was clear to him that he taken the best years of her life and offered nothing in return. She was back living with her parents now, the twenty-eight-year-old daughter of a publican, serving bar snacks and pulling pints with that fixed, cheery look he knew so well, the one that was a mask for disappointment.

As Robbie continued with his morning chores, bestrewing the near corner of the field with fresh hay for the sheep and checking their water trough, the thought of Rachel's imminent arrival – the prospect of being viewed through her eyes – made him see with a new and shocking clarity that he had somehow slipped into becoming something he had never quite intended. Visions of his own future had always contained a wife, a family, a warm, well-ordered home. Staring at his cottage now, noting the missing jigsaw pieces in the roof, the crumbling corners of the chimney stack, he felt the same lurch of affection that had prompted him to bind his soul to a building society some five years before. But he felt a sense of shame as well, since he knew that its shambolic state reflected some deep failing within himself, some inability to grasp the business of living and mould it into the shape he wanted. The fact that Polly lacked it too probably lay at the heart of all their problems. While adept at teasing damp wood into a roaring fire or cajoling sheep through a foot-bath of copper sulphate, Polly had always looked to him to provide any spark of inspiration where their relationship was concerned. She was a follower, not a leader; someone who needed to feed off another's imagination in order to give the appearance of having any herself.

Like me with Rachel, he thought glumly, pulling the hose from the trough and heading back towards the house, his heart curling with fear at the thought of her, of how she might judge him and all that he had become.

Rachel spent the first part of the drive trying, and failing, not to think about babies. Not so much their physical attributes as what they represented, what effect a child would have on her life. Most important of all, becoming a mother would provide some other peg on which to hang her emotions and hopes, something entirely separate from her career. Though she had not yet made up her mind whether it would be courageous or cowardly to resign from McKenzie Cartwright, the idea of a long-term future there had been soured for good. Not just because of Cliff Weybourne, but also because she was now resolved upon the business of changing her life. Getting in touch with Robbie was all part of this new confusion of change, she told herself, deccelerating sharply in order to move across into the exit lane. In the midst of such imponderables the thought of a baby was soothing: it was her secret hope, her hidden jewel of a plan that meant in the long run nothing else mattered at all.

As the West Country drew nearer, so did images of the past: Robbie, shared holidays, favourite films and old jokes, spun through her mind on a carousel of dazzling speed and intensity. Memories from her early working days soon joined the fray – the pleasing terror of delivering her first presentation, the disappointing boredom of attending her first shoot – all those hours spent in a show-case house in Richmond while scores of people debated the best ways of illuminating a can of furniture polish. She recalled one fresh-faced account director in particular, who, on one memorable occasion, had dared to arrive late for a big meeting on the grounds that his seven-week-old daughter had chosen that morning to offer up her first smile. Rachel, then a twenty-something hot-head, hungry to prove herself in a man's world, had experienced a barely disguised impatience at the blatant soppiness of such an excuse. Remembering that impatience now, she felt ashamed. It had taken bravery, she realised, to bring this tale of fatherly ecstasy into the boardroom, to own up to priorities other than those typed on the agenda sheets in front of them. The couple of women account handlers at McKenzie Cartwright who had children would never dream of doing anything similar, she thought sadly. It was more than their jobs were worth.

It was only after she left the motorway and began trying to decipher the scrawled directions on the piece of paper beside her that Rachel allowed herself to focus properly on the potentially awesome business of a reunion with Robbie Dexter. She would have been far more afraid, she realised, if she had not seen him on the television, looking somehow more glamorous than she remembered him, more rugged and more mature. She had forgotten what a nice voice he had too – low and slow – and how all his movements were unhurried and deliberate, as if originating from the most deep-seated self-belief; a quality towards which she felt more urgently drawn for the fact that it was so terribly absent in herself.

As Robbie had promised, there was a dead-end sign ten yards past the Fox and Hounds on the left. Her car crept along the narrow lanes like a sleek black cat, unaware of the eyes observing its progress, eyes belonging to people like Polly Drayton as she stood at the window of her bedroom above the front bar, chewing the dry ends of her hair, smelling the chip fat on her skin and clothes, its oily stench mingling with the debilitating self-hatred of frustrated love.

Rachel made the last turn, noting as she did so the hand-painted sign saying, Station Cottage, half-buried by brambles – as Robbie had warned her it would be – its arrow pointing skywards, as if the residence it described was to be found smothered under pillows of grey cloud. Rachel took several deep breaths to clear the tightness in her chest as she drove the last few yards, steering her car as best she could between the hard mud gullies forged by tractor wheels. As she rounded the first bend, the cottage suddenly came into view, its bricks looking somehow less red, less spruce than they had appeared on screen. A profound sense of unreality threatened to overwhelm her then, an absurd notion that she was about to step onto a film set and play a role for which she had no script. She parked behind Robbie's mud-splattered white van, remembering with a heart thud how they had once made love on the front seats of something similar, how they had laughed at the uncomfortable inconvenience of the gear stick, how triumphantly reckless they had felt afterwards.

Robbie was putting the hoover away when he heard her car pull up. It lived, suspended by an old and noble hook, at the top of the cellar steps, amongst a jungle of brooms, buckets and used dusters. The hook, which Robbie had hammered in himself during a patch of zealous domesticity shortly after moving in, chose that moment to rebel at the considerable weight to which it had been unwisely subjected for far too long. With a resounding crash, the hoover toppled down the cellar steps amidst a billowing cloud of dust punched out of its overstuffed bag, taking in its wake two buckets, three aerosol cans and the only broom without a loose handle.

'Fuck.' Robbie started down the steps after it and then changed his mind. The hoover had done its job. It was impossible to think beyond that moment to the unimaginable point of ever needing it again. There was just time to wash his hands at the kitchen sink before she knocked at the door. In his terror he tripped on the loose flagstone by the dresser as he left the kitchen, lunged sideways and hit his shoulder on the wall, knocking a faded print of an English beach badly askew. He was still adjusting it when the front door swung open to reveal Rachel Elliot framed in its archway. A Rachel of softer lines and wider eyes. A Rachel who was taller than he remembered and slimmer too, but otherwise so exactly the same that for a moment he was too shocked to speak.

'Hello, Robbie.' The apparition came to life, smiling broadly, so broadly that he guessed she was as afraid as he was. With so much fear, it was hard to separate out the pleasure. As to resentment, he found there was none at all.

'Rachel – you made it then.'

She walked towards him, across the brown rectangle of carpet that he had been hoovering just minutes before, playing with the shoulder strap of her handbag, her eyes darting around to cover up the awkwardness of the approach. Robbie stood with one hand still on the picture frame. She looked so fresh and elegant. His usual dirt and disorder wouldn't have suited her at all, he thought, remembering how he had hurled the jumbled contents of the spare room into the attic, where the debris of his life lay in incoherent unattended heaps that grew larger and more bedraggled as the years went by.

She stopped and cocked her head at the picture. 'That's about right I think. No – perhaps a shade to the left. That's better. Do I go in here?' She stopped short of him and stepped through the doorway that led into the kitchen. Robbie followed, ducking automatically under the low beam, cursing himself for having failed to kiss her. There followed a curious wave of sadness, a mixture of nostalgia for what they had lost, and of apprehension for what might lie ahead. It made him wish for a moment that she had not come.

'It's lovely, Robbie, lovely.' Rachel peeled off her gloves as she walked round the room, inspecting pictures and cupboards like a prospective house-buyer, the points of her heels clacking smartly on the cracked, freshly washed tiles. Too timid, now that the moment had come, even to catch his eye, such businesslike curiosity was her only refuge. She felt brusque and unnatural, but quite powerless too. To be so close to Robbie again was far stranger than she could ever have imagined. He was so familiar, yet so unknown.

'Robbie – I—'

'Would you like a tour of the estate, then?' He rubbed his hands together and then eyed her footwear doubtfully. 'But it wouldn't be a good idea in those, I'm afraid.'

She looked down at her brown suede shoes and wiggled her toes, wanting to make light of her silliness for having worn such things, for having allowed herself to be guided by vanity rather than good sense.

'I'm sure I've got a pair somewhere that would fit you – boots, coats, scarves, brollies – you name it – I've got hundreds of the damn things – breed on their own I think.' Relieved to have something practical upon which to exercise his concentration, Robbie began rifling through a large wickerwork basket at the far end of the kitchen, flinging out items of footwear and clothing between sentences. After some to-do and more than a little awkwardness, Rachel settled for a pair of scuffed black boots.

Though they were an obvious choice, it gave Robbie an unexpected jolt to see them on Rachel's feet. They were an old pair of Polly's, abandoned upon receipt of the new fur-lined leather ones he had given her the Christmas before last. Polly had always had a bit of a thing about cold feet; poor circulation, she said, like her mum.

Walking round outside, Rachel took off the glossy, Cossack-style hat which she had retrieved from the back seat of her car and tossed her hair at the sealed grey of the sky, enjoying the prickle of cold on her scalp. A formal introduction to some outhouses and several chickens required a leap across a muddy ditch, about three feet wide. There had once been a footbridge, Robbie explained apologetically, referring to a soggy plank that had finally caved in the winter before. But Rachel laughed away the necessity of such a thing. It suited her mood perfectly to have to jump across. Better still, a slightly awkward landing on the other side provided the perfect pretext for hand to meet hand, for real contact to be made at last. There was no lingering over the moment, but each felt better for it having happened, as if reassured by the solidity of their own bodies in the midst of so much emotional uncertainty.

Rachel couldn't help thinking the Charollais very ugly when seen close-to: they had piggy eyes and Roman noses which gave them an air of what struck her as quite inappropriate haughtiness. But they trotted over to Robbie with an eagerness that was almost endearing, their short stout legs working hard under the tumescent woolly bulk of their bodies. Robbie's assurance too, was curiously impressive, she decided, watching him move amongst the surging animals, rubbing foreheads and patting backs as if they were a pack of friendly dogs. Rachel stood a little to one side, hands thrust into the pockets of her coat, happy to play the spectator.

'It's feeding time at the zoo, I'm afraid,' he called, striding deeper into the jostle of sheep, tugging at ears and tail stumps and bending down to inspect hooves. 'They need supplements at this time of year. Most of them are pregnant, you see, so they need more than this old field can provide – but not too much, mind you, or they'd grow too big and then we'd have a hell of a time at lambing.'

'Lambing?' Rachel's imagination flashed with images of Christopher Timothy elbow-deep in the rear end of something bovine. 'Is that soon, then?'

'Not till mid-April probably. I was late with tupping this year. There's a while to go yet.'

'Why are you looking at their feet?'

'Foot rot. That warm spell before Christmas – all that rain and so on – gave us a hell of a time of it.' He was bending down, talking into the ground, so it was hard for her to catch every word. '. . . Better now it's colder . . .'

Rachel's own feet were beginning to feel icy and more than a little damp, thanks to deep dry cracks in the soles of Polly Drayton's boots. She hopped from one leg to the other, hugging herself, having to work harder now at looking interested.

'Bloody creatures. I'll have to get the clippers out again.' Robbie clumped back across the field towards her, irritation etched across his face. 'If it isn't one damn disease it's another—' he checked himself. 'You poor old thing, you look frozen. Let's go inside. The sheep can wait for once. I'll make a pot of tea and stoke up the fire. We could have toast and jam – if you like,' he added shyly. 'There's not much for supper I'm afraid – just cold meat and so on – I'm still not much of a cook.'

'That makes two of us.' She laughed, and linked her arm through his for the walk back to the house. 'It is *so* good to see you Robbie Dexter.'

He squeezed her arm with the fingers of his spare hand. 'And it's good to see *you*, Rachel Elliot.' He paused for a moment, before adding, 'Weird, but good.'

'I thought you'd have a family by now,' she said quietly.

'Yes, so did I.' He let out a short laugh.

'Not met the right person?'

'Something like that.' He thought of Polly and children. The subject evoked a blurred string of unhappy recollections, conversations meandering across the years, getting nowhere. Polly refusing to talk properly, refusing to do anything but dismiss the idea with that bitter scorn of hers, the one she used when she was most afraid. But then children had never been exactly high on Rachel's list of priorities either, he thought, casting her a wary look and doing a quick mental calculation of her age.

Tea was drunk to the ice-breaking accompaniment of an album of ancient photographs, many of them so bad that it was easy to laugh at the past, at the fatter faces, the longer hair, the endless cigarettes and arms round friends whose names they couldn't remember. But steadily the photographs evoked other images too, more emotional ones that filled Robbie with longing and Rachel with shame. It seemed incredible that she had turned this man away, expelled him from her life for qualities which she now so longed to know again.

Meanwhile, Robbie studied the blister caused by ironing two double sheets and four pillow cases, all of them quite bone-dry and pitted with ancient creases, and dared to wonder whether such industry had been necessary after all. Rachel was still sitting down the opposite end of his ragged brown leather sofa, but her stockinged feet, once tucked under her, had slowly been working their way down the sofa towards him. When the tips of her toes arrived they sought warmth in the lee of his left thigh. And when at last his hand dared to close round the toes, they pressed into his palm at once, full of sweet resilience and promise.

22

Anita blew an extravagant kiss at herself in her dressing-table mirror and smiled. The scarlet lipstick, purchased only that morning, made her teeth look gratifyingly white, and somehow sharper. She pressed a clean tissue to her lips and examined the imprint for a moment before dropping it into the wastepaper bin beside her. Leaning forward, she tugged at the short front tufts of her hair to make them look more spiky – scowling at the swathe of grey as she always did – but none the less thinking that she looked vaguely vibrant – provocative even, she decided, puckering her lips.

It was a long time since she had so looked forward to a party, or indeed had a party to look forward to, she thought bitterly, her mind performing a quick flashback over the meagre contents of their social life that year. The Robsons' New Year's Eve thrash represented quite a highlight, a pitiable fact for which Anita blamed her husband, since she believed there to be a direct correlation between the frequency of Giles's trips abroad and the steady dwindle in the number of invitations that came their way. Once, a million years ago it seemed, there had never been enough evenings to go round. Now, any evening invitation lit up the diary like a beacon, terrible evidence – as if Anita needed such a thing – that their life really had slipped into a new and infinitely bleaker gear. In spite of countless sympathetic protestations to the contrary, wives on their own were not in much demand round the symmetrically arranged dinner-party tables of north London hostesses, she had discovered, especially not ones with a tendency to use four letter words after the fifth glass and to stub cigarettes out beside the wreckage of what had once been a perfectly formed bread roll.

Anita tweaked out a last rebellious eyebrow, scowling at the twinge of pain. God, it would be brilliant, after two weeks of behaving herself impeccably, to drink without counting the glasses or – worse still – worrying about who else might be counting them. No one cared about such things on New Year's Eve. It would also be brilliant to see the delicious Will Raphael again. Having engineered his invitation to the party herself – Sally Robson was beautifully accommodating about such things, even going so far as to phone her the moment he replied – she was determined to make the most of it, determined, more specifically to punish Giles, towards whom she was currently feeling more vitriol than she had experienced in a long time.

They had had bad patches before. She had been known to joke to friends like Rachel that the entire marriage had been nothing but a bad patch. In truth, matters usually reached some sort of nadir, a crux of awfulness, at which point they would both turn to each other in a frenzy of regret and promises to try harder in the future. For a while things would be riotously cheerful, then calmer, then tricky as the whole hopeless cycle started again. However tired Anita was of the cycle, there was something about the predictability of it all which made it bearable; it meant that nothing lasted for ever, neither the good nor the bad. But in recent weeks something had changed. Giles wasn't playing the game any more. Nor did Anita feel certain that her drinking was to blame. Giles was used to her ways; he knew she always pulled herself together in the end. Sometimes, she even believed that her drinking made him nicer to her, gentler, more conciliatory.

Giles had spent the entire Christmas hiding behind the inane and incessant flow of conversation generated by his parents, leaving his wife to supply any necessary responses. It wasn't that he wasn't being nice. He wasn't being anything. His gift to her had been a Smith's token and a book on birds. He knew she hated birds.

The thought that her husband might finally have given up on her was not so much depressing as intolerable. If the bastard was having an affair, she would not go quietly, she vowed; she would make him pay. She slammed her powder compact back down on the dressing table, causing a mini storm of brown specks to fly into the air and settle in a dusty film across the green leather top of her jewel case.

The plot concerning Will Raphael – the bold idea of trying to nudge fantasy a little way into the realms of reality – had sprung partly from this enraged resolve, and partly from a chance encounter with an article in the hairdresser's during the lead-up to Christmas. Not having realised that the man had a career of such distinction, Anita was instantly impressed. Fame could be quite an aphrodisiac, she found, if allowed to be.

Under the discreet aural camouflage of whirring hairdryers, she tore the article out with the intention of slipping it into Rachel's Christmas card. Instead, it remained in her coat pocket for a few days, before graduating to the innermost zipped compartment of her purse, assuming qualities akin to that of a secret memento along the way. Then Giles returned from his December trip in a shroud of impenetrable silence. On his first night back – when, historically, absence sharpened the pangs of lust if nothing else – he huddled away from her with his knees to his chest, responding to all enquiries with inarticulate grunts that were to set the pattern for the rest of the month. So it was that the bad patch had grown and stretched and become something disturbingly new, something that called for action.

The article sat beside Anita now, propped up between a bottle of Chanel Eau de Toilette and a box of Tampax. A small but full-length version of Will Raphael was staring at her from amongst the creases, leaning against the dark railings of what looked like a fire escape, arms crossed, and a quizzical look on his face, as if he had just asked a question and was still awaiting the answer. His hair looked much darker and sleeker than she remembered it, brushed straight back off his face in tidy waves and curling neatly round his earlobes.

'I just photograph what's there,' declares portrait photographer, Will Raphael, who has recently received commissions from the MP Howard Graves and the acclaimed film actor Rupert Cheshire. After the great critical success of a private exhibition last summer, thirty-eight-year-old Raphael is currently putting together a book of his work, featuring some of his more experimental techniques. The book is to be called Images

In Time *and is due for publication next autumn (Cauter and Prowse £24.99). 'Novelists get many hours of concentration from their readers, but a picture hung in a gallery is lucky if it gets a couple of minutes,' he argues, 'so I thought a book would give me a better chance of getting inside people's heads.' Will Raphael, who lives alone in a basement flat in Chelsea, claims only to have time for his work. When not helping in the management of the film editing company Filmstyle, which he and several partners set up eight years ago, he is always behind a camera. 'Taking pictures is my hobby as well as my work,' he declares, 'so I'm very lucky.'*

At the sound of a wailing child approaching the bedroom door Anita hastily tucked the article into the satiny interior of her evening bag, alongside a stick of eyeliner, a fresh packet of cigarettes and a small gold comb that had come free with the lipstick.

Rachel, seated at her own dressing table, had seldom prepared for an evening's entertainment with less rigour. Although her body clearly had made the journey back from Devon, it felt as if her mind was still there, drawn to the compelling events of the last few days like a moth to a light. Staring at her reflection, she was startled to see how well she looked. Even her lips burned with colour. She touched them for a moment with her fingertips, remembering the astonishing familiarity of Robbie's mouth, so strange beside the shyness and the sense of daring as they slipped between the icy sheets of his creaky iron bed, not wanting to hurry, but hurrying none the less, because it was cold, because a certain haste seemed necessary to make up for the interruption of the years.

Slowly, almost lazily, Rachel ran the mascara brush through her lashes. Her pupils remained glassy, still seeing nothing but the images in her head. Robbie had fallen asleep almost immediately afterwards, one arm tightly round her and the other thrust up under his pillow. She had lain awake, smiling at the dark outline of the lightbulb overhead, listening to the creaks and whispers of the cottage, still too full of wonder to feel sleepy. As the weight of his embrace grew uncomfortable, she tentatively began to shift her position. The idea of being hugged to sleep, though attractive, was not one that she had ever found very practical. Her right arm was quite dead. After a few minutes of some courteous but quite ineffective nudging, she grew more assertive, remembering that nothing woke Robbie once he had fallen asleep, that even trips to the lavatory were a form of sleepwalking of which he had no recollection in the morning.

To feel nothing but friendliness towards a bare bulb, swinging gently on the curling snippets of a Siberian wind, was for Rachel – lover of warmth and creature comforts of every kind – such a bizarre experience that she felt it could only bear irrefutable testimony to the rightness of the course on which she had now embarked. Any concern about other aspects of the indisputable squalor of their surroundings had also been greatly assuaged by Robbie's profuse apologies on the subject, together with his detailed descriptions of all the renovations and decorations that were in the pipeline. There were architect's drawings of how the kitchen would look, he told her, once the wall to the outside toilet had been knocked down and the boiler had been moved upstairs. Somewhere he had a book of fabric samples for the bedroom and sitting room curtains. He would value her opinions on everything, he admitted shyly, on the morning of their second full day together, when the banishment of the dreaded Errol to a dark shed had afforded them something approaching a civilised stretch of sleep.

'I'm hopeless with curtains,' she replied, smiling and stretching, savouring the thrilling suggestion of a shared future that this simple invitation allowed. 'A mad woman called Priscilla did my place up for me – you ought to see it . . .'

'Is that a promise?' He came to sit on the edge of the bed and brushed back a few strands of hair from her cheeks.

They had made love without taking any precautions at all. Robbie had clearly assumed that she was on the pill – as she had always been before – and Rachel, after a few minutes' tussle with her conscience in the privacy of the bathroom, had sealed her cap back into its compact and given her hands a vigorous washing with soap and hot water. The washing gave her time to think, time to marshal her considerable capacity for logic against the forces of guilt raging on the other side:

At almost forty, every cycle counted, she reminded herself. In addition to which, her confidence in a future with Robbie was growing by the minute. If, by some cruel twist, such a future was snatched away from them, she could – she would – cope on her own. She hid her cap under a wadge of cotton wool in the bottom of her vanity case, where it remained for the duration of her stay.

But resolve could not entirely smother the rumblings of her conscience. The underlying deceit of her actions at times distracted her so much during their love-making that she felt like an actor playing a part. There were moments when she was convinced Robbie sensed it too, when his eyes fixed hers with a questioning frown, his silence probing her expression for answers. It was tempting then, locked in the cocoon of physical intimacy, to tell him everything. But still Rachel held back, fearful of marring their reunion by bringing too much to bear upon it too soon. Recollections of her showdown with Nathan fuelled this reticence, criss-crossing her mind like shadows from another life.

They spent the last evening lying on their elbows on either side of the fire, their feet towards the hearth, their free hands linked, bridging the space between them. Their faces were lit only by the flickering glow of the flames, an orgiastic dance of yellow and orange, enlivened and applauded by the cracks of sound exploding underneath. The next day Rachel would leave, to get back to a party – to a life fast losing its allure. While Robbie, with equal reluctance, would have to face three days' worth of demands and messages on his answering machine, the horrors of unsorted bills and estimates, together with the devious weaknesses of forty-two pregnant sheep. The hovering dread of such realities, only a few hours away, charged the atmosphere between them with a fresh intensity, oiling the wheels of intimacy and tightening their reluctance to part.

'Do you remember me swearing I'd never become a godmother?' Rachel ventured, wanting to at least tiptoe round the subject burning in her heart. 'Well I've got four now – godchildren, I mean . . . Robbie?'

He was staring at the carpet, his head bowed at such an angle that the large curls on top of his head had flopped down as a mask for his face. 'Robbie? Are you OK?' She craned her neck for a glimpse of his expression.

'I'm brilliant.' When he looked up she was shocked to see that there were tears in his eyes. 'I love you Rachel.' It was the first time he had said it. 'There's never been anyone else that mattered.' The words rushed out of him. 'I thought I had got over you, but now I realise I was just waiting for you all along, that I would always be waiting for you.'

'Oh, Robbie.' She squeezed his hands, wishing she could suffocate the small part of her that did not like the tears. This was what she had wanted to hear, she realised, what she had been working towards ever since her audacious phone call inviting herself back into his life. It seemed unforgivable in the extreme that a small bubble of disappointment at having got her way so very very easily should choose that moment to burst and scatter inside her, a silent explosion of ingratitude.

'And you'll come to London soon?' she urged, wanting to make up for it.

Robbie nodded, sitting up and reaching for his boots from the hearth. They were heavy leather ones with thick rubbery soles and laces up to the anklebone. He stuck the tip of his tongue into the corner of his mouth as he struggled to pull them on over his thick socks. 'And I'll sort that bastard out for you while I'm at it, Cliff whatever-he-is.'

Though Rachel had derived considerable relief from telling her tale of sexual assault to a sympathetic audience, she had not found Robbie's show of male bravado on the subject particularly consoling. 'Oh, forget him,' she said airily, 'he's not worth it, I promise you.'

'But to think of that bastard daring to lay a hand—' He tugged sharply on his laces. 'It makes my blood boil. I always said it was no place for a woman.'

'I beg your pardon?'

He dropped the laces. 'I just meant – after what you told me – you might be best off resigning after all.' There was a glint of panic in his face, the worry of a child who fears he may have stumbled into saying the wrong thing.

'I may yet do just that.' She smiled, wanting more than anything for his look of anxiety to dissolve.

Robbie returned his attentions to his boots, his square face creasing with concentration as he focused on the unaccomplished chores listed inside his head.

'Is that scowl for me or life in general?'

'Sheep.' He grinned and pushed back the unruly mop of hair that lived along the dark ledge of his eyebrows. 'A few things to do.' Reaching for his sweater from the sofa – a shapeless, stained sack of a garment which had clearly seen many years of service without too many interludes amongst soap suds – he clambered to his feet. 'Could you wrestle with that chicken, do you think? Or we won't be eating much before midnight. There's a few dried herbs and so on in the cupboard. Though Phil Giddings' stuff is usually very tasty. One benefit of life in the sticks—' he shot her a smile of pride, '—no supermarket food in this neck of the woods.'

Rachel, who found the sight of the saggy pink corpse on the draining board far more alarming than the hard, neatly packaged creatures she occasionally selected from the freezer section of her supermarket, had tackled her allotted her job with determination, if little relish.

Back in London now, she smiled to herself at the memory of that last evening meal: dry pinkish meat and half a pack of frozen vegetables. Robbie had eaten eagerly, while she lanced peas on the prongs of her fork and chewed without tasting, her appetite quite dulled by excitement.

Rachel blinked her reflection back into focus, feeling the faint stickiness of the mascara as her upper and lower lashes touched before being pulled apart again. She did not want to go to the Robsons' party. She did not want to see Anita or Giles or any of the half-known acquaintances who would be there. She wanted to go back to Drakeshead, back to Robbie's roaring fire and glacier sheets, back to timeless afternoons of toast and sweet tea, to all the new and wonderful possibilities of sharing dreams instead of struggling along with them alone.

Polly Drayton sat at a dressing table too that night, her flat face flushed with heat from the crowded bar below and from the two double gins that Mr Bernard, the retired polo player, had bought her, flirting badly as he always did after a pint or three. New

Year's Eve was always something of a party, with free drinks flying all over the place.

She was supposed to be helping out in the kitchen – as well as serving at tables – but had sneaked upstairs for a breather. Robbie would be along later, she was sure of it. Now that the black car had gone, there was nothing to stop him. There were no other local parties that she knew of – and nobody liked to spend New Year's Eve on their own.

Polly chewed her lower lip as she studied her reflection. The colour in her cheeks belied the slump of her face, a slump of deep resignation, borne of a life lived entirely without the luxury of self-esteem. 'Expect nothing and you won't be disappointed,' her mother liked to say – folding her chunky arms and sticking her chin out with the certainty of one well acquainted with the truths of such a philosophy.

But she had expected something from Robbie Dexter. And who wouldn't, after seven years?

'She got her hopes up and gave herself too freely,' Mrs Drayton had declared several times during the past few weeks, broadcasting her views with the determined defiance of one proud of a reputation for calling a spade a spade. 'We warned her, but she wouldn't listen.' Polly, invariably within earshot of such confidences, would slink away, her ears burning with shame, her mother's words echoing after her. 'No good crying over spilt milk, that's what I say. Plenty of other fish in that particular sea and some with more security to offer too. Not a bad man that Robbie Dexter – I'll admit I always liked him – but he's got his head in the clouds half the time – running round after those blessed animals when he should be building up his business.'

It was true, Polly knew that. But truth had nothing to do with what she felt inside. She would have died for Robbie Dexter. She loved his crumbling cottage and messy life. Perhaps because it made her feel less of a mess – less of a burden – herself. He was always so grateful for any help she gave – unlike her parents who expected her to work all the time, as if it was some right granted to them upon her birth. A long time ago, she had sometimes dared to answer them back, confident that time would bring some sort of escape; but as the years closed in, narrowing the

- Amanda Brookfield

prospects of a grown woman with three CSEs and nothing but twelve years of working the deep fat fryer to her credit, she grew more timid about holding her own. Her parents were all she had, all that she could be sure of, especially now.

Hearing the crunch of feet on the gravel outside, Polly ran to the window for a peak between the curtains; but it was only Bob and Sharon Tayer who ran the newsagent's down the road. Their laughs and greetings mingled with the muffled hubbub from the bar below as they opened the door and were welcomed inside.

'Polly! What the devil are you playing at up there?' The cannon of her father's voice boomed up the stairs. 'Table eight is threatening to walk out and Eric says if he doesn't get any help in the next five minutes he's going too – for good this time.' Eric was their chef, whose threats to leave multiplied during the course of each year that he stayed.

As the door flew open, Polly cowered against the window, her heart racing, her face a picture of guilt.

Her father, largely silent, as always, before the fog-horn opinions of his wife, had been curiously tender with his daughter during recent weeks, not saying anything directly, but sometimes using a new tone of voice which resonated with some of the compassion he felt but did not know how to own up to. 'What are you up to girl?' he said softly, staying by the door. 'Your mother's going mad downstairs. One more minute and then down, OK?'

Polly nodded, this sudden gentleness making her want to cry.

Much later that night, when the doors had at last closed on the ex-polo player, whose mother had come from the Argentine and who had spent two hours commemorating the fact with sonorous renditions of the tango, Polly stole out into the night. Robbie had not come. She needed to see again that the black car had gone.

The air was crisp and still, each hump of mud, each blade of grass brilliantly dusted with frost, creating a dim iridescence to light her way. Though her fingers and face were soon numb with cold, her feet remained warm in the fur-lined nest of her boots. There had been no present from him that Christmas, she thought miserably, pushing her hands deeper into her pockets

- 182

and increasing the length of her stride so that she skidded slightly on the frozen ground.

There was no sign of her car. Polly sighed with relief, but walked on, feeling that her mission was still not quite accomplished. A thick layer of frost masked the windows of Robbie's van, each an inviting square of white, chaste and perfect as a field of freshly fallen snow. With a glance over her shoulder, Polly pulled off her mitten and began to work her index finger across the rear window, the letters forming easily upon the bed of brittle crystals. *I AM DYING*, she wrote, heedless of any possible charges of melodrama, responding only to the real desperation strangling her heart.

Then she stood for a moment staring at the cottage, praying that the black rectangle of his bedroom would blink open with light, that some deep, telepathic power might bring him and everything they had once shared back to life. But all remained quiet, apart from the infinitesimal creaks and whispers of freezing vapour and burrowed animals. Even the field was silent, all its occupants having been moved earlier that evening to the barn behind the house, where a scattering of straw awaited them together with several buckets of the expensive pellets on which pregnant ewes were said to thrive. Evidence of the invariably hazardous transition from field to barn lay all around her in the form of frozen piles of what she had originally taken to be mud, but which she now realised were sheep droppings.

Polly bent down and, with gloved hands, picked up as much as she could of one heap of frozen excrement. Empowered by fresh resolve, she then marched across to the front door of the cottage, where she forced what she could of her grim parcel through the letter flap. Then she rang the bell, holding the button down as hard as she could and counting to ten, before running off into the night.

Since Piers Robson was a political journalist of only moderate reputation and his wife, Sally's, contributions to interior design magazines had become so freelance as to be practically nonexistent, the lavish splendour of their parties was always something of a shock.

Anita, taking in the elegant structures of sea food and exotic salads – each one an architectural masterpiece in its own right – the massive flower arrangements, interlaced with twists of mistletoe and dangling lanterns, felt unashamedly envious. The venue this year was an entire restaurant on the south side of the Thames, its tables carefully arranged so as to allow a large space for dancing without impeding access either to the bar or this extravaganza of food. Outside, a few of the hardier guests were already braving the covered walkway, admiring the prospect it afforded of several of the capital's most famous monuments, lit up along the river banks with picture-postcard perfection.

Beside her, Giles was pulling at the joints of his fingers, making little clicks that set her teeth on edge. He had been doing it ever since he got in from work an hour or so before, when she had hissed that there was no time for a bath and he had turned and slouched back downstairs, looking at the floor. Filled with impulsive shame at her bossiness, Anita had darted forward and kissed him fiercely on the cheek. 'I'm sorry, love. I didn't mean to shout. It's just that the twins were so awful this afternoon – massive overdoses of sugar at a quite unspeakable party featuring somebody called Melody Man who was so boring even the dog fell asleep – and then they cried because that new girl Chrissie was coming to sit and not Moira who irons, who they like so much more.' The stiff silence of her husband made her back down further still. 'Look, have that bath. Have a sleep. Do what you like. It won't matter a bit if we're late.'

'No. I don't care.' He had sat down on the bottom stair and pulled his coat onto his lap from where he had slung it across the bannisters. 'Whatever you want, Anita.' Then the baby-sitter had emerged from the sitting room, releasing a deafening noise from the television as she opened the door. Instead of being brave and saying something, Anita followed Giles out to the car, where the expense and general failings of all their baby-sitters served as conversational fodder for the journey. If, that is, the intermittent growls provided by her husband could be said to qualify as conversation. They now stood side by side amongst the other first arrivals, scanning the half empty room for familiar faces, the few inches separating them feeling vast and unbridgeable.

Rachel arrived a little after nine o'clock, her departure from the flat having been delayed by a call from her parents wishing her all the best for the New Year. They never stayed up to mark the occasion themselves, thanks to a lifelong aversion to champagne and a dogged belief in the rejuvenating effect of every hour of sleep gained before midnight. Her father barked out a sentence or two of greeting before handing over to his wife, who launched into a lengthy account of their American Christmas. Duncan and Mary Beth's hospitality had known no bounds. They had seen the Bolshoi at the Kennedy Center, attended Midnight Mass in the cathedral and glimpsed the tail of the presidential cat during a tour of the White House. Craig and Billy, apart from a little over-excitement on Christmas Day, had behaved like angels. They were missing the little darlings already. If only air travel wasn't so expensive they'd fly out every few months or so. Grandchildren were so special – such a treat – it was quite cruel to miss so much of it by living so far apart.

Rachel waited patiently for a suitable lull in these eulogies before daring to offer any information about herself.

'I had a wonderful Christmas.' She paused before blurting, 'I'm seeing Robbie Dexter again. I thought you'd like to know.'

'Robbie Dexter? After all these years? I don't believe it . . . but darling, that's marvellous. Is it – I mean – is it serious?'

'Serious?' Rachel smiled to herself at the crudity of the question. 'Yes, I suppose it is.'

'We were so very fond of Robbie, but then you know that. Well, well, that's the best news I've had in a long time. So when are you both coming to pay us a visit? Is he still designing gardens and things? We'd so love to see him again, your father and I. Come any time – absolutely any time – though the weekend after next would suit us best.'

'The weekend after next,' explained Rachel patiently, 'would be hard. I've promised to go to Devon. But Robbie will be coming up to London soon – let's arrange something then. A Sunday lunch – you could come to me for a change.'

'That would be nice dear. Only give us plenty of warning, won't you? You know what your father's like – needs everything organised well in advance.'

'Of course,' Rachel murmured, privately thinking how adept couples could be at blaming each other for their own foibles. But it was good to hear her mother's pleasure, good to feel that, just for once, there was an aspect of her life capable of causing some genuine parental satisfaction.

'Hang on a minute, while I tell Dad.' Her mother raised her voice to an unnaturally high pitch in order to compete successfully with the television. 'Rachel is back with Robbie, dear,' Rachel heard her call. 'Robbie Dexter. We're going to see them both in two Sundays' time. Won't that be lovely?'

While recognising that her mother was demonstrating nothing but the jubilation which she herself had sought to provoke, Rachel none the less cringed inwardly. The business with Robbie still felt so new and delicate that it was hard not to flinch at having it bandied about by other people. Even telling Anita about it on the phone during the drive back that afternoon had initially felt almost like a betrayal. Being Anita she had jumped to all sorts of conclusions, most of which – infuriatingly – contained too many grains of truth for Rachel to utter any convincing denials.

'It'll be wedding bells and christenings before we know it – ooh goody, new clothes . . .'

'Anita, really, you're impossible.'

'But you're not denying it, I note. Robbie Dexter, eh? The guy

I never got to meet – well, who would have thought it? Are you bringing him tonight?'

'I wish I could.' Rachel sighed. 'It's going to be one of those commuting things for a while yet . . .'

'Until I get my fancy hat, you mean?'

'Anita, stop it. Apart from being bloody cheeky, you're tempting fate. How are you anyway, you sound good,' she added carefully.

'Not pissed, you mean.'

'I didn't say that.'

'You didn't have to.' There was a pause. 'As a matter of fact life in the Cavanagh camp seems to have hit a new all-time low—'

'Anita, I'm sorry.'

'Don't be. I'm getting quite used to it myself. I'm going to use it as an excuse to misbehave dreadfully at every opportunity.'

'Like tonight, you mean?'

'Most definitely.'

'But not so much we won't be able to have a proper talk, I hope. I've got to stop, I'm almost at the North End Road.'

'So long as it's not about me,' Anita replied, laughing.

Rachel had collected her coat ticket and was just bracing herself for the uniquely dreadful moment of having to enter a room full of smoke and crowded people – a moment which grew no easier with the years – when a finger tapped her on the shoulder. She spun round to find herself staring into the bespectacled face of Luke Berenson, the vicar's son towards whom her mother had nurtured such hopelessly misguided aspirations a few months before.

'Small world.'

'Yes, isn't it?' Although quite pleased to see him, something in Rachel recoiled. Recollections of their curiously intimate autumnal walk brought with them an unwelcome sense of vulnerability. I want to call Robbie she thought, glancing round for a public telephone and saying, 'How are things with you?'

'Not too bad, thanks.' He pushed his glasses up his nose and cleared his throat. 'That is, if you discount the fact that I'm not on speaking terms with the old man, but then that does have its advantages.'

They both laughed, recalling the shared horrors of their lunch together.

'I'm here with my new partner, Alan Raymond. He's a journalist. We're not staying long – going to another party afterwards.'

Rachel was on the point of responding to this happy piece of news when her eye was caught by a tall, dark-haired man handing in what looked like a trench coat. His hair had been cut so short that for a moment she didn't recognise him.

Luke turned politely to follow her gaze. 'Someone you know?'

'Oh no – I mean, barely. Shall we find ourselves a drink?' She turned hastily and led the way towards the teeming throng in the large room behind them, some instinct impelling her to lose herself within it before Will Raphael had time to catch them up. As they entered, Luke was accosted by a ginger-headed man wearing a lime-green bow tie and matching handkerchief, who propelled him away to meet someone else. Left to her own devices Rachel found herself a drink and then began surreptitiously scouring the room for Anita. After the intense intimacy of the last few days the amorphous, impersonal mass of humanity swarming around her felt painfully alien.

'I got the distinct impression I was being run away from just now. Was I right?'

He was wearing black trousers and a plain white collarless shirt held together with small, ivory-coloured oval buttons which caught in the beams of the ceiling spotlights.

Rachel opened her mouth to deny the allegation, but found the truth coming out instead. 'I'm sorry – I don't know why – I'm feeling decidedly unparty-like I'm afraid. Probably shouldn't have come at all . . .'

'Believe me,' he put in dryly, 'I know the feeling. I only came because I had my arm twisted.'

They each took sips of their wine and studied their fingers for a moment.

'Devon was clearly a success.'

'What do you mean?'

'Your face, it's full of . . . not colour exactly but . . . there's a sort of glow. Fresh country air maybe?' He cocked his head at her and smiled. 'Though now it's because you're blushing.'

'Really, I must say . . . I mean, why do I get the impression that you get perverse delight from making me feel uncomfortable?'

'And why is it that I get the impression you are unhealthily unused to being teased?' He smiled and shook his head. 'I'm sorry. You're quite right. I've no business being so familiar. Teasing is for one's closest friends and I barely know you.'

'Quite.' She took a sip of her drink, wishing she was one of those people who could stand next to someone and remain silent without it feeling awkward. 'As a matter of fact,' she found herself saying, 'my stay in Devon has made me think that it might be fun to move out of London for good, leave the rat race and so on.'

'Really?' He raised his eyebrows. 'You strike me as the sort of person who would be quite lost without the rat race – and I don't mean that as an insult,' he added hastily.

'I shall endeavour not to take it as one then,' she replied, resolving to change the subject one last time and then make an excuse to get away.

'How is your little boy – Jack, was it?'

'He's good, thank you.' His face broke into a broad smile, in one move eradicating every trace of rigidity, but still leaving Rachel with the impression that each flicker of emotion was under masterful control. There were black flecks in the brown of his pupils, she noticed, tiny dark smudges which perhaps accounted for the intensity of his stare. 'But he's not my boy, I'm sorry to say, he belongs to my sister, Anna.'

'Oh, I see,' she replied quickly, not seeing at all. She almost asked if he was married, but checked herself. Single people could not ask such things, at least not without creating certain resonances.

'I had a wife once,' he said, 'but no children.'

'That was lucky.'

Across the other side of the room the disco had started up. A few eager couples were already shuffling under the strobe lights, their limbs looking twitchy and disjointed, their expressions frozen and robotic.

'Christ, *there* you are – the only two people I want to see at this horrid party.' Anita pushed between them from behind, neatly linking her arms through theirs. 'Mr Will Raphael because I'm a shameless flirt and Rachel because I want to hear all about Robbie and be made *furiously* jealous. Finding true love so late on in the game is simply not fair. Most of us found it so long ago that we've forgotten what it felt like. I've certainly forgotten what Giles feels like lately . . .' She completed the sentence with a musical laugh.

'Hello, Anita.' Rachel kissed her cheek, wondering how much of the manic cheeriness was put on and how much came from a bottle. 'Can we talk?' she whispered.

Anita pulled her hand free and leant on Will. 'Oh, I'm right off talking, I'm afraid. Never does any bloody good.' Alcohol had helped to dull the sharper angles of her mood, although disappointment still raged inside, like the irrepressible nausea that came with one of her migraines. Getting Sally to invite Will Raphael to the party had been the easy part, she realised; now that he was here she had no idea what to do with him, beyond a sudden and quite irrational desire to get him away from Rachel. Rachel, who was going to make babies and live happily ever after with Robbie Dexter, for Christ's sake. Rachel who, having decided she wanted true love and the works, had clicked her fingers and got the lot.

'I'm going to be bold and ask you to dance, Will. Rachel won't mind, will you Rachel? If you see Giles, tell him I've left him for a tall dark handsome stranger. Tell him he can keep the kids but I'd like a standing order for the mortgage and the school fees.'

Will allowed himself to be led away, but not before throwing Rachel a glance of good-humoured apology as he went. He really was quite impressively tolerant, Rachel thought, smiling after them but feeling worried. It was so impossible not to worry about Anita these days. Things could not carry on at such a pitch for much longer. Some awful climax was coming, she could feel it.

It was quite a relief to slip into the cool confines of the phone booth. As she searched her handbag for coins, Rachel found herself thinking about the rat race and wondering whether she needed to be a part of it or not. She pictured Robbie's cottage, not as it was, but as it could be, her imagination moulding order and beauty from amongst the chaos. She could live there, all right. Of course she could. She pressed several coins into the slot and waited for the dialling tone. Imagining Robbie as a permanent fixture in London was altogether harder. Even the features of his face shimmered and creased like a broken reflection. Her fingers hurriedly pressed the numbers. She needed to speak to him. She needed to hear his voice for it all to come back into focus.

'I thought you were just going to take my photograph.' Rachel shuffled in the armchair in which she had been sitting for some fifteen minutes and made a face.

Will, perched on a stool a few feet away with a pencil and a large sketch pad, glanced up. 'I am. Sometimes I do a few drawings too. It helps me focus on what I want. Angles and lighting and so on.'

'I can't believe I agreed to do this.'

He smacked his pencil against his pad and laughed out loud. 'The power of alcohol for you, maybe?'

'Nonsense. I wasn't that bad . . .' She stopped, scowling and blushing at the recollection of the headache she had endured on New Year's Day. 'Well maybe I was,' she muttered, thinking at the same time that her presence in Will's studio in fact had something to do with how kind he had been to Anita.

The phone call with Robbie, a lovely long talk full of mutual longing and half-articulated hopes, had left her quite elated. She had floated back into the arms of the party in quite a different mood, full of energy and a sense of celebration. A few glasses and idle conversations later she found herself seated before a plateful of food at a round table of lively people that included both Will and Anita. Giles had apparently gone home, an action to which his wife referred with mounting venom and wit as the evening wore on. At the approach of midnight, ice-buckets of champagne were distributed generously to all the tables, encouraging the tide of unbridled – and quite un-British – camaraderie that was sweeping through the room.

'Any resolutions, then?' Rachel asked Anita, chinking her glass with her fork to get her attention.

'Not bloody likely.'

'I've got one,' piped a small man with a beaky nose, putting his hand up like a child in a classroom.

'Let's hear it then, darling,' drawled Anita through a mouthful of smoke.

'To personally harass as many women as possible.'

'That's a split infinitive,' shouted someone, 'you can't have that.'

'Yes he can,' replied Anita, reaching across to pat the man's hand and assure him he could personally harass her any time he wanted.

'You wouldn't like it,' Rachel had heard herself saying, 'I mean . . . it happened to a friend of mine – a . . . a . . . close friend . . . not nice at all.'

'Well, I think it would be heavenly to be harassed,' declared Anita, trying and failing to catch the eye of Will who was sitting opposite.

'What happened to this friend, then?' Will asked, leaning forward and resting his chin on both hands.

'Nothing. She'd like some revenge, but can't think how. She wants to resign but thinks it might make her look guilty. Can't face a court case. Usual sort of story.' Rachel clapped her hand to her mouth. 'Oh God, I'm being boring. Sorry everybody, sorry.'

'Darling you're not, you're being sincere, which is another thing entirely, but quite unforgivable all the same.' Anita blew her a smoky kiss and they all laughed. Then it was time to stand up and link hands for 'Auld Lang Syne'. They sang gustily, repeating the first two lines of the song over and over again since they were all anyone could remember. Afterwards, neighbour embraced neighbour, the man with the reedy voice kissing Rachel on the lips, while Anita made a smacking sound at the air beside her ears, clinging on for a few seconds of tipsily sentimental affection. As Will left his side of the table and approached them, Rachel found herself studying the dark shadows across his cheeks and round his mouth with something like anticipation. But instead of a New

Year's greeting, he asked again if she would sit for a photograph. Then Anita was between them, bestowing Will with a festive embrace of such ferocity that Rachel could see the whites of his nails as he prised himself free.

'Yes, OK then,' she had said, raising her voice and her glass, as the floor heaved beneath her feet.

'Hang on a minute.' Will put his pencil behind one ear and clambered down from his stool. 'What are you up to over here?'

'Up to?' She tensed as he adjusted the angle of her face and then her neck. His fingertips felt cool.

'Relax. Look at me. No, don't stare, just *look* – not through me, but at me. Engage my face – pretend for a minute that you know me.'

Rachel, stiff with self-consciousness, swivelled her attention from the intimidating vulture of a tripod to the face now just a few inches from hers. With his dark hair cropped so short at the front, his eyes, with their curious mixture of jet and brown, were even more prominent – quite impossible not to stare into when viewed so close, though she did her best. There were faint webs of laugh-lines in each corner, she noticed, pulling his expression towards amusement even when he was being most serious. His nose looked longer close-to, and very straight. 'But I don't know you,' she said hopelessly.

'No, I suppose you don't.' He grinned and sat back on his haunches, studying her for a moment in a way that was both critical and unsettling. 'But I think I'm beginning to know you, a little.'

'Oh, do you now?' She crossed her arms and sucked in her cheeks.

'Hands in your lap, please. There, like that. But you don't like to be known, do you Rachel Elliot? You're like me. Full of secret spaces.' He was back with his pad now, sitting on the very edge of his stool, one leg caught up in its struts, the other just reaching the ground. His pencil made small scratching noises as he worked.

'I don't know what you mean.' It was hard to sound indignant and dignified at the same time. The sense of unease with which she had approached this appointment, after a gruelling few weeks of going through the motions at work, increased to new proportions. Without weekends in Devon she would have gone insane. But Robbie had been too busy to see her that weekend, so there had been no excuse to cancel. He was going to make up for it by coming to London next time, he promised. And about time too, she had teased, making him cross.

In one swift, impatient movement, Will slid off the stool, walked once round her chair and went to sit on the window seat which overlooked the wharf below.

'This isn't working,' he muttered, staring out of the window with a sigh. 'You're like a . . . a cardboard cut-out. All hard edges. Tight as wire.'

Rachel reached down for her handbag at her feet. 'Well, I am sorry to have wasted your time,' she said with icy sweetness. 'I did warn you – cameras and I have never enjoyed the most fruitful of relationships.' She strode towards the door, wishing her heels didn't clump quite so noisily on the bare boards of his studio and trying not to be distracted by any of the curious statuettes and canvasses that she passed along the way. The place was like the storeroom for a gallery of modern art, except for the daylight pouring in through the windows along its river-facing wall, a white wintry light from a sky that glittered like a polished stone.

'Oh, come back here,' he called lazily, not moving. 'Come back and talk – have a coffee – a biscuit – if that's allowed.'

She stopped and turned. 'What do you mean, if that's allowed?'

'You just look like the kind of person who counts her biscuits, if you don't mind my saying so.'

There was an impudent gleam in his eye, though his mouth did not smile. It was a beautiful mouth, she saw suddenly, full and shapely, almost feminine. The thought, bolting into her mind from nowhere, was so absurdly inappropriate that she nearly laughed out loud.

'I eat when I'm hungry.' She hitched the strap of her handbag further onto her shoulder and crossed her arms. 'A biscuit would be quite nice, actually.'

'Good,' he said softly, leaving his window seat and strolling over to a cluttered trestle table in the far corner of the room that housed, among many other things, a paint-splattered metal kettle and a large, lidless jar of instant coffee. While the water boiled he tipped generous heaps of granules into two tea-stained mugs. 'Let's just talk.' He held out the steaming mug of oily black coffee like a peace offering.

'Talk?' She forced out a laugh, nervous of his calm. 'I thought I was here to have my photograph taken. It was your idea, remember? I agreed because it was New Year's Eve and I'd had five glasses of champagne. And because . . .'

'Because?'

She took the coffee and shrugged. 'Oh bloody hell, I don't know. What do you want to talk about anyway?'

'You.'

She shrugged again, determined to convey carelessness even if she could not feel it. 'Nothing to say. I've had a worryingly easy life. I work hard. I live well.' She started on a tour of the room while she talked, taking sips and blowing at imaginary swirls of steam. He stood leaning up against the wall beside the trestle table, one leg bent up behind him, the sole of his shoe pressed against the scuffed wall behind.

'And you want to move to the West Country?'

She spoke carefully, wishing suddenly that she had told Robbie about Will Raphael and the improbable business of agreeing to sit for a photograph. A combination of embarrassment and caution had prevented her. Robbie could be quite jealous, she had found, sometimes about the silliest things. 'Yes. Well, like I said, I'm thinking about it. I'm thinking about a lot of things at the moment. I feel it's time to move on . . . make a proper life-change . . .' His silence impelled her to continue. 'I've met someone – Robert Dexter – Anita mentioned him. We knew each other before – a long time ago. It was my fault it ended. Now we've got the chance to try again.' Rachel stopped in front of a picture of a woman, propped up on an easel, half-hidden by a writhing figurine modelled entirely out of rusty nails. It was the same woman who had appeared on the Christmas card. 'Who's this?'

'That is . . . that was my wife.'

'Oh, I see.' She hid her face in her coffee mug for a moment, before deciding that silence was probably the most tactless response of all. 'Does she still live in London?'

'No, she's dead.'

'Oh no . . . sorry . . .'

He hadn't moved. 'She was a cellist. She killed herself four years ago. Valium and gin. We had been married a year. She suffered from depression.' Though his voice was matter-of-fact, something about the stillness of his pose conveyed the impression of effort – of anguish – behind these words.

'How sad.' Rachel, wanting to save him further pain – not to mention discomfort for herself – opened her mouth to change the subject; but he hadn't finished.

'Sometimes I still feel guilty – that I wasn't enough. That I wasn't enough reason for her to live. If it wasn't for Anna – my sister – and Jack, I might have resorted to valium myself. Though Anna is a mess too,' he went on quickly, 'a typical anorexic dancer – which is probably why I like a woman who's not afraid to eat biscuits.' He chuckled, breaking the tension and coming towards her holding out a tin. 'Chocolate chip cookies. I take full responsibility apart from the black fingerprints, which belong to my nephew. Jack doesn't like cooking, but does a good line in bowl-licking and biscuit-counting.'

Rachel, subdued by the intimacy of his revelations, took one and ate steadily.

'By the way, I've got something for that friend of yours.' He began shuffling through a pile of papers beside the kettle.

'For Anita?' Rachel was intrigued.

'No, that other friend. The one who was sexually harassed.'

'Oh, her,' she said quietly, biscuit clogging her throat. 'I can't think why I mentioned it – talk about the wrong moment . . . Once, centuries ago, I used to have a sense of humour, you know,' she muttered. 'Anita was quite right to put me down.'

'Personally, I think your sincerity is one of your most endearing qualities,' he replied, using that tone he had, the one that left her quite unsure as to whether he was mocking or being kind. 'But if this doesn't kick-start the sense of humour you claim to have mislaid, then I'm afraid nothing will.' He held out a photograph, adding, 'It's for your friend – to help her get that revenge you mentioned.' There was a mischievous I-know-you-know-I-know look in his eyes that made it quite impossible to hold his gaze.

The photograph was of Cliff Weybourne. He was sitting on a sofa wearing nothing but an orange party hat, a pair of pink and blue striped boxer shorts and tartan socks. Aside from the lopsided smirk on his face, the most dominant feature of the picture was his stomach, which was as large as that of any expectant mother in her ninth month, but with the unattractive addition of a matting of thick, dark hair. Wedged between the second and third fingers of his right hand was a long, fat, freshly lit joint; a heavy swirl of smoke poured from its ashen tip. His left hand was buried wrist-deep in the ample cleavage of the woman seated next to him, like greedy fingers thrust into a bag of toffees. Best and most impressive of all in Rachel's eyes, was the expression on the woman's face: not so much boredom as complete indifference. Almost as if she did not know that the hand was there at all.

'It's fabulous,' she whispered, giggling in spite of herself. 'Where did you get it?'

'Ah, now that's a long story. A friend of a friend. A wild party. It doesn't really matter, does it?' He had come to stand beside her and was admiring the image over her shoulder. 'All that matters is that it is put to some worthwhile use. The lady is the wife of someone, by the way.' He paused. 'It won't destroy lives or careers, but for a spot of retribution I'd say it was just the thing.'

'It's brilliant,' murmured Rachel, grinning at the picture and then catching her breath as the full implications of this inspired act of generosity sank in. 'But hang on – how did you know – I mean, I never said it was Cliff . . . did I?'

'Let's call it a lucky guess.' He gently removed the photograph from her hands and slipped it into a brown envelope.

'And . . . well . . . isn't he a friend of yours?'

'Cliff Weybourne? A friend?' He shook his head, laughing. 'Christ, if I had friends like that I'd be seeing a shrink. No, no. No way. I've run into Weybourne several times through work projects, that's all. The man's a shark. I have as little to do with him as possible. I only ever come to your place to see Steve Betts. Which gives me an idea.' He tapped the envelope with his fingers. 'I'm sure Steve would be willing to blow this thing up to poster size – so that everybody might have a chance of appreciating it. It would only be fair, don't you think?' His eyes twinkled.

She clapped her hands, laughing. 'Oh, absolutely. Or,' she paused, as fresh inspiration took hold, 'what about a Valentine's card – an enormous, life-size Valentine's card, from an anonymous admirer?'

'Now you're talking.' He came over to collect her mug. 'I had a feeling you'd know what to do with it.'

'Yes, well—' she began sheepishly.

'She's a very close friend, I know, as close as friends get. And I've a notion you make a habit of helping close friends.'

'I . . .'

'I'm just glad I could help. Shall we return to some serious work now?' He made a grand gesture of invitation at the armchair. 'If madam would care to step this way?'

'Yes, she would. And – thank you, Will. Thank you very much indeed.'

He began inserting a film into a polaroid camera. 'Don't mention it. Now then, I'm just going to shoot a roll of this first, then we can get down to business.'

He took a series of trial pictures while Rachel picked crumbs out of the lambswool fluff of her jumper, brushing the smaller bits down onto the lap of her new, blue – too blue – jeans. Dress casually, he had said. Not such an easy task for a woman whose wardrobe reflected what she now recognised as a history of woefully inadequate leisure time. She had bought the jeans for Devon a couple of weeks before, on the lunchtime of the day she agreed to be the Head of Account Management, a day when she had needed to take her mind off things. Cliff Weybourne was skiing at the time, which had helped. But she had still felt awful.

As Will began arranging various foil reflectors and lights around the chair, a creeping unease stole over Rachel, a sensation of sitting alone on a stage, waiting for the spotlight to fall.

'Perhaps I should have taken those lessons after all,' she remarked, with a lightness she did not feel, 'then I might have a clue what you're doing.'

'Perhaps. I did my best to persuade you, you might recall,' he added with a wry smile. 'I dared to tackle that dense communications network of yours, the one you hide behind.'

'The one I what?'

'Forget it.' He was all businesslike again, almost brusque. 'Now face me, chin down a bit, that's it.' Leaving his post by the camera, he went to fiddle with the sugar-paper backdrop of yellowy cream that he had hung behind the chair. Then, quite without warning, he stepped silently up behind her and placed both hands on her shoulders. Using his palms, he began to press in slow hard circular motions across the top of her back, his fingers kneading so deep into the bands of muscle that it almost hurt. Rachel opened her mouth to say something, but then closed her eyes instead. When the hands were removed – a little later and with as little warning – she experienced a fleeting but quite extraordinary sense of loss, followed by a feeling of weightlessness, as if she was floating several inches above the seat of her chair. He remained standing behind her. She could hear him breathing, not because it was loud, but because the vast room suddenly seemed quite still, a frozen moment, captured in the flying poses of his sculptures, in the inscrutable expressions of the faces on the easels and walls.

'You are in knots, Rachel,' he said quietly. 'Stop trying to be brave all the time. Fear is a necessary part of the sensation of being alive. Sometimes we have to let it show. We have to own up to it or it drives us mad.'

Then he went and stood behind his camera, saying nothing more – not even instructing her how to sit or look – filling the silence with whirs and clicks from the tripod, while Rachel sank down into the soft embrace of the armchair, feeling unnerved but strangely elated. What a bloody cheek the man had. Quite unanswerable. She stared into the face of the camera boldly, unblinking. Knots indeed. She flexed her upper back, feeling still where his hands had worked, remembering with a twist of shameful pleasure how good it had felt, the releasing emptiness afterwards.

But it really wasn't worth mentioning to Robbie, Rachel decided, as she hopped from one leg to another in front of the ticket barrier the following weekend, waiting for the first sight of his curly head amongst the sea of faces streaming down the platform towards her. It was just a weird thing that had happened – too weird to try to explain – irrelevant the moment it was over. Will Raphael had not touched her again – had hardly come near her in fact – except to compare diaries for dates as to when the photo might be ready. Then he had held the door open for her and stood at the top of the stairs as she descended, hands pushed into the pockets of his trousers, his expression so unreadable that she suspected he might be masking disappointment in her as a model, that she had not lived up to whatever unimaginable expectations he had had in mind.

Robbie saw her first and waved hard, boyish glee radiating from his big square face. He could still have been a student, Rachel thought affectionately, taking in the weathered duffle coat and knee-bagged cords. There was simply no vanity to the man. Twiddling the duffle buttons, she lifted her face for a kiss.

A few yards behind them, Polly Drayton, her straggly hair bunched into a tight ponytail that tugged the skin back from her temples, watched them embrace and walk away before handing her own ticket to the man at the barrier. Robbie had invited her to London, she told her parents that afternoon, for a long weekend. Make or break sort of thing. See if they could sort something out after all.

'And I thought he had a new woman,' said her father, 'that's the story at any rate. A London lady.'

'That's just his sister, the one that went to Canada. She's back in London. We're going to stay with her the first night. After that it's a posh hotel. Five star with an indoor pool, Robbie says. Breakfast in bed with the newspaper if you want it. We might stay there all week.' The lies, once they started coming, flowed with silky ease.

'And how are we supposed to manage running this place while Lady Muck gallivants in London, that's what I want to know?' complained her mother, but good-humouredly, as if she might be persuaded that enjoying oneself was a forgivable crime after all.

Polly was in no hurry. She knew where Rachel Elliot both lived and worked – one sortie into Robbie's kitchen while he was out doing an estimate for the new owners down Sandy Lane had sorted that out. In the midst of so much clutter and mess, it hurt more than anything to find the woman's name – her numbers and addresses – so carefully written out and fixed to the middle of the fridge door with a magnet that Polly herself had given him. A sheep magnet, with a red ribbon round its neck.

Rachel and Robbie, busy with the greetings that precede proper conversation, did not notice the hunched, plump figure sprint across the road towards the buses, her half-empty rucksack jigging on her back like a swaddled child, her ponytail bobbing with jaunty defiance at the inky night sky.

'Do you want the good news or the bad news?' Rachel burrowed her face into his shoulder, savouring the solidity of him.

'Oh, only the good please.'

'We're going out to dinner – there's a really nice Italian place within walking distance from my front door.'

'Sounds great. I'm starving.' He patted her hand. 'Go on, hit me with the bad.'

'My parents are coming to lunch tomorrow. Sorry.'

'Your parents? Well, you did warn me.' He kissed her nose. 'We'll survive. They were OK, if I remember correctly.'

An unexpected ripple in the harmony of such exchanges occurred a little later in the evening, towards the end of their meal, when Rachel offered to pay and Robbie, fuelled with pride and too much wine, resisted vehemently.

'I know you earn more money than me Rachel – a lot more – but that does not mean you should pay my way. I've got enough to have a good time now and then, I promise you. I haven't been in a dole queue since college . . .'

'I know Robbie, I know. I just wanted it to be my treat tonight. I mean, you've come all the way up here and—'

'*My* treat, to make up for being apart on Valentine's Day,' he insisted grandly, signalling to the waiter with a flourish.

But the restaurant did not accept his credit card and his cheque book turned out to be in the side pocket of the bag which he had deposited at the flat.

'But I guess you might not be richer than me for very much longer,' he remarked stiffly, as they headed back up the street towards her flat. 'I know you've said that it's a question of getting the timing right, but the sooner you leave that horrible agency the better, if you ask me. Then we'd be on more of an even keel, eh?' Rachel's outward response to this was an encouraging smile, while inwardly she quailed. Did Robbie mean resign from the agency, or from work in general? Having so recently recovered from one minor upset, she was unwilling to risk another. So she let the matter pass.

In the light of such uncertainties, Rachel also elected not to mention a conversation she had had with Jimmy Chartsworth on the Monday of that week, informing her of a cabal of dissatisfied directors like herself who were hatching a plot to break away from McKenzie Cartwright and form a small agency of their own, an agency where discretion and personalities mattered, where artistic and moral values could be maintained at levels to which they had all originally aspired. The thrill of such news had almost caused her to abandon Cliff's Valentine surprise; though she relented when she saw Steve Bett's masterful transformation of the card. It was for a friend of Will's, she had explained, a friend with a grudge. Anything for a friend of Will's, he had said simply, offering a wry smile that confirmed better than words ever could that she had allies in the business after all, that she had not been suffering entirely alone.

The card was so large that it had taken two secretaries to transport it from reception to the bar, where a Valentine's Happy Hour was in full flow. The sight of Cliff Weybourne's face when he tore off the tissue paper, when laughter froze to horror, was exactly the therapy Rachel had craved and would, she knew, be a source of satisfaction for years to come. *To My Valentine*, it said in large letters across the top, *I've always loved a party animal*. To Cliff's credit, he had tried to laugh, though it looked more like gagging and no noise came out at all. He left the bar shortly afterwards, unwisely leaving his gift propped up by the juke-box, where it still remained, enhanced by a few creative additions with biros and fibre-tipped pens. A bubble coming out of the woman's mouth now said: *If you ignore a gorilla it eventually goes away*.

When she told Robbie about the incident, he laughed, but doubtfully. 'Where did you get such a picture, anyway?'

'I've friends in the right places,' she replied quickly, putting her hand in his coat pocket and lacing her fingers in his.

'I hope this doesn't mean you won't resign after all? What with this and accepting that promotion you might feel tempted to stay.'

He was walking so fast that she had to keep lengthening her stride to match his. 'I honestly don't know, Robbie. Things are up in the air at the moment.'

She thought about wanting a baby and clenched his fingers even more tightly inside the pocket. Why was finding the right moment to tell him so hard? Why was she only able to progress things inside her head?

'It's just that I feel like I'm playing second fiddle to your job,' remarked Robbie, while she searched in her bag for her keys.

'Don't be silly,' she replied, slotting the key home and thinking how much more fragile his ego was than she had at first judged, how little it seemed to have evolved over the years.

There followed a brief half-hour or so of silent friction, one of their first. In order to overcome it, Rachel found herself slipping into the role of the little woman, curling up in the broad circle of his arms like an animal seeking protection. Robbie had responded instantly, his confidence blossoming with every stroke of her hair.

I could live like this, she'd thought, nestling closer, relishing the intimacy, telling herself that it did not matter if its origins were a little contrived.

26 $

At some indefinable point the weekend slipped out of Rachel's control. While Robbie lay in bed with the papers, swooning at the treat of not being roused by the needs of poultry and sheep, she found herself wrestling with a spitting shoulder of lamb in her kitchen, some ill-founded notion of wanting to feed her parents in the manner to which they were accustomed having prompted her to attempt dizzy heights of culinary achievement from which she usually had the wisdom to refrain.

Thanks to carrots with tiny, suspicious looking drill-holes in their sides and roast potatoes which stubbornly refused to show so much as a hint of a tan – even after two hours on the top shelf of the oven – a good portion of Rachel's morning was spent in the kitchen. When her parents arrived they greeted Robbie Dexter like a long-lost son, monopolising him with so many questions about his life that she almost felt neglected, and had to remind herself that such adulation should make her glad.

Sheep dominated the conversation, without one single ironic reference to the disappointingly fatty joint which formed the centrepiece of their meal. Rachel, absorbed in ragged, inexpert carving with a blunt knife, kept her thoughts largely to herself, thinking as she finally sat down that what remained of the bone looked as if it had been the subject of a vicious brawl between two starving dogs. Robbie, oblivious to such niceties, ate heartily, two platefuls of meat and vegetables doing nothing to dent his appetite for the board of cheese and biscuits that followed.

'You'll take care of Rachel, won't you now Robbie?' said Margaret, popping a single grape into her mouth. 'We can't help worrying about her, can we Henry?'

'Mum . . . for goodness' sake,' began Rachel.

'Oh, don't you worry, Mrs Elliot. Rachel's already thinking of packing in work. Did she tell you?' Wafery splinters scattered as he bit into his cracker and cheese.

'No, she didn't.' Her mother beamed. 'It's always been such a demanding job – she works far too hard, we've always said so. Never has time for any fun – until now, of course. Thank goodness for you Robbie, thank goodness.' As she leant across the table to pat his arm one of her bangles skimmed the top of the butter. Rachel, observing the minor mishap, immediately resolved to keep it to herself, childishly relishing the thought of a surprise grease stain appearing somewhere on her mother's turquoise twin-set later in the day.

It was something of a relief to be summoned away from the table by the telephone.

'How's it going?'

'Oh Anita, it's you. Fine, I guess. I'd forgotten how much they adored him – it's quite sickening really.'

'And the course of true love continues to run smooth?'

'Apart from the occasional loop-the-loop.'

'What did I tell you? You'll be needing best men and god-mothers and things soon.' She sounded gloomy.

Rachel sipped the wine which she had brought with her and leant up against the wall, wishing guiltily that she could feel as sure about such things in her own heart. All that she so badly wanted was now within reach. Not just motherhood, but love on a grand scale. Robbie hadn't asked her outright, but the hints were certainly starting to come thick and fast.

'I really ought to get back to them all.' She sighed. 'Poor Robbie – he's managing awfully well.'

'You couldn't get away for a couple of hours today or tomorrow, could you?' Anita, remembering the grey parcel of a husband slumped in bed upstairs, spoke now with real urgency.

'Oh Anita – you know I'd love to – but this weekend it really would be hard.'

'Giles has left me.'

'He's what?'

'Left me – mentally speaking. He's turned away, gone for good.'

'You mean you two haven't made it up yet?'

'No, Rachel, this is different. Much much worse. He barely moves. He doesn't speak.'

'Is he ill, for God's sake?'

'I don't know. He says not. But he's like a . . . zombie. I'm wondering if he's fallen in love – not married love, but the crazy kind, with someone who's not yet old enough to be sour and cynical. Someone who doesn't drink,' she added very quietly.

A burst of laughter sounded from the lunch table. 'Have you asked him if there's someone else?'

'Of course – millions of times. He denies it. He denies everything. I tell you, Rachel, I'm at my wit's end. It's like living with a corpse. And to make matters worse I've been given my first serious piece of work in centuries. Post-natal depression – right up my street – good money, too. Only I can't do it – I can't concentrate on anything with Giles like this. I think I'm going to do something desperate if I'm not careful.'

'Now calm down. Call a doctor. Get someone to look at him.'

'Doctors don't come round these days, unless you're dying. Nor can I give a man who weighs thirteen stone a fireman's lift to the car. The bugger. I hate him. Do you know that, I really hate him.'

'Nonsense.'

'You sound like his mother.'

'I'm sorry, I don't mean to. I just don't know how to help . . . except perhaps . . .'

'Go on – say it.'

'You've got to stop drinking, Anita. It's gone way too far this time.'

There was a silence. 'You have no idea Rachel . . .' her voice trembled for a moment before she wrenched it back under control. 'Stop fussing, will you? Run along and plot weddings and babies then, and leave those of us who've done all that to sort ourselves out. It'll be funerals next. I want Mahler at mine, by the way, and a video recording of Elvis singing 'Love Me Tender'. Oh yes, and that lovely poem that they did in the Four Weddings film – the one that made everyone cry. I want Giles to read it.'

Rachel laughed as she was meant to. 'OK, I'll see what I can do. Now go and write about post-natal depression and I'll call you on Monday to see if things are any better.'

Robbie shot her a look of relief when she reappeared – a fleeting arrow of complicity which cheered her greatly as she set about clearing away the plates and making coffee. Later, her mother came to help with the washing up, while Robbie and her father lounged in the sitting room discussing the pros and cons of garden gnomes. Rachel had forgotten how much they had in common.

The women in the kitchen, the men digesting their meal, she thought, trying not to mind. Her father's pipe smoke curled round the hangings and corners of the flat, a blue snake of a shadow that transported Rachel back to earlier times in earlier kitchens. The boys playing elsewhere. The women with their hands in the sink.

'That nice Luke Berenson has found himself someone, too,' remarked her mother in cosy way, rubbing invisible flecks off the side of a saucepan and searching for an appropriate cupboard in which to stow it. 'His father came by for sherry last Thursday, or was it Wednesday . . . ?' She paused, saucepan in hand, to ponder the point. 'He says Luke's been coming home a lot less as a result, but there we are. Can't have everything, can you? I expect he'll meet her soon enough.'

Rachel, recalling the ginger-headed journalist with the vibrant bow tie, suppressed a smile.

'Such a nice man. I'm so glad for him. I do hope they get married.' Her mother clutched the dishcloth to her chest and smiled dreamily, while Rachel marvelled that the unromantic terms of reference under which her own marriage had evolved should not have dulled her appetite for believing in such things.

So well did Robbie entertain her parents that they did not leave until late afternoon, after a walk down to the Embankment and two pots of tea. Rachel closed the door with a groan of relief and kicked off her shoes. Robbie, who was in the sitting room watching a rugby match, held out his arm to her when she came in, though his eyes remained fixed on the screen.

'Got you to myself at last,' she murmured, suppressing a

twinge of resentment at the thirty or so rugby players now distracting his attention.

A few minutes later there was a long ring on the doorbell.

'Oh shit, they've forgotten something,' she moaned, casting her eyes round the room for a glasses case or a stray glove. Since there was no answer on the intercom, Rachel made her way to the front door in her stockinged feet, hugging herself against the cold and thinking uncharitably about the incompetence of the old.

Standing on the step outside was a white-faced girl with a greasy ponytail, wearing a purple anorak and a handsome pair of brown leather boots.

'I've got something for Robbie,' she said, thrusting a flat brown envelope into Rachel's hands and backing away.

'Do you want to see him?' asked Rachel without thinking, concerned by the look of pinched misery on the girl's face.

Polly took another step backwards and shook her head. How could he want someone so middle-aged, she was thinking, even if she had got pretty eyes?

'No message to pass on, then?' Rachel's patience, worn thin by the wind that whipped round their ankles, was in danger of giving way to sarcasm.

'Just give it him, would you?' The girl gestured with her head at the envelope. 'Say Polly brought it,' she called, running away down the steps.

'Right you are.' Rachel slammed the door and marched back down the hallway, cursing the way the weekend was developing and thinking not for the first time how much sweeter and simpler life seemed in Devon, with nothing but sheep and chickens to get in the way of things.

That night they almost argued.

'Why didn't you tell me about her?'

'Because she is nothing. Because there is nothing to tell.'

'Well, Molly—'

'Polly.'

'Polly clearly wouldn't agree with you. She looked in a terrible state too, all teeth and eyes. When you said there'd been a girlfriend over the last few years I had no idea she still lived so close to you, that she still was involved with you—'

'Well, I'm not involved with her.' Robbie, recalling the messages on his windscreen and the strange objects which had been forced through his letterbox during the course of the last few weeks, resolved to say as little as possible. Rachel, in her current mood, would not react well to news of sheep shit landing on his doormat.

'And how the hell did she get here? I mean, has she been following us or something?' Rachel shivered. 'I find the whole thing really spooky and horrible.'

They were lying in bed, surrounded by the debris of a disappointingly soggy pizza take-away, most of which had been consumed by Robbie, while Rachel picked at flakes of burnt onion and nibbled all the crusts.

'And I can't understand why you don't open that bloody envelope. I just couldn't do that – I mean, just out of curiosity I would have to open it. I know you say it will be nonsense of some kind, but I'd still like to see what *kind* of nonsense.'

'I've told you. Forget the whole thing. I'll sort it out when I get home. I promise you, I had no idea Polly was up to this sort of thing.'

'What sort of thing? You haven't opened her letter, or whatever it is.'

He sat up and threw his hands down onto the bedcovers. 'Look, I've told you, forget the letter. I don't want it to ruin our weekend.'

At the realisation that this was precisely what it was doing anyway, they both fell silent.

'Sorry,' Rachel whispered. 'Just jealous, I suppose.' It seemed simpler to say this, when in fact it didn't feel like jealousy at all. More like frustration. Or plain annoyance.

'I'm glad you're jealous,' Robbie replied gently, getting back into bed and pulling her hands to his mouth. 'It means you care. It means what I've always wanted to happen is finally happening.'

'And what was that?' she murmured.

'Oh, I think you know, Rachel Elliot,' he whispered, kissing her fingers between words, and pushing her back onto the bed. 'I think you know.'

Tell him now, chanted a voice inside her head, tell him now about wanting a child. The voice was so loud she was almost suprised he didn't remark on it himself. It occurred to her in the same instant that the reason she had not yet managed such a confession might be related, not to a fear that Robbie would object, but that he might just be thrilled beyond words. Appalled at herself, she hugged him harder, squeezing the thought away.

Rachel picked up the two transparencies lying on her desk and held them to the light for a minute before putting them down with a sigh. At this particular juncture in her life it was hard to care deeply about the destiny of a tube of skin-tinted moisturiser, especially one clad in a lilac bikini, frolicking in the spume of a fake wave. It was part of an American press campaign which Frank Alder was under pressure to test in the UK. Hopeful of taking at least some of the Mallarmé account with her to the break-away agency, Rachel was doing her best to cooperate. But it was difficult to concentrate. Things were moving so fast. Work that week had been structured round a series of hurried and secret meetings between her, Jimmy and the handful of others involved. A high-powered creative team had verbally agreed to come too. Three of the media buyers were interested. Premises had been found and several clients warned. It was almost time, but not quite. She had even asked Jimmy about the possibility of part-time. He had said they'd do anything to have her along, which was nice.

The failures of the weekend had also unsettled her. Worse than their silly spat about the Polly girl was her absurd inability to talk to Robbie about anything that mattered. Thinking back, Rachel felt positively ashamed of herself. Robbie was ideal in every way: He would make a good father. He loved her. And she loved him, in her own way. But here she faltered, aware that her feelings of tenderness towards Robbie had a worrying habit of expanding to satisfying proportions only when he was absent. It was two days since his visit to London and already she was longing to see him again, longing to sort out the future once and for all. Next time there would be no wavering, she told herself. Next time she would tell him everything.

Impatience had a lot to do with her confusions, Rachel decided – impatience not only with the cumbersome process of changing jobs, but with her body too. It was almost March. Given the instantaneous ease with which she had once conceived quite by accident, she found it impossible not to feel somewhat cheated that so many weekends of healthy, unprotected sex should have produced no results. Not even a measly false alarm. Coping with uncertainty had never been one of her strong points, she reflected grimly, returning her attentions to the transparencies and frowning in a fresh effort to concentrate. Getting pregnant would have simplified and crystallised things far sooner, she was sure. It would have brought matters to a head, instead of allowing them to flounder on the rocks of this unbearable – and wholly irrational – hesitancy and indecision.

These unhappy musings were interrupted by Naomi Fullerton, who burst into her office looking determined, though not altogether friendly, in a voluminous Laura Ashley dress and a thick gold hairband that made Rachel think of halos.

A concerned Melissa bobbed up behind. 'Sorry Rachel, she just—'

'It's OK Mel, Naomi's an old friend. No calls for a while, all right?' she called, as the door closed.

The two women hugged.

'Couldn't you wait till Easter to see me, then?' teased Rachel, smiling with genuine pleasure, but concerned by Naomi's expression. Though she was smiling back and her eyes were their usual glossy brown, her skin looked grey and saggy, as if transplanted from another face entirely.

'What are you up to these days, Rachel? It's been so long.'

Rachel, wondering what Naomi would say if she confessed that wanting a child was making her ruthless and selfish beyond repair, that she was currently toying with the idea of sharing a family and a future with a man who yet knew nothing about such plans himself, nodded her head slowly, saying she was fine. 'Not looking forward to forty,' she added with a grimace, 'and I'm about to start a new job.'

'Really? I thought you loved it here . . .'

'Yes, well I did . . . but I . . . fell out with a couple of colleagues just before Christmas. It made life hard,' she went on carefully, thinking with irrepressible satisfaction of the new, emotionally deflated version of Cliff Weybourne with whom they had all recently become acquainted. 'So, I've decided to move on.' She put one finger to her lips and glanced at the door. 'Still very hush-hush, so not a word.'

Naomi burst out laughing. 'As if I am likely to run into someone whose career path crossed with yours.' She began walking round the room, examining pictures and objects, her hands clasped behind her back, the tips of her suede heels sinking into the lush blue pile of the carpet. Rachel stood watching, noting the way the shiny ribbons of hair streamed from the teeth of her hairband and wondering why she had come.

'It's quite something to see this for myself,' Naomi said at length. 'All that I could never have. All this.' She held out both arms and let them drop heavily to her sides.

'You have come all the way from Suffolk to see my office?' Rachel, now seriously worried by the expression on Naomi's face, hoped to tease.

'Graham has left me,' she said, scowling at the square panels of Rachel's ceiling for a moment before going back over to the windows. 'After fifteen fucking years and four fucking children, Graham has left me.'

'Oh Naomi . . .' Rachel started forward, but Naomi held up her hand, warning her to keep away.

'No sympathy, please. He's been having an affair for two years with a primary school teacher with unshaven armpits and two studs in her nose. If I hadn't been so busy being grateful for the nose-dive in our sexlife, I might have noticed earlier. But one sees what one wants to see, I suppose. I've never been that keen on sex, I'm afraid. I was actually grateful.' She gave a short laugh. 'The children did wear me out so.' She rested her cheek on the palm of one hand and gazed unseeing into the washed-out blue of the sky. 'I thought it didn't matter. I thought we had enough other things – the children, the house and so on. I was wrong. Graham says he's in love. He's moved into her house – a horrible box on the edge of the estate. He says I can have whatever I want.' She turned and looked hard at Rachel, who was leaning back on the edge of her desk, still trying to absorb the fact that the one relationship she had always assumed would last had so spectacularly fallen apart.

'And right now,' Naomi went on, 'all I can think is that I gave up all this—' she swung her arms at the room again, '—that I gave up my career to be the kind of woman he wanted.'

'But you've got the children . . .' ventured Rachel gently.

'Oh yes, I've got the children all right.' She sighed. 'And I love them. But it's a burden, love, you know; it ensnares you. I shall be financially indebted to a man whom I no longer love – and who certainly cares nothing for me – until little Helen is through university. That's eighteen years away.' She reached for her handbag, which she had slung over the back of a chair, and pulled out a hand mirror. 'I'm staying with my parents here in London while I work out what to do.' She pinched her cheeks and pressed her lips together.

'You've left Suffolk for good?'

'Don't look so incredulous, Rachel, for God's sake. He is living a few miles down the road with a woman he's been screwing for years.' She spat out the last sentence, curling her lip in disgust. 'The whole bloody county knows about them. I cannot carry on living there. I've got my pride.'

'Jesus, the selfish bastard,' Rachel said, half under her breath, trying to reconcile the big friendly bear of a man she had half-known for two decades with this version of love-sick deception and injustice.

'I do have one favour to ask you . . .' Naomi was already at the door, clearly ready to leave.

'Of course – anything. Look, don't go. We can have an early lunch or something.'

'No thanks. I've got an appointment with a lawyer.' She put her head round the door and called to someone. 'I've left three with my mother, but she finds it hard going. I wondered if you could keep an eye on Jessica for a couple of hours, just while I have this meeting. I won't be able to concentrate unless I'm on my own.'

At this point Rachel's seven-year-old goddaughter appeared in the doorway, tugging at her white knee socks and looking suitably solemn.

'Jessica,' Rachel exclaimed, holding out one hand. But the child stayed close to her mother's floral smocked dress, her dark eyes wary. She wore an Alice band, an elasticated version of her mother's headgear, except the hair which tumbled out of it was wavy and much darker.

'Go on, Jess. It's Aunt Rachel. I won't be long. You said you'd be good, remember?'

At this last admonition the child shuffled forwards, but still clinging to a panel of her mother's voluminous dress.

'Please, Jess, let me go. I'll be late.' Naomi pleaded with her eyes at Rachel, who grabbed one of the transparencies and flicked on her desk light.

'I could do with some help actually, Jessica. I've got to decide which of these pictures is better. It's going to appear in hundreds of magazines – and I just can't make up my mind. It's a funny picture. Come and see. Tell me what you think.'

As Jessica approached, Naomi winked and slipped quietly out of the door.

Robbie held the black-and-white image up to the kitchen window for perhaps the twentieth time that week and frowned. He had known the brown envelope would contain something appalling, but still he was unprepared for this. Blurred, but unmistakable. A foetus. How many weeks old, he had no idea. Its head looked elongated and its feet were small, fuzzy claws. It looked as though it was holding itself, as if its arms were wrapped around its middle. For comfort perhaps. To one side trailed a thin white line, a small stream of light from the middle of its belly. He squinted at the image, trying to make out some genitals amongst the blur. It was impossible not to be curious, after all, in spite of the awfulness of it all. Unimaginable awfulness. He wondered if Polly had told her parents yet, whether she planned to at all. He wondered if she had been in London to have an abortion. His hopes surged and dived at the thought. The white skeletal thing in front of him looked horribly formed already. He did not want it. He did not want the horrible muddle of it. But he did not like the idea of the creature ending up as medical waste either. Thoughts of hooks and blood and mess filled his mind. He closed his eyes and put the picture down. Then he thought of Rachel and great heaving sobs punched his chest.

The ring of the phone forced him to swallow his tears and compose himself. It was Polly's mother. She sounded surprised to hear his voice. Why hadn't Polly rung to say when she was returning? A long weekend together in London was all very well, but as parents they had a right to be kept informed. It wasn't right and he could tell her so from them.

'I think she's still in London . . .' he faltered, his mind racing for a way out, but impeded by visions of Polly lost in unfamiliar streets. Hopeless, hopeless Polly, on her own. And pregnant. Oh God.

'What do you mean "think"? Aren't you together, then?'

'She decided to stay on – for a bit – to – er – think.'

'To think?' Mrs Drayton's snort was audible. 'Well, she's a bloody fool. You're both bloody fools, for that matter. In my day something was either on or off – none of this shillyshallying around when nobody knows what's going on. And where's she doing this thinking, anyway?'

'At a friend's.' His voice was weak with the effort of lying.

'Well tell her to get a bloody move on, will you? There's work to be done down here, not that that's ever bothered *her*.'

For the rest of the day Robbie worked feverishly, ploughing through paperwork, returning unanswered phonecalls and tending to the herd. With lambing only a few weeks away some of the ewes were already getting uncomfortable; they had that listless and bemused look about them that he had come to know so well. Instead of filling him with excitement, he was haunted by apprehensions of what might lie in store. He found himself remembering Polly the year before, staying till long after the vet had gone, tears rolling down her face at the hopeless distress of the two ewes nuzzling still-borns, refusing to move till their mourning was done.

Though keeping so busy eased the passing of the day, as Robbie lay in bed that night, the worry solidified into something indigestible. Polly alone in London. Bearing his child. Oh, God. Worst of all, he was powerless. Everything rested with Polly. Until she came home there was nothing he could do. No one he could talk to. He pulled the covers over his head and tried to focus on Rachel. But the image of her kept slipping from his grasp, teasing him like the echo of a lost thought.

Will was just packing up to leave when there was a knock on his door.

'Come in,' he called, expecting it to be one of the artists who shared the studio downstairs, who frequently put their heads round the door for teabags or opinions of one kind or another.

On the table beside the kettle sat a plastic bag full of groceries. He was eager to get home, to stir-fry himself something healthy, read a novel maybe, drink a few beers. Having until recently believed that he had lost the art of pleasurable anticipation for good, to look forward to such things – to realise that he could once again enjoy the world outside his studio – was something of a revelation.

Anita coyly put her head round the door. 'Can I really?'

Will's heart plummeted. 'Anita,' he said flatly, 'what a surprise. I'm afraid I was just leaving.' He began flicking switches on the wall beside him, extinguishing several strips of light down the far end of the room.

'Oh no, please, let me just have a little look.' She skipped unsteadily across the wooden floor, swinging her bag like a schoolgirl. 'I want to see some of your work. I really do.'

'Well you'll have to make it snappy, I'm afraid.' Will remained where he was, tidying boxes of film on top of a filing cabinet, determined to appear as discouraging as possible without actually being rude. 'What are you doing in these parts, anyway?'

'Seeing you, silly.'

He jangled his keys at her. 'Come on Anita, I'm locking up. We can talk on the way downstairs. I've really got to go.' He flicked off another light to emphasise the point.

Anita had now thrown herself into the chair in which Rachel had sat, hitching her silky red skirt well above her knees in the process. 'Don't you want to take a snap?' She pouted and wriggled deeper into the chair, revealing a slice of white thigh, dimpled beside the silky edge of her stocking. 'I'll be ever so good, I promise,' she simpered, her self-esteem sufficiently heightened by vodka for her to be undeterred by the expression on Will's face. She made a big show of uncrossing and crossing her legs, seeing herself suddenly as a woman of superstar attractions; a Sharon Stone-like figure, hard-edged, self-assured, sexy. Giles had always had a thing about Sharon Stone.

'Anita, stop mucking around will you?' Will's annoyance had increased at the sight of her slumped in the chair. Rachel's chair. He had borrowed it on a whim from downstairs, inspired by the thought of her slim frame being hugged by such a thing, knowing how its old dark leather would embrace her, how it would set off the fair frame of her hair and skin, how she would look lost but comforted all at the same time, fragile but safe. He had the finished photographs to prove it. No clever tricks required at all.

'You'd come running if I was Rachel, I'll bet.' Anita pulled herself upright and fumbled for a cigarette. 'Fancy the bloody pants off her, don't you?'

'Yeah, I do actually,' he agreed cheerfully, crossing his arms and leaning back up against the wall.

'Well, you haven't got a hope, darling.' Anita picked a grain of tobacco off the tip of her tongue and blew a plume of smoke towards the wall of windows on her left. 'She's found true love you know.'

Will, secretly thinking that what he had seen of Rachel's behaviour suggested she had found nothing of the kind, crossed the room to check a couple of window locks. Anita followed him with her eyes.

'The hunk from Devon. Mr Robbie Dexter. Landscape gardener and sheep farmer extraordinaire. Talk about a ghost from the past.' She made a face and strolled across to the wall of windows. Outside, night had transformed the river from its daily grey into a shimmering banquet of jagged black and gold. 'Bonking and babies. That's all Ms Elliot has on her mind, these days.' She fired smoke at the pane of glass and closed her eyes as it swept back over her face. Her head was beginning to pulse uncomfortably. 'Any chance of a drink?'

'Babies?' Will took a step backwards.

'A last-minute scramble against the proverbial ticking bloody clock, I suppose. Ah, the joy of being female.' Anita sighed and closed her eyes, adding absently, 'Would never have thought it of Rachel though . . . I even tried warning her off. But you know. Rachel, once she's made up her mind . . .'

Will was jangling his keys again, much more loudly this time. 'You should try to stop being jealous of her,' he said shortly, 'it doesn't get you anywhere, you know.'

Anita turned slowly. 'Me? Jealous of Rachel?' She started laughing and then checked herself. 'I've been jealous of Rachel for as long as I can remember. Most of our lives are an accident. But Rachel's has been *designed* – by her. What Rachel wants, Rachel gets. And what's worse I like her for it – I *admire* her.' She wanted to leave suddenly. She needed a drink. It had been a crazy idea to come in the first place. Crazy. The man was no fun at all.

'And you think she'll have children just as easily?'

'Of course,' she sneered. 'A hunk like Robbie – they've been at it like—'

'Yes, I get the picture thank you,' Will cut in, seizing her firmly by the elbow and steering her towards the door. He thought of the photograph, ready now to show her, and wondered whether it wouldn't be simpler just to post it after all.

'Not a fucking taxi in sight,' Anita complained, as they tumbled out into the dark narrow alleyway to the rear of the warehouse that housed his studio.

'Can I drop you anywhere?' he offered, his voice edged with a weariness he was now struggling to hide.

'How very kind.' She got into the passenger's seat, opened her packet of cigarettes, saw there were none left and threw it petulantly onto the floor. 'Anywhere you like.'

'I'll drop you at Victoria,' he said, 'from there it's all up to you.' After a moment or two of silence he could not resist saying, 'I don't think Rachel Elliot has had that much of an easy life.'

'Oh, don't you now? What an intriguing opinion.' She retrieved the packet from the floor and began dismantling it. 'And on what vast knowledge do you base these views of yours?'

Will hesitated. 'You don't get where she has without a fight. She's worked hard for what she's achieved. She's made sacrifices . . .'

'Oh please, my heart is bleeding.'

'Are you always this pleasant about your friends or is it simply because you're so drunk you can't think straight?'

Shocked into silence by the veracity of this challenge, Anita folded her hands and studied her knees. 'Life's crap right now,' she said hoarsely. 'My husband has lost interest in me—'

'That would be Giles, would it?' put in Will, eager to develop these first threads of sobriety into something resembling a conversation.

'He's not been himself for so long . . .' her voice tailed away. 'I keep thinking I should get him to see a doctor – but he's so bloody obstinate—'

'I'm sure you can persuade him if you try. Make it happen.'

'I will, I will.' She clutched what remained of the cigarette packet between both hands, squashing its edges.

'Good. Well we've sorted something out then.' Will pulled into the taxi rank in front of Victoria station and put on his hazard lights. 'And good luck with your writing.'

'My writing?' She let out a curt laugh. 'And what do you know about that?'

He shrugged. 'Only that you're quite good at it, if Rachel is to be believed – which I rather think she is.' He smiled at her then, his wide mouth curling upwards in a way that transformed his entire face. 'Like I said, good luck, Anita.' He reached across her and opened the door.

She put one foot on the pavement and turned back. 'Thanks Will . . . and sorry for being a bore . . . and for coming on . . . so strong. I just want . . . I just needed . . . to feel . . . I mean, Giles hasn't exactly been much of an ego-trip recently,' she finished meekly, pressing her fingertips to her temples, where the drumming was worst.

'Drinking certainly won't help matters, you know. And anyway,' he leant back and made a show of scrutinising her appearance, taking in the cropped inky hair with its sweep of grey, the over-made-up face that hid a generous smile and pretty, feline eyes, 'I'd say you've absolutely no worries in the looks department—' he caught his breath, 'oh, not for a decade or two at least.'

'Well, thanks for that.' She laughed weakly, before levering herself out of the car.

It was only as he drove away that Will realised he had left his bag of shopping on the table in his studio. He slammed both hands on the steering wheel in irritation. But his appetite had vanished anyway. Anita Cavanagh's life may be salvageable, he thought grimly, but his certainly wasn't.

After a couple of hours in his flat with a book which had seemed compelling the evening before, but which now struck him as trite and absurd, Will felt more than usually restless. The can of tomato soup, which had assumed the role of supper, had left him both thirsty and hungry for real food. He tried calling Anna but got a baby-sitter instead, a flurried-sounding girl that made him worry for Jack. He had to fight the urge to drive round there himself. With there being just the two of them, it was so hard not to give in to the temptation to be over-protective. A grandparent or two would not have gone amiss, he thought sadly, tenderly recalling parents whose advanced ages had often seen them mistaken for grandparents themselves.

The impulse to call Rachel, an impulse which beat constantly at the back of his mind, was becoming increasingly difficult to suppress. He could tell her about the photograph, he argued to himself, how well it had worked out, suggest a meeting even, present her with a copy in person. His heart soared and then sank the moment after. It would be pointlessly frustrating – enriching an increasingly treasured library of images maybe, but only driving him madder in the end. There was nothing to be done now, he had to remember that.

He remembered instead the tight, hard shoulders beneath his hands, the confirmation of all that he had suspected: such energy contained inside, such control, such longing. The thought that he might have the power to unleash some of that energy, to tease some of that brilliant spirit out and make it less afraid, was as alluring as the thought of opening himself up to her. They were a pair, he felt – two people who longed to be known but were scared of it too, scared of the vulnerability that ran alongside.

He found himself staring at the large black-and-white photograph half-sticking out of the folder in front of him: Rachel's face, the far side cast in shade, the near side in light, her eyes bold but questioning, her body curled away from the lens, as if to say, keep your distance, I'll have none of you.

'Bugger it.' He swung his legs up onto the table and leant back with both hands clasped behind his head. But the grey, intelligent eyes followed his, challenging him from under the heels of his boots. He had to force himself to look away, to study instead the familiar contours of the room – a vast rectangle which he loved, containing only one chair, one table, three vast pictures and two luminous blue lights that made the soft polished wood of the floor glow with shadows and life. The only other piece of furniture was a baby grand in the far corner, on which sat a photograph of Ginnie, poised at her cello, her chestnut hair tumbling down her back, her favourite black velvet concert dress pressed against the bony contours of her knees, her heart-shaped face composed and smiling. A Ginnie that may once have existed, thought Will grimly, though it was hard to recall her now. Their marriage had been a calamity all of its own, long before the depression and drugs took hold. Time had woven a film of tragedy over events, especially in the eyes of other people, but in reality there had been only ugliness, bitter and ignoble to the last. Nothing had been enough in the end, not medicine, not therapy, not music and certainly not love. Will grimaced at the recollection of the last of his wife's lovers, the one she'd wooed and spurned most blatantly of all, spilling the guts of their emotions for daily scrutiny and consolation, too imprisoned by her own world to care about destroying his. It was only then that he had fully realised the awful power that the sick wield over the healthy, especially for those versed in the blackmailing potential of a bottle of pills. Was it any wonder then that he should now find himself so drawn to a woman of such contrasting self-containment; a woman who, no matter how much she gave away, would always hold as much back? A woman who would find a way through, whether he was there or not.

A few minutes later Will was striding away from the ornate

black railings that marked the entrance to his basement flat, heading in the direction of the more salubrious part of Chelsea in which he knew Rachel Elliot lived. It would help to get the image out of his mind, he told himself, if he physically removed it from the premises. He would post the photograph himself, by hand. Far better than horsing around with a meeting. Who was he trying to fool, anyway? If he had ever entertained any hopes, Anita had quashed them all for good. Best to get rid of the damn thing and be done with it.

It was a cold night even for late February. He zipped his jacket up to his chin and increased his pace. Overhead, a creamy coin of a moon dodged behind lacy clouds, as if coy of its glory. Will, in no mood for moons, however glorious, kept his eyes on the ground, watching his long legs cover the ground as if they moved of their own accord.

When he reached the steps to Rachel's block he was careful not to pause for an instant, not wanting to imbue the moment with pointless sentimentality of any kind. Taking two steps at a time, he sprinted to the top and carefully eased his delivery through the wide handsome brass flap, before turning to descend.

It was only then that he noticed the figure hunched, knees to chest, on the bottom step. Though London was awash with homeless of all ages, Will was nonetheless surprised to find one who had not even bothered with the scant shelter offered by a doorway or a wall on such a chilly night. He noticed too, a stiff bunch of hair sticking out of one side of the anorak hood. Young hair. Female hair.

Reaching into his pocket for change, Will approached.

'Would this be of any help?' He held out what he had, about six pounds in all.

'No thanks.' The girl sniffed.

Will was almost offended. 'Go on, take it. Can't do any harm.'

'I'm waiting for someone.'

'Oh, I see.' He eyed the grubby anorak and mud-stained boots doubtfully. 'They're coming tonight, are they?'

She shrugged. 'Soon. It's the weekend isn't it? They always meet at weekends.'

'It's Wednesday,' said Will gently, sitting down beside her.

'He'll be here,' she said, but with less conviction. After five days on her own Polly was running out of steam. She had thought it would be easier, that she would know just what to do. Instead a fog had settled inside her head, blocking everything but the cold. 'He'll be coming to see her,' she said, mechanically this time, her voice colourless.

'Who?'

She jerked her head at the door behind them. 'Miss Rachel fucking Elliot, that's who.' Her lips were covered with small cracks which looked ready to bleed when she spoke. 'He loves her. My Robbie loves her – and I—'

'And you love him? Is that it?'

She looked momentarily amazed and then scowled. 'So?'

Will tucked his hands up under his armpits and pressed his knees together, wondering how many nights she had spent sleeping rough. 'I think I might know how you feel,' he ventured.

'Sure you do.'

'How about a warm bed for the night?' he suggested suddenly.

'A bed with you?' She frowned, suspicion flashing in her eyes.

'I'm talking about a bed of your own,' he explained quickly, smiling to make her less afraid. 'I've got a spare bathroom too – well a shower anyway.' He stood up and tapped his watch. 'He's not coming tonight, I'll bet you. It's far too late – see?' He held out his wrist. 'And it's Wednesday. Far better to have a hot bath and a good night's sleep. I don't live far away.' He got up and held out his hand. 'I'm sure we can sort something out between us. And a good breakfast always cheers things up, don't you find?'

She eyed him from under a tangle of hair, looking so wary he almost laughed.

He held up both hands in a show of surrender. 'Please trust me. I'm a friend of Rachel fucking Elliot's. And I know she'd hate to have someone freezing on her doorstep.'

'Serve her right,' muttered Polly. But she got up all the same and followed Will back to his flat, clutching her knapsack protectively to her stomach and trailing half a pace behind him like an errant child.

'Mum says Dad is a spoilt bastard.'

'I'm sure she didn't . . .'

'She did. I heard her. On the phone to Granny.'

Rachel and Jessica were sitting on a bench in St James's Park enjoying their second meeting of the week, thanks in part to the demands of Naomi's lawyers and partly because Rachel had so much enjoyed herself the first time. They were eating ice creams, towering peaks of soft vanilla pitched at dangerous angles from the flimsy cones. Their main course, at her goddaughter's pleading, had been a hot dog, smothered in squirts of ketchup and rings of white onion. Rachel, to her intense surprise, had enjoyed it enormously, spurred on by the elation of a companion who clearly regarded rubbery frankfurters as forbidden fruit of the most indulgent kind. They weren't allowed hamburgers either, Jessica had confided wistfully, on account of all the mad cows.

'Mummy says brain-rotting would be too good for Daddy.'

'Oh dear, I'm sure she doesn't mean it.'

'Oh yes, she does.' Jessica took a long searching lick of ice cream. 'She hates him now.'

Subdued into a compassionate silence by such frankness, Rachel reached out a cautious hand. Patting it briefly, as if her godmother was the one in need of consolation, Jessica sidled several inches closer along the bench.

'Lucky you, Aunty Rachel, not having a husband.'

She couldn't help laughing. 'Oh I'm afraid I still have all the same kind of problems.'

'Do you love someone, then?' Jessica had reached the cornet, which she was nibbling with two incongruously large front teeth, her reward, as she had solemnly informed Rachel, for never having eaten more than three sweets in a row.

'I think so.'

'Does he live in your house?'

'No, he lives miles away, in Devon. I'm going there this week-end actually,' she added, thinking wistfully of the unsuccessful phone calls which had cast such a shadow over the week – stilted conversations that seemed to find no common ground at all, with Robbie wheedling for reassurances at every turn. Fuelled by guilty realisations as to quite how selfish she had been – how singularly calculating, if she was honest – Rachel had met these needs as best she could. But uncomfortable echoes stirred at the back of her mind; echoes of a version of Robbie she had known once before, a Robbie who had ended up pleading for her love like a beggar with an empty bowl. 'He's got lots of animals,' she went on brightly now, aiming to keep Jessica's interest. 'Sheep and chickens.'

Jessica screwed up her nose. 'Yuk. I only like cats. Sheep and chickens are silly.'

They were distracted from this discouraging veer in the conversation by the arrival of a swarm of pigeons, whose beady eyes had been attracted by the possibility of food. Jessica threw a small crumb, picked carefully off the edge of her cone, and watched with detached interest at the ensuing squabble for the spoil.

'Time to wander back, I'm afraid,' said Rachel, glancing at her watch.

'Oh please, not yet.' Jessica jumped off the bench, scattering birds as she charged off along the path.

Rachel followed, equally reluctant to leave the park. Although it was cold, a white disc of a sun was bravely pushing its way through the grey landscape overhead. Here and there along the path, clusters of snowdrops huddled at the foot of trees, together with a few clenched crocuses and a scattering of noble daffodils, leading the late march against winter. 'Wait for me,' she called, running to catch up, her scarf unwinding and flying out behind like a banner. Jessica had been distracted by the sight of a ball lodged between the roots of a tree. A bright red ball covered in yellow dots. She charged towards it with a whoop of delight and kicked it to her godmother.

By kicking with the toe of her shoe, Rachel managed a high arc of a return-shot that landed right at Jessica's feet. The next time she used the inside of her foot, teetering slightly on her heels as she swung her leg backwards, but making contact with enough force for the ball to do a gratifying bounce off a nearby tree before rolling back onto the ground. Heedless of the mud clods attaching themselves to the heels and undersoles of their smart shoes, the two of them threw all their energies into the game, using scarves and gloves as goal markers and taking it in turns to have shots.

'Hey, that's mine,' shouted a little boy appearing from nowhere, his face and the tips of his ears pink with exertion.

Rachel, bracing herself for an outburst of some kind, was most impressed to see her godchild pick up the ball and take it over to the boy at once. 'We were only having a little play,' she explained. The child smiled with relief, which was when Rachel recognised him.

'It's Jack, isn't it?' She looked round nervously to see who had charge of him.

A young woman with long black hair came jogging over to them, wearing a coat that reached almost to her ankles and shiny silver trainers with three-inch rubber platforms. She was tall and wiry, with watchful black eyes and a pointy nose. The mouth and smile were just like her brother's though, thought Rachel, as she hastily introduced herself, explaining in the same breath that they had to walk all the way back to Covent Garden and only had ten minutes to do it in.

'We're going there too,' exclaimed Anna Raphael, her angular face softening the moment she smiled, 'I take a dance class in Floral Street – Sloane Rangers trying to tone up their thighs.' She made a face and then looked apologetic. 'It's not too bad, really. Though Jack wouldn't agree. He gets so bored, don't you Jack? But it's the holidays,' she added with a sigh, 'so I've got no option.'

Smalltalk about children and the unseasonably cold weather saw them to Trafalgar Square, whereupon Anna declared,

'Assuming you're the Rachel Elliot I think you are, I've just got to thank you for what you've done – for Will, I mean.'

Rachel thought she had misheard over the roar and choke of the traffic. 'I beg your pardon?'

'You've no idea.' They were crossing towards Long Acre, each holding the hand of a child as they pressed through the lunchtime crowds.

'You mean sitting for him?'

Anna didn't seem to be listening. 'He's a different man since you came on the scene – I can't tell you.' She let got of Jack's hand to hoick her black tights further up her long legs, revealing a silvery plastic mini skirt that matched her shoes. 'I just thought I'd mention it. We've got to turn off here. Jack, come on.' She held out her hand.

'But I'm not . . . on the scene,' Rachel began, but Anna was already striding away, the wide panels of her coat flapping, the little boy having to trot to keep up with her.

The first thing Rachel did upon getting back was to look again at the photograph. It was surprisingly nice. Her face looked more creased than she liked to imagine it, but then she was beginning to get used to that. And her smile, which was wide without looking in the least bit smug, somehow made up for it. She liked the position in the chair too, the way one leg was bent up under her and the other just touching the floor; it looked relaxed but confident. In fact, she looked exactly as she would have liked to look, though she could never have engineered such a result herself. She propped the photograph up beside a jar of ground coffee, pondering again why Will had made the delivery in person, but not rung the bell; why there was no accompanying note, not even a compliment slip; why his sister should make baffling remarks about her 'being on the scene' and then rush off without explaining herself.

I'll take it to Devon, she thought suddenly, seizing the picture and carrying it through to the bedroom where an open suitcase lay on the bed. Robbie would like it. But at the recollection of Robbie's emotional fragility on the telephone that week, she slipped the photograph into a drawer instead. There were more important subjects that needed explaining first, she told herself, her heart thumping. Trying to explain Will Raphael would only complicate things. All that mattered was sorting everything out with Robbie.

As Rachel prepared for bed that night, it was not Robbie or preoccupations about motherhood that occupied her mind however, but godchildren. Getting to know Jessica might prove to be the one good thing arising from an otherwise abysmal set of circumstances she reflected ruefully, smiling to herself at the recollection of their time in the park. They had arrived back so late and so muddy that Rachel had found herself making excuses to Naomi like a child herself. Melissa had been surprised too, laughing out loud at the state of Rachel's expensive leather shoes and producing a damp cloth for the smuts on her tights. The pleasure of it all had taken her completely by surprise. It had made her think properly about her other godchildren, about how little she knew them, about how unforgivably ungrateful she had been all these years.

Before going to sleep that night Rachel wrote to Joy, sitting propped up by pillows with a malt whisky in one hand and her writing pad pressed against her knees.

What must you think of me – so many months since your letter and not a peep. I shall look into the Good Housekeeping *thing very soon, I promise. And I should be more than happy to contribute to the PG Tips supply and anything else you want. Just send a list. I do hope Tony has found some time to do a bit of work on your house by now – all that rain and wind sounded dreadful.* She paused for a moment, taking a thoughtful sip of her nightcap. *You're too brave all the time, do you know that? Sometimes you just have to admit that life is full of crap and then you feel a thousand times better for it. Tony might be a bit more sympathetic too if you actually tell him what you're really feeling.* She stopped again, thinking of the original author of such advice, and how hopeless she was herself in such matters. *It's been quite a hectic few months what with one thing and another. The long and short of it is it looks like I might be settling down with someone at last – an old old friend called Robbie Dexter, whom you might remember from way back. We've both grown up a lot since those days and now I really do think we could work out a future together. Part of this life-change (you see, you're not the only one!) is that I am leaving MC to work three days a week for a brand new agency being formed by a few other dissatisfied colleagues. We're going to concentrate not just on advertising but also on new product development – something in which I have always been particularly interested. But anyway, enough of all that. I'll keep you posted.*

One more thing. About Leo, she paused, wanting to get it right, wanting to convey that she sought far richer rewards than the mere assuaging of some godmotherly guilt, *'if ever you felt like coming over here for a break (and maybe some shopping!) why not bring my godson and leave him with me? I'm not saying I could cope for days on end, but I would so like to get better acquainted – before he's lost to rave music and drugs and women half my age. Let me know what you think.*

She looked at her watch before dialling Washington. The rings were much longer than on English telephones, she noticed, winding the flex round her index finger while she waited.

'The Elliot residence,' came a voice at last, whose sing-song intonation Rachel recognised as belonging to Carmen, the housekeeper.

'It's Rachel, Dr Elliot's sister, calling from London. Is Duncan there? Or Mary Beth?'

'Oh no, Miss, they not here. They skiing in Vermont.'

'With the children?'

'Oh yes, Miss.'

'Could you say I called?' She hesitated, impeded by doubts about Carmen's skills as messenger. 'Could you send them my love?'

'Your love OK. I send it.'

Well, that seemed clear enough. Rachel, replaced the phone with a smile, enjoying the suggestion that love could be parcelled and mailed like a free sample of washing powder.

That left one more call. Rachel braced herself, wishing at the same time that she didn't have to and vowing to get Anita back on the wagon, no matter what the cost.

'Hello, who is it please?' The voice was small and very sleepy.

'Charlotte? Goodness me, what are you doing up at this time of night? Is Mummy there?'

'Mrs Hershey's here from next door.'

'Oh, I see, well can I speak to her then?'

'She's asleep. She's got the telly on, but she's asleep. I know because I've poked her and she didn't move. She's very fat.'

'Well Charlotte, sweetheart, I think you had better tiptoe back to bed, don't you?'

There was the sound of a door slamming followed by a series of rustles and squeals.

'Rachel?'

'Anita? I've been trying to call for days but you're never in. Your baby-sitter's gone to sleep.'

'I know. She always does. She's a last resort, Mrs Hershey, but she is genuinely fond of the children. Listen, Rachel, you'll never guess. Giles really is ill.'

She sounded relieved.

'What with?'

'They think it might be ME. They're keeping him in for observation. I've just come from the hospital.'

'But that's dreadful—'

'I know, I know. But it's also wonderful – I mean at last there's an explanation, don't you see? These past few months have been hell. I really thought it was the end of us, I really did Rachel – I've started imagining all sorts – you know he did once have a fling or two, back in the early days – so I thought, right here we go again, only this time I didn't feel like I could cope with it. So to find out that he is *ill* – that he probably has been for months – is amazing. And do you know,' her voice quavered, 'I haven't had a drink since Monday. I've signed up at last with the dreaded AA – and I'm not talking about servicing cars—'

'Oh Anita, well done.' Rachel sat up in bed gripping the phone, wanting to praise her to the skies but fearful of being tactless.

'It's not so bad, at least not as bad as I thought it would be.'

'That's the best news I have had in months.'

'Yeah well, I figured Giles and I couldn't fall apart at the same time. And Rachel . . . I want to apologise . . .'

'Whatever for?'

'For being a pig and a bloody nuisance. Thanks for sticking by me.'

'There's absolutely no need to thank me for anything,' she

retorted at once, though inside she was glad. 'Tell me more about Giles – they think it's ME?'

'Possibly. We'll know more after they've stuck a few more needles in him. Poor love – it's no picnic. But at least we're *doing* something about it. And the children are being sweet, making get-well presents out of loo rolls and bits of string and generally cheering us up no end. Weirdest of all, the work keeps pouring in. My post-natal depression piece clearly hit the spot. There's a new features editor, which helps. I'm on wife-beating now, with euthanasia in the pipeline. So things really are looking up. If I could get some decent childcare my life would be complete.'

'About childcare,' put in Rachel tentatively, 'could I help out sometime?'

'Why, Rachel, how kind.' She sounded genuinely touched.

'I'm not sure I'm up to the twins,' she went on quickly, not wanting to raise any false hopes, 'but I'd love to see a bit more of Charlotte—'

'She'd love that—'

'Not right away I'm afraid, but when this new job starts and I've settled into some sort of routine for dividing myself between Devon and London . . .'

'That's still on then, is it?'

'The job change?'

'No – yes – I meant Robbie, actually.'

'Of course it is.' She couldn't keep the edge out of her voice. 'Why shouldn't it be?'

'Don't get all bristly, I was only asking.' Anita waved a ten-pound note at Mrs Hershey who had appeared in the sitting room doorway looking puffy-eyed and flustered. 'When the hell am I going to meet him, that's what I want to know? It's been months.'

'Oh, soon enough,' replied Rachel quickly, 'there'll be plenty of time for all that.'

'By the way, what were the results of your modelling session with the delicious Mr Raphael like?' Anita hoped she sounded detached. It would be a while – if ever – before she confessed to Rachel about visiting Will at his studio. She had told Giles though. And in spite of the shame it had felt good to share a confidence with him again, good to have a husband cast in the role of ally as opposed to enemy.

'Oh, fine,' answered Rachel airily, equally anxious to sound nonchalant and dismissive, but for rather different and infinitely more complicated reasons. 'Not bad at all, in fact.'

Robbie stepped into his boots, icy from their night in the draught by the back door, and made his way across the yard to the wood shed, a leaning, doorless contraption which had once served as a pigsty. It had been quite a week. Aside from problems in his personal life, the job down Sandy Lane was turning into a fully-fledged disaster. He had made the mistake of contracting out the work and was suffering the consequences. The whole bloody garden would have to be replanted and properly drained at his own expense.

The only good piece of news was that Polly had finally called her parents from London the night before, sounding cagey, complained Mrs Drayton, but promising to be home by the weekend. Upon hearing this Robbie had felt relieved, but terrified the moment after. He thought of the smudged image of their baby, now buried in the bottom of the black wheely bin behind the wood shed, and wished that the truth was as easy to hide. Borrowed time was all that remained now. He hurled the head of the axe at the logs in front of him, unblinking as the wood chips flew, seeing only the splinters of his hopes.

'Surprise,' called Rachel, a little while later, having parked at the front and crept stealthily through the house.

'Surprise,' she called again, more loudly this time, her spirits dampened both by the mess she had encountered in the cottage and the manic intensity with which Robbie continued to swing the axe.

Robbie spun round, dropping the implement to the ground, a look of shock and then gratitude sweeping over his face.

He moved towards her at once, arms outstretched, staggering slightly, like a drunk man.

'Steady on, you'll squeeze the breath out of me,' she gasped, her ribs hurting in the crush of his embrace.

'Oh God, I've missed you so much.' He was almost sobbing.

'Yes, well I've missed you too,' she replied briskly, pulling back to inhale a lungful of air. 'Lovely to be out of London. I thought I'd take the day off and surprise you. Things at work are totally mad at the moment – but I can tell you about that later,' she added hastily, seeing the expression on his face. 'Any chance of a coffee break for the workers?' She had hoped to extract a smile, but he only grunted, slinging an arm across her back to steer her inside.

'Do you like my jeans? I thought they might be quite suitable for egg-foraging. I'm going to be a tower of strength this weekend – you won't recognise me.'

Filled with the sense that she was for some reason having to keep the lines of dialogue open and mystified as to why, Rachel chattered on in a similar fashion while Robbie excavated mugs and teaspoons from the heaps of crockery stacked around the sink.

'Robbie, is everything all right?' she blurted at last, unable to ignore the strangeness of his mood any longer, a strangeness which she knew had been brewing all week.

He slowly raised his eyes from the mug which he was clasping to his chest with both hands. 'No, I guess not. It's . . . it's been a bad week. Big trouble with a job on the other side of Drakeshead. Cock-ups all round. Lambing due any week now . . .'

'Oh dear, poor you,' she said feebly, feeling useless. 'Well, just set me to work about the place. I'd love to be of some help, if I can.'

'Christ, Rachel,' he put down his mug and placed a hand, clammy from cradling his hot coffee, on top of hers, 'I don't know what I'd do without you. You know that, don't you?'

Such intensity again. It didn't feel right, somehow. 'Of course I do. Now tell me what I can do.'

Shortly afterwards, however, both Rachel's capacity and enthusiasm for assistance of any kind were delivered a major setback by a fist-sized puddle of black ice in the back yard. Her left foot slipped awkwardly, bringing both her and a basket of kindling heavily to the ground. Twigs and pieces of wood scattered for yards around, like debris after an explosion. It was only when she struggled to her feet and the pain seered upwards from the arch of her foot into the region of her ankle bone, that she realised the full extent of her injuries. She hobbled gingerly back inside, where Robbie was seated at the kitchen table, gloomy-faced before the contents of a beige folder marked 'Sandy Lane'.

He was at once all flustering concern. A tender examination of the swollen ankle was quickly followed by the triumphant extraction of a large bag of frozen sweetcorn from amongst the icy peaks of his small freezer. Rachel pressed the bag to her foot, grimacing at the ache of cold it produced and doing her best not to spill corn from the various puncture-holes which materialised in its sides.

'Ice cubes would be better of course, but I just don't use the things. Sorry.' He shrugged helplessly, torn between offering more comfort and getting on with the pressing demands spread out on the kitchen table. 'Would you like a cup of coffee? Tea? A biscuit?'

'That would be lovely. A cup of tea. And a biscuit,' she added, her mind flitting to Will Raphael and having to be tugged back again.

'Now keep your foot up – higher – that's it – right on top.' Robbie adjusted the angle of the chair on which he had placed a cushion embroidered with the words 'Home Sweet Home', and kicked a few grains of corn in the direction of the overflowing waste-bin beside the fridge.

'You get on with whatever you've got to do,' ordered Rachel, filled suddenly with an unforgivable urge to be left alone. She took the sagging bag from her foot and dumped it beside the packet of digestives which Robbie had thoughtfully placed within reach. 'I know you're busy.'

'Well, if you're sure you wouldn't mind . . .'

'Of course not – don't be silly.'

'I really ought to get over to this place.' He gestured with his head at the folder. 'Make a start on damage limitation.' He hung his head in miserable apology.

'Go on, go. I'll be fine. I can look after myself. It's just a bloody nuisance. I'll man the phone – make myself useful.' She waved a digestive at him. 'You run along. I'll still be here when you get back.'

'Is that a promise?' Though he meant to tease, the worry edged through.

'Sure it is.' She reached for a magazine from a nearby pile and raised her mug in salute.

His farewell kiss, soft with apology and passion, did little to lift her spirits.

'By the way,' she called, when he had left the kitchen and was on the point of opening the front door, 'that girl – Molly – Holly – or whatever it was. Is that all sorted? Has she been any more bother?'

'No bother at all,' he called back at once, before plunging out through the door, head bent against the wind.

There were a lot of phone calls, the first one coming just seconds after the sound of Robbie's van had melted away. Rachel's tea, which was too milky for her tastes anyway, gradually acquired a head of scum while she fielded questions about turf-laying and ponds and pergolas, assuring each caller that Mr Dexter had their business well in hand and would be in touch personally later on that afternoon. After an hour or so, when the rumble of her stomach told her that it was well past lunchtime and the beige folder was surrounded by scribbled messages, Rachel decided she had earned a rest. Having turned on the answering machine, she levered herself through into the sitting room, taking the magazine and pack of biscuits with her, lured by the idea of reclining on something more welcoming than the bare wood of Robbie's kitchen chairs.

The room smelt of cold ashes and old leather. Though the storage heater by the sofa felt warm, it appeared to be having little effect on the temperature of the room. The remains of a fire sat in the grate, a charred log amidst several dunes of grey sand. Piled on the hearth were some of Robbie's freshly cut logs, together with a newspaper and a grubby, misshapen box of matches. I'll make a fire, thought Rachel, inspired both by her chattering teeth and because it was something to do.

The paper burned well, curling hungrily round the amputated

stumps of branch, and radiating lovely jets of warmth. Rachel, perching awkwardly on the floor, blew on her knuckles, staring into the blue heart of the flames until her eyes grew glassy. But before long, all the promising flames had shrunk down into derisory black heaps that left her feeling inept and cross. With her ankle now throbbing badly, she retreated to the sofa, burrowing under a pile of cushions and trying not to look at her watch. It was hateful to be so helpless, so bloody uncomfortable. Since the only reachable diversion was the magazine, Rachel comforted herself with that, doggedly working her way through an article on the Swedish timber industry, before arriving at a more promising headline that ran: *WHY IS THIS SO RARE?* The words were superimposed on an enlarged image of what looked like a long-tailed tadpole nosing up against the fuzzy edge of a huge circle. In smaller writing underneath she read: *Scientists are telling us that conception is becoming increasingly rare. Growing numbers of couples are seeking infertility treatments. Is the human race on its way out?* Shivers of schadenfreude tiptoed down Rachel's spine as she feasted on the heart-rending testimony of couples labouring under the burdens of low sperm counts, irregular ovulations and thickening womb linings; couples who had taken out bank loans for treatments with names that read like dialogue from a sci-fi horror movie: gamete intrafallopian transfer, intra-cytoplasmic sperm injection, surgical sperm retrieval. *Prospects for success are grim and hard fought*, Rachel read, shamelessly scrutinising the strained expressions on the faces of those courageous enough to be photographed. These people were in another league, she realised with a start, another world entirely; they were strapped to a treadmill of clinical dependence to which she knew she would never dream of subjecting herself, whatever the circumstances.

Her eyes left the page and flicked across to the charred pyramids in the grate. Was her desire to have a child so deeply rooted after all? It had offered a way forward, a bridge to a future that had otherwise seemed unimaginable. Yet recently the idea of motherhood brought as much fear as it did longing. As much uncertainty as confidence. And as Rachel huddled under the heap of cushions, her fingers stiff with cold from holding the magazine, she wondered for the first time whether this was natural, or whether it was an indication of something to which she should pay more attention.

By the time Robbie returned, a couple of hours later, she had fallen into an uncomfortable doze, in which she seemed to be forever clutching at thoughts that slipped from her control, sliding out of reach, like feet on ice. She awoke with a jolt at the slamming of the front door. In a few weeks she would be forty. Her fertility curve, according to an unforgiving chart in the article, was on a nose-dive towards zero. No wonder nothing had happened yet. Perhaps nothing ever would. She retrieved the magazine from where it had slipped down the side of the sofa and skimmed the last paragraph. She could hear Robbie calling her, the heavy thud of his feet on the stairs.

There is an all-too prevalent notion, encouraged by developments in fertility research, that we somehow own our bodies, that we should be able to programme them as we please. When in fact the human body, in every respect, is a complex mystery of chemical, biological and psychological elements, the combination of which may always prove ultimately resistant to control or manipulation of any kind ...

'Rachel – there you are – why didn't you answer? Christ, it's dark in here.' He switched on the light.

She struggled onto her elbows, frowning at the glare, the magazine slipping from her knees to the floor. 'Robbie – sorry – I was half asleep.'

'How's the leg? I'm sorry I was so long.' He crouched at her feet, resting his head on the arm of the sofa like a penitent hound. 'Have you been terribly lonely?' He leant forward and planted a gentle kiss on her sore ankle. 'I stopped off and bought a Chinese take-away on the way home. We could eat now or heat it up again later. What do you say?'

'Sounds great,' she whispered, while inside there raged a new confusion of sadness.

'I'll light the fire.' He sprang to his feet and set about constructing an expert wigwam of wood and paper, using small twiggy branches that he snapped off the bigger logs. 'Have you finished with this?' He held out the magazine. 'Only there's not much paper.'

'Yes,' she said quietly, leaning her head back against the arm rest. 'I've finished with it.'

'You look tired,' he murmured, coming to kneel behind her head and placing his hands on her shoulders. His fingers smelt of smoke.

Feeling tears push against her lids, Rachel kept her eyes closed.

'Bad luck about the ankle.' He began to massage her shoulders, pushing and pressing in flat repetitive motions that seemed to make no contact with the shapes inside. 'Is that nice?' he whispered.

Rachel, gulping silent tears, could only nod. While inside her head the images soared out of control – sensual images that had nothing to do with Robbie or what she now realised was the fiction of their future together, but which transported her back instead to the deeper comfort of another chair and to hands that had touched more than the surface of her body, pressing into the very heart of her in a way that she had tried not to think about, but which had left her at once deeply attracted and deeply afraid.

These hard, concentrating palms of Robbie Dexter knew nothing of her, she realised. They never had. They never would. She had made the most terrible mistake, led on by an emptiness which had nothing to do with him, and probably little to do with having a child either. An emptiness to do with being almost forty and on her own. She had been taking stock, she realised, and getting it all wrong.

But the crime of having rekindled feelings which were no property of hers, of having materialised like some shining angel with a false heart, was not something to which Rachel felt able to confess at once. Instead, despising herself for the coward that she was, she made room for Robbie on the sofa, shifting her leg gingerly when he pressed up against her and breathing appreciatively when he began to kiss her neck in that way he always did, when more serious intimacies were on his mind.

'I've been hopelessly forgetful about the pill,' she lied a few minutes later, dreading his reaction, but needing to be true to herself on at least one level that afternoon.

'I'll see what I can find,' he grunted, pulling away and shuffling out of the room with his shirt hanging out and his hands holding up his trousers.

Rachel lay quite still, staring at an orange smudge on the back of the sofa, while the darkness outside deepened and the eager young flames matured into the subtler, redder glow of a true fire. Inside, her shame burned and curdled with an intensity of its own. She had plundered a life, seen what she wanted to see instead of the man himself, all the while feeding her imagination with impossible unrealities that bore no relation to the truth. Wanting to love someone was not enough, she realised, no matter how much will power one had, no matter how momentous the other issues involved. Feelings, like babies, she thought grimly, watching the last corner of the article burn, could never be manufactured with any certainty, no matter how hard one tried.

Robbie unearthed a slim pack of condoms from behind a dusty bottle of bubble bath on top of the bathroom cupboard. Only two left. Not used since Polly. The dull ache in the pit of his stomach tightened into something more painful. Putting his lips round the tap, he drank greedily, as if pain was a thirst that could be quenched like any other. Perhaps he should warn Rachel the damn things were unreliable, he thought bitterly, taking the packet with him and padding back downstairs. Tiny splinters of wood caught on his socks as he descended, as if not only his conscience, but the very bones of the house were trying to hold him back.

31

Towards the end of the following week the cat returned. Rachel spotted it sitting in a circle of early evening sunshine, its dainty pink tongue licking one paw with the bored insouciance of a secretary filing her nails. When she opened the sitting-room door it slipped in at once, pausing to brush against one of her crutches before trotting into the kitchen and mewing at the fridge.

'Are you here to stay or just passing through?' she demanded, reaching with difficulty onto the high shelf where she had stowed the tins of cat food. 'Not that it matters, seeing as I've no plans to leave.' The cat emitted a throaty purr, weaving in and out of her legs like a dancer. 'It's all right for cats to pop in and out of lives,' she went on, wrinkling her nose at the jellied chunks as she spooned them into a saucer, 'but definitely not for humans. Believe me, I know, I've tried it. A bloody disaster from start to finish.' The cat rubbed its cheek hard against her hand as she lowered the saucer to the ground, its engine of a purr shifting up a gear. 'So you do as you please,' she murmured, noting how it seemed to grin as it ate, liking the way it glanced up every now and then to see if she was still there. 'You make the most of your cat-freedom.'

The weekend in Devon had flopped badly. Under an umbrella of flimsy excuses, she had left on the Saturday, surprised by Robbie's lack of resistance, but grateful for it too. Apart from a last-minute flurry about whether a left leg was required to drive an automatic car, the departure had gone smoothly enough, each promising to be in touch, to fix another weekend soon. There had been a great silence ever since, like the stillness preceding calamity. She ought to call, she knew. Or write, maybe. Dear Robbie, sorry but I think we both know it's not going to work out after all. Apologies for wrecking your life – again. All the best, Rachel. PS. I've been suffering from delusions brought on by a confused desire to have a child. PPS. But I'm not even sure about this any more.

Manoeuvring her way through to the study, Rachel sat down at her desk and began sorting disconsolately through an unpromising pile of mail shots and unanswered bills. It was time to get her life back in order, time to accept that she would be going on alone after all, that there would be no long-term rural idyll and probably no child. It would be a relief, she realised, to let the idea go one day, to release herself from the cycle of hope and apprehension that she knew would persist in some form for the remaining years of her fertility.

The prospect of three weeks' holiday and a new job beckoned. Tomorrow she would struggle through the swing doors of McKenzie Cartwright for the very last time. Alan Jarvis had accepted their resignations with stoical calm the day before, only the pulse in his lower left jaw suggesting commentary of a more emotional kind. Rachel had been the last to file out, swinging with as much dignity as she could through her crutches, which were too big and dug cruelly into her armpits. At the last moment he had summoned her back, his face clenched and pale.

'Just tell me one thing.' He stood stiffly, hands clasped behind his back. 'Does this have anything to do with that incident . . . the problem with Cliff? Is this some kind of twisted revenge?'

Hesitating, wanting to be honest, Rachel experienced a wave of affectionate pity for the man. To lose several million pounds' worth of business to mutinous employees was hard on anyone, no matter how arrogant their nature, or how solid their power-base. The news that Frank Alder was to entrust her with a large slice of Mallarmé's NPD work had cut particularly deep, she knew.

'Once, I would have liked it to have been,' she said cautiously, 'but, no, it's not revenge Alan. Just a coincidence of events. I was invited to leave and it felt the right thing to do. For what it's worth, I am sorry for the trouble caused.'

'And I'm sorry,' he growled, adjusting his tie. 'I should have listened to you. Weybourne will be gone himself before long. Talking to other agencies already, apparently. He's after power and little else. Whereas you . . .'

'God knows what I'm after,' she cut in with a laugh.

'You're good, that's what you are. And I should have made damn sure I kept you.'

Rachel shifted on her crutches, thinking that recriminations would have been easier than this.

'Go on. Buzz off and clear your desk then. And good luck. You deserve it. What happened to your leg, by the way?'

'I slipped on some ice.'

'Ice?' He raised one eyebrow at the sun streaming in through the window, catching dust motes in the slant of its beams.

'It was icy at the weekend, remember?'

'So it was,' he muttered, shaking his head, 'so it was.'

As he held the door open for her to pass, something made her stop and kiss his cheek. 'Just to say thank you,' she said, smiling, 'no harassment intended.'

'None taken,' he replied with a laugh that began quietly, but which grew louder as she progressed down the passage, causing looks of bafflement amongst those working nearby.

Her diary, sandwiched between a brochure on Bermudan tourist attractions and an old letter from Joy, was the most unexpected find of the day. The sight of it, after so many months of neglect, caused a wrench of guilt, followed by a quite irrational curiosity, as if she was on the verge of discovering something new. But all she found was a maddening evasiveness – half-truths and brave announcements that she wished she could disown. She had wasted far too much energy trying to persuade herself of things, she realised, instead of attempting to understand them. The last entry provoked the harshest self-recriminations of all: *Still no reply from Nathan . . .* Rachel sighed deeply and closed the book. Nathan Kramer. What a mess. What a cock-up. And here she was again, in the thick of something equally hideous with Robbie. Almost forty and still ballsing everything up. It was pathetic. She tossed the diary into the bin beside her – already brimming with discarded envelopes and information on cruises and pension plans – and reached angrily for the telephone. She would finish it properly now, she had to. It was the least she could do.

As her fingers touched the telephone it rang, giving her such a shock that she leapt back in her chair, knocking both crutches to the floor with her elbow.

'Robbie? This is too incredible for words. I was just going to—'

'To what?' It was Robbie's voice all right, but a strangled version she had never heard before. 'To tell me you loved me?' he sneered.

'No, I—'

'Oh come on, Rachel. You claw your way back into my life, make out like we're going to live happily ever after—'

'Robbie, calm down. I've something important to say – to explain . . .'

'About Mr William Raphael, by any chance? Yeah, I thought that might shut you up a bit. I can put up with a lot, Rachel – getting me to meet your parents, all that horsing around with promises about giving up work and moving out of London – I can cope with that. But not with this other stuff.'

'What other stuff?' she whispered, incredulous and afraid.

'If it wasn't for Polly you might have got away with it, too.'

'Polly? Got away with what, for God's sake?'

'Don't fuck me around,' he growled. 'I may not be the most successful man on earth, but I still have the right to be treated with decency . . . from you of all people. Was there someone else when you pulled out the first time, eh? All that bullshit about needing space . . . Was there a Mr Raphael in the wings then, too? One in London and one in the country. Very nice too.'

'Robbie, you've got it all wrong,' she said quietly, shocked both by his anger and this twisted fabrication of events. 'There's nothing—'

'Oh shut up, Rachel, just shut the fuck up.'

'This is ridiculous . . .'

'Not any more it isn't. It's over.'

Having been so preoccupied as to how best to bring about this very outcome herself, Rachel was nonetheless reluctant to submit to such garbled accusations of betrayal. She had betrayed Robbie all right – and herself too for that matter –

but not, so far as she knew, through any connection with Will Raphael.

'What's Polly got to do with all this?' she asked quietly.

'Polly's the one that opened my eyes, that's all.'

'What has she said?' Rachel persisted.

'She was sitting ouside your flat one night—'

'Outside my flat?'

'When your lover came to call – last week, when I was safely tucked up down here – played the good bloody samaritan, by all accounts, the bastard, just to quiz her about me, no doubt. Even put her up for a couple of nights . . .' Robbie's voice tailed off for a second. This was the part of the story he was least happy about. From what he could gather, Will Raphael had not only looked after Polly for three or four days, persuading her to set her parents' minds at rest with a phone call, but he had even paid for her ticket home on the train. '. . . during which time Polly found out quite a bit about you and him. She's no fool, you know. She even found a fucking picture of you in his flat . . .'

'The photo? I can explain about that—'

'Don't bother,' he snapped. 'And don't get in touch again – not next week, not next year, not next century. I won't be duped a third time.'

'But Robbie . . .' But the line had gone dead, leaving Rachel staring into the speaker-holes in stunned disbelief.

'Well done,' breathed Polly, placing a timid hand on Robbie's knee, letting it lie there, limp but persistent, ready as always for him to take up if he chose.

Robbie pushed the telephone out of reach and took a swig of beer from the bottle in front of him. 'Bloody woman,' he muttered, 'I should have guessed – I knew something wasn't quite right . . .' Catching sight of the pained expression on Polly's face, he stopped. 'Thanks again Pol, for telling me, for putting me right. I'd be lost without you, you know that.'

Blushing with pleasure, Polly took her hand away and set about preparing supper. They were having fish fingers, eight for Robbie and five for herself, together with mashed potato and frozen sweetcorn from a very battered bag she had found wedged in one corner of the deepfreeze. A bottle of ketchup and two sets of knives and forks were already on the kitchen table, like the old days, she thought, breathing hard. Already the weight of the child in her womb seemed to press against her ribs, pushing up rather than out as she always imagined it would, making her feel wheezy and full. Five months gone. Five long months since a moonlit October night up against the back wall of the pub, near the vent that poured steam from the kitchen, billows of greasy vapour that bounced and curled around them before dissolving into the dark. A crude thrusting and groping; beery breath and mawling hands. No sweetness in revenge after all, she had thought even at the time, as comparisons with Robbie's big, tender hands had sprung inevitably to mind and Felipe the polo player crooned obscenities into the gaping front of her shirt.

'He's kicking, if you want to feel.' She approached, spatula in one hand, the other resting on the underside of her belly.

'Where? I can't feel a thing.'

'Down a bit. There.'

Robbie, detecting a brief fluttering under his fingertips, smiled up at her. To find himself relieved that there had been no abortion after all had come as quite a surprise. As had the reactions of both Polly and her parents. Mrs Drayton, whom he feared most, had made stout, supportive declarations about infants of her acquaintance born before wedlock and young couples who took their time. They supposed marriage was on the cards and Robbie had no intention of disillusioning them. It was assumed he would stand by her. And so he would. Rachel's duplicity had made that easier at least. He couldn't love her now, nor ever again. The future looked all the clearer as a result.

He had wanted to punish her, though. Not just for having an affair, but for being so toweringly capable and intelligent, for making him so cruelly aware of his own failings and chaotic ways. With Polly it didn't matter. With Polly he was the toweringly capable one, deferred to in everything, without the shadows of unspoken criticism to darken each day. The last few months had wrought a terrible pressure, he realised now, all that nagging, unacknowledged worry about how to make Rachel happy, about living up to expectations; expectations that were all the harder for being imagined but never explained.

The fish fingers, burnt round the edges as he liked them and smothered in tomato sauce, tasted good.

'Our baby, eh?' he said, his eyes flashing, his mouth twitching to a near-smile.

Polly looked down at her plate. Felipe had dark hair and brown eyes. He was quite fair-skinned too, which was good. She wouldn't have stood a chance otherwise. She scraped some sweetcorn into her pile of potato, moulding it into a lumpy cake with her fork. 'We're all yours,' she said simply, while the baby danced a celebration of its own inside. Remembering the kindness of Mr Raphael, Polly kept her eyes on her plate, for a moment guilty at how she had snooped around his flat when he was out, how she'd kept her big jumper on to hide the lump in her stomach. She had wanted his help all right, but not all those opinions as to how to live her life. Mr Raphael had said she should leave Robbie alone, that loving someone meant wanting them to be happy with whatever they chose. While pretending to agree, deep down she knew he was wrong. She had a right to happiness too, a right to use whatever she could to get it.

Making out that Will was sleeping with Rachel had been a stroke of inspiration for which Polly was still congratulating herself. They were friends after all; so it was only a slight fudging of the truth. And then there was the photograph – a very nice one she had to admit – sitting in a drawer all on its own, as if it was something special. The pieces had started to fit together then, like they were meant to, like they were clues towards an answer. It had been the best – the only – way to be sure of getting Rob. It was all too perfect for words, like a miracle. Like Felipe taking a job at those stables in Sussex, safely far away, out of her system for good.

'Baby and I will be always be here,' she said, brushing some dry wisps of hair off her forehead and smiling back at him. 'Your own little lamb at last, eh Rob?' She pushed back her chair and began clearing away the plates, stopping only to plant a kiss on top of his head, before running a bowl of washing-up water and plunging her hands into the warm foam.

FOR THE ATTENTION OF WILL RAPHAEL:

I have been trying to get in touch with you for several weeks now and am beginning to think you must have left the country. Or perhaps your answering machine – whilst appearing to be in perfect working order – is in fact not working at all? Or perhaps you have suffered a severe and terrible accident and are, as I write, lying in hospital paralysed from the neck down hoping that somebody will pull the plug out? Forgive the cynicism, but I'm more than a little baffled, not to say confused.

I might not find your reluctance to get in touch with me quite so peculiar were it not for the fact that several people seem to be under the illusion that we are close friends. (This is embarrassing, but I am determined to go on. I hate unsolved mysteries for one thing and for another, I am resolved – partly on your advice, I have to admit – to spend the second half of my life being altogether more forthright and honest.) I like the photo very much, by the way. But perhaps you don't. Perhaps that's why you have failed to return my calls . . .

You once implied that I hid behind a mesh of electronic communications systems. Might I be so bold as to suggest that you are now doing the same? Might I be equally bold and say—

Rachel paused, fingers poised over the computer keys, wondering how far she dare go. After three idle weeks she was feeling wonderfully mellow. Free time, such an enemy for so much of her life, was at last something she was learning to savour rather than fear. While she relished the challenges of a new job, the prospect of two extra days to herself each week was equally sustaining. It would mean more time for friends and hobbies, more time to be a godmother, to house-hunt for the cottage she wanted, somewhere in Wiltshire, or Dorset maybe, a spot where the cat could have more than a few yards in which to hunt without dodging irritable bus drivers and speeding cars. For the animal was showing every sign of staying now; like a human putting down roots, it had established its own routines, complete with preferred snooze-spots, mealtimes and flavours of food. Though it was often absent for half the night, slipping out of the cat-flap Rachel had had drilled into the lower section of one of her beautiful sitting-room doors, she would always wake to find it curled up by her feet, its stomach heavy with the night's prey, its whiskers twitching at its dreams.

Since the night of Robbie's call Rachel had made several efforts to get in touch with Will Raphael, all of which had met with a recording of his voice or no answer at all. While a part of her recoiled at the unseemly notion of appearing pushy, her curiosity remained as strong as ever. At least she told herself it was curiosity, though her stomach performed rebellious acrobatics of its own, and the tall, dark-haired strangers who now peopled her dreams had a worrying propensity for emerging from behind cameras, with dark eyes that laughed away her fear.

The cat landed neatly beside her right elbow and mewed at the screen before extending a tentative paw towards the coiled flex protruding from the back of it.

'Push off, Hamish, this is serious,' Rachel scolded, giving him a fond nudge with her arm. The christening of the animal had happened almost imperceptibly, the name tripping off her tongue one evening without any forethought at all. Hamish was perfect, she had felt at once, for one so upright and independent, with such a clear agenda of his own.

As Rachel raised her hands to continue typing, the cat placed himself between her and the screen, disdainfully running its abundant tail under the tip of her nose.

'Push off, you.' She picked him up and dropped him to the floor. 'I've nearly done. I'm trying a spot of man-chasing here and it's bloody hard-going. Not something I've ever been very good at.'

* * *

—that I would like to meet up for a drink, preferably sometime before the next millennium, that is if you could possibly fit such a thing into your action-packed social calendar.

I'm between jobs, so please contact me at home.

With very best wishes,

Rachel (Confused of Chelsea)

PS. Do you know a Polly? If yes, I would appreciate details.

Although Rachel had originally intended this communication as a fax, she ended up sealing it in a long white envelope and delivering it to the pillar box at the end of the road that very evening, scurrying through the wet night like a thief.

'And that's all I can do, Hamish,' she declared upon her return, brushing her palms together as if dismissing the matter for good. 'And don't look at me like that. Your position in this household is secure, I assure you. Neither man nor child shall separate us, though I'm not saying I might not expect a compromise or two along the way.'

The cat, clearly unimpressed by such ideological guarantees, gave her an arch look and headed for its door-flap, diving out of sight with dainty precision, its tail giving the merest flick of a farewell, as it disappeared into the night.

33 ∫

'Are you sure you don't mind dropping her back?' Having used her teaspoon to skim the chocolatey froth off the top of her cappuccino, Anita eyed the brown peaks appreciatively before depositing them in her mouth.

'Of course not – so long as Charlotte can put up with me for that long.' Rachel cast a sideways glance at her goddaughter's crumb-encrusted face and smiled. 'You will hold my hand if it's scary won't you? I'm not very used to monsters in the cinema.'

'They're not *real* monsters Aunty Rachel, only people dressed up.' Charlotte's face, bulging with half-chewed pain-au-chocolate, twisted for a moment with genuine concern. 'It's all pretend.'

'I'll try to remember,' she promised, winking at Anita.

They were sitting at a table outside a tea shop in the King's Road, making the most of a mid-April heatwave before Rachel treated Charlotte to a PG-rated box-office hit entitled, *The Grange Goblins*, while her mother pursued a much lamented search for shoes.

'So how are you, Rachel?' Anita asked with a directness that reflected the new-found confidence in herself and life in general.

'Talking to the cat, but otherwise OK.'

'You've got a cat,' exclaimed her goddaughter, 'you lucky lucky thing. Mummy *promised* me one for my birthday.' She fired an accusatory look at her mother before seeking silent solace from her pastry.

'Don't exaggerate, Charlotte. I said *maybe*, if Dad agreed.'

'And how is Giles?'

'So much better – though there's still no definitive diagnosis of anything. Personally, I think it's just plain exhaustion. All those years and years of travelling and stress finally catching up with him. His latest plan is to take a year's sabbatical – write the definitive journalist-in-the-front-line book – interviews with terrorists and bullets grazing earlobes – you know the kind of thing. Apparently two publishers are interested already.' She fiddled with the handle of her coffee cup, her mind skipping from happy recollections of the recent and highly satisfying resumption of her married sex life to a less easy consideration of such matters where Rachel was concerned. The Robbie Dexter business had dealt her quite a blow, she knew, though, typically, she had barely admitted as much out loud. 'Any explanations from the elusive Mr Raphael yet?'

Rachel shook her head and frowned at something across the street. 'I think he must be away on business . . .' The lack of reply to her most recent – most direct – plea for a meeting still rankled.

'Must be.'

'I'm certainly not going to try any more. He'll begin to think I'm interested, or something.'

Anita, while privately concluding – on the basis of several recent conversations – that for Rachel to describe herself as merely 'interested' was a close call for the understatement of the century, hid her smile behind the rim of her coffee cup.

'And Robbie's all right, is he?' she enquired airily, spitting onto her paper napkin before beginning an assault on the brown stains covering her daughter's cheeks and chin.

'I assume so. I haven't heard a word.' Rachel signalled to the waitress for the bill. 'Odd really. I almost feel as if it never happened, as if I dreamt the whole episode. Wish to goodness I had,' she added gloomily, making a face at Charlotte who was fighting the napkin.

'And the new job? I want all the gory details.'

Rachel's eyes lit up. 'It's fabulous – such fun. There's so few of us and all wanting the same things.'

'Not one teeny weeny disagreement about logos or the colour of the walls?'

'Oh come on, *please*,' interrupted Charlotte, consumed now

by boredom and certain that she had been politely silent for quite long enough.

Anita opened her mouth with a reprimand, but Rachel got there first. 'Poor Charlotte, we grown-ups are so dull, aren't we? Come on then,' she held out her hand, 'lead me to those goblins.'

Anita waved them off down the street, marvelling not for the first time at this new and infinitely more relaxed version of her old friend, wondering how much of it was connected to frustrated desires to be a mother herself. She would probably never know, she mused with a sigh, reluctantly acknowledging that some questions could never be asked after all, no matter how tender the intent nor how many years of shared intimacy had gone before.

Rachel hastily let herself into her flat, all thoughts of goblins superseded by crazed and leaping hopes for the envelope in her hand. It must have come by the second post. He had written at last, just when she had given up hope.

She forced herself not to hurry, propping the envelope up against a jar of spaghetti while she poured herself a glass of wine and refilled Hamish's saucer of milk. Was it wicked to savour such a moment, she asked herself, carrying the letter through into the sitting room and choosing a Chopin piano concerto as the appropriate foil for her mood? She was thinking of learning the piano. It was to be part of the second half of her life, something she had always wanted to do. Much more up her street than photography, she thought wryly, attending to the envelope at last.

His handwriting was conspicuously beautiful, thick-nibbed, black and smooth, adding a grandeur to her name and address which was somehow flattering. Unable to wait a moment longer, she ran her finger under the flap and pulled out the single page contained inside. Her stomach tightened as she began to devour the words.

Friday, May 3rd

My Dear Rachel,
I am sorry I have not replied before. My failure to do so arises not, as you so sweetly suggest, from being bed-ridden in an intensive

care ward, but from a deep conviction that it would be unwise for us to develop our relationship any further. We both have other commitments which I believe should take priority.

As to the opinion of others regarding my affection for you, I can only blame the human predilection for gossip and speculation. Some people seem to think that photographers enjoy intimate relations with all their models, which, alas, is not the case. (I too am very happy with the picture, by the way.)

I did make the acquaintance of someone called Polly a little while ago. She claimed to be a friend of your Mr Dexter. By sheer coincidence I found her in a state of considerable distress and did what I could, which wasn't a lot. As far as I know she was posted safely home to her family. I hope that answers your query.

To know what you want out of life is a rare gift and one that I believe you have. I hope everything works out exactly as you plan. You deserve to be very happy.

> *Yours apologetically and affectionately,*
> *Will*

'Bugger, bugger, *bugger*.' Rachel screwed up the letter and hurled it across the room, where it bounced once before rolling to a stop beside the glass door of the cabinet that housed her music system. He could go to hell, she told herself, wishing she believed it, wishing she could despise the man as much as she did the feelings that were surging inside.

She was still brooding over the matter – and cross at herself for doing so – when her mother phoned half an hour later.

'How are you, dear?' asked Margaret Elliot in a tone that cunningly suggested her own welfare and not her daughter's to be in need of tender enquiry. She had taken news of the split with Robbie very badly. No matter what Rachel said, she persisted in regarding the failure of the relationship as temporary – something that could be overcome with determination and patience, like a patchy marriage.

'Brilliant, thanks,' replied Rachel firmly.

'I just wanted to say happy birthday for next week and to ask if there was anything special you had in mind. For a present, I mean. It is a special occasion after all, getting to forty.'

'Oh anything, honestly Mum. You choose,' Rachel added, doing her best to sound grateful. 'A book or something would be nice.'

'I thought maybe a token to spend at Marks and Spencer . . .'

'Perfect. I'd love that.'

'Only, it is easy to send and of course you can pick what you want . . .'

'A token would be just the thing. How's Dad?'

'His back's bad, but then he will spend half the day on his knees in the garden.'

'Bad time for weeds, I suppose,' she sympathised, eager to keep the conversation on such wonderfully manageable tracks.

'Well, of course it is, but I think we should pay someone to do the garden these days. We're not getting any younger after all, and it would only cost a few pounds a week, but your father won't hear of it.'

'Sounds like dear old Dad.' A wave of cheerfulness came at her from nowhere. Will Raphael could stay behind his camera lens if he wanted. She had got over worse disappointments in her time. Besides, there was just so much grovelling a girl was prepared to do. She tore off a wedge of bread from a fresh loaf in front of her and pressed it between her fingers. Something flashed in the garden. Hamish's green headlamp eyes perhaps. Rachel craned her neck for a better look, pulling the telephone flex taut. She would mind terribly if the cat left now, she realised, thinking in the same instant how unfair it was that loving something inevitably brought the fear of losing it – how unspeakably vulnerable it made one.

'Your father and I have had our rough patches,' her mother was saying, 'but where there's a will there's a way.'

'Yes, Mum.' Rachel, recognising the preamble to the very lecture she had so dreaded, took a large bite of bread and closed her eyes. She chewed slowly, letting the familiar intonations wash over her, deliberately focusing her mind on the salty softness of the dough. She was eating more these days, not in any frenzied way, but out of a new, keener appreciation of food and the natural call of her own appetite. Beside the loaf was a machine for making fresh pasta and two new cookbooks, one of them open at an enticing picture of dressed crab meat surrounded by lush slices of avocado pear.

'. . . So all I'm saying is there's no harm in offering to try again. There's no point in being obstinate about these things, Rachel—'

'Like Dad, you mean?'

'I beg your pardon?'

'Dad's obstinate about everything. I expect I get it from him. Lovely to talk to you, Mum, but I've got to dash – something's boiling over on the stove. Bye.'

Rachel replaced the receiver with calm exultation and ripped off another hunk of bread. Chewing and frowning, with one hand holding back the heavy sweep of her hair, she willingly surrendered all her mental energies to instructions for dissecting the delicate innards of a crab, on how best to keep the white meat separate from the brown, without splintering the brittle labyrinth inside.

As a particularly bad wave of nausea took hold, Rachel pulled over onto a double yellow line and stuck her head out of the window, breathing in deep lungfuls of smoky Balham air. Across the road, a pair of teenagers sitting on a wall eyed her curiously as they took it in turns to swing round the slim trunk of a small tree, shaking its armfuls of pink blossom so that they shimmered like dusty gems in the dim evening light.

The hangover, instead of easing as the day progressed, was still uncurling, snaking its coils round the perimeter of her head and pushing deep into the shaky pit of her stomach, where it did battle with a fizzy cocktail of analgesics and several pints of liquid that had left her feeling bloated and unrevived. The pain was worse than being forty, she thought meekly, hating these unseemly after-effects, but none the less recalling the previous evening's celebrations with a surge of affection.

Thanks to a spot of last-minute coincidences of strategy and timing, the party had comprised a total of four women: Anita, who had done all the organising; Naomi, who had leapt at the chance of a night off from her domestic problems and Joy, who had taken Rachel at her word and channel-hopped for a short holiday with little Leo. Since there were many other people Joy wished to visit, she had stayed with Rachel for only twenty-four hours, leaving her alone with her godson for just one afternoon. All Rachel's hopes and apprehensions about this spot of child-tending had focused on the cat, since Leo, now aged almost one and packaged like a miniature sumo warrior, tackled all objects – inanimate or otherwise – with a careless, bear-hug affection capable of causing serious harm.

Throughout their first few minutes alone Hamish was lunged for, squeezed and rubbed with such alarming zest that Rachel feared all her worst imaginings would be realised. Having failed with distractions of every kind, she waited grimly for Hamish to flee or draw out his claws. It was a while before she realised that he would do no such thing. Observing the cat's endurance and patience, admiring the way the paws warned but did not harm the child, she had the feeling that he had seen it all before, that somewhere in its unknowable past an infant of similarly good but potentially injurious intentions had been artfully entertained and kept at bay.

Just as fresh worries were surfacing about Joy's complicated set of instructions concerning bottles and naps, Leo disarmed her completely by picking up a book and climbing aboard her lap. Here he settled down like an animal himself, eyelids heavy, his silky white hair flopping endearingly into his eyes. Rachel forgot the clock then, together with all the other details with which she had been briefed for his afternoon routine. As they studied baleful cows and lions that smiled, Rachel nuzzled the sweet smell of his soft head, remembering her tentative cradling of the baby version of this same child the summer before, and the wound of longing that followed. The longing was still there, but the intensity had dulled. Four godchildren was quite a clutch. They had been there for her all along and she hadn't even realised. All the fun and none of the heartache; perfect parenting. Almost.

Rachel swallowed a few gulpfuls of water from the bottle on the seat beside her. The A-Z was open at the right page. Nearly there now: third left, fourth right and right again. *'Only call if you can't make it,'* Anna Raphael had said, her voice casual but firm. *'I've been meaning to invite you over for ages – there's something I want to ask your advice about – 8 o'clock Saturday – 32 Egremont Road.'* The phrases relayed by her answering machine played back disjointedly inside Rachel's head. She had meant to phone anyway, not to refuse necessarily, but to find out a bit more before going. But then Leo and Joy had arrived and things had got rushed. Then it had been too late to back out anyway, irrespective of headaches and gloominess about birthdays.

A bus arrived and the two teenagers got on it, all thoughts of ghostly-faced middle-aged women panting like dogs out of car windows clearly far from their minds. Although it was nearly eight o'clock, Rachel could not muster the enthusiasm to hurry. She thought again of the dinner the night before, of all her female friends' persistent and predictable protestations of envy at her life, the griping about husbands and the juggles of domestic life. Godmothers had it easy, they teased, especially ones with highly paid, part-time jobs and filofaxes full of the names of eligible men. Rachel had played along, happy to accept the safety offered by these familiar and affectionately constructed guidelines, not out of any cowardice but on account of the fresh flower of self-certainty that had taken root inside.

Looking back with the lucidity of hindsight, Rachel was beginning to believe that the upheavals of the last few months were not so much hormonal as part of a fundamental need for softening and change on a grand scale. A need for other people, perhaps. There had been a void at the heart of her, she realised now. A void certainly manifested by her crazed resolution to become a mother, but which would not necessarily have been filled if she had been successful in her quest. Parenthood was not yet impossible. But in the meantime there were other things, she thought with relief, surveying the pink-cheeked faces of these mothers of her godchildren with affection and then exchanging a glance of more penetrating empathy with Anita. It was a special pleasure to discover that vulnerability did not necessarily mean weakness, that to lean on people a little was allowed.

As she settled back into the seat of her taxi, waving at the receding figures of her friends, Rachel felt, for the first time in ages, as if the best part of her life might still lie ahead of her. There was no one else she would rather be after all, she thought gratefully, sinking down into the seat of the taxi with a sleepy sigh, as snippets of narratives from her friends' lives echoed inside her head. Such strife, such chaos. She shuddered. Not for her at all. Then an image of Will Raphael wheedled its way in alongside. She shuddered again, but this time for a different reason. I'd take strife and chaos for him all right, she thought, smiling grimly in the dark, wishing she could fully accept that on that score at least, fate had already played its hand.

Anna Raphael was wearing dungaree-style shorts, made of faded denim and covering a grey T-shirt that looked several sizes too large. Gracing her feet were a pair of heavy-soled boots and socks that bagged round her ankles. Her dark hair had been swept into a loose ponytail that was spilling out of control, a soft, striking frame for the pale triangular face which creased with pleasure as she opened the door.

'Oh, you're here. Great. Come in.' Without further explanation she led the way to the back of the house, past a stack of boxes and a child's bicycle. Her walk was at once poised and full of energy, in spite of the boots or perhaps because of them, marvelled Rachel, following on behind. Part of her own long cotton skirt caught on a bike pedal as she sidled past; her legs buckled and she staggered for a step or two as a fresh wave of confusion and nausea hit home.

'I shouldn't have come,' she said weakly, recovering her balance and stepping through into a large kitchen, which clearly functioned as several other things as well. A small oblong table, set for two, separated the cooking units from a sofa and a portable television, balanced rather precariously on top of an overflowing bookshelf. Toys dangled from drawers and containers on every side.

'Sorry about the squash. We tend to live in this room, especially in the winter. I know it's summer, but I haven't spilled back into the front yet. A drink?' She was bent in an exact rightangle before the contents of her fridge, her back flat, her legs straight, her neck turned with swan-like grace towards her guest.

Rachel shook her head doubtfully. 'I was forty yesterday and am still suffering the consequences, I'm afraid.'

'Oh, you poor darling. But I've got just the thing. Hang on.' She skipped out of the room, returning a few moments later with two large round pink capsules which she handed to Rachel together with a tumbler of water. 'I use these when my back's buggered. They're just muscle relaxants – but work wonders for sore heads too. Go on,' she urged, seeing Rachel's hesitancy, 'they're quite legal. And then we can start on this.' She set down a bottle of champagne and began peeling back its metal cap. Her fingernails were badly bitten, Rachel noticed, torn and pink round the edges.

'Champagne?' Rachel's stomach twisted.

'Absolutely.'

'Are we celebrating something?'

'I don't know, we might be . . .' The cork shot across the room and bounced off the television screen, while the exploding contents of the bottle were messily steered in the direction of the two glasses on the table.

Suddenly the weirdness of it all was too much, the confusion raging inside her head nothing but a source of irritation. 'Look, what the hell is all this about?' Rachel burst out, folding her arms and standing squarely in the middle of the kitchen area. 'To be quite frank with you, the last thing I feel like is champagne – or being sociable in any way, for that matter. Of course I'm flattered that you asked me over and everything—'

'Crap,' retorted Anna amiably. 'You just didn't get around to cancelling, I bet.' She was pouring out the champagne now, waiting for the bubbles to subside so that she could fill the glasses to the very top. The pink band responsible for the ponytail had slid further down her head, so that only a small portion of it remained reined back off her face. 'You've every right to be pissed off, especially if you've got a bad head. How is it, by the way?'

Rachel started to scowl and stopped in surprise. 'A bit better actually . . .'

'They work fast. Come and sit over here and I'll tell you what this is all about. And do try not to be cross,' she added with an impish grin.

Curious in spite of everything, Rachel went obediently to the sofa, which was surprisingly comfortable, and without thinking took a sip of champagne. The bubbles burst pleasantly at the back of her throat. A wonderful smell was emanating from the oven. Melted cheese of some kind . . . something with garlic.

Anna got out a small tin and began rolling a cigarette, her stubby fingers expertly packing and patting as she talked. 'I just wanted to consult you about Will, actually. He's been a miserable sod recently and I know it's because of you—'

'Me? What have I—?'

'And I just think if a sister can't help a brother out on something like this, then who the hell can?'

'Something like what?'

'I know I'm hardly the one for personal relationships,' she stuck the white stick of a cigarette in her mouth and began searching the pockets of her dungarees for a light, 'but one thing I do know is . . .'

She was interrupted by the doorbell.

'Oh shit.' She slotted the cigarette behind her ear and bounded from the room, the heavy rubber soles of her boots squeaking on the linoleum floor.

To Rachel's horror she did not return alone. Her brother was walking one step behind her, talking animatedly until he stepped into the kitchen.

'What the hell—' He stopped in the doorway, looking from one woman to the other, his face a picture of awkward bewilderment. 'I mean, I didn't know you two knew each other—'

'We don't at all . . . I was just . . .' Rachel got up and made a big show of hunting for her handbag.

'Anna . . .' There was a warning note to his voice, and his eyes, as they turned to confront his sister's, were intent with stern, unspoken meaning. 'I had no idea you were expecting another guest.' He shot Rachel a polite smile. Insultingly polite, she thought, now rummaging manically under cushions and soft toys.

'Don't worry, I'm just going.' She had at last spotted her bag dangling from the back of one of the dining chairs.

'No, no. You're not going anywhere,' squealed Anna, waving her arms. 'Neither of you are.'

'Well somebody clearly isn't expected to stay for dinner,' remarked Rachel, staring hard at the table. All eyes followed her gaze: two wine glasses, two plates, two sets of cutlery.

'It's me,' declared Anna stoutly, pulling the pink band out of the last straggle of her hair and shaking her head defiantly. 'I'm not staying. I never was. You two are. Don't say a word, either of you. Don't you dare.' She held up her hands and began backing out of the room. 'Lasagna in the oven. Garlic bread too. Red wine. Salad. If you can't think of anything to say to each other put the telly on and call it baby-sitting. I'll be back by midnight.' And she rushed away, leaving the two of them alone with nothing but the echoes of the slamming door and their own embarrassment for company.

'How very awkward, I'm so sorry.' Rachel had made it as far as the kitchen door, bag now safely slung over one shoulder, coat in hand. Time seemed to have slowed to a malevolently teasing crawl. 'I'm parked right outside,' she muttered, for something to say, part of her recoiling at the sight of the dim, cluttered hallway through which she still had to pass, as if it were some kind of hazardous rite of passage, something she might not manage. Questions beat inside her head, but she thrust them aside. There were too many other feelings raging for courage to play a part. No matter what she might feel, it was clear that her unexpected presence in the house of his sister had caused this man nothing but pain. He had flinched at the sight of her. She did not dare to ask him why. There was just so much rejection a girl could take.

'You look well, Rachel,' he said as she took the first step into the hallway. 'Weekends in the country clearly suit you.'

'The country?' She turned back.

'Devon.'

'I don't go to Devon any more.' She gripped the strap of her bag. 'Robbie and I are no longer together. The Polly girl told him we were having an affair.'

'She what?'

'It doesn't matter, really. It was all over anyway – should never have started in the first place – my fault entirely.' She forced herself to look into his face. His expression was set and grim. A dark stubble covered the lower section of his cheeks and chin, a shapely shadow of a beard that rather suited him, she thought, transferring her gaze to the oven where a red light was winking at them. 'In fact, I'm not well at all . . . I'm forty – I mean, I have – I had – a horrible hangover. And I think the lasagna wants to come out.' They both looked at the flashing light for a moment and then simultaneously moved towards it. When their elbows touched he jerked his arm away and stood to one side, while she wrestled inexpertly with oven gloves and doors.

The lasagna bubbled and steamed, its top layer looking enticingly crispy and brown. Beside it was a long tin-foil parcel of garlic bread. The bottle of red wine standing beside the hob had been opened, Rachel noticed, and its cork laid neatly to one side.

'I can't imagine what Anna thinks she's playing at,' Will blurted, running his hands through his hair and staring in despair at the dish of sizzling food. 'But . . . I guess . . . it would be a shame to waste it?'

Rachel, still holding the oven gloves, felt a sudden rush of lucidity. Time was ticking by at its usual rate once again. It made it easier to be honest. 'Your sister is clearly under several misapprehensions concerning your feelings towards me. So she arranges this ambush.' Rachel gestured at the table set for two. 'It is hideously embarrassing, because, as we both know, you have in fact been trying for several weeks now to avoid contact with me altogether – a minor detail in this sorry episode of which dear Anna is as yet unaware. Perhaps you would be so kind as to set the record straight, once and for all, when she returns? No harm done.' She held out her hand for a businesslike farewell, a concluding seal on their mutual confusion.

'Oh, but there is harm done,' he whispered, taking her hand and then not letting go. 'Terrible harm.'

His grip was cool and firm; she could feel the shape of each finger curved over her knuckles. 'No, really, I'll get over it. It's all been a bit of a mess. Thirty-nine was definitely *not* my year,' she added with a short laugh, 'crises on every front in fact – but forty's looking better – a shaky start maybe but . . .' she babbled on, hardly knowing what she was saying, torn between the sense that she should remove her hand from his and the stronger impulse to leave it where it was. 'If I've been bothering you, I'm sorry. Hounding men is really not my style . . .' She wrenched her fingers free and relocated the strap of her bag.

'I ought to explain,' he faltered. 'It's not that I'm not interested; it's . . . it's far worse.'

'Worse? . . . Look, please, you don't have to explain. I'd really rather not know.' She forced a smile. 'I have got the message, as they say. And now I really am going.'

The strap of her bag caught on the bike handle this time, as if it too was playing the intolerable game of trying to prolong her stay in the house. Then she couldn't manage the door handles, of which there were several, none of them, apparently, having any effect on the lock. At some point during these latter struggles Will came up behind her. He reached round to open the door and set her free, but then she somehow got caught up in the withdrawal of his arms. There was no hesitation in his embrace then, no signs of lack of interest, no awkwardness at all.

'Are you deliberately trying to confuse me?' Rachel gasped, pulling away at last. 'I mean, is this a game, or what?'

'Let's eat,' he said, taking her by the hand and leading her back.

His silence, as he served up the food, induced her to talk, to provide some structure for what was taking place. 'I've decided you're a typical artistic neurotic,' she declared. 'It's the only possible explanation for such extraordinarily erratic behaviour. Am I right?' She bit into a slice of garlic bread, holding her chin out over the plate to catch the crumbs. But on glancing up, she saw that his face, instead of reflecting her own gathering excitement, was suffused with discomfort. It was all too delicate, Rachel thought helplessly, so wanting to get it right, but feeling herself blunder at every turn. Perhaps she was going too fast, she scolded herself, remembering the dead wife and conjuring fuzzy, romantic images of a woman with a cello and tumbling pre-Raphaelite hair.

'There is something you have to know, Rachel.' Will spoke very precisely, laying down his knife and fork and placing his hands palms down on either side of his plate. 'It is the reason why I have been trying not to see you. It's got nothing to do with what I feel, I . . .'

The tension was unbearable, so much so that she felt compelled to break it. 'AIDS?' she suggested, with a sharp laugh.

'I've actually been checked out for that one,' he replied with a rueful smile. 'A while ago now, mind you, but my sexual activities since then would hardly warrant a re-trial.'

'What, then? You're a closet paedophile?' Rachel helped herself to a clutch of lettuce from the bowl in the centre of the table and raised a mouthful of food to her lips. Cheerfulness was edging back, bubbling back up in that silly, irrepressible way it had. Because of the kiss.

'Rachel, I can't have children. Ever.'

She lowered her fork, still laden with food and crossed her hands in her lap.

'Absent "vas deferens". Which is to say, no sperm ever make it past first post. It's congenital. I found out with Ginnie. It was one of the things that depressed her.'

'And you decided,' her voice was trembling now, 'you decided that because of this we should not see each other?'

'It did not cross my mind so much at first, but then Anita mentioned that you wanted a child and—'

'Anita?'

'I just felt I had no right to step in and waste your time . . . I know a bit about wanting a child . . . about how the idea can take hold, eat away at people. I knew you didn't have much time left . . .' he added quietly.

'You knew a lot, didn't you?' she said icily, pushing away her plate.

He threw up his hands. 'Oh go on, get it over with, walk out of the fucking door. I knew you would. I knew it.'

She stood up. 'Yes, I shall walk out of the fucking door, not because of the uncooperative nature of your anatomy but because of the audacity – the arrogance – of your decision that my wanting a child should rule you out of my life. You don't know anything about my feelings on the subject and neither,' she banged the table with her fist, 'for that matter, does Anita.'

Leaving was easier this time: no straps catching on bike pedals, no knee-weakening nausea. Once at the front door she masterfully jiggled every handle in sight until it swung open, releasing her into the welcome cover of the dark night. She turned right and strode towards her car, not looking back. A whipping breeze caught under the panels of her skirt as she groped for the car keys, her eyes bleary with tears of rage and disappointment.

How dare he? How dare he have decided for her? Of course she minded. She minded like hell, about everything. She slipped the key into the ignition and pressed her foot on the accelerator, bracing herself for the engine to throb into life.

Will watched her leave through a chink in the front-room curtains. As the wind ruffled her hair and ballooned her skirt around her knees, he had clenched his fists and teeth from the sheer effort of not running after her. He had not felt such affinity for another human being for a long long time – had never thought to again. But at least she now knew why, he consoled himself, as she disappeared from view. At least, when her anger subsided, she would see that it was from caring too much rather than not at all. Though he had long since been forced to come to terms with his own sterility, Will never questioned his right to subject her to such grim realities. It was up to Rachel to choose. And choose she clearly had, he thought wretchedly, rubbing his hands up and down his arms, shivering though he wasn't cold.

From his position in the bay window he could not quite see her car. There had been no noise from the engine. Or had there? The wind was stronger now, noisily buffeting the tarpaulin that covered next door's motorbike, rattling dustbin lids and loose panes. She must have gone already. He craned his neck to see, pressing one cheek hard up against the cold glass.

'Mummy?'

'Jack? What's up?' He turned at once and hurried over to the child standing, frowning and pale, in the doorway. 'Mummy will be back soon. You come with me now.' He scooped him up in his arms and carried him through into the warm kitchen, where he dimmed the lights and stroked his hair. 'A bad dream, was it?'

Jack nodded, snivelling and rubbing his eyes.

'The one about the dragons or the nasty dog?'

There was a hiccough followed by an incoherent reply.

'Want some milk? OK, but Uncle Will needs two hands for that, so why don't I put you down over here.' He set the child gently amongst the sofa cushions and pulled a book at random from the nearest toy box. *'Peter Pan.* He's ace against pirates – and dragons and dogs for that matter. Give me a minute and I'll read the words.' While waiting for the milk to boil, Will pulled a mug from the cupboard where Anna kept Jack's things. A faded Winnie the Pooh, suspended amongst a cloud of bees by a balloon string, eyed him with cheery hopelessness as he dolloped in a teaspoon of honey and stirred the milk. Warm, but not too hot. Will knew the score. He stirred with exaggerated diligence, deeply grateful, that evening of all evenings, to have someone to worry about other than himself. Anna's instincts were good, he thought grimly. Spot on, in fact. She just hadn't known the whole story. She had assumed – as indeed he once had – that Rachel had got beyond babies.

By the time he returned his attentions to his nephew, the child was asleep, his head lolling on a cushion and the book clasped to his chest like a loved toy.

When the doorbell rang, Will moved slowly, telling himself it was Anna back early and having forgotten her keys as usual.

'The bloody car won't start.' Rachel was fidgeting with the buckle on her bag, her eyes directed somewhere around his knees. 'Flat battery. I just need a phone.'

'A phone, of course.' He stood back and opened the door wider. 'Come in.'

'I'm still cross.'

'I know.'

'And I've got four godchildren and a cat.'

'I've got a nephew. He's in the kitchen.'

Still she stood on the doorstep, knowing that going in, however valid the pretext, would be the start of something irrevocable.

'I'm forty and a typical spinster. A spinster with inclinations towards broodiness. How does that sound?'

'Perfectly horrible. Are you coming in, or what? It's turning nasty out there.' Seizing both her hands, he pulled her across the threshold so roughly that she almost fell. He kicked the door shut behind her with his foot, slamming it so violently the floorboards shook beneath their feet. 'Got you,' he whispered, pulling her to him and kissing her hair.

'Only till I'm rescued by a nice man from the Automobile Association. Their technicians are uniformly gorgeous, you know, and known to go for the older woman . . .' She made a show of trying to pull away.

'Really . . . ?' The circle of his arms was immovable.

'Is that the lady who's good at football?' piped a small voice behind.

'Is it? I don't know – probably.' Will dropped his arms, laughing. 'She's full of hidden talents, I'm sure. But right now she needs to borrow our phone. Shall we let her?'

'Only if she reads a story,' Jack replied, sensing some game with his uncle and wanting to play his part.

'This is a plot,' Rachel protested, smiling at both of them. 'It's a conspiracy. You're all in it together. I don't stand a chance, do I?'

'I certainly hope not. The telephone is this way.' Will led her back into the kitchen, where Jack now hovered by the sofa, watching them curiously. 'Have a drink while you're here. Red wine, or maybe champagne?'

'I might just have a drop of champagne, thank you – only because it would be a shame to waste it.'

'Absolutely. A terrible shame. And perhaps you could see your way to reading an abridged version of *Peter Pan* before you leave?'

'Oh, I think I might manage that.'

'One phone call, one drink, one bedtime story. Then we'll let her go, shall we Jack?'

'Maybe,' the child replied, cocking his head in thought before adding brightly, 'unless she wants to read another one.'

Will eyed Rachel, now looking businesslike, with the receiver to her ear. 'I wouldn't bank on it if I were you.'

Rachel put down the telephone and picked up her glass. 'It's engaged,' she lied, thinking that even fate needed a hand now and then, to push things on their way.

MARRIAGE GAMES

In loving memory of my dear father

Special thanks must go to my sister, Fiona Ballantine Dykes, and to Sara Westcott and Christine Goodall for all the time and trouble they took in advising me over subjects on which their knowledge vastly exceeded mine.

A fresh fall of snow, faintly blue under the velvet glower of the night sky, masked the ancient uneven cobbles of Torbridge's market square. In its centre, the weathered frame of the poultry cross seemed to sag under the weight of the whiteness layered on top. Only the dim strains of the string quartet performing in the domed apse of St Cuthbert's church penetrated the muffled stillness of the scene. As the last chords were stroked and held, the town hall clock struck an imperious chime, as if to assert itself against the silent mountain of Torbridge cathedral towering behind, its giant illuminated triangle quite dwarfing the chattering clusters as they spilled out of St Cuthbert's cosy Norman doorway into the square below.

'Christ, I hate concerts in churches,' declared Juliet Howard cheerfully, linking arms with her husband, and blowing on the knuckles of her other hand. 'Frozen bum, frozen fingers and a streaming nose. Even my hair feels cold,' she added with a sniff, tugging the black velvet rim of her beret to a more rakish angle over her left ear and putting up the collar of her coat so that her frizz of bleached curls bunched round her neck like a scarf.

'No you don't,' soothed James Howard good-humouredly, patting her hand. 'Besides, a little discomfort is good for the soul – not to mention some fine music. I thought it was fabulous. Great acoustics.'

'Hmm,' murmured Juliet, who nurtured a fond scepticism for her husband's judgment when it came to the echoing qualities of draughty old buildings, and musical excellence of any kind. His throaty performances in the shower each morning could make even their children – undiscerning musicians of nine and seven years old – go bolting for cover under the bedclothes. Their intermittent support of the Torbridge winter concert programme stemmed, as Juliet well knew, more from a keen sense of the social role expected of a local GP rather than from any real desire to feed a musical habit that had latched on to Pink Floyd a couple of decades before and never quite let go. Such wifely wisdom in no way diminished Juliet's respect or affection for the man to whom she had been married for ten of the twelve years they had been acquainted. As if to underline this fact for herself, she curled her left hand up into a fist and pressed it into his large warm palm. James responded at once by closing his fingers round the fist and giving a tender squeeze. The gesture was an old friend, an echo of a mutual attraction which time had mellowed, but never yet called into serious question.

'Oh look, there's Ben and Isobel – do let's catch up and persuade them to have a drink.' Juliet wriggled her hand free and started to elbow her way through the throng loitering round the railings guarding the haggard stone front of the church.

Isobel Tarrant was walking half a stride behind her husband, absently placing her feet in the imprint left by his heavy-soled shoes while she thought about the music and the snow and the mystifying fact that profoundly beautiful things were somehow sad. Her head was still ringing with sound and her throat ached from the lump that had blocked it from the start of the final slow movement, when the man on the viola closed his eyes and kept them shut till the last reverberation of the final note had died away.

To Isobel, snow was a treat at any stage of the winter, let alone in mid-January when there was nothing to look forward to but weeks of damp drizzle and false starts to the spring. The recent weather had thrilled the girls too, making them late for school that morning because of snowballing and having to stop at every wall and gatepost to shovel white clods off the top. Both sets of mittens had been so sodden by the time they reached the playground that Isobel had taken them home for a spin through the tumble-drier, providing company for a consignment of towels and a beloved bed-toy of Sophie's that had been salvaged from an altercation with a leaky felt pen and which went coarse and bobbly if left to dry on its own.

Ben Tarrant was the first to stop and turn to acknowledge the Howards, merely grinning and shrugging his broad shoulders so as not to have to remove his hands from the ragged but warm interiors of his anorak pockets.

'Hey, you two. Good, wasn't it? That violinist . . .' He rolled his eyes in admiration. 'So much talent. And only nineteen. I think these winter concerts get better every year.' Famous himself for a lively ability at the piano – reserved for increasingly infrequent displays during late evenings in the company of friends – Ben Tarrant pronounced such views with a confidence that was both well received and quite uncalculated.

'I liked the viola best,' murmured Isobel, recalling again the enchanting concentration of the player, how each twitch of his face had altered with the mood swings of the music, how the tips of his slim fingers had seemed to tease out the notes by touch alone. The violinist had been too much of an extrovert for her tastes, swaying all over the place, like a kite straining to get off the ground; all elbows and showing off.

'Can we continue this discussion somewhere warm?' suggested Juliet, tucking her hands under armpits. 'Like the Stag, for instance? If we hurry we might even persuade them to serve up a plate of chips.'

'Did you walk?'

The women had fallen into step behind the men, their conversation creating wispy swirls of vapour that rose on the cold air.

'I did, yes. But Ben came on his bike straight from school, as usual. I wonder where he left it?' As Isobel paused to look back in the direction from which they had come, she was struck again by the stark beauty of the square under its vast duvet of snow. 'I say, isn't this lovely?' she sighed. 'The children are behaving as if they've never seen the stuff before. For the first time in months they wanted to be outside instead of watching the telly. We spent all afternoon building a lopsided snowman with mean eyes and a leering grin.'

'Lovely,' echoed Juliet, with a dismissive sniff, 'for anyone considering retirement to the North Pole. I tell you, it's like Ice Station bloody Zebra where we are, but with none of the heroics. The school bus got wedged between snow banks at the bottom of our lane and James's car made one measly whir before subsiding into an icy silence that made him very late and horribly cross.'

Isobel smiled. 'Serves you right for moving out of town and becoming dependent on such things.'

'And the AA wouldn't come because we'd broken down outside our own home instead of half a mile down the road.' She beat her hands together, scowling good-naturedly at Isobel, who was laughing. 'What on earth kept Ben in the staffroom on a Friday night anyway?'

'Play rehearsals. What else?'

'Already? But it's months till his play, isn't it?'

Isobel sighed. 'It'll be at the last weekend of term, as usual. But Ben says it's got all the makings of a complete disaster . . .'

'Well, bollocks to that,' interrupted Juliet brightly, 'it's what he always says. It's what directors are supposed to say, it goes with the territory,' she added, by way of an oblique reference to her own considerable – if somewhat distant – experience of thespian life. 'Do you remember last year and the Miranda whose voice broke?'

Isobel giggled. 'From treble to bass in one week . . . oh, poor Ben, he agonised for nights about what to do. But no, this time it really does sound bad,' she persisted earnestly and with a loyalty which Juliet, in her more critical moments, could find quite infuriatingly dogged. 'Julius Caesar is being played by that boy who got suspended last term – Giles Turner – the one found having glue hallucinations on a bench in the close. Do you remember? Terribly talented but difficult as hell, Ben says. He's sort of taken him on,' she added, her heart twisting with a familiar confusion of pride and resentment at the relentless alacrity with which her husband was drawn to such causes.

The Stag was a low-beamed den of a pub with horse brasses and prints of milk carts and old shopfronts decorating its walls. Since it was Friday night at an hour when Torbridge's one theatre and two cinemas had ejected full audiences into the streets, the single-roomed bar was more packed than usual. After having jostled for drinks, Ben led their small party, with some triumph, to a single empty stool and sufficient space to stand right beside the fiery mouth of a huge hearth. Juliet, at first eager to toast herself before the flames, was soon stripping off layers and fanning her cheeks with her concert programme. They piled their coats and sweaters in a precarious tower on the stool and took it in turns to stand in the hottest spot.

As Juliet set off to retrieve her order of chips, James embarked on a funny story about a bashful patient with haemorrhoids. At the punch line Ben laughed more heartily than his wife, who caught herself savouring an old gratitude that she had had the sense to register herself at the practice in Farley Road once it became clear that the Howards were to become close acquaintances. Stethoscopes and friends didn't go together, she felt, although James was undeniably marvellous with the girls, and Ben had no qualms whatsoever about consulting his keenest squash rival on the rare occasion when he admitted the need of medical intervention beyond that offered by the bathroom cabinet.

'Oh dear, now I've offended Isobel,' remarked James, running his hand through his handsome grey-blond hair in a show of despair. At fifty, he was considerably older than his wife and most of their friends, but never in danger of showing it. Thanks to a genuine fondness for ball games and a lifetime of caution about desserts, his waistline was still so trim that he had recently taken to tucking his sweaters into the waistband of his trousers in order to advertise the fact.

'Don't be silly,' she replied quickly, feeling caught out. 'I'm quite used to you and your stories, James.'

'I certainly hope so.' He looked almost serious for a second. 'I should hate to lose the respect of your wife, Ben—'

'What makes you so sure you had it in the first place?' The two men were still laughing when Juliet returned. 'Did I miss something funny?'

'I was just telling them about—'

'Oh no, not again,' groaned Isobel, helping herself to a chip from the heap on Juliet's plate. 'Stop him, Juliet, please. It's all about a poor man with piles . . .'

'Don't be tedious, James,' Juliet scolded, passing the plate round. 'Anyway, I want to hear more about this play, Ben. Isobel says it's bound for disaster.'

'Well, thanks for the wifely support, darling.'

'I only meant that you had said it was . . .' she began, but he had already turned away to answer Juliet.

'. . . a Brutus who can't act, a Caesar who won't act and a Mark Antony who thinks he can act but can't at all. Only a couple of months till curtain-up and I've got a field trip to Wales to contend with as well.'

'Have you?'

'The lower sixth spring term treat in Pembrokeshire. Remember?' Ben shook his head in wonder at his wife's forgetfulness.

'Oh, of course,' Isobel murmured absently, suddenly feeling awash with tiredness.

'Don't worry, Isobel, I have to phone Vera at the practice to find out what's going on in James's life, don't I, darling?'

'She certainly doesn't,' retorted her husband with mock indignation. 'Keep your wife informed of your movements at all times, Tarrant, it's the secret of a happy marriage, I assure you.'

'Oh, we already know the secret, thanks, James,' quipped Ben, slipping his arm round Isobel and pulling him to her. Caught off balance, she half stepped, half fell against him and clung to his shirt for a moment to steady herself. He took her hand and lightly kissed the fingers. 'You look tired, my love. Do you want to go home?'

'No, I'm fine, as long as you are, Ben,' Isobel lied, defeated as always by his tenderness, and wishing that such shows of affection could be both more frequent and more dependable. Having accepted the offer of a second glass of wine, she concentrated on maintaining an expression of interest while Juliet embarked on an entertaining but lengthy account of the healing power of aromatic oils, the latest in a long string of flirtations with life-enhancing hobbies. As her thoughts drifted, Isobel found herself trying to imagine what it would feel like to be as confiding as Juliet, who released anxieties about husbands, children and life in general with an ease that was almost gleeful. Whereas in her own case, to talk so freely about Ben would, she knew, feel like disloyalty, or, worse still, an admission of defeat.

Aware of Ben laughing, as the two men sparred happily on familiar topics, Isobel experienced a sudden spurt of envy towards James, for the casual friendship that he could enjoy with a man whom every instinct in her being still loved, but whose friendship seemed to be slipping from her grasp. From there, her thoughts plummeted towards the even more unsettling notion that friends like the Howards, so casual, but seen so often, might in some way have contributed to such problems, by minimising the need to confront them.

In a bid to divert herself from such gloominess, Isobel proceeded to offer a volley of penetrating questions on the subject of aromatherapy, now so excelling in the art of appearing interested that she quite forgot to listen to any of Juliet's answers.

Meanwhile, the mask of snow outside was beginning to melt, sliding with slow elegance from roofs and crevices throughout southern England. By morning all that remained of Torbridge's postcard prettiness was a gravelly sludge, pushed into ugly drifts along pavements and walls by car wheels and hurrying feet.

Ben Tarrant threw a piece of blue chalk at the boy reading a magazine under his desk and emitted a rumbling growl. The child jumped visibly as the chalk landed squarely on the tarbrush crown of his head before bouncing once on his desk and then rolling on to the floor. Titters of amusement rippled round the classroom.

'Perhaps Marcel Proust back there could spare some time to share with us his views on the infinitely fascinating subject of glacier formations. How the thing moves, for instance. You may use the blackboard – and that writing aid now situated near your trailing shoelaces. If I draw a boulder – here' – Ben drew a ragged circle in the centre of the board – 'perhaps you would be so good as to describe for us how the ice gets past it?'

The boy slouched to the front of the class and stood for several moments staring disconsolately at the ring of chalk.

'Take your time, Martin,' said Ben, pretending to shake himself awake. The rest of the class laughed again, more loudly this time.

'Does it sort of melt, sir?'

Ben folded his arms and cocked his head. 'Yes,' he said slowly, 'it sort of does.'

'And then it freezes again round the other side of the rock, sir, I think. But I haven't the foggiest how to draw it.'

There were more muffled giggles which Ben silenced with a stern look. 'You seem to have grasped the basic principles quite well, Martin, by miraculous osmosis, I'd say, given that you have been so ungraciously distracted by other literature since the start of the lesson.'

'Yes, sir. Sorry, sir.'

'OK, go back to your seat. And Martin . . .'

The boy stopped and turned, fresh worry creasing his freckled blushing face. 'Yes, sir?'

'My chalk. Do you think I could have it back?' Ben smiled, aiming to convey that the sin had been forgiven, but still hoping that the memory of the discomfort suffered for it would be sufficient to prevent similar occurrences in the future.

At the sound of the bell for lunch, desk lids slammed and the room emptied in seconds. Ben sighed and began slowly rubbing his dubious representation of a boulder off the blackboard. He worked with unnecessary diligence, erasing every trace of chalk, distracted now by the concern that he might have been too harsh. The boy's parents had separated the year before and a slow deterioration in concentration had been in evidence ever since. Fifteen was a tough age, he reflected grimly, a watershed time when even the most promising pupils could drop beyond reach of reason or help, overwhelmed by adolescent confusions or peer pressure to be defiant and lazy.

Perhaps getting Martin involved in a spot of set-painting would help, he mused, putting down the board rubber and absently dusting white streaks of chalk on to his trousers. God knew, they needed all the help they could get. He wrote the boy's name on a scrap of paper to remind himself and opened the first of a tall pile of blue exercise books which he needed to return to their owners that afternoon. A sausage of an ox-bow lake greeted him, floating between two smudged blue felt-pen streaks.

Use coloured pencils, please, he wrote, before scowling at the miniature spider writing that accompanied the drawing. Tempted to put a red line through the lot, he resisted, knowing both that his impatience rose from his own fatigue more than anything justifiable and that, if deciphered, the spider scrawl could comprise comments that were lucid and sometimes illuminating. *Well tried,* he wrote after a few minutes, before putting down the pen and rubbing his eyes with his fingertips. With the bustle of the morning behind him, a terrible tiredness began to take hold. He felt as if he could sleep for ever. Pushing the books back to one side, Ben crossed his arms on the desk and laid his head upon them with a heavy sigh. Specks of colour danced before his eyes, jigging to a half-remembered tune from the concert the week before. For a few minutes he grappled with the sensation of being pulled in several conflicting directions at once; as the music merged with the sound of school bells, images of Isobel joined the fray in his head, her lips pursed with disappointment, her lovely eyes twitching with unspoken challenges that he recognised but for which there seemed to be no appropriate response. Then, at last, a glorious blackness took hold, pulling him down into a pleasurably vacant womb of a world where nobody required anything of him at all.

Having made a mug of coffee, Isobel took the brochures upstairs with her to the small attic which they had converted into a cubby-hole of a study bedroom the year before. It took several minutes to clear a space for herself on the desk, minutes which she did not resent at all, since they delayed still further the moment when she would have to try and pretend to herself that she was being serious. A moment which she had been avoiding all morning, first by returning a couple of children's books to the library and then by an impromptu and not altogether necessary cleaning of the lavatory. She had frowned as she scrubbed, holding her long auburn hair back from her face with one hand and rigorously jabbing the brush up round and under the rim with the other. Then a splodge of something suspiciously sticky had caught her eye round the back under the pipes and before she knew it she was on her knees with a J-cloth and a bottle of Jif. Though such frenzied activity might have fooled any onlookers, Isobel herself knew very well that she was merely taking a cowardly detour round the large white envelope which had been forced through their narrow letterbox that morning. Housework had never been a major priority in her life, not even before she had acquired the assistance of dear Mrs Beety, who behaved as if the very foundations of human happiness were threatened by fluff balls or undetected grime of any kind.

With the desk cleared, there was only the view of neighbouring rooftops and terraced gardens to distract her, together with the couple of framed photographs that lived on either side of the letter-stand. Ben and the girls building sandcastles on a

Suffolk beach; the wind blowing their hair in flat strands across their faces, their eyes screwed up against the glare of the sun; brandishing spades and buckets in cheerful salute at the camera. The image provoked a lump of nostalgia which Isobel impatiently swallowed away. That particular day had been as fraught with petty domestic dramas as any other, she recalled wryly. Ben in a bad mood as he invariably was when they stayed with her parents, smiling through gritted teeth while they waited for her mother to find her reading glasses and her father rootled about in the back of the garage for a fishing rod that would never get used. By the time they set off it was almost lunch-time; the girls, still at an age when food dictated states of euphoria or despair, had bickered and moaned so relentlessly that they had undertaken a lengthy diversion round a sleepy village in search of ice creams. Though eventual success in this quest had produced silence for the remainder of the journey, the price paid was a punishingly tight-lipped grandmotherly anxiety about children being given sweets just before a meal and the notion of ice-cream dribbles staining the upholstery of the car. The sandcastle episode had taken place just a few minutes after they had all finally staggered through some grass-tufted dunes on to the beach, when all adult parties had thrown themselves into the taxing business of having fun. It seemed to Isobel now that even as she had taken the picture she had felt the duplicity of it, the play-acting rigmarole of snapshots and smiles.

The other photograph, which was much older, showed her, sitting on a five-bar gate in muddied wellingtons and a crumpled T-shirt and shorts. Ben had taken it one glorious September afternoon on their honeymoon, when they had just tumbled out of a draughty Cotswold bed and breakfast, groaning at the heaviness of the fried food in their stomachs and teasingly chiding each other for their shameful failure to commune with anything but themselves. Her hair was tied back in a loose ponytail that had broken free round the sides. She was grinning broadly, her head cocked towards one shoulder, her eyes locked with quite audacious intensity on the centre of the lens, or rather the person behind it. Looking now from one photo to the other, Isobel was struck, more forcefully than ever before, by the great chasm of experiences that divided them. She would not look like that now if Ben were to take her picture, she reflected sadly. She would look questioning and unsure. But Ben never did take her picture. These days their albums were full of photos of the girls. These days she felt increasingly as if she were waiting for affection from her husband, like a dog begging for scraps from a table. Still so eager for a show of love, but powerless to inspire it.

And they had begun so well. Isobel closed her eyes, letting the nostalgia flood through her, knowing from experience that it would run its course if allowed to. Ben's affection had seemed infinite, enough for lifetimes and more. A shiver of recollected ecstasy tiptoed from the nape of her neck and down her spine. Ben Tarrant. She would have died for him. Robbed grannies. Gone to hell.

Isobel seized the honeymoon photograph and scowled at it, hating the image for reminding her of what she missed, of what she had hoped their marriage would be. Of what it had been. She rubbed her temples, trying and failing to pinpoint the origin of her husband's declining interest, knowing only that it had worsened considerably in recent months. Impatient with herself, she turned both photographs to face the window before tearing open the flap of the white envelope and tipping its contents out on to the desk. *Open University: Courses, Diplomas and BA/BSc Degrees*, she read, before her eyes skipped to a scrutiny of the collage of pictures below, in which earnest-looking men and women of politically correct skin colours and sexes assumed false poses round charts and test tubes and books.

Absently twisting one tress of hair round her index finger, Isobel creased her brow in concentration, wishing she could muster something approximating to enthusiasm for the subjects and vocations described inside. Instead, the sense of pointlessness that had inspired her to reach for the loo brush rather than race to study prospects for self-improvement mushroomed obstinately inside.

She had known pointlessness before, as a student; a more angry, energetic kind, generated by three years of trying to develop a liking for the law and a lack of funds with which to enjoy the distractions offered by London in her spare time. With her finals behind her and a resolution never to open a legal book again, the future had shimmered alarmingly out of focus. A cousin of her mother's invited her to New Zealand, a godfather talked about introducing her to colleagues in Hong Kong. While Isobel feigned interest in such possibilities, in her heart she knew she was waiting for something else, something altogether more momentous, to vault her into the gaping next stage of her life.

She met Ben Tarrant thanks to a flatmate's undeclared passion for a wiry, blond German who spent his spare time shifting scenery and painting backdrops for a motley group of part-time thespians in East London. Much against her better judgment, Isobel allowed herself to be coerced into offering moral support for the development of this unpromising relationship by attending a lesser-known Lorca play in a dingy basement theatre next to a warehouse on the Old Kent Road. Isobel's own love life had been disappointingly uneventful since a brief and ugly fling with a tutor who turned out to be in possession not only of a wife, four children and a dog, but also of a notoriety of which everyone had apparently been aware but herself. The episode had done little to endear her to the course. Nor had it heightened the dubious attractions of her male fellow students, most of whose lives seemed to revolve around an unrestrainable passion for beer and ball games.

Ben Tarrant stormed into her consciousness in the few instants it took him to stride into the spotlight on the stage. He was tall, with glossy dark hair and startled blue eyes that looked almost comical under the heavy line of his eyebrows. Isobel, sliding forward on to the edge of her seat, was at once transfixed, not only by his physical presence, but also by the unintelligible Spanish poetry tumbling with evident sing-song fluency from his wide, agile mouth. All the pretension of performing such an incomprehensible play in a hot shoe box of a theatre on a sticky August night was forgiven in an instant. And when her companion suggested they gatecrash the cast party scheduled to take place afterwards, Isobel's initial reluctance to do so arose only from a regret that she should be wearing her most unflattering knee-bagged jeans, instead of the newish purple dress hanging, with most of her clothes, round the dado rail skirting the high-ceilinged wall of her Camberwell bedsit.

As she later discovered, Ben Tarrant liked the faded jeans

almost as much as the shimmering conker colour of her long
hair and what some regarded as the unhealthy pallor of her
skin. He said that with the light behind her she looked as if her
head were on fire. She was wearing a T-shirt saying 'Save The
Whales' and a thin gold bangle that fell down her forearm every
time she tried to tuck some flyaway wisps of hair behind her
ears. The trainers on her feet were flecked with dried mud and
there were ink stains on her two middle fingers. Then involved
in a highly unsatisfactory liaison with a woman addicted to the
transforming powers of curling tongs and self-tanning lotion,
Ben was instantly charmed by such scruffiness. While Isobel,
never having met a man so clearly aware of his abilities and yet so
reluctant to admit to them, was equally awestruck. The discovery
that he had a Chilean mother and had spent his boyhood in
South America added a wonderfully exotic edge both to his
appeal and Isobel's determination to become better acquainted.
Incoherent with ardour and too much wine, the pair of them
had flirted outrageously, much to the disgust of the lovelorn
flatmate, whose own romantic expectations had been dashed
by a rival with studs in her nostrils and electric-blue hair.

From such unglamorous beginnings, however, had sprung a
connection of more lasting quality, based not simply on mutual
physical attraction, but on instinctive feelings quite unlike anything Isobel had experienced before or since. Wonderful when
it worked, but hopeless when it didn't, she reflected sadly,
abandoning the desk and shaking her head at the realisation
that not understanding something rendered one powerless to
mend it.

When Ben left for a teaching exchange at a school in Madrid,
just a few weeks after their first meeting, she had accompanied
him. After an intense and idyllic twelve months spent mostly
in each other's company, they returned to England and got
married. By the time Ben had successfully nailed the job of
geography master at Torbridge Cathedral School, Isobel was
several months into her first pregnancy, struggling to readjust
both to a cold climate and the realisation that her husband had
many things in his life to attend to other than her.

The sound of yapping drew her to the window. Down below
she could see a wiry terrier sniping at one of Druscilla Carew's

treasured cats through the hole in the bottom of her front fence. After a few moments Druscilla herself scurried out through her front door, clapping her hands and making small screeching noises designed to attract her pet back into the safety of the house. She was dressed in one of her pastel-coloured track suits, with pom-pommed slippers on her feet and a large velvet bow tied on the crown of her head. Like an Easter egg, mused Isobel, trying and failing to skip out of view.

'Halloo, up there!' Druscilla shrieked, waving hard. 'I've been neglecting you, I know . . .'

Isobel stepped back into the frame of the window with an acknowledging smile and wave.

'. . . simply *must* have one of our chats soon . . . been far too long.' She scooped up the cat and retreated back inside her house amidst a flurry of coughing, designed to remind anyone within earshot that pets were the cause of both her greatest allergy and her greatest love.

'But not long enough,' muttered Isobel to herself, turning her back on the window and returning to the desk with a sense of stoical determination that had seen her through many a crisis in the past.

Juliet Howard stood for a few moments at her bedroom window, watching the young man pushing a wheelbarrow of stones down her garden path. In spite of the foul weather, he wore only a T-shirt and a pair of paint-encrusted jeans. His long, bushy blond hair was tied back in a ponytail, revealing earlobes pierced with gold and silver loops. He walked nicely, she decided, with that faint roll of the hips which she associated with masculine confidence of the most enticing kind. His fellow workers, with whom he was responsible for repointing the outer walls of the house and constructing a large semicircular patio in the back garden, were far less gratifying to have around; all bottom cleavages and ugly pot-bellies that hung below the hem-lines of their T-shirts.

Turning her attention to the blobs of hand cream in her hands, Juliet started to massage them into her palms. She hummed quietly under her breath as she did so, savouring the prospect of day ahead: a morning at her aromatherapy course, a sandwich with one of her fellow students – granary with bacon and avocado inside, or maybe egg mayonnaise. She licked her lips. Then some shopping – just the top-up kind round Torbridge's central square mile – before picking the children up from school and ferrying them home for *Blue Peter* and her non-beef version of spaghetti bolognaise. Tilly would groan and Eddie would have seconds, she thought with one of those pangs of fond maternal indulgence that came so easily at a distance, and could be so elusive when the little darlings were actually around.

Having combed the zigzags of her perm into a more satisfactory shape, Juliet set about applying her make-up for the day. One of the more obvious pleasures arising from their recent move out of Torbridge had been the discovery of the school bus. Though occasionally envious of Isobel Tarrant's ability to look fresh-faced and windswept without trying at all, Juliet herself was as likely to leave the house without lipstick and mascara as she would have been to parade naked up the aisle of the cathedral. But then Isobel, at the measly age of thirty two, was almost ten years younger, she reminded herself with a sigh that was accepting rather than envious. Juliet was far too fond of Isobel to let jealousy get in the way. Besides which, there were other aspects to the woman which she would not have wanted for the world; like her shyness amongst crowds, and the flickers of unhappiness that sometimes glazed her eyes when she imagined she was alone. Juliet, on the other hand, not only adored people, but had also developed a singular capacity for being cheerful in the face of almost anything. Not even growing old was going to get her down, she decided, working creams and powders into her face with a practised efficiency that bore testimony to her days on the stage; days on which she frequently looked back with affection, but no longing at all. Apart from a Pam Ayers-style voice-over for a commercial for clotted cream, she had never really earned any serious money. By her mid-thirties it had been nothing short of a relief to give up the struggle with agents and diets and surrender at last to the tug of marriage and motherhood with James. Dearest James, waiting patiently in the wings for two long years, putting up with all those premarital tantrums and panics, and then agreeing so readily with her plea to abandon his lucrative Holland Park practice and make a fresh start. As things turned out, Torbridge life had suited them both beautifully right from the beginning. Bumping into Isobel Tarrant so early on had helped enormously, Juliet reflected, smiling at the recollection of the antenatal class in which they had met and the repugnantly zealous representative of the NCT, who breast-fed a precocious two-year-old during sessions and handed out price lists for birthing pools together with sachets of raspberry leaf tea. United by near-hysterical aversion to such things – confessed to over coffee and wedges of cheesecake in Royles Coffee House afterwards – the two women had struck up a friendship that had lasted ever since.

Juliet sighed contentedly as she applied a final stroke of pink dust across the cheekbones which, she knew, would hold her face in place for many a year to come. The sight of her full-length image in the mirror on the landing, however, brought a less rapturous sense of wellbeing. She did a little shimmy to recover some of her sense of self-worth, before reminding herself that the loss of figure had been traded for regular indulgences of her favourite foods and two enchanting children. And my husband still loves me, she thought suddenly, her heart surging with fondness and her legs tripping down the stairs in a rush of schoolgirl eagerness to be on her way. As she stepped outside into a blaze of unexpected sunshine, it occurred to Juliet that she was probably as happy as she had ever been in her life; that, apart from the patio, things were pretty well complete. The thought made her feel both pleased and faintly worried. To want for nothing but a patio was, she suspected, not terribly admirable; not something she was sure she would own up to, not even to Isobel, to whom she told most things.

At the sight of the bushy-haired workman tipping something sludgy into the skip parked outside their front door, all such potentially self-critical thoughts flitted out of Juliet's head. She tooted twice as she drove off, enjoying the look of pleased surprise that preceded the impish smile he offered in return.

James Howard studied his list of patients booked in for the morning and groaned quietly. He was in no mood for Arthur Hackett's rickety hips, Mrs Reeves's gluey sinuses, or the obese

Grigson boy's fantastical abdominal pains, invariably brought on by the prospect of the classroom and the enticing alternative of keeping his mother company behind the sweet counter in the mini-market next to the chemist.

It was harder to feel inspired these days, he thought wearily, recalling with a small twist of envy the evident passion of the young quartet to whom they had listened the week before. Such intensity and commitment. Such fiendish energy. James stooped to check his appearance in the small mirror that hung behind the door in reception, running a small black comb through his handsome sweep of hair and baring his teeth to check for specks. The sight of his reflection did lift the doctor's spirits a little; many a fifty-year-old would, he knew, have been glad of the solidity of his hairline and the way the tiredness round his grey eyes manifested itself in small lines that could look quite becoming when he smiled. That he felt heavier and moved more slowly these days was due not so much to additional kilograms as a fundamental sense of prudence. He could still beat Ben Tarrant on the squash court, but only once in a while and only because the dear man had a habit of throwing himself at everything without reference to logic or intelligence. The thought made James smile. He liked Ben enormously, without believing – even after almost nine years' acquaintance – that he knew him very well. Several shared family holidays in a variety of cottages and caravan parks had brought them to a state of mutual affection that never seemed duty-bound to develop into anything else. Which was precisely what he liked about it, decided James, slotting his comb back into the pocket of his white coat and returning to his desk.

In contrast, the superior intimacy evident between their wives had at times made him uneasy. Not just because it was clear that Juliet did most of the talking, but also because Isobel Tarrant seemed to be one of those quiet, unknowable women, content to sit well within the shadow of her very able husband and to let everyone else commit to the risky business of expressing opinions. That she had opinions, James was in no doubt; though he had yet fully to decide whether such reticence made her interesting or merely devious.

As he scrolled through files on his computer screen, James

found his mind drifting from the welfare of his patients back to a vivid snapshot of his wife's best friend, tipping water over herself early one sticky morning in Brittany the year before, when the rest of the campsite was still asleep. James, peering out from a small smeary caravan window for an early weather check, had, somewhat to his surprise, found himself spying with all the guile and curiosity of the true voyeur. She was too slight and freckled for his tastes, hollow-cheeked and pale, with an almost childlike slimness to her arms and legs. James had always preferred his women to come in larger portions, to have bodies that could quiver and crush, with flesh that could cushion his. Yet there was something about the sight of Isobel that morning, ladling water over herself from a bucket, that was mesmerising. Her hair, usually so red, blackened under the water, until it dripped down her back in long dark tails that soaked through her shirt. He could see the pink of her skin, protected so studiously during the day with creams and covers and shades, pressing through the damp white cloth. So delicate compared to the deep honey tan of Juliet, he had thought, tearing his eyes from the window for a moment to check that the splayed body of his wife still heaved with the deep sighs of genuine sleep. When Isobel had finished with the water, she bound her hair in a tight towering turban with a towel, so tight that it slanted the corners of her green eyes and showed a line of chalky whiteness along the top of her forehead, where the sun hadn't reached the skin.

Such was James's immersion in this reverie that he jerked visibly when the phone rang. More disconcerting still was the fact than the voice on the other end proved to belong to Isobel Tarrant herself. Blushing profusely, James had leapt to his feet to take the call, knocking over his mug of coffee in the process.

'Isobel – bugger – sorry. Hello. I've just spilt a drop of coffee. Not at all, no . . . just a drop . . .' He mopped with his handkerchief as he talked, failing to notice the brown stream trickling down the desk leg and forming a dark puddle on the green-carpeted floor. 'To what do I owe the pleasure?'

'James – sorry. This is a real cheek. The receptionist said you were fully booked, so I thought I'd make a direct appeal. Could you squeeze Megan in later on this morning? It's probably just the start of a bad cold – we got caught in all that dreadful rain at the weekend – but she's so floppy and hot that I can't help being worried. And she says she's got a horrible headache, which of course makes me think of meningitis, though she can still look up and down which is supposed to be the main thing, isn't it?'

James could not help smiling at such a wonderfully simplistic mode of diagnosis for a disease which even the most competent doctor could struggle to detect. 'I doubt it's meningitis, Isobel.'

'I was wondering if I could bring her in when you've finished all your appointments. If you call me I can be there in five minutes if I come in the car. But of course I'll understand if you're too busy. Now that she's older we don't get same-day appointments any more, which I quite understand. Like I said, it's probably only a bad cold . . .'

'I'll come myself,' he said kindly. 'As soon as I'm done here. Will you be at home?'

'Oh no, I didn't mean to put you out in any way—'

'It won't be putting me out at all, Isobel, honestly,' he lied, spurred on by a sudden impulse to atone for the thoroughly uncharacteristic bout of daydreaming that had preceded the phone call. He looked at his watch and frowned. 'But I've got to get on now, I'm afraid. I'll see you around lunch-time. Junior Disprin and lots of liquid in the meantime.'

Having wrung out his handkerchief over the bin, James then returned to his desk and pressed the buzzer that would indicate he was ready, for by no means the first time in their long acquaintance, to discuss hip replacement surgery with Arthur Hackett in the certain knowledge that the old man would limp away refusing to commit himself to anything of the kind.

3 ∫

'You're delivering a speech, Leon, not reading out a shopping list,' wailed Ben, rolling his eyes in despair. The group of boys gathered on the stage at one end of Crofton College's impressive oak-panelled hall giggled and exchanged glances while the would-be Mark Antony frowned in genuine surprise.

'But I thought you said I was to sound gentle, sir . . .'

'Gentle, yes, but firm. You want this lot to trust you. You're trying to win them over. You want them – improbable though it may seem – to think you are noble, so that they realise quite how dishonourable Brutus has been.'

'But he says Brutus is honourable, sir,' replied the boy, pointing at the page in front of him with a wide-eyed desire to be helpful.

'Yes, Leon, I am well aware of that.' Ben spoke in a tone of weary patience. 'But he means the opposite. He's saying Brutus is honourable, but by describing Caesar's virtues he is communicating precisely the opposite sentiment. OK?'

'Right you are, sir.' The boy shrugged, clearly mystified by such a perversely complex interpretation of something potentially so very simple.

Ben concentrated on pushing back the cuticles of his fingernails in order to prevent himself from interrupting the speech again. He studied the white flecks on his nails and told himself to pour more milk on his cornflakes while Mark Antony delivered a new version of instructions to his countrymen, this time employing a loud, clipped tone suggestive of little more than a desire to make his voice echo round the hall. They were already fast approaching the point, as Ben well knew, when any wise director resorted to encouragement rather than overt criticism of any kind. Egos mattered terribly, especially amongst teenaged boys. Experience had taught him that a little self-confidence could uplift even the most abysmal performance.

Leon was barking 'my heart is in the coffin' and pointing for no discernible reason at a portrait of the lugubrious face of the school's founder when Ben, with equal illogicality, remembered Aunt Violet. Or rather, he remembered that he had forgotten her.

'Isobel, darling, can you do me a huge favour.' Overwhelmed again by the grogginess that had prompted his unscheduled nap during break that morning, Ben leant back against the wall beside the pay-phone and ran his hand across his eyes.

'I expect so,' Isobel replied cautiously, wanting to please but made wary by the breathy impatience in his voice.

'It's Aunt Violet. Would you have time to drive over and see her?'

'Aunt Violet? Today? Oh, Ben, don't be ridiculous.' Ben's spinster aunt, who had recently suffered a stroke, was a relatively new addition to the Tarrant family duties and one about which Isobel retained well-aired and highly negative views. To ship the poor dear, after years of voluntary and mutually satisfactory exile in the wilds of Scotland, to a nursing home on the far side of Ilcombe seemed to her to constitute nephewly philanthropy of the most misguided kind. Not only had she quailed at the responsibility on her own account, but she also felt that Aunt Violet's very small contribution and involvement in Ben's childhood did not warrant such a massive return of effort. That the old dear had clearly lost touch with most of her mental faculties only reinforced such views.

'I've just remembered that I forgot her birthday—'

'Ben, you said you were going to deal with all this sort of thing—'

'I know, I will, I just forgot this time. Please, Isobel. Couldn't you pop over with a card and some flowers or something? . . . please.'

'You could phone her. Extend your greetings in person.'

'It's not the same . . . she hates the phone . . . and probably wouldn't recognise my voice.'

'Well, she probably won't recognise it's her birthday either,' snapped Isobel with a cruelty she did not quite feel.

'Oh, darling, please.'

'But Megan's not well and Mrs Beety has only just got here—'

'Then surely you could leave Meg for a couple of hours with Mrs Beety?'

'Well, I suppose I could, but James has kindly agreed to come round . . .'

'When?'

'Lunch-time,' she mumbled, wishing she had the courage to lie.

'So there is time, then?'

'Yes, I suppose there is,' she conceded, wondering if she were being kind or merely weak for caving in and thinking that once upon a time he had at least pretended that the demands of her life were of parallel as opposed to subordinate importance to his.

'Ben, we need to talk,' she stammered, interrupting the warm expostulations of gratitude that followed.

'What about . . . ? Hang on, the money's going to run out. I've got to go. I left a rehearsal in full swing. Thank you again, Isobel, I really appreciate it—'

Isobel stared for a few seconds at the receiver in her hand, before returning it to its slot on the wall beside the kitchen window. Appreciation isn't love, she thought glumly, rummaging in drawers for a box of chocolates she knew she had but couldn't find. Had her husband's affections slumped to the point where he could only feel positive emotions towards her if she actually did things for him, she wondered, but not during the times in between? Isobel paused, chocolates now in hand, thinking again that gratitude wasn't love, that it was unsustaining and one-dimensional and led nowhere.

As the car lurched reluctantly out of its parking space, Isobel found herself drawing somewhat hysterical and uncharitable parallels between her husband's aunt and her eldest daughter's guinea pig. There had been promises to assume responsibility there too, she recalled with a sigh, waving at Megan's pasty face framed in the sitting-room window and doing a mental calculation as to exactly when anyone but herself had last cleaned out the smelly interior of the hutch, or filled the small plastic feeding bowl with nutrients of any kind. Though Aunt Violet did not require quite such personal or frequent attention, she reflected wryly, her very presence, just thirty minutes' drive away, was somehow just as insidiously demanding.

I don't have a life, Isobel decided with a certain sense of self-drama, as she sat waiting for a space in the traffic streaming round Torbridge's busy ring-road roundabout; I have everybody else's. 'Good for guinea pigs and decrepit great-aunts,' she muttered, hooting at a motorcyclist who swerved in front of her, and blushing at the gesture she received in return.

Any idealistic hopes that the burden of visiting an ancient aunt might be redeemed by a sense of having done some good, of having brought a little happiness into an otherwise clouded and diminishing life, had been dashed almost at once. On their very first trip to the home, made jointly with Ben on the day following Aunt Violet's arrival from the North, it became clear that the old lady was either too mentally damaged, or too riddled with the self-centredness peculiar to old age, to disclose any emotions beyond a liking for boiled sweets and large-print true romances. She liked watching boxing on the telly too, Isobel had since discovered, but was seldom allowed to by her more queasy fellow residents.

'You look peaky,' announced Aunt Violet in a querulous voice, waving a lacy handkerchief at the sight of Isobel and then looking round as if in search of a more pleasing view.

'Happy birthday.' She kissed the sagging powdered cheek and held out the present. 'Ben is sorry he couldn't come himself. He'll be over soon.'

'I don't know a Ben,' she retorted, ignoring the box of chocolates and turning her attention to the large window beside her chair.

'Pretty, isn't it?' murmured Isobel, following the old lady's gaze to the tall silver maple that swayed in the gusty breeze outside. 'It'll be flowering before too long, I expect, with spring just around the corner.' Since the chocolates had been ignored, she delved into her bag for a packet of wine gums.

'How lovely,' exclaimed Aunt Violet, her face breaking instantly into an enchanted smile at the sight of the tube of sweets. Though the white fortress of her false teeth was flawless, the structure moved slightly under the pressure of her lips when she talked. She had been quite beautiful once, Isobel could see, though the face now, beneath its mask of glistening powder, was furrowed with wrinkles and splodgy liver spots. Most disconcerting of all were her eyes, of faded turquoise with pupils as sharp as stones, and the heart-shaped curve of her upper lip, which that morning had been clumsily accentuated with a daub of pearly lipstick.

There were several smudges of pink on the teeth, Isobel noticed, watching the smile broaden as the packet of pastilles was handed over for unwrapping. Experience had already taught her to resist the temptation to offer help. Whatever insanity afflicted the old bird, her pride, cruelly, had survived it intact. Isobel concerned herself instead with the dancing maple in the garden outside, studying the grace of its gnarled branches while, in the lap beside her, the knotted fingers struggled for command over the tiny twists and folds of the sweet wrappers.

Another resident came into the room, moving slowly with the help of two sticks, her head bent towards the floor in concentration. Her legs, Isobel noticed, were not much thicker than the sticks themselves. At the sight of Isobel and Violet her face lit up.

'Ah, a visitor!' she exclaimed delightedly, pausing to rest on her props.

Violet shrugged and turned her back on the door, hoicking her cardigan over her shoulders with a loud, contemptuous grunt. 'They're all women here, you know. No men at all,' she confided in a whisper of foghorn proportions.

Isobel smiled apologetically at the woman in the doorway, who nodded and went to sit down in an armchair next to a table of newspapers and magazines.

'Do you know any men?' asked Violet suddenly, feverishly gripping Isobel's arm, her eyes ablaze.

'I know my husband,' replied Isobel gently, wondering as she spoke whether this was in fact true. 'Ben Tarrant, your nephew. The one you used to visit sometimes at boarding school. His father Albert was your brother. He went to live in Chile.' Isobel spoke very slowly and clearly, as she might address a foreigner with a limited understanding of English.

Aunt Violet was nodding her head. 'Albert left the Diplomatic

Service, to marry that woman. Silly boy. He's dead now, of course. Everyone is, you know,' she added archly, popping a second sweet in her mouth and giving it a noisy suck. 'That's why I'm here, of course; to die.'

Isobel looked at her hands and smoothed at imaginary creases in her brown corduroy skirt.

'I was born in Dorset, you know,' Aunt Violet proceeded airily. 'As a little girl I grew up in Poole, near the sea and all those heavenly white rocks.'

'Poole's not far from here at all,' exclaimed Isobel, with an eagerness that betrayed her discomfort.

'Silly Albert, staying away like that. And she died too, you know.'

'His wife?'

'That's what I said. The wife, Louisa. Died in a car crash.'

'I know,' said Isobel gently, remembering how moved she had been the first time Ben had referred to this childhood tragedy, using the steely tone of voice that he reserved for any references to his family. With his subsequent exile to boarding school in England at the age of seven, had come an estrangement from his father from which neither of them had ever quite recovered. Albert Tarrant's death, several years before they met, had been a relief, Ben said, the final cutting of a tie that had never meant anything anyway.

'I visited them once, you know . . . such heat . . . and the insects . . .' Aunt Violet sighed and pressed her handkerchief to her cheek, her eyes suddenly dreamy, lost in the kaleidoscope of her past.

Isobel sighed too, feeling helpless and a little bored.

'Isn't it time you were going?' Aunt Violet declared a few moments later, just as Isobel was wondering if she might venture the same opinion herself.

'Yes, probably.' The prospect of escape caused a rush of guilty tenderness. 'Don't forget the chocolates, will you? They're for your birthday.'

'Birthdays are hell,' came the retort, delivered through half-closed eyes that revealed tiny rivulets of blue where the morning's smudge of eyeshadow had collected. 'And if you meet any men, remember not to chase them. They don't like that, though they pretend to. And for heaven's sake do something with your hair,' she hissed, as Isobel scurried away, minding and wishing she didn't that the lady in the corner had probably heard every word of these curious farewells.

As she hurried across the gravelled driveway to her car, Isobel found herself putting her hands to her head, raking back the long tresses of her hair and pushing her fringe out of her eyelashes. But the wind only whisked it back again, tossing it round her ears and eyes so that she could barely see to put the key in the lock.

4 ∫

At a quarter to four, the Torbridge school rush-hour traffic was at its worst. Another good reason never to move out of town, thought Isobel with a scowl at the car clock as she realised that by the time they had had tea with the Howards and driven home again, it would be at least six thirty. She had done nothing about supper and the girls were bound to need cajoling through their homework. Sophie, who was six, was studying the body. Why did poor children look so fat? she had enquired at breakfast that morning, her mouth bulging with Coco-pops as she squinted at a pot-bellied famine victim pictured on the front of the newspaper. Isobel stumbled through several answers about air and emptiness before conceding that she could not offer a precise explanation as to why the human stomach should behave in such a contradictory fashion. 'And couldn't Father Christmas have left them some food?' had been the more challenging follow-up, much to the silent but manifest disgust of her elder, more worldy-wise sister. In the interests of protecting such endearing naïvety for another twelve months at least, Isobel took rather longer to complete her answer, right up to the end of the walk to school, in fact; by which time Megan, squirming at her sibling's relentless inquisitions, had wrapped her scarf around her ears by way of a protest. All that could be seen were her angry blue eyes, so like Ben's under the dark arches of her brows, and the tip of her nose, still pink from quite the worst cold that Isobel could remember. At the grand age of nine, she was showing increasing signs of tolerating rather than enjoying the company of her younger sibling. A fact which Sophie, a much more precocious and volatile six-year-old than

Megan had ever been, seemed to interpret as a challenge to be as annoying as possible at every opportunity.

On the back seat boredom had prompted a potentially explosive discussion concerning ownership of a comic whose battered covers had been littering the car for weeks. Sophie, having won possession of what remained of its pages, was in the process of rolling it up in preparation for use as a weapon. Unable to face the prospect of the rumpus that would ensue, Isobel, by endangering all their lives for several seconds, managed to turn and swipe the disputed item from her daughter's hands, tearing several more of its pages in the process.

'That's enough,' she shouted, venting rage that was as much connected to the traffic as her offspring. 'You two do not deserve to be going to tea with anybody. You have been behaving like animals and I'm sick of it. If you don't start being more considerate towards each other then I shall have to think up some serious punishments . . .' She faltered for a moment at the thought of quite what such castigation might entail. 'My big sister was my best friend when we were little,' she added weakly, thinking as she spoke that this was not an outright lie since she and Angela had always managed a façade of respect for each other's differences in preference to an open declaration of war.

'But she's not your best friend now, is she?' mumbled Sophie. 'Tilly and Ed's mum is.'

'That's right, Juliet is my best friend,' conceded Isobel, thinking somewhat ruefully that intimacy with a workaholic sister, whose prime passions were money markets and Swedish exercise machines, was not something that could be expected to come naturally to anybody.

The submissive silence behind her made Isobel feel guilty for her outburst. The children were the only people she dared to shout at, she realised with a start, the only people whose love she trusted with enough conviction to know that something as futile as a raised voice could do nothing to jeopardise it. When it came to Ben, she only shouted inside her head, where it was safe to make a noise, where nothing could be said that would make things any worse than they were already.

The Howards, on the other hand, had never been shy of the

occasional display of mutual antagonism. As their handsome new red-bricked Georgian home came into view, Isobel was reminded of several public marital spats about wallpaper designs and the space required to accommodate a downstairs lavatory. The house, which had been half restored by the previous owners until their funds had dried up and they were forced to sell, was set half a mile down the back route to Ilcombe village, along a pretty road lined with silver birches. By the time Isobel reached the Howards' drive their silvery trunks were gleaming in the late afternoon sun, casting a light that seemed to come from within the trees themselves rather than from the sky.

Was it simply a question of self-confidence? Isobel wondered, as she edged cautiously between the two gateposts, whose separating width seemed to narrow mysteriously as she approached. Was Juliet able to bare her teeth at James just because she possessed enough conviction – in both herself and her marriage – to do so? But then Juliet had other helpful character traits in her favour, she reflected; like a cunning knack for owning up to any doubts or shortcomings with such cheerful and open resignation that they instantly seemed irrelevant or endearing. In fact, thought Isobel, praying through half-closed eyes on her wing mirror's behalf as she edged forward, the only thing that ever seemed to cause Juliet any genuine exasperation were the eccentricities of her offspring – a pleasant, if boisterous, pair whom their mother had cast into the rigours of full-time school with a much-advertised and unabashed relief.

Isobel jerked up the handbrake, and winked at Megan's sulky reflection in the rear-view mirror. By contrast, motherhood was the one area of her own life with which she felt entirely at ease. From the first scissor-thrust of pain that would, some eight hours later, result in the birth of Megan – so different from the quick wrenching of the miscarriage the year before – Isobel had known instinctively that childbirth was something she would manage rather well, something she could even excel at. Mothering had followed with as much ease, all the well-publicised difficulties, like shortage of sleep and adapting domestic routines, being underpinned by a fundamental sureness of touch; a self-belief that came from nowhere and which she recognised as being as much a gift as the children themselves.

Miscarriages happened all the time, Isobel reminded herself, as the ache swelled inside. Caught by surprise, a part of her regarded the strength of the emotion with something like curiosity. So many years on from the event, such stabs of grief were fortunately few and far between. Unstrapping her belt in a businesslike way, she turned and managed a grin at the girls.

'Out you get.' But for a moment all she could see was the space on the seat between them. They were nearing the anniversary. He would have been ten; a big brother, tall and dark like Ben and Sophie.

'Mummy, are you going to cry?'

'No, Sophie, I am not,' she retorted, making a silly face and then smiling more genuinely as the pain eased away.

'I'm lusting after one of the workmen,' declared Juliet cheerfully a little while later, after the children had demolished platefuls of crusty jam sandwiches and two-thirds of a large chocolate cake. 'The short one with the deliciously long curly hair,' she went on, enjoying the expression on her friend's face as she ploughed up a blob of buttery icing from the rim of the cake board.

'Oh, Juliet, really, you're impossible.' Isobel shook her head with a smile and set about clearing dirty plates and mugs from the table.

'I've told James, naturally.'

'Naturally.'

'He took it very well. I think he finds it reassuring to know that the menopause has not yet affected my libido.'

'The menopause?'

'Well, not yet, I know. But it looms, my dear, it looms.' Having seen to all the excess icing on the board, Juliet embarked on a modest assault of the cake itself.

'Anyway, James says sex in the head is quite normal after a certain age.'

'Sex in the head?'

'Fantasy for the faithful, you know.'

'Oh yes.' Isobel, scraping crumbs into Juliet's large green plastic dustbin, wondered if the way she felt about Harrison Ford at the end of *Witness* counted. She didn't experience many sexual longings these days, except towards her husband, which she suspected wasn't what Juliet meant at all. And even then they weren't fantasies so much as memories, of how things once had been, when any faltering in their sex life had been something to apologise for instead of ignore. The steady decrease of physical intimacy between them – dwindling in recent months to barely any contact at all – was something which Isobel found hard to regard in any terms other than those of personal failure. Ben's angry reticence on the rare occasions she had dared to broach the subject had only driven the wedge between them deeper still. A deadlock of silence had been reached in consequence; an unwilling surrender, on her part anyway, which brought some relief, but considerable anxiety too. Sex had once seemed so very important. To have given up fighting for its reinstatement into their married life seemed the worst defeat so far.

'By the way, do thank James for coming to see Megan the other day.' Having loaded the dishwasher, Isobel returned to the table with a cloth and began steering crumbs into manageable piles. 'I was out, unfortunately – but Mrs Beety said by the time he got there she was, needless to say, sitting up looking horribly perky – though it really was flu and quite a bad bout at that—'

'Stop clearing up, for God's sake, Isobel,' interjected Juliet through a mouthful of cake. 'You're making me dizzy.' She had now cut herself a proper slice and was eating it with a fork; chiselling off mouse-sized mouthfuls, so as to delay the sad prospect of its disappearance for as long as possible.

'James mentioned he'd paid a house call. He adores playing the good Samaritan, it's how he gets his kicks. He's an old-fashioned dear at heart, you know, loves all that Dr Finlay business – doing his rounds with a black leather case and an avuncular smile. Loves hearing about his patients' private lives and all that. It's why he left hospital medicine so early on and opted for the GP routine.' She gave her fork one last lick and sighed. 'There was no real follow-up, he used to say.'

'Well, I was extremely grateful, so please tell him. The antibiotics did the trick at once.'

'So much gratitude – it'll go to his head.' Juliet got up to put the cake out of reach. 'They've got a date on Crofton College squash courts tonight, our men, haven't they,' she said absently, before being distracted by the view from the window above the sink. 'I say, do look at the children, they're playing like lambs.'

Isobel went to stand beside her. Although it was already quite dark, their four offspring, whose many years of acquaintance was no guarantee of harmony of any kind, had unanimously insisted on going outside. They were playing tag round the piles of rubble and mud, completely ignoring the swing and the spacious stretch of lawn beyond.

'We ought to go,' murmured Isobel, trying and failing to think what might be extracted from the fridge to form the basis of an evening meal. Megan being ill had thrown the whole week off course. She had achieved nothing positive at all, apart from visiting Aunt Violet. She opened her mouth to confide as much to Juliet and then closed it again, unwilling to sound as if she were angling for sympathy.

'What about a Greek island for our hols this year?' announced Juliet suddenly, reaching for a pile of magazines stacked on top of the fridge. 'It would be wonderfully hot and you can get villas at quite reasonable prices if you share. I've got a brochure here somewhere,' she muttered, flicking with some impatience through old copies of *Good Housekeeping* and unread parish magazines. 'It's almost spring after all, and you know how these things get booked up. Make a change, don't you think?'

'Yes, maybe. I'll talk to Ben about it.' Isobel smiled to make up for the lack of conviction in her voice. Attracted though she was to the idea of allowing Juliet to organise them all for a third summer in a row, other deeper instincts told her that to accept such an invitation might be unwise. A proper family holiday alone could be just what she and Ben needed. 'Might be a bit too hot,' she ventured, by way of further justification for her reticence. 'Oh, and good luck with your dashing workman,' she teased, mainly to change the subject, as she was pulling on her coat. 'Though I thought James still kept you far too happy to think about such things.'

'Oh, don't worry, James makes me deliriously happy . . . at least twice a year.' Shrieking with amusement at her own wit, Juliet disappeared to the back of the house to summon the children.

'I'll never get used to your living out here,' Isobel complained, as they sorted through the satchels and precarious items of artwork piled round a spindly chair in the hall.

'Well, you'll just have to move closer, then, won't you,' retorted Juliet, unable to stifle a tut-tut at the wedges of mud being scattered by the Tarrant children's shoes across her newly laid parquet floor.

Knowing this to be a remote possibility, Isobel kept her response to a smile, wondering all the while if the subtle but growing distance evident between her and Juliet was purely geographical, or whether it related to more complicated matters, like specks of mud on hall floors and worrying about the bricks of a house instead of the things it contained. She would hate to leave Torbridge, even if Ben could have afforded it. Unlike Juliet, who had always regarded even the short walk to St Leonard's as painful aerobic exercise, she loved having no need of a vehicle beyond the demands of Aunt Violet and the supermarket. She loved too, for equally passionate but less easily explained reasons, the fact that her husband still cycled everywhere on a bicycle with two working gears and a rusting mudguard.

Isobel had successfully negotiated her way back out on to the road when Juliet scurried out of the front door and through the gates, rubbing her elbows against the cold. 'By the way, I forgot to tell you – that week Ben's going camping in the wilds of Wales . . .'

'They go to a youth hostel, but never mind . . .'

'I was just going to say that it looks like I might be away then too.'

'Lucky old you. Whatever for?' Isobel hoped she didn't sound envious.

'A girl called Shelley, who's in my aromatherapy class, has invited me to go on a course with her – aromatherapy and reflexology, which is all about feet.' Juliet made a face. 'Bound to be interesting, though. Apparently it's in a fab hotel just outside Peterford. Quite a drive, but a great excuse to remind James of why he needs me,' she added, flexing the pretty crescents of her eyebrows at the dark sky, oblivious of the elegant silver birches swaying beside her, their limbs shimmering in the paltry half-light of the moon. 'Anyway' – she was now hopping from one foot to the other in an attempt to ward off the cold – 'I thought you two ought to get together, seeing as Ben's away as well. Being over the weekend and so on, it might be nice to organise something for the children.'

'Juliet, go inside this minute, you're freezing to death. We can talk about this on the phone.'

'I was only going to say Torbridge Theatre's putting on *Wind in the Willows* that Saturday afternoon – might be a nice treat for the children . . .'

'Sounds great. Now go inside,' commanded Isobel, winding up the window.

'I'll get tickets, then,' Juliet called, stepping back into a pile of workmen's sludge on the roadside, which caused her to think rather less enthusiastically of the youth whose charms she had been praising so freely just half an hour before.

5

Ben took his hands off the handlebars and settled back in his saddle to enjoy the rush of freewheeling down the tarmac slope that led from the main school, past the rugby pitches, to the sports hall. *La Traviata* pumped through the headphones of his Walkman. The music heightened the thrill of the ride: the black sky, the brilliant patterns of stars, the energising bite of the air. Ben breathed deeply and closed his eyes for an instant. Of all Verdi's operas, this was by far his favourite. A light pressure from his left thigh and he was taking the bend. Across the playing field on his right he could see a single light on in the science block. Dick Caulder, no doubt, the only member of staff ever to work as late as he did. Though in Caulder's case everyone knew it was a question of killing time, until the caretaker locked up and there were no more excuses to prevent him going home. Mrs Caulder had died the year before and the poor man was still in shock. Other staff said it was just as well there were no children. But Ben wasn't so sure. Sophie and Megan lit up his world in a way that he found both awesome and quite indescribable. His family was everything, he thought with a gulp of sentiment, a concrete backdrop without which he would function with even less coherence than he did already.

A squirrel scuttled across his path, making him swerve and almost fall. In the same instant the battery in his front light flickered and died. Unwillingly, Ben replaced his hands on the bars. He wanted to live after all. He had a squash match to win, a play to produce, a field trip to organise, a family to return to. The handsome square clock set in the stone façade of the science buildings warned he was already five minutes late – enough to make James irritated but not irredeemably so, thought Ben, grinning to himself as he brought his bike to a skidding halt outside the double swing doors that led past the swimming pool to the squash courts.

Apart from the thwack of rubber on wood and squeaks from the soles of their shoes, the two men played in a silence that was fraught with an intense but quite unmentionable sense of serious competition. The tactical pattern of their games seldom varied: Ben set the pace and did all the running, while James made up for their fifteen-year age difference and his own relative slowness with brazen cunning. On this occasion, however, Ben found his usual fount of energy seriously lacking. Rather than owning up to it, he fought on, charging from wall to wall with ever-diminishing hope or sense, feeling like some insect flapping against the confines of an airless box, the victim of some cruel schoolboy game. Smiling at defeat over the handshake afterwards felt unbearably hard, as did the inevitable gloating banter that accompanied their stroll back to the changing rooms. It was a relief to step under the hot jet of the showers. Ben turned his face up to the coursing water, full of frustration at himself, not for losing – which happened from time to time – but for minding so badly, for failing to be amused by the predictability of James's pleasure.

'How's Megan?' enquired James, stepping out of the next-door cubicle and wrapping his towel around his waist.

'Megan? Fine. Why?' Ben was already pulling on his clothes, tugging them impatiently over the numerous sections of his body that he hadn't dried properly.

James rolled his eyes in despair. 'Your daughter was ill last week, Tarrant. I had to pay a house call. Ring any bells?'

'Oh, of course – Isobel mentioned something about you coming round.' He wrestled his jumper over his head and began combing his fingers through his hair in a vain attempt to smooth down the wet curls. 'Meg's fine. Bit of a cold. Bolshie as a bloody teenager. God knows what we're going to have to put up with in a few years' time. She'll be consulting you about contraception before we know it,' he added, wrenching the show of good humour from somewhere deep inside.

'And Isobel's all right, is she?'

'Isobel?' Ben dropped his hands from his head and glanced up in genuine surprise. 'Isobel's absolutely fine,' he replied carefully. 'Had a bit of a cough a week or two ago, if I recall . . .'

'Good, good.' James slipped on his watch and busied himself with stuffing his sweat-soaked clothes in his holdall. 'Just thought she wasn't looking quite herself, that's all. A bit pale.'

Ben laughed. 'Isobel's always pale. She eats red meat like a Trojan. Hey, how about a drink?' he added, in a sudden burst of determination to blow his ill-humour away.

James, though sorely tempted, managed to refuse. 'Promised I'd be back by eight – more than my life's worth to be late.' He shot Ben a wry grin. 'Bitter experience and all that.'

Though Ben knew that he too should be getting home, his thirst remained quite unassuaged by the water fountain outside the sports hall. As he wheeled his bike back up the path, he found his gaze wandering once more across the playing fields. The light was still on. If Caulder didn't leave soon he'd be kicked out by Macgraw, the school's crusty old caretaker, who was thirsting for a pint himself by eight o clock.

When the sitting-room clock struck nine, Isobel's feelings towards the tired tail-end of stew she had rushed to unearth from the ice-packed recesses of her deep-freeze turned from apology to righteous indignation. Though hungry, she decided not to eat, as if such punishment of herself might punish Ben too, through guilt if nothing else. He had said nothing about being late. After his squash games he was usually back by eight at the latest. She stared at the handsome gilt-edged face of their carriage clock for a few minutes, thinking about her parents, who had given it to them as a wedding present, and wondering whether to call them or not. It would be a useful thing to do to fill the time; possibly pleasant too if her mother was in the mood to chat. Which she usually wasn't, she reminded herself, returning to the kitchen. A second glass of wine seemed a surer form of consolation for an evening that was turning out to be unpleasantly empty. A documentary on heart transplants saw her through the next hour, together with another glass of wine, drunk guiltily now, since she usually waited for Ben before opening a bottle at all. At ten o'clock she found herself peeking out of the sitting-room curtains at the empty street outside. A pretty dusting of frost covered the pavement and cars. A streetlamp flickering on and off a few yards past Druscilla's house lent a certain eeriness to the scene. Isobel dropped the curtain with a shiver and retreated once more to the back of the house and the uninspiring challenge of clearing a swathe through the clutter on the kitchen table. Even if supper never took place there was still breakfast to consider. The mess depressed her spirits further. The whole house needed a thorough sorting out, she told herself, staring morosely at the haphazard but cosy arrangement of the room and finding it impossible to imagine having things any other way.

A few minutes of prodding disconsolately at the lumpy contents of the saucepan convinced Isobel that her hunger had genuinely evaporated anyway. Having turned off the stove, she found herself traipsing to the bookcase that lived squashed up against the umbrella stand in the hall. After a moment, she pulled out the slim pocket-book-sized photo album, which she kept tucked between some old theatre programmes and a book called *Meals in Thirty Seconds* – a slim, useless directory which she had bought for Ben as a joke shortly after their return from Spain.

There weren't many pictures and what few there were had the blurred, overexposed look of bad flash photography. Being neither equipped nor in the mood to wield cameras themselves at the time, the nurses had performed the honours, explaining softly that parents were usually grateful in the end, even the ones that said they wanted only to forget. Isobel liked the one in the blanket the best, the brown pixie face peeping over the top of the silky trimming, as if he were merely dozing. On the opposite page she had stuck the death certificate, together with a tiny handprint – again done without request or fuss by one of the nurses – and his identity tag. *Toby Tarrant*. For a while Isobel felt nothing, which was disappointing. To fuel her emotions, she plyed her memory, dredging up every last detail, right down to the glassy eyes of the pale nurse, and the earnest young doctor who had talked so unfeelingly and at such length about the needs of a uterus to expel an 'infected product'. In cases of listeria infection, survival at twenty-four weeks was highly unlikely, it was explained, time and time again, until the words sounded meaningless. The blanket picture had been taken right at the end, before the portly hospital chaplain floated in offering kindly, hushed condolences and leaflets on bereavement.

Isobel rocked slowly, still on her knees beside the bookcase, holding the album to her chest, inviting her heart to burst and feeling some frustration at its failure to co-operate. During the months following their loss, crying alone was something at which she had become rather proficient; partly because she grew embarrassed at her own aptitude for tears, and partly because of the alienating effect it gradually seemed to have on Ben. As the weeks went by, the increasingly detectable effort behind his attempts at sympathy during her bouts of weeping undermined any solace he sought to provide. Though he would sit with one arm draped dutifully round her heaving shoulders, Isobel sensed something in his silence that felt like impatience, as if one surreptitious eye never left the clock; as if he were merely sitting it out rather than riding alongside. Sometimes, during the bad early days, she had even caught herself wondering whether these stoical silences in fact contained any recognisable human emotions at all. Such crises of hostility passed, however, aided both by the speed with which she got pregnant again, and the realisation that the person least likely to be equipped to offer any help was the one closest to her own suffering. In the end, time had proved the most effective aid to convalescence, assisted greatly by Juliet Howard, whom she had met while attending breathing lessons for Megan.

After a while – and somewhat to Isobel's relief – the tears came. Self-inflicted pain, but nonetheless carthatic for that, she told herself, letting the sobs take over, and rather relishing the images of sweet baby innocence that danced across her mind. She thought of the approaching anniversary and wept harder. For years now, the date had passed unnoticed save by her and Ben. Though he probably only remembered it because she reminded him, Isobel reflected bitterly, gripping the book in her lap more tightly and vowing, with a sniff of self-pity, never to mention the subject of their lost firstborn again. Somewhere in the midst of this last indulgence, however, burst the uncomfortable realisation that she was crying not about the miscarriage at all, but about Ben himself and the fact that he seemed to have stopped loving her. The effect was sobering. Finding a wife in a gibbering heap on the hall carpet would do little to increase a husband's waning ardour, she scolded herself, slamming the album shut and roughly shoving it back into its slot.

The familiar creak of the rusty hinge of their front gate roused Isobel still further from this nosedive into self-inflicted misery. Hurriedly, she tugged at her hair and wiped her nose with the back of her hand in a bid to appear welcoming; self-disgust having by now dispelled all other, less friendly emotions. I just want him to love me, she thought weakly, splashing water on her face from the kitchen tap before returning to the hall, the picture of fresh-faced fortitude. If they had weathered losing a baby, they could certainly weather whatever storm was besetting them now, she told herself, wondering whether she had it in her to smile as he opened the door.

Ben Tarrant had always made a meek and rather endearing drunk, particularly when his handsome features were suffused with the smiling penitence of one who, even as he crawls for remission, does so in the delightful certainty that forgiveness is just around the corner. Such was the expression on his face as he approached his front door, having, with considerable difficulty, locked his bike to the railings separating their scrawny rose beds from Druscilla Carew's. The simplest movements were becoming tantalisingly hard, Ben observed, recalling with some indignation all Caulder's game attempts to assist him in the challenge of mounting his bicycle in the empty carpark behind the Red Lion pub. The recollection of the demise of his front light had eventually provided an honourable pretext for admitting to the necessity of wheeling as opposed to cycling the bike home. He had set off very carefully, taking the dainty, exaggeratedly high steps of one whose perceptions of ground level have been somewhat distorted by the effect of six pints of real ale on an empty stomach. He crossed roads only when little green men indicated that he was permitted to do so, even though this necessitated standing on one empty street corner for so long that a watchful policeman reached for his notebook.

At the sight of Isobel, who opened the door while he was still waiting for the keyhole to co-operate with the modest demands of his key, he experienced a rush of choking and largely incoherent remorse.

'Darling – so late – so sorry.' He put his arms round her and pulled her close. She could smell the beer on his breath and the pub smoke in his clothes. 'Got sidetracked – sorry.'

'Did you have a drink with James, then?' she asked, melting at such penitence, but feeling that a little frostiness was called for all the same.

'No, with Dick Caulder. Chap whose wife died, you know. Dreadfully cut up. Can't bear to go home, poor devil. Kept him company.' Ben threw his coat on to the hall chair and stifled a burp. It took revenge a few moments later in the form of noisy hiccoughs, which had an annoyingly deflating effect on the gravitas of anything he tried to say.

'Poor Mr Caulder,' she murmured, leading the way into the kitchen in search of water.

'Sorry for being late, love,' he muttered, shuffling after her and proceeding to take grateful gulps of water between hiccoughs.

Watching him, Isobel could not help smiling.

'Still love me?' He cocked his head at her sheepishly.

'Yes, silly,' she whispered, stepping into his outstretched arms.

'Christ, I love you Isobel, so very much,' he rasped, spilling water on the floor as they kissed.

'We can't go on like this Ben . . . we need to talk . . .'

He had to lean on her for the walk upstairs.

'To talk . . . absolutely . . .'

A few minutes later he was sound asleep, leaving his wife to converse with the muffled clicks issuing from the airing cupboard on the landing. The clicks, which were generated by their old but perfectly functioning boiler, had so unnerved Megan at one stage of her early childhood that she had gone to sleep for weeks with sections of her nightie stuffed into her ears.

Alone in the dark, all Isobel's doubts resurfaced, charged by the unhappy acknowledgment of the fact that it had taken alcohol to prompt the kind of passionate declaration for which she had been longing; the kind of declaration to which once, a long time ago, she had been treated almost every day. The past rose like a wall again, reminding her of what she had lost, not as a mother, but as a wife. She missed the certainty of his love. The intensity of it. I need to feel that I am loved, she thought hopelessly, all inward recriminations that such emotions might be naïve as well as self-indulgent for middle-aged housewives with busy husbands doing nothing to blow any of them away.

She started to count the noises coming from the boiler in the hope of lulling herself to sleep. But that night, the clicks, usually so steady and companionable, seemed to have a menacing ring, like the inexorable countdown to calamity.

6 ∫

Torbridge library was housed in a smudgy red-bricked Victorian building that was said to have once been an asylum for the mentally insane. While its interior had received enough coats of pastel paints over the years to obliterate any trace of this disturbing history, there was still something ominous about the high metal balustrade that ran round its perimeters and the poky windows of its upper floors, where the less popular subjects like philosophy and economics were housed. Isobel, whose patchy interest in literature had never quite recovered from the interruption of motherhood, had only really become familiar with the place on account of the children. During earlier, difficult days, before videos and board games had been sufficient child-care props for wet afternoons, she had frequently wheeled prams and pushchairs the mile or so from her front door to the library's imposing entrance, grateful for the change of scenery, if nothing else.

On visiting the library a couple of weeks after her husband's unscheduled drink with Dick Caulder, Isobel found some of these early memories coming back at her with unusual poignancy, reminding her of other ways in which times had changed. There had been workshops on puppets and mask-making, she remembered fondly, and rowdy percussion sessions with a girl with café-au-lait skin and glittery blue nails that curled over her fingertips.

Peering through the glass doors of the children's section on this occasion, however, she could see that the place was deserted apart from a lanky-haired woman breast-feeding a baby, and a ruddy-faced toddler rolling and moaning round the floor space at her feet. It was almost lunch-time – not the hour for small children to visit libraries, Isobel reminded herself, withdrawing to the adults' section and rummaging in the side pocket of her handbag for the list she had forced herself to compose during a brief session in the study that morning.

19th Cent. eg Jane Austen, George Eliot, Thomas Hardy, Charles Dickens Literature & Gender eg Wilkie Collins, Ibsen, Louisa May Alcott, Tolstoy

Such were Isobel's modest extrapolations from the description of a course under the Arts and Languages section, entitled *Approaching literature: authors, readers, texts.* The course was coded A310 and, if Isobel understood the accompanying symbols and numbers correctly, it cost three hundred and twenty pounds, took one academic year to complete and would give her sixty points towards the three hundred and sixty required for a fully fledged degree. Since it sounded like quite a mountain to climb, and a potentially pretentious one at that, she had come to the library with the vague aim of getting a better feel for precisely what she would be letting herself in for. The other option – suggested in one of her booklets – of seeking guidance from a member of staff at her nearest Open University Regional Centre, was simply too daunting to contemplate.

Isobel had alighted upon A310 for the embarrassingly pedestrian reason that most of the names of the authors were recognisable. That this was thanks largely to a spate of recent dramatisations of the classics on television did not exactly fan the embers of her self-conviction over the project. 'You're doing it for something to do,' sneered a voice inside her head, while another countered, more reasonably, that this was better than doing nothing at all. So it was with some trepidation that Isobel approached the section headed *A – D Fiction* and began skimming her eyes along the shelves in search of the works of Jane Austen. When *Pride and Prejudice* had been on the telly she had got as far as hovering in front of the stack of reissued paperbacks on the bestseller stand in Smith's, tempted but resisting, hating the notion of being driven towards a purchase like a sheep being herded into a pen.

If only they hadn't all written so much, she thought with a

sigh, her courage faltering as her trailing fingers reached the fat spines of Eliot and Dickens, while the sneering voice reminded her that these days it was all she could do to flip through a magazine from the weekend papers before falling asleep. A book Juliet had recommended at the end of the summer still sat beside her bed, underneath a travelogue about the Himalayas given to her by her parents that Christmas; it had breathtaking photographs, but tiny compressed lines of print that made her squint. Juliet's book was one of a series written by an author whose chief protaganist was both a female detective and a gourmet cook. Every murder was intricately and skilfully tied up with food, the blurb said, which put Isobel off for a start; though Juliet had been so enthusiastic she still felt she ought to read the thing before handing it back.

Archibald Heighton-Jones, the new young curate at St Cuthbert's, who was not as engrossed as he would have liked to have been in some haphazard research for an ambitious sermon on the subject of poverty, caught sight of Isobel and wondered if he dared offer a nod of greeting. Though she was by no means a regular churchgoer, he knew her well enough by sight. He knew several other things about her too: that she had two daughters, one dark and one with copper curls, who attended St Leonards, the Church of England school on the road past the old bus station; that her husband was head of geography at Torbridge's illustrious Crofton College; and that they lived in Fox's Crescent next to the mad lady with the cats. Whether such information, acquired indirectly and even a little deviously, constituted a sufficient pretext for a direct approach, however, was a matter on which Archie felt altogether less certain. Pressing his index finger to the bridge of his long nose, as if literally to pin himself to his task, he sighed heavily and returned his gaze to the atlas open on the table in front of him. Beside his books lay a blank sponsor form for a twenty-five-mile walk in aid of breast cancer. Flora Dobbs, who organised the St Cuthbert's flower rota, a woman of intimidatingly vast proportions, had asked – or rather commanded – that he offer his support, regaling him with details of sick and dying victims with a directness that had been both harrowing and a little embarrassing. Submission had offered the only immediate release. Though in the longer term he had found himself more ensnared than ever: with the common bond of the walk to bind them, the woman now assailed him at every opportunity, summoning him to teas and Sunday lunches with a voracious enthusiasm that made Archie afraid. No young curate was safe with such widows around, he decided, with a shudder of pity for the husband whose uncooperative heart valves had apparently released him to an early grave. The thought caused Archie's eyes to stray from his papers again, whereupon he discovered – with a flush of alarm and pleasure – that the object of his earlier speculations was staring right at him.

Isobel nodded and smiled, recognising at once the new addition to the bottom ranks of the complicated religious hierarchy that governed all matters relating to St Cuthbert's. As he eagerly nodded back, she caught herself wondering fondly whether the defiant springiness of his ginger hair stemmed from defeat or a lack of vanity.

'It's Isobel, isn't it?' ventured Archie, scraping back his chair so loudly as he stood up that several studious faces glared in his direction. He considered holding out his hand, but at the last minute changed his mind and stuffed it into his jacket pocket instead. He was never sure about shaking hands, or kissing for that matter, which seemed to be of increasing vogue amongst the most lightweight acquaintances. He still found the Peace in church awkward enough, though had high hopes of it improving alongside his familiarity with St Cuthbert's parishioners. 'A lover of literature, I see,' he said, indicating the books in her basket and inwardly kicking himself for saying something so inept and pompous.

'Oh no.' Isobel smiled and shook her head. 'Though I'm considering trying to be. I'm thinking of doing a course – improving my mind,' she added with a self-deprecating grin that made Archie sure her mind needed no improving whatsoever.

'What's that, a sponsor form?' She cocked her head at the piece of paper dangling in his left hand.

'Oh, this . . .' He frowned at the form, as if its presence between his finger and thumb was a matter of pure coincidence. 'This . . .'

'Breast cancer. What a worthy cause. Would you like me to sign?' She set her basket on the table and began digging in her handbag for a pen, irritably pushing her hair out of her eyes as she did so. 'Do you promise not to do more than twenty-five miles? I mean, is it safe for me to say ten pence a mile? . . .'

It was a moment or two before he realised she was teasing him. 'Oh, I promise – don't worry at all – I'm a devilishly slow walker – probably won't even get that far.'

'Let me see, that will make my final bill – oh, heavens – two pounds fifty. That is right, isn't it? It's not twenty-five pounds? I'm so hopeless at decimal points . . . I just know I've got a pen in here somewhere,' she murmured, seizing a battered tampon by mistake and hurriedly burying it again.

'Good heavens, use mine,' exclaimed Archie, handing over the Biro with which he had been making notes and happily wringing his hands while Isobel wrote her name and pledge in neat capitals.

'I'm completely useless at sums of any kind,' he volunteered cheerfully. 'And my general knowledge is lousy too.' He nodded at his books and papers. 'Can't write a thing without help. But I do think it's so important to get the facts right.' He scowled, his thoughts straying for a moment to the exact whereabouts of Zaire, one of the many reasons for his presence in the library. Somewhere amongst his possessions was an atlas, but his digs were so small that he had had to ship a lot of things back to his parents in Cheshire. Most of the books and ornaments he had kept were still in boxes as it was.

'But I bet you know the Bible,' said Isobel kindly, responding to the look of dejection that flashed across his face. 'All that time at theological college or whatever.'

'Oh yes, I know that pretty well. Though how to use it – with people, I mean – is – can be – tricky.'

'I'm sure it can.'

'Have you read this?' Seeing she was about to go, Archie seized a book at random from the collection in her basket.

'No. Have you?'

'Well, no . . . but I've heard of it . . . of course . . . *Anna Karenina* . . . ah yes, very famous.'

'All I know is she gets married and then commits passionate adultery with a glamorous count.'

'Does she? Oh dear.'

'Lives in sin and causes a frightful scandal,' continued Isobel matter-of-factly, taking the book from him and returning it to her basket. Upon glancing up, she was astonished to find that the young priest was blushing; his ears were a particularly vibrant red. 'Well, I'd better get on . . .' she murmured, not knowing whether to be impressed or concerned by evidence of such fragile sensibilities.

'Thank you for your support,' he whispered loudly, flapping his sponsor form in appreciation as she moved away. 'And best of luck with all that reading.'

'Thanks,' she mouthed back, feeling an absurd spurt of encouragement and wishing that Ben's reaction could have been as simple and positive. Instead, he had grilled her about her long-term motives and the time and money it would involve, echoing all the reservations she had been fighting to overcome herself. Every trace of the tipsy affection demonstrated on the night of the squash game had clearly been blasted away by the headache to which he awoke the following morning. Ever hopeful, Isobel had taken care to be obviously tender herself for the next few days, showing in every word and look that a show of love would be welcome, that her affection only needed the light of his to be sparked into life. But Ben, if he noticed such invitations, gave no indication of doing so, coming home each night with ever-darkening looks and a briefcase full of marking for the following day.

He had left for Wales that morning, amidst the usual last-minute flurry of sandwich-making and locating vital, missing items. The disappearance of his cagoule from the peg in the hall caused such a stir of ill-temper that both girls were drafted to join in the hunt. Just as they were all on the point of giving up, Sophie extracted it with a triumphant squeal from the bottom of the old crate in which Isobel kept their wellingtons.

'It must have fallen in.'

'Must have,' he muttered, glowering at her before turning a beam of gratitude on his gleeful daughter.

Outside, some drifting grey clouds were beginning to drizzle with rain.

'At least they can't go without you,' Isobel reassured him, by way of reference to the white minibus parked outside their own front door.

Ben hugged the girls goodbye and swung his rucksack over one shoulder.

'I'll come out and wave you off,' she volunteered, grabbing an umbrella.

She stood, within the safe dripping circle of her brolly, while Ben stowed away his belongings, ignoring all attempts of hers to shield his head. Soon, his hair was soaked to a shining black and the shoulders of his jacket were sodden.

'Don't forget your picnic.' She held out a plastic box containing four beef sandwiches and a pear. She raised the umbrella several inches so that he could step under it to say goodbye. 'Give me a ring, won't you?'

'Of course, but you've got the number of the hostel in any case.' His voice was impatient, his mind already on the few days ahead, on the taxing but rewarding business of herding a group of seventeen-year-olds round cliff-faces and pubs.

'Yes,' she murmured dutifully, all the while thinking that if past years were anything to go by, there was never a good time to call. And if he ever got around to phoning her it was usually quite some time after she had fallen asleep.

'See you Sunday night, then. Have fun at the theatre or whatever. Look after the girls. And if Miss Harris rings about any costume problems tell her I don't want to know.'

Isobel had nodded, wishing he would hug her instead of talking, and wondering how long a love that got nothing in return could last. Even a very deep love, which had started with all the blinding conviction of a religious conversion.

The memory of her husband's brief kiss of farewell was not inspiring, reflected Isobel gloomily, dumping a pile of books beside the computer on the librarian's desk and thinking that the rain on Ben's face had left more of an impression than the touch of his lips on her cheek.

Druscilla Carew was practising the tango with a cushion clasped between her arms when she caught sight of Isobel Tarrant between a gap in her net curtains. Pretty hair, but such a dismal taste in clothes, she thought, sliding one step closer to her unsuspecting neighbour, who was clutching a pair of secateurs and staring doubtfully at the brown stumps of rosebushes in their adjoining shoe box of a front garden. Such was Druscilla's pity for these poor mismanaged plants that she had on occasions been known to nurture them with some secret recipes of her own. Tea leaves and milk in particular. Without such clandestine care she was certain they would never have produced any buds at all. Withdrawing her eyes from her window for a moment, Druscilla stamped her left foot back alongside her right and brought her warbling accompaniment to a vibrato flourish of a finale, squeezing the cushion to her chest like a lover.

'Now don't look so jealous and silly,' she scolded, addressing a honey-coloured Persian cat draped across the closed lid of her piano. Wagging her index finger at the animal, she left the room in search of the pink scarf she had knitted herself that winter by way of an inspired precaution against the cold. The wool was a delicious furry fluorescent pink, spangled with myriad flecks of silver. The pattern had included a hat too, but Druscilla distrusted hats; even the prettiest ones seemed to squash all the bounce out of her hair and make her scalp itch like the devil.

'Isobel, how nice.'

Druscilla's head appearing so suddenly over the flimsy wind-blown fence dividing their properties made Isobel jump. She was wearing her awful scarf – a neck brace of candy floss, as

Ben had so wickedly dubbed it – and clashing gashes of scarlet across her lips.

'How are you, Druscilla? Enjoying all this sunshine?' Isobel squinted up at the inky blue which had appeared as if by magic that morning, its dazzle quite making up for the grey blur of all the weeks that had gone before. 'Spring is here at last,' she murmured, continuing to lop off any stems that didn't look a perfect green.

'The girls on holiday yet?'

'Oh no, not for a while . . .'

'Time for a cup of coffee?'

'I don't think so, I'm afraid, Druscilla. Thank you – sweet of you to ask – but I've heaps to do.' Isobel paused in her snipping in order to make a show of looking at her watch.

'You're cutting too low,' exclaimed her neighbour, wringing her hands in a drama of compassion.

'Oh, they'll survive,' replied Isobel with an airiness she did not quite feel and, driven by some wicked instinct, starting to cut lower still.

Druscilla turned away and picked up a black cat for comfort. 'On your own, then?' she remarked slyly. She had witnessed Ben's departure the previous morning for herself, from the slit in the curtains of her front bedroom window.

'Yes. Ben's taken his upper-sixth group to the Welsh coast to study rock formations and things. Lots of limestone layers and so on to help them through their A-levels.'

'I could bring the coffee out here,' declared Druscilla suddenly, as if the response to her earlier invitation had never been made. 'It's really quite nice, isn't it? Milk no sugar, I know,' she added briskly as she trotted back inside her house, leaving Isobel to roll her eyes heavenward, cursing whichever omniscient creature had been responsible for awarding them such a co-resident in an otherwise very amicable and undemanding street. Being an end-of-terrace house, they at least enjoyed the luxury of having no one to worry about on the other side; though Isobel sometimes thought it would take quite a lot more than that to make up for the dubious neighbourliness to which she was habitually subjected by Druscilla.

The object of these uncharitable speculations returned a few minutes later with two cups, which she set down on the pinewood bird table that formed the centrepiece of her own contrastingly ordered front garden. 'And here's some change for the children.' She pressed two warm fifty-pence pieces into Isobel's hand. 'I know it's not much these days . . .'

'Really, Druscilla, you shouldn't.' Isobel tried to hand the coins back, but to no avail.

'They're lovely girls and they deserve it.'

'Well, thank you, they'll be thrilled,' replied Isobel, staring at the money, while she struggled to reconcile the small confusions of distaste and gratitude caused by such unexpected and inappropriate generosity. She offered Druscilla the first genuine smile since their exchange had begun, wishing she could bring herself to like the woman more, wishing she could feel warmth rather than distrust at all her prying conversational ways. She appeared well intentioned enough, though there was something sinister about the scaffolding of dyed black hair, back-combed to such an unnaturally high distance from its roots that there were visible gaps between each strand, like spaces in a wood of trees. Her eyebrows were starkly blackened too, thick grimaces, half an inch or so above the faint mousey line where nature had clearly destined the original articles to be. But then there was no crime in heavy make-up, Isobel quickly reminded herself, thinking fondly of Juliet cursing into a matchbox-sized mirror on the wall of a caravan the summer before. Juliet refused to approach even a swimming pool without lipstick and lashings of non-drip mascara.

'I expect you miss that friend of yours, don't you,' commented Druscilla with quite unwitting perspicacity a few moments later. 'The one that did those adverts for that butter spread?' She hummed the tune as a reminder, heedless of the fact that Isobel was more than familiar with the main commercial triumph of Juliet Howard's career. 'Where's it they've gone?'

'Ilcombe.'

'That's right – lovely. Pity for you, though . . .'

'Not at all. It's not far. The children still go to St Leonards and next year Eddie will start at Crofton, where Ben teaches, so I'm sure we'll still see lots of each other.'

'Should have had boys really, shouldn't you,' Druscilla exclaimed with a sudden cackle, only just struck by the irony of which the Tarrants themselves had long been aware, that the generous discount offered to children of teachers at Crofton College was quite irrelevant for a family of female offspring.

'We should,' replied Isobel, biting her lip, glad that her delightful neighbour had arrived after the birth of Megan rather than before. 'Careless of us, wasn't it,' she added with a light laugh, while inwardly she quailed at the thought of the conversational possibilities Druscilla would have found in a subject so inviting as a miscarriage.

'Well, I can't stand here chatting,' declared Druscilla abruptly, seizing Isobel's mug and flinging the dregs on to her lawn. 'Some of us have work to do.'

'Don't let me keep you,' murmured Isobel, trying not to feel indignant at the insinuated reprimand. Quite what such work was supposed to comprise remained a mystery, since the woman was clearly well into her fifties and seldom left the house except to buy tins from the mini-market two streets away, or to walk one of her cats round the cathedral close. The religious atmosphere was good for their souls, she said.

After her neighbour had gone back inside, Isobel dawdled in the front garden for a few moments longer, taking deep breaths of the fresh sun-filled air and marvelling at how bound to the seasons human moods still were. Perhaps Ben would call that night, she thought, her spirits lifting still further, buoyed both by the weather and the ease of loving someone at a distance. She wondered what he would have made of her reading till the small hours, as she had the night before, drawn in by the quite unexpected pleasure of encountering Jane Austen first hand. Having opted for *Pride and Prejudice* for the shamefully simplistic reason that it looked a more manageable length than some of the others, and because, thanks to the TV, she was at least familiar with the cast of characters, the enjoyment had come as something of a shock. Even the Mrs Bennet character, whom she had found so grating on-screen, made her laugh out loud. What struck her most forcefully, however, were the social constraints endured by the characters, the painful infrequency with which anyone could truly speak their mind. Thank God for telephones and liberality, she had thought, turning out her bedside light at last and hugging generous wadges of the double duvet round her chin. Whereupon it occurred to her that even without nineteenth-century codes of behaviour to bind them, most humans were still busy performing daily social rituals that did little to illuminate the machinations going on inside their heads.

The character of Darcy accompanied Isobel on the gentle slide towards sleep. Not because she found the literary version any more appealing than his soaked-shirt screen counterpart, but because it vexed her that a fictional hero could get away with appearing romantic by saying practically nothing at all; when in real life such emotional reticence and simmering silences felt only worrying and unkind.

8

'I've put the tickets in an envelope on the hall table. The plate covered in tinfoil is some old bits of lettuce and carrot for Eddie's rabbit and the bowl with clingfilm on is the stew for you. I've mashed some potatoes and left them in the saucepan ready to heat up. Add a dab of butter and milk too, remember, or it will be too lumpy and dry. And a sprinkle of nutmeg is nice, if you can be bothered, which I expect you can't. The microwave is still being funny, but if you press the button twice it usually works. If the children demand waffles for breakfast there are some in the deep-freeze, between the fish fingers and the pizza with the olives on top. I've put out a cheque for the milkman and given the children their pocket money. If Eddie asks to let that creature of his loose in the house again, by the way, the answer is no. I'm still finding those horrid little pellets from the last time, when he *promised* it wouldn't happen.'

'Eddie's rabbit broke a promise?' murmured James absently, his attention more engrossed by the local paper than his wife's instructions. He would muddle through somehow. At least, being a weekend there were no challenges relating to urgent time-keeping or the mysterious intricacies of school uniform and lunch boxes. 'Perhaps we could skin the rabbit and grill it instead of the waffles,' he went on, warming to his theme. 'That way no rabbit dropping could ever darken our doors – or should I say floors – again.'

'James, don't be vile.' Juliet planted an affectionate kiss on the top of his head and took a bite from the piece of toast on his plate. 'Are you going to miss me?'

'Dreadfully.'

'You're not, are you? You're going to be a slob and enjoy every moment.'

He winked at her for a reply before returning his attention to the paper. 'Someone wants to turn St Cuthbert's into an arts centre.'

'Hasn't Torbridge got enough of those?'

'It's got enough churches too, for that matter.'

'I must go.' She looped her green silk scarf round his neck and used it to pull his head close to hers. 'Now, you be good. Not too many sweeties in the theatre and be nice to Isobel.'

'I'm always nice to Isobel.'

'I know, but extra specially.' She kissed him on the lips and then lightly on the nose. 'She's got that forlorn look about her at the moment. I don't think she's eating enough.'

'I'll buy her an ice cream in the interval . . .'

'James, do try and be serious for one second.'

He held up his hands. 'I will, I will. Isobel will receive all my kindest attentions. I thought myself that she wasn't looking well – I mentioned it to Ben, as a matter of fact . . .'

Juliet snorted. 'Ben, bless his cotton underpants, wouldn't notice if Isobel was at death's door. He's an undeniably wonderful man – infinitely handsome and full of talent' – she sighed – 'but really too wrapped up in his own world sometimes . . .' She stooped to examine her appearance in the hall mirror, batting away a few corkscrew curls that had flopped below her eyebrows. 'She couldn't be brooding about the miscarriage again, do you think? . . . It's *so* hard to ask about these things . . .'

'The miscarriage?' James put down the paper. 'But that was decades ago.'

'I know, James, I know. But Isobel's the type. It was around this time of year, you know – I forget which date exactly now . . . It was only a thought,' she muttered defensively, prompted by the look of incredulity on her husband's face. She pressed her lips together and pouted at her reflection. 'I'm probably wrong. As you so rightly say, my sweet, it was a long time ago. For all I know Isobel is suffering from constipation or lack of sleep. I hardly see her these days. How do I look?'

'Ravishing.'

'I'm going to say goodbye to the children. I won't phone

tonight, in case it upsets them. I've left the hotel number by the bed.'

'Remind me exactly what you are going to be doing this weekend?' he said softly, putting his arms round the comfy spread of his wife's waist and squeezing hard.

'The Hotel Primavera near Peterford, to learn about oil and feet.' She made a face.

'And how much are we paying for this privilege?'

'Peanuts, darling, I promise,' Juliet replied hurriedly, trying to prise herself free. 'It's all part of my education. Think of all those lovely massages you're going to get,' she added impishly. 'I'll need to practise an awful lot if I'm to qualify.'

'Is that a promise?' he murmured, nuzzling her neck and enjoying the way she squirmed to get free. 'Don't go, my sparrow.'

'Got to,' she whispered, reluctantly pushing him away and disappearing off in search of the children.

Such fond farewells left James feeling more bereft than he had expected, especially since Tilly, who was usually as tough as nails, decided on an outburst of tears that took almost an entire pack of chocolate biscuits and half a video to resolve. Eddie, meanwhile, groaned antagonistically at the cartoon princesses frolicking on the screen, before shuffling up to his room in disgust. Perhaps it was going to be a long weekend after all, he mused with a sigh, checking the carriage clock on the sitting-room mantelpiece for a countdown to the theatrical extravaganza promised for the afternoon: five hours, with the small challenge of lunch to get through in between. Daunted by hazy recollections concerning the quite separate roles required of Tupperware and pudding basins, James found himself toying with the idea of eating out instead. Pizza Hut maybe. The prospect raised his spirits sufficiently for him to treat himself to a biscuit and to embark on one of the many unread medical journals piled on the coffee table beside him. He had got as far as 'Craniosynostosis – premature closure of different cranial joints may . . .' before being interrupted by the observation that his daughter was feeding biscuit to a rabbit, and that his son was hanging over the banisters bellowing something incoherent about a missing piece of Meccano.

*   *   *

They had reached the far side of Ilcombe Woods before James realised that the theatre tickets remained in the silver saucer on the hall table; at which point not even the thought of a lifetime's supply of aromatic massages could appease his attitude as regards his wife's absence. Juliet, as his son took pleasure in reminding him, would not have forgotten the tickets, nor indeed the whereabouts of a Meccano spanner. Their mother had turned domestic organisation into an art form, agreed James acidly, as they doubled back into the busy traffic from which they had just emerged. To intensify their father's suffering still further, the children responded to this additional postponement of lunch by groaning for food. A packet of extra strong mints, unearthed with some triumph from the dusty recesses of the glove compartment, offered little consolation. Were they behaving badly, or was he simply too old to be a father? brooded James, reversing out of their drive after their unscheduled return home with such aggression that he only just managed to avoid collision with a passing cyclist.

'Wicked, Dad,' gasped Eddie, in ill-judged appreciation of the brake screech that accompanied this manoeuvre.

It was unusual for James Howard to harbour any misgivings at all about his suitability and skills as a parent. The relative lateness of his acquaintance with the delights of fatherhood had been quite deliberate, stemming not only from a wise caution about being the author of such lifelong ties, but also from a hearty enjoyment of bachelordom. In his heyday as a young doctor he had experimented with partners like a lover of exotic food, trying out new colours and flavours in an endless quest for surprise and gratification. With several London hospitals and hordes of pretty nurses on which to feed, such appetites were richly served. It was only when Juliet crossed his path, a delectably curvaceous package of good humour and sensuality, then shackled to a nearly famous actor with a bald head and short legs, that James became convinced he had finally encountered a creature who could satisfy his tastes and needs on a long-term scale. That he had been forced to work for her attentions only sharpened this conviction. His capacity for jealousy had been tremendous, both on account of the actor – who took some time to absorb any scenario that did not include himself – and the demands of Juliet's career as a whole, then bird-hopping along between disappointment and relative success. In his more honest moments, James recognised that such jealousy had probably been far more instrumental in his agreement to whisk his wife away to premature retirement in Torbridge than any serious concern for his own career path. Sometimes, he even caught himself missing the emotional trauma of the early days, when the mere sight of her strutting her stuff on stage had been enough to fill him with paroxysms of possessive envy and pride. More prosaically, James was also beginning to feel some nostalgia for the repeat fees and other haphazard payments which had constituted his wife's income at that time. Endearing though it was, Juliet's enthusiasm for channelling her creative energies into courses on basket weaving and body massage was beginning to tell on the family expenses. Even the sight of the prices printed on the theatre tickets prompted James to embark on a quick mental recap of what they had spent on the house and what Eddie's fees at Crofton would add to their outgoings over the coming year.

The package had been placed, somewhat unimaginatively, in a litter bin between the multistorey carpark and the start of the cobbled shopping precinct that led down towards the theatre. More imaginative were its contents, which contained enough explosives to kill the homeless old man who had the misfortune to be poking round the contents of the bin when the bomb went off, and to injure all those strolling past within a radius of twenty yards. It was a small device by modern terrorist standards, but nonetheless shocking for that.

Isobel and James, sitting amongst hundreds of other families enjoying the sight of Toad disguising himself as a washerwoman, gasped in unison as the noise and tremors shook the theatre. It was so loud, but over so fast. For a few moments there was complete silence. The actor playing the part of Toad stopped in mid-speech, his lacy bonnet flopping comically over one half of his face, his white dress barely concealing the checked plus-fours underneath. In the next instant, no doubt compelled by ancient adages about shows and going on, he attempted to rediscover his lines. But his voice was quickly drowned by the murmurs of fear and speculation, which rose to a crescendo as the unmistakable sound of Torbridge's emergency services could be heard, whining into action outside.

Toad pulled off his hat and looked to the wings for inspiration. All about them children were asking questions in breathy, high-pitched voices while their adult escorts grabbed hats and coats and began herding them along the rows towards the aisles. An atmosphere of contained panic prevailed. Just as the murmurings reached a fever pitch all the lights on the stage were flicked on and the theatre manager, looking somehow noble in his black tie and shiny patent shoes, appeared before them clutching a microphone.

'Ladies and gentlemen . . . children . . . please stay in your seats. It appears that some kind of explosive device has gone off in the arcade outside. The police are dealing with the situation and have appealed for calm. They are arranging an orderly evacuation of the town centre and have asked all of us to await their instructions. Please refrain from crowding the exits and return to your seats. The police are trying to clear the area outside and will be here shortly.'

'There could be another,' shouted one man.

'We're sitting ducks,' yelled a woman two rows further on.

These discouraging comments were greeted by swelling murmurs of assent.

For the first few minutes Isobel was too busy stonewalling Megan and Sophie's frightened questions to take stock of her own responses. Beside her, James was doing the same with his two. Not wanting to alarm their charges more than necessary by appearing to hurry, they had only just risen to their feet when the manager appeared on stage. At his words most people were obediently returning to their seats, though a shameless few stayed where they were, guarding their proximity to exit signs with defiant eyes. An unnatural hush descended then, while the audience waited for the cavalry – in the unlikely form of Torbridge's local police force – to appear on the scene. Isobel got out a bag of toffees she had been saving to quell any restlessness during the second half and offered them down the line of children occupying the four seats between her and James. Having thus brokered a temporary silence, the two of them exchanged a look of deep concern, a sense of mutual responsibility preventing them from voicing their thoughts out loud. Everyone was talking in whispers. A woman in the front row started her children off in a shrill chorus of 'Ten Green Bottles' which quickly died out for lack of support.

'Are we going to be blown up?' enquired Sophie at length, sucking noisily on her sweet.

'Shut up, stupid,' retorted Megan, digging her in the ribs and prompting a howl.

'No, Sophie, I don't think so. We've just got to wait a little bit until the police come and tell us we can leave.'

'Where are the police anyway?'

'Coming,' Isobel whispered, listening, as most of them now were, to the muffled sounds emanating from the street outside and imagining the worst. She glanced across at James, who appeared grim-faced but calm. He turned and caught her stare, his grey eyes full of reassurance.

'We'll be out in a jiffy,' he said quietly, giving Eddie's flat head a pat and then reaching his arm along the backs of the children's seats, towards Isobel. Still holding her gaze, he held out his hand for hers. Without a word they linked fingers tightly. A cordon to protect the children, thought Isobel, shifting her eyes to the row of subdued heads between them and feeling the physical strength of the hand that held hers. But she felt something else too, something not protective at all. His thumb was stroking her palm, lightly and gently, soothingly, under cover of their knotted fingers.

A man in one of the circle seats stood up and asked loudly if there was a doctor in the house, because his wife had fainted.

James got to his feet at once, dropping Isobel's hand, ready to declare himself; but a woman seated nearer got there first.

'Perhaps I ought to volunteer my services outside,' he whispered. 'God knows how bad it is.'

'But you might be needed in here. Anything could happen—'

A buzz of relieved approval travelled round the room as a policeman at last strode on to the stage, the smart cut of his uniform bringing a much-needed sense of order and control. A few hearty souls clapped. They were thanked for their patience and reassured of their safety. The bomb had resulted in one fatality and a score of injuries. A helpline had been set up for those anxious to enquire about relatives. They were instructed to leave the theatre in an orderly fashion by the main exit and turn right into King Street instead of left towards the mall. Those with cars trapped in the affected area were warned they would have to be patient. Reassured by both the calmness and clarity of this address, the audience formed tidy lines and filed out of the theatre like lambs. Outside, several police personnel, aided by bollards and fences of orange tape, steered them down King

Street, away from the pedestrian precinct. Thanks to James's earlier reluctance to cater for lunch, they were able to make their way to his car, which he had left down a small alleyway that ran between the back entrances of Pizza Hut and a department store. Isobel's car remained imprisoned but unharmed, on the lower ground floor of the multistorey carpark, just a couple of hundred yards from the scene of the explosion. She asked to be dropped home, but James would not hear of it. Not till they knew exactly what was happening, he argued, driving right past the end of Fox's Crescent and heading for the short cut to the ring road south. Inwardly, Isobel was relieved. After putting on such a brave front to the girls, she was aware of her own fears bubbling unexpressed inside. Her hand trembled as she tried to pull the seat belt across her and Sophie, who had insisted on sitting on her lap.

'Here, let me help – it's devilishly stiff.' James reached across her and tugged hard. 'All right?' he asked, touching her arm lightly as he straightened himself.

By the time they reached Ilcombe the car radio had informed them that the bomb was suspected to have been the inspiration of the IRA, though the only warning call received had been an uncoded message to a local newspaper a couple of minutes before. Much was made of the merciful safety of the cathedral and several other buildings of antiquity which had remained intact. It was a miracle too that more people had not been wounded or killed, said the report several times, given that the bomb had been planted on a busy spring Saturday afternoon.

'Bastards,' muttered James, winding down his window and scowling at the chalky green landscape flying by. Isobel stared out too, clasping Sophie's bony ribcage and thinking that the brightness of the day had been somehow deceiving.

With Isobel's help, the four children were fed rounds of sandwiches and mugfuls of hot chocolate. Afterwards, they were granted the unprecedented treat of sucking lollies in front of the television, while James and Isobel retreated to the kitchen.

'A drink, I think.' James tipped the dregs of his tea into the sink and reached for two tumblers from the dishwasher. 'Speaking as a doctor, I would recommend brandy. Sound OK to you?' He turned to check on Isobel, who was sitting at the kitchen table with her head in her hands. 'Hey, are you all right over there?'

She nodded, but kept her face down to hide the fact that she wasn't all right at all.

James, torn between appropriate and inappropriate responses to such distress, gave her time to collect herself. He poured two generous brandies and flicked on the small radio that lived on the shelf above the microwave, so as to be sure not to miss any of the evening news.

'Do you want to call Ben?' he asked, lowering the volume and approaching with a glass held in each hand. A telephone call to Juliet during tea had met with a few gratifying expostulations of horror, before she reverted to a detailed account of the riveting events that had filled her own afternoon.

Isobel lifted her face and took a deep breath. The skin around her eyes looked tight and drawn, accentuating the striking darkness of the lashes and the clear pools of green inside. She must have had a haircut, James realised, registering for what felt like the first time the startling colours of the features usually left skulking under a fringe.

'Oh dear . . . I feel quite shaken up.' She smiled apologetically and took a sip of the brandy, closing her eyes as she swallowed.

'So do I,' he confessed, though he knew his own inner trembling stemmed not so much from terrorist activities as the peculiarly charged atmosphere that seemed to be forming in his kitchen.

'Do you want to call Ben?' he asked again, more quietly.

'Yes, yes of course.' Isobel cleared her throat. 'I've got the number here somewhere . . .' She pulled a small brown diary out of her bag and went to the phone which lived on the wall beside a framed watercolour of Torbridge cathedral.

Ben was not at the hostel, and the manager, who sounded unfriendly, claimed no knowledge as to when the party might return. When Isobel explained the reason for her call he grew marginally more co-operative.

'Could you just pass the message on that I'm all right – that his wife is all right . . . oh, and that I am at the Howards'.'

She had to repeat the name and spell it out several times.

James, watching from across the room, smiled and rolled his eyes.

After she had put the receiver down the shakes came back again, together with a sudden urge to cry. She took a sip of brandy and swallowed hard.

'You, my dear, are in shock,' said James gently, steering her by the elbow to the battered two-seater sofa that lived where Juliet eventually planned to have a Shaker dresser installed. He sat next to her and after a couple of minutes lifted her spare hand and pressed it between his. They remained side by side in silence, each absorbing the unmentionable fact that their shock extended to matters other than bombs and wondering what, if anything, to do about it.

10 $

Ben picked up a smooth flat stone and hurled it at the water. It flew fast, bouncing three times with small elegant splashes before finally sinking into the sea. Behind him, six boys, clad in windbreakers and hiking boots, were sketching the textured lines of the cliffs that towered over the shingle. Limestone and shale in cross-section. A geological snapshot of history, Ben liked to call it, a glib enough phrase that had served him well for several years in succession now, but which did nothing to communicate the awesome power of the place, the way the stone thrust itself out of the ground, how it seemed to breathe through the cuts and fissures of its craggy face.

Grey and huge, the sea boiled with energy, the waves slopping round the jagged edges of the coastline like dull soup. A band of brilliant blue stretched across the far line of the horizon, but immediately overhead the sky remained overcast and leaden. Ben, more than familiar with Welsh coastal predilections for rain, did not mind unduly. There was a drama to the place that warranted such elemental accompaniments. Besides, it was good for the boys to get their necks wet, he thought with a chuckle, hurling one last stone before turning back to check on the artistic progress of his charges.

'Come on, you lot,' he shouted cheerfully, 'we're not here for a picnic.' He stopped behind one boy and nodded approvingly at his drawing. 'Got your inclines and anticlines nicely under control, Lewis, well done. Don't worry about every limestone fragment lying on the beach, though.' He gestured at the cliff-face. 'It's that lot we're worried about for the time being. We've got an intraformational clast in turbidite to delight us before tea,

73 •

remember, so don't put your brains or your pencils away just yet. Not entirely necessary to the curriculum, but tremendously interesting and only half a mile down the coast, so we couldn't miss it, could we, Harrison?'

'No, sir, absolutely not.'

'And how's the headache?'

'Headache, sir?'

'Anyone who requires Coca-Cola for breakfast has a headache. Next time you decide to smuggle bottles of beer under your bedclothes, consult me first, there's a good lad. I was extremely disappointed not to be invited along too.'

Harrison nodded eagerly, his regard for the geography master soaring to new heights.

'And what does intraformational mean, by the way?' added Ben slyly.

'It's all about the stuff coming from the rock in which it's found.'

'Not the most eloquent of answers, but it will do. Yes. If by stuff, as you so inspiringly put it, you refer to pebbles and other sedimentary inclusions. The one we're going to look at was eroded by a turbidity current from the sea floor, rolled up like a sausage roll and deposited on the beach. There is even some coarse sediment within the roll itself – a filling for the Swiss roll, so to speak. Dawson, if your stomach rumbles any louder I'll need a loudspeaker.' He clapped his hands. 'Right, let's go. And if you get wet socks it's your lookout.'

They set off along the shingle, the boys following the master with an enthusiasm that complimented him far better than composed classrooms or an absence of ink-blots in their workbooks.

Much to the boys' delight, Ben was the one who slipped on a slimy rock and got his feet wet. Though he made a show of complaining, it was for their benefit alone, because he knew it would make them laugh. Unpleasantly chilled toes and a faint squelch to each footstep taken thereafter did nothing to dampen his energies when it came to explaining the mysteries of collapsed breccia and turbidity currents. Nor did a sizable blister on his big toe prevent him from leading the challenging climb to the cliff-top for a better view of the impressive coastline and the sea beyond.

On their way back to the minibus, which he had parked by a deserted caravan and a dilapidated billboard advertising hot dogs, Ben's eye was caught by a flash of pink amongst the clusters of grey and black stones lining the path that led up from the sea. On further investigation he discovered a stone of pale pink crystals that bore no relation he could think of to the geological rock formations in evidence around them. The mystery of its presence pleased him as much as its colour and shape. Closer inspection revealed that, if held at a certain angle, the rock could be said to resemble a heart, albeit a rather lopsided one. Ben opened his mouth to call the boys over, but then changed his mind. He dropped the stone into the deep pocket of his anorak instead, burying it under his gloves for safe-keeping and imagining how Isobel's face would light up when he gave it to her. An anniversary present, maybe, he mused, distracted for a second by the visual image of the crystal dangling on a gold chain against the freckled cream of his wife's skin.

'Mars bars all round,' he announced, hurling confectionery into laps behind him before steering the minibus on the enjoyably bumpy ride back up to the main road. Since hunger dictated a fairly lengthy pit stop for food, it was gone ten o'clock by the time they got back to the youth hostel. The boys, worn out by an early start and a day of hiking along a wind-blasted coast, meekly took themselves off to their beds, all thoughts of beer or any other rebellious activities for once far from their minds.

On account of the bottle of single malt kept hidden behind a flowerpot on the lower shelf of the reception desk, the hostel manager was not entirely lucid about the by now well-publicised events that had taken place in Torbridge that afternoon. Despite the advantage of having seen not only the early but also the late evening news, he could provide Ben with little detail beyond the fact that his wife had telephoned to say that she was all right. Ben looked at his watch, torn between phoning Isobel and waking her with unnecessary drama. She hated being woken up, he knew, never having quite mastered the art of picking up the thread of sleep once it had been interrupted.

'Did she say anything else?'

The man frowned and ran his hand over the length of his face, lingering over the grey bristles protruding from his chin.

'Ah,' he exclaimed in triumph, after a few moments, 'she said she was staying the night with friends.'

'Friends . . . which friends?'

'I'm afraid you've got me there.'

'Not the Howards, was it, by any chance?' suggested Ben, suddenly recalling his family's plans for that afternoon.

'That was it.' The man banged his hand down on the counter. 'Got it in one. Howard. Like the castle.'

Phoning so late seemed even less acceptable when it wasn't even to his own home.

'Bugger,' he muttered, seizing his room key and traipsing up the narrow stairs.

The blister, having been ignored for so long, had shed its flimsy layer of skin and started to bleed, leaving a small dark stain on his sock. Ben rinsed it in a basin of water before stepping under the inadequate tepid dribble that passed for a shower in the bathroom at the far end of his corridor. He shivered as he made his way back to his room, a towel no bigger than a dishcloth clasped round his waist, his wet feet slipping on the cold linoleum floor.

The Hotel Primavera had an endearingly dilapidated air about it, like a lord fallen upon hard times. Less enticing was the adjoining and sadly incongruous honeycomb of modern conference rooms in which Juliet and her fellow course members spent most of Saturday, improving their knowledge of the properties of essential oils. Having approached the weekend in something of a holiday mood, Juliet was determined not to have her spirits dampened by ugly surroundings or anything else. Shelley, on the other hand – her companion and the architect of the entire weekend – arrived in a foul temper that intensified as the day wore on. Long before the news of Torbridge's bomb had cast a shadow over the proceedings, she had found fault with most aspects of the amenities – the new wing's over-zealous heating system and the discomfort of the green plastic lecture chairs coming high on her list of complaints. It was all horribly reminiscent of school, she moaned, posting her tray of untouched dinner through a hatch before joining Juliet in the queue for the coffee dispenser. Juliet, who had only narrowly avoided the temptation to have a second plate of chicken fricassee, and who had enjoyed a healthy portion of jam sponge pudding and custard, murmured unconvincing platitudes of concurrence while wondering – for by no means the first time since their arrival – if she dared to slip away in search of brighter company.

Sunday morning brought little evidence of a change in Shelley's mood. While picking at a breakfast of grapefruit segments and natural yoghurt, she regaled Juliet with stories of her troubled night, spent, she claimed, alongside a cardboard apology of a wall listening to the mysteriously incessant gurgling of a fellow

77 •

guest's lavatory cistern. Juliet, accommodated in a bed just a few feet across the same room, felt almost guilty for having slept so soundly, her dreams dimly woven with the soothing poetry of the after-dinner lecture on oils. There had been a table of samples to try afterwards, each with beautiful italicised labels, describing the powers of the fragrant liquids inside: *Myristica fragrans: oriental, rich, sensual, spicy and warm. Rosa damascena: floral, rich, rosy, sweet, tenacious. Citrus limonum: clean, fresh, lemony, light, penetrating. Jasminum officinale: exotic, exquisite, long-lasting, rich* . . .

By the time they filed out of breakfast to powder their noses before the Sunday morning introductory session on reflexology, Juliet was beginning to experience some sympathy for the husband whose faults her new young friend had found time to introduce into her catalogue of woes against life in general and the domestic arrangements of the Hotel Primavera in particular. While waiting for Shelley to complete her ablutions in their shared cubby-hole of a bathroom, she caught herself tempted by the idea of going home early. After all the fascination of the aromatherapy lectures she couldn't help thinking that learning about feet would feel like something of a comedown. Besides which, there was the awful business of the bomb, depicted in some detail on the front pages of the paper that had been slipped under their bedroom door that morning. Seeing it reported in black and white like that, with pictures of Torbridge's familiar shopping arcade covered in broken glass and people clutching hands to bleeding faces, brought home to Juliet the full enormity of what had happened. She was almost cross with James for sounding so calm over the telephone the day before, for playing it down. Prompted by such sentiments, together with the somewhat tardy realisation that she could have lost her entire family, Juliet decided to call home. She tried the number several times, turning her back with a tremor of disgust at the uninhibited view of her room-mate leering into their bathroom mirror as she sawed floss through the gaps in her large handsome teeth. When her fifth attempt still met with no answer, Juliet slammed the phone down impatiently and suggested they pack their bags.

Shelley, whose English originated from the Midlands, but who laid claim to some exotic-sounding Jamaican ancestry, tossed her beaded black hair and flashed the whites of her eyes at such a suggestion. 'No way, Juliet, no way.' She dropped her coil of floss into her make-up bag and clipped it shut. 'You and I are staying till the end. Otherwise I would have spent a sleepless night for nothing, wouldn't I?'

'It was only a thought . . . and you don't seem to be exactly enjoying yourself . . .'

'Whatever gave you that idea?' Shelley replied imperiously, flashing one of the large, gleaming smiles than had drawn Juliet to her in the first place. 'I'm away from Stuart, aren't I? That's a holiday in itself, I assure you, girl.'

Juliet, who had found a few moments in which to miss the eminently huggable, heat-radiating presence of her husband in her measly pallet of a bed, shook her head in a show of hopeless but relenting despair. It was only a few more hours after all. 'Come on, then, let's get on with it.'

Something in the weariness of Juliet's tone seemed to bring her companion to her senses. By the time they left their room to head into the rabbit-warren of corridors said to contain Lecture Room B, Shelley was cracking jokes about the eccentricities of their fellow students and confessing to an ambition to set up her own beauty therapy business. Not even the difficulty of negotiating a maze of ambivalent arrows and noticeboards soured her mood, though both women felt some embarrassment when they stumbled into a room of Japanese executives and had to be directed back the other way.

The woman in charge of the reflexology session was strikingly rotund, and encased in a long woollen tunnel of a dress that give little indication where the various sections of her ample anatomy began and ended. Before starting to speak, she pushed up the sleeves of her dress to her elbows, revealing forearms as round as pumpkins and a small tattoo of a serpent where one might have expected a watch.

'Have I got any sceptics?' she asked, flexing her hands across the impressive plateau of her chest. 'Because if I have, I can guarantee there won't be any by the end. Money back if you're not satisfied. How's that?' She beamed, taking a moment to study some of the faces among her audience. 'Now then, I want everybody to pick up their chair and make a stack of them against the wall over there. We need some space here. Right, good, that's it. Now take your shoes and socks off – or garters or stockings or whatever the hell you're wearing.' There was an outburst of embarrassed tittering, which she silenced with a clap of her hands. 'Hurry up, we haven't got all week. Good. Now, turn to the person next to you – introduce yourselves if you have to. Then sit down opposite that person – anywhere on the floor, that's it – and place your feet in each other's laps. Toes don't bite, you know.'

More embarrassed laughter; while Juliet experienced an uncharacteristic stab of modesty at having to expose her veiny white feet, thinking they looked old and positively ugly beside the creamy brown smoothness of Shelley's extremities.

'Feet are one of the miracles of the body,' continued their instructor, sorting out a few stray recruits who had not yet managed to locate partners, 'since they comprise a very small area and yet can accommodate even the most excessive weight. Their wondrous strength and mobility are achieved by the arrangement of the bones, muscles and ligaments of which they consist. In fact they contain one quarter of all the bones in the human body, not to mention nineteen muscles and one hundred and seven ligaments. Each foot is made up of twenty-six bones. Now, pick up one of your partner's feet and feel the toes. Don't be shy. Firm but gentle handling is the secret, ladies – and gentlemen,' she added, nodding and smiling at the small cluster of men working together in a group near the door. 'You will feel three bones – which are called phalanges – in each toe, apart from the big toe which has two. Leading back towards the heel we have five metatarsals – each one relating to a toe. The remaining bones are tarsals, all with names that I won't mention at this point, though if you help yourself to the literature I'll be handing out at the end of this session you'll find drawings and descriptions of them all. My object today, ladies and gentlemen, is to teach you not only some of the basic theory of reflexology – a rather misleading name, incidentally – but also to give you an inkling of the power of this treatment, through instructing you in a few basic techniques to try out on each other. The potency of this therapy is considerable and – I cannot stress this too strongly

– should be respected as such. The zones of the feet relate to different zones in your body. By over-stimulating one or the other, you could do more harm than good. Reflexology is about restoring the overall balance within our systems – chemical as well as psychological; through the correct massage we can expel toxins, restore natural equilibrium and iron out areas of stress and pain. It is essential to know what you are doing and the effect it might have. Practised wisely it is a formidable tool, a powerful form of healing, which has been responsible for helping millions of people over countless centuries . . .'

Juliet and Shelley exchanged amused grimaces of incredulity, further strengthening their new-found amity.

'I shall also be telling you of several case histories relating some quite astonishing cures to well-known and very grave diseases . . .'

Not such a bad way to spend a morning after all, mused Juliet dreamily, kneading the soft smooth ball of Shelley's right foot while enjoying similar attentions to her own. The physcial pleasure was something of a revelation; almost sexual, she decided, eyeing her partner through half-closed eyes. She and James never bothered with feet. But perhaps they should, she mused, thinking with some affection of her husband's ticklish, hairy prehensile toes and rather relishing the challenge of taming them. He would protest, of course, she thought, smiling to herself as her imagination spiralled down a sensual sidetrack of its own.

On Monday morning, after she had walked the girls to school, Isobel turned and set off at a brisk pace back towards home. Several loads of washing lay strewn across the girls' bedroom floor and in Ben's half-unpacked rucksack on the landing. A shopping list needed writing for her weekly trawl round the supermarket. Open University application forms sat gathering dust accusingly on the desk upstairs. A busy week beckoned, yet she felt none of her customary enthusiasm to greet it.

On reaching the beginning of Torbridge's main shopping precinct, she hesitated just for a moment before turning her back on her usual route and heading towards the shops. The orange tape cordoning off the immediate area affected by the explosion fluttered in the breeze, as if straining to be free. Though the worst of the mess had been cleared up, fragments of broken glass still littered the pavement, glinting in the spring sunshine like crystals. Shoppers were making the small detour round the flimsy fencing with barely a head-nod of acknowledgment, steering prams and buggies round the larger of the shards of glass and tugging toddlers to heel. The world had accommodated this small insult to its surface, and moved on.

Different but the same, thought Isobel, pausing to stare in wonder at the jagged hole in the pavement and the broken and boarded windows of the shopfronts immediately behind. Beyond these, it was business as usual in the multistorey. She had rescued the car on Sunday morning, dropped off by James, who sat waiting with his engine running at the exit to check that they emerged safely, before hooting his horn twice and driving off. She had tooted back, her heart quickening at the sight of him, or more accurately, at the almost forgotten sensation of being worried about at all.

Nothing had happened and yet everything had changed. Something invisible yet momentous. Isobel gazed on at the cavity in the ground, trying to recall the exact moment this alteration had taken place, trying to reconcile the James Howard of the past with the creature who had emerged over the weekend. Thrusting her hands deep into her jacket pockets, she strode away from the scene of devastation, angrily listing in her head all the components of his character that she had never liked: his intimidating self-confidence, the excluding displays of male camaraderie, not to mention his typically crude medic's sense of humour. Try as she might, however, none of these considerations could erase the peculiarly charged images of their recent encounter. A handle had been turned, a switch pressed, a door opened . . . It was flattery, Isobel told herself, increasing her stride still more as she turned down the cobbled street that led towards the cathedral: flattery in its purest, most pathetic form. Her friend's husband was flirting with her and she was enjoying it. Despicable. Unforgivable. Fantastic. She continued to scold herself as she walked, trying and failing to quash the excitement fluttering inside, the image of his grey eyes burning into hers.

Staying for the entire night had been the children's idea. They made a den of sleeping bags on the floor of Eddie's bedroom amidst toppling piles of books, torches and other provisions declared to be vital for the night. They cleaned their teeth and licked down the tangles in their hair, before appearing in the kitchen in a strange assortment of nightwear, clutching pillows to their stomachs and promising to behave; so beautifully naïve that it made Isobel argue all the more determinedly against agreeing to their request. But James had caved in almost at once, conceding with wide-eyed innocence that a Saturday night spent under the same roof could certainly do none of them any harm.

And no harm had been done, Isobel reminded herself, stopping to stare into a shop window, but seeing only her own reflection. White-faced, blurred edges, like a picture waiting to be completed. For nothing had happened. Nothing at all. They had nibbled at cheese and fruit, sipped wine and talked, seeking refuge from awkwardness in anecdotes about the children. Even the most mundane subjects seemed to burn with new meaning. Then James, for the first time in all the years she had known him, brought up the subject of her miscarriage, probing gently as he might have physically examined a wound.

'Must have been very hard.'

'Yes . . . yes, it was. But we pulled through it – I did lots of crying and so on, like you're supposed to . . .' She pulled a face, but he did not smile.

'It's soon, isn't it? The anniversary, I mean.' So distracted was James by her fingers fiddling absently with a piece of cork beside her wineglass that he had to fight the temptation to seize them in his own. There were faint freckles on the knuckles of her hands, he noticed, pretty pinpricks of ginger. It took all his self-control to command his own hands back into his lap, to return his concentration to the conversation. All his keenest instincts told him that in raising such a topic he had stumbled upon a key, an entry into the kind of emotional terrain that could lead to the intimacy which had become his goal. He wanted badly to get it right.

Isobel nodded, flashing a smile of pleased surprise at this startling feat of memory. 'The third of March.'

'Next week, then?'

She nodded. 'Some years I hope I'll forget. But I never do.'

'And you'd probably never forgive yourself if you did.'

His eyes seemed more deeply set into his face than she'd noticed before, and such a compelling, steely grey that she wondered how a careless glance had ever passed between them. I've just never looked at him properly till now, she marvelled, struggling with the urge to hold his gaze but finding it hard. Seen close to, his hair was more white than fair, and beautifully smooth, brushed back off his face in a way that flattered the strong lines of his jaw and cheeks. Even his mouth looked different, Isobel observed, not merely thin as she had always seen it before, but delicate and sensuous, the lower lip being noticeably fuller than the upper, except when stretched into a smile.

Observing how her mood had softened, James continued to

talk gently about bereavement, embarking on a moving account of the loss of his parents, who had died within a few months of each other many years before.

'The mourning doesn't end, you just learn to accommodate it.' Much to his amazement – and gratification – real tears pricked his eyes. He blinked to emphasise their presence.

'God, that's so right.' Isobel sighed, dropping her gaze to the table, unwittingly granting him the opportunity to admire the transparent delicacy of her eyelids and the dark lashes that were such an unusual complement to the glossy copper of her hair. 'My parents are alive and kicking in Suffolk, as you know.'

'Yes, yes, of course they are.' James found his attention focused on the fingers once again. Slim and papery white, like chalk. He wanted so badly to touch her, to move the situation on, to take the next stage in these extraordinary proceedings by storm. But all his antennae warned him it was still too soon. Isobel Tarrant was such a fragile thing in many ways, so delicate and complicated. Years of acquaintance had taught him that much if nothing else. He knew it wouldn't work unless she met him halfway. 'A little more wine?'

She cast a regretful eye up to the pretty hand-painted saucer of a clock on the wall behind him, wondering at the unnatural speed with which its arrows seemed to have flown past the roosting hens and grinning pigs decorating its rim.

'Better not.' She stretched her arms and opened her mouth in a display of fatigue that cheered him greatly for being so unconvincing. James played along with a yawn of his own, all the while feasting his eyes on her pale slender limbs, inwardly scolding and congratulating himself in equal measures. He had not looked for this, after all. It had just happened. A gift on a plate. Maybe even just a game, he decided, escorting her up to the spare room, talking all the while about landing lights and burglar alarms. Before Isobel closed the door, he handed her a spare toothbrush and a nightie of Juliet's, a white lacy one she never wore, as if that made the crime of imagining some other woman enfolded within it a little more forgivable.

Pulling the crisp white garment over her head a few minutes later, Isobel felt all the irony of borrowing such a thing in such circumstances. Through the wall she could hear the muffled sounds of James preparing for bed, the run of a tap, a door closing. The children were at the end of the corridor, sprawled amongst the covers of their makeshift camp, arms and legs flung out across discarded comics and games. The area occupied by the two younger ones was surrounded by soft toys, hugged and abandoned with an affection that yet knew no fear of consequences. James and Isobel had watched the sleeping four in silence for a few moments, before tiptoeing round the room, tugging covers over limbs and tucking pillows under heads. Such traditional parental rituals had helped to fortify their self-control, easing the tricky transition from corridors to beds.

'Sleep well,' he had murmured, as she closed the door, only the haste with which she did so suggesting that the action shut out emotions of an altogether more inadmissible kind.

The relief offered by sliding into the cool cocoon of the bed was brief, however, her sense of safety short-lived. Sleep was out of the question. Instead, Isobel put the light back on and lay staring at Juliet's violet wallpaper and freshly glossed skirting boards, as if by fixing upon such things she might cling on to her faltering sense of the real world. Less easily contained, was the glow of excitement burning inside, fuelled by the long-forgotten sensation of being the object of such attention. Too exhilarating to relinquish at once, she told herself, putting out the light and wishing she could click her own emotions on and off with as much ease. Alone again in the dark, with no physical distractions to get in the way, she was overpowered by a sense of her own latent wickedness and the realisation that sin could occur in the mind long before the deed.

But I love Ben, she thought bleakly, wondering if it was simply her own frailty that made the sustainability of such emotions feel so increasingly one-sided and hard. He hadn't even bothered to telephone, she reminded herself, turning on her side and pulling her knees up to her chest. It occurred to Isobel in the same instant that perhaps what she loved was not the Ben Tarrant she knew now, but the memory of the man she had once known, when his enthusiasm for life had included rather than defied her own.

Angrily, she wrenched back the bedclothes and padded over to the window. Peering through the pretty yellow curtains, which she herself had helped Juliet choose from a chic furnishings shop in Torbridge Arcade, Isobel made fresh resolutions for the days and weeks to come. Sanity would be restored by the normality of the morning, she reassured herself. James would be embarrassed and cold. Ben, returning the next night, would be refreshed and – possibly – pleased to see her. She would nurture every grain of affection; she would try harder; she would make things work between them no matter what it took.

The outskirts of Ilcombe were too far into the depths of the countryside for streetlamps. Only the silvery cuticle of the moon served to cast any light in the darkness below. A shadow passed along the furthest verge of the lane, before turning into the hedge. Something tall and grey. Isobel shivered and withdrew, scolding her imagination for seeing demons where there were none.

Back in bed, she told herself that James Howard's apparent intensity was part of a similar confusion, that it was purely a figment of her imagination, that she was a sad emotional wreck of a housewife looking for daydreams to illuminate a life dominated by domestic appliances and the preparation of meals. Such arguments buoyed her for a time. Until she was struck by the strongest sense of him lying awake and thinking of her just a few yards away. They were in each other's minds, she could feel it. The sense of intimacy was tangible. They had performed the first rituals in a game that could progress even when they were apart. She could feel his desire seeping into the room, destroying all her common sense, promising her something she had thought never to know again.

'Penny for them?'

'Oh my . . . Reverend Heston-Jones – you startled me – I—'

'It's Heighton-Jones, actually, but call me Archie, please. Enjoying the sights of the close on this fine spring morning? It really is irresistible, isn't it – everything in bud, the cathedral so spruce and majestic after its clean-up, all these gorgeous old houses. I like Lady Lacy's the best, I think. Though I wouldn't say no to this one either,' he added with a hearty laugh and a nod at the archbishop's fifteenth-century residence, glimpsed behind a handsome elm tree on their right. 'I know it's wicked, but I was so pleased to be assigned to Torbridge instead of some inner city hell-hole. Oh, don't get me wrong, I'll get to hell-holes in time, but it is a bit of a flying start to be somewhere so jolly glorious. How long have you lived here?'

'Me? Oh, let me see . . . about ten years.' Jolted from her reverie, Isobel was somewhat startled to find that she had already passed under the arch at the end of Mayers Street and into the close itself.

'Where were you before that?' Archie was not so much walking along beside her as bouncing on the rubber soles of his brown leather shoes, hands clasped behind his back, dodging shallow puddles like a child playing a private game. Instead of his habit, he was wearing ill-fitting jeans and a tweed jacket that did little to enhance the aesthetic appeal of the rather grey-looking dog-collar clinging to his neck.

'Spain,' Isobel murmured, with the surreal sensation that she was referring to the life of another person. 'Ben taught in Madrid for a year. Then he got a job at the Cathedral School. Then Crofton College.'

'And here we are,' Archie exclaimed, clapping his hands with delight.

'Well, I'm afraid I ought to be getting back,' she began, despairing of shaking him off any other way and realising that if they walked the entire circuit round the cathedral it would take at least another half an hour. 'Good to see you again.' She stopped and held out her hand.

Archie looked disappointed for a moment and then hit his head in a show of such vehement self-reprimand that Isobel flinched.

'Crumbs, silly me. What I *meant* to say was could I call round to collect my sponsor money some time?' He flushed, clearly embarrassed by the request.

'Of course . . . but look, I can pay now.' She began to unbuckle her handbag.

'Oh goodness, don't worry now, please . . . I haven't got my form or anything.' He held out his empty hands helplessly. 'And when I call I might just ask you to sign the petition too, if that's all right.'

'Petition?'

'About closing St Cuthbert's. Somebody on the council has

proposed it for an arts centre. Reverend Tully says it will probably all come to nothing, but you never know. So I've started getting signatures. Without St Cuthbert's I'd be out of a job,' he added, looking crestfallen.

'I'm sure that won't happen.' Isobel clipped her bag shut and offered her most reassuring smile. Priests, like policemen, were getting younger, she thought wryly, feeling suddenly much better, much more herself. 'Call round any time, won't you?'

'I surely will.' He grinned and waved his hand at her before hastily stuffing it in his trouser pocket as if it had misbehaved. He was a pathetically awkward sod when it came to women, but Isobel Tarrant made him worse than most. Something about the dreamy green eyes and flaming hair, he reflected, still grinning as she walked away, and thinking that even God could forgive a healthy appreciation of such assets. And who could control dreams anyway? Archie reasoned, suppressing the rather less virtuous images that hovered on the edges of his mind, trailers from various fitful nights over the preceding weeks. There had to be some compensations for a mattress with a gash down its middle and a pillow like a starched napkin. So compact was Archie's two-roomed flat that even when lying in bed he could see the edge of his small fridge and the silver curve of the kettle glinting beside it. With his first few months behind him, the novelty of such squalor was wearing a little thin. Almost worse than the lack of space were the vagaries of its ancient electrical system, which shut down in protest if called upon to supply power to more than a couple of appliances at any one time. The tactics required for a successful negotiation of the kettle, the toaster, the radio and his electric razor each morning were particularly testing. Recently, he had even fallen back on the old and much-abhorred labour of wet shaving in order to reduce the hazards.

It was altogether easier to feel tolerant about such grievances when he was at some distance from them, he realised with a sigh, pausing to admire the gargoyles ranged to one side of the cathedral's west door. He loved the ugliness of them, the suggestion of lewd humour beneath their contorted expressions. To have such portraits accommodated in something so majestic was, in his view, utterly marvellous. The church itself should be the same, he thought suddenly, able to house everything under its broad wings, ugly or beautiful, good or bad. Pleased with the idea, he burst into an ear-piercing whistle of the Magnificat sung by the choir of St Cuthbert's the previous Sunday, causing a couple of startled pigeons to retreat in alarm to the stalwart arms of a nearby oak.

'But Isobel, I haven't seen you for *months*,' complained Juliet, breaking off half a biscuit from the plateful left out beside the tea bags for the workmen. 'Not since my weekend away and that hideous bomb . . .'

'That was just last week,' Isobel reminded her, but thinking to herself that it did indeed feel like much longer ago.

'—If I didn't know you better, I'd say you were deliberately trying to avoid me.'

'Avoid you?' she echoed, in a small voice. 'Don't be a twit. Tell me about your course. Was it worthwhile?'

'It was fabulous – that is, once Shelley decided to start enjoying herself. I had no idea the woman could be such poison. Really – spending time with someone is such a revelation, don't you think?'

'Yes . . . indeed it is.' Isobel could feel the blood rush to her cheeks. She reached out and touched the prettily serrated petals of one of the dozen carnations that had arrived that morning. Just when she was beginning to convince herself that Saturday night had all been meaningless, a bubble of nothing, blown away as quickly as it had arrived. There was no note, just twelve tall white flowers, their simple beauty throwing Ben's contrasting forgetfulness into cruel relief. He hadn't mentioned the anniversary at all. Isobel reached out and stroked the petals again, as if seeking consolation for the expected – but nonetheless bitter – disappointment of this omission.

'So you didn't get along with Shelley,' she murmured, distracting herself from the absurd temptation to tell Juliet that James had sent her flowers, to scotch the whole terrible situation before it could advance into more dangerous terrain.

'Oh, we were bursting with mutual affection by the end. Turns out the poor girl's a slave to PMT – I just wish she'd said something earlier. The course itself was marvellous . . . I say, are you all right, Isobel? You sound a bit . . . distant.'

'Do I? Sorry. Bit of a headache . . . and the weekend did shake all of us up rather . . .'

'So it seems. James hasn't been himself at all ever since.'

Isobel felt her mouth go dry. 'Hasn't he?'

'I suspect he's punishing me for going away. Men are such babies.' She uttered a short laugh, before adding in a gloomy voice, 'So much for absence and fondness.'

The comment transported Isobel back to Sunday night and all her hopes for Ben's return from Wales. Though he looked well – wide-eyed and faintly tanned – whatever good humour the trip might have generated had clearly been sapped by a disastrous journey home. Bad traffic and several engine seizures on the part of the minibus – each requiring desperate and inexpert probing on the hard shoulder of busy motorways – had meant that he did not get back until almost midnight. When they hugged he felt stiff and reluctant. They talked about the bomb, but only briefly. Evidently exhausted, Ben had kissed each of his sleeping daughters before crawling into bed and closing his eyes. Lying tense and expectant beside him, all Isobel's penitence had shrivelled to a hard sense of injustice. She had spent all day tormenting herself with the crime of having encouraged intimacy with another man. Filled with remorse, she had washed her hair and soaked her body in a perfumed bath, feeling all the while as if she were cleansing herself at a far deeper level, preparing and wanting to love, and be loved. To find the inspiration behind such actions, the prime sandbag of her self-discipline, slumped in bed beside her, offering one dead, draping arm by way of a token caress of welcome, was not heartening. He does not love me, she thought, curling her freshly scented body away from his and thinking with new and bitter resignation that, without reciprocation of some kind, it was impossibly hard to feel love in return. And when, a few minutes later, the figure of James Howard had tiptoed into her mind, his eyes glistening with desire, his large doctor hands reaching out for hers, she welcomed him in, telling herself that such mirages of passion were the least she deserved in the circumstances.

Juliet was still talking about James. 'He's been thoroughly hateful about the course. Playing the pompous doctor. He simply refuses to admit that any good can be done beyond the boring bounds of conventional medicine. He says that alternative healing methods are mostly a load of bull, that they corrode the world's faith in real medicine, that they encourage gullible people to take silly risks and to refuse treatments that could otherwise save lives.' She paused for an indignant sigh. 'Not even the case history about multiple sclerosis – which I must tell you some time because it is *truly* amazing – would budge him. Obstinate bugger. I hate him sometimes, you know, I really do. He even had the cheek to say I was wasting money to have fun – or almost said, which was just as bad. Worse, in fact. And that got us on to money in general, which is never a good idea in our household. I told him to fuck off, too, which probably didn't help,' she added meekly.

'Oh dear,' said Isobel, wishing she could summon the wherewithal to offer help or advice.

'But still, at least we've got all that kissing and making up to look forward to, eh?' She offered an uncertain laugh.

The sensation of struggling so badly in conversation with Juliet was not a pleasant one. No matter how much Isobel reminded herself that there was nothing tangible for which to feel guilty, the guilt persisted nonetheless, and so vividly that she feared drawing attention to it simply by using the wrong tone of voice. While not exactly avoiding the Howards, she had certainly felt little inclination to encourage a meeting with either of them. Instead, she had spent the last few days concentrating so hard on being normal that even the most mundane actions were beginning to feel strange.

'Of course, we'll be coming to Ben's play,' went on Juliet, leaping with characteristic energy into new tracks of conversation, 'but that's weeks away, and I would so like to get the four of us together before then. How about dinner over here? You could all stay the night if you're worried about driving.'

'Ben's so busy,' faltered Isobel, staring hard at the carnations.

'Bollocks to that. We all need to relax sometimes – you can tell that husband of yours so from me. How does next Saturday night sound? I'll cook something really special – give us all a treat—'

'I think Ben may have a rehearsal . . .'

'Well then, tell him he can arrive afterwards. We'll eat late,' declared Juliet stoutly, determined, now that she had hit upon the plan, not to be swayed from it. 'If you're staying the night, it won't matter when the hell we finish, will it?'

'I suppose not,' Isobel admitted, squeezing the telephone flex round her fingers and telling herself that she couldn't hide away for ever. With Juliet and Ben there as well, the situation between her and James was bound to feel more normal; maybe even disappear altogether. 'But I don't know about staying the night . . .'

'But darling, it's only common sense. The children loved all sleeping in a heap – James said so – and you and Ben can push the beds together in the spare room . . . or were you horribly uncomfortable when you stayed? James should bloody well have given you our bed and slept in there himself. The smell of paint must have been awful. But it's all gone now, I promise.'

Overcome by the misguided absurdity of such speculations, Isobel almost laughed out loud.

'I'll take that pregnant pause as a yes,' declared Juliet, pleased as always to have a social event of some sort for which to shop and prepare. 'And any chance of a coffee tomorrow, after my aromatherapy class?' she added slyly, some sixth sense picking up on Isobel's reluctance to see her and pushing against it.

'No, Juliet, sorry, I . . . well, I've got this Open University stuff to plough through – I'm looking at some sample essay questions, some of the texts and so on . . .'

'I can't think why you've got it into your head to go back to school – you've got quite enough facts in your head as it is. One degree is more than enough, in my view . . . unless – I say' – she switched to her most teasing voice – 'we're not trying to recapture our lost youth or anything unwise, are we? Rose-tinted memories of all that slog in libraries and so on. It's all crap, you know. The past is usually best left to its own devices. We couldn't get it back if we wanted to and even if we could it would be a disappointment. It's *designed* to be looked back on,' Juliet concluded firmly, thinking with some pride of her own undeniably dignified exit from London life and how good she was at not missing it at all.

'I'm thinking of the future actually,' replied Isobel quietly, 'of what might lie ahead . . .'

'Well, you could fill the immediate future by agreeing to have that coffee with me for a start—'

'Oh . . . but I've also promised to visit Aunt Vi—'

'But you only just saw the wretched woman,' wailed Juliet despairingly.

'That was a while ago now—'

'You're a slave to your own conscience, Isobel, and quite put the rest of us to shame. One day you must learn the art of giving yourself a little pleasure as well as the rest of society, or you'll end up bitter and twisted and sticking hatpins in models of your friends. Let yourself go a bit, girl. There, that's Auntie Juliet's thought for the day. Now, how about agreeing to let me have a shot at your feet?'

'My feet?'

'Reflexology is the most amazing thing – you'd love it, I promise.'

'I'm far too ticklish.'

'A massage, then. I've got some lovely oils and I desperately need the practice,' Juliet added, wondering whether Isobel was being hard work or whether it was her. 'I know what, come early on Saturday and I'll do it then, before our dinner, while the children run riot in the garden. Don't argue, I've made up my mind.'

Isobel replaced the phone with a sigh and leant over to sniff the sweet scent of the flowers. After giving the matter some thought, she carried the vase through to the mantelpiece in the sitting room, telling herself that if Ben remarked on their presence she would tell the truth and face the consequences. But he probably won't even notice them, she reflected glumly, trying disconsolately to nudge the stems back into the elegant arrangement she had managed in the kitchen.

14

Ben Tarrant had always thought of himself as strong, not just physically, but deep down inside, where it counted most. That he had grown up largely on his own, at a school several thousand miles away from a father he hated, was not something to which he usually referred, either in his own mind or out loud to other people. He knew that the experience, hateful though much of it had been at the time, had helped to form him, that it lay at the heart of his inner resources. He also regarded himself as fortunate for never having doubted what he wanted to do with his life. Teaching, as well as being satisfactorily contrary to the more financially ambitious aspirations of his expatriate father, had always been the only thing that appealed. Perhaps on account of the relative turbulence of his own childhood, Ben's enthusiasm in this regard was almost a need. He knew instinctively how to get the best out of his pupils, how to nurture every precious glimmer of interest and fan it into knowledge and intelligence. He had always recognised this ability as a vocational thing, even more of a genetic gift than an athletic body and a passably handsome face.

Recently, however, he was beginning, for the first time in his thirty-five years, to wonder whether his inner strengths were quite as inexhaustible as he had always assumed. He could never recall feeling so tired. Not even the break in Wales, once an oasis of refreshment in a busy term, had worked its usual magic. Upon his return there was so much to catch up on, both inside the classroom and out, that he could barely bring himself to start. Not only did he feel as if he were drowning in paperwork, but the school play was draining every ounce of energy and patience in a way that felt worrying and new. The pleasures once inherent in committing to such enterprises were as weak as borrowed memories.

And then there was Isobel. His touchstone. His unchangeable fall-back of common sense and good humour, the one who, by her quiet, unquestioning devotion, fuelled all his conviction in himself and in what he was trying to achieve. She was shutting him out. Every time he looked at her was like having a door slammed in his face. I am unhappy, said her eyes, and I'm blaming you.

And so she probably should, reflected Ben grimly, absently running one finger along a hairline crack in the corridor wall as he traipsed down the main body of the school to answer a summons from the headmaster. He watched his feet as he walked, carefully avoiding chips and ink stains in the scuffed parquet and puzzling over the depressing fact that recognising his culpability in the curious downward spiral of his married life should offer up no starting point for remedying it. There was a fine line between relying on a wife and neglecting her, he thought wryly, nodding his head to himself in acknowledgment of the fact that he had almost certainly blundered across such boundaries, but knowing too that in his current state of mind he lacked both the energy and inspiration to atone for it.

Burdened by the lucidity of such harsh self-analysis, Ben found himself making slow and faltering progress towards the fine oak-panelled study from which Dr Peter Abbott, surrounded by auspicious photographs of his predecessors, directed operations for the successful running of Crofton College. In spite of a rather forbidding physical presence, he was a warm-hearted and open-minded man, whose habit of incorporating impromptu discussions into the busy timetables of his staff was not something that any of them usually resented. Least of all the head of his geography department, who nurtured hopes of exerting a similar style of leadership himself one day.

In a bid to shake off some of his dark mood, Ben paused to admire a colourful classroom display on the life-cycle of the tapeworm. *An invisible enemy*, said the headline, its words hugging the bulging head of a smug-looking parasite, whose multi-segmented body was sheathed within the intestines of a large, placid-faced cow. Thinking gloomily that invisible enemies took many forms, Ben nodded a brief farewell at the ruminant, whose expression he rather liked, and forced himself to hurry on his way. It was just a question of regaining mastery over his own feelings, he told himself, tightening the knot in his tie and increasing his stride; just a question of crushing all the pointless self-doubt back into its rightful, subjugated place. Isobel had not married him for his weaknesses, he reminded himself, throwing back his head and striding, jaw clenched, down the last few yards of the school's long central corridor. He would give every matter its proper attention in due course, his wife included. But both Ben's resolve and his stride faltered somewhat at the question of exactly what such attentions should involve. A hero in a book would organise a spring weekend in Paris, or tickets to the opera, he mused bitterly, thinking in the same instant that heroes in books didn't have overdrafts and a terror of appearing weak. The thought drove him on to unhappy reflections on Isobel's recent frenzied interest in literature. For, in Ben's view, this discovery of the pleasures of reading was neither a coincidence nor a cause for celebration. Whatever vocational quest Isobel claimed lay behind her visits to the library, it was painfully apparent to him that she was holding books to her face like a shield. Whenever he was around these days, she seemed to be reading, hiding behind the covers, as if to shut him out, to emphasise their separateness.

Once, a long time ago, he remembered sadly, Isobel had been proud to boast her preference for home-making as opposed to the more socially acceptable postgraduate practice of pursuing a career. Only a joint venture with him would lure her into the rat race, she used to say, or possibly sorting through stained clothes and chipped crockery in aid of a good cause. For a moment Ben wondered if he could blame Juliet – these days attending courses with the same kind of frequency that she visited the hairdresser – for his wife's recent show of self-improving zeal. But he quickly brushed the notion aside. It was impossible to compare the two women. Fond though he was of both the Howards, Ben had never doubted that Isobel was in another league. As indeed their love had been, once upon a time, he thought hopelessly. His throat tightened so much that for a moment he couldn't breathe. It took a monumental effort of self-will for him to raise a clenched fist and rap smartly on the headmaster's handsome panelled door. Two sharp orderly knocks, beating the hopelessness away.

'Ben, thank you for coming. Take a pew.' Peter Abbott gestured at the studded leather chair facing his desk.

'No, I'm fine, thanks, Peter. Slightly behind schedule, in fact.' He looked at his watch and scowled.

'Coffee?'

Ben shook his head.

'I'll come straight to the point, then.' Peter Abbott walked round to the front of his desk and leant back against it, careful to nudge a silver Victorian inkwell out of the way beforehand. 'The fact is, there's been something of a complaint from a parent. Concerning one of the boys on your field trip.'

'What sort of complaint?'

'Hard to categorise, I'm afraid.' He frowned, flexing the imposing grey bushes of his eyebrows and crossing his arms across his broad, pin-striped chest. 'Misguided infatuation probably describes it best. Nothing we can't sort out, I'm sure.'

Ben's pulse quickened. When he spoke his teeth felt as if they were sticking to the insides of his lips. 'Misguided infatuation?'

'Take a look at these. The shorter one is from the parents to me, the longer is what prompted them to write in the first place. They found it under Lewis's pillow at home.' He picked up two letters lying on the top of the correspondence in his in-tray and handed them across to Ben. 'It's got to be looked into, I'm afraid, Ben. These things always do.'

'Jesus Christ,' gasped Ben, looking up after a few moments, 'this is . . . absurd.'

'I couldn't agree more, but the parents – understandably – are anxious.'

'They actually think I would encourage this . . . this drivel?'

'I know, I know, it's unthinkable . . .' Peter Abbott sighed, but his steady brown eyes never left the face of his employee.

'Bloody hell.' Ben hit the letters with the back of his hand. 'This is the last thing I need, I can tell you.' He could feel indignation rising like panic in his chest. 'How dare they think that I would encourage improper affections from a child . . .'

'Now calm down a minute.' Only Peter Abbott's raised left eyebrow indicated his surprise and disappointment at the suggestion of hysteria in Ben's voice. The man was exceptionally talented in every respect, quite capable of running his own school before long, if he played his cards right. 'Let's keep things in perspective. I'll talk to Lewis myself first. Perhaps you would write to his parents. I've already had a word on the phone. He's an only child, as you probably know; blessed with a father who seems to spend half his time flying off to visit oil rigs in North Africa. Not so surprising that he should have latched on to you by way of a substitute.'

'Though it's hardly father–son material, is it, Peter?' muttered Ben, his face sagging with a despondence that he no longer had the energy to hide.

'No, indeed it isn't.' The head took the letters back and removed his spectacles, taking his time to fold and stow them away into the breast pocket of his jacket before speaking again. 'And Lewis seemed perfectly normal on the field trip, did he? No – er – incident that might have been a trigger for this outpouring of passion?' He smiled, to indicate his trust in the answer.

'Jesus, no.'

'Right. Good.' He rubbed his hands together. 'Let's get the matter sorted, then.' Prompted by the look on Ben's face, he added, 'There are other more pleasant aspects to being a role model for these hooligans, Ben, don't forget that.'

Ben tried to smile by way of acknowledging the compliment. But as he turned to leave the room, it occurred to him that the resilient confidence of which he had once been rather proud was in danger of seeping away, leaking out of him from the sheer force of being pulled in so many different directions.

'Steady on, there, old fellow,' exclaimed Caulder, as Ben barged into him on the other side of the door.

'Sorry. I'm late. Sorry. Always fucking late,' he growled, striding back down towards the hall.

'No matter,' humphed the elderly science master, standing back to let him pass and shaking his head in amiable despair. He was a good man, Tarrant, one of the best, in fact, but very tetchy lately; very tetchy indeed.

Guilt could make one do strange things, Isobel reflected, pulling up outside the newsagent's in order to buy her husband's aunt a packet of peppermints. As well as the sweets, she bought a large print paperback entitled *Mistress of Destiny*, whose cover featured a full-breasted woman nose to nose with one of the chiselled-faced heroes which had proved such a success on previous occasions. If I bump into Juliet, she thought, then she will see that I am telling the truth, that I am too busy visiting decrepit relatives for idle chat in Royles over cappuccinos and wedges of gateau.

The fact that another bouquet of flowers had been delivered to Fox's Crescent that morning had greatly aided this drive towards virtue. They were more ostentatious than the first lot, all crimson and pink, with fat speckled stamens and wide silky leaves. Overtly sexual, in fact, decided Isobel, telling herself she should be appalled, but managing only to feel secretly thrilled instead. But such flowers definitely needed hiding, she had realised, her heart skipping a beat. Even Ben couldn't fail to notice the flamboyance of their lush red curves and fat green stems. So she put them on the wide window ledge in their little box of a spare room, taking the precaution to pull the curtain half across so that, should anyone open the door, the only evidence of their presence would be a pungent aroma, as unsuspicious as the sickly sweetness of a newly opened air-freshener. Only as Isobel closed the door behind her was she struck by the potentially awesome significance behind such a simple act of deception. It was almost interesting that such a very small – and ostensibly harmless – deed could feel so very wicked.

It wasn't Juliet she bumped into, however, but James. James, whom she had spent all week dreading but hoping to see, by scurrying round Torbridge like a nervous thief, steeling herself for chance encounters round every corner, and then sighing with gratitude and dismay when none occurred.

They caught sight of each other just as Isobel had returned to her car. James, *en route* for a meeting at Torbridge General Hospital, had parked a few yards further up the road in order to post a letter. There was no avoiding each other. He waved at once and began to walk towards her. Torn between beating an unseemly retreat into the safety of her vehicle and yet wanting to appear attractively unflustered, Isobel found herself leaning against the passenger door in the most unnatural of poses, the pages of Aunt Violet's book flapping unhelpfully in the gusty breeze.

'Isobel, how are you?' He was all warmth and confidence, even kissing her on the cheek. He was wearing a grey double-breasted suit flecked with blue and a light pink shirt. His tie was a daring swirl of pink and grey; a tie that Ben would have consigned to the bin, observed Isobel wryly, but which for James was the perfect finishing touch. He would look just as clean-cut and dashing at sixty, she realised, self-consciously putting her fingers to where his lips had touched her skin and offering him a nervous smile in return.

'I'm fine. How are you?' Her voice was unnaturally bright, while her eyes surreptitiously searched his face for signposts as to how they should proceed.

'The Open University has a broader curriculum than I thought.' He winked, gesturing at the paperback with his chin.

'You mean . . . oh this? Oh no, it doesn't – I mean, this is for Ben's aunt. I'm on my way to visit her.'

'Sounds grim.' He made a face.

'She's OK,' replied Isobel quickly, unsure as to whether she was defending Aunt Violet or herself.

'Did you get the flowers?' he whispered suddenly.

'Oh God – I mean, yes, I did, thank you so much, James – they were lovely, but no more I think, don't you? I just feel . . .'

'No more.' He smiled gravely, casting glances between the polished tips of his shoes and her face. 'I can't stop thinking about you, Isobel,' he whispered. 'It's hell.'

'Oh dear.' Though it was what a part of her had been waiting to hear, the disclosure of such intimate information threw Isobel into fresh confusion. 'We're coming to dinner next weekend. Juliet wants us to stay the night. Did she tell you?'

'She most certainly did.' James threw back his head and laughed, pushing his hands deeper into the pockets of his trousers and showing two impressive archways of teeth.

'Don't laugh,' she urged, glancing nervously about them. 'It's awful – I mean, I feel awful. Well, to be honest, I don't know what I feel . . .'

'I know what I feel,' he interrupted with sudden and sober urgency, every trace of amusement wiped from his expression. 'I know what the hell I feel and it's driving me mad. I know you feel it too, Isobel, I know you do.' He slapped the roof of her car, taking a step towards her. 'I can't carry on like this . . . thinking about you all damned day . . .' He was speaking through clenched teeth. '. . . imagining . . . you and me.' He swallowed hard.

'Don't,' she whispered, steering her shaking fingers towards the door handle. 'Don't . . . there's nothing . . .'

'There's everything,' he said hoarsely, touching her shoulder, moulding his hand round its hard curve.

Compelled mostly by a terror of being observed, Isobel somehow wriggled free and levered herself into the car. She did not look up again until she was safely ensconced behind the steering wheel, key ready in the lock, her left hand gripping the handbrake.

James remained on the pavement watching her, feet planted squarely apart, both hands still thrust into his trouser pockets, a look of shameless intensity on his face. If anything her obvious nervousness made him more determined, more excited. It felt like a long time since he had wielded such power over his wife. A long time since he had wielded power over anything.

'Isobel!' exclaimed Aunt Violet, throwing wide her mottled, bangled arms and pressing soft jagged pink lips to her forehead. 'How lovely – how absolutely divine. My dear girl, sit down, sit down and tell me all your news.'

The nurse, who had warned Isobel that her patient was

having something of a good day, winked briefly as she closed the door.

'I brought you these.' Isobel held out the book and pepper-mints.

'But how kind,' exclaimed Aunt Violet in the high tremulous voice she reserved for special occasions. Making no attempt to examine the gifts, she fixed her eyes upon her visitor's face instead. 'But my dear girl, you look exhausted and so terribly ... *worried*. I do hope it's not on my account. I love being here – quite the right thing to do. The North was never my *thing*. I should have left years ago ... but change takes such courage, don't you find? But I always loved my visits to England,' she continued merrily, throwing back her head and pressing her hands together. '—I used to take Ben out on weekends, you know, whisk him off to London and the theatre ... Ah, but those were gay times ...' She fanned the air in front of her face, flapping both hands, while her habitual head-nod ran wild, as if keen to offer its own independent support of such enthusiastic emotions.

'And you also left Scotland to visit your brother sometimes, didn't you?' put in Isobel, in a bid to appear interested, want-ing, if only for conscience's sake, to see this charitable chore through to the best of her ability. For a moment it seemed as though the question had snapped the chain of lucidity. 'Your brother Albert, the one who settled abroad,' she prompted gently.

Violet's crinkled eyes darkened and then grew dreamy. 'Once or twice ... such a journey. But blood is thicker ...' She sighed and started to fidget at the hem of her dress. As the material jerked in her hands, Isobel glimpsed a wide ladder in the thick brown tights; a terrible staircase of veiny white flesh that made her swallow hard and look away.

'Such a fool, Albert was, such a dear fool ...' She was muttering to herself now, her voice reduced to a series of sniffs and tut-tuts. 'Falling for that Louisa ... just a girl herself ... and a foreigner too. Leaving us all like that ... without a thought for anyone else.' She snorted, before adding more matter-of-factly, 'She couldn't cope when the baby arrived, of course, which was why Albert asked me to visit.'

'That was nice of you,' murmured Isobel, trying and failing to conjure an image of her husband in a pram.

'He was the spitting image of his father. But had his mother's eyes.' Aunt Violet continued, her tongue darting out to retrieve the saliva that had a habit of collecting in the creases round the corners of her mouth. 'Dark Latin eyes . . .'

'So sad that Louisa died,' said Isobel softly, concerned now by the look on her companion's face, the way her jaw was sagging. 'They sound like such a perfect couple—'

'Perfect? They were a disaster,' retorted the old lady indignantly. 'She broke Albert's heart, you know, not once, but many times.'

'Did she?' responded Isobel, mildly intrigued by these disjointed revelations in spite of herself. Ben's own memories, infrequently though they were raised, had always begun with the fatal crash and his father's decision to send him away to England.

'May I have a peppermint now?'

'Of course, they are for you – to eat whenever you want.' Isobel pressed the cool, liver-spotted hand in hers, inadvertently moved by the childishness of the request. 'I brought them for you, remember? And the book.' She patted the cover on the window seat beside them. 'Would you like me to read to you for a while?'

At this, some of the haughty bitterness with which Isobel was more familiar flooded back into the old lady's face. 'Certainly not. Stupid as children, most women. Dressing up and flirting when they shouldn't. Like that one.' She shot an arch look at the provocative image on the book cover. 'In my day we were gay, but never . . . wicked.'

'Is it wicked to flirt?' asked Isobel with studied innocence.

'Louisa was the one to answer that question.'

'Why, what did Louisa do?'

'She was Ben's mother.'

'I know . . . I was just wondering what she was like—'

'So many questions – it's rude, you know, to ask so many personal questions. You should mind your own business, young lady. Who let you in? This is my bedroom . . . my bedroom.' Aunt Violet gripped the arms of her chair and struggled to lever herself upright. Isobel got up to help, but was pushed rudely away. 'I'll ring if I need assistance, thank you. I have servants, you know.'

Isobel remained standing, debating how best to take her leave when her identity had so obviously been mislaid and suppressing the impulse to take offence.

'Could you bring cigarettes next time?' The thread of hostility had been lost. She was all chiming bangles and fluttering smiles again. 'Those pretty cocktail ones – colours like rainbows with heavenly gold tips on the end. Perfect for parties, don't you find?'

Isobel nodded and smiled, though she was sure a no-smoking policy reigned throughout the home. 'I'll see what I can do.'

Once outside, a reluctance to return to the tensions awaiting her in Torbridge made Isobel stroll away from the driveway towards the sloping grass viewed from Aunt Violet's bedroom window. While much of the grounds surrounding the home was rambling and overgrown, the central lawn was kept trimmed and spruce for those still hardy enough to venture beyond the confines of their rooms. Though mowed to a tidy half-inch, the grass proved to be riddled with moss and weeds, a kaleidoscope of different greens that closed round the edges of her shoes like the pile of a soft carpet. After a few minutes she sat down on one of the many benches parked within easy walking distance of the house. A few yards to her left, two peacocks were fanning their tails at each other round a laurel bush, jerking their velveteen necks and looking indignant every time a gust of wind threatened to bowl them over from behind. An old lady swaddled in scarves and furs as protection against the light spring breeze appeared from round the other side of the house. She paused unsteadily, watching the birds' comical courtship for a few minutes before edging her way back along the gravel path by which she had come.

Ben could bring cigarettes if he wanted, decided Isobel crossly, suddenly furious at herself for not having had the courage to tell Juliet outright that she did not wish to meet, for having succumbed to the base and pathetic impulse of manufacturing excuses to account for her time. A screech from one of the peacocks made her jump. The old woman had unnerved her, she realised, leaving the bench and hurrying back towards her car. Those faded eyes could look so horribly beady at times, so disconcertingly knowing. It was almost as if she had recognised her confused state of mind, and had wanted to punish her further with a few timely revelations about the past. Isobel kicked angrily at a pebble on the lawn. Whereas the very last thing she needed was to be furnished with details of the apparently sad subject of her husband's parents' marriage. To feel any curiosity on the subject was irritating beyond belief. She could feel it blocking her mind, preventing her from quite cutting off the tendon of emotion that still bound her to the man she had married. A man who no longer loved her, Isobel reminded herself, opening the car door and throwing her bag inside. The least – the best – thing she could do for all their sakes was to learn not to feel anything in return.

Virtue was no good unless it extended to the head as well as the deed, Archie told himself, as the sight of Fox's Crescent induced a frenzy of butterfly wings to beat against the walls of his stomach. In one hand he held a folder of papers relating to both his sponsored walk and the on-going threat to St Cuthbert's. In the other he clenched a Biro which, every few minutes or so, he ran round the inside of his dog-collar to ease the itching. The skin there was a mass of red bumps; not spots exactly, more like a rash, but painful as hell. It did not help that the day was turning out to be curiously warm for early-March; a flagship for summer glories ahead, perhaps, thought Archie grimly, consigning the Biro to his mouth and resorting to his nails.

Archie had spent a dispiriting morning knocking on doors and pressing bell buttons. Many parishioners had not been in and those that had had not exactly greeted him with the warmth he had hoped his smiling, well-intentioned presence might inspire. Anything overtly connected to the Church seemed to make people feel guilty, he had discovered, especially if money was involved. Though the sums relating to his sponsored walk could hardly be described as bankrupting. Thirty-four pounds was an almost embarrassing total compared to the amounts raised by some of the other volunteers. The walk itself – once he had managed to shake off the cloying attentions of the irrepressible Flora Dobbs – had not been too bad at all. The rain held off for the first couple of hours and by the time the drizzle did set in, he was enjoying some lively conversation with a group of Macmillan nurses who had driven from a hospital a hundred miles away to participate. They had insisted on him accompanying them for a celebration drink in a pub afterwards, where they quaffed pints of beer and cracked increasingly risqué jokes through screens of low-tar cigarette smoke. Archie, somewhat alarmed by the force of personalities and ribald humour emerging from the staid mackintoshes and wellingtons that had kept him company through the afternoon, had speedily finished his own pint and slipped away.

Getting close to people was unbelievably hard, he mused sadly, thinking not only of his ineptitude with the nurses, but also of his experiences on doorsteps throughout the morning. Humans were so wary, so painfully suspicious of hidden agendas; when all he was after – all that he longed for – was not to make converts or hear penitent excuses about church attendance, but to be taken on as a friend and confidant. Someone to be trusted. Was it nineties cynicism or was it him? he wondered glumly, running his Biro with a satisfying click along a set of railings to his left. Perhaps he just didn't have the right personality. A cat, roused from a snooze on a dustbin lid, arched its back in disapproval at the noise. As Archie reached out a hand to soothe it, the animal sprang away, disappearing through a gap in a hedge.

Being so hatefully baby-faced and freckled didn't exactly help, Archie reflected with a sigh, catching sight of his reflection in a car wing mirror and glancing quickly away. Nor did having two parts to his surname. Heighton-Jones somehow didn't sound humble enough for a priest. Yet it was a name to which he felt greatly attached, both on account of a generous affection for his parents and the interesting eccentricities of the ancestors from which it derived. Abandoning any part of it would be tantamount to an admission of defeat.

People could take him as he was or not at all, he thought with a surge of defiance, his expression lightening at the sight of Isobel Tarrant's front door. Three Easter chicks made from pipe-cleaners and cotton wool dangled precariously from the door knocker. So precariously that he took the precaution of rapping on the wood beside them instead. When there were no sounds of response from inside he submitted to the temptation of peeking through the letterbox. A couple of envelopes on the doormat reinforced his disappointment. Though it did justify another visit, he thought slyly, straining his neck to see down the hall.

'I'm afraid she's out, Reverend. Shopping, I think. She usually goes to the supermarket on the ring road.'

'Oh, hello there.' The blood rushed to Archie's cheeks as he hastily straightened himself and turned to face Druscilla Carew. 'Yes, yes, I'm afraid that does appear to be the case.' Only the knowledge that all members of the Lord's flock were equally deserving provided Archie with the resources to smile. Mrs Carew had not been on his calling list. Not even for saving St Cuthbert's. There was something alarmingly voracious about the woman, a sense of unappeasable appetites behind the sticky lips and pillar-box smile.

'Anything I can help with?' Her dark eyes alighted upon the papers in his left hand.

'A signature would be marvellous.' He trotted over to the low fence with studied jollity and a heavy heart. 'We're trying to save St Cuthbert's from the arts people.'

'I've just made some macaroons. Would you like one?' She took a step back from the fence and crossed her arms.

Archie patted his stomach, which had a tendency to cave inwards no matter the quantity or density of anything fed into it, and shook his head in a show of regret. 'That's very kind but I'd better not . . .'

'Fiddlesticks. You're all skin and bone. If you eat one of my macaroons I'll sign anything. I forbid you to refuse.' Her eyes blazed from under their heavy canopies of purple and blue eyeshadow. 'And we'll have a coffee,' she commanded, waving a heavily ringed hand at him by way of an instruction to follow her to her front door. 'It'll have to be instant as my percolator's broken. Clogged, I think. Perhaps you would have a little look at it for me?'

'But I'm useless with machines,' protested Archie meekly as she disappeared inside. Muttering expletives to himself, he looked round for a way out. But the street was empty. Apart from a small sparrow with its eye on a crumb at the base of Druscilla's bird table. Though tempted, the sight of the priest's tall figure striding in that direction himself made the creature judge the risk too great. By the time the front door had closed and silence had descended once more, a fat magpie had got there first, alighting upon the morsel with a croak of triumph that set the sparrow hopping in dismay.

Isobel put down her book and brushed the flaky crumbs from her chest. Though a double-sized croissant filled with cheese and bacon had seemed like an inspired subsitute for her usual apology for a lunch – picking at leftovers from the fridge on most days – it had left her feeling faintly sick. She had stopped in a roadside café on her return journey from the supermarket, driven both by genuine hunger and a lingering reluctance to return home. Being between places had suddenly felt potentially liberating; like a pause between sentences, time just to be. The café was new and smelt of chip fat mixed with fresh paint. The only other customers were two lorry drivers and a motorcyclist with a purple birthmark splashed across his left eye and down one side of his nose. The tray of croissants had looked sorely neglected, as had the spinach quiche beside them and a full tureen of orange liquid, which the girl said was carrot and mandarin soup, made fresh the day before.

Having recently progressed from the sedate drawing-room dramas of Jane Austen to the altogether more tempestuous world of *Anna Karenina*, Isobel had at first found some trouble in adjusting. Especially since Anna was clearly one of those infuriating women bent upon a course towards self-destruction, no matter how friends or fate tried to intervene. Yet after a few chapters she had nonetheless become intrigued by the woman's avalanches of passion, towards her lover, Vronsky, in particular. The eroticism of it was breathtaking. It made everything they did forgivable. It made the jealous, vicious rages of her husband despicable. Though wronged, the husband had so far gained the least of Isobel's sympathies. In her view, Anna deserved to keep her child and to have her lover as well. It was obvious that she should, yet equally obvious that such an outcome was not to be. Isobel, wiping the grease off her fingers with a tissue, found herself wondering whether it was just a trick of art that adultery could seem justifiable. Or whether it was the certainty of doom that made it so redeeming.

She sighed and dropped the tissue into her empty coffee cup.

Ben, continuing in the acerbic vein with which he had taken to delivering most remarks, had recently commented that if she read any more she might consider running an Open University course instead of applying to join one. Suppressing the faint hope that such reactions might evince a husbandly jealousy of some kind, Isobel had managed to contain herself to a pursed-lip silence of a response. She did not feel able to stop reading. As well as granting some genuine enjoyment, she was aware that the self-absorption it required presented a legitimate distraction from the failure going on around her, and from the hateful and unrewarding business of trying to prevent it.

She pressed the tissue with the back of her teaspoon, squeezing it into a soggy brown ball, while dwelling on how increasingly incapable her husband seemed of loving anything, except perhaps his work. He had agreed to dinner with the Howards, but only after considerable debate. In fact, so reluctant had he been, so contortedly hesitant, that Isobel had found herself urging the invitation upon him without any of the reserve she had originally felt herself. He didn't even want to spend time with friends now, she thought miserably, let alone with her.

As she brushed a few remaining crumbs off the ripped cellophane cover of her library book and got up to return to her car, it was the recollection of her chance meeting with James that Isobel found the most sustaining. Remembering the pleasure and interest written so plainly across his face during their encounter outside the newsagent's, she smiled and felt stronger. There was someone who would appreciate her all right. Even if he wasn't supposed to.

The difficult, the impossible question of what to do next remained unanswered. As she drove slowly back towards Torbridge, Isobel's gaze kept leaving the road and scanning the hills and tree clumps on either side of her, as if their chalky faces might hold decipherable answers to such a dilemma. On the skyline to her left a lone skeletal tree crouched like a human begging for forgiveness. With a shiver of apprehension Isobel averted her eyes. There was always prettiness too, she assured herself, heaps of it, if only one looked hard enough. All around her spring was unfolding with fairytale perfection; lambs were finding their feet; fields were lush with sprouting tufts of grass; clusters of bobbing flowers lined the roadside. Though summer was many months off yet, the countryside already seemed enveloped by its promise; all its tight, bright colours throbbing with the ripeness contained inside. Like an unwrapped present, she mused. Like her and James: poised for fulfilment. Erotic images began to seep into the tangle inside her head. Images that took all her common sense and self-discipline to force aside. In a way, the situation was perfect as it was, Isobel realised, and a part of her longed to keep it that way. Unwrapped parcels had a horrible tendency to lose their allure, the shapes inside never turning out quite as one had dreamed. It was wonderful being wanted without having given in to it. It was wonderful too to feel such things and yet still be able to say, hand on heart, I have done nothing wrong. Except perhaps to hide a bunch of flowers. It meant she could enjoy the consolation of desire – of being desired – with none of the sin. Isobel gripped the wheel, telling herself that any woman in her shoes would feel the same, that any human would nurture these pleasures as some compensation for the coldness now endured within the sanctuary of her own home.

On the Saturday of the Howards' invitation to dinner Ben woke early, his head aching from a fitful sleep. Through bleary eyes he studied the sleeping figure of his wife, his heart filling with a sort of sad longing, as if she were some priceless thing he desired but could not touch. Her lips were relaxed and slightly open, as though ready for a kiss; one thick tress of auburn hair was flung to one side across the pillow; copper on white. Ben stroked the wisps near his face with the back of his hand. She opened her eyes and for a moment their gazes connected. Then reality broke through, bringing with it an awareness of where they were, of unsolved problems, of distance.

'Have you got to go into school?'

'I told you, I've got the first run-through in costume this afternoon.'

'I meant this morning . . .'

'It's my turn to invigilate prep for the boarders.'

'Could you drop Megan at her flute lesson on the way?'

'I mustn't be late—'

'Don't bother, then. We'll manage.'

She kicked off the bedcovers and stretched, reaching her arms up towards the bedstead and screwing up her eyes as she yawned. Her green nightshirt rode up over her shins, revealing bony knees and a slim, creamy portion of thigh. Beside her Ben closed his eyes, leaden with sleepiness now that the day had arrived, and hugged the covers round his face like a child with a comforter. All Isobel could see was a small segment of one cheek, darkly unshaven against the white sheet, and the solid curve of his right arm now clutching the area of duvet she had vacated. The hairs lay flat and dark along his forearm, save for the smoother, lighter band of skin left by his wristwatch. She could see the exaggerated lump of his wrist bone, a famous family trait which he had pointed out to her himself, shyly, on the first night they spent in the same bed. 'If that's your greatest fault then I'm on to a good thing,' she had teased, tracing the shape with the tip of her finger and loving it already because it was a part of him. How uncritical they had been then, how forgiving, how generous. Staring at the lump now, she was struck by the incongruity of it, the curiously inelegant start it made to the long, strong hand; a hand, she thought grimly, which once would have chosen to caress her in preference to a padded bedspread. Tentatively, she reached out to touch him; so tentatively that the moment her fingers made contact with his arm he twitched away, imagining in his sleepiness that he was shaking off a single stray hair or a nervous shiver within the layered mysteries of his own skin.

Ben left the house some twenty minutes later, his face still puffy with fatigue, his hair ironed into odd shapes through nocturnal tussles with his pillow. The girls danced in circles round him, while he grappled with chain locks and bike wheels. They leapt on his back and hung on his arms, squealing with threats never to let go. Somehow Ben seized them both at the same time, spinning them round in a carousel of flaying limbs and laughter till they begged for release. Isobel, watching from inside the hall, hugged herself against the stream of chill morning air, while a terrible envy welled inside. That he could be so unchanged for their children only heightened her own sense of alienation and loss. By the time Ben looked up to wave, she had retreated into the bathroom to wash and plait her hair.

Her fingers worked deftly with the thick wet strands, while her eyes gazed defiantly at her reflection in the mirror. Her mood hardened still further as she rummaged through shelves and cupboards for clothes. Aware that she should not mind what she wore – that it would be wrong to mind what she wore – only increased Isobel's mounting concern for her appearance. She wanted to compose an outfit that would do for the day as well as the evening. I am going to dress for James, she realised with a start, discarding a handsome but dull brown dress in favour of a calf-length bottle-green skirt and a creamy cotton shirt. It had a wide lacy collar and crisp broad cuffs, fed by billowing sleeves that were pleated attractively at the shoulder. Shoes were harder. It wouldn't do to look too dressy. Having settled on a pair of low-heeled old black favourites, she looked up to see her youngest daughter, indignant and pink-faced, surfacing from amongst the heap of bedclothes.

'I was hiding and you didn't even notice,' she wailed.

'But Sophie, darling, you were so terribly good and still, how could I possibly have known you were there?'

Partially mollifed, Sophie flung herself across the bed on to her elbows and stared sulkily at her mother. 'Are you going to a party?'

For a moment Isobel felt caught out. 'Don't be silly . . . I mean, we're going to Eddie and Tilly's house, remember?' she added, recovering herself. 'The grown-ups are having a special dinner and we're all staying the night. Mummy thought she would look a little smart for once.' She tossed her plait over her shoulder and began punching air into pillows. 'Off the bed now, or I can't make it.'

'I think you always look smart – and *very* pretty,' announced Megan, bounding in barefoot through the doorway and slipping into a dusty pair of court shoes, which Isobel had excavated from the back of the wardrobe. 'Why don't you wear these?' she enquired, balancing with difficulty on the high heels. 'They're beautiful.'

Surveying her eldest parading Lolita-like round the bedroom made Isobel laugh in spite of herself. 'Because nowadays if Mummy wears those for more than ten minutes at a time the circulation stops in in all her toes.'

'What's circulation?' asked Megan, now eyeing her dramatic footwear more doubtfully.

'It's the blood going round our bodies. Every little finger and toe needs it otherwise it falls off . . .'

'Falls off?'

'But only if the blood can't get to them for quite a long time,' explained her mother quickly, suppressing a smile.

Megan kicked off the shoes and began a worried inspection of her extremities, before being distracted by the more rewarding pastime of studying her hair for split ends and seeing if any might be encouraged to split a little further. Behind her, Sophie, endeavouring to do a headstand in the middle of the bed, yowled with frustration each time her skinny legs toppled out of control.

Watching the pair of them, Isobel experienced a rush of sentimental love. Were the girls really all that kept Ben with her now? she wondered, reaching out to stop Sophie's knees from a collision with her sister's head. The idea prompted a motherly hug of such inappropriate intensity that Sophie, sensing an emotion that made her afraid, scowled and squirmed away. Long after her daughters had chased each other out of the room, Isobel stayed where she was, twisting a fold of sheet between her fingers and wondering how long they could all go on as they were.

Ben cycled fast, barely pausing to check for traffic at the end of Fox's Crescent before swerving left in the direction of the town centre. A small detour took him past Torbridge's famously irresistible Old Bakery where he bought a large Danish pastry by way of breakfast. As he left the shop, already chewing hungrily, he was confronted by James, looking spruce and clean-shaven in a padded green vest of a coat and rust-coloured corduroy trousers. He clicked his heels and saluted when he saw Ben, who, for no explicable reason, felt his heart sink ungratefully in return. He hastily raked his fingers through his hair and wiped the crumbs from his cheek with the back of his hand.

'James . . . on Saturday duty are you?'

'Only in the domestic sense.' James grinned and waved an empty shopping basket at him by way of an explanation. 'On a mission in aid of our revels tonight. Fresh rolls – some of this establishment's finest – half a dozen eggs and . . . buggeration . . . what was the other thing?' He began patting his pockets in search of a list. 'Wrote it down somewhere . . .'

'Milk?' suggested Ben, for no reason other than the fact that it popped with enticing coherence into the fog of his head.

'Milk. That's it, exactly. You're a genius, Ben. Four pints. Three semi-skimmed, one completely skimmed. Juliet's trying to keep us all fat-free,' he added, rolling his eyes at the sky in a show of amused tolerance that bore little relation to the real state of affairs at home. Juliet was on her high horse and would not get down. It did not help that he was aware he had put her there, through irritation at all the absurd hocus-pocus about feet and flower oils, and – rather less complicatedly – because of Isobel. Unfortunately, the tentacles of such unresolved conflicts seemed to have probed every other aspect of their existence too, instilling a general negativity about domestic life, which was for James quite unprecedented and highly unsettling. The approaching evening with the Tarrants had been the only shaft of light in what would otherwise have been a very dark tunnel indeed.

'How was Wales?'

'Wales?' For a moment Ben's mind refused to move on from milk. Then he remembered all the problems connected with the boy Lewis and frowned. The child had been removed from the school; behaviour that suggested the parents remained suspicious in spite of all Peter Abbott's reassurances to the contrary. Without such unfaltering support from his headmaster, Ben was not sure how he would have coped with the situation at all.

Another customer leaving the bakery murmured an 'excuse me' and stepped between them. The interruption gave Ben a moment to collect his thoughts. 'More to the point, how are you . . . ?' he burst out heartily. 'I mean . . . Christ, I haven't seen you since the damned bomb – haven't thanked you properly for fielding Isobel and the children – that was very kind, James, very kind indeed . . . it will be months before the girls are properly over it . . . hope they catch the bastards.'

'Got a couple of Irishmen in custody apparently – heard it on the news this morning.'

'Really? Well, that's marvellous . . . look here, James, I've got to go – late as usual.' Ben smiled weakly. Remembering his half-eaten pastry, he took a large bite. 'See you tonight, of course,' he muttered, ineptly fielding crumbs with his tongue.

'Absolutely.' James gave Ben an affectionate pat on the shoulder, declaring, 'I'm looking forward to it enormously,' and thinking to himself that this was true, even if the prime cause for such zest remained as wholly inappropriate fodder for conversation with Isobel's husband. 'Look like you could do with a night off, mate, to be honest,' he added, on a spurt of sincerity that may well have derived from the uncomfortable duplicity of such notions.

'I'm fine. Only a few weeks till the Easter break – I'll catch up on myself then.'

'Lucky sod,' growled James cheerfully before disappearing inside the shop. He chose a selection of brown and white bread rolls and a sesame-seed baguette for good measure. By the time he re-emerged, Ben and his bicycle were at the far end of the street. Raising his arm in salute, though there was little chance of the gesture being received, James was struck by how small and curiously vulnerable Ben Tarrant looked. The thought was at once novel and vaguely disturbing. A weak man was harder to respect, easier to beat. Not just on the squash court, but in other areas too. A small, unforgivable sense of power tightened in the pit of the doctor's stomach as he embarked on a deliberately unhurried drive back to Ilcombe. A power that thrilled as much as it disconcerted. Of course it was wrong to lust after another man's wife, but it was exciting too. Especially if the wife concerned responded with such charming and eager perturbation. James slapped the steering wheel hard several times, inwardly riling against the social constraints of his immediate situation, and more deep-seated, less easily defined disappointments to do with the pattern of his life in general.

'Do you ever miss that first flush of being in love?' The question slipped out of its own accord, oiled by the smooth pummelling of Juliet's hands across her back. The entire length of Isobel's body felt drowsy and warm. The heavy scent of roses, which had at first struck her as merely cloying, now tasted like the sweetest air; each inhalation seemed to drug her mind with fresh colour and depth.

Having expected only the unease of guilt, Isobel had been somewhat overcome by the pleasure she had experienced upon seeing Juliet again. Their friendship came into its own, fuelled by the separate but related difficulties each had endured during the preceding weeks. While the children stampeded upstairs to begin constructing dens for the night, Juliet had shooed Isobel into the spare room for her promised introduction to the delights of aromatherapy.

'All that brooding over one sentence, one word, one inflection? All that navel-searching over which feelings one should have and how intensely?' Juliet snorted. 'Not bloody likely.' She ran her thumbs down Isobel's spine, from the nape of her neck to the small of her back, pushing hard. 'I'm a bit off love in general at the moment, to be honest.' She brushed a few stray zigzags of hair out of her eyes, using the back of her hand so as to avoid the oil gleaming in her palms, and gave a dismissive sniff. 'And lust for that matter.'

'What, even with that Adonis bricklayer of yours?' teased Isobel lazily, her mind cruising soft, insouciant seas of crimson and orange.

'*Especially* with him.' Juliet paused to sprinkle a few more drops of oil on to her hands. 'Not even that scrubbing board of a stomach moves me now.'

Isobel giggled. 'Harsh words indeed. What crime has he committed?'

'You mean apart from leaving a superglue-like trail of cement and filth through the house when I specifically told them all to use the side door? Oh God, and the downstairs loo . . . by the time that lot have finished with it in the morning . . .' She groaned. 'Cigarette stubs floating in the bowl, half a roll of paper gone . . .'

'I get the picture,' interjected Isobel, feeling, as she so often did with Juliet these days, that she was being entertained rather than spoken to. 'Reality strikes again.'

'You're telling me. But listen to this, you haven't heard the worst of it.' She lowered her voice. 'I was standing in my bedroom the other day, doing my face in the mirror by the window. Still in my petticoat. One eye done, hair its usual morning haystack, when suddenly there he was, standing in the doorway behind, staring at me . . .'

'There who was?' enquired Isobel, incredulous.

'The handsome one. The workman with the ponytail. Only suddenly he didn't look handsome at all. He looked greedy and hopeful. And in the same moment I saw myself as he must: a plump middle-aged woman looking for a bit of young stuff on the side . . .'

'Oh, come on now . . .' Isobel tried to lever herself up off the bed, but Juliet pressed her down.

'Stay where you are or the effect will be ruined. I knew at once that it was entirely my fault. I batted my eyelashes once too often and he thought he really stood a chance. But it was quite a shock, I can tell you.'

'So what did you do?'

'I told him to get the hell out of my bedroom, that's what I did. And he scampered off like a naughty schoolboy. I haven't managed to feel the same about him since.'

'I'm not surprised.' Isobel couldn't help laughing.

'Now you see, I couldn't tell James about that.'

At the mention of James, Isobel felt the breath snag in her throat. 'And why not?'

'Not in his present mood. He'd get angry – with me and that silly boy, probably. That is, if he could get angrier than he is at the moment.'

'What's he angry about?' asked Isobel in a small voice.

'Oh, nothing much.' Juliet's tone was airily dismissive. 'Me. Aromatherapy. Reflexology and any other perfectly good healing practice which is not scrupulously itemised in medical textbooks. I've decided that eventually I want to train in reflexology as well, you see. It's just too fascinating for words. We've had some fearful rows about it,' she added ruefully. 'Personally, I think it's a gender thing. We women believe in the mystical stuff – healings and happenings that cannot necessarily be explained – and men don't. The darlings are just so hopelessly calculating and analytical . . .' She sighed again. 'What does Ben think about things like that? Could I convert him with a massage or two, do you think?' She karate-chopped her way across Isobel's shoulder blades to emphasise the point.

'Ben? I'm not sure,' faltered Isobel, thinking that she was in fact more certain of her husband's views on Juliet's penchant for creative hobbies than she was of most things.

'I'll ask him tonight.' Juliet studied her palms, which were looking warm and very red. 'And you see if you can cheer James up a bit for me, will you? This is quite the sulkiest I've ever known him.' She clapped her hands together, clearly ready to move on to other subjects. 'Now . . . I want you with your forehead down so I can get at your neck. And let's keep this beautiful plait safely out of the way – God, this mane of yours is glorious . . . that's it. I need you centralised. There we are. How are you feeling, by the way?'

'Wonderful,' mumbled Isobel, wondering quite how she was supposed to continue breathing with the flat of her face buried ear-deep in pillow.

'Rose oil is by far the best, in my opinion,' went on Juliet from behind. 'The most expensive too, mind you. The Egyptians swore by it. It's supposed to be a mild sedative, an antidepressant, a soother, a spirit-lifter and – oh yes – an aphrodisiac, especially for women. Isn't that incredible? Should I warn Ben?' she enquired slyly. 'Or don't you do it in other people's houses?'

'Mind your own bloody business,' retorted Isobel, managing a brief muffled laugh before burrowing deeper and more gratefully into her pillow. A white lake with grey specks floated into view. She squeezed her lids tightly but the image remained. Cold and empty. My husband flinches at the touch of me, she remembered, the misery of it connecting somehow to the drab screen fixed like a mask before her eyes. She pressed her head deeper still into the bed, wishing she could stifle such knowledge away.

'Keep still, for God's sake,' scolded Juliet. 'This last bit is so important.' She began kneading authoritatively along the slender ridge of Isobel's neck, pushing up under the base of the skull in a way that felt curiously wholesome and yet unpleasant. Then she took hold of Isobel's head in both hands and gently stretched it towards the bedstead, as if trying to lengthen the spine itself. The sensation was so unsettling that Isobel opened her mouth to protest. In the same instant Juliet released her head and lightly scraped her nails down her back and legs, stopping at the tips of her toes. 'There,' she whispered, tucking the towel back round Isobel's shoulders and ankles. 'You mustn't get cold. Stay like that for a bit while I clear up.'

Isobel kept her eyes closed, floating again in a pinky darkness of her own, while Juliet bustled softly between the bedroom and adjoining bathroom. 'You're looking fabulous, by the way, Isobel,' she announced, drying her hands on a small yellow hand towel. 'I've been meaning to say . . . I was quite worried about you a couple of weeks ago, but now you're all lit up. I love that shirt too. Heavenly sleeves. You haven't acquired a lover by any chance, have you?' She held the garment against herself for size and did a small twirl round the end of the bed.

'A lover?' Isobel turned over slowly, keeping the towel up round her chin.

Juliet carefully hung the shirt on the back of a chair. 'Or is it this Open University lark that's giving your cheeks such a glow?'

Isobel groaned, despising the relief that flooded through her on being so swiftly diverted to safer ground. 'Hardly. I can't decide whether to make a formal application or not. To be honest, I dread the thought of having to write essays again, when I suppose all I really want to do is read the books.'

'Well, read books, then. Bugger the course. Cup of tea?'

'Time for a drink, Tarrant?'

Ben looked up from his desk to find Dick Caulder peering at him over the rims of his half-moon spectacles.

'I don't think so, Dick. Sorry.' He shot him an apologetic smile before returning his attention to the pile of rehearsal notes in front of him. He was marking the lighting cues – each one of which had been disastrous – with angry slashes of red felt pen. 'I should have left already,' he added, since his colleague showed no signs of moving away. 'We're out to dinner in Ilcombe tonight. Old friends. I was going to cycle but' – he frowned at his watch – 'on second thoughts I'll call a cab.'

'I could drop you. Ilcombe's on my way.'

'No it isn't.'

'Well, not far off.' Dick jangled the change in his pockets. 'I'd like to, Ben.'

Ben sighed, threw down his pen and leant back in his chair. 'You're an obstinate sod, aren't you?'

Dick Caulder grinned. 'I'll get my coat, then, shall I?'

Some twenty minutes later they were standing elbow to elbow in front of two pints of toffee-coloured real ale, sharing a bag of bacon-flavoured crisps.

'I haven't eaten since this morning,' Ben confessed, tearing the bag apart and pressing out the last of the salty crumbs inside.

'How'd the rehearsal go?'

'Middling to bloody awful. Though I suppose some of the little buggers know their words now. And most of the costumes worked, after a fashion. Julius Caesar – the infamous Giles Turner – is finally coming good too. In fact, it looks as if he'll end up carrying the whole show. There's a sort of atmosphere when he's on, a feeling of suspense, a sense of danger even . . . or maybe desperation is starting to play tricks on my imagination.' He laughed uncertainly and took a large mouthful of beer.

'Sounds most promising to me.'

A comfortable silence ensued, during which the two men sipped their drinks and contemplated the colourful array of bottles and labels on the wall behind the bar.

'I've been seeing one of those what-do-you-call-thems . . . a counsellor,' announced Caulder, just as Ben was on the point of draining his glass and suggesting they leave. 'Therapy.' He scowled and pressed the bridge of his nose.

'Because of . . .'

'Agnes – the wife – dying. Yes, because of that. Thought I could cope, but I coudn't. Anxiety attacks started. Saw my GP, got referred. Simple, really.'

'And has it helped?' Steered by compassion for the unimaginable effort of making such an admission, not wanting to make it any harder than it was already, Ben began an engrossed inspection of his wedding ring, pulling it to the hump of his knuckle and back again.

'Do you know, it has. Can't think why, really. Just someone to talk to. Used to talk to Agnes all the time, I suppose . . . kept ourselves very much to ourselves. Too much probably. Not great ones for friends or socialising. Find myself talking to the shrubbery these days – are you into gardening, Tarrant?'

Ben shook his head, smiling apologetically.

'Neither was I at your age. Agnes did the lot. Now I spend half my spare time out there. Roses are my speciality. I've planted a whole bed of Rugosas called "Agnes" in her honour. Sentimental, I know, but I can't tell you how it's helped. Big flowers, thorny stems – just like her,' he chuckled quietly, 'all heart and bark . . .' He clamped his teeth together to hide a momentary tremble in his jaw. 'They'll look a treat in May.'

'Dick . . .'

'Oh, I'm not saying I don't get down – I miss her like hell most days – most nights too . . . but it's' – he hesitated, searching for the right word – *'manageable* now. I know I can live with it. Nice lady counsellor I got. Kind without going overboard. No pressure either, to say anything really. Or even to keep going. Unshockable too, which was nice. When I think of some of the things . . .'

They were on their second pints now. A couple more empty crisp packets had joined the heap of old cigarette stubs in the massive pewter ashtray in front of them.

'All I'm saying is, it gets such a knocking – all this business of people seeing shrinks instead of talking to each other – but it can really help. Anybody. It can help anybody.'

It took a while for Ben to realise that instead of being in the role of sympathetic listener, as he had, perhaps arrogantly, assumed, he was himself being given some veiled advice. The realisation shocked him so much that he could think of nothing appropriate to say at all. It was like being found guilty of a secret crime. And for his accuser to be a man towards whom he had grown accustomed to feeling nothing but pity was at once humiliating and deeply humbling.

Caulder was still talking, more quietly and more directly now. '. . . the Lewis business hasn't helped, I know, though believe me it will blow over. Has already. The boy's a twit and his parents no better. But coming on top of everything else . . . I've been watching you for a while now, Ben, seeing how much you've taken on, the extra hours you give to every damn project, every ass of a boy . . . not spending enough time at home . . .'

Inside, Ben felt as if one single remaining thread was holding him together, that if Caulder said anything else that was either true or kind, he would collapse into a state of total incoherence.

'I've got her card, if you're interested.' He put something in the nearest pocket of Ben's anorak. 'Or just throw it away, of course. No more said on the matter, if you don't want to. Entirely up to you.' He slipped off his stool and dangled his car keys in front of Ben's still-unregistering expression. 'Better get you to this dinner, mate, or you'll be in the dog-house in no uncertain terms. Mind you, I even miss that,' he added, leading the way to his car, 'damn fool that I am.'

Walking into the Howards' sitting room that night reminded Ben of walking on stage. Except the audience was closer and participating volubly. Their chorus of reassurances that being late did not matter at all only served to convince him that it in fact mattered very deeply. Juliet, kissing the air beside his ears with theatrical noises of welcome, looked the most obviously flustered of the three. 'Isobel warned me from the start that you'd have a horrid rehearsal to get through first. Was it ghastly? You look quite washed out,' she chattered, not looking at Ben at all, before hurrying into the kitchen to put the starters in the microwave. 'I warn you,' she called gaily through the open hatch connecting the rooms, 'I take no responsibility for the state of the meal.'

'Ben's a good cook, he can take over,' quipped James, winking over the top of his glass.

Isobel, beaming to make up for the disheartening look of bewilderment on her husband's face, the dishevelled state of his hair and clothes, shrugged hopelessly, as one might shrug at the endearing misbehaviour of an errant child. 'He is a good cook, you're right, James,' she declared firmly and falsely, crossing the room to bestow a kiss on Ben's cheek. As she did so she smelt the beer on his breath, the unpleasant aroma of smoke in his clothes.

'Good rehearsal, was it?' she murmured, all her loyalty crushed by this evidence of duplicity.

'Fine.' He switched his attention to James, who was now offering him a flute of champagne.

'We're at least a bottle ahead of you, old friend, so drink up.' As James handed the drink over, his eyes found time to flick to Isobel's face. Her expression was unreadable, disappointingly so. 'How's your glass, Isobel?' he urged, wanting to draw her gaze to his.

'It's OK, thanks.' She offered him a flutter of a look, an embarrassed, reluctant acknowledgment that made the hairs on the back of his neck stand up. James took a step nearer. He could smell her perfume; sweet musky roses. Anything could happen, he thought breathlessly, a heady sense of freedom exploding in his mind. He had quite forgotten how acutely attractive the perception of such possibilities could be, how bloody intoxicating. His present life seemed positively deprived in comparison, all his existing relationships nothing but uninspiring cul-de-sacs of familiarity.

'I thought about inviting some other people, but decided it was so long since the four of us had got together that I'd keep it cosy.' Juliet, revived by the pretty sight of her dinner table and the benevolent smile fixed on her husband's face, raised a glass in toast to them all. 'Welcome. To friendship.'

'To friendship,' they echoed, while each in his heart questioned the meaning of the word.

Ben found his stomach quailing at the sight of the milky flesh of the scallops that formed the centrepiece of their first course, the humps of their brilliant orange tails swelling somehow obscenely out of the generous lakes of Juliet's heavy cream sauce.

'Freshly caught this morning,' she whispered, tracing the line of his gaze and misinterpreting its cause. 'They're a bit like oysters, you know,' she continued, raising her voice so as to include James and Isobel. 'That is, they are said to have aphrodisiac properties . . . like rose oil.' She gave Isobel a pointed look.

Isobel dutifully opened her mouth to pronounce upon the delights of aromatherapy massage, but James got there first with a good-humoured groan.

'Not those bloody oils again. Juliet's obsessed by the damn subject. Thinks she can cure the ills of the world . . . I'm not saying a good massage isn't relaxing – whatever part of the body is involved' – he paused to chuckle and dab his lower lip with his napkin – 'but as to actually healing, in the sense that an antibiotic goes about its work . . .' He stabbed a scallop with his fork. 'Well, frankly, it's ridiculous. Don't you think, Ben?'

'Probably.' Ben, fighting an overwhelming sense of alienation, of not belonging or knowing anybody in the room, had to force his attention to the subject. 'Though my Aunt Violet used to swear by lavender oil for cuts and bruises.'

'There. See?' Juliet pointed across the table with her fish knife. 'I told you, it's been going on for generations.'

'And how is your aunt?' asked James, ignoring his wife and turning to Ben, still smiling but with an icy edge to his voice. 'I'm sometimes grateful that all our own dear ancients are pushing up the proverbial daisies. Such a worry, old people, aren't they? Especially when they're not even immediate family. So time-consuming, all those visits . . .' As he spoke, his knee brushed against Isobel's. The movement was so swift and subtle that a moment later she was wondering if she had imagined it.

'Aunt Violet is family,' replied Ben slowly, managing to fuel his irritation into the grip on his wineglass.

'So, no regrets about taking her on, then?'

'Taking her on?'

'The move to the home.' James chewed lazily on a crust of sesame seeds, unaware of the latent hostility in Ben's tone. Only Isobel recognised it.

'Aunt Violet's a dear old thing,' she interjected hastily, 'no trouble at all.'

'As a matter of fact, she did more for me than most parents,' said Ben, his emotions back under control and his spirits lifting at the smell emanting from the casserole dish Juliet had set down on the place mat in front of her. The dizziness in his head told him that he was badly in need of food, real food. 'Isobel is marvellous about visiting her. It's harder for me to find the time. And to be frank, it's bloody depressing.'

'But not depressing for Isobel?' chirruped Juliet, thinking she was being clever, thinking that it was high time one of them made a show of sisterly support.

'Of course.' Ben swallowed. 'Though Isobel didn't know her before, when she was still . . .' To his horror, he felt a lump block his throat. Images of Aunt Violet, gusting into school occasions, decked in embarrassingly flamboyant hats and trailing cigarette smoke, her voice zigzagging shrilly across crowded rooms, flooded his mind, bringing with it an absurd sadness. He had hated her. Partly for being so conspicuous. Mostly for not being his mother. 'As I said,' he resumed, in normal tones, 'Isobel is marvellous. I am deeply grateful to her, in many ways, but especially with regard to the burden of my aged and cranky aunt.' He lifted his wineglass, his dark eyes glittering at his wife across the table. Though the ostensible subject of this tribute, Isobel sensed only a coldness at the heart of it. While their hosts cheered in support, she realised with fresh force that her husband was a stranger to her, that he had been for some considerable time.

Several stories of Juliet's about an ancient acting acquaintance with four miniature poodles and a penchant for vodka saw them through to the cheese. By which time all four members of the party were, to varying degrees, enjoying the peculiar lack of inhibition generated by the consumption of alcohol. Shielded by an increasing sense of unreality, Isobel found herself waiting for the by now regular contacts from the warm knee beside her, each more prolonged than the last. Nor did it come as any surprise when James's hand sought hers under the generous canopy of Juliet's treasured damask tablecloth. His fingers felt cool and very sure of themselves. It's only holding hands, she reassured herself, while the squeezing and stroking to which her fingers were being treated blatantly suggested intimacies on a far grander scale. Whilst not exactly unpleasant, it was the absurd audacity of such behaviour that struck Isobel more forcefully than anything. Across the table, the glazed look in Ben's eyes seemed merely neglectful. While beside him Juliet was drooping visibly, dry squirls of her hair trailing amongst abandoned crumbs of cheese and wholemeal crackers.

A little later, while Juliet clawed ineffectually at the cellophane on a box of mint chocolate sticks presented to her by Isobel that afternoon, James found the wherewithal to produce a jug of coffee. Back in the dining room a sense of disintegration prevailed. Juliet's half-hearted plea for Ben and Isobel to entertain them at the piano was quickly swept aside by her husband. Much to the relief of the Tarrants themselves. Never had Isobel felt less capable of steering her clear but subdued soprano through their limited repertoire of theme tunes. While Ben, too, felt quite unequal to the challenge of justifying his reputation for ingenious improvisation at the keyboard. So great was the weight of sleepiness now pressing upon him, that he only managed to keep his eyes open with the accompanying facial support of a frown. He reached an elbow towards the table, but found only empty space. Inside, melancholy pressed like a need for air.

'Funny how the past always looks so much better,' he said quietly, snapping his stick of chocolate in half and laying the pieces side by side. His head was full of Aunt Violet again, of her dogged loyalty to his father, of a guardianship bestowed not for love of a child so much as an obstinate family duty. 'No matter what you felt at the time.'

'Oh, I don't know,' murmured James, 'the future can look pretty rosy too.'

Isobel fixed her eyes upon the candle sputtering low amongst a flower arrangement in the centre of the table. There was yellow and green at its heart, she noticed, and a small core of blackness. It never occurred to her that Ben could be referring to his childhood. He means to hurt me, was all she thought. He is trying to tell me that we have nowhere to go. With what felt like enormous courage, she forced her eyes to leave the flame and meet her husband's, to face the rejection that awaited her there. But all that greeted her were the scruffy dark curls of Ben's head. With the grateful closing of his eyes, his chin had tipped down on to his chest; his cheeks sagged visibly with the relief of release.

'Poor love,' crooned Juliet, nearly asleep herself. 'Let's get him upstairs.'

'I'm fine,' retorted Ben, jolting awake and looking round the table with a kind of rage, his eyes bloodshot and heavy-lidded.

'But we're all going to bed, Ben, my sweet,' cooed Juliet, patting his hand. 'We're all in a hopeless state . . .' She levered herself out of her chair, yawning deeply and shaking her head. 'Just clear this lot . . .'

'I'll do it, my love,' offered James slyly, adrenalin inspiring sobriety. 'Isobel will help, won't you, Isobel?'

She nodded meekly, not trusting herself to speak. It felt suddenly as if events were in control of her, and that only by submitting to them would a resolution ever be found.

20

Druscilla was watching television in the dark. A group of men with shaved heads and earrings were talking about parenthood and the rights of homosexuals to adopt a child. A woman waved a microphone between them, interjecting questions which seemed to have little effect upon the general course of the conversation. Druscilla was studying the woman's scarlet bubble of a mouth, intrigued both by its vibrancy and elasticity, when she heard the noise outside. A cross between a clang and a thud that made her jump. Driven more by curiosity than concern, she edged her way to the front window and peered into the night. The row of terraced houses across the street huddled shoulder to shoulder, like dark sleeping giants. With what moon there was veiled in cloud, only the streetlamps cast any light on the scene. There was no sign of movement or life outside; only the sense of it. One of Druscilla's cats hopped on to the window sill and ran its tail across her face.

'Did you hear it too, my pet? Did you? Clever girl. Yes, she is. Mummy is going to see.' She scratched the smudged white face with the tips of her scarlet nails. 'You stay here and watch these lovely people,' she instructed, lifting the cat on to the armchair in front of the television and pulling a rug off the back of the sofa to wrap around her bare shoulders. Though it was well into the small hours of an evening that she had spent entirely alone, Druscilla was wearing her best frock, a long pinky silk affair which she had rescued from a charity shop a few years before. A floppy cotton rose was stitched at the centrepoint of its plunging neckline, while remnants of lace trimmings hung like streamers from its arms and hem. Druscilla found it impossible not to feel glorious in such a thing. Marvellous tonic for a sleepless night, or a pick-me-up for one of those rare low spots, when the past came at her like a dark avalanche, when even the cats seemed to embody spirits of people she longed only to forget.

Outside, the cold paving stones sent icy charges through the slim soles of her pumps. The scrape of a dustbin lid made her start and spin round. 'Come out!' she shrieked, waving the umbrella that she had taken the precaution of bringing with her like a sword. A small fox scurried away across the road. I am fearless, she thought excitedly, jigging on her frozen feet and la-la-ing in celebration. She was dancing towards the Tarrants' front door, conducting herself with the umbrella, when the sudden grating of an opening sash window momentarily stole some of the valour from her heart.

'Who is it?' called an angry voice which she recognised as belonging to Mr Coombes, head of the impossibly hostile family who were her neighbours on the other side.

'Only me. Druscilla Carew,' she trilled back. 'I heard a noise.'

'Do you have any idea what time it is . . . ?'

'I think it was a fox . . . but the Tarrants are away tonight, so I'm taking a little look . . .'

'Bloody woman,' muttered the man, yanking his window shut and wondering, not for the first time, what had to happen before a citizen could be locked away for being certifiably insane.

'Silly, silly bugger,' whispered Druscilla to herself, pushing open the Tarrants' front gate and scowling at the rusty squeak of its hinge. Having got this far, it seemed only right to make a proper investigation. It was just her poor toes that were really starting to suffer from the cold. The rest of her was tingling almost pleasantly, adding to the delightful sensation of being exaggeratedly alive, of being ready for any foe, invisible or otherwise. What if I did scare away a burglar? she thought, skipping through wet leaves up to the front doorstep, imagining how pleased Isobel would be, how wonderfully grateful. The notion was so sustaining that she extended her exploration to both sides of the house, even peering through the crack in the side door across the alley that led round the back. But there was nothing to see, save for the faint dark outline of the tree swing and the small garden shed beyond. After a few moments

Druscilla made her way, with a little less exuberance, back round to the front gate. She had almost reached it when her eye was caught by something white, half hidden by earth and twigs. She stopped at once, thinking it might be an item belonging to one of the girls, a mitten maybe, or one of Megan's pretty white socks. Instead, she found herself retrieving a small calling card, with a tiny pink rose embossed on the top left-hand corner and a couple of lines of writing – smudged and muddied almost to the point of illegibility – across its middle. Curiously consoled, feeling that she had found at least some kind of a memento of her night's adventure, Druscilla tucked it into the deep cleft between her breasts before hurrying back to her open front door.

She would tell Isobel about her vigilance anyway, she decided, stirring large quantities of sugar into hot milk as she returned to her armchair in the sitting room. Not to blow her own trumpet, but just because it would be neighbourly to do so. Burglars were everywhere these days, like those horrid bombers. Nobody could be too careful. Pleased to see the earringed men had been replaced by James Stewart in a bow tie, Druscilla curled up happily under a blanket, pulling a cat inside it for added warmth. She placed the card on the arm of the chair beside her. *For Isobel. My darling, no words can say what I feel*, it said, which was nice, Druscilla decided, giving the card a little pat. Very nice indeed.

Archie slid two more pieces of bread under the grill and poured himself a second glass of milk. While inconceivably hard for a sandwich, the bread made fine, if slightly brittle, toast; more than adequate as a vehicle for the unsurpassable luxury of his mother's home-made damson jam. Since the heat control on the grill functioned only in the sense that it moved rapidly to a blinding maximum, Archie kept a close guard. Turning away for just a second too long had, on countless occasions, proved fatal for many a promising sausage and fishcake, not to mention loaves' worth of healthy bread. Scraping out every last blob from under the lip of the jar, he spread the red jelly thickly across both pieces of toast, swirling his knife around in small circular motions so as to mix in as much as possible of the melting butter.

He ate very quickly, taking enormous mouthfuls, oblivious of the specks of yellowy pink dotting his chin. As soon as he had finished Archie felt sad, partly because of the empty jar, and partly because of the half-written letter awaiting his attention on the small lumpy Formica table in front of him. There was nothing to do but return to it now. He would not be able to sleep until it was done. It was already two o'clock. He had to be up before daylight to help Reverend Tully at the early Sunday service, a prospect for which he was struggling to experience any enthusiasm at all. There had been the grand total of eight communicants attending the previous week, and that included old Terry, whose reasons for huddling by church radiators were rarely spiritual and who smacked his lips shamelessly after receiving the sacraments. In a few years there would be no one at all, thought Archie grimly, visualising the grey bent heads of this early congregation with a new cynicism that he hated but could not dispel.

Taking his milk, he slumped back down at the table and glowered at his attempts to end the only serious relationship he had ever had – or had expected to have – in his life.

Dear Bridget,

You're probably wondering why I have not been in touch for a while. I am very busy here, as you know, but I'm afraid there are other reasons too. No, I have not met someone else, if that is what you are thinking. But I have decided that you should not 'wait' for me any more. I don't think I'm going to be ready to settle down – with anybody – for a long time to come, if ever. Knowing how much you want to start a family and so on, I think it only fair that you should feel free to see other people.

The worst thing about all this is the thought of hurting you, Bridget. You are the most perfectly good and kind person I have ever met – I mean that – and deserve to be really happy. It's just that I no longer believe I am the right person to bring you that happiness . . .

Which was the gentlest way he could think of saying precisely the opposite, acknowledged Archie wearily, rolling the pen between his palms as he agonised over how to start another sentence. He had known Bridget Evans since his teens, had shared with her the awkwardness of first kisses, of holding moist hands in cinemas, between whispered promises of inexhaustible love. While many friends of the time had been enjoying similar experiments, Archie and Bridget differed in that they did not move on to fresh partners and oaths, but remained a pair. They had – with only a trace of smugness – shaken their heads at the fickle emotions of their peers, secure in the knowledge that they were working towards something infinitely more long-lasting and worthwhile. By the time Archie left Cheshire for theological college, leaving Bridget to embark on training as a speech therapist, marriage had been openly discussed and postponed for the next stage of their respective careers. During the ensuing few years they had seen each other when they could, often with months passing in between. Their loyalty in the face of such absence – not to mention abstinence – was something of which Archie had once been fiercely proud. He felt a great well of gratitude too, for the early inflaming zeal of Bridget's support, especially early on, when so many acquaintances had scoffed at his choice of career.

Archie dropped the pen and clasped his head in his hands, recalling with despair the sweet naïvety of all their promises. The jewel of her virginity for his. Not a jewel now, he reflected grimly, but a deadly weight, a millstone of unignorable preoccupation and guilty desire. Sex had never been allowed to be the focus of their relationship. Sometimes Bridget allowed his trembling fingers to explore the soft pointy contents of her bra. She would keep her eyes closed while he probed and stroked, assuming a look of serene forbearance that made him anxious not to linger over such activities for unseemly periods of time. Where such sacrifices had once seemed inspiring, Archie had recently been confronting the growing realisation that there was another kind of love he wanted more; a love fired by a passion that could not have waited as they had, a love that embraced the sort of searing sexual images that fuelled his shame-ridden nightly fumblings with the flies of his pyjamas and a box of tissues. Confessing such habits to Bridget was unimaginable; far, far more frightening than facing – as he did on each occasion – the wrathful disappointment of the Lord. Even less admissible, to himself or anyone else, was the way the long red hair of Isobel Tarrant seemed to weave its way through his private mental library of erotica, at once strangling the life from him and quickening the pulse of his desire.

> *Please try and accept what I say,* he wrote desperately, his Biro skidding across the page. *I am not worthy of you. God, more than anyone, knows this to be true. Show the same faith in me you always have. Trust me.*
>
> *As I have told you many times, you will make the most wonderful healer – and mother. Good luck, Bridget, and be happy.*
>
> *Please do not reply to this letter. Nothing you say or do could possibly change my mind. But I'll always treasure what we had.*

Signing the letter presented fresh dilemmas. While 'Best wishes' sounded false and cold, Archie feared that anything to do with 'love' might be misinterpreted as reason to hope. After sucking the tip of his pen for quite some considerable time, he simply wrote his name in the middle of the space below the last paragraph. As an afterthought he drew a thick line underneath his signature, pleased with the air of finality that it gave the page.

21

It was almost dawn when Isobel crept into the Howards' spare room. Ben lay sprawled half in and half out of the covers, one arm flung out across her side of the bed, as if inviting an embrace. All trace of rose scent had vanished. Instead, the faint, sweet smell of alcohol lingered on the stuffy air, mingled with the garlic that had formed the mainstay of Juliet's venison casserole. Mechanically, without making any attempt to be particularly quiet, Isobel peeled off her clothes and slipped into her nightie before going into the small adjoining bathroom to clean her teeth. Her eyes, framed by smudgy lines of mascara, looked unnaturally wide and still, as if shocked into a state of inexpression. Great straggles of hair had worked their way loose from the plait and hung limply down her neck and cheeks. In spite of the clammy efficacy of the Howards' central heating system, so unlike the haphazard – and strictly pre-midnight – warmth of their own home, Isobel's face looked cool and pale. Only her lips glowed. Scarlet mouth for a scarlet woman, she thought, working the toothbrush with slow but vigorous strokes, until the white froth streamed down her chin.

They had waited a long time, attending to abandoned lumps of meat and stale breadcrumbs, wiping gravy droplets off place mats and rinsing wineglasses. They worked efficiently and in a silence filled with the strain of listening for evidence of movement upstairs. Though she had felt steady and sober, Isobel knew she must be drunk. The drudgery of their work dissolved in the dizzying significance of each moment. James, gliding from chore to chore, stepping round chair legs and through doorways with all the self-conscious precision of a dancer, did not seem like James at all, but a partner in an elaborate game. With every circuit between kitchen and table he came nearer. As the silence from upstairs drummed in their ears, so the tension grew, hardening the possibility of what lay ahead into the unavoidable. With only one more plate to go in the dishwasher, Isobel found herself clinging on to it, staring at the green-and-gold diamonds edging its rim until their bright points zigzagged before her eyes. She was trying to tie a rubbish bag, her fingers slipping on the greasy overstretched plastic, when James stepped, for the first time that night, into the full frame of her gaze. 'Let me,' he murmured, his eyes holding hers while he deftly knotted it shut and reached for the handle of the back door. 'Come,' he said simply, carrying the bag in one hand and three of her fingers in the other. 'Come with me.'

They kissed standing next to the Howards' tall handsome black wheely bin, the icy night air pressing through their clothes, their lips dry with cold. His intensity was at once frightening and irresistible. All teeth and tongue and hot breath. Alien and ravenous. When she tried to arch away he pressed his hands into her lower back and pulled her closer, bending the curve of his body into hers. While a part of Isobel's mind floated free, shaking its head in horrifed incredulity at their imprudence, another infinitely less cerebral part luxuriated in the unabashed greed of his embrace. She had forgotten the sensation of being desired, how intoxicating it could feel, how deeply empowering. After a few moments, disjointed and distracting images from the past bird-hopped in and out of her consciousness: echoes of similar emotions experienced during happier times. Isobel redoubled the passion of her responses in an effort to dispel them, angry that not even betrayal could set her free from the blind alley of such retrospective longing.

James, struggling with the vagaries of an unfamiliar bra strap, had his sights set on rather more immediate preoccupations. And when thoughts of his own spouse did at last break through, it was to savour the tantalising comparisons between one woman's body and another's. What he had forgotten was the rich diversity of such terrain, the hidden secrets in every store. More than the childlike slimness, her sweet flowery scent, the cool, tight texture of her skin, it was the sheer unfamiliarity of Isobel that excited

James the most. In the instant the clasp of the strap gave way a hot rush of excitement charged his veins as powerfully as any drug. And like any addict at last succumbing to his vice, he found himself marvelling at the self-restraint than had allowed him to forgo such delights for so long.

Shaking her hair free of the green slide that had controlled the bulk of the plait, Isobel bent over to brush out the tangles. She worked with almost brutal insistence, barely flinching as knots were caught and pulled. And even when every thick rusty strand was smooth and clear, she brushed on, as if trying to smooth out the last of the ridged markings left by the plait, keeping her head bent towards the floor till the blood rang in her ears. When she finally crawled into bed the steely light of the March dawn was already visible through the central chink in Juliet's fresh yellow curtains. Gently, she tugged the covers from Ben's clenched hands and tucked them round herself with exaggerated care. She lay on her side and watched his sleeping face, the dark handsome curl of his eyelashes, the soft full line of his mouth, and remembered a time when she had been naïve enough to believe that the tenderness reflected in such loved and loving features was a possession she could rely on. Instead of being something that could be withdrawn, a gift snatched back, leaving her bereft and alone and uncomprehending. Isobel caught her breath, panic at what had happened to them, at what it was driving her to do, punching her lungs.

Yet, in spite of James's at times frenzied persistence, they had not made love, not quite. It was too much for Isobel, even in her befuddled, peculiarly sensitised state of mind, to commit adultery either up against an icy wall next to a dustbin, or on the cosy sofa where she had nibbled peanuts and reassured Juliet about the resilience of game casseroles just a few hours before. Instead, James had cajoled her into a pledge to meet during the coming week, at a time and place to be arranged round the non-negotiable commitments of school runs and surgery hours.

'I'll sort something out and let you know. Promise me, Isobel, promise me you'll be there.'

'But where?' she had asked faintly, playing for time.

'I don't know yet – like I said, I'll sort something out. I'll call you.'

'I don't know, James, I don't know . . .' She prised herself free and sat up on the sofa, hugging her knees. 'This can only lead to . . . to harm . . .'

'And pleasure,' he interjected gruffly, reaching out to stroke her hair. 'And not necessarily to harm . . . no one need ever know, Isobel.'

She shook her head. 'People always know . . . in the end.'

'Look, let's just meet once,' he pleaded gently, his hand moving down to the nape of her neck. 'Let's just treat ourselves to a few wonderful hours . . .' For a moment a lump of emotion blocked his throat. 'And then it need never happen again. We could simply . . . treasure it . . . keep it as our secret. You never know,' he added with a soft, confident laugh, 'it might be an unmitigated disaster.'

'I suppose we could . . .'

'Of course we could,' he interjected softly. 'It would settle what we've started – give it a natural end – see it through . . .'

'It'll change everything—'

'Everything's changed already, Isobel, whether we make love or not. Everything changed from that one extraordinary afternoon, when I looked at you and realised—'

She pressed her hand to his mouth. 'Don't say any more. I'll wait to hear from you. I'll meet you if I can. Just once.'

'Just once,' he echoed, smiling at her, deafening and quite unutterable celebrations exploding in the privacy of his head. 'Christ, Isobel, I don't know how I'm going to wait . . .'

'We'd better go upstairs. The children will be awake soon.'

'Oh God, what an awful thought.' He rolled his eyes and grinned, unable to hide the boyish jubilation bubbling inside. While Isobel, following him upstairs, had felt only a deep stillness, the slow-motion calm of surrender.

The next morning old patterns of amiability dictated that the Tarrants, instead of rushing home, as they both secretly would have wished, stayed for an hour or two after the mêlée of breakfast. While Ben, gaunt and black-eyed, retreated behind the Sunday papers, Juliet put on a display of unnatural perkiness before subsiding, quite suddenly, into a deep chair in the sitting room, slumped vacantly over a colour supplement article on breast implants. James remained with Isobel and Ben in the kitchen, refilling coffee cups and quizzing Isobel in a self-consciously interested way about the literary textual choices offered by the Open University. The four children meanwhile, clearly sensing that some level of adult responsibility had been withdrawn for the morning, grazed freely on prohibited snacks from the larder, in between constructing an elaborate system of corridors and walls using all the Howards' smartest cushions and chairs.

'Juliet said you've agreed we'll go to Greece with them this summer.' Ben wound down his window, ignoring the chorus of protest from the back seat, and tipped his face towards the rush of cold air.

'No, I haven't.' Isobel curled both hands into fists, emptying the fingers of her gloves.

'Well, she's under the impression that you have.'

'I agreed to think about it, that's all.'

'You'd hate Greece.'

'I know. That's why I agreed to think about it.'

'Why didn't you just say no?'

She shrugged, wondering herself why the simplest answers were sometimes so hard.

'We can't afford it anyway.'

'No, I know.' Isobel slid her fingers back into their slots and folded her hands. 'Shall we go to Suffolk, then?'

Ben scowled. 'I suppose so.'

'They'll need fair warning . . .'

'It's March, for Christ's sake. Are you telling me your parents need to know things five months in advance?'

'You know what they're like,' she murmured, reminding herself of James in a bid to feel strong. He had squeezed her arm when they performed the ritual of goodbye pecks on the doorstep. Only the merest hint of pressure, but with an effect not dissimilar to that of a small electric shock. She wondered how he would contact her, what he would say, whether she would be brave enough to carry out her promise. It took a certain courage to give in to temptation, Isobel thought suddenly; it wasn't just about selfishness and being unhappy.

'I need a proper holiday,' Ben was saying. He had wound the window back up and leant back against the headrest, his eyes barely open, only one hand on a central spoke of the steering wheel.

'Yes, of course,' she replied automatically, not concentrating. 'It'll be the Easter holidays before we know it.'

'Can we have an egg hunt?' piped a voice from the back.

'I expect so.'

'Chocolate is bad for you,' declared Megan with a pout. 'It makes you spotty.'

'Does not.'

'Does.'

'For Christ's sake shut up you two, just shut up, shut up . . .' Shocked at the pitch of his own voice, Ben swallowed the anger away. The girls, crushed into immediate silence by the volume and rage of such an uncharacteristic outburst, exchanged looks and shrank into their coats. Only by the greatest effort of self-restraint did Isobel allow herself to show no flicker of reaction at all. Instead she stared, unblinking, at the dots of moisture just beginning to fleck the windscreen. It was clear to her that the anger, though ostensibly aimed at their children, was all for her. He hates me, she thought, feeling lucid and brave. Nothing I do matters. Nothing could make it any worse.

22

A service in the cathedral never failed to cheer Archie up. It was so much easier to feel sure of God beneath the vaulting beauty of its ceilings and with the cherubic-faced choir's fluting trebles spinning their way through Tallis or Byrd. Sitting in the splendour of one of the ornately carved choirstalls, Archie attended to each note and word with grateful wonderment, feeling his spirit soar heavenward on the echoing clouds of sound. Though well aware that religious faith should stand on firmer ground than the sensual spectacles of ceremonial beauty, Archie consoled himself with the argument that every career needed a little inspiration at times. God understood, he was sure. A cathedral was like the Rolls-Royce of religion, he mused happily, but better because it was available to everyone. The thought led him on to a series of absorbing analogies between other, less dramatic places of worship and equivalent vehicles. St Cuthbert's was a Volkswagen Beetle, he decided, rusting round the edges but endearing to the last. So engrossed was Archie by this theme that he quite forgot to listen to the Bishop's ennobling address on the importance of spiritual pilgrimage and opening windows on to the soul. He was juggling, a little sleepily, with a confused carpark's worth of cars and associated buildings when a pointedly loud amen from a more attentive neighbour alerted him to the fact that the service had moved on and that small snoring sounds might possibly have been emanating from the recesses of his nose.

'Thanks be to God,' he muttered to himself, groping for the fat tapestried hassock at his feet and clasping his hands for added effort in prayer.

'A prayer for unity,' began the Bishop, using the dignified vibrato which Archie had been dismayed to observe overtook most of God's servants when called upon to cope with the cavernous acoustics of the cathedral. At least his own tremulous tones – unsteady still before the smallest of congregations – could never be accused of sounding false or insincere. He squeezed his eyes shut to narrow the focus of his concentration. The carpark shrank into a black dot. Unity. Archie mouthed the word, wishing the black dot would allow itself to be superseded by something more appropriate, or at least charitable. Instead he saw his letter to Bridget, felt again how it had fallen from his fingertips into the postbox, so quiet and weightless for such a loaded thing.

After the service he skipped tea in the chapter house and found himself instead hovering in front of the noticeboard by the main entrance. The new Canon Residentiary had put up a notice about a breakfast project for the homeless, to be served out of the cathedral hall on weekday mornings. A pencil hung on a piece of string beside a large empty piece of paper inviting names of volunteers. Archie ran his finger round the inside of his dog-collar and sighed. It was a good idea. A great idea. But so hideously early. The only decent sleep he got these days was in the couple of hours before the shrill dawn chorus of his two alarm clocks.

Someone approached the other end of the board and set about pinning a small yellow poster into a space beside a faded notice about donations for Rwandan refugees.

Glad of the interruption to the ever-faltering engine of his conscience, Archie strolled over for a better look.

> *Crofton College presents:*
>
> *JULIUS CAESAR*
> *by William Shakespeare*
>
> *Saturday 6th April*
>
> *Seats: £5.00*
>
> *Tickets available from School Secretary or call 01867 422091*

It was only when the man turned round that Archie recognised him as Ben Tarrant. He was quite imposing when seen close to, with his tall figure and hooded black-browed eyes. He was wearing a shapeless grey sweater and a blue scarf wrapped several times round his neck and chin. That his face clearly had not seen a razor that morning only struck Archie as adding to the impressively casual and rugged look of the man. Of course Isobel would love such a person, he thought miserably, taking a step backwards and feeling suddenly gauche and pitifully young.

'Hope that's all right there,' growled Ben, responding only to the clerical dress of the young person hovering next to him and nodding his head at the board. 'I believe the school secretary has cleared it with whatever powers have to be consulted about such things.'

'Oh no – I mean yes, I'm sure it's fine there. Absolutely fine.' Archie nodded hard and approached the poster for a better look. '*Julius Caesar*, eh? Never seen that one. Or read it for that matter. Is it the one where everybody dies?'

'Quite a few people do,' replied Ben, smiling, 'but I think you may have *Titus Andronicus* in mind. That's the play where you really can't move for bodies by the end.'

'Ah yes, probably.' Oh no, and he's nice, thought Archie miserably, torn between lovelorn curiosity and a violent urge to run away. Instead, he found himself saying, 'I think I know your wife,' which he hadn't meant to at all.

'Isobel? And how is that?' Gripping his bunch of papers more tightly to his chest, Ben plunged his left hand deep into his coat pocket where, beneath two used hankies and several sweet wrappers, he felt the cold bobbled edge of something hard. His fingers closed around it. The pink stone from Wales. He had forgotten all about it.

'I've been bothering her for money, I'm afraid. Sponsorship – a charity walk thing. You might tell her I'll be calling again soon,' added Archie eagerly, as if such openness could somehow atone for the other less innocent enthusiasms firing his heart. 'I'm after signatures too at the moment. Fighting the good fight for St Cuthbert's. Some people on the council want to turn it into an arts centre.'

'I thought it was one already,' murmured Ben, squeezing the stone so hard that he could feel it cutting into his skin.

'Well, it's used for the odd concert and so on . . .'

'Oh, I see. Well, good luck. Are you coming this way?' Ben gestured with an inviting smile at the massive oak door behind them, something in the troubled expression on the young curate's face compelling him to be kind.

Once outside, they fell into step on the narrow tarmacked path that cut through the cathedral's manicured carpet of grass towards the cobblestones of the main gateway. Though a quick walker, Archie found himself hurrying to keep up with the long strides of his companion, the panels of his black tunic catching irritatingly round his ankles.

'So you're based at St Cuthbert's?'

'First posting, so to speak.'

'I thought of going into the ministry once.'

'Did you really?'

Ben flashed a self-deprecating smile. 'Only briefly . . . hard to believe, eh?'

'No, I didn't mean that at all . . .' Archie stammered, cursing himself for having sounded so surprised.

'It was only a teenage phase. I chose teaching instead . . .'

'Yes, I know. Geography, isn't it?'

'Yes.' Ben nodded, worrying suddenly about the tinderbox of rumour, whether the Lewis story had, after all, spread beyond the padded safety of Peter Abbott's study. 'That's right. And drama too. Do you think you might come to the play, then?'

'I'll certainly try. I say, have you got loads more of those to stick up?' Archie pointed at the wodge of yellow notices under Ben's arm. 'I'd be glad to help. I'm sure I could get rid of a few for you.'

Ben stopped walking for a moment. 'If I wasn't hung over and if it didn't look as if it was going to rain any minute' – he cast a rueful glance at the sky – 'I might just have been able to refuse such a generous offer . . . but as it is, I should be delighted.' He took a few pieces of paper off the top of his pile and handed them over.

'Oh, heavens, I can do better than that.' Archie helped himself to a generous sheaf. More generous than he had intended, as it happened, though having taken them it felt impossible to hand any back.

'Oh, really . . . thank you . . . er . . . Reverend.'

'Heighton-Jones – Archie.' He held out his hand. 'It will be a pleasure, honestly. I could do with a walk – wear me out for bedtime,' he added, darting off while Ben was still formulating a suitable reply.

'I'll warn Isobel you'll be round, then, shall I?' he called after a few moments.

'Absolutely. Thank you,' Archie shouted back, waving his stack of yellow notices in salute and making fresh vows of purity and penitence in his hopelessly wayward heart.

A quarter of a mile down Chapel Street, beyond the butcher's where they made vegetable sausages, was a small boutique which Juliet usually did her best to avoid. It was run by two beautiful, long-haired women, with permanent honeyed suntans and long pearly nails. The window of their shop never contained more than one mannequin, its implausibly sculpted body decked in one simple dress or suit, often barefooted, with perhaps only a string of pearls for decoration. The attraction for Juliet was not simply the sartorial elegance offered by such classical, understated styles, but the treatment that went with it. It was a charade, she knew, the two assistants purring round customers like cats, stroking the soft natural fabrics of the wares with their pretty talons and innocently batting their almond eyes at prices that would feed ten starving families for a month; but she loved it nonetheless. It was how shopping ought to be, she had enthused to James, when he ventured into the place with her to watch the investment of a generous birthday cheque (and a little bit more) a couple of years before. He had sat in an armchair shaking his head or nodding as she paraded in and out of the one fitting room, like some kind of indulgent lord overseeing purchases for his mistress. Afterwards, Juliet had skipped out of the shop with all the glee of a spoilt teenager, bags flapping against her legs as she danced on tiptoes to plant smudgy kisses of gratitude on her husband's benevolently smiling face.

It was an altogether less carefree frame of mind, however, which drew Juliet to Chapel Street mid-morning on the Tuesday following their dinner party with the Tarrants. She had spent the previous hour and a half at the hairdresser's, having her roots done, with a quick trim for good measure. Consultation with the stylist, Sylvie, had resulted in the joint view that the growing-out look of the latest perm in fact suited her rather well – all smooth on top with long tumbling curls lower down. It was quite Sarah Miles-like, Juliet decided, cocking her head at her reflection and trying to recall the exact film she had in mind. She had rather modelled herself on Sarah Miles at one stage – during her English Rose phase, when she'd gone all out for an Ophelia with a wonderfully inspiring director called Michael Jacobs, who had drunk himself to death a few months after the production ended. The memory was not a happy one. Not simply because of her failure to land the role and the subsequent demise of the charismatic Mr Jacobs, but because – as the hairdresser's mirrored walls reminded her – any passing resemblance she bore to Hamlet's luckless girlfriend was being cruelly and inexorably buried by the passage of time. Juliet scowled at herself and gave an extra pound to the girl who had washed her hair.

'I've got all morning,' she confided, as the sleeker of the two assistants in the boutique offered to take her coat amidst apologetic murmurings about the temperature of the room. 'It's lovely,' Juliet reassured her, rubbing her hands at the greenhouse warmth and beginning a slow tour of the largest of the circular rails. She ran the back of her left hand across the clothes as she walked, not yet really looking. The quiet swish of the materials was somehow thrilling, as was the sense of barely having begun. It was like standing on the edge of pleasure, brimming with the bliss of anticipation. She pulled idly at a panel of a long beige skirt on a small rack in the corner.

'Now that *is* special,' crooned the girl, deftly slipping the hanger off the rail and holding the skirt against her own enviably slim frame for her customer to admire. 'It's loose, but so smart. Stunning with one of those jackets over there, especially the darker blue. Though Miriam swears by the brown, don't you, Mirry?' Her colleague obligingly groaned her concurrence.

'Which jackets?' murmured Juliet, turning her head slowly, savouring every moment. The girl seemed to glide across the carpet ahead of her.

'With your eyes you'd want the blue, I think.' She held up a long smart navy jacket, with large pockets and wide lapels.

'Though you've got the sort of colouring to get away with either. It's a sort of chocolate brown, see?' The other jacket was in her hand now. 'More of a county look, you might say. Whereas the blue somehow has more of the town about it, don't you think?'

'Doesn't it just.' Juliet stood back and folded her arms. 'I'll try on both, shall I? Size fourteen, if you've got it.'

The girl drew in a breath of disbelief. 'I'd have sworn you were a twelve. Are you sure?'

Not even the knowledge that such doe-eyed incredulity constituted flattery of the most despicably calculating kind marred Juliet's determination to enjoy the compliment. Everyone needed lying to sometimes. 'I'll try both sizes, then, shall I? Oh, and I'll need a shirt or two, size fourteen,' she added, patting her chest with a rueful smile. 'Something in silk would be nice.'

'Is madam buying for any particular occasion?'

'Not really.' Juliet pushed all ten fingers up through the curly mop of her hair, before dropping her arms to her sides with a theatrically wistful sigh. 'I just felt I needed to clear out a few cobwebs. Spring does that to one, don't you find?'

'Oh God, yes.' The girl led the way into the compact, brightly lit changing room and hung the clothes on the line of hooks beside a full-length, gold-framed mirror with sunflowers painted in each of its corners. 'Shout if you need any help, won't you. I'll be just outside.'

Juliet needed a lot of help, as it turned out. Not just with skirts and jackets, but with trousers and shirts too. Being unable to choose between colours planted the alluring idea of covering all options by buying more than one of each. Though all size twelves had, discreetly, to be withdrawn from the running, the teeth of each zip on their replacements slid into place with such sweet, snug smoothness, while their buttons slotted so easily into their respective holes, that Juliet began to feel like a gambler on a roll. Everything looked perfect. When some billowing pantaloon-style trousers – not her usual thing at all – proved an inch or two too long, a pair of high-heeled Italian leather shoes were deftly slipped under the door of the fitting room. With their assistance, the wide hems of the trousers floated as prettily as their designer had intended, just an inch or so from the ground; most of the soft creamy leather of the shoes was denied the possibility of public admiration as a result, but with the happy side effect of adding greatly to the perceived length of the wearer's legs.

'I look yards taller,' exclaimed Juliet happily, wriggling her toes in celebration, 'and these darlings are as comfy as slippers. Who would have thought it with such a heel?'

Her assistant, now on her knees at Juliet's feet with a shoe-horn, sat back on her ankles and shook her glossy head in wonder. As well she might. For just a few feet to her right, the pile of this unusually amenable customer's 'probables' had swelled to dramatic proportions; price tags dangled like Christmas tree decorations from amongst its multicoloured folds. The shoes were added to the heap, together with the pantaloon trousers and the last-minute addition of an irresistible suede waistcoat with a string of gold buttons down its front and two pretty finger pockets in its sides.

At the till Juliet almost faltered. But only for a second or two. While the girl unsnagged tags and totted up prices, she slipped her credit card out of her purse and gripped its hard edges tightly between her fingers. When the final numbers appeared in the small window facing her, she did not even blink, though her heart raced for an instant or two. She handed across her card in a kind of trance that lasted all the way home.

Strangely, having unloaded all her bags from the car, she felt little inclination to examine her purchases further. Instead, she pushed them under the bed, feeling suddenly hollow inside. Kicking off her shoes, she flopped on to the bed, still unmade from the night before, and lay on her back staring up at the ceiling. A hairline crack ran from the corner of one window right across to the lintel above the door. Had it been there all along or had she simply not noticed it before? All was quiet outside. The workmen had not been for a day or two, even though piles of bricks and sand still defaced the once immaculate lawn of the garden. They were doubling up on another job, she was sure. The floor of crazy paving was laid, but the low wall that was to surround it still awaited construction, as did the pathway destined to run round the side of the house and up through the middle of the lawn to the attractive log cabin of a garden house at the far end. She ought to phone the men on one of their mobiles, find out exactly what was going on, put some pressure on, remind them who was in charge. James might be cross if there was still no sign of further progress by the weekend. At the thought of James the trance-like feeling came back again. The ceiling crack melted into a faint blur. Then she remembered the bags of new clothes packed beneath her under the bed and allowed herself a small smile of terror. He would go mad.

For a few minutes Juliet toyed with the notion of ringing up the shop and grovelling for a refund. On the grounds of diminished responsibility. Or foolhardiness. Or an impending war with her spouse. But there's a war anyway, she reminded herself, shrugging away the idea and getting off the bed. Started deliberately by James, she was sure, though quite why remained a mystery. Juliet crossed to the window and frowned at the half-finished state of the garden below. Time would sort it all out, no doubt, as it always did. Meanwhile, since all her attempts at reconciliation had been so hurtfully rejected or ignored, she resolved to fight her corner as hard as she could, with every weapon at her disposal. Juliet gripped her elbows with her hands as tears pricked her eyes. Including money. For a moment the realisation of her own strength burst into the hollowness inside, before dissolving into disappointment. How absurd, she thought, that loving someone could impel such an overpowering need to defeat them.

24 ∫

As the last and latest addition to an already overcrowded list, James could not help regarding the presence of Archie Heighton-Jones in his consulting room as something of an inconvenience. In less than an hour he was due to meet Isobel in the carpark of a roadside hotel in which he had already taken the liberty of booking a double room. It was a large and impersonal-looking hostelry on the stretch of the Drayford Road beyond Ilcombe, of the kind whose prime source of income was tourists and itinerant executives with small expense accounts. A venue, in other words, of the safest kind. He had a bottle of champagne concealed in a thermal bag under the driving seat of his car, together with a small box of Black Magic chocolates, which he had bought along with his paper *en route* to work that morning.

'How can I help?' he began briskly, tweaking the crease of his trousers as he sat down and uttering a brief, silent prayer of gratitude for not having been born with the affliction of the springy, carrot-coloured hair smothering the head of the young man seated opposite him.

Archie, whose nervousness had been greatly enhanced by a considerable stay in the waiting room, glanced at the doctor's sharp grey eyes for just a moment before reverting to a keen examination of his knuckle-bones. A recently acquired twitch, an annoying blip of a pulse just below his right eye, doubled in ferocity under the bold, enquiring gaze of the doctor. Though outwardly friendly, James Howard was not – as Archie sensed at once – empathetic. He frowned hard in an attempt to swallow the facial convulsions above his right cheekbone, which, though barely detectable to a casual observer, felt grotesque to Archie himself.

'I'm not sleeping very well . . .'

'Since when?' James was already punching the keyboard of his computer.

'I don't know . . . I suppose for a month or so.'

'Ever happened before?'

'No . . . no, not like this.'

'Got anything on your mind?'

Archie let out a nervous laugh at the utter inadequacy of the question. 'This and that . . . you know.'

James dropped his hands to his lap and turned back to face the young man, in the same instant flexing his mouth into the most avuncular of smiles. So stretched were his lips that they almost disappeared into the skin surrounding them.

'Are you – I hope you don't mind my asking – are you employed?'

Archie hesitated. He had changed out of his cassock before coming to the surgery. An absence of obvious symptoms made him wary of drawing attention to himself. After filling out the various forms required of new patients, he had hovered behind a large rubber plant, planning fictitious aches and pains in his defence, should the need arise. For a clergyman to admit to an inability to sleep seemed to Archie's exhausted mind to be tantamount to admitting that he had lost touch with his God, or, worse still, that he was being punished by him. The nature of many of the feverish thoughts peppering his periods of insomnia did little to dispel such notions.

'Yes,' he ventured at length, 'I'm a member of the Church . . . a curate.'

James raised his eyebrows. 'Really? How interesting. Been in Torbridge long?'

'Six months. It's a two-year job.'

James increased his smile. 'And are you finding it a particularly stressful one?'

Archie shook his head miserably. 'No. It's not like that at all. Everything like that is fine.' He wrung his hands and clenched his teeth, fighting the urge to confess to the extent of his misery. 'I've recently split up with my girlfriend,' he stammered at length. 'I suppose that might have something to do with it.'

James let out a long, knowing 'ah' and leant back in his chair, in the same moment pulling up the sleeve of his jacket so as to get a clear view of his watch. 'These things pass, you know, with time.'

'It's just that I feel so tired – I can't think straight – nothing feels normal – I mean, it – that is, the tiredness – it's just really beginning to get me down.'

'Of course it is.' With the end of the consultation in sight, James was fired with new energy to be kind. 'Insomnia can be devilish.' He swivelled his chair back round to face his desk and reached for a prescription pad. 'A couple of these a night should help. Just to see you through. Stop the moment you want. If you run out, come back. They are addictive but only if used unwisely.'

'Addictive?' Archie looked up, his tic fluttering like mad, a little creature trapped inside the skin below his eye.

'Don't look so worried,' said James, now at his most jovial. 'Your body has lost some of its natural rhythm, that's all. These—' he held out the paper for Archie to take – 'will help get you back into the swing of things again. Until the next girlfriend maybe . . .' James winked as he stood up, though in his heart he felt nothing but pity for the evident gaucheness of the young priest. Sexual naïvety was such a burden, he reflected with some complacency, holding wide his door and nodding Archie through. The thought led on to a few moments of indulgent speculation about the afternoon ahead. Though many problems might beset his meeting with Isobel, the sexual side of things, he felt sure, would not count among them. He would see that she was not disappointed; and since giving physical pleasure had always – in James's considerable experience – been the most efficient route to enjoying similar sensations oneself, he had high hopes on his own account. Such was the intensity of these musings that his fingers actually trembled as he set about tidying the papers on his desk. Isobel Tarrant, of all people. He whistled softly to himself. There would be guilt, of course. He could feel it already, crouching just around the corner, ready to pounce. But Christ, it would take a lot more than that to deter him now, James realised, giving his computer a companionable parting pat and heading for the door.

*   *   *

Archie, who, in spite of all his apprehensions, had been secretly hoping for more of a heart-to-heart with whichever of the Stanton Street practice's various GPs was allocated to him, trailed out of the surgery and across the road to the chemist with little sense of relief. To be a twenty-two-year-old servant of God, tortured by an unforgivable obsession with another man's wife and with a dependency on sleeping tablets, was not exactly an ideal condition for fuelling faith or self-esteem. As he pushed open the chiming door of the chemist, tears of self-pity pricked his eyes, blurring his vision and sense of balance so badly that he tripped on the step down and almost collided with a laden display stand of bath caps and corn pads.

Later, as he waited his turn to be served, a little girl with a chalky face and a thunderous cough began playing peek-a-boo behind the tails of her mother's raincoat. Using his prescription paper as a mask, Archie found himself returning the compliment, until the mother was smiling too, while a lilac-haired old lady, sitting on a stool beside a hedgehog of lollipops, silently clapped her delight. And when the pharmacist handed him his prescription, the pills looked so small and innocuous – taking up barely a third of the tiny brown bottle – that Archie found some of his misgivings evaporate. A good night's sleep would be a hell of a treat after all, he thought to himself, however unnatural the method of obtaining it.

All morning Isobel looked for a sign that she should not keep her appointment with James. If Ben is nice to me, then I won't go, she told herself. But Ben, for whom the emotional effort of getting through each day had now reduced his conversational skills to a series of monosyllables, showed no indication of being nice to her or any other object in his path. Fire-fighting invisible terrors inside his head, he pedalled off to school with his forehead creased against the wind, his hands white on the handlebars. In the briefcase strapped to the rack behind him was, among other things, Dick Caulder's card with the counsellor's name on it. Throughout the ride Ben's head throbbed with the pulse of this new dilemma. At every other lamppost he changed his mind. It felt too desperate for words even to be tempted to pick up the phone to such a person. Worse still, it felt like failure.

Men like him – educated, sensible, able men – should be able to sort their own lives out, he scolded himself. They should not need to pay someone to listen and nod at their problems. Whereas the wretched Caulder had at least had good reason, Ben felt all the awkwardness of possessing nothing solid to lay at a therapist's door beyond a general, debilitating feeling that control over all quarters of his life was slipping away, that the once clear waters of his future had turned to mud. If it wasn't so sad it would be laughable, Ben mused bitterly, slowing down at the sight of a phone box, but then pedalling past it twice as hard. How long, he wondered, before other people started to notice that his once unquenchable well of energy and confidence had become nothing but a sham? And Isobel . . . Ben clenched his face, as if gripped by a sudden spasm of pain. For he feared for her opinion of him most keenly of all. That such fear had already produced the most painful alienation they had suffered to date was bad enough. Their marriage was on hold, he knew, waiting for such a time as he had the energy to attend to it. And attend to it he would, he promised himself, for by no means the first time; just as soon as he felt a little better, just as soon as some of his inner strength had returned. When he was more like his old self again; the one that his wife had loved.

The steepening gradient of Crofton Hill forced fresh reservoirs of energy from his legs. On meeting this by now familiar physical challenge, Ben found himself wishing that he could flex a comparable muscle over other elements in his life. It was almost comical, he thought grimly, flicking up the gear switch to make himself work still harder, some part of him relishing the pain, that a creature of such apparent physical resources could be the vehicle of so much weakness inside.

Throughout the walk to school, meanwhile, Isobel remained fully prepared for one of the children to develop a sudden illness which would require hospitalisation or bedside vigilance at the very least. Given the approaching tryst with James, it seemed only right that God or sod's law should intervene to remind her of her rightful duties as a wife and mother. But both Sophie and Megan skipped along pavements and zebra crossings with uncanny zeal, pigtails and satchels flying, as if their sole desire in life that morning was to get into their classrooms and release their parent to her fate. They were so early that the playground was virtually empty. Isobel hung around for several minutes, half hoping to catch the arrival of the school bus and the Howard infants, as if the sight of them might act as an emotional deterrent for what lay ahead. In the end her own children shooed her away, rolling their eyes in embarrassment at such an unnecessary and uncharacteristic show of solicitude on their behalf.

Rain, Isobel told herself, as she turned on her heel for the walk home; if it rains then it means I'm not supposed to go. But, even as the thought entered her mind, the grey scudding clouds which had shrouded the early disc of a sun were being tugged away by a friendly spring breeze. By mid-morning Torbridge was basking in its first truly yellow sunshine of the year, to a backdrop of magnificent, unqualified blue.

After a frenzy of domestic chores, Isobel decided to pass what remained of the time by embarking on an examination of an arts study pack that had arrived from the Open University the day before. It was entitled *Words* and came with a cassette tape and a cheery introductory leaflet that promised access to academic material without the burden of exams or having to submit written work to tutors. Though Isobel read and reread the sentences, their significance eluded her. In the last few days she had been too distracted even for fiction. *Anna Karenina* and several other worthy works sat gathering dust on the table in the hall, waiting for her to have the spurt of energy required to return them to the library. It felt as if she were now too caught up in the tangled thread of her own life to expend the emotion necessary to the enjoyment of reading about anybody else's.

Isobel was also beginning to see that all her indecision over the Open University was linked to issues of a far more fundamental kind. So many years had passed without having to confront the muddle of her own ambitions. Ben's needs had always led the way in that regard, not because he had been a bully, but because she had wanted them to; because, if she was honest, she had been only too grateful to seize upon the abdication of self – of responsibility for the wavering course of her own life – that marriage to him had involved. Looking back, Isobel saw more clearly than ever that their union had only ever worked because of the mutual devotion that had empowered it. Without that there was no point or logic to their relationship at all. Without that she had nothing, except the children, already beginning to be baffled by a breakdown of something they could not understand, something that was only beginning to be tangible now that it had ceased to function.

Abandoning the desk, Isobel retreated back downstairs for her umpteenth trip to the bathroom. If I'm pink and blotchy I won't go, she told herself, casting a sly glance at her reflection in the mirror as she washed her hands. But her face was its usual pallid self, set off particularly that morning by the bright auburn tumble of her freshly washed hair. The pupils of her eyes looked particularly wide and black, dark holes in the usually predominant green. I'll go, but only to talk, she promised herself, retreating into the bedroom where she struggled to avoid the lure of the full-length mirror in the corner. She had forgotten the torture of feeling so self-conscious; the concentrated deviousness of dressing to please while aiming to look as if one had barely tried at all. Not that Ben would have noticed, she thought grimly, taking James's hastily scribbled note from the drawer of her bedside table and tearing it into long strips: *The Cobbler's Inn*, it said, *Drayford Road, 1 o'clock Wednesday. Please be there. I think I love you*. The pieces of paper fluttered from her hand and into the tin wastepaper bin behind the bedroom door. Quickly she set about camouflaging them with various discarded tissues and old envelopes, telling herself as she did so that deceit was not really so very difficult, but that it needed to be worked at, like any other activity that felt new and strange. But after a few moments she fell to her knees, removed the old tissues and placed the torn pieces of James's note back on top again. It would be easier to be found out, she thought desperately, for an instant wanting only to fast-forward this terrible, leisurely crumbling of her life to a point where the worst had happened instead of being yet to come.

25

A tiny spider was making its way down the steep white rock-face of Aunt Violet's hair, dangling precariously between one flat curl and the flabby lower section of an earlobe. Did ears grow bigger with age? Isobel wondered, unconsciously fiddling with the pearl studs in her own small, neat lobes and trying not to stare at the minute creature's daring acrobatics. Whether to mention the spider or not had been bothering her for some minutes. Like a snowfall of dandruff, or a rebellious bra strap defying the confines of a sleeveless shirt, it was not a matter easily raised. The thought did occur to her of reaching across the distance separating their two chairs – one deft sweep of her hand and it would be gone. But bridging such distances was a challenge at the best of times, especially with someone like Aunt Violet, whose hands fluttered like wings as she talked, as if to beat people back, warning them to give her space.

Instead, Isobel tried to concentrate on the old lady's face, quite animated that afternoon and flushed with genuine colour beneath the dusty beige dunes of her face powder. As on her previous visit, Aunt Violet was talking a lot, spilling snatches of anecdotes about ancient friends and places, leading herself in circles that were almost charming but mostly nonsensical. Sitting in the chair opposite her, conducting an unconvincing charade of reactive interest, Isobel grew increasingly aware of the fraudulence of her position and the suspect motives that had impelled her to make the visit at all. As the old lady talked on, she could feel her own thoughts slipping the safe moorings of her surroundings and drifting into the more treacherous current of the events that had preceded her arrival;

events connected to the clean but dingy hotel room in which she had found herself undressing before the admiring eyes of a man married to a woman who was supposed to be her friend.

To begin with, it was the thought of Juliet that had given Isobel the courage to say no, to back into the room with her hands like shields in front of her, keeping James at bay while she muttered apologies for having come at all. In spite of being so eager to touch her in the corridor, he had merely folded his arms and watched her retreat. Kicking the door shut behind him, he stood quite still, studying her in intent and unhurried silence until her withdrawl was halted by the wall on the other side of the room. Isobel pressed her palms and back up against it, as if willing the busy floral patterns to swallow her from sight. Between them stretched the bed, its crisp white bedspread yawning like a blank page.

'It's all right, Isobel, I know what you're feeling.' His voice was gravelly and sure. It soothed her. 'I feel it too. It's all right. Don't be worried. Don't – for heaven's sake – be scared, about anything. We're both in the dark here. We're both struggling to know what to do; whether to follow our hearts or our heads. I'm not in the habit of this either,' he added, rolling his eyes in distaste at their surroundings and shrugging helplessly. 'If I had my way we'd be alone on a desert island . . .'

'But we're not on an island, are we, James? We're here . . . in real life . . . in this vile, poky room. Oh God, I shouldn't have come, I feel so dreadful.' She turned her back on him and leant against the wall, resting her head on her arms.

'Hey, take it easy. Nothing has happened, remember? And nothing has to happen, Isobel, if you don't want it to. Let's just talk. I brought this.' He produced the bottle of champagne and the chocolates, his face a picture of apology. 'For you . . . I had to bring you something,' he stuttered, while his heart hammered at the thought of the condom in the small back pocket of his trousers.

'Thank you,' she whispered, managing to smile, marvelling now at the dubious strength that had empowered her this far. She watched as James nimbly uncoiled the wire from the top of the bottle and began easing the cork out with his thumbs. She noticed for the first time how beautifully manicured his nails were, trim white tips and tidy white crescents.

'Oh Christ, we're going to need some glasses. Could you look in the bathroom?'

The sight of the cork edging its way towards explosion urged Isobel to hurry obediently across the room. The bathroom was green and tightly packed. Barely an inch separated the shower curtain from the lavatory cistern, while the curve of the basin rim only just allowed a clean opening of the door. On a shelf beneath a small square mirror were two beakers sheathed in transparent plastic. Isobel took them at once, not daring to look up, not wanting to see her reflection for fear of what it might reveal.

'I found these.'

'Well done . . . closer – come closer, quick.' James laughed and held the bottle at arm's length. 'We're almost there. Are you ready? There we go.' He whooped with satisfaction as the cork flew across the room and the champagne spilled into the plastic cups. He took one from her and raised it high, staring her in the face until she met his gaze. 'Not so troubled, please, my lovely Isobel. We're here. That's all that matters for now . . .'

'If only it was.' She sipped the champagne and sighed, closing her eyes. 'I can't . . . go through with this after all, James, I'm so sorry.' She sat down on the bed next to him, stretching out her legs in front of her and staring at her shoes. A last-minute change from trousers to a skirt had resulted in faint sock lines round her ankles, just visible through her tights. Instead of minding, she felt brought down to earth by the sight of so humdrum and inelegant a physical detail. It made her feel unalluring and quite safe. 'I think I've only just realised the full enormity of what's been going on,' she continued matter-of-factly, wiggling her toes, 'of what it would do – to Juliet especially—'

An imperceptible tightening of James's jaw preceded his response to this confession. 'Of course, of course,' he interrupted. 'Though, for what it's worth, I don't think Juliet would spill too many tears . . . I mean, she's no stranger to, er . . . how shall I put this . . . ?' He took a swig of his drink, scowling as the bubbles filled his nose. '. . . marital transgressions?' He swallowed hard. 'Yes, I think that just about sums it up.'

'Juliet?' Isobel was genuinely astonished.

'The actress in her, I suppose,' continued James, now affecting a pained nonchalance which a less vulnerable or confused observer might have judged as being a little overdone. 'Needs attention. Misses the limelight,' he added, thinking to himself that the lie was so good – so plausible – that it almost had a right to be true. 'I've tried to analyse – to understand it – a thousand times.' He shook his head. 'I only wish I could lump my feelings for you in the same bracket. But Isobel . . .' Slowly he reached his hand to her face, stroking her cheeks and lips with the tips of his fingers. Isobel watched the hand approach as if it were an object quite beyond her control. When his skin touched hers, she closed her eyes, unexpectedly reassured by the simple pleasure of the contact. 'What I feel for you,' he murmured, 'I never thought to experience again. You light up my life . . . just the thought of you . . .' He stopped touching her face and picked up her hand, slotting his fingers through hers.

'But Juliet . . .' she whispered. 'I can't believe . . . I mean, she always seemed so . . .'

'I probably shouldn't have told you. It's not relevant,' he continued earnestly, 'it's got nothing to do with my feelings for you . . . I want . . . oh Christ . . .' He dropped her hand and turned abruptly away, his voice cracking with emotion. With hunched shoulders he gripped his plastic cup in both palms, staring dejectedly into the lemony bubbles.

For a moment Isobel thought he was going to cry. The notion that she had reduced him to so vulnerable a state made her feel both culpable and tender. 'I am so sorry,' she whispered, putting her cup down on the thinning carpet and reaching an arm across his back.

'I think we need each other,' he murmured, responding to the touch of her arm with an embrace that was far more fervent than anything she had anticipated and which tipped the precarious balance of control entirely, and finally, his way.

She let the weight of his body press her back on to the soft lumpy mattress of the bed, while the wallpaper trellises of flowers surrounding them danced before her half-closed eyes like the twisting spirals of a pretty cage.

'You don't seem yourself,' snapped Aunt Violet, the edge in her voice bringing Isobel back to the present. The old woman cocked her head quizzically. 'You're not listening,' she accused with a sniff.

'I'm sorry . . . I'm . . . a little tired today. Sorry . . . please forgive me.' Isobel reached out to pat the veiny hand nearest to her, but found it withdrawn before she got there. A trivial rejection which somehow sharpened her sense of wrongdoing; not just about seeing James, but for not having driven straight home afterwards; for yet again complicating her duplicity by drawing Aunt Violet into the tightening circle of deceit. She folded her hands back in her lap, wondering if the old lady sensed her lack of affection, whether she somehow intuited that she was being used as an unwitting alibi for the whereabouts of an ineptly adulterous housewife.

'Too many parties, I expect.'

'I beg your pardon?'

'Being tired – too many parties.'

Isobel managed a weak laugh. 'No – no such luck, I'm afraid.'

'Ben's mother was a great one for parties. Oh Lord, yes. How that girl could dance.' She clapped her crooked hands. 'And the dresses . . . my dear, you should have seen the dresses – thirty or forty at least . . . and hatboxes too . . .'

'Really,' murmured Isobel, working harder to be polite, longing now to get away, especially from the possibility of any more intriguing tidbits about the Tarrants' family history. It only brought the sense of Ben closer, and she wasn't ready for that. By deceiving him she had quite destroyed her curiosity.

'One for every lover, Albert used to say – though he wouldn't throw them out, you know . . .'

'I really think—' Isobel stood up.

'One for every lover,' repeated Aunt Violet more harshly. 'Louisa was a tart.' Her head was doing its nodding trick, jerking in crazed agreement with itself. 'Deserved everything she got. I say, would you like to see some photographs?' With the invitation her voice switched to the sweet, silky tones that had greeted Isobel's arrival, while the rheumy eyes flickered with traces of a disturbingly girlish pleading, each one like a glimpse of the person lost inside.

'Perhaps we could ask for a cup of tea?' suggested Isobel faintly, wondering suddenly at the maze of subterranean motives that had impelled her to make the visit, whether it was an alibi she had sought, or some kind of self-inflicted punishment. It did not help that James's champagne was now wreaking its revenge, enhanced by the stuffy temperature of Aunt Violet's bedroom. Her tongue and gums felt sticky with thirst, while a painful pulse was gathering speed and intensity in her temples.

'Tea?' Aunt Violet's voice was scathing. 'The servants are instructed to bring tea at four o' clock.'

Isobel picked up her bag. 'Well, in that case, perhaps I'd better—'

'My albums are up there, on the shelf. Right behind you.' She waggled a finger at some high point behind Isobel's head. 'I want the red one.'

'Ah yes, the photos.' Isobel, feeling hysteria threaten, rubbed the palms of her hands together in a desperate parody of enthusiasm.

Aunt Violet's twisted fingers twitched with painful inefficiency at the edges of grey tissue paper interleaved between the pages of the old album. The fact that countless photographs had come loose did not make the task of studying them any easier. Unstuck corners fluttered to the carpet like confetti. Isobel, standing silently at her shoulder, gripped the edge of the chair in a bid to control both her impatience and dismay. The pictures were all from days prior to Albert Tarrant's posting to South America, prior to his encounter with Louisa da Costa and subsequent decision to make his life and living permanently overseas. Most of the images were too smudged or faded to be appreciated for any reason beyond sentiment; private ghosts from a private past.

'Here we are,' trumpeted the old lady suddenly, stabbing at a photograph of a woman posing with a baby in front of the broad, sweeping feathers of some pampas grass. She let out a humph of satisfaction. 'The tart herself.' Isobel recognised Louisa at once, from the one picture Ben displayed of his parents, a formal shot of their wedding day, which lived on top of the crowded bookshelf in the hall. She was undeniably beautiful, with raven hair and wide, challenging black eyes that stood out despite the blurred and browning look of everything around them.

'And is that Ben?' she asked in a final bid to appear appreci-ative, pointing to the moon-faced infant propped, rather stiffly, in Louisa's arms.

'Ben? Good heavens, no. That's the other child, the one that died.'

'Whose child?'

'Louisa's. Though whether poor Albert was the father . . .' Violet sniffed and closed the book.

Isobel knelt down beside her. 'So Ben had a . . .'

'Shh.' A spray of saliva accompanied the reprimand. 'Family secrets, my dear.' She glanced nervously at the door, before whispering, 'Baby girl – died in the crash and a good thing too.' Pressing her lips together, she tilted her head back and closed her eyes. 'We might ask for tea now, don't you think?'

'Tea?'

'Got to go, have you? Always rushing off.'

'Yes, yes, I must.' Isobel's voice had shrunk to a monotone, an instrument for saying anything that would allow her to leave. 'I have to collect my children from school,' she lied, reaching for her bag. Sophie and Megan were both at friends' houses and required nothing from her for several more hours. 'They hate it if I'm late.' Quickly she brushed her lips across one soft, shrunken cheek.

'My cigarettes – where are they? You said you'd bring some, remember?' The accusation exploded out of her with such force that for a moment Isobel was almost afraid.

'Next time,' she faltered, moving towards the door.

'Don't bother – I haven't smoked for years.'

She was rescued from the incongruities of these farewells by a buxom, steely-haired nurse who bustled in carrying a tray. 'It's tea and tablets, Mrs T, and I won't take no for an answer . . . I heard all about what happened yesterday, you naughty girl . . .' She winked at Isobel, who managed an unconvincing smile before hurrying down the stairs.

The confusion of emotions that accompanied Isobel on her drive back to Torbridge was quite unlike anything she had ever experienced before. To have discovered on that day – of all days – that the fateful crash had deprived her husband of a sibling as well as a mother was ironic to the point of farce. It didn't matter, she told herself. It was no longer her business – or her right – to care about such things. That Ben had never told her himself clearly meant that he didn't think so either.

It was almost a relief when fresh surges of guilt began to override the finer points of such sentiments. Isobel clenched her teeth together and drove faster than felt either safe or normal, inwardly cursing the fact that a spouse's neglect should turn out to be no proof against the emotional consequences of seeking solace from other quarters.

The only redeeming feature of her circumstances was that she was beginning to feel, not love exactly, but certainly a great well of tenderness towards James Howard. And he loves me, she reminded herself, clinging, with unconscious desperation, to the padded leather of the steering wheel, as more intimate details of their recent encounter flooded into her mind.

As she turned off the Drayford Road towards Torbridge, the spire of the cathedral rose into view on the skyline, pushing up from amongst the chalky hills like the blade of a knife. In the same instant Isobel remembered that, in spite of all her resolutions, she had promised to meet James again. Her eyes glazed over from staring at the view ahead; the tarmac seethed like a black river, the cathedral blurred and divided. The car seemed to hurtle forwards of its own accord, gobbling up the old Roman road like a creature bent upon destruction.

A couple of weeks later it was the turn of Druscilla Carew, returning from an excursion to Drayford's celebrated Roman ruins, to admire the view of Torbridge cathedral afforded by the most ancient of its approach roads. Though she sighed with delight as the familiar prospect came into sight, it was out of satisfaction with life in general rather than from any appreciation of Gothic architecture. In fact Druscilla could not remember when she had last spent a more exciting few hours. The remains themselves had been a bit of a disappointment. She had only signed up for the trip because the nice young priest who failed to fix her percolator had mentioned it, and because she fancied getting out of Torbridge for a change. She had been meaning to visit the place for years, just as she had always fancied booking herself on one of the guided tours they did round the cathedral. It was the tourists who put her off, as well as laziness about paying attention to the countless historical things within her daily reach.

There had been three Americans in the group and a large herd of Japanese, whose rendering of English seemed to Druscilla to be quite indistinguishable from whichever oriental dialect they used to communicate amongst themselves. Having accepted the small disappointment that Archie Heighton-Jones was not to be among the party after all, she resolved to keep herself to herself. A resolution to which she managed to remain loyal, even when the American with the big moustache smiled in a way that showed he wanted to talk. She bought a *Daily Mail* at the bus station and kept her nose buried in it all the way to the Drayford Road, by which time she felt so sick that only by an intense study of the passing scenery did she manage to persuade the contents of her stomach to remain where they were.

Though their guide boasted that very little restoration work had been done on the site, Druscilla, surveying the faded, incomplete maps of mosaic flooring, separated only by knobbly knee-high divisions for walls, could not help thinking that a proper rebuilding of the place would have made the visit far more worth everybody's while. As soon as the guide released them, she retreated into the café for an early lunch and then spent the rest of their allotted time browsing through boxes of trinkets in the gift shop. Unenticed by key-rings of Roman generals and posters showing aerial views of crumbling stones, she treated herself to a cat calendar and a small bag of potpourri that smelt of lilac and roses. By the time the rest of the group had got to the shop, Druscilla was already back in the coach, doing the coffee-break page of her paper and sucking, rather noisily, on the liquorice straw of a sherbet lemon.

On the return journey it was one of the American trio, a wide-hipped lady with braces and bleached hair, who confessed, loudly, to feeling ill. Shortly after one roadside stop, during which she gulped air from the open door of the coach, she began retching into a plastic carrier bag held, rather gingerly, by the man with the bike-handle moustache. Druscilla, having so narrowly avoided a similar affliction herself earlier on, could not help feeling rather smug, and somewhat entertained. I ought to get out more, she thought happily, while the woman sobbed for access to a bathroom and the guide entered into frantic whispered consultations with the driver. A few minutes later they pulled up on the grass verge opposite an ugly roadside hotel, where several vehicles were already packed on to the adjoining piece of fenced tarmac that served as a carpark. The coach driver grudgingly flicked on his hazard lights and lit a cigarette, while the guide ushered the two Americans over the road. The rest of them, who had been asked to contain any urges relating to basins and lavatories until their arrival at Torbridge bus terminal, sat and waited.

Idly chewing the last coil of her liquorice, Druscilla stared after the hobbling American lady and her two escorts. The woman looked ugly and stupid in her view, and the man unhappy. Probably why he had smiled so invitingly at her, she decided, with a small pout of satisfaction; though she had never liked moustaches, or Americans either for that matter. She was on the point of dismissing the pair from her thoughts completely and returning to the testing top left-hand corner of the coffee-break crossword when her eye was caught by two figures emerging from a side door of the hotel. For a moment she could not believe her eyes. But the auburn hair, streaking out behind in the whip of the wind, was unmistakable. As was the well-groomed figure of the man whose arm was round the woman's waist, his fingers curled protectively round her hip bone. At the sight of them Druscilla experienced a profound and quite unexpected stab of jealousy. Dr Howard was undeniably handsome; well preserved and distinguished-looking with sleek dusty grey hair and wonderfully penetrating eyes. Just the kind of man, she thought wistfully, whom she might have gone for herself, once upon a time. After one hurried farewell kiss – lips on lips, Druscilla noted, with mounting excitement – they got into their respective cars and drove away in opposite directions; for camouflage, no doubt, she decided, swallowing the last speck of her liquorice and dabbing her lips with a tissue.

Upon getting home, Druscilla positioned herself – and a full box of After Eights – in a comfortable chair by the bay window of her front room. Every few minutes she dipped one of the slim chocolates into her mug of coffee before sucking it, relishing the way the sweet minty juices slid between her teeth and on to her tongue. Untouched envelopes of chocolate lay in several saucers scattered round her feet, awaiting the arrival of the other members of her household, currently occupied with more obviously feline pursuits outside.

She had suspected the existence of an admirer for some time. Husbands like Ben Tarrant didn't send bouquets – at least, not two such large ones – in the space of one week. And then there was the note too, Druscilla remembered with a heart-flutter of excitement, the tiny trophy she had unearthed from the damp ground inside the Tarrants' front gate. Abandoning her vigil by the front window, she fetched the old biscuit tin from the middle shelf of her small kitchen dresser and tipped its contents on on the carpet. Amongst the heap was a ball of rubber bands, her wedding ring, a set of miniature screwdrivers, a broken but favourite earring, four curtain hooks, a tube of hand cream and several business cards advertising the services of taxi firms and carpet-cleaning companies. But no sign of the flower note. Druscilla frowned and sat back on her heels. It was unlike her to lose track of something so intriguing. She tried pressing the tips of her fingers to her temples and concentrating hard with her eyes closed, taking herself back to the small hours of the night when she had been so disturbed by a noise outside; but beyond images of Cary Grant and her lovely dress she could remember barely any details at all. Cross with herself, she swept the pile of papers and trinkets back into the tin and pressed the lid shut, banging her fist impatiently at the bent edge of one corner.

Outside, a car drew up and a door slammed. On tiptoes, her spirits recharged in an instant, Druscilla stole towards her window. Isobel was walking slowly towards her front gate, hands in her coat pockets, her eyes on the pavement. There was no sign of the children. Slipping her feet into her trainers, new pink ones with purple arrows on the sides, Druscilla trotted into her kitchen to fetch a bottle of milk before returning to the hall. As soon as she heard Isobel's door slam, she carefully let herself out and scurried across the few yards separating their houses, her laces trailing in the dirt.

'I've got some extra,' she declared, waving the milk bottle, which was barely a quarter full, and pushing past Isobel the moment she opened the door. 'I know you're always short, with the girls and so on. Can't give too much to my pussies,' she continued, sidling down the hall, 'upsets their stomachs so – though chocolate doesn't, which is odd, don't you think? I'll pop it in the fridge for you, shall I?'

Isobel had been on the point of running a bath. As always, the smell of James was in her skin and hair, the taste of him in her mouth. Even the air in the car seemed to hold his scent for hours afterwards, as if breathed out by the corrupted pores of her own body. Driving home, she would wind the window right down in an effort to get rid of it, breathing in lungfuls of fresh cold air like an ex-smoker trying to destroy evidence of a relapse. The sight of Druscilla Carew on her doorstep was so unexpected, so utterly disheartening, that for a moment all sense and strength drained from her. It was only when she followed the woman into the kitchen and saw her sitting at her table, clearly bent upon staying, that some of her wits returned.

'Thank you for the milk, Druscilla, but I'm afraid I can't offer you a cup of tea. I'm *extremely* busy, as it happens . . . so if you wouldn't mind . . .' Any normal person would have understood the intention of such a politely unfinished sentence. But her neighbour merely rolled her eyes and gave a delicate pat to the hard, hairsprayed crust of her hair.

'I know you're *busy*, my dear Isobel, very *busy* indeed.' Something about Druscilla's tone sent a ripple of apprehension down Isobel's spine.

'Was there something you wanted?' she asked faintly.

'To congratulate you, my dear,' exclaimed Druscilla, with genuine warmth. She had never liked Ben Tarrant. He never had time to chat or smile. When the girls were small and still crawling, she had seen him shoo her cats from their garden, muttering about the little messes they sometimes deposited on the lawn. But never his wife. Isobel was quite different: much more tolerant and kind. Quite deserving of a lover in fact. 'I just wanted to say . . .' She beamed. '. . . that in my opinion it couldn't have happened to a nicer person.'

'What couldn't have happened?'

'You and Dr Howard. It couldn't have happened to a nicer person. There was me, wondering who the admirer was – all those heavenly flowers – but I'd never have guessed, honestly, I wouldn't, not in a million years. You dark horse, you.'

'Oh dear.' Isobel sat down and put her hands to her mouth, staring at the gleeful face opposite her in disbelief. After each tryst she found that guilt turned quickly to remorse. Regardless of the pressure of both conscience and common sense, she also continued to dread the prospect of confession, of pushing the whole pitiable state of their marriage on into its next, inevitable phase. Sometimes, between meetings with James, she would even catch herself grasping at the pathetic straw of a hope that the situation between her and Ben was in fact salvageable after all, that, with a little more patience on her part, some sort of acceptable *modus vivendi* might be found. The thought that her odious neighbour was now in a position to jeopardise such hopes

– or to make things even worse than they were already going to be – was almost more than Isobel could bear. Yet she couldn't tolerate the thought of begging to her either, of being in thrall to such a woman. 'Druscilla, I would really appreciate it if . . .'

'My dear girl, your secret is safe with me.' Clearly delighted with the situation, Druscilla hopped to her feet, and began clumsily filling the kettle from the tap. Jets of water spurted across the breadboard and on to a roll of kitchen paper on a holder attached to the wall behind. 'I think it's all heavenly. I saw you this afternoon, in case you're wondering. I went on a tour to the Drayford ruins – not worth a visit, by the way – and then was fortunate enough to catch sight of you and Dr Howard during a stopover on the journey back. Such a coincidence – I love coincidences, don't you? You were in the carpark of that inn place on the Drayford Road, saying goodbye . . .' She wriggled her shoulders. '*Very* romantic it looked too, you lucky things . . . that husband of yours never deserved you, you know . . .'

Isobel flinched. 'I think you'd better go, Druscilla.'

But her neighbour was in full flow. She pressed the switch on the kettle and took two mugs down from the cupboard. 'The only decent thing to come out of my marriage was money. Not a lot, but enough.' She dropped a tea bag into each mug. 'Mind you, I paid in other ways. Oh yes, I paid dearly . . .'

'Druscilla, please go. I want you to go.' Isobel stood up, her chair screeching on the tiled floor. 'I want you to go.'

'Goodness, you are all fizzed up, aren't you? Well, I'll leave you in peace, then. Want to freshen up, I dare say . . . but if *ever* you want to talk . . .' She nudged Isobel, who swayed against the side of the table. At the kitchen door she paused and frowned. 'I've got a little something to confess too, as it happens . . .'

Isobel gripped the edge of the table, dreading what might come out next.

'. . . that is to say, I possess something that belongs to you – a little love note, I suppose you'd call it.' She pressed her fingers to her mouth to suppress a giggle. 'Must have dropped out of one of those pretty bouquets Dr Howard sent a few weeks back. I found it by your front gate, all covered in leaves and dirt and goodness knows what. I forgot all about it until today . . . can't quite lay my hands on it at the moment, but when I do you will be the first to know. All property should be returned to its rightful owners, don't you think?' She winked, before turning and heading towards the front door. Isobel, now clinging to the merest thread of self-control, sat on the bottom stair and watched without blinking as the crack of daylight widened and Druscilla stepped into it. 'Such lovely wording it was too.' She wrinkled her nose in an effort to remember the exact phrase. 'No words can say what I feel . . . yes, that was it.' She sighed happily. '*So* nice to know that romance isn't completely dead in this unfriendly world of ours, at least not for some . . .'

She was still talking at the front gate, when Isobel finally dragged herself from the stairs in order to close the door.

27 ∫

Ben, much to his amazement, was having something of a good day. That his long-postponed phone call to Dick Caulder's counsellor – hastily made from a call-box during break that morning – might have had something to do with this turn of events did not escape his attention. In the end, it was something of a relief to have taken the plunge. Not only did it put a stop to the dreadful tug-of-war going on inside his head, but it had also been far less painful than he had feared: no probing questions, no sense of that distinctly female greed for emotional details that he felt in no position to release. Instead, the woman, whose name was Ione Brown, had suggested meeting for a preliminary session, to explain who she was and how she worked. Asking nothing about why he wanted to see her, she simply took his name in a friendly sort of way and issued directions for finding her consulting rooms. She was lucky enough to have a spare slot that evening, she said, owing to a cancellation. He could come at eight o'clock, if he liked, and they would take it from there. Without really thinking beyond the fact that he wanted the phone call to be over, Ben found himself agreeing.

After giving the matter some thought, he decided to telephone Isobel with a white lie of an explanation as to why he would be home even later than usual that night. He had no wish to tell his wife – or anyone else, for that matter – about Ione Brown. Investigating the possibility of such help was bad enough, without the added horror of advertising the fact. When, after several attempts throughout the afternoon, there was still no reply from home, Ben couldn't help feeling a little relieved. He wouldn't offer any excuses unless directly called upon to do so, he decided. One more late night could hardly make things between them any worse or better than they were already.

The run-through that lunch-time was the best yet. The lighting was more or less sorted – at last – and some final touches to the scenery had worked to marvellous effect. For the first time since the outset of the project, Ben found himself almost looking forward to the rehearsal due to take place the following night – a sort of critical preview, to be attended by Peter Abbott and a few other key members of staff. Instead of working during his free period that afternoon, he treated himself to a browse amongst the staffroom newspapers. Flicking through a weekly supplement on jobs, his eye was caught by a boxed bold-print advertisement at the very bottom of the page. A small private school called Fairlands required a headmaster. Located in Hampshire with two hundred pupils. On any other occasion in recent months Ben would have shaken his head and moved on. But thanks to the unexpectedly pleasing pattern of the day so far, he found himself scribbling down details on the back of an envelope and filing it away in his briefcase.

Upon catching sight of the boy Lewis skulking behind the headmaster's new red Volvo, this new-found and highly precarious lightness of spirit almost disappeared. Ben had to clench his fists to prevent himself from turning and scurrying away. Though it was seven thirty and quite dark, Lewis's pale face and extraordinary halo of curly yellow hair were plainly illuminated by the glare of the security light at the entrance to the school drive. It was unfortunate hair for any child, thickening as opposed ever to increasing in actual length, and retaining a colour that looked chemically enhanced on even the most sunless of days. Ben, who was heading for the metal bike rack half hidden by the bushes on the far side of the drive, paused only for a moment before quickening his pace. There was no avoiding being seen. A meeting – a chance to talk some sense into the lad – was what he had been arguing for all along, he reminded himself, striding into view with a decidedly grim expression of welcome fixed to his face.

'Evening, Lewis.'

'Oh, sir – good evening – I was hoping to catch you – I've been waiting. I recognised your bike.'

'The smart one, eh?' replied Ben, his mouth relaxing into a more genuine smile, all his apprehensions dissolving at the obviously embarrassed confusion of the boy. He was still only a child after all. 'Two gears, half a mudguard and a generous coating of rust in preference to paint.'

Lewis laughed and looked relieved. 'I've come to . . . say sorry. I mean, I know I've caused the most frightful bother . . . to you especially.'

Ben knelt down and fiddled with his bike lock. 'No harm done, in the long term. Got to keep a hold of your emotions a bit more . . .' He stopped in mid-sentence, wondering suddenly whether such advice was either true or wise.

'Yeah.' The boy looked at his boots, which were round-toed and big-soled. 'But if I feel things, they just sort of come out. But that letter – well, I'm really sorry . . . I mean, I was never going to send it or anything. The last thing I wanted was for my parents to find it . . . when they did they just flipped,' he added in a small voice.

'It's all right, Lewis. It's done with. Enjoying your new school?' Ben stood up and looped the chain and padlock round the handlebars.

He made a face. 'Not much, but we're moving to Scotland. Dad's going to work on rigs in the North Sea. Mum doesn't want to go.'

'And what about you, what do you want?'

He shrugged and shuffled his feet. 'Don't care really.' He bent down and scooped up a handful of loose stones.

'Oh, you must always care, Lewis,' Ben said gently, inwardly marvelling at the ease with which such pearls slipped out, given his hopeless management of his own emotions. He wheeled his bike up to where the boy was standing and held out his hand. 'Goodbye, Lewis, and good luck.'

'I think I'm gay,' the boy muttered, biting his bottom lip and throwing a chip of gravel at the grass verge.

Ben sighed. 'Well, it's not a crime, you know. Nothing to be ashamed of either.'

Lewis threw another stone which bounced off the security light lamppost with a resounding clang. 'I somehow don't think my dad would agree with you . . .'

'Dads can be a problem,' admitted Ben with a rueful smile, 'and mums too for that matter. Just be sure what you want in yourself and the rest will fall into place. OK? Now I'm afraid I've got to go – I've got an . . . appointment. How are you getting home?'

'Bus.'

'Well, we could walk to the bus stop together, then. Unless you've got other plans?'

Lewis beamed and shook his head. 'I could push your bike for you, sir.'

'I'll manage, thank you. I'm not a bloody geriatric, you know – at least not yet, anyway.' He shot a sideways grin to soften the rejection. Kindness, but not too much, he thought grimly, fearing for the future of his young companion.

'I don't know why I've come, actually – I mean, I'm almost certain I shall be wasting your time. It's a bit like putting off booking the doctor and the moment you get round to it your symptoms disappear like magic. Then you feel a right fool.' Ben laughed, aware that he sounded nervous.

Ione Brown smiled. 'It's the people who rush to the doctors with the slightest symptoms who are usually the malingerers. Come in and take a seat. Help yourself to water whenever you want. And I'll begin by telling you a little bit about how I work, my costs, cancellation policy and so on.'

She had one of those faces that had reached a stage of ageing beyond which it was hard to imagine anything else. Deep laugh lines radiated from the corners of her eyes and mouth, but they had the effect of softening her appearance instead of making it more severe. Though he put her at around forty, she could just as well have been thirty-five or close to fifty. Her hair, cut in a short, chic style round her ears, was very black. Apart from some pale lipstick, she appeared to be wearing no make-up at all, while her clothes, a calf-length black skirt and cream polo-neck jumper, were equally inconspicuous. Everything about her demeanour, as a person, as a female, was – Ben felt at once – wholly open and quite without expectation.

In the same soft tone of voice which she used to explain that each session would cost him twenty-five pounds and last for fifty minutes, Ione Brown proceeded to enquire whether Ben could tell her something about the events that had led him to request the appointment.

He struggled hopelessly to answer. 'Oh God, I don't really know, honestly I don't.' He ran both his hands through his hair and studied the flecks in her grey carpet. 'I mean, to tell you the truth, today has been great. A really good day. The first for a while, in fact . . . but apart from that – oh hell, it's probably just a mid-life crisis – usual cliché at my time of life, I suppose. I'm thirty-five.' He offered her a wry smile which was not reciprocated.

'Nothing's a cliché if you feel it.'

He cleared his throat. 'No, I guess it isn't.' He coughed again. 'I'm here because – well, to be frank, a friend recommended you to me. His wife died and he had trouble coping afterwards.' He clapped his hands together. 'But my wife hasn't died – I'm happy to say. In fact, everything in my life is in pretty good working order, except that recently I've felt . . . oh Christ, it's hard to put into words, but . . .' He leant forward in his chair, shamed now by his stammerings into wanting to explain properly. 'I've always been the kind of person who has coped with life. Not just coped, but done pretty well. I don't mean to sound arrogant or anything, but I was thrown into the deep end quite early on – my mother died in a car crash and I was sent to boarding school in England – we lived in Chile – and so I learnt how to get on with things. Did well at school, good at languages, drama, decided to be a teacher – never wanted anything else . . .' He paused, worried that he was boring her. But upon glancing at the counsellor's face he could identify nothing but sympathetic interest. She was leaning forward on her desk, her hands folded neatly across a pad of paper. 'And then I met Isobel.' He hesitated again, remembering with an unexpected rush of pleasure the intensity of that time, the blind, arrogant certainty of all the feelings they had shared. 'And we lived abroad together for a year – she dropped everything to come with me.' He shook his head and smiled, remembering the episode as if in wonderment. 'After getting back to England we married, moved to Torbridge – I worked as a junior master at the cathedral school for a few years, Isobel miscarried our first baby, but we went on to have two lovely girls, now nine and seven . . . the point is, nothing has gone wrong in my life. I mean, I'm now at Crofton College – head of my department – I still love my wife, I adore my children and yet recently . . . I've just been feeling that I can't . . . hold it all together like I used to . . .' He poured a glass of water, disturbed to feel his hand shaking as he did so. 'I'm so damnably busy,' he growled, holding the glass, but not drinking from it. 'I direct school plays too – I'm in the middle of one at the moment, first night this Friday – and well, I guess it's all just been getting on top of me. Too old or something, maybe. There, you see' – he took a gulp of water – 'I told you, a mid-life crisis.' He shot her a look that was meant to be challenging, though it faded fast.

'You sound as if you don't think you've any right to feel like this.'

He scowled. 'No, now you mention it, I don't think I do. I've got everything a man could want – a career, a family, a roof over my head – nothing to feel dissatisfied about at all. A charmed life. Isobel and I haven't been getting on brilliantly recently, but that's because of me . . . because of me feeling like this.' He threw up his hands. 'It's hopeless. I don't see how anyone can help, it's up to me to pull myself together.'

'I don't think that a man who has lost both his mother and his first child could be described as having led a charmed life.'

'Oh, and there was a baby sister too, by the way,' he snapped. 'Let's add that to the catalogue of woes. She was in the car crash too. Just a few months old. I was seven, so there wasn't much sibling bonding to shout about . . . but, don't tell me, I know,' he jeered, 'I feel guilty for her death, do I?'

'Do you?'

'No.' He stuck out his chin. 'Nor do I feel guilty about my mother, in case you're wondering.' Aware that he was sounding increasingly aggressive, Ben took a deep breath to calm himself before continuing. 'It was a very long time ago,' he explained patiently, using a tone of voice he might have employed for an eager but slow-witted pupil, 'at an age when a baby sister was something either to ignore or envy. And my dear mother – from what little I can recall of her – was not what you might describe as the hands-on type of parent. Hordes of servants and so forth.' He laughed quietly. 'Her company was something of a rare treat for all of us, my father included . . .' Ben paused. 'His response to being widowed was to send me to school in England. Which distressed me a little at the time; but then I got used to it – loved it in fact. The school was in Surrey, acres of grounds and all that sort of thing. A maiden aunt used to come and take me out for cream teas.' He stopped, suddenly aware of how intently she was listening to him. 'No, I did not get on with my father,' he added wearily, 'but that's not a crime, is it?'

'No, it's not.'

'I learnt self-sufficiency at an early age. It's something for which I've always been profoundly grateful.' He paused, before murmuring, 'Funny how the worst things that happen to us can also turn out to be the best.'

There was a long silence during which Ione took a sip of water from a glass beside her telephone. 'How did you feel about losing your first child?' she asked gently.

'You make it sound so dramatic. It was really only a miscarriage—' Ben stopped, realising that he sounded unfeeling. 'I'm not saying I wasn't sorry; of course it was awful, but much more so for Isobel, obviously . . .' Aware of the attention of the counsellor, he felt obliged to offer some justification for such opinions. 'I mean – hell, she was carrying the damned thing, feeling it kick and all that stuff. She had to go through the agony of giving birth to something that was barely alive.' To his amazement and horror he found he was crying. Right out of the blue, without having received any warning signs at all. Beside the jug of water was a box of tissues. 'Bloody hell. Sorry.' He blew his nose. 'Hang on a minute, that's what I'm supposed to do, isn't it?' he sneered. 'Therapy in action. Wow. Grown men weeping.'

She remained quite still and silent while he collected himself. Then she said, 'It sounds as though it was very hard for both of you.'

'Isobel was devastated, of course. She cried a lot – even after we discovered she was pregnant again. To be honest, I got . . .' He paused. 'I was going to say angry, but of course I don't mean that; but it did get to the stage where I felt that being so sad wasn't getting her anywhere . . . wasn't getting us anywhere. And it was hard for me too, I suppose, feeling the same things but in such a different way . . .' He slapped his thigh. 'We were lucky enough to have another baby on the way, for God's sake . . .' His voice softened. 'Little Meg.'

'The first pregnancy . . . was it a girl or—?'

'A boy,' he put in quickly. 'Toby. Of course, we still remember the anniversary and all that.' He offered her a tight smile. 'My dear wife has this irritating habit of starting to remind me about it weeks beforehand – like she's scared I'll forget or something. It pisses me off so much that sometimes I pretend I have . . . but not this year.' He frowned and shuffled forward to the edge of his chair, locking and unlocking his fingers. 'This year it was the other way round: her turn to say nothing at all, leaving me to wonder what kind of game she's playing, whether it's to get at me or whether it's a sign that she really wants to be allowed to let that chunk of our past go . . .' He frowned to himself and shook his head. 'She never mentioned it once this year,' he repeated absently, 'not even when I sent flowers.' He looked up. 'So I said nothing either. Funny the games people play, isn't it?' he added with a brief laugh. 'Especially the ones who've known each other a long time. But then you'd know all about that, wouldn't you?'

'Tell me more about Toby. Was there a funeral?'

'Christ, no, we thought it was a bit early for that kind of palaver. Twenty-four weeks. They took photos and so on. The hospital chaplain did a blessing. Then they took him away for cremation. Burnt in a hospital incinerator, no doubt, along with all the other medical waste that week.' He caught his breath and stopped for a moment, breathing hard. 'Oh, and there was a post-mortem.' He raised his voice a little in an effort to quell the new tremor pushing up from the back of his throat. 'Listeria, they said. We'd been on holiday to France that year. Lots of soft cheese. Baguettes and pâté and all that sort of thing . . . it was just before all those food poisoning scandals really hit the headlines. Edwina's eggs started it off, didn't they?' He chuckled quietly. 'Isobel wouldn't go near anything produced by a chicken or a cow for years afterwards – well, certainly not until after Sophie was born anyway.'

'I'm not surprised,' Ione murmured. She let out a small sigh and then raised her eyes to meet his. 'I am very much aware that some of what you have said may have been painful for

you, Mr Tarrant, and that this may feel like a difficult moment
to stop. But I'm afraid we're in danger of running out of time.'
She paused to cast a rueful glance at the clock on the wall above
the door. 'You've mentioned a lot of important things that have
happened, though obviously I realise that there are many areas
we haven't begun to cover. How do you feel it has gone?'

Ben was somewhat taken aback, both by the formality of this
address and because his fifty minutes seemed to have sped by so
fast. He couldn't help feeling a little rebuffed, offended even.

'Do you feel sufficiently encouraged to return?' As she opened
her diary she offered him a warm smile. 'Naturally, it is entirely
up to you to decide.'

Ben stood up, suddenly exasperated. 'Excuse me, but what's
the point? I mean, what can you do for me? What can you
possibly do to help?'

She remained sitting, her brown eyes steadily meeting his.
'Maybe nothing. Maybe something. From what you have said,
it seems to me that ever since you were a child you have always
had to be strong. Though you claim to have found this easy,
it means that there may be losses in your life that you have
not resolved properly. The result of that can be that smaller
subsequent losses, or distress of some kind, may trigger reactions
that are quite out of proportion with the events themselves.'

'You mean it's all catching up with me?'

'Something like that.'

'It sounds too simple, too pat.'

'Often the truest things are the simplest.'

'But do you think it's really worth me coming back?'

'It's up to you – whether you think you might gain anything—'

'Bloody marvellous,' he interrupted. 'I'm supposed to be the
patient, aren't I? Yet I don't get told what to do.'

'Precisely.'

'Well, what do you recommend, then?' he asked, more
meekly, but unable to resist adding, 'That is, if you're allowed
to express an opinion.'

'Six sessions over a period of six weeks. From next week I
shall have a free slot on Thursday evenings at seven o'clock.'

'I'll think about it.'

'Fine. Call me when you've decided what to do.'

Cycling home afterwards, Ben felt a mounting astonishment and dismay at the way he had behaved, not just because of the crying, but also because he had allowed his life story to sound so dramatic. Some families didn't cohere and his had been one of them. Baby Lisa, or 'the little bastard' as his father – on the infrequent occasions when he had referred to her brief existence at all – had so endearingly liked to call her, had been banned as a topic for discussion not so much out of sadness as Albert's sense of family shame. Aunt Violet, like Ben himself, had been sworn to secrecy. A pointless secrecy in Ben's view, but one that over the years had evolved into a habit rather than a challenge. Not telling Isobel had never felt like a big deal. Apart from other considerations, he had also been reluctant to stimulate any more pity from her than the details of his colourful family background had already. Ben had always hated pity, regarding it as the most belittling of responses, from loved ones or anyone else.

Instead of capitalising on his earlier good mood, the immediate effect of the counselling session therefore, was to throw him into deeper confusion. His head was buzzing with images from the past, not so much from his childhood, as from the early years of his marriage: images of little Toby in particular, what he had felt at losing him. Or rather, what he had tried not to feel. Being strong had appeared as his obvious, allotted task, he remembered, the one useful thing he could do in the circumstances; the thing he could do for Isobel. At the thought of his wife, a hand tightened around Ben's heart. Talking about her behind her back like that, pouring so much into the grey expectant silence of Ione Brown's small consulting room, felt like betrayal. It was Isobel he should be talking to, he realised hopelessly, not some empathetic stranger with a heart-warming smile.

By the time Ben got home, however, Isobel had already gone up to bed. He made himself a sandwich, which he ate along with two bananas and an overripe tomato while watching the late evening news. He started a can of beer but abandoned it after a few swigs. A pleasant exhaustion began to seep through him, relaxing his body like a warm bath. While a bespectacled weatherman pointed at cut-out rain-clouds and frothing satellite pictures, Ben's head flopped from side to side in a faltering attempt to resist sleep. In his mind he could see Isobel, but far away, a speck at the end of a tunnel. And he was running towards her, shouting at her to wait, that he was on his way. Though he ran his hardest, the speck grew ever more tiny until its existence was the merest pin-prick, something to be believed in rather than seen.

Upstairs, meanwhile, the object of Ben's dreams lay hunched in a stiff representation of sleep, listening for, yet dreading, the footfall on the stair, the creak of the loose floorboard on the landing outside their room. And when it did not come, when minutes became hours and still it did not come, something in her gave up and was replaced by the steel of resigned resolution. If James wanted her he could have her, she thought, biting the knuckles of her hand. Anything was better than not being wanted at all, than living with an absence of hope as well as love.

28 ∫

My Dearest Isobel,

   Has it really only been a matter of hours since our last meeting? How the time drags when we're apart. And yet how it flies when we're together. To say I'm missing you does not begin to do justice to the intensity of my feelings . . .

James smiled to himself as he paused to dip his fountain pen in the pot of ink. It was hard to recall when he had last felt so happy, so excited, so . . . alive. He held up the page, admiring the rich, thick squirls of his handwriting. Though it was only ten o'clock, Juliet had already gone to bed, early nights having become something of a habit of hers in recent weeks. As this was the only evidence of wifely withdrawal since the start of his affair with Isobel, and since each retirement was embarked upon with the tenderest of goodnight kisses, James had not yet allowed himself to worry over the matter. In many ways he was grateful: such behaviour generated an atmosphere of affectionate distance which suited both his mood and his capabilities perfectly. They had stopped rowing too, which was nice.

All I can see is your face, all I can feel is your body . . . James hesitated, wondering how erotic or risqué he dared to be. Matters had reached a very delicate stage. The last thing he wanted was to scare her away. *I need you,* he wrote, crushing more wildly erotic expressions of passion that flitted into his mind. Better to play it safe, he told himself, pausing again, this time to extract a minute hair from the gold nib of his pen.

*As I keep saying, we need some time away together. I know your
reservations. I know that, like me, you are steeling yourself for the
right moment to break the news. But don't you feel it would do
us both good to think through such a prospect together, in peace
somewhere? What about it, Isobel? A few days away, on our own.
Wouldn't that be wonderful? Could your parents perhaps look after
the children? I don't mean to appear hasty or presumptuous . . . I'm
just so desperate to get you away from everyone – from everything –
to get you to myself. After that . . .*

James stopped and frowned. For the truth was that, while
implying to Isobel – because she clearly needed to hear it –
that any future they chose was theirs for the asking, he had
not really thought things through properly on that score at all. It
was too difficult for one thing; and for another, he was enjoying
himself too much. If he had one criticism of his mistress it was
that she could not lose herself entirely to the moment. Their
physical compatibility was unquestionable; all those weeks of
fantasising and flirting had resulted in the most satisfactory
of sexual relationships. Left to his own devices, James would
have been happy to have let things coast for a while, to delay
rocking the boat on any front until it was absolutely necessary.
But Isobel's thought processes had quickly raced to a point way
beyond such easy options. What would become of them? she
wanted to know, almost from the start. Where would it all lead
in the end? Sex had to be part of something, she said. It had to
lead somewhere lasting and worthwhile. James's face softened
at the recollection of the sincerity of her pleadings, how she
warmed to his declarations of love. All wide-eyed and fearful.
Like a child. It was impossible not to feel passionate about such
a creature. With a frown he forced his attention back to the
business in hand, bracing himself for the direct approach.

*Since so much is at stake, I feel increasingly certain that we owe
it to each other to take some time out to think things through
clearly, without the pressures of time and guilt breathing down
our necks. We may have a future together, Isobel, and I for one
need a bit of space in order to contemplate how best to achieve
that . . .*

Having laboured sufficiently over the pretext for the point he was trying to make, James's handsome writing doubled in speed and flourish.

If you could escape to Suffolk for a few days, I've heard of the perfect place we could go. A wonderful country hotel; discreet and luxurious. And not at all far from where I believe your parents live. I think I shall probably be completely frank with Juliet – tell her straight out that I need some time to myself to think about our future. What you decide to tell Ben is of course your business and I would not dream of interfering. No aspect of this is remotely easy for any of us. But then of course you know that. Just as I think you know that we are very good together, Isobel, that we deserve a chance to see things through. I'm not so foolish as to make false promises about exactly what the future will hold, but I just know that everything will work out all right in the end. Because all this was meant to be.

Pleased with this last sentence, James was for a moment tempted to leave it at that. But the opportunity for a little more romance got the better of him.

This was intended as a love letter, but I'm not sure how I've done. I'd forgotten what love felt like. I don't feel hungry or tired. I don't feel anything except a burning desire to be with you. Nothing else matters. I just can't care about anything else in the world . . . I'll call you soon, my love, during a 'safe' time. I'll be delivering this by hand. I'm thinking about Suffolk already, longing for it . . . don't let me down.

Yours devotedly, James

After reading it through James wondered whether he should tear it up and do a new version that was slightly more ordered and well argued. He really had set his heart on a few days away and would be extremely disappointed if she refused. Upon a second reading, however, he convinced himself that a slight incoherence was part of the letter's charm, and that anything better structured would be in danger of seeming glib or insincere. He sealed it and addressed it by hand, before slipping it amongst some papers in his briefcase. He would deliver it the next day, at an hour when he could be sure Ben's bicycle would be absent from the tiny box of a front garden in Fox's Crescent.

At the thought of Ben, James flinched, as a twinge of something like compassion momentarily pinched his heart. It was quickly overcome by impatience. From what he could gather from Isobel – who volunteered very little on the subject – the man had been ignoring the poor girl for months. As a result James had – somewhat conveniently – decided that Ben Tarrant was one of those secret bullies, lovingly protective towards their spouses in public, but with an altogether more hostile agenda reserved for the home.

As he moved quietly around the ground floor, turning out lights and checking locks, James felt indignation mounting on his lover's behalf. He wouldn't dream of treating Juliet in such a manner, he thought, or decided to think, until the ambiguities inherent in such emotions caused him to pause, hand poised over a light switch, in order to ponder such contradictions more deeply. Although he had implied to Isobel – many times – that he wished to abandon his marriage, in his heart James was not as sure as he claimed. Juliet understood him in ways he could never imagine another woman doing. She laughed when he farted or belched. She tickled him if he snored, and rolled her palms around his shoulder blades when he was tense. Such familiarity had taken years to construct. He couldn't imagine it with Isobel. More importantly, he didn't much want to. His relationship with her seemed to exist on a purer, higher plane, quite apart from the real world. And, in spite of all protestations to the contrary to his lover, a considerable part of him wanted to keep it that way.

'Hello, Mum, it's me, Isobel. How are you?'

'Wait a minute, I can't hear a thing.' Betty Hitchings scowled, as she always did if her presence in the kitchen happened to coincide with the over-ebullient spin cycle of her washing machine. There was one long final vibrating whoosh followed by a relieving silence. 'Thank God for that. Your father's shirts in their final throes. The belt on the machine is about to go, I just know it. But will he look at the damn thing . . . ?' Aware that she was in danger of sounding disloyal, Betty checked herself, before rushing on with more conventional expressions of greeting. 'But how are you, darling? How are the children?'

'We're all fine,' replied Isobel carefully, wondering, now that she had got this far, how much she was actually prepared to reveal. She had never been a great one for heart-to-heart talks with her mother, as much from her own reticence as a distinct sense that neither of her parents wished to be drawn into the role of confidant, that to do so would overstep some traditional boundary line that they wished to preserve. They could be sympathetic when the need arose, but always in a brisk no-nonsense way, faintly suggestive of impatience.

'How's Dad?'

'Grumpy. He's on a diet.'

'Again?' Isobel tugged a tired grape off its stalk and squeezed it between her thumb and forefinger before placing it in her mouth. She was sitting on the edge of the kitchen table, her feet lodged between the slats of a chair.

'Doctor's orders. High blood pressure and so on. Got to cut down on his cholesterol.'

'Poor Dad.'

'He'll survive. We're eating a lot of pasta and fish. I've lost half a stone.' She laughed. 'Which is more than can be said for George. He's in the garden now, digging fiendishly round the roses in the hope of shedding a few pounds before lunch.'

Isobel laughed too, enjoying, in spite of her own preoccupations, the familiar snapshot of her parents' married existence. Was it resignation or faith, she wondered, that had kept them together for so long? What did love become after thirty-five years?

'I say, how's that university course of yours going?'

'It's not,' replied Isobel flatly, pulling at a loose thread in one of her socks until it broke.

'But you sounded so excited . . . all those books . . .'

'I've given up, actually – on the idea of literature, anyway. It was too much like . . .' She hesitated, remembering her recent frustrations with Anna Karenina and various other heroines on the reading list, how absurdly glorious their creators had made them seem, when real life was not glorious at all, but full of belittling detail and doubt. '. . . escapism,' she ended lamely. 'I'm thinking of doing something more practical. The OU have just introduced a Spanish course – it's a new thing. Seeing as I got the hang of the basics all those centuries ago in Madrid, I'm toying with the idea of applying to start in September.' It was hard to inject any conviction into her voice. Present circumstances had deterred her from mentioning such plans to Ben. September seemed worlds away, on the other side of an abyss.

'How splendid,' exclaimed her mother in a way that Isobel knew was intended to communicate enthusiasm, but which only managed to sound patronising instead. In spite of all her efforts to the contrary, Betty Hitchings retained a fondness for the most archaic of attitudes towards the concept of women and work. Though both daughters had attended reputable universities, it remained evident that she regarded all female education as a prelude to marriage and little else. That her high-flying merchant banker of an eldest child was still showing not the remotest hint of a nesting instinct or anything related was, as the entire family knew, a growing source of secret maternal disappointment.

'I know it's very short notice,' blurted Isobel, unable to sustain small talk for a moment longer, 'but I was wondering if you and Dad were busy this weekend and next week . . . ?'

'The Birketts were due to come and stay, but they've cried off – Donald's rheumatism, Caroline says, though I suspect it's because they couldn't face the journey. It is a hell of a way for them to come and Caroline herself only has to look at a car seat and her back seizes up . . . why do you ask, dear?' she added suddenly, a note of something like suspicion edging into her voice.

'I know it's short notice—' faltered Isobel.

'Were you and Ben thinking of coming to stay?'

'Sort of . . . well, yes . . . and I was also hoping to leave the girls with you for a couple of days next week.'

'Is term about to end?' Betty squinted at a calendar of seascapes pinned to the back of the door beside her.

'Not quite. They officially break up next week . . .' Isobel cast her eyes down to James's letter which was sitting next to her on the table. With one hand she folded it back in two and pressed her fingers hard along the crease. 'But I was thinking of breaking the habit of a lifetime and pulling the girls out of school a little early . . .'

'Whatever for? Surely Ben's got to see out his term too. Has he done that play of his yet?'

Isobel, in danger of getting riled, had to remind herself that her mother was not being deliberately obtuse, that all the responsibility for the difficulty of this conversation rested entirely with her.

'No, that's this weekend. Final dress rehearsal tonight . . .' She sighed. 'Look, it's hard to explain properly, Mum, but the fact is that I need – Ben and I need – a little time apart right now.'

There was a stunned silence.

'We . . . things have not been good recently—'

'What sort of things?'

'Like I said, it's impossible to explain.' Isobel had now folded the page of James's letter into a tight, fat square. 'All I'm asking is whether I could come over with the children for a little while and perhaps take a couple of days on my own next week, to go away somewhere . . .'

'On your own?'

'To think,' put in Isobel quickly, wanting to avoid an outright lie. She wasn't ready to mention James yet, not until they knew exactly what their plans were. 'I need time to think about what to do.'

'Have you two had some sort of tiff?'

This was such a monumental understatement that for a moment Isobel was tempted to laugh out loud. A tiff sounded feisty and amusing. A tiff happened between two people who could still talk to each other, who still ate meals together. 'I'm afraid it's all much more complicated, Mum,' she replied quietly, the anguish plain in her voice.

'Of course you can come and stay,' came the barked reply, as Betty Hitchings slipped into full crisis-management mode, using a tone that transported Isobel straight back to all the landmark traumas of childhood, traumas usually associated with Angela, who had generally taken it upon herself to pioneer the reprehensible antics of adolescence. 'Where are we? Thursday afternoon. Right, then, come tomorrow if you want. We'll expect you by lunch.'

'Thank you,' Isobel whispered, despising the pang of nostalgic longing that burst inside, the brief, false relief of being a child again, of having parents to rail against instead of the inadequacies of oneself.

'Of course your father and I will do anything we can to help. But do try and sort it out in the meantime, the two of you, won't you? Running away never solved anything, you know. And think of the girls . . .'

Isobel, who had recently been thinking of little else, closed her ears to the gently scolding lecture that ensued. Telling Sophie and Megan was easily going to be the worst part of all. She dreaded their bewilderment. Though they saw too little of Ben, their devotion to him was absolute, she knew. They were fond of James, but only as a doctor who gave them lollipops for being brave, and as a grown-up with a high tolerance for tickling games and losing count of the number of biscuits consumed between meals. How they would feel about him moving into their lives on a more permanent scale was hard to imagine. As indeed it remained for Isobel herself. Try as she might, she could not picture how a reshuffled future might look, how it would feel, day to day. She was intent on pushing things that way because all her instincts told her that it was the only thing to do; the only way of redeeming anything from the situation at all. And because James, though baulking like her at the prospect of all the upheaval and hurt, seemed to be growing increasingly desperate to have her to himself. It was impossible not to be flattered by the intensity of his ardour, impossible – much as she hated to acknowledge the fact – not to be grateful for it.

'We'll come tomorrow, then,' she pressed on, swallowing her doubts and focusing on the burgeoning need to get away from the stranger who had once been her husband, away from the collapse of all that she had once held so dear. 'Be there by lunch-time,' she echoed, quailing inwardly, though her voice held firm.

'And stay the whole of next week?'

'If that's all right.'

'But you'll be going off for a couple of days on your own somewhere?'

Isobel swallowed. 'That's the idea. If it's OK with you.'

'To think.'

'Yes, to think.'

'Where?'

'Where what?'

'Where exactly is all this thinking going to take place?'

'I don't know, I've not yet sorted everything out . . . it doesn't really matter, to be honest.'

Her mother humphed. 'Well, all I can say is I'm very sorry indeed.'

'So am I, Mum, believe me.'

'I thought we might go to Granny's for a while.'

'For Easter?'

'No . . . starting tomorrow.'

'You mean miss school?'

'Just a few days . . .'

'Yippee times a million.' Sophie, who was supposed to be holding the frilly paper trim of her Easter bonnet in place until the glue dried, let go in order to clap her hands. Since a greater quantity of adhesive had found its way on to her fingertips than on to the cardboard contours of the hat, the lacy strip of paper was soon hanging in several soggy pieces between her palms.

'But why?' Megan, old enough to be more suspicious, ruled a careful line underneath the last of a set of perfectly formed fractions and closed her book. 'You don't believe in missing school. Ever.' She folded her arms. 'You made me go back when I still had all those scabs.' The recollection of this indignity deepened the pained expression on her face.

'You weren't infectious,' began Isobel, feeling diverted and hopeless.

'No, I was hideous.'

'Darling, it was years ago . . .'

'Only a little bit over two years ago. I got the first spots on Christmas Day, remember?'

Isobel smiled and reached out a hand to stroke her eldest's mop of dark hair. Even after several months of being commanded to 'grow out', Megan's fringe had still somehow only managed to reach the corners of her eyes, from where it flopped, with regular and infuriating persistence, into her long dark lashes. She was glowering from behind this new protection now, exercising a sullenness that had something to do with being almost ten and something less easily defined to do with the expression of unnatural cheeriness imprinted on her mother's face. 'I don't want to go to Suffolk. It's horrid except in the summer. All cold and windy. And Grandpa makes us help in the garden.' She scowled.

'But Granny will take you to the library and that adventure playground with the tree-house and the long curly slide—'

'And to the place with the penguins,' squealed Sophie, for whom a trip to the aquatic wonders of East Anglia's Sea World the summer before remained one of the unparalleled highlights of her existence.

'But why?' persisted Megan, unappeased.

'Because I need . . . a little holiday . . . and because I think Daddy probably needs a little holiday from me,' stammered Isobel, wringing her hands, wishing she felt more brave, wishing she could think of some acceptable way of explaining that their father no longer loved her, that not being loved had made her embark on something so imprudent and out of character that she might have to spend the rest of her life trying to make up for it.

'That's stupid.' Megan slammed her hands on the table and ran from the room, banging the door behind her.

Sophie, worried now by her sister's outburst, stared despondently at the bits of paper sticking to her fingers. 'It's all gone wrong,' she wailed, plucking furiously, and quite ineffectually, at the hardening lumps of white glue.

'We'll start again, darling. Don't cry,' said Isobel brightly, close to tears herself. 'I've got loads more paper. We'll make another edging and stick that on instead. Mum can do the glue next time and you can tell me exactly where to put it. And when it's dry we'll paint it – pink and yellow, just like you wanted.' She pulled the sobbing child on to her lap and held her tightly, while silent tears of her own trickled into the copper curls burrowing beneath her chin.

Now it's really begun, she thought grimly, clenching her jaw to steady the tremor in her lower lip. All that remained was telling Ben. She wished she could feel defiant at the prospect instead of merely afraid. Only his not loving her had made the affair with James possible. Yet even the knowledge of this truth offered little comfort. At best Ben might feel relief that she was offering him a way out of their marriage. At worst what had appeared only as cold indifference might be transformed into the most derisory form of hate. But there was nothing left for such hate to destroy anyway, she consoled herself, reaching round Sophie for the scissors and beginning to hack at another paper strip.

Thinking of James did provide some solace, though their conversation earlier that afternoon had not been without its tensions. When she broke the news about Druscilla Carew he let out an expostulation of such outraged dismay that Isobel found herself abandoning all her own worries on the matter in order to insist on its insignificance. Everyone would know anyway soon, she reassured him, while her own stomach twisted at the thought.

'Yes, I suppose they will.'

'In fact, I've decided to tell Ben tonight . . . about going away . . . about you. I've done what you suggested in your letter. We're leaving to stay with my parents tomorrow.'

There was a fractional hesitation. 'So you really are going to tell Ben, you brave thing . . .'

'When are you going to break the news to Juliet?'

'Not sure. Soon. Maybe tonight as well . . .'

'Then we'd be doing the hardest part together . . .'

'Yes, that's true . . . no reason to hang on any longer, I suppose, especially not with nosey neighbours starting to talk . . .'

'I don't care what anyone thinks,' blurted Isobel. 'All that matters is . . . trying to do the right thing, trying to be happy . . .'

'Oh, and we will be, I promise you,' he whispered. 'The place I want us to stay in is exquisite; near the coast, between Ditton and Wetherall, only twenty miles or so from your parents' neck of the woods. "Le Relais", it's called, a couple of miles in from the main coast road. Three stars in the Michelin, a health spa, luxurious suites, total seclusion . . . just what we need.'

'Sounds lovely,' said Isobel quietly, winding the telephone flex so tightly round her fingers that their tips turned a yellowy white.

'Look, why don't we agree now to meet there on Monday evening at, say, seven o'clock? I'll make all the arrangements, they're bound not to be busy mid-week. I'll book us in for three nights, just the two of us, what do you say?' His voice bounced with enthusiasm.

'OK . . .'

'I'll only call in the meantime if there's a hitch.'

She was silent for a moment.

'Will you be able to find it? Are you with me, Isobel?'

'I am, James, I am. Monday at seven. "Le Relais". I'll be there, I promise.' Though more muted in her reaction, Isobel too was now longing to get away, not so much to be with her lover as to have time and space in which to reflect, to regroup for the unspeakable difficulties that lay ahead.

The old lady pointed to the 'closed' sign and shook her head. Ben tapped his watch, to indicate that there was still a full minute to go before half past five, and mouthed 'please' with as much charm as could reasonably be mustered in the circumstances.

'I shouldn't,' she tutted, opening the door. 'He'll go mad.'

'I won't keep you long – thank you so much.' Ben stepped past her, smiling with relief. He had half an hour before he was due back in school for the final rehearsal. With the first night only a day away, all he wanted was to see it through.

'Who is it?' growled a voice from a room behind the counter.

'It's a gentleman, dear, he says he won't be long.' The woman winked at Ben and began stabbing at a tray of silver trinkets with a feather duster.

'He'd better bloody not be.' A stooped old man with a shining bald pate and pebble spectacles appeared holding a mug of tea. Through the open door behind him, Ben could see a small television set and a tartan two-seater sofa. His voice had a gentle Northern ring to it, while his eyes glittered with humour behind the thick lenses of his glasses. 'What can I do you for, then?'

'It's this,' said Ben at once, pulling the pink crystal from his pocket and placing it on the counter. 'I want it made into a piece of jewellery. A friend of mine said you might be able to help.'

'Friend? What friend?'

'A Mr Caulder. He teaches—'

'Ah, Dicky, yes – know him well, of course. His lady wife helped in the shop from time to time . . . tragedy her passing on like that . . . terrible tragedy.' He puffed out his cheeks, which were pink with tiny broken veins. 'Not that we've any call for part-time staff these days. I don't care what those politicians say about this feel-good factor business – whatever it is, none of it's bloody coming our way. Is it, Kitty?'

'No, dear.'

'Interesting rock.' Pushing his glasses on to his forehead, he plugged what looked like a small telescope to his eye socket and screwed his face into creases as he studied it. 'Where did you find this, then?'

'Wales. Near a beach. It's been in my coat pocket for weeks . . . been meaning to do something imaginative with it, but I've been so busy . . .'

'Pretty.' The man sniffed. 'And what were you wanting – a brooch, was it?'

'Or . . . I thought maybe a pendant,' ventured Ben, eyeing a glass-topped case of chains in the cabinet next to him. Isobel never wore brooches. 'Could a sort of ring be put round it, with a loop to hang on a necklace?'

'It could.'

'I'd need a chain too.'

'You would.' The man put his telescope in a drawer and got out a pad of paper. 'Sure you don't want a brooch, then?'

'Absolutely.'

'As you wish.' He did a few dark scribbles on the pad with a blunt pencil. 'Like to please, don't we, Kitty? Do you want to choose a chain, then?'

'I'll have that one, please, the one with the smallest links.'

'Got a train to catch?' chuckled the man, raising one grey bushy eyebrow at his customer's evident impatience to be gone. He coiled the chosen necklace into a tidy pile beside the crystal. 'It'll cost you thirty pounds in all and I'll need a deposit. A fiver will do. Be ready by the end of next week, I should think.'

'Great. Thank you very much.' Ben turned to go.

'Don't you want an inscription?' It was the woman, Kitty, who had abandoned her cleaning and was sitting on a small upright chair beside the door, fanning her face with her duster. 'An inscription's always nice, I think.'

'Now, now, Kitty, the gentleman knows what he wants.'

'An inscription – what a good idea.' Ben returned to the counter. 'Round the side maybe, engraved in the ring . . .'

'It'll have to be short,' put in the man, scowling.

'Just "Isobel", I think.' Ben hesitated, blushing slightly, much to the delight of his audience. 'No, hang on . . . how about "Isobel, my love"? Yes, that's it. Is there room?' he added anxiously.

'I should think so. It'll add a tenner to your bill, mind.' The old man smiled. 'Write the name down, then, so I've got the spelling. Full of possibilities is Isobel, like Catherine – or Ewan, for that matter. A right bugger is Ewan, spelling-wise.'

As Ben hurried outside, the shop door jangled shut behind him. He was in a small side street right on the outskirts of Torbridge, full of small, struggling local shops and huddling terraced houses. He was going to have to cycle his very fastest in order to get back to school in time for the run-through. As he swung his bike back on to the road he caught sight of the old lady, Kitty, smiling and waving from behind the smeary pane of the shop window. Ben waved back, his heart thrilling with goodwill towards her and mankind in general.

His two hours of fitful armchair dozing the night before had been followed by a brief but refreshingly dreamless sleep. He had woken with something resembling a sense of purpose, though still accompanied by the feeling that he was clawing his way back from the edge; that every tiny movement mattered desperately in relation to how things would turn out in the end. Snatches of his conversation with Ione Brown criss-crossed lazily through his morning sleepiness, now bringing small surges of comfort as well as amazement. Understanding the past might help the present after all he mused, if tackled in the right way. As the face of the counsellor blurred into Isobel's, he reached an arm across to her side of the bed. But all it found was the warmth of where her body had been. He let his arm rest in the empty space for a few minutes, hardly breathing as he strained to hear the dim sounds of female voices emanating from the kitchen below, of taps running, of cutlery clinking against crockery. And as he listened his heart swelled with love and a new determination to put things right, without further recourse to third parties of any kind.

By the time he got downstairs his family were already halfway out the door. Megan was playing the flute in school assembly and had to be there early for a practice. As he kissed the girls goodbye, he tried desperately to catch Isobel's eye, wanting to communicate at least something of his new-found hope for them all. But she was busy with satchel straps and lunch boxes, dodging behind their daughters as if seeking to shield herself from his reach. She did not meet his gaze until they were at the front gate, and then only fleetingly – more of a blink than a look – before quickly swivelling her face to the road ahead.

All day Ben had been haunted by this farewell glance, by the sheer dismissiveness of it. It made him impatient to get home, impatient to challenge and obliterate the reason for its existence. Instead of dreading the evening's rehearsal he longed only for it to be over. In the meantime, finally doing something about the crystal had made him feel a little better, not because he was naïve enough to believe that Isobel could be wooed back with sentimental gifts, but simply because he knew that at last he was doing something positive. A step in the right direction, albeit taken invisibly and alone.

Pedalling furiously back through the winding side streets of Torbridge, taking every short cut he knew, Ben found his mind skipping to absurdly idyllic images of the little prep school in Hampshire. He had telephoned for the application forms that morning. They would be interviewing throughout the first half of the summer term and would have a decision by the middle of June, the school secretary informed him briskly, before slipping her mask to reveal that she had once had a nephew who sang with the Torbridge choir and retained fond memories of Royles cream teas. Ben had felt ridiculously buoyed by the news, as if such irrelevant connections somehow boded well on his behalf. Remembering the conversation as he rounded the final bend towards Crofton College caused him to break into exuberant song, a silly ditty from one of the girls' tapes that set the handful of boys still loitering on the pavement outside the school's large iron gates giggling into their collars.

Juliet, speeding in the opposite direction on course between retrieving Tilly from a birthday party and Eddie from the scouts, was far too preoccupied to recognise the hunched, dark-headed figure on a bike who slowed and then accelerated over the zebra crossing a few yards from the entrance to the school. Of more immediate concern to Dr Howard's wife were the fresh salmon fillets which had sat in the blast of the car heating for far longer than was good for them, not to mention the bloodied bag of steak, and the tub of hand-whipped ginger ice cream she had bought from the small expensive deli by Mayers Gate. At Tilly's vociferous insistence, they were listening to an Enid Blyton story on the cassette player, an improbable narrative about cave tunnels and treasure, whose literary merits did not stand up well to the pressures of repetition. Tilly, who knew all the words by heart, had turned the volume up and was chanting along with it, omitting nothing, not even the unconvincing barking of Timmy the dog. That Juliet succeeded in maintaining a stoical silence throughout this ordeal was due not so much to motherly tolerance as to a heightened reluctance to provoke confrontation of any kind. Another battle awaited her, for which she knew she would need every ounce of mental reserve.

The Barclaycard bill had arrived that morning, together with a polite letter pointing out that they had exceeded their credit limit for the month and requesting immediate settlement. Thanks to some generous adjustments made during a particularly heavy phase of purchasing shortly after moving house, the limit referred to was a hefty five thousand pounds. The amount by which the bill exceeded this was half as much again. The only resource containing anything like this sum of money that Juliet could conceive of was a special savings account for school fees that James had opened a few years before. Without understanding all the details, Juliet knew that it was an account with a time lock on it, that touching the funds before Eddie was thirteen was not supposed to be allowed and would almost certainly incur financial penalties of the most crippling kind.

Thinking about the showdown ahead made Juliet curiously eager as well as afraid. Preparing for it, as she had done all that day, had reminded her of the once-familiar rigours of facing an opening night, steeling oneself both for certain terror and the possibility of exultation. There would be an argument, of course, ostensibly about the money, but at heart about much more serious things. She knew it was going to take all her cunning and skill, not only as an actress, but as a woman and a wife, to steer them safely through to the other side.

James was having an affair, of that she was now certain. So certain that she no longer even bothered to look for lipstick impressions on his collars or telltale receipts in his suit pockets. It was infinitely more mundane aspects of his behaviour which had aroused her suspicions; like the alacrity with which he had taken to getting out of bed in the mornings, the smug expression on his face as he groomed his hair, the inane whistling as he skipped downstairs for breakfast. Equally remarkable was his recent predilection for relating the events of his day with quite unprecedented and unnecessary detail, as if driven by a sudden need to account for his time. And now a mysterious three-day conference had materialised, only several days away, based at some hotel in East Anglia. James's account of the agendas to be discussed had been thorough to the point of tediousness: a series of seminars and plenaries on the future of the NHS, workshops on fund-holders and trusts, lectures on and from health authorities. He had also taken the trouble to remind her – not once, but several times – that he had once attended something very similar in the past. Juliet, remembering the event to which he referred, had only just managed not to mention that James's involvement on that occasion had been for one day only and that the date had been entered into the diary several months beforehand. Tempting though it was to make him squirm with a few prescient enquiries on the matter, instinct warned her it would be unwise. With his defences up, her husband's conscience would be far harder to assail; she wanted him soft and unsuspecting, malleable in every conceivable way.

By far the hardest aspect of the situation had been containing her curiosity as to the identity of the other woman. To know such a thing would, Juliet knew, make James unforgivable. Far better to keep the enemy a blur, to beat it back before it came sufficiently into focus to represent something so personalised as to be relevant or threatening. What limited speculations she had allowed herself had quickly resulted in the conclusion that it was probably someone much younger. Prime among suspects was the busty new receptionist at the practice, whose arrival James had for some reason failed to mention, and who answered all calls with the silky innuendo of a female overpowered by a nauseating confidence in her own magnetism. But the girl was so absurdly young and pretty that Juliet simply could not imagine her falling for a fifty-year-old, even a relatively dashing, well-preserved one, with a twinkle in his eye and most of his hair still rooted to its follicles.

All the perishables sweating in the plastic bags upon which Tilly was resting her small feet were for supper that night. They would start with the salmon, bathed in a vermouth and cream sauce. The steak would follow, bloody and soft in the middle, just as he liked it, nestling between fist-sized grilled mushrooms and the pretty peaks of a parsnip purée. For dessert she would sprinkle shavings of fresh ginger on the ice cream and decorate the rims of the plates with wafer-thin lemon biscuits that melted on the tongue. As these prospects drew closer, Juliet grew calmer, almost forgetting the initial panic that had overwhelmed her when she recognised the credit company's envelope lying beneath the letter flap on the hall floor, covering the *W* of the *WELCOME* stitched into her doormat. She had stood staring at it for a good two minutes, while her polished parquet floor heaved beneath her feet and the terracotta tints of her walls danced with dizzying black spots. When at last the figure on the bill had been confronted, if not exactly digested, she had rewarded herself with a deep bath, extravagantly scented with the last drops of her best rose oil. She lay in the water for nearly an hour, topping up the hot and inhaling the perfumed steam with long slow breaths that gradually cleared her mind. Afterwards, steaming gently, her flesh mottled pink with heat, she had swept her wet hair into a turban and sat on their bedroom window seat in her dressing gown, letting her breath cloud the view of the garden below. After a few minutes she rubbed a porthole in the misted pane with her fist, and gazed out at their neat arrangement of lawn and shrubs, thinking incredulously of a time, not so very long ago, when all but a patio had seemed to sit between her and the attainment of worldly bliss. The stonework was completed now. Only a dusty circle of leftover sand remained as evidence of all the weeks of wheelbarrows and upheaval. The finished article, with its neat arched inset for a barbecue and low surrounding wall, looked so solid that it was hard to recall the scruffy flowerbeds and shrivelled hedge that had once occupied the same ground.

The view blurred and disappeared as the warmth of Juliet's breath steamed the porthole closed again. It wasn't love which lasted, she thought bitterly, shaking her hair out of the towel and crossing to her wardrobe, it was marriages, sustained by a memory of love. Though uncharacteristically bleak, the notion did nothing to discourage the slow surge of determination now mushrooming inside. If anything it encouraged it. It was a question of understanding the rules, Juliet told herself, as she tugged clothes off hangers and rummaged through drawers. Even if that meant accepting that there were no rules at all.

She got dressed in a plain blouse and shirt for the day, but laid out an altogether different costume for the evening. From the bags still buried under the bed she unearthed the pantaloon trousers, shoes, a cream tank top of knitted silk and the waistcoat with gold buttons. On top of these she placed the least comfortable but most exotic of her bras, an article which, thanks to a heavy dependency on hidden wire, succeeded in pushing her breasts up and together at the same time, presenting them for attention, like ripe fruit on a plate. Last touch of all were her G-string panties, bought during a bygone era of tight trousers, when the curve of her bottom was something she sought to show off rather than disguise. With her clothes sorted, Juliet immediately felt better. Moving now in a brisk, motivated way, she fetched her vanity case of oils and set out a small army of bottles on her dressing table. She paused to trail two immaculately painted nails over the lids and labels, nudging them into new positions as if they were pieces on a chessboard. After a few minutes she settled upon a bottle labelled 'Essence of Nutmeg Oil' and carefully unscrewed the lid. The sweet, nutty aroma smelled good enough to eat. Tiny writing on the side of the bottle confirmed her confidence in her own choice: *Analgesic, aphrodisiac, calming, comforting, elevating, euphoric, narcotic, soothing, tonic (nerve and heart). Mix 3 drops with 1 tbs of sweet almond oil before use in massage.*

'Perfect,' she murmured, closing her eyes, willing herself to believe that with such props all would yet be well in her life. Instead, she saw James as he once had been, felt again his early adoration of her, all that jealous obsession with her body, the dogged patience in the sidelines of her life, his jubilation when, at last, she totally succumbed. Such memories brought both Juliet's fears and her anger more sharply into focus. It was not the shame of a younger rival that scared her so much – though that rankled – as the threat of being left alone. She had done her time as a single woman, experienced enough of its dubious freedoms to know that it was a territory to which she never wished to return. Especially not as an older – as an uglier – woman. For, having tasted some of the power that goes hand in hand with beauty, Juliet knew too well how such influence diminished with age. She could not believe she would find such a husband again. Losing James would mean losing not only security and companionship but also her self-esteem. A disaster from which she had the self-knowledge to realise she would probably never recover.

By the time she got home with her purchases, Juliet had the structure of the evening laid out in her head like a battle plan. Having hurried the children through their homework and shooed them to bed without baths, she set about preparing the food, humming quietly to herself as she moved around the kitchen. When every ingredient had been seasoned or chopped or garnished, she decanted a bottle of claret and set the table, putting a pretty vase of freesias between two fresh red candles. She would feed his senses till they burst, overload him with pleasant sensations until the guilt, the doubt, choked in his throat. She would defeat him with kindness, smother him with spoiling, churn up so much gratitude and pleasure that he would wonder how he ever could – ever should – leave such a marvel. Then would come the money, the trickiest – but potentially the most effective – element of all. The debt had to be both forgiven and recognised for the weapon it was. She needed James to understand that if he wronged her she would bleed him dry, that he could never afford to leave her anyway, because she had him by the balls.

Sometimes Druscilla lost the thread of why she did things. There was an airy space inside her head, a vacuum whose emptiness could feel quite a burden, but which at other times served to make her feel uniquely disconnected and free. She had tried to explain it to a doctor once, a long time ago, during the last and worst of her breakdowns. He said having one's face used as a punch-bag left many legacies and that in time the blankness would go away, be filled, like skin closing over a wound. That he was wrong did not bother Druscilla unduly, since as the years wore on what occurred inside her head seemed of increasing inconsequence to anyone but herself. And sometimes it was quite nice not to know why one did things, not to have to bother with the tedium of understanding and logic. At least that was the explanation she gave herself for deciding to give the flower card not to Isobel, as she had promised, but to Ben Tarrant instead.

The note had emerged on Wednesday evening, crumpled but still legible, from down one side of an armchair during a bout of nocturnal spring-cleaning. It stuck to the powerful snout of her dust-buster, vibrating like a trapped leaf until she prised it free. *For my darling, no words can say what I feel.* She read the message out loud several times to the mouth of her Hoover, trying out different inflections and waggling its black head as if hopeful of a reply. Before going up to bed she Sellotaped the card to her front door, as a reminder to return it to its rightful owner in the morning.

After all the exertions of her night, however, Druscilla ended up sleeping through most of the following day. And when she did finally stir from her bed, in order to consume a large bowl of Weetabix and clotted cream, it was already dark. She had just resigned herself to a deferment of her duty when she heard the familiar squeaking of Ben Tarrant's bike brakes in the road outside. The next thing Druscilla knew she was rushing outside in her wellingtons and dressing gown, waving the note at him like a mad thing.

Seeing his neighbour approach in such a crazed fashion caused Ben a moment or two of serious concern. The woman was clearly deranged; but quite harmless, he thought wryly, returning her extravagant gesticulations with a modest wave of his own and an expression that he hoped passed for a smile.

'Out for a run, Druscilla?'

'Only to catch you.'

'Really? I am honoured.' He nosed the wheel of his bike between the gate and post guarding his front garden, his mind still preoccupied with the minor problems needing to be ironed out before curtain-up the following night.

'Isobel is seeing Dr Howard.' She tapped her nose with the note and winked.

'Yes,' drawled Ben, wrestling with his bike, 'we still see a bit of the Howards . . .'

'I mean really *seeing*.'

'Absolutely – of course they are. Now if you'll excuse me.' His left pedal had caught on the gatepost.

'Here's a note from him to her. It came with some flowers.' She thrust the card into his fingers and bolted back inside her house, her heart racing in sudden awe at her own audacity. I've done her a favour, she told herself, when some of the adrenalin had ebbed away, and a small worry surfaced as to which of the Tarrants she might have damaged the most.

Ben studied the writing on the card, chuckled and shook his head. He had just finished locking up his bike when Isobel opened the front door. For a moment the two of them looked at one other, their usually furtive stares emboldened by the dark. Isobel was in leggings, barefooted, with a long dark green shirt that reached to her knees. Her hair was a cloud of orange against the light in the hallway behind. Ben, struck afresh by the beauty of the woman he had married, found himself momentarily at a loss for words.

'Who was that?' Isobel asked, clenching her knees to hide the tremble in her legs.

'Our dear neighbour.'

'What did she want?' She clasped herself with her arms as the shivering moved up her body, dizzy with dread at the thought that Druscilla might have decided to share her sordid secret with Ben after all. It would have been too cruel, that night of all nights, when she herself was primed to tell the truth. She tried to read Ben's expression in the dark. I don't know him any more, she thought desperately, watching him pull the tarpaulin over his bike and noting that he seemed agitated, if not exactly angry.

'She was gabbling about us and the Howards. About you and James, to be more precise.' Ben paused on the doorstep. He wanted very much to say that she was beautiful. But there was so much distance between them still, it was hard to reach across it. He took one of her hands, aware that his head had emptied of all the things he had planned to say. 'You feel cold. Let's go inside.'

'Gabbling?' Isobel whispered, wondering at his calm and allowing herself to be led into the sitting room. Her fingers felt cold and limp in his warm palm.

'Too ridiculous.' He was smiling. 'Implying all sorts of things – some erotic fantasy maybe? But then you know the poor creature better than me . . . always had far more patience in that department . . .' He was rummaging in his pockets, shaking his head in despair. 'She gave me this.' He produced the small white card, no bigger than a bus ticket, and held it up.

Isobel took one step backwards and slowly lowered herself into a chair. 'What is it?' she whispered, knowing already.

'It's a message I wrote to you . . . with the flowers I sent . . . must have fallen out, I suppose . . .'

'You?' There was the briefest, sweetest moment of relief.

'You know I did,' he said gently, coming over to her and crouching at her feet. 'For the anniversary. You put them on the mantelpiece. Carnations . . . Isobel . . .' He tried to pick up her hand but she tugged it away. 'There's so much that we . . . that I . . .'

'You sent the carnations,' she repeated stupidly.

He was looking at the carpet. 'I know I've been hopeless . . .

I don't blame you for not saying anything, for wanting to . . . punish me. I'm aware that I've not exactly made life easy for you recently . . .' He tossed the card on to her lap and got to his feet, determined not to be deterred by the expression on her face. 'Don't think I don't care, Isobel, because I do, very deeply.'

'Care about what?' The handwriting on the card, Ben's handwriting, blurred and shifted before her eyes.

'About everything.' He began pacing the room, clenching and unclenching his fists. 'I've been doing a bit of thinking recently . . . about us . . . about why things have become so . . . hard. Mostly it's my fault, I know . . . I allow myself to get too involved at the school, take on every lost cause that's going . . . and this term has been particularly hard . . . there was one incident especially that almost . . .' He broke off, for a moment overcome by the realisation of quite how long it was since he had shared anything with her at all. Even before the recent bad patch, everyday life had swept them along in its current, creating a semblance of progress and cohesion where in fact there had been nothing of the kind. 'Christ, Isobel, I don't know where to start,' he burst out, running both hands through his dark hair in a gesture of frustration and excitement, utterly overwhelmed by contradicting sensations of empowerment and ineptitude.

Isobel, watching him, felt only the cold brush of despair tiptoe up her back. He had sent her flowers. Flowers for their baby. She hadn't even realised. He was still talking, words pouring out of him.

'I've been feeling so desperate, Isobel, for so long now . . . I didn't want – didn't dare – to tell you . . . I suppose I was afraid what you would think of me if I owned up to some of the things . . .' He was standing with his back to her, one hand holding on to the edge of the mantelpiece above the fireplace. 'Nothing can change overnight, I know that, but at least now I'm beginning to feel that I understand what's been going on, where it all started.' He paused. 'It goes way back, you see. You shut me out.' He swung round to face her, not aggressively, but with the light of inspiration in his eyes. 'When you had the miscarriage . . .'

'The miscarriage?' Shock had slurred her senses.

He shook his head. 'I know it sounds crazy, but hear me

out, please. You see, you were the one who did all the crying, everybody wanted to know how you felt, whether you were coping. Nobody worried about me.' He let out a short laugh. 'Do you know, I actually think I was jealous of you. All those tears you could cry, leaving me without any power to help, without any bloody role at all. Part of me hated you for it. Isn't that terrible? I hated you for suffering so well . . . and then the girls came along, so quickly, taking all your attention, taking you away . . .'

'And does part of you hate me now?' She spoke in a monotone, keeping her eyes fixed on a scuff mark above the skirting board, willing him to answer that he did, in order to take some of the pain of what awaited them away.

'Christ, no. Isobel, no.' He was too absorbed in the effort of unleashing his own emotions to observe the unnatural stillness of her pose, to see that his words were making no impact on her expression at all. 'No, I mean, I got over that – whatever it was. We both got over it, but maybe a little too . . . separately. And it did change things.' He was pacing the room now, lecturing more than talking. 'It pushed us apart. Or at least, it pushed me away from you, back to the old self who had learnt to believe that life was a war that had to be waged alone . . .' He let out a brief self-deprecating laugh. 'Except I'd rather lost the knack . . .' He stopped walking and sighed deeply, shaking his head and looking at the carpet. 'There are other things I should have told you,' he went on gently, 'not because I want sympathy but because, as my wife, you have a right to know.'

'What things?' she whispered, watching her hands twist in her lap and thinking of Aunt Violet.

He swallowed hard. 'There was a baby – my half-sister – who died in the crash that killed my mother.'

Isobel bit her lip, staring only at her twisting hands. Much as such confessions would have meant to her in the past, they could have no significance now. She hooked her fingers together, as if clinging on to the thought.

'It became a big family secret,' Ben continued, interpreting her silence as shock. 'Father's orders. Perhaps keeping it was my way of making up for hating him so . . .' He shrugged. 'I should have told you. I should have told you a lot of things. I didn't because I didn't think it mattered. I thought by keeping silent I could leave it all behind . . .'

'I know all about that . . . about the accident.' She spoke as coldly as she could.

'You know?' He was incredulous.

'Aunt Violet told me.'

'And you never said anything?'

'You never said anything, Ben.' Her voice edged up a note or two, for the first time belying the outward calm of her face. 'You never said anything about anything, until now . . . now, when it's . . . too late.'

'Too late?' Her tone puzzled him. He had imagined something more along the lines of relief, of gratitude even. Wasn't this what all women wanted, what Ione Brown wanted, being true to one's emotions, excavating them from all the dark corners inside? 'Isobel, I'm trying to . . . explain myself to you . . . trying to say I'm sorry. I know I've been difficult to live with, but at last I think I'm beginning to understand why. I'm beginning to understand myself.'

'So you've sorted out the puzzle of your life, have you?' she sneered. 'Well, bully for you, Ben Tarrant. Congratulations. X plus Y at last equals Z.' She was almost shouting. 'But what about me? Where do I fit into the equation? Is my life just supposed to slot into place too now? Is it? And if so, how?' She folded her arms and glared at him, her eyes blazing with anger and tears.

'Isobel, my love,' he whispered, taking a step closer, 'I'm so sorry, I . . .'

'Shut up, shut up,' she screamed, putting her hands to her ears. 'Don't touch me, don't come near, it's all too late, it's all over, it's all over . . . don't be kind, don't you dare be kind to me now, not after all this time . . . please.' She was sobbing, rubbing her eyes with her fists and shaking her head. He tried to touch her but she pushed him away.

'Don't do this, Isobel, please, not now . . . now that we're talking at last . . . sorting ourselves out . . .'

'No, Ben, you're wrong. It's got nothing to do with us, it's all you. You, you, you.' She pushed the wet ends of her fringe from her eyes and took a deep breath. She felt beyond crying suddenly, beyond feeling anything at all. 'And while you've been sorting yourself out, I' – she paused for an extra breath of air – 'I have been having an affair. With James Howard. I was going to tell you tonight anyway.' She got up from the chair and straightened her skirt, tugging it down to her knees. 'I think I might have a drink. Would you like one?' But she didn't move and neither did he.

There was a long moment of silence.

'You've what? . . . You mean Druscilla . . . ?'

'She saw the two of us together.'

'How long?'

'A few weeks.'

'Do you love him?'

'He loves me.'

'Do you love him?'

'He's been very kind, he . . . yes, yes, I love him.' She spat the words across the room. 'He has made me feel . . . oh, never mind. What does it matter? We need to separate, Ben, we have needed to for a while now. I've made arrangements to go to my parents tomorrow . . .'

'How could you?' The question was little more than a gasp. 'How the bloody hell could you . . . with James, of all people?'

'Who would you have preferred, Ben?'

He wasn't listening to her. 'I mean, Christ, Juliet is . . . was your friend . . . how could you?' There was disgust in his voice now. She could hear it blocking his throat.

'I'm not proud . . .'

'Oh good, well at least that's something.' He nodded his head in mock approval, his dark eyes now glittering with all the antipathy she had expected. 'The lady is not proud.'

Isobel reached for her jacket, slung across the back of a nearby chair. 'I do not expect your forgiveness, Ben. I shall never expect that. But a little understanding maybe . . .'

'Understanding? Of your desire to screw a friend of ours? Now that's really rich. Life may not have been the proverbial bed of roses round here, but . . .'

'No, it certainly hasn't.' She pulled on her jacket and tugged open the door. 'All you're feeling now, Ben, is what you've been suppressing for months, for years . . . I'm just helping you admit it. Regard it as a favour.' And with that she strode out of the house, slamming the door.

Druscilla took one timid peek through her curtains before retreating, with some dismay, into the deepest of her armchairs. Imagining more responsibility for such neighbourly goings-on than was in fact the case, she clutched a cat to her chest for comfort, nuzzling its fur with her face. Though the creature purred its appreciation, these gestures of affection were followed by a volley of such virulent sneezing that it leapt from her lap and took refuge under the piano.

Isobel walked fast, her hands clenched in the pockets of her jacket, her eyes fixed on the paving cracks beneath her feet. In the quiet of the night, with the darkness all around her, she felt as if she were taking steps merely to keep her balance, like a runner on the moving pad of an exercise machine. Above her, as always, the cathedral spire towered over the skyline of the buildings, its illuminated glory urging attention and reverence. But Isobel did not even glance upwards. She was too locked in her own mind to possess the energy for bestowing the visual world with any meaning at all.

Though she tried to think of James, clinging to the idea of him, images of Ben kept breaking through; disconnected snapshots, bright frozen stills from times long past, from Spain, London, Torbridge. They had begun so well. A charmed love. Only when this carousel hit the episode of her miscarriage did the whir in Isobel's mind slow and clear. Was Ben right? Had things really not been right since then? Had it really been so long? She frowned from the effort not of remembering but of focusing. Usually, looking back to those dreadful months, she thought only of the child she had lost, of her own emptiness. Now she forced herself to recall exactly what Ben had been like, how they had been with each other. She saw him holding the tiny swaddled bundle, heard again the brush of the chaplain's skirts as he left the room, the aching silence afterwards. Then she remembered Ben's dry, dazed eyes, his passive hopelessness, and experienced in the same instant a rush of hatred so strong that the bitter taste of it flooded her mouth. The vehemence of the emotion, never before admitted, shocked her. It was a hatred not just for his helplessness, Isobel realised, but for his very presence. A violent selfish questioning of his right to be there at all. As if her own grieving had indeed been deeper, truer, more worthy in every way. The emotion ebbed away, but the shock remained, fused with a retrospective guilt: for having felt such things of her own husband; for not having loved or wanted him at such a time. Schooled in the belief that an alliance like theirs was an indomitable thing, that any personal crisis could only make them stronger and more devoted, such awfulness had been impossible to own up to, she realised, even to herself. The only faint consolation was knowing that Ben had experienced something similar; that they were jointly guilty both of such feelings and the failure to admit to them.

Making sense of the past offered no remedies for the present, she reflected bitterly, seeing someone approach, and cutting down a side street towards the town hall and Torbridge's main square. The figure had looked familiar. A teacher from the girls' school maybe. Isobel feared recognition above all things; she dreaded the need to talk, to give some explanation for her dishevelled presence out alone so late at night. A light rain had started, a soft drizzle that glittered in hazy clouds beneath the orange glow of the streetlights. When she got to the old black railings skirting St Cuthbert's, Isobel paused, pretending to search for something in her pocket, unnerved by a new set of footsteps half a beat behind hers. But it was only an old man out with a bow-legged hound, both waddling in comic and unconscious symmetry, their noses to the ground. Isobel was about to head for the benched shelter offered by the pleated stone roof of the poultry cross when she noticed that the gate into the churchyard was slightly ajar, as was the door of the church itself. The rain was sharper now, falling not as a mist but in needles of seemingly vicious intent. Seeking shelter rather than religious inspiration, Isobel pushed the gate open and hurried down the short path towards the door.

Archie was on his hands and knees in the vestry swearing profusely, and quite inventively, when he heard the faint but unmistakable groan of St Cuthbert's door hinge being pushed a few inches against its will. Suppressing un-Christian fears as to the likelihood of whoever had entered the church carrying a sawn-off shotgun and a history of acrimony towards ginger-headed priests in jeans and dog-collars, Archie paused only for a moment before continuing with his search. He had lost his crucifix, a small plain silver one which Bridget had given him years before, saved for with money from her Saturday job in the shoe shop. In the light of recent decisions regarding his personal life, mislaying such a thing had seemed so hugely symbolic that Archie had been momentarily tempted not to undergo any search at all. But in the end sentiment had triumphed, boosted by distaste for the sight of the chain dangling empty on his bony white plateau of a chest. The depressing chaos of his bedsit had multiplied dramatically in consequence. Even though two hours of intense investigative activity had thrown up nothing but a handful of loose change and a mysterious, unmissed key.

Searching St Cuthbert's was a last resort as well as a welcome diversion from the still-unsolved problem of how to endure the night. The sleeping pills acquired from Dr Howard worked so well that all Archie's initial relief had quickly been superseded by a terror of dependency. A new routine had established itself in consequence: a routine that involved a prolonged and fatally strained effort to fall asleep, followed by a miserable and uneasy surrender to the promise of oblivion contained in the innocuous white tablets. The result was an entirely new brand of grogginess as company for his working day, a sensation not entirely dissimilar to the challenge of swimming through glue. His eye twitch could now only be held in check by the most exaggerated of frowns. The strain of looking as if he were pondering some universal dilemma whenever anyone was within visual range of his cheekbones was really starting to get him down. He was beginning to feel as grotesquely conspicuous as one of the cathedral gargoyles he had once so admired. Though nobody said anything outright, Archie now flinched at every snigger from the motley gaggle that passed for St Cuthbert's choir, and at every one of Reverend Tully's repertoire of unreadable stares.

Archie was just toying with the unattractive notion of running his hand along the two-inch gap of cobwebbed grime under St Cuthbert's vast wardrobe of clerical vestments when he heard the muted but instantly recognisable sound of someone crying.

Not the sobs of a distraught, machete-wielding male, nor even of an alcohol-sodden mendicant, but – unless his hearing deceived him – of a distressed female.

Filled in equal measure with shyness and charitable zeal, Archie sprang to his feet and tiptoed back into the main body of the church. Here was someone to help, someone to remind him that there were sorrows other than his own. When, from behind the safety of a wide, fluted pillar, Archie established that the someone in question was none other than Isobel Tarrant, a whole host of new emotions flooded his mind. Among them a wicked and most unpriestly excitement that caused him to press his palms together and squeeze his eyes in silent gratitude to the Lord. She was in trouble and God had steered her his way. It was unbelievable. Like a bloody miracle.

Some element of these thrills faded as he made his approach. She looked so forlorn, her hair sticking in wet strands to her cheeks, the shoulders of her thin jacket visibly soaked. And when she looked up, impelled to do so by his polite annunciatory cough, Archie could not help but notice that her face registered nothing but dismay at the sight of him. Her eyes, usually such a crystal green, were red-rimmed and bloodshot. Her lips too looked peculiarly red against the ashen pallor of her skin. The sense of having intruded was so strong that instead of offering help he found himself apologising.

'Sorry . . . I couldn't help . . . I heard something. I was in the vestry.' He wrung his hands and clenched his face tight against the pulse of his tic.

Isobel got out a shrivelled tissue and dabbed her nose, shaking her head.

'There's a box of Kleenex in the vestry,' he ventured, thinking at the same time that any self-respecting hero would have been in possession of a large starched white handkerchief. 'Shall I fetch it?'

She shook her head again and began tearing at the edges of her tissue.

'I say, would you just like to be left alone? I don't have to lock up yet. You can stay for as long as you want – for hours if you like. Won't bother me at all. Loads to do, you see' – he gestured vaguely over his shoulder – 'so you just do as you please.' He turned to go, but stopped. 'Though I know that sometimes people think they want to be left alone, but they don't really, not deep down. I'm like that – pretend I'm fine when I'm not, because . . . well, I suppose because it's kind of embarrassing sometimes to admit to not being fine . . . it's like it's your fault for making a mess of things . . . not that I mean to imply—'

'I'm leaving my husband.' She shoved the tissue into her pocket and shook her hair back in a gesture all the more poignant for its failure to convey defiance.

'Oh dear, oh dear.' An absurd, despicable seed of hope burst inside.

'For all the wrong – but right – reasons.'

'Sounds complicated.' Archie hazarded a small smile, which met only blankness. Now that she had stopped crying she appeared to have gone into a sort of daze.

'It is rather,' she murmured. 'But then love is complicated, isn't it?'

Archie, thinking of Bridget, and his feelings for the woman before him, nodded slowly. Emboldened by the progress of their conversation, he then sat down, not next to her, but one pew away, facing back in her direction. 'It certainly is.' A silence followed during which he racked his hopelessly uncooperative brain for a sentence that might sound wise or endearing. But all he could think of was the outrageous turn of his own emotions, the hope that if he helped her, if he could make her grateful to him in any small way, she might start to feel something in return. 'And there are so many different kinds, aren't there?'

'Kinds?' Isobel stared at him vacantly. She was beginning to feel cold and very tired.

'Kinds of love,' he stammered, his confidence faltering. 'There are different kinds of love . . . for different people.'

'Oh yes . . . how very true.' She stood up stiffly. 'I think I'd better go.'

'Are you sure? I mean, don't you want to talk some more?' He stood up too, careful not to look at her too hard, partly out of shyness and partly to keep the unattractively twitching side of his face out of her line of vision.

'There's nothing to say.' She shrugged her shoulders. 'I have to leave Ben, that's all.'

'Don't you love him, then?' blurted Archie. He did not want her to go. He felt as if they were poised on the very edge of intimacy, that this was his one brilliant, God-given chance to get close to her. Really close. He couldn't bear to feel it slipping away.

She laughed softly. 'Oh, I love him all right. But I've made it so he can't love me . . . I've committed myself to someone else . . . like I said, it's complicated . . . to let another person down too would just make things even worse, don't you think?'

Archie didn't know what to think. He felt a terrible urge to cry. She was walking towards the door, her hair spilling beautifully over the edge of her collar. He wanted to lunge for it, bury his face in it, tell her what he felt. She stopped by the font and for a moment he thought she was going to dip her fingers and cross herself. Instead she bent down and picked something up off the floor. 'Look, a little crucifix . . . someone must have dropped it. Here.' She held it out for him. 'I expect it's being sorely missed.'

He took it from her without a word.

'Heavens, I owe you some money, don't I? That sponsored swim you were doing . . .'

'Walk. It was a sponsored walk.'

'I completely forgot. I'm so sorry . . .' She patted her pockets.

'Don't be . . . for goodness sake, it doesn't matter. It was ages ago.' Something in his tone made her let the subject go.

'I'll be off, then . . . thank you so much, for . . . talking.'

He shrugged and smiled, not trusting himself to speak. As she disappeared through the door, he remained motionless, his fist clenched around Bridget's crucifix, welcoming the tiny stabs of pain as its edges dug into the flesh of his palm. He opened his mouth for an echoing howl of self-pity, but closed it again abruptly. For inside, deep down below the sadness, he felt the feeble glow of a warmth that had been absent for a long time, the dim small light of God's presence, crouching in the darkness of his heart, waiting only for the breath of his faith to fan it back to life. He dropped the little cross in amongst the change in his pocket and trudged back to the vestry to retrieve the keys and begin locking up.

33

Crofton College's *Julius Caesar* was a triumph. The old formula of adrenalin and terror worked its habitual magic on the cast, sharpening the boys' senses and giving an edge to their performances which none of their rehearsals had ever achieved. The pupils and members of the staff attending on the Friday night hammered their applause with such enthusiasm that the actors filed back on stage for two extra curtain calls. On Saturday, when the school hall's handsome oak doors were thrown open to the general public, the atmosphere on stage was nothing short of electric.

Only the director of the show remained unmoved. Watching from the wings, armed with a prompt-sheet and catch-phrases of encouragement, Ben operated throughout both evenings with robotic detachment. The success, so longed for and worried over, felt utterly hollow. Recalling how much it had once seemed to matter filled him with a mixture of incredulity and shame. All that mattered was Isobel, and she was gone. His sense of loss was even worse than the knowledge of her betrayal. Memories of other losses, triggered by the gentle probing of Ione Brown, now slouched out of the shadows in which he had endeavoured to confine them. A pattern was emerging. A pattern that made losing a wife seem painfully inevitable.

Saturday's performance progressed even more smoothly than the first night, animated by a spirit all its own. After a while Ben folded his prompt-sheet away and sat on an upturned crate with arms folded, watching the proceedings from behind the gauze of his own inner despair. Snatches of phrases drifted off-stage and into his consciousness, sounding unfamiliar and fraught with new meaning.

I have not from your eyes that gentleness and show of love as I was wont to have . . .

You are my true and honourable wife, as dear to me as are the ruddy drops that visit my sad heart . . .

. . . if you have tears, prepare to shed them now . . .

'Sir? Do you have a safety pin? The hem of this dress is right down again – I'm scared I'll trip . . .'

It was little Jamie Oates, a rosy-cheeked fourth-former whose initial vehement reluctance to take the part of Caesar's wife, Calpurnia, had been magnificently overcome, to the admiration even of his peers.

'Of course, Jamie, of course,' Ben whispered, patting the boy's head. 'Let's find Miss Harris, shall we? She's got a whole box of the damn things.'

Thanks to a series of such minor demands upon his time, Ben managed to keep a tighter hold on his concentration during the second half. Through a chink in the curtains he squinted at the blurred sea of faces in the audience, unable to stop looking for a glint of Isobel's red hair, even though he knew she was not there. She had fled to Suffolk the previous morning, taking a small holdall for herself and two big suitcases for the girls. Megan and Sophie had tumbled into the back of the car still dazed with sleep, moaning about the cold and the prospect of a long journey. He had kissed them lightly, feigning insouciance, since it was the only protection he could offer, not trusting himself to hug them for fear of breaking down. While Sophie appeared to have swallowed the story of going for a holiday with their grandparents, Megan's black eyes seemed to acknowledge that the break foreshadowed separation of a more terminal kind.

The only red hair that Ben was able to identify was the distinctly unalluring carrot mop of the young clergyman who had been so generous about distributing publicity posters a few weeks before. He spotted him towards the very end of the performance, sitting in the middle of the front row, frowning in grim-faced concentration and absently chewing his nails while Brutus movingly begged for his servant's assistance in running on his own sword. It was only during the final blast of applause, when Ben was leading the last bow on stage, that his eye was caught by two other familiar figures down the far end of the front row, both clapping manically, their hands raised high above their heads, their mouths fixed in grins of appreciation. The Howards. Their knees and elbows touching. He saw James mouth the word 'bravo' before bending his head near Juliet's cheek to catch something she was saying. For a moment the vision of such marital unity was reassuring. Maybe – for some perversely female and whimsical reason – Isobel had been lying? Maybe there was no affair at all? The hope, desperate and pitiable, swelled and died. Ben took a step backwards and dropped his head by way of a bow, before turning with outstretched arms and a mask of a smile to congratulate the cast, holding hands in lines behind him. Then Miss Harris swung the heavy curtains across the stage, muffling the handclaps, which faltered, before finally dying away.

Though Juliet was annoyed with James for wanting to leave so promptly, she did her best not to show it. Determined to nurture their newly brokered peace – still so fragile and tentative – she allowed him to lead her through the mêlée in the hall with as brief a backward glance at the stage as she had once granted her own career. Being in an audience always got her fired up, even when it was a mediocre school play with ill-fitting costumes and scenery done in poster paints. Listening to Calpurnia had been hardest of all. She had had to force herself not to mouth the words, which she had delivered herself many times, croaking most of them through a severe chest infection that lasted for the entire six weeks of a provincial tour. The memory of the cough helped quell any inclination towards nostalgia. As did the diversion of trying and failing to trace Isobel Tarrant in the crowd.

While the crush was bearing them towards the doors, she nudged James in the small of his back with her handbag.

'It really is very odd, don't you think?'

'What, my love?' With so many people about them he could barely turn his head. 'What is odd?'

'That Isobel is nowhere in sight. Whatever can have happened to her? Do you think she's ill? Perhaps we should call in on our way to the restaurant?'

'If she is ill, she won't want us barging in, will she?' James worked his elbows to show that the impatience in his tone related purely to the number of people pressing round him. 'And it would make us late for our table. I could do with a bloody drink after this lot,' he added through clenched teeth, as someone's stiletto ground into the soft leather of his shoes.

'Anything you say,' Juliet murmured, pressing herself against James with unnecessary pressure and using the moment to run her fingers down the back of his right thigh. Believing once more that she held all her husband's dear, predictable emotions in the palm of her hand, she badly wanted to keep it that way. Though things looked set fair, one could never be sure. Indeed, being sure had almost been the death of them, she reminded herself, hooking one finger through a loop in the waistband of James's trousers and giving it an affectionate tug.

A few feet behind them, Archie too had been unable to prevent himself from looking for Isobel in the press towards the exit. He kept catching the eye of Flora Dobbs instead, resplendent in pink and pearls, and fluttering her programme over surrounding heads at any face she recognised. It was heartening to see that most, like him, seemed content either to ignore her or to keep their responses to a muted flutter in return. She had been more predatory than ever since the completion of the sponsored walk, with quite unnatural effusions over the paltry sum of money he had raised and earnest invitations to tea. All Archie's initial guilt about resisting such attentions was diminishing by the day; he was beginning to realise that even priests had a right to say no to people, to preserve some private space of their own.

Having enjoyed the play far more than he had anticipated, Archie was toying with the idea of hanging back to offer Ben Tarrant his congratulations. For once, his hesitation stemmed not so much from shyness as the dubious itch of curiosity that the prospect of such a meeting aroused. He couldn't help wanting to know whether Isobel had really left after all. While the rival man in him longed to see how Ben wore his suffering, whether he cared at all.

As two boys in uniform started to stack chairs and retrieve abandoned programmes, Archie found himself offering to help. By the time they had cleared the hall, quite a party had developed on stage. Music was spitting from a ghetto-blaster, while members of the cast, their faces still smeared with make-up and their costumes in varying states of dishevellment, were swigging from plastic beakers and plunging their hands into bags of food. Archie was on the point of slipping away when Ben Tarrant's voice boomed out across the hall.

'Gatecrashing our cast party now, are you, Reverend?'

Several spotlights were still on the stage and Archie had to raise his hand to his eyes to get any sort of view of Ben at all. 'No, I didn't mean . . . I was just helping clear away . . .' He had to shout above the pulsing rhythms of the music. A couple of boys behind Ben had linked arms and were springing round in circles. 'Thanks anyway.'

'But you've earned it, Reverend . . . very helpful you've been . . . practically a member of the cast. Come on up here, for goodness sake. My wife gatecrashed a cast party to meet me, you know, many moons ago.'

Deliberately ignoring the reference to Isobel, Archie approached slowly, wary not only of being an outsider, but also of the raucous cheerfulness in Ben's voice. It erased all his curiosity in an instant.

'I didn't mean to . . .'

'Shut up, man, and come up here.' He slapped Archie's back as he arrived on stage. His dark eyes blazed with an unnatural light. His smile was tight and fierce. 'There's only orange juice and cider, I'm afraid – not bad in combination actually – and heaps of crisps. Mostly pickled onion flavour, it would seem. Help yourself. And ignore this lot. They'll probably get drunk and then throw up into each other's laps. All part of the ritual. Yours truly has the delightful task of making sure they don't murder each other . . . until the parents return to pick up the pieces. Miss Harris has – with suspicious convenience – developed one of her migraines . . .' Ben appeared to sway slightly as he peered at his watch. 'Bugger . . . one whole hour to go . . . but nice to have another grown-up around.' He handed Archie a cup and steered him by the elbow to a couple of upright chairs in the wings. 'Let's keep an eye on things from here, shall we? Oh, and drink up, we've got litres of the stuff to get through. Think of it this way: the more we drink the less they will.' Ben let out a dry laugh and tipped the contents of his beaker down his throat.

'It was very good,' said Archie quietly, taking a tentative sip of his own drink. 'The play, I mean, not this.'

Ben laughed again, too loudly. 'Glad you thought so. Great stuff, wasn't it? A few young Kenneth Branaghs in our midst after all, eh? The head was relieved, I know that.' He tapped the side of his nose conspiratorially. 'Got to keep the head happy in my business.'

Ben appeared to be even drunker than Archie had first thought. He was talking so fast and furiously that he began to be afraid what the poor man might say. To be so contrastingly sober felt advantageous in a cruel, horribly voyeuristic kind of way. But at the same time there was no question of leaving, not only because of the powerful force of Ben himself, pinning him to the chair with conversation, but because of the largely unattended carousing boys, many of them clearly in a far worse state than their master.

'I say, a pair over there are smoking. Should we . . . ?'

'Oh, let the devils smoke . . . they all do anyway . . .'

While on a mission to find an unopened bottle of cider, Archie mustered the courage to suggest that cigarettes should be enjoyed outside, in the safety of the school grounds. To his astonishment the culprits obeyed at once, reappearing a few minutes later looking windswept and smug. Pleased to see that Ben had closed his eyes, Archie settled back in his chair with a handful of crisps.

'What's your view on adultery, Reverend?'

Caught with a mouthful, Archie was grateful for having a legitimate reason to hesitate. 'I think it's a pity . . .' he managed at last, his throat clogged with salty crumbs.

'Could you do it? Could you screw another man's wife?'

Archie blushed crimson, feeling suddenly quite transparent, as if Ben had guessed the truth of his feelings for Isobel, and was venting some of his own bitterness by deliberately making him squirm. 'I . . . I'm afraid we all could. Probably.'

'And what does your God say about that, eh?'

'He forgives us.'

'Oh, bloody marvellous.' Ben began a slow clap, looking round for an audience that wasn't there, since most of the boys had disappeared to take advantage of Archie's impromptu off-site smoking regulations. 'And what about us poor mortals? Are we just supposed to take the forgiveness route too?' Ben sat up and glared at him, his face twisted with anger and pain. 'My wife's left me, you see, Reverend, so I'm doing a spot of research into the matter. Turns out she's been fucking – sorry, having an affair – with another man, something of a family friend as it turns out . . .'

'I really don't think . . .' Archie stood up.

'Oh, come on, surely you can do better than this, Vicar. If God doesn't come up with some decent answers then therapists are going to steal all the business. The couch is the modern alternative to the confessional, you know. Feels good too, for' – he drew in his breath – 'oh, at least four, maybe five minutes afterwards. But understanding things can't stop them *happening*, can it? Especially for those of us who've reached the understanding stage rather late in life.' Ben picked up his empty cup and crushed it between his hands. He had said as much to Ione Brown the evening before, when her quiet acceptance of his decision to pull out of any further sessions had provoked him into being unforgivably rude. Instead of confessing to the very real fear of making himself even more vulnerable to her than he had already, he had launched into an emotional diatribe against professionals who peeled back the onion skin of other people's lives and constructed nothing in their place. She said that such construction was for him to do and people like her could only help to point the way. At which point he had disgraced himself and all his arguments by slamming the phone down and sobbing into a cup of cold tea.

'Don't you think you've had enough . . . ?' suggested Archie gently, now seriously worried by the expression on Ben's face.

'Enough? Oh yes, I've had enough, all right.' Ben lunged for the bottle of cider and made an ugly show of swigging from it, spilling a few drops on his shirt front in the process. 'And I suppose Isobel had too, one way or another . . .'

'She must have had her reasons, I suppose,' Archie muttered, flicking away a crisp with the tip of his shoe. He wondered where she had gone, but did not dare ask. Since their encounter in the church his feelings for Isobel had reached a new pitch of confusion to do with trying to adore something that was so plainly imperfect. His fantasies did not work so well with a woman who cheated on her husband.

Ben let out a short laugh. 'I'm sure she did. I'm sure she did. Reasons to do with me, no doubt . . . I never stopped loving her, you see, I just forgot I needed – forgot how – to show it . . .'

'Perhaps if she realised that—'

'What, and then I just forgive her, do I?' Ben clicked his fingers. 'Just like that.'

'Perhaps she has to forgive herself first,' suggested Archie quietly, responding to an uncharacteristically intuitive flutter of inspiration that blew across his mind from nowhere, as sweet and subtle as the whispering in his heart after Isobel had left the church. With it came a vivid recollection of her crumpled misery. She had not seemed like a woman in love, with herself or anyone else. It struck Archie in the same moment how curiously coincidental it was to have stumbled into intimate conversations with both Tarrants within such a short space of time. Curious to the point of being designed. Ordained. The ember of faith flickered again inside, helping to ease the pain of what he was relinquishing. Fantasy was a figment of the imagination after all, he reminded himself, fuelled by the dubious powers of enzymes and hormones, and the unfathomable mysteries of human psychology. He did not know Isobel Tarrant enough to love her. He never had. The best – the most Christian – tribute to his affections would be to help her in any way he could. 'I think forgiving oneself can be the hardest thing of all. We can't move on until we've done it . . .'

'Maybe not,' drawled Ben, staring hard at his companion, wondering through the fug of his unhappiness how young freckle-faced curates acquired such wisdom. 'That's quite a twitch you've got there,' he remarked suddenly, which stopped Archie in mid-yawn, bringing a blaze of colour to his cheeks.

He quickly slapped both hands to his face and attempted a casual laugh. 'Oh, it's nothing really . . . gets a little worse when I'm tired . . .'

'Eye-strain,' muttered Ben, rolling down the sleeves of his shirt and beginning, ineffectually, to try to rake some order into his hair.

'I beg your pardon?'

'Eyestrain,' he repeated, more loudly. 'See an optician.' He stood up, now diverting his attentions to the untucked ends of his shirt. 'Look here, sorry if I've been, you know, aggressive . . .' He rocked back on his heels and caught hold of the edge of his chair to steady himself. Behind him, his students had collapsed into stupefied and silent cameos of disarray. A few had even fallen asleep. The tape of music had stopped and been left unreplaced.

'You haven't been aggressive . . .'

'Bloody liar,' growled Ben, glaring in a way that managed to convey affection.

Archie grinned back at him. 'Would you like me to stay until the parents—?'

'No, no. Run along, please.' Ben picked up an empty cardboard box and embarked on a slow, shuffling tour of the debris littering the stage. When Archie started to help he found himself seized quite roughly by the elbow. 'It's OK, Reverend, I can manage now. You're a good man, a very good man, but I want you to go home. I know I'm pissed, but I can manage – I'd prefer to manage alone. You've been a big help but now I want you to bugger off,' he whispered, but so kindly that Archie knew he was being thanked.

He strolled the mile or so through town back to his digs feeling more at peace with himself than he had for months. Instead of bolting inside, he paused before putting the key in the lock, and gazed up at the vivid, surreal triangle of the cathedral spire towering above him, noticing for the first time the halo of fuzzy light that clung to its outline, like a shadow illuminated in the dark. The surge of joy that flooded through him almost knocked him off his feet.

Though sleep remained its usual elusive self, there was no suffocating panic that night. For once the darkness seemed full of comfort and companionship. After a while an easy stream-of-consciousness-style prayer began of its own accord, focusing not on himself, but on the Tarrants. Archie had forgotten the exquisitely uplifting pleasure of genuinely wanting someone else's happiness more than his own. Riding on the crest of such sensations came the relief of knowing that he had moved on at last, that he was no longer locked in a time warp of self-obsession and disappointment, that he was ready to get on with the job of helping rather than needing help. With a little easy detective work he would find Isobel – wherever she was – and tell her exactly how things stood. They were both evidently wretched without each other. He would offer his services as a go-between, someone neutral who could make both positions clear. All Archie's own longings paled into insignificance beside the Christian nobility of what he intended to do. He would reunite the Tarrants even if it killed him. He could feel God willing him on inside.

Slipping into the usually irritating straitjacket of her parents' domestic routine had proved strangely comforting. It removed the pressure of trivial decision-making and provided them all with a structure to get through the day. The girls responded particularly well to the extra attention and discipline, which made Isobel realise how badly she had allowed things to slip at home. Mothers weren't designed to have emotional crises, she reflected ruefully, while gazing at but not reading the Sunday newspapers during a rare spell alone; there simply wasn't the time. Her parents had taken the children to church, leaving her with meticulous instructions concerning potato-basting and the preparation of vegetables. The carrots had to be sliced thinly instead of chopped into her usual careless chunks, and the French beans, once topped and tailed, were to be cut into equal halves. Instead of offering her customary resistance to the inflexibility of such absurd family codes of culinary practice, Isobel agreed with a meekness that highlighted her greediness for a spell of abdicating control.

The relief of leaving Torbridge – of leaving Ben – was immense. Though his pinched face still haunted her, she was grateful to be removed from the incessant, hopeless need to try to do something about it. For there was nothing to be done. She had done him a terrible wrong. Not just by throwing herself at James, but by misreading the entire situation so badly from the start. That she had failed to acknowledge the flowers he sent on the anniversary of the miscarriage – to have assumed they were from another man – was so awful that Isobel could still hardly bring herself to think about it.

But behind such regrets resided a deep anger. The memory of Ben's neglect of her, the months of coldness, however justified she now perceived some of the causes to be, still stung. He had been selfish, of that she had no doubt, brooding over his own troubles without any thought as to how it felt for her, being left alone on the other side of his silence. That this silence somehow related to problems brewing from as far back as the outcome of that first disastrous pregnancy was something with which she was still struggling to come to terms. Having assumed all along that she was the one labouring to absorb her grief, it was something of a shock to discover that Ben was as deeply – but so differently – wounded himself. She realised now that all his clumsy impatience with her misery, his apparent eagerness to get on with their life, had blinded her to everything else. She even wondered whether the arrival of Megan, such a distracting joy at the time, hadn't come too soon; whether having a second baby so quickly had helped to hide the fact that they weren't yet fully – or jointly – over the loss of their first.

Isobel sliced the carrots viciously, wishing she could stop her thoughts wheeling backwards when all she wanted was to focus clearly on what lay ahead. She had James to think of now. Their tryst, only a day away, loomed large, filling her with a confusion of hope and dread. Though she still grasped at the possibility of their sharing a future together, the reality of it seemed more and more improbable. Only the wildest, most ardent love could propel such a drastic rearrangement of their families. And while she feared that James's emotions reached such a pitch, she was growing increasingly aware that her own fell far short of it. Realising the extent of her misjudgments as regards Ben had made everything much harder, much more complicated. There was no justification any more, no self-righteous zeal to fuel her betrayal. Yet James loved her. He wanted to make a life with her. Could she let him down as well?

She was staring out of the kitchen window, transfixed by the resilience of a bright regiment of tulips under the incessant siege of a stinging wind, when the church party returned.

'How's the gravy?' enquired her mother at once, expertly looping her apron over the robust perm of her hair and seizing the oven gloves from off her daughter's shoulder. 'Did we make a roux?'

'No, we did not. Sorry, we forgot. We're quite hopeless,' apologised Isobel, rolling her eyes comically for the girls' sake and then doing her best to listen to their two simultaneous but conflicting accounts of the morning's religious adventures. All younger members of the congregation had been presented with crosses made from palm leaves. Competitive efforts to describe this high point, however, resulted in the precious articles themselves being used as martial aids across the kitchen table.

'Now, now, you two, that's enough,' shouted Isobel, losing her temper at last, and shooing them out of the kitchen.

'Stir the gravy, there's a dear,' said her mother, handing her a wooden spoon. 'George is on sherry. Do you want one?'

'No thanks.' Isobel concentrated hard on her allotted task, inwardly marvelling at her parents' studious inability to refer directly to the reason for her visit. It was almost as if by ignoring it they hoped to trivialise the matter sufficiently for it to disappear altogether. All her tentative attempts to explain the severity of the situation had so far been greeted with tuts and arm-waves of dismissal, together with mutterings about it being nobody's business but their own. On the couple of occasions she had steered the girls to the telephone to ring Ben, her only punishment for not grabbing the receiver herself was two raised eyebrows of disapproval and knowing parental glances batted across the room.

Watching her mother scamper between sink and oven now, Isobel was uncertain whether such stoical reticence was something for which she should experience gratitude or vexation. That her parents both cared very deeply about what was happening was not in question. All their pink-cheeked Sunday morning vigour sprang, she knew, not from the fresh East Anglian air, nor from the stirring words of their local priest, but from a state of suppressed emotion. How would such feelings be vented, she wondered nervously, when it became clear that their daughter was already involved in a relationship with another man? The thought made her stir the gravy so vigorously that several thick chocolate-coloured drops splashed on to her mother's immaculate white hob. For all their funny ways and implied criticisms, her parents had, she knew, grown quite fond of Ben. More significantly they both shared a puritanical like-it-or-lump-it approach to matrimony, treating all deviations from such a creed – by friends and public figures alike – with impatient and withering contempt.

'So you're off tomorrow, are you?' Her mother stabbed the shoulder of pork with a two-pronged fork and levered it on to a serving dish.

'Yup.' Isobel found a small lump of flour and chased it around the edge of the saucepan with her wooden spoon.

'I see. And back on Wednesday. And we're not to know where.' She set the serving dish on the table and put a carving knife beside it.

'If that's all right. I'm sorry, it's just . . .'

'Fine. We'll say no more about it, then.' Betty Hitchings took off her apron and folded the oven gloves into a neat rectangle before disappearing to summon her husband and granddaughters to the table.

35 ∫

Ben spent most of his Sunday sleeping off an excruciating headache and trying to resist phoning Isobel. It was up to her to take the initiative, he told himself, thinking at the same time how much he would hate to be ensnared in conversation with either of her parents. So far the girls had phoned him twice, on each occasion giving hurtfully cheerful summaries of how they were spending their time and with no suggestion that they should hand the receiver over to their mother. She had obviously briefed them well beforehand, Ben decided grimly as he tussled with the double duvet, sticking arms and legs in wild and unnatural poses in a vain attempt to find a position conducive to sleep.

Eventually, hunger lured him downstairs, where he finished off the last of the bread and cereals on which he had been subsisting since Isobel's departure. Though the fridge was quite empty, he had not yet been able to find either the time or the inclination to shop. Having plied his system with instant coffee, he forced himself to tackle the correspondence which had been accumulating on the hall table, an unpromising pile of brown envelopes whose sole redeeming feature was the application form for the headmaster job in Hampshire. For a few brief moments Ben allowed himself to be seized by the conviction that the post offered the way out of all his dilemmas, a way forward on his own. He kissed the form and waved it over his head in an attempt at celebration that quickly fell flat. Not so much because of the realisation that there would be scores of other excellent candidates, but because it dawned on him that he was still banking on Isobel coming too. The emptiness of the house curled round him like the breath of an icy wind. She was gone, but he was the one in exile. Forgiveness was all very well, he thought miserably – recalling snatches of what the kindly priest had said – but not always relevant. Isobel wasn't available to be forgiven. She had run away, to plan a future that did not include him. The thought of James Howard – a thought which Ben realised he had subconsciously been doing his best not to confront head-on all day – hit him like a punch to the stomach. Convinced he was going to retch, he hurled himself dramatically in the direction of the sink, where he stared at the soggy remains of some cornflakes clogging the plug-hole and waited. But nothing happened. The feeling ebbed away, taking with it the nausea, and leaving an expected residue of puzzlement. The Howards had looked conspicuously united. Was the hypocrisy of the man so developed that he could behave like that in public with his wife when he was planning to leave her? The thought created a quite absurd combination of hope on his own behalf and apprehension on Isobel's. Loosening his grip on the edges of the sink, Ben returned to his seat at the kitchen table, telling himself that his wife deserved everything she got and it was no longer his business to worry about her. But his emotions continued to disobey him, spurred on by two slanting and smudged rows of old-fashioned typing informing him that his pendant was ready for collection sooner than expected and asking that the balance of thirty-five pounds be paid as soon as convenience allowed.

Seated only a few yards away, at her own kitchen table, Druscilla was studying a list of properties to rent by the sea. Brighton seemed to hold the most possibilities in her price range, though many of them were flats with shared gardens. The property agent, after raving about the dearth of rentals in roads like Fox's Crescent, hadn't seemed nearly so enthusiastic or friendly in person. At the memory of the man's visit the day before, Druscilla shuddered and gripped the edges of the paper more tightly. She hadn't liked the way his beady eyes had appraised her home, sniffing at things she held dear, pushing round her private space as if he had a born right to be the judge of it; all the while committing indecipherable mutterings into his little tape recorder. The cats hadn't liked it either, especially when he spent so long in their room, nudging cushions and mattresses out of the way in an attempt to assess the state of the walls.

Though Druscilla had told the animals – and the property agent – that a change was as good as a rest, that she had always wanted a spell by the sea, that most likely they would all return after six months and carry on just as before, the truth was very different. Nothing would ever be as before. Life had turned sour, as it always seemed to, in the end. And so suddenly too. The first phone call had come on Friday morning, when she was rushing round looking for empty plastic bags to take to the shops. There wasn't any noise exactly, nor even any breathing; just the sense of someone there. A few moments after she replaced the receiver it rang again. When she answered, more gingerly this time, she was greeted only by the same thick silence. The experience was so unnerving that she fled from the house without any bags at all. And without her handbag too, which proved rather more of an inconvenience, though thankfully her keys had been in her pocket. The comfortable vacuum of her existence had been broken, and Druscilla felt all the terror of it. Just when she was feeling safe the phone would ring again; and though she told herself to ignore it, somehow she was unable to. Suspicions as to the origin of the calls had initially focused on the Coombes – her neighbours to her left – who had never been polite enough to hide their dislike of her and whose stair-pounding made the precious pictures on her walls vibrate. But then a less easily contemplated possibility had planted itself in her mind, arising from the deep dark waters of her past and the knowledge that nothing – that nobody – could be run away from for ever.

The sudden inspiration of dialling 1471 was rewarded only by the disheartening message that the caller's number had been withheld. She thought of contacting the police, but rejected it in the same instant. Bitter previous experience had taught Druscilla to expect no favours from such people. Nor did the idea of changing her number offer much hope. He – for she was sure it was a he – knew where she lived, she felt certain. In thinking through her limited options for escape, Druscilla was alerted for the first time to the alarming degree of her own alienation. Only Isobel Tarrant had ever found time for a smile and a word, and now she had gone, taking her beautiful children with her. The conviction that her involvement had triggered this departure did little to lighten Druscilla's state of mind. Whatever had possessed her to give the note to Ben she could not now imagine. At the sight of him over the last few days, all stormy-looking and striding, she scuttled back from the window, fearful of whatever daggers of blame his expression might hold. Though she did not really think him the type for hate-calls, she had nonetheless whispered his name a couple of times into the silence on the telephone, just in case. With such preoccupations it took all Druscilla's determination to digest small print about gas central heating and ventilated lavatories and to scrutinise the tiny, inadequate photographs of places that might provide a new refuge. Many of the nicer-sounding ones said pets were not welcome, which made her so cross that she put a big black cross in the margin together with three exclamation marks of disapproval. She had just completed a series of these when the shrill ring of her phone set her nerves fizzing with apprehension. Taking deep breaths, she tiptoed into the hall, picked the receiver up very slowly between two fingers and slipped it under the hairsprayed curtain of her hair and on to her ear.

'Hello. Anybody there?' said a cheerful male voice.

Druscilla was so relieved that for a moment she could not speak. She nodded vigorously instead, putting her hand to her throat as she fought to catch her breath.

'Hello?' said the voice again, less certain this time.

'Who is it?' enquired Druscilla, looping the flex round her fingers.

'Reverend Heighton-Jones . . . I popped in a couple of weeks ago . . . you kindly treated me to some biscuits. I spilt a few coffee grains on your kitchen floor,' he added meekly, by way of a further prompt into the silence on the other end of the line.

Laughter, the hysteria of relief, burst into Archie's right ear. He held the receiver at arm's length for a moment, shaking his head in despair. The woman was a complete crackpot.

'Oh, Reverend,' she cooed, 'I can't tell you what a nice surprise this is . . .'

'Sorry to disturb your Sunday afternoon, Miss Carew—'

'Call me Druscilla, please.'

'Ah yes, Druscilla, exactly . . . the thing is . . . I was just wondering if you would happen to know of anyone who could put me in touch with one of your neighbours.' He coughed nervously. 'I need to get in touch with Isobel Tarrant and did not want to bother her husband . . .'

'She's left him,' interrupted Druscilla flatly.

'Yes, I am aware of that . . . but do you know where she—'

'What do you want her for, Reverend?' she asked slyly, some of her old curiosity blossoming at the scent of intrigue.

Since it felt impossible to explain the ambitious philanthropic reasons for wanting to contact Isobel to anybody, let alone her inquisitive neighbour, Archie made the sign of the cross on his chest and told an outright lie. 'I have a couple of books that belong to her, that's all. I'd like to know where to send them.'

For a moment Druscilla toyed with the deliciously meddling idea of confiding the name of Isobel's lover to the vicar. She drew in her breath and managed to swallow the temptation away, aided considerably by a recollection of recent events. 'I can't say for sure, but I believe she has gone to stay with her parents in Suffolk. I don't know the address, but maybe directory enquiries could help . . .'

'What is their surname?'

'Now I'm afraid you've got me there . . . I've no idea.'

'Oh dear.'

He sounded genuinely forlorn. 'The simplest thing would be to ask Mr Tarrant himself . . . or . . .' Druscilla hesitated. 'I suppose you could always try her friend, Juliet Howard, who lives in Ilcombe.' She spoke very slowly and carefully, inwardly congratulating herself on her powers of discretion. She would not betray Isobel again. 'Her husband's Christian name is James. I expect they'll be in the book.'

'I might just try that, then. Thank you so much for your time . . .'

'Vicar?'

'Yes?' Archie spoke with blatant and quite un-vicarly impatience, oblivious of the lifeline his phone call presented.

'Well, goodbye, then,' she muttered, deterred by his tone of voice.

'Goodbye, Miss Car—, I mean, Druscilla. And thanks awfully.'

When the other calls started again a little later, Druscilla took the phone off the hook before making herself a mug of hot milk and taking her black pen and list of properties upstairs. The three cats curled amongst the chaos of bedclothes blinked lazily at her as she came in, their claws sliding out like knives as they stretched.

'It's no good looking like that, my lovelies,' she scolded, pulling a wide-cabled jumper on over her clothes and negotiating a space between them on the bed. 'There'll be none of Mummy's milk for anyone that sulks. We'll find a lovely place to hide, you'll see,' she crooned, stroking each animal as it lapped from her mug, before taking a greedy slurp herself and feeling comforted as the warm liquid snaked its way down inside.

On seeing no evidence of James's car, Isobel decided to while away the time by going for a walk. She was almost one hour early and did not relish the idea of checking in on her own. With the clocks having been put back over the weekend, it was not yet dark. A suggestion of summer seemed to lie in the cool brightness of the evening and in the way the sun warmed the colours of the grass and trees. Le Relais, which she had vaguely heard of but never visited, looked more like a grand family home than a five-star hotel. In the centre of the semicircular gravelled drive in which she had parked was a small round fountain comprising a single cherub blowing water from a long horn. The entrance to the hotel itself was a narrow porch, tumbling with the green ropes of ripening wisteria. On either side of it an immaculate jigsaw of grey stone formed the walls, interrupted only by dark-timbered windows, each one adorned with its own flower box of exploding colour.

On walking back out of the gates, Isobel passed the rustic arrow of a signpost she had almost missed from the road, with the words Le Relais carved across its middle. Understated to the point of illegibility, the sign of a truly affluent business, she thought wryly, crossing the road towards a five-bar gate and the start of a promising pathway along the edge of a field. She quickly discovered that the evening was colder than it looked, especially when the sun dropped behind the rim of a distant wood and brisk wind appeared from nowhere, edging its way up under the hem of her coat and in through the cracks in her clothes. She bunched her hair about her ears for warmth and curled her fingers tight inside her pockets. She would walk to the end of the next field, she decided, before turning back. But as she pressed on, her determination not to return until James had arrived began to be superseded by a greater concern that he might appear in her absence, see her car and worry where she had gone. The end of the second field was further than it looked and the ground was growing unpleasantly muddy. After a few yards of stepping from tussock to tussock in the interests of preserving the appearance of her shoes, Isobel at last acknowledged the pointlessness of her journey and turned back. It was already a quarter to seven. The sun was gone for good now and had been replaced by a menacing steel wall of cloud. A few minutes later a drizzle started, compelling her into a fast walk that gradually became a run, as a dim panic welled up inside. Earlier indulgent sentiments about not trampling upon the fragmentary carpets of bluebells were all quite forgotten as she raced back along the last stretch of path, her hands and face still icy but her body growing hot from the exertion of running. Poor James, she thought, her heart thumping. The decision she had prepared for him was bad enough; not even being there when he arrived would make it look as if she didn't care at all.

A pretty string of yellow lights lit up the hotel sign and a nearby tree. There were others along the gutter line of the main building, like a trim of gaudy icing round a cake. Eagerly, Isobel sprinted the last few yards across the road and up the drive, pausing only to brush her loose hair behind her ears and to wipe her face with the back of her hand. She almost laughed at the thought of what a sight she must look, wondering with some hysteria whether James would mind, whether it might make the blow she was about to strike any easier to bear. He was the kind of man, as she had discovered, who appreciated perfume and hair that behaved, the kind of man who liked high clean heels and painted nails. Only very recently had she realised that the small extent to which she had obliged such tastes had been nothing but an act, nothing to do with how she wanted to live her life at all. Never my kind of man, she reflected bitterly, marvelling not for the first time at how unhappiness had so utterly warped her perspective on the world.

It took several minutes for Isobel to establish that James's car was still not resident in the drive. A smudged chalk board saying *Extra Parking To The Rear*, propped casually amongst some bushes, offered fresh hopes that were quickly dashed upon the discovery that the space referred to contained nothing but an old wooden handcart and a tractor wheel sprouting pansies. Faced with little alternative, Isobel scurried back round to the main entrance and went inside. A cosy sitting room of a reception area greeted her, complete with a roaring fire and cartoon hunting prints on the walls. The instant she entered, a well-groomed young man in a dark suit appeared from nowhere, crooning banalities of welcome and commentaries upon the ugly turn in the weather. 'I presume madam would like to check in?' he said, keeping his eyes on her as he reached out to press the bell on the unattended reception counter to their left.

Isobel nodded uncertainly, wondering suddenly what name James might have used on her behalf.

'Our receptionist will be with you in just a moment. Will you be wanting a table at dinner this evening?'

'I – I'm not sure. I should think so.'

'Excellent.' The young man slipped a gold pen out of his breast pocket and swung his clipboard into action. 'Will that be a table for one, madam?'

'Er . . . two. A table for two.'

'At what time?'

'Eight thirty,' she hazarded, seeing from the handsome grandfather clock beside the door that it was already almost a quarter to eight.

'We shall look forward to it,' he announced, carefully returning the pen to its lodging place and clicking his heels. 'And here is Elspeth to take care of your room reservation.' Looking perceptibly relieved, he sped away down the corridor, ducking under a low beam and a sign saying *Restaurant & Bar*.

Elspeth, who wore a badge advertising her name in gold letters, offered Isobel a stiff grin of welcome and reached under the counter for a large leather ledger.

'Could I have your name, please?'

'Howard,' replied Isobel with considerably more confidence than she felt, stepping forward to tinker with a small stand of pamphlets detailing sites of local interest.

'Ah yes, here we are. Two nights, double—' The girl stopped

mid-sentence and frowned. 'That's odd, it appears to have been cancelled.' She smiled apologetically. 'I've only just come on duty, I'm afraid, so I'll have to find out what's going on. I'm sure we've still got a room if you've changed your mind.'

'Cancelled?' repeated Isobel, staring at her stupidly, a colourful fact sheet about a nearby stately home dangling from her hand.

'Oh, hang on a minute . . . my colleague has left me a note here explaining all about it. Don't worry,' she added, seeing the expression on Isobel's face, 'I'm sure it will all be fine.' Her voice had a pretty Welsh lilt to it that was somehow soothing. Isobel relaxed a little and smiled back.

'What does it say?' She put down the pamphlet and rested her elbows on the counter.

The girl's pale young face creased into a frown. 'It says there's a letter for you . . . oh yes, here we are.' She produced a long white envelope and handed it across. 'Came by courier this afternoon apparently, a little after the reservation was cancelled. But like I said, we've lots of room at this time of year . . .'

But Isobel was already turning away, staring dumbly at the slanting loops spelling out her name. Slowly she made her way to the armchair in the furthest corner of the room and sat down. For a moment she was tempted to drop the letter into the flames unread. It was obvious what it would say. It was obvious he was not coming. Any relief she might have felt was overcome by horror at her own obtuseness; not only for having failed to guess this outcome herself, but actually having worried – of all things – about being late. On closer inspection the roaring fire turned out to be a gas-fired simulation of the real thing, complete with faked coal embers and crumbling logs. Quite unsuitable for burning letters or anything else.

'Excuse me? Would it be possible to turn the heat down a bit?'

'Of course, madam.' Elspeth scampered out from behind the counter and fiddled with an artfully concealed panel of knobs in the skirting board. 'If you need anything further, madam, don't hesitate to ring,' she added with a look of pity that made Isobel quail inside. 'A drink perhaps . . . or a cup of tea?'

'I'll let you know . . . thank you.'

When the girl had gone, Isobel ran her finger under the envelope flap and pulled out the single folded piece of paper inside.

Seeing the body of printed script she felt the first prickings of real disappointment. The handwritten opening and closing only added insult to injury, like the two-word scrawl on Christmas cards from friends one never saw.

Monday, 8 April
My Dear Isobel,
What will you think of me? If I wrote sorry a million times I know it would still not be enough. Believe me when I say I wish with all my heart that it could have worked. You are such a special person. I can only say how privileged I feel to have been allowed so close to you.

She groaned quietly to herself. It was going to be even worse than she had imagined.

It would be hard to explain all the detail of what has occurred during the course of the last few days. Suffice it to say that Juliet and I seem to have reached a new understanding with each other. Please find space in your heart to wish us well.

I thought about phoning you at your parents', but was worried I might stir up yet more trouble, since I know you had not explained the situation in full to them. Biking over this letter seemed the only safe way to get in touch. Since the hotel is only a relatively short drive from your parents' place, I know you will not be stuck for somewhere to go once you have received it.

We had a good time, Isobel. Can we remember it that way?

I'm afraid I have to end by requesting one humble favour. Juliet, while being cognisant of the fact that our marriage has come through something of a 'bad patch', is not to my knowledge aware of our affair. She has her suspicions, I know, but none of them focus on you. Would it be too much to ask you to assist me in keeping our secret from her? It would make things very hard for me otherwise.

I can only wish sincerest good luck to you and Ben. I am sorry that you are both so much further down the road towards separation. But perhaps it was meant to be and will turn out for the best. Who knows, maybe we can all become good friends again one day!

With all fondest wishes,
James

Isobel left the hotel without bothering to inform Elspeth or any of her colleagues. Instead of turning back in the direction of her parents' village, she headed east towards the coast. The rain seemed to be coming horizontally at the car, and with such force that her windscreen wipers barely had time to clear a view before it was shattered by a fresh onslaught. She drove slowly, partly because of the weather and partly out of shocked preoccupation with what had happened. Abhorrence at the cowardice of James's chosen method of dealing with the situation was exceeded only by disgust at herself. At the thought of all her recent agonising over how to protect his feelings she almost laughed out loud. James Howard had the welfare of his own emotions well in hand, she thought grimly, and required no help from her or anyone else in looking out for them.

Telling Juliet was not something she would ever have seriously contemplated anyway, for the simple reason that it would have caused additional and unnecessary pain. Although a more vulnerable creature might have needed warning about the finer features of her husband's personality, all Isobel's instincts and knowledge on the subject of Juliet Howard reassured her that she would be more than equal to the task of coping with James, on this and any such similar occasions in the future.

Since she had already resolved not to return to Torbridge until the following week – and then only to pick up a few more belongings – the chances of running into either of the Howards were mercifully thin. Testing though it would be for all concerned, Isobel had decided to prey on her parents' hospitality for a while longer. It was the only way of creating the time and space in which to work out how she and Ben would lead their separate lives. Tempting though it was, common sense warned her that too much had been destroyed for her to grant herself the indulgence of thinking in any other terms.

A lively and unexpected chat with a young curate from St Cuthbert's with an unpronounceable surname had livened up Juliet's Sunday evening considerably, though it did bother her later that night and during the course of the following day that she had failed to quiz him more directly about his reasons for needing to contact Isobel. News of the Tarrants' break-up, received via James that afternoon, had left Juliet feeling somewhat shaken, not to say offended. For Isobel not to have given even so much as a hint as to how bad the situation was cut very deeply. As her one-time closest friend, Juliet felt she had every right to feel thoroughly cheated.

Such disappointments had been partially made up for, however, by James's surprise announcement on Monday morning that he would not be attending the conference after all, but would take a couple of days off work instead. He spent an hour or two pottering in his study, before salivating over the simple tuna salad she prepared for lunch and then surprising her for a second time by declaring his intention to collect the children from school and take them to a Disney extravaganza at the cinema. Suppressing motherly knee-jerk reactions about such indulgences being more appropriate for birthdays or weekends at the very least, Juliet had pronounced herself delighted and settled down to enjoy an indolent afternoon.

Since she never quite bridged the distance between sofa and ironing board and then managed to fall asleep in front of *Oprah*, it turned out to be even more indolent than she intended. Worried that she would not even have supper ready by the time James and the children returned, she scurried round her pretty pine kitchen, hurling chicken legs, vegetables and stock cubes into a casserole dish with unseemly haste. As she did so, Juliet found her thoughts flitting back to the milestone of a meal she had prepared with such contrasting care the week before. It had been so much easier than she had expected, she reflected, with a happy sigh, pouring in a generous splash of red wine before fitting the casserole lid and placing it in the oven. Almost as if James had been looking for a way out. She paused, knives and forks in hand, as details of the evening came back to her, feeling again the excited terror with which she had played her part.

The candles on the table had surprised him, as had the lingering kiss with which she greeted his arrival at the door. Aware that he was appraising this new turn of events, taking in the stunningly provocative look of her clothes, the delicious smells seeping out from under saucepan lids, she had said nothing at first, but simply taken him by the hand and led him into the kitchen.

When he tried to speak she put a hand over his mouth, whispering, 'Not now, just enjoy.' He sipped the whisky she gave him, eyeing her with curiosity over the rim of his glass, watching as she moved around the room, stirring and tasting and adjusting all the elements of their meal. Aware of his eyes, aware of his interested bewilderment, Juliet savoured every moment. As the sense of expectation mounted, so did her confidence in her own desirability. It was a long time since she had tried to seduce her husband.

When she saw the whisky was almost gone, she turned and faced him, leaning forward on the back of a chair so that her breasts pushed upwards through the flimsy material of her shirt and the longest, loosest curls of her hair fell forward over her shoulders.

'The children are asleep, the meal is ready when we want it . . .'

He protested then, shaking his head and smiling. 'I don't think . . .'

'I'm going to remind you why you married me,' she said quietly, taking him by the tie and leading him up the stairs, 'before you've had too much good wine and food to appreciate such things.' He had giggled like a guilty schoolboy, offering up protestations, but weakly and through smiles, so that she knew that the first hurdle had been overcome. Before making love she massaged him with the nutmeg oil she had prepared, kneading and teasing his flesh with slow suggestive movements, relishing in spite of herself the feelings of power flowing through her palms. Through a great effort of will, which good sense warned her she would have to learn to exercise many more times in the future, Juliet managed during the course of this exercise to keep all images of possible rivals firmly out of her mind. If she wanted him enough, she had to forgive him, she reminded herself, abandoning the oil and tipping her head forward so that the curly tips of her hair floated across his back.

When at last they arrived back in the kitchen, in dressing gowns and exchanging the flushed happy glances more commonly associated with young lovers, she had lit the candles and set about serving up the first course of her tremendous meal.

'Am I missing something here?' James asked after a while, laughing softly as she poured a teaspoon of wine into his glass for tasting. 'Is my birthday early this year?'

'No, it's more important than that.' For the first time nerves threatened to have an adverse effect on her performance.

'More important, eh?' He raised one eyebrow and smacked his lips appreciatively at the claret. 'I say, that's good.'

'We are celebrating the first day of the rest of our marriage,' she declared, aiming for a tone that she hoped sounded both solemn and fond. 'I know I've been losing you and I want you back.'

'Losing me?' James, who had gone along with the evening so far with a combination of tolerance and pleased surprise, experienced his first frisson of real worry. It dawned on him that his wife might have a hidden agenda of some kind, that a little more than the easy reassurance of sex was required of him.

Her round blue eyes, glittering under the clever enhancement of eyeshadows and coloured pencils, never blinked. 'Yes, losing you. And . . .' She paused for full effect. '. . . you have been losing me.' Juliet paused again, thinking that a lover of her own would have been easier to confess to than the piece of paper folded under the lee of her side plate. 'I have been very unhappy, James. And when I am unhappy I do foolish things . . . like spend money.' She put down her knife and fork and slowly pulled the bill out from its hiding place. Her nails, richly red and round-tipped, looked striking beside the whiteness of the paper.

'What's that?' he whispered, now scowling with worry.

'This?' She dangled it between thumb and forefinger over her plate. 'This is the evidence of my unhappiness, James. I want you to be understanding about it. I want you to recognise the part you played in bringing it about.'

'What on earth . . . ?' Before she could stop him he had reached across the table and snatched the bill from her. For the first few moments he just gasped, his jaw agape in a caricature of horrified dismay.

'A woman scorned,' she said quietly, threateningly. 'And if you leave me ever again – in any sense of the word – I will make you pay. I promise you, James, together or apart, I will make you pay. I swear it.' Having delivered her ultimatum, Juliet allowed her voice to quiver more endearingly during the course of the next sentence. 'Because I love you, you old fool. And I will fight to the death rather than surrender you to anyone else. Because' – her voice was higher now, cracking with emotion – 'because we are good together, we know how to make each other happy, because I wouldn't be with anyone else for the world. And I'm sorry – desperately, desperately sorry – about the money. I was just so miserable and alone and trying to cheer myself up and get at you all at the same time . . .'

James, struggling with the shock not only of a demand for several thousand pounds, but also of the implicit revelation that she knew of his affair with Isobel, took an unseemly gulp of claret and shook his head from side to side. 'It's just so much. What did you . . . ?'

'It was clothes,' Juliet muttered through a hiccough of a sob. 'Most of them are still in bags with the receipts . . . I've asked if they'll take them back and they said maybe. They don't usually give cash refunds,' she added meekly, beginning to clear a space for dessert, 'but said they might be able to make a bit of an exception with some of the more costly items.'

'Well, that's something, I suppose.'

She shot him an anxious glance, unsure whether he was expressing genuine relief or merely being sarcastic. But James was the picture of distress, shaking his head as he clasped and unclasped his hands.

'What I'm saying, I think, is that I'll be good if you will,' Juliet continued quietly, setting out the swirling finale of ginger ice cream decorated with biscuits and then going round behind him to place her hands on his shoulders. 'I don't know who she was and I don't want to know. As far as I'm concerned it's over. And I'll try to get some of the money back, I promise,' she blurted, 'and if I can't, I'll earn it. Even before I qualify I can start to charge a little for a massage, begin to build up a clientèle . . . Shelley wants us to go into business together, run our own beauty therapy shop . . .'

'Steady on there . . .' he interjected, sounding decidedly unsteady himself. 'One thing at a time, eh?'

'Do we forgive each other, then?' she asked in a small voice, sliding her fingertips down into the front of his dressing gown and resting her chin on his shoulder.

'Oh, Juliet, I—'

'Just say yes and we need never talk about it again.'

'Yes,' he growled, taking her hands and pressing them between his own. 'Silly sparrow, of course I love you.'

'Always?'

'Always,' he agreed, telling himself in the same instant that the business with Isobel had probably run the most stimulating part of its course anyway, and wondering how many other husbands would be let off so lightly for sexual misdemeanours. It was only money after all, and maybe not even too much if the shop did the decent thing. A small price to pay for a marriage that he now realised he had never really wanted to jeopardise in the first place.

Juliet smiled to herself as she recalled the way they had both tucked into their ice-cream desserts afterwards, marvelling at the wonderful simplicity of knowing what one wanted and recognising the most effective way of bringing it about. And they had felt so close ever since, not in a fake forced way, but really deep down inside, where the bedrock of their commitment lay. The only pain was the vigilance, she reflected with a sigh, as the crunch of rubber on gravel alerted her to the fact that the cinema party had returned. She tweaked back the dining-room curtain and watched James get out of the car and clap his hands with impatience at the children. She would always be watching him now, she realised with a start, not just with her eyes but with her instincts, listening for the inflection that sounded wrong, for the first pulse of unnatural affection that would warn her that it was all happening again. It was not a happy thought and she made up for it in the vehemence of her greeting as he stepped through the door, gripping his neck so tightly that he let out a small, surprised cry of pain.

Ben stood at the end of the bed staring down at the motionless figure of his aunt. Her frail frame caused barely a ripple amongst the bed covers. On her bedside table was folded a small white handkerchief with a lacy trim and a full glass of water. Slowly he let his eyes roam around the rest of the room, taking in the modest array of belongings and mementos on the shelves and dressing table. Like a selected museum of relics. Even the brush-and-comb set, arranged at perfect equidistance from the hand mirror, looked like articles on display rather than existing for any practical use. Seeing their familiar mother-of-pearl backs and the single tooth missing from the comb, fourth from the end, Ben felt the first tremor of real emotion. Aunt Violet had had tremendous hair; long and fair and thick as a horse's tail. She had brushed it one hundred times a night, occasionally before his sleepy, mesmerised eyes, beating it down in strong swift movements and then whipping it up and round her clever fingers into a sort of knot that managed to stay in place until the morning.

'Can she hear us?'

'We think so.' The nurse smoothed an imaginary crease from the counterpane. 'Unless she's asleep, of course. Sometimes it's hard to tell. But she does speak from time to time. Cup of tea?'

'No thank—' began Ben automatically before realising that a cup of tea was in fact exactly what he wanted. 'That would be great. Milk, no sugar.'

When they were alone Ben approached the bedside cautiously. Watching his aunt drawing small, barely audible breaths through the crack between her thin grey lips, he felt all the pointlessness of even beginning to try to make up for all his ingratitude, for his inability to act upon the extraordinary surges of passionate admiration that seemed to characterise his affection for her. She had found him hard to love too, he knew; the role of surrogate mother, forced upon her by the selfishness of an absent but adored brother, never having suited her very well.

He felt angry at her too, for choosing such an inconvenient time to start her dying, for adding to his wretchedness about Isobel. For making him feel so damned guilty.

A small groaning noise was coming from the back of her throat. Repelled, and a little scared, Ben bent over and picked up three of the limp, lumpy fingers lying near him and held them lightly in his. 'I'm sorry,' he muttered.

The nurse bustled back in carrying a cup of tea and a small plate of biscuits. 'Thought you looked like you could do with something,' she said with a bright smile, 'it being most folks' suppertime. Stay as long as you like. There's a phone booth downstairs when you want to call a cab for your return journey – down the corridor to your left, past the sitting room. If we had the space I'd offer to make you up a bed for the night, but I'm afraid we're chock-a-block at the moment. There's always an armchair if you fancy a doze. I'll be downstairs if you want me, or you can find Nurse Dudley who's on duty down the corridor – third on the left past the lift.' She paused to cock her head fondly in the direction of the patient, now silent once more beneath her grey shroud of a counterpane. 'A dear, really, beneath all that huff and puff. Has she no other relatives?'

Ben swallowed. 'Just me.'

After the nurse had gone he couldn't bring himself to hold the fingers again. The least he could do, he felt, was not be a fraud, not make a big show of something he could not quite feel. Instead, he crossed to make a closer study of the bookshelves, sipping his tea and wolfing biscuits with a relish that felt quite inappropriate. It was nine o'clock on Monday evening and, as the nurse had correctly guessed, Ben hadn't consumed anything by way of a meal since lunch. Though he had managed two bags of shopping on the way home from school, he had made little headway in unpacking them. The call from the home telling him of Aunt Violet's stroke had interrupted a catnap in front of the early evening news, a guilty, fitful doze which had served as a diversion not only from the mayhem of the kitchen, but also from the increasingly burning need to speak to Isobel. He was missing her more every day. And the girls. It seemed incredible that only five days had passed since they had left. It felt more like a lifetime. The Easter holidays, now only one day away, loomed large, shimmering with difficult and unresolved dilemmas.

While waiting for a taxi to whisk him to his aunt's beside, temptation had vied with self-pity, as Ben tussled with the decision as to whether or not to dial the number in Suffolk. A dying aunt was a fair pretext. But then, it was his aunt and not Isobel's. He knew only too well how she had always resented visiting the home; and with the easy vista offered by hindsight, Ben could well understand why. Another responsibility taken on and shirked, he thought regretfully, picking up the receiver and slamming it down again, as all his longing hardened into bitterness towards himself.

Amongst Aunt Violet's books were several that looked familiar, including a large leather-bound atlas with a torn spine. Putting down his cup, Ben reached up and carefully slid it from the shelf.

To My Darling Vi,
    You see, the world is not so large after all,
    Your devoted brother, Albert. Christmas 1956

Seeing his father's extravagant handwriting, sweeping across the flyleaf with all the brash confidence that had made him as resented as he was successful, caused his son an unexpected shiver of pain. He closed the book abruptly, suppressing and despising the sense of quite illogical expectancy which the sight of Aunt Violet's possessions had triggered in him. There were no keys to understanding life, except within one's own head. If the last few months had taught him anything it was that. The image of Ione Brown flickered in his mind, bringing with it the usual confusion of anxiety and gratitude. Talking to her had opened a lid that would not now be closed. The Pandora's box of his past. Self-knowledge till the cows came home, he thought grimly, slotting the atlas back into place. And none of it had so far done anything to make him – or anyone else – any happier. Being repressed and dysfunctional had been far easier, he reflected with a wry smile, as he turned away from the bookshelf and reached absently into his jacket pocket. His fingers closed around the brown envelope he had collected from the jeweller's that afternoon.

'Bloody thing,' he muttered, tearing open the envelope and pouring the chain into the palm of his hand. Closing his fingers round it, he quickly crossed the room, lifted the lid of a small green suede jewel box and dropped the pendant inside. Briskly dusting his hands together, as if to dismiss the matter and his own sentiments for good, he returned to his aunt's bedside.

'Who is it?' she croaked, making him jump.

'It's me, Ben, Aunt Violet.' He sat down and patted her arm. 'How are you feeling?'

'Who?'

'Albert's son,' he reminded her quietly.

'Where's that girl?'

'Which girl would that be?' He wondered for a moment if she was referring to one of the nurses.

'Lovely hair. Red hair. Nice voice.'

'Isobel?'

'Where is she?'

'She's . . . not here.'

'I want that girl who visits. I've not been nice to her—'

'Oh, I'm sure you have.'

She was twitching the sheets with her hands and jerking her head. Her eyes fluttered open and closed again, as if searching for something they could not see. Alarmed, Ben pushed the red button in the wall above the bed.

'She seems a little upset,' he explained apologetically, when the nurse hurried in. 'I wasn't sure . . .'

'What have we here, then . . . ?' The nurse lifted the twiggy wrist for a pulse and punched some air back into the pillows.

'She's been asking for someone . . .'

'Has she? Well, that's nice. Is it someone you can contact?'

'Er . . . maybe.' He coughed and mouthed the words 'How long?' across the bed.

The nurse shrugged sadly. 'Hard to say,' she whispered. 'Days maybe . . .'

'I'll certainly do my best, Aunt Violet,' Ben said loudly, picking up his coat from the back of the chair. 'Will you call me if there's any change?' he added in a whisper to the attending nurse, before gently easing open the door and slipping outside.

It was a relief to leave the room, though the smell of medicine and floor polish was, if anything, even stronger in the corridors. As he passed the open door of the sitting room on his way to the telephones, Ben saw two rows of empty armchairs being lectured to by a man on the television. He hurried past, averting his gaze, suddenly dreading his own fate as an old man.

39

It rained all night, not just across East Anglia, but over the whole of southern England. Archie, sitting on Tuesday morning in the luxurious rear seat of a coach that had more features than the interior of an airplane, shook his head in wonder at the streaks of silver flooding cutting through the fields flying past his window. Thinking of the summer to come and the drought that had so preoccupied weather experts the year before, he said a short silent prayer about rainfall and reservoirs, before extracting a cheese-and-pickle bap from the bag on his lap. He had found himself in a state of almost constant prayer over the last couple of days, jumbled stuff, mostly about gratitude for being grateful. God didn't mind jumble, he was sure of that. He could feel the pleasure of him burning inside now, like hunger, only stronger. After his recent sustained inability to feel anything except misery, the wonder of it was breathtaking.

Almost equal pleasure had been derived from addressing the more practical problem of his eyesight. A half-hour visit to the Chapel Street optician's the previous afternoon had resulted in the acquisition of some gratifyingly erudite, wire-framed spectacles, containing lenses empowered to accommodate the very different requirements of his eyeballs. The eyes had been working against each other, the optician explained cheerfully, blinking over the top of his own tortoiseshell frames, resulting in prolonged and considerable muscle strain. After only a few hours, Archie had noticed a difference: the twitching still came and went, but less regularly and with none of its customary ferocity. With the curious cohesion that life sometimes allows, this diagnosis had been followed by the first good night's sleep that he had known in months. The small brown bottle of Dr Howard's little white pills was now set to gather a nice coating of dust on the window sill above his bed. Though Archie planned, eventually, to consign them to the grimy interior of his kitchen bin, he had decided for the time being to let them play the useful role of psychological fail-safe, a safety net should the need arise.

Having seen off the bap in four or five mouthfuls, Archie reached into his bag in order to pull out his latest acquisition from the library. Though a trifle bashful at the thought of being seen in possession of a book like *Anna Karenina*, his new-found confidence made him determined to give the thing a go. Any enquiries on the subject would have met with a stout defence of a curate's right to improve his knowledge of Russian classics. But what Archie really sought was more understanding of the emotional complexities of Isobel Tarrant in particular and the female psyche in general. The memory of his first proper meeting with Isobel in Torbridge library was still vivid; especially the carelessly bright way in which she had mentioned the book's theme, and his own absurd shyness in trying to respond. Any assistance Tolstoy might offer on the perplexing question of fully fledged female passion could, Archie believed, only strengthen his capacity to handle the meeting that lay ahead. Quite what Isobel's parents were going to make of a Torbridge priest striding up to their front door he hardly dared imagine, though he had deliberately worn full battledress – as he fondly called his cassock – in the vague hope of giving himself something of a flying start. As the moment drew ever nearer, he cowered most at the prospect of confronting Isobel, worrying that she might think him interfering instead of kind. Defused though his passions were, Archie could not bear to think of her not liking him at all.

Druscilla Carew's recommendation had proved a highly fruitful means to information. Juliet Howard not only surrendered the address of Isobel's parents without a moment's hesitation, but also seemed extremely eager to discuss her friend's circumstances in some detail.

'Yes, she's gone to her parents, without a word to anyone.

James only found out quite by chance. That's my husband. He's a doctor at the Stanton Street practice.'

'Ah,' said Archie, some of his enthusiasm for conversation instantly dampened by the revelation of this minor social connection. While not consciously apportioning blame to anyone but himself, he retained few positive memories of his consultation with James Howard.

'The marriage has broken up. Been on the rocks for months – she had a lover, apparently,' went on Juliet. 'A lover, for goodness' sake. Isobel Tarrant. None of us can believe it.'

Archie tried to interrupt her with a view to concluding the discussion, but Juliet had swept on.

'And those poor, poor girls, caught between them, as the children always are in these circumstances. And such a *nice* family too . . . positively frightening to see it all fall apart . . .'

'Absolutely,' Archie had cut in with mounting desperation, sensing all the impropriety of discussing the Tarrants' misfortunes in such gleefully scandalised terms. 'And thank you so much. Goodbye—'

'Goodbye, Reverend . . . what was it?'

'Heighton-Jones.'

'Ah yes. St Cuthbert's, did you say?'

'That's right.'

'So they haven't yet managed to pin African face-masks round the apse?'

'I beg your pardon?'

'Totem poles instead of altars. I thought you were under threat from the ethnic arts people?'

'Oh no, I mean, yes, we were. Plans have been shelved. We've been saved – for the time being.'

'Wonderful. I hope we meet in person soon. Though we usually go to the cathedral – if we go at all . . . Goodbye, Reverend. So nice to have talked to you.'

Remembering the conversation, Archie squirmed in his bus seat. She might be a friend of Isobel's, but he hadn't liked the sound of her at all.

To Archie's dismay, he found his new novel hard going, largely on account of the unsympathetically extravagant emotions of Anna herself. As the coach sped on, its fat wheels spurting like water mills through the dripping roads, Archie found himself concentrating less on the rollercoaster ride of Anna's sensibilities and more on the simple pleasure of skimming his newly reinforced eyes effortlessly over the lines. So accustomed had he become to the blurring and jumping of letters on a page that being restored the simple gift of perfect sight felt nothing short of miraculous.

After an hour or so he gave up completely and pulled out his second and final sandwich – the one he had vowed to keep until lunch-time – and told himself he would eat half. It was beef and horseradish, on a doughy bread with crusty doorstep edges. He chewed quickly, staring with a wild and happy heart at nothing in particular while the rain coursed down his window. Views of pretty floods or anything else had been blotted out by the grey curtain sweeping from sky to earth. But I still know the prettiness is there, he mused, lingering on the notion with pleasure, sure that he had found yet another small but revealing analogy for the visibility of God to troubled souls. There but sometimes hidden, he murmured, stifling a fruity burp and settling back to close his eyes.

Spending Monday night in a seaside bed and breakfast did little to raise Isobel's sense of optimism for her own future. She felt washed up and quite beyond repair. The thinking time – once so longed for and talked about – had produced such vague and fruitless circles of regret and self-recrimination that she left her room shortly after dawn in search of distractions. It did not feel possible to go scampering back to her parents just yet, like the failed child that she was. Instead she had a greasy cooked breakfast and a mug of lukewarm coffee in a café that smelt of fish and then set out for a stroll along the beach. Apart from a bounding Labrador, being roared at by a distant owner, the sands were empty and grey. The waves snarled at her as she walked by, like foaming animals straining at the leash. After a while, she took her shoes and socks off and walked with her feet in the icy water, wishing the numbness could seize her heart as well as her toes. Staring out towards the grey bands where sky met sea, she found herself understanding the attraction of stepping into it, of wanting to merge with the nothingness that it seemed to contain. The incoming tide embraced her ankles, then slid back towards the sea, pulling the sand from under her toes and leaving the instep of each foot stranded on little humps that dissolved beneath her weight.

From nowhere the Labrador appeared at the water's fringe, its tail flicking water as it pumped the air, its drooly jaws clamped round a large stick. It plunged towards where Isobel was standing and deposited the stick a few feet from her left hand. For a moment she watched absently as the piece of wood bobbed and started to float away on the swell of a receding wave.

Seeing its toy in danger of disappearing, the dog gave a frantic yelp of encouragement.

'Oh, bugger it,' she muttered, reaching for the stick and hurling it as far as she could back towards the shore. In the exertion of doing so, she lost her balance and fell backwards. For a moment there was nothing but cold and shock. Then the palm of one hand met the hard pebbly ground and in an instant she had levered herself upright again. Amazingly, only one leg, half her back and an entire arm suffered the calamity of being entirely drenched. The dog, having retrieved its trophy, raced away towards the sound of a piercing whistle, leaving Isobel to wade back on to dry land, now laughing breathlessly – and a little hysterically – at her own foolhardiness. A trail of dark drips marked her path across the beach and back up to the road. Her hair, dampened and frizzy from the moist salty air, stuck in clumps to her cheeks and neck. Catching sight of her reflection in the polished glass of an amusement arcade a few minutes later, Isobel clapped her hand to her mouth in a mixture of horror and real amusement. No wonder she had been getting strange looks. A few yards on from the arcade was a hairdresser's. With a rush of determination to achieve at least one positive thing that morning, however superficial, she pushed open the door and stepped inside.

In spite of the look on the girl's face, she stuck to her guns. 'I want it all off. Right down to the last inch. And I'm a bit pushed for time.' She smiled briskly and looked at her watch. 'So if you wouldn't mind . . .'

'If you're sure . . .'

'I'm sure, thank you.'

'Would you like to keep the hair?'

'Keep it? Whatever for?'

'To make a hairpiece, or as a memento . . .'

Isobel laughed. 'Oh God, no, I wouldn't. I don't want any mementos at all, thank you.'

The hairdresser, who was usually renowned for her sales patter with even the most awkward customers, remained quite silent while she saw to Isobel's request. Sensing an agenda that was quite out of her realm, she kept her eyes on her scissors instead of her client's sodden clothes, trying to keep her expression impartial as each coil of shining copper flopped noiselessly to the ground.

Before embarking on the drive back to her parents', Isobel changed into dry clothes and bought a large green headscarf from a charity shop. As well as introducing her to the phenomenon of cold ears, to have so brutally cropped such an obvious asset felt like an act of honesty; anyone could see now that she had nothing to hide behind, no camouflage for her insecurity. That is was indisputably ugly felt most important of all.

'Ugly on the outside, ugly on the inside,' she declared to the wing mirror, grimacing at the egg shape of her skull and the crimson tips of her ears. Her eyes, exposed in the bare pale frame of her face as never before, glittered with new resolve. 'Not the Ophelia sort anyway,' she muttered, giving the sea a parting scowl as she turned along the road that led away from the coast. At the thought of seeing the girls, Isobel allowed herself a broad smile; her first for days. Both the traffic and the weather deteriorated steadily as she continued her journey inland. On the final stretch of motorway, she was caught up in a tailback of traffic that lasted for several miles. Impatience at this unforeseen delay was instantly humbled by the sound of sirens wailing in the distance. The line of cars on her side of the road was completely stationary, while on the other side there were no vehicles to be seen at all. Leaning back against the headrest and half closing her eyes, Isobel prepared to wait. A minute later she opened them again, her attention caught by a stunning scissor of azure blue opening in the sky ahead, directly above where she imagined the cause of the delay to be taking place. With the rest of the world still so thunderously black, it looked like a crevice of light in a darkened room.

After a good half-hour the traffic started to move again. The cars appearing on the other side accelerated away with evident relief. A couple of miles later bollards, police signs and a scattering of broken glass told Isobel that she was about to pass the scene of the accident. Feeling she shouldn't look, but wanting to anyway, she glanced left and saw a coach tipped over on its side. Two badly dented cars were behind it. To her right, several yards' worth of snarled metal road fencing told a little more of the story. The number of uniformed helpers and official cars parked round the damaged vehicles underlined still further the grave scale of what had occurred. Shaking her head in dismay, Isobel sped into the clear road opening ahead of her, empowered by a fresh sense of her own good fortune. Remembering the bleakness of her thoughts on the beach that morning, she felt quite guilty. There was so much to live for after all, even for foolish women with broken marriages and pitifully hazy notions as to the nature of their own ambitions. It was just a question of seizing this new phase in her life by the scruff of its neck and shaking some sense into it, she told herself, pushing off her headscarf and stroking the soft brush of her hair. She would get over Ben, with time. Maybe, one day, she might even be able to laugh at the calamitous sequence of misunderstandings and misfortunes that had driven them apart, at the awful fiasco of seeking answers in the arms of someone like James Howard.

The crevice of blue had opened into a great canyon. The stream of yellow sunlight pouring from inside made the dark wet roads shine like polished obsidian. For the last couple of miles Isobel drove faster than she should have, spurred on not just by the brightness of the day, but by the pleasurable prospect of surprising the children by her early return, of putting some of her new determination to the test.

'Now that's what I call odd,' remarked Juliet, flicking the page of newspaper in front of her with her fingertips and then scowling at the jagged shoreline of her week-old nail varnish. It was Wednesday morning, and James, having enjoyed two days in the company of his family, was returning to work.

'Hm?' Never at his conversational best before eight o'clock on any day, he glanced first at his wife, then at the kitchen clock and finally at the egg still submerged in frothy water in a saucepan on the stove. Having safely waved the children on to the school bus, Juliet, attractively enveloped in her peach housecoat, had confessed to a firm but loving intention to provide her husband with the nourishment of a cooked breakfast. Keen as they both still were to foster every show of affection, no matter how mundane or small, James had falsely pronounced himself delighted at the prospect and had been regretting it ever since. 'How long did you say it would take?'

'Four and a half minutes. Two to go,' she added, keeping her eyes fixed upon the paragraph of newsprint in front of her. 'This really is too much . . .'

'What is, my love?' he asked dutifully, after casting a surreptitiously sceptical glance across the table. Juliet was not often absorbed by newspaper headlines, least of all those splashed across the inside pages of the *Torbridge Gazette*. 'Another bomb?' For a second or two his thoughts lingered with something like nostalgia on Torbridge's brush with terrorist explosives earlier in the year. He remembered holding Isobel's hand, the look of surprise in her wide green eyes.

'James, are you listening?'

'Loud and clear.'

'It's all about that vicar chap, the one I told you about – the one who rang on Sunday night. Listen.'

DEATH MYSTERY OF TORBRIDGE VICAR

The only fatality of yesterday's Suffolk motorway coach crash has been identified as Reverend Archibald Heighton-Jones, a twenty-two-year-old curate from Torbridge's own St Cuthbert's. His parents were called to Barstone Hospital to identify the body, which they have taken to their parish in Cheshire for burial. 'He was a fine and holy man,' commented Reverend Tully, 'called to God far sooner than any of us would have hoped or expected. Our hearts go out to his friends and family.' That his employee had apparently claimed to be too sick to attend to his parish duties in Torbridge that morning was a matter on which the Reverend was unprepared to comment. A fellow passenger confirmed that the young trainee vicar was carrying no luggage apart from a picnic lunch, a pair of spectacles and the novel Anna Karenina. *So it seems the secret of the itinerant vicar is one that he will carry to his grave. His replacement at St Cuthbert's has yet to be announced.*

'Poor chap. And a man of passions, obviously, if his taste in reading is anything to go by.' James left the table to peer anxiously at his egg, too distracted by such pressing dilemmas to make any connection with the red-headed curate who had consulted him about insomnia a few weeks before.

'Of course, of course, but don't you see?' Juliet was so excited she could hardly speak. 'It all fits.'

'What fits?' James retorted with some impatience, now seriously concerned both for the welfare of his breakfast and his time schedule for the morning.

'All that stuff about wanting to send her books was nonsense. He was going to visit her.'

'Visit who?'

'James, don't be dim. Isobel. He was going to visit Isobel Tarrant.' Juliet slapped the table with the palm of her hand and pushed past him to the saucepan. 'There's no other explanation.' She transported the egg, its surface turbulent with cracks and entrails of yellow and white, to a rabbit figurine of an eggcup, before – somewhat unnecessarily – batting it on the head with a teaspoon. 'Everyone's saying Isobel had a lover. Well, I think it must have been this priest. He had a lovely voice – and no doubt a lovely body to go with it.' She handed him his breakfast and folded her arms with a challenging humph of satisfaction.

James quickly busied himself with picking off fragments of shell. 'Don't be ridiculous, darling – I mean, really . . .' Inside, the yolk was dry and quite solid, as was its surrounding cushion of white. As he chewed he could feel little bits of it sticking between his teeth.

'It's the only scenario that makes sense. Listen.' Juliet held up her fingers and counted off each component of her theory. 'The two of them have a clandestine affair; when Ben finds out, Isobel panics and runs off to her parents'; then the vicar – lovelorn and despairing' – she rolled her eyes with relish – 'calls me to find out where she is and goes running after her. And ends up getting killed for his pains. It's too romantic for words, like something out of a great tragic' – she spread her arms for added emphasis – 'love story.'

James opened his mouth to scold his wife for being so absurdly imaginative and then closed it again. He ran his tongue round the clogged edges of his teeth before smiling. 'You are a genius, my sparrow, did you know that?'

'Yes, I did, actually.' She sat back down beside him and sighed deeply. 'It just goes to show, you never have a clue really what's going on in other people's lives. You think you know someone and then' – she clicked her fingers – 'pow, you discover something that makes you realise you never did at all.'

'Like the Tarrants, you mean,' he said carefully.

'Exactly. All that time the four of us spent together . . . it's weird . . . it's like we never really knew each other at all.' She sighed again. 'But I do miss her – Isobel, I mean. We did have a lot in common, once upon a time.'

James abandoned his egg to put his arms round her. 'You've got all your Ilcombe friends now and that Shelley woman.'

Juliet pushed him away with a brusque kiss and began clearing the table. 'Of course I have. I'm not complaining. I'm very happy with my lot – now.' She shot him a little look as a reminder of the subject she had vowed never to mention again, before picking up the newspaper and folding it in half. After only a moment's hesitation she then turned and dropped it into the bin, where it subsided amongst an avalanche of eggshell and yolk crumbs.

Though reputedly still breathing, Aunt Violet was showing few signs of life by Wednesday afternoon when Isobel raced up the green-carpeted stairs two at a time for her turn at the bedside. The physical deterioration was a shock. Her skin seemed to have shrunk to her bones, sinking round each curve and nodule of her skeleton like shrivelled clingfilm. Without the support of dentures, the jaw and cheeks looked pitifully deflated; quite incapable of defiance, thought Isobel sadly, recalling all the acerbic comments to which she had once been subjected with a surge of affection. After the nurse had left, she stood quietly by the bed for a few minutes before retreating to a chair to fiddle with her rings and wonder quite what she was expected to do.

Thanks to her hair – or rather the lack of it – her homecoming in Suffolk had proved something of a trial. Though her parents managed to contain their astonishment with a few murmurs and a stoically tight-lipped determination not to appear shocked, both Sophie and Megan howled at the sight of her and for quite some time afterwards. The news about Aunt Violet did little to alleviate such tensions. Though it felt churlish, Isobel could not repress a certain incredulity at having been summoned to the bedside, Aunt Violet's rambling and spiky conversation having done little to suggest that she might ever be called upon to play such a potentially dramatic role. The fact that her last few visits had served as a loose geographical alibi for meeting James Howard added a further twist of complicating guilt to these emotions. Remembering how beadily the old bird had eyed her sometimes – her uncanny knack of saying the most unsettling things – Isobel had even caught herself wondering if she was being called to attend a dreadful final tribunal of some kind; whether she was to be subjected to quavering judgments for having allowed old bad cycles of hurt and betrayal to recur.

In spite of such apprehensions, there was never any question of her not complying with the request. Her only condition was that Ben should be contacted and warned off being there himself. Though her parents clearly thought this an unnecessary cruelty, Isobel remained adamant. She feared what might happen to all her new-found courage at the sight of him; she feared, above all, the thought of his disdain, of seeing once more the look of repulsed disappointment that had burned in his eyes upon the revelation of her affair with James. Seeing her daughter's determination, her mother had finally agreed to phone Ben to make the terms of the visit clear. But as she left the room to do so, the grim expression on her face revealed for the first time the full extent of Betty Hitchings' consternation at what was taking place and her despair at being so powerless to do anything to prevent it.

Upon seeing the old lady, Isobel had immediately felt ashamed of all her earlier apprehensions. What little remained of Aunt Violet's energies was clearly being channelled into far more fundamental matters than delivering tirades upon the misdemeanours of relatives. Feeling both relieved and strangely let down, she eventually abandoned her chair and began to wander round the room much as Ben had the day before, tinkering with ornaments and speculating about their origins and the sentiments attached to them. When she reached the dressing table, Isobel picked up the comb and gently ran her thumb down the uneven row of teeth. Pushing her headscarf back off her head, she stooped in front of the mirror and slowly pulled the comb through her hair, still intrigued by the way the crop of her fringe now grew vertically upwards, like the glossy bristles of a soft brush.

Two cups of tea and one hour later, Isobel felt she had earned a stroll in the grounds. As she walked, she peeled off her scarf and cardigan and slung them across her handbag. The day had warmed up considerably since her arrival, though the manicured lawn and rich foliage surrounding it still gleamed from their recent rich diet of rain. After making two circuits, her eye was caught by a gap in the hedge and a narrow path that seemed to lead towards some greenhouses, their glass roofs just visible through the trees. Upon following the path, however, she found herself being led round the back of the greenhouses, past a large compost heap and out into a scrubby area of land that contained the fenced-in square of an old tennis court. Tufts of grass and dandelion clocks had pushed their way up through the lines in its rugged face and one net post slanted dramatically towards the ground, like the death-dive of an uprooted tree. Isobel pushed her way inside through a broken gate and began an idle tour of its perimeter, keeping half an eye open for rotten balls and wondering how many decades had elapsed since any had been in use.

When Ben got his first proper view of his wife she was leaning with her fingers looped through the rusty mesh of the fencing surrounding the court, staring outwards. A woman in a cage, was his first thought. And in the same instant he felt a searing stab of responsibility for the part he had played in putting her there. Only then did his senses register the full horror of her hair.

Unaware that she was being observed, Isobel abandoned her pose and absently kicked at a stone with the toe of her shoe. She watched as it bounced along the faint dusty image of a baseline and out through the open gate by which she had entered. When she saw Ben, she stopped abruptly and threw down her bag.

'You weren't supposed to be here.'

'I know.'

'You promised.'

'I know. I lied. I wanted to see you.'

'Well, now you've seen me.'

'You've cut your hair.'

'Full marks for observation.' She reached down and tugged her scarf free from the tangle of her bag straps. Letting Ben, of all people, see her ugliness was hard. Worse than standing naked before the scrutiny of strangers. He had loved her hair. Once, a long time ago, he had held strands of it to his face as he slept. Isobel twisted the scarf round her hands and wrists, glowering at the effort of not putting it on. 'It's my head.'

'Yes,' he said quietly, 'I know. How are you?' He plunged his hands in his pockets and looked at his shoes, as if such distraction might make the burden of any answer she had to offer easier to bear. 'How is . . . James?'

Isobel rolled her eyes and picked up her bag. 'I've no idea. He's back with Juliet.'

'I see,' he whispered, wishing she did not look so sad.

'Apparently she knows nothing of my involvement with James and I for one am more than happy to keep it that way. Seeing the threat I must have – however briefly – posed to their marriage, it seems the very least I can do.'

'And what about our marriage?' he faltered, still seeing only her sadness and hating James Howard for being the cause of it.

'I think that was a casualty long before any of . . . this, don't you?' She cleared her throat and tightened her grip on the strap of her bag. 'Now, if there's nothing else . . . I have come here – in case you had forgotten – to comply with the dying wishes of your aunt. I know we have a lot to talk about, but if you don't mind I'd rather not do it here.' She swept past him and began marching back towards the house, half hidden through the screen of trees behind them.

'Wait – Isobel, I . . . I've got your post.'

She stopped and turned, her voice scornful. 'My what?'

'Post,' he repeated faintly, feeling pathetic as he reached into his jacket pocket for the couple of letters that he had grabbed as he was leaving the house.

'You could have sent them on . . .' she began; though the remark did not prevent her from coming back towards him, holding out her hand. 'Thank you.'

'She looks bloody awful, doesn't she, the old thing?'

Isobel nodded.

'Has she said anything to you yet?'

'Nope. Can't think what it was all about.'

'She said something about not being nice to you . . .'

'Did she?' Isobel was so surprised she smiled. 'Well, I . . . how funny and how unlikely.'

'Wasn't she nice to you?' he asked, with real concern in his voice. 'You never said . . .'

'I never said a lot of things, and neither did you . . .' she began, before checking herself and letting out a small sigh. 'Oh God, I don't know . . . I suppose she sort of picked on me a bit, let off some steam – nothing serious at all.' She shrugged. 'Funny old thing. Who's the other Isobel, by the way?'

'The other Isobel?'

Admitting to her nosiness made her flush. 'I was rooting around in her jewel box and . . . well, I found this pendant thing inscribed to an Isobel. I couldn't help wondering who she was.' She shrugged and turned to leave him once more. 'I thought you might know. It doesn't matter.'

Ben opened his mouth twice before managing to project any sounds from it. 'No, there's only you. Only one Isobel.'

Something about his tone made her stop and look back.

He cast his eyes to the ground, suddenly overcome with emotions for which he could find no adequate verbal expression. But she still loves James, he reminded himself, clenching his jaw to steady his voice. 'The contents of all her jewel boxes will go to you anyway – and the girls, of course. There's no one else. There'll be no money to speak of – it all went on paying for this place.' He nodded in the direction of the house.

'Well, that's nice,' Isobel murmured, realising for the first time that she had been so absorbed by her own emotions that she had failed to notice his. He looked neither bitter nor disappointed, as she had expected, but preoccupied and utterly downcast.

'You'd think dying might provide some answers to *something*,' he burst out, spreading his arms in dismay. 'I mean, when I got here I actually found myself hoping for a better understanding of . . . oh Christ, the past, I suppose, and why everything happened as it did . . . but in fact it's just a bloody anticlimax, isn't it? There's nothing to understand, no deathbed epiphany, no visions for anybody except perhaps bloody John of bloody Gaunt—'

'John of Gaunt?'

'In *Richard II* – prophetic urge as he's dying – mind you, that doesn't do any bloody good either—' Aware that he was ranting, but that she was listening, Ben careered on, all his instincts telling him that though the door was closing fast, he might yet slip his foot into the gap to stop it shutting completely. 'The bad stuff just happens,' he continued, 'and before I've always let it – not fought it – or at least fought it inside by pretending it wasn't there. And I kind of thought you'd taken me on those terms, that you had fallen for this unbreakable, self-driven thing, and so I guess I wanted to keep it that way, because if you saw the mess inside you wouldn't . . .' He broke off, angry with himself for the tremor in his voice. 'So I kept a tight control over myself and part of that was controlling you, not letting you . . . flourish.' He threw his hands up in despair at the inadequacy of the word. 'I trapped you as much as I trapped myself.'

Isobel, shuffling her clutch of letters, swallowed hard, though her mouth was quite dry. Having expected any angry rantings to be on the subject of James or marital infidelity, she was astonished at the turn the conversation was taking, and fractionally encouraged too.

'I drive people away from me, don't I?' he snarled, his dark eyes blazing. 'Apart form my pupils, of course. But then they're easy because they go home at night, taking most of their troubles with them. But people that matter, I drive away. It's my big speciality. Like my father—' He caught his breath before continuing, his voice tight and calm. 'For whom, as you know, I was barely able to feel any affection at all.' He shook his head. 'God, how the past throttles the present . . .'

'Only if you let it,' she put in quietly, picking at the corner of a stamp.

'The only person I've ever felt really close to . . .' He swallowed. '. . . is you . . . until . . .' He clapped his hands, making her jump. '. . . our baby . . . there's another death that didn't make any sense – life's full of the bloody things, had you noticed?' he added, flashing a dark smile. 'And all I could do was feel jealous of your sadness – God, Isobel, you were so bloody good at being sad.' He laughed bitterly. 'Jesus Christ, it's funny, it's actually very funny.' His laughing echoed round the empty tennis court beside them. 'Because you see I've learnt how to be miserable now, all right. But now is too late . . .' He threw his head back, whooping at the sky.

'Stop it, Ben, please,' she begged, appalled.

Putting his hands up, he made a show of trying to swallow the laughter away. 'Do you know, I have even been driven to seeking professional help – I actually saw a counsellor who confirmed all my worst fears—'

'A counsellor?' Isobel was so surprised she dropped her letters.

'Amusing, isn't it? What's even better is that this one and only session – this great hopeless bid for psychological self-reform – took place just the day before you elected to break the news about dear James. I mean, if that isn't funny I don't know what is.' But he wasn't laughing any longer. All he could manage was an attempt at a smile, which Isobel, staring hard at a tree as she braced herself for the barrage of recrimination that would follow, failed to observe.

But instead of recrimination, there was silence.

'The fact is I want you back, Isobel, and don't know how the hell to go about it, how to persuade you that I'm worth a second shot, that I'm worth more than . . . James.'

'More than James?' she repeated dumbly, her mouth dropping open in disbelief, while her heart leapt with a hope she had thought to have abandoned for good. 'I need persuading of that, do I?' she went on archly, recovering herself. Though, as she stooped down to retrieve her letters, she was careful to keep her chin to her chest so that he would not see the wobble in her lower lip.

'Don't you?'

The scurrying figure of a nurse suddenly appeared in the shrubbery behind them, waving her arms and shouting.

'Oh, there you are . . . could you come? We think . . . it might be time . . .'

'Oh heavens, we'd better be quick.' Isobel, with a spurt of guilt, began to trot back up the path.

'We had indeed,' he called, striding after her. 'Who knows what dying revelations we may have missed – more family scandals, buried treasure or hidden deeds to magnificent homes . . .'

'Ben, shush,' she scolded, having to suppress a smile as they caught up with the nurse.

'So you two found each other, did you?'

'In a manner of speaking,' said Ben, giving Isobel a funny look which she pretended not to see.

'I'm so sorry, but your aunt seems to have taken a turn for the worse. You'd better come with me.'

43 ∫

But Aunt Violet was to prove as uncooperative in dying as she had in living. Conceding, almost apologetically, that the immediate crisis seemed to have passed, the nurse left the old lady's chief mourners-in-waiting eyeing each other with some awkwardness from opposite sides of the bed.

'This will only be my second death,' remarked Isobel after a while, 'of someone to whom I feel any attachment at all. That's quite lucky, I suppose, isn't it, for a person who's been on the planet as long as I have?'

'All of thirty-one years, isn't it?'

'Thirty-two.'

'Ah yes, thirty-two.'

'Do you believe in heaven, Ben?'

'Not for a moment.'

'Not even for Toby?' It was the first time she had said the name out loud to him in years.

'Well, all I can say is, if that's where he is then I only wish we could warn him who's on the way,' he replied, making a face at the figure of his aunt, whose shallow breathing was now being conducted with her chin thrust at the ceiling, as if to facilitate the passage of air.

'This is awful. I'm not sure I can bear much more.'

'You're not thinking of going, are you?' he said quietly.

'Maybe.'

'Please don't. I . . . need you, Isobel.'

'I was just beginning to adjust to the idea of not being needed at all, by anyone ever again. And of not needing anyone myself, for that matter,' she added, frowning at him.

'But Aunt Violet might give a sign any minute – something to show why she wanted you here. You obviously meant a lot to her.'

'Don't you dare start flattering me now, Ben Tarrant,' she retorted, leaving the bedside and wandering over to the dressing table. Seeing the chain of the pendant hanging out of the jewel box, she pulled it free and dangled it at him.

'This was what I was talking about. *Isobel my love*, it says.' She squinted at the tiny print inlaid in the silver. 'And it's even spelt my way too. Don't you think that's peculiar? A pretty heart shape . . . and it's got a sort of shiny new look to it too compared to all the rest of this stuff.' She fished out a pair of enormous pearly paste baubles and held them to her ears. 'What do you think?'

Ben scowled furiously shaking his head. 'You look like a tacky Christmas tree.'

'How sweet of you to say so.'

'But the hair's growing on me, though, if you'll pardon the expression.' They both laughed, and then shot guilty looks at the bed.

'This won't do at all,' she whispered, spinning the chain round her hand and suppressing another smile.

'This will do just fine,' he countered, sitting back in his chair, savouring the realisation that he did not need to own up to the ownership of the rose crystal, that he could woo her without needing to resort to sentimentality or dramatic gestures of any kind. All that they had once shared was still there, dormant, but wonderfully alive. 'In some countries they dance at gravesides every year to celebrate the life of the person who's gone. They drink vodka and tell rude jokes.'

'Do they, now?' She slipped the necklace over her head and made a face at herself in the mirror. 'Well, the vodka part sounds promising.'

'Isobel . . .'

A look from her almost silenced him. A look generated by the fear that they would get it wrong, that some slip of a remark would throw them off course again.

'Would you like to live in Hampshire?'

'I very much doubt it.'

'I'm going to apply for a job . . . headmaster of a small prep school . . . I couldn't do it without you.'

'I want to study Spanish with the Open University.'

'You could do that too—'

'All those smelly little boys.' She screwed up her nose.

'And smelly girls too – it's mixed.'

'Oh God, look, she's moving her mouth, Ben – she's trying to say something.' Isobel leapt back across the room and bent her head near the withered face. As she leant over the bed, Ben took the opportunity to seize her hand.

'I'm sorry for what I did to you – to us – Isobel—'

'Shush, I'm trying to listen,' she whispered, trying and failing to tug her hand free.

'I know how much of it was my fault—'

'If you carry on like this I'll think I deserve no blame at all,' she retorted, looking up at last and relaxing her fingers in his.

They kissed, with some awkwardness, across the bed, and with such absorption that when Aunt Violet did at last open her mouth to embark upon a dying utterance, they did not even notice. The nurse, appearing a few minutes later at the open door behind, blushed scarlet and tiptoed away to tell her colleagues. A lively and impromptu tea break ensued, during which a range of ribald but by no means ill-intentioned opinions on the unexpected nature of the visitors' behaviour were gleefully exchanged. Beneath the sheer thrill of these speculations hummed a deep gladness, which the nurses themselves would have found hard to define, but which perhaps derived from a general sense of the irrepressibility of the human spirit.

An air of something like triumph lingered in the hushed, scrubbed corridors of the home, even after Ben's bashful but solemn face appeared round the office door to announce that his aunt seemed finally to have breathed her last. While the nurses moved around the bed, the Tarrants stood a little to one side, their heads bowed in respectful silence. After a moment or two they linked fingers, tentatively at first, but with increasing confidence, until their two hands were as tight as a clenched fist. Within the small circle of this private embrace each sensed a world of forgotten possibilities, a world powered with enough determination and desire not only to accommodate the burdens of the past, but also to allow stirrings of hope for what might lie ahead.

AMANDA BROOKFIELD

THE LOVER

After twenty years of contentedly playing the role of home-maker and mother, Frances Copeland's life is shattered by the sudden and premature death of her husband. Aged forty-three and with two near grown-up children, the solitude of bereavement hits particularly hard, forcing her to reassess both her own personality and the shape her life has taken.

When the chance of a fresh start presents itself in the form of a man seventeen years her junior, Frances's own reservations about pursuing such a love affair seem to be confirmed by the judgemental attitudes of those nearest to her. Obsessed by this predicament, she fails to observe the crises evolving in the lives of her children, until a tragic accident brings her to her senses.

A FLAME PAPERBACK

AMANDA BROOKFIELD

SINGLE LIVES

Having secured a lucrative contract as a newspaper columnist, the only thing missing from thirty-three-year-old Annie Jordan's life is romance. In spite of numerous partners, her glamorous flatmate Marina seems to be suffering from the same problem. As does Jake, their easy-going gay friend, a mediocre actor tiring of the blind alley of sexual promiscuity.

Yet love, when it comes, brings as many problems as it solves. When pressure mounts in her personal life Annie begins to lose any sense of where reality ends and the contents of her column begin. Shadows from an unhappy childhood, together with the confusing and secretive behaviour of a new neighbour, contribute to the impression that the tenuous threads holding her life together are breaking apart.

A FLAME PAPERBACK